Ethoria's Chronicles

Book I

Ethoria's Chronicles

Book I:
The Shadows of the Past

Michael Kostin

ICLS International, Inc.
HARVARD, ILLINOIS

First printing 2004

ISBN 0-9727012-4-9
LCCN 2002117538

History of Ethoria
(as recorded by Zermun the Wise of the City of Azor)

THE ANCIENT TIMES

No one knows for sure when or how the world of Ethoria came to exist. The first accounts tell of the Ancient Times when lands were settled and ruled by a mysterious and powerful race, called the Keepers. No descriptions or images of those people have survived through time. Yet it has been rumored that they resembled humans in form and wielded great powers (often referred to as Magic), which allowed them to shape the world and life as they desired. Using those powers, the Keepers built their cities, leveled mountains, created oceans, and grew everlasting forests, thus shaping much of present Ethoria.

THE FIRST TURMOIL

Although it was unclear how long the ancient civilization prospered, it was eventually shattered by a civil war, known as the First Turmoil. A group of the Keepers rebelled against the popular rule and seized control over several cities, establishing a new nation. The conflict lasted for many years and ended with the defeat of the mutineers (also known as the Fallen Ones). Those rebels who survived the many battles were captured and sent away into the barren wastes of Northern Ethoria, where only ruins of once magnificent cities remained. There the Keepers created a natural prison by sealing off the half-frozen region by creating an impassable range of mountains, which came to be known as The Land's Edge.

THE SECOND TURMOIL

Alas, the prison could not hold forever and years later the Fallen Ones returned. Using much of the same powers that had made the mountains, the rebels blasted a portion of the Land's Edge and through a wide passage (The

Shadow Pass) stormed into southern Ethoria, thus setting off the second civil war, called the Second Turmoil.

THE DEMISE

In due course the second civil war ended with yet another defeat of the Fallen Ones. But it was a sour victory for the Keepers as most of their kin had perished on the fields of battle. The surviving rebels fled back beyond the Land's Edge, but the remaining Keepers found themselves weak, their numbers dangerously reduced, and their powers diminished. Nonetheless the once mighty people started to rebuild their nation. After repairing their damaged cities, the Keepers turned to the Land's Edge, where the open passage still stood. Although they did not have the power to erect more mountains, the Keepers mustered enough magic to construct a grand wall that ran from west to east, blocking the pass. The fortifications were immense and have survived the passage of time to stand as the only reminder of the Keepers' existence in Ethoria. The wall itself came to be known as the First Barrier.

Alas the construction of the massive battlements drained the Keepers of the last drops of their powers and soon they found themselves unable to sustain their immortality. After ages of life, the Keepers finally faced death and with it their own extinction. Soon there were only few of them left. Many died, but some chose to prolong their existence by bounding their Spirits to the many lakes and ponds scattered across the world. For them it was a way to live, and so they did, remaining in an astral state forever.

THE OLD EPOCH

As the Ancient Times ended the Old Epoch began. It was unclear as to when the last of the walking Keepers left Ethoria. Once they did, the world saw a rise of new races. In the end, two peoples—the A'als and the Dark Ones—populated the lands. While the Dark Ones always remained a mystery, much was known about the A'als. Slender, tall, and graceful, the human-like people came to Ethoria from beyond the foothills of the Great Plains, spreading quickly across the world, populating the lands, and founding many cities. They were the first to record the history of Ethoria, and also to create the first calendar, known as the Ispa Crom.

The Golden Age of the Old Epoch: The first period of the Old Epoch was believed to start with the founding of the first A'als kingdom. Sometime during that period, the A'als' Empire was born and extended quickly, conquering much of Ethoria and seizing the First Barrier. It was also then the A'als' armies went beyond the Land's Edge and started to explore the northern wastes. There they found yet another race, called the humans. The men were primitive, lived in small tribes, and spent their time hunting and gathering amidst the icy lands. Unable to defend themselves from the superior armies of the A'als, the humans gave up easily and soon most of their tribes were conquered, their people brought back into Ethoria as labor.

The Cursed Age: While exploring the North, the A'als eventually met a strange force that emerged from the farthest reaches of the ice-clinched region in the mountains of Vudor (the world beyond the living world in A'als' tongue). The resisting side was made mostly of human kin, but unlike the weak tribes closer to the Land's Edge, these men were well armed and their leaders wielded great powers of Magic. This proved devastating for the unsuspecting A'als, who could do little but retreat, chased back by a horde of men, wolves, and other unknown creatures. The A'als tried to make a stand at the First Barrier, but their numbers were too few, and before long the Northern Horde streamed into Ethoria, devastating everything in its path. The War of Tears began and lasted for many years.

In the end the victory belonged to the A'als. The Horde was defeated and its supreme leader, the Master of the Old, or Rackshahan, was slain. Yet the aftermath of the war was horrifying, and to prevent new invasions from the North the A'als decided to keep the Barrier Wall manned at all times, protecting the Shadow Pass. They also pledged never to cross into the Northern Wastes again.

The Age of Blood Wars: After the war the A'als nation changed. As many of the clans' leaders had fallen during the many battles, a lot of old clans disappeared and new clans emerged. Along with them came a fight for power and soon a split that ripped the nation in two, the A'als and the D'ars. While the origin of the conflict between the two had long been forgotten, the A'als and the D'ars fought constantly, their confrontation coming to be known as the Blood Wars. This warring period lasted for thousands of years and ended with the defeat of the D'ars, who fled into the mountains of the Land's Edge, never to be seen again.

The A'als' civil war had similar results as the war among the Keepers. Much of the land was destroyed and too many of the A'als were dead. With most of the cities in ruins the A'als did not have enough strength to rebuild their empire. The humans also had grown stronger during that time and started to populate more regions, settling among the remnants of the destroyed sites.

While human expansion continued, the A'als retreated further east and settled in the depths of the Ancient Woods, known as the Great Forest.

THE NEW EPOCH
First Age of the New Epoch

0 (N.E.)...Rural, the first human city-state, is established. Its founding brings the beginning of the new period in history, known as the New Epoch. It is from that moment the first human calendar begins, starting with the year 50, since it takes that long for the first human king, Anderic Oregi, to pass his seat to his son, Anderic Semoi.

50 (N.E.)...Rural captures more land, becomes the first human kingdom, and is renamed Titul (in the old tongue, meaning a human parish).

550 (N.E.)...Titul grows to include the present realms of Normandia, Westalia, and the Northern Empire.

1500 (N.E.)...The first clash between the armies of Titul and the A'als—some of whom still dwell in the plains of present-day Magnicia—is recorded. The humans win the initial battle, but more A'als come from the Great Forest and push the humans back. A series of campaigns follow and become known as the Wars of Green Leaf.

1680 (N.E.)...The conflict produces no winner, no ground is gained, and no cities are captured. So at the end of the Fourth War, the humans and A'als finally sign a peace treaty, whereby they agree the humans will occupy all the lands west of the Great Forest, and the A'als will rule over the Great Forest and the lands further east. It is also agreed that no human will enter the Great Forest without prior permission from the A'als. The Pact of Free Hand is signed. A'als leave Ethoria's grasslands and humans spread across the world.

1900 (N.E.)...Human population grows and men now occupy all the lands around the Seven Seas. Titul becomes but a formal name for a collection of hundreds of smaller nations, which soon begin to squabble among each other over territory and resources.

1900–2250 (N.E.)...Many smaller wars are fought. In the end three winners emerge: 1) A newly reformed nation of Titul that occupies the northwestern and northern parts of Ethoria; 2) Rimal (a land of meadows), a new empire that holds the eastern regions; and 3) Sirum (Sands) that rules the southern parts. The fourth realm belongs to the A'als, who continue to dwell within the Great Forest.

2250–2520 (N.E.)…A period of peace and stability. The world is established and all the realms prosper. But it soon comes to an end.

2521 (N.E.)…An enemy emerges from beyond the Land's Edge. Through the unprotected Shadow Pass another horde of invaders streams from the North and attacks the human settlements near the mountains, thus marking the start of the Great War.

2521–2542 (N.E.)…The Great War rages throughout Ethoria. The Northern Horde advances mightily as it did during the reign of the A'als. Led by a great leader, who claims to be the Master of the Old reborn, the attackers sweep through Ethoria like a wild fire.

Titul falls first, then Rimal. In one year the fighting reaches Sirum. When much of its resistance is dealt with, the Horde suddenly turns south and pushes into the sands of the Sarie Desert. But that proves to be a mistake. Within the next ten years the Northerners battle heat and sand, trying to push further south. However, unable to overcome the natural obstacles, the invaders have to turn back.

Its numbers cut in half, the Horde finds its way back into Ethoria. By then though, the battered human realms have rallied their forces to meet the offenders one more time. Gathering under the banners of General Rass Moir Al, a great human force is assembled. And in the year 2542 (N.E.) the human army meets the Horde on the banks of the Amber River. The battle then rages for two weeks and the humans emerge victorious. Most of the enemy is slain and those who survive flee back into the desert, later founding the small nation of Bahagor.

2542–2558 (N.E.)…After the war people come together to rebuild their shattered world. When many of the cities are restored, new nations are born and their kings decide to man the Barrier Wall to protect Ethoria from any further incursions. At the same time the human rulers also decide to construct another Barrier, some leagues south of the first one, so as to ensure the protection of the world. To watch over the two massive walls, they build a citadel, called the Great Fortress.

Alas, much of the old human world is lost. No longer do three Empires rule Ethoria. And so ends the First Age of the New Epoch. As the first stone is laid in the foundation of the Second Barrier, the new period begins, the Second Age of the New Epoch.

Second Age of the New Epoch

0 (S.A.N.E.)...The construction of the second Barrier begins.

0–560 (S.A.N.E.)...During this period the new nations reshape the borders of the world. Sirum is restored after the war, but then splits into three realms: Alabia to the southwest; the Great Amber Empire, the heir of the old Empire, occupying much of the land; and Zamal to the southeast. Later Zamal crumbles and becomes a collection of many small kingdoms, known as the Free Cities. Rimal is completely destroyed during the war and gives way to four new realms: Lombardia, Gremias, Azoros, and Dvorenia. Titul is dead. Nothing is left of its cities or its populace. For some years the lands are empty, but then are resettled and so the following nations are born: Westalia, Normandia, and Magnicia.

561 (S.A.N.E.)...The present Ethoria is formed and will remain so almost unchanged until the present. Still there are some events that are worth mentioning.

572...After a bitter rebellion Zamal's dynasty is eliminated and the realm falls apart.

575...Dvorenia's kings reaffirm their honoring of the Pact of Free Hand and prohibit any human from entering the Great Forest, even though not a single A'al has been seen since the end of the Great War. (It is rumored that the D'ars' royals had strange visions that warned them to take such steps to save their realm from destruction).

578...Wild tribes of humans, known as the Grass Folks, leave the Great Plains and invade southern Ethoria. In just a few seasons they reach the borders of Dvorenia, but then are pushed back by the allied forces of Ethorian nations. Although the invasion is successfully repelled, Azoros suffers greatly. Its ruling family is killed and in its place come four new rulers who form the Four Houses, each favoring one of the allies that have driven back the invaders. House of Glory rules the city of Nacitav and is close to Dvorenia. House of Pride controls Oniram and is favored by Gremias as well as the remnants of the old ruling family. House of Valor rules Omoc and is supported by Lombardia. House of Coin has the city of Azor and is allied with the Great Amber Empire.

A loose confederation, Azoros does not have a single ruler or a standing army. Instead it is controlled by the Houses, which hire mercenaries to protect their interests. As a result Azoros keeps a strict state of neutrality and never takes part in any conflict.

591...The realm of Magnicia expands east. Its lore of Magic powers is unmatched. No other nation can even think about challenging Magnicia. Yet the wizards of the realm cannot take their magic too far from the cities, which serve as pools of energy, thus limiting their ability to expand. As a result internal conflicts start to brew.

650...The Great Amber Empire allies itself with Gremias and attacks Dvorenia, eager to get access to its lumberyards near the Great Forest. The war that follows is known as the Summers War as the fighting takes place mostly during the summer seasons.

656...The Campaign against Dvorenia ends with a Dvorenian victory. As a result, Gremias loses most of its eastern territories, and the Great Amber Empire has to pay restitution so that the Dvorenian armies do not invade its lands.

673...The Unification Campaign begins. Normandian kings decide to expand their territory and begin to annex some of the empty lands near the Land's Edge and the Seven Seas. The kingdom grows quickly, its borders soon reaching Lombardia to the east and Westalia to the west.

678...The Unification Campaign ends in success, making this the birthdate of Normandia as a solid nation. Unified under the Vans royal family, the realm is composed of fourteen provinces, but the number is later reduced to ten.

684–690...The rapid expansion of Normandia causes Lombardian nobles to become anxious, and soon they mount an offensive to drive the border further west from Lombardian major cities. So the first Border War between Lombardia and Normandia begins.
691–694...The second Border War begins. (Both wars bring little change and the borders remain the same.)

701–722...Magnicia is ravaged by a devastating Civil War. Followers of two different schools of Magic clash in a horrifying conflict. The war is bitter and brutal. Others nations do not dare to interfere but just watch as the two sides try to score the victory. Alas the many battles reveal no winner. But the nation itself falls in disarray. Much of the land is scorched, cities lay in ruins, and many of Magnicians have died. Those wizards who have survived the conflict soon find themselves alone and leave the battered realm for other kingdoms, carrying with them the few magic crystals that are essential to channeling the power. But the crystals' supply is soon depleted and so the Magic leaves Ethoria forever.

723–726…Taking into service many of the Magnician wizards, Lombardia finds itself with an advantage over its neighbors and immediately acts on it, declaring war against Gremias. The campaign is quick and victorious. Gremias loses one third of its territory and surrenders in the summer season of 726.

727–730…Taken by the success of the Gremias campaign, Lombardia turns to its longtime rival, Normandia. Due to the fact that the wizards have drained most of the energy during the previous conflict, by the start of the second war Lombardia finds itself fighting a conventional war. But with its armies less organized it cannot stand against better-trained Normandian troops. As a result, after two years the campaign ends in a complete Lombardian defeat. It loses two thirds of its northern territories and much of its fighting forces. Many Normandian lords want to destroy Lombardia completely, but their resources are strained and so in the year 731 the Normandian king, Eter the Brave, signs a peace treaty. As for the captured lands, Eter the Brave realizes that he does not have enough men or gold to control them. So instead of unifying them with the rest of his domain, he creates a new nation, which serves as a buffer zone between Normandia and Lombardia.

732…The year when the Northern Empire is born. It is split among five dominant families, and to rule over them a king is chosen from a bloodline of the Amber Empire's dynasty as the most neutral candidate. The same year the Great Amber Empire is attacked by Bahagor. Although the attack is repelled, the Empire begins to fortify its southern borders. As a result it withdraws from the Great Fortress and stops sending supplies there.

738…Following the earlier example, Alabia, Gremias, and Dvorenia also refuse their aid to the Great Fortress.

742…Lombardia also stops sending help to the Barrier.

752...By this time, Normandia, the Northern Empire, and Westalia are the only nations that continue to support the Barriers.

753...The Northern Empire makes a claim to parts of Lombardia south of the Bound. The negotiations bring no result and the Annex War begins.

755...Westalia and Normandia also find themselves in dispute over several leagues of land. War spreads to these lands.

756...Westalia is forced into signing a peace treaty and Normandia acquires Bois Province.

757...Lombardia loses the war to the Northern Empire and with it lands south of the Bound. The Border Regions are born.

758...After all the wars, Normandia is the only nation sending aid to the Great Fortress. The same year Ethoria sees the birth of several isle nations, which rebel against Lombardia after its defeat in the war against the Northern Empire. The largest of the new kingdoms is the Claw and is ruled by a religious order called the Dores. Its followers isolate themselves from the rest of Ethoria and only a handful of outsiders are allowed to enter. Some believe that the Dores possess secrets of Magic and do not want to share them with others, but its is only a rumor.

763...The First Caves are uncovered inside the mountains between the two Barrier Walls. Parts of some ancient mines, the tunnels are filled with gold and iron. But more important is the red ore discovered here, a material lighter and stronger than usual ores, one that can withstand twice the pressure as normal steel. Perfect for making weapons and armor, the red ore quickly becomes a precious resource and its discovery marks a new age for the Great Fortress. Since Normandia is the only nation still supplying the Barriers with men and food, it becomes the first realm to control the mines. Soon enough though other kingdoms become interested in controlling the supply of red ore, and with tension mounting, Normandia finds itself on the verge of another war, with most of the realms allied against it.

To resolve the problem, Normandia is forced to give up its rights to the mines. The Great Fortress Region is then declared an independent realm and the mines are to be split among the nations. Yet after a few years, the new rulers of the Great Forrest, the supervisors who had once commanded the garrisons, deny access to the mines and thus become the sole owners of the red ore supplies by the year 779.

1030…In secret the Normandian king meets with the Supervisors of the Great Fortress and strikes a deal, whereby in exchange for several mines, Normandia will supply the two Barriers with labor, which is in demand there.

1031…The first caravan of Normandian workers or guards arrives at the Wall.

1100…Production of the red ore grows fast and soon Normandia finds itself unable to recruit free people to go to the Wall. A new system is then designed. Instead of hiring workers, Normandia sends criminals to serve their time at the mines. So the Barrier Duty is born. About the same time, the Great Fortress sees a change in the Supervisors' ranks. New casts are born, each with a distinctive color assigned to it.

1132…Normandian influence over the Great Fortress grows strong once again. Other nations become more restless.

1148…The Northern Empire is the first to try to fight its way to the mines. But its troops cannot pass through the Second Barrier Wall. With the help from Normandia, the Great Fortress holds off the imperial army until the imperials are exhausted and seek a peace treaty, which is signed. Afterward the Northern Empire joins Normandia in exchanging labor for ore.

1175…Westalia tries to negotiate better terms for the supply of red ore, but Normandia intervenes and the second Westalian War begins. Also known as the Border War, the conflict ends in 1180 with the defeat of Westalia, which not only loses its territory but also access to the Great Fortress.

1215…Ethoria's Chronicles begin.

Races and Peoples of Ethoria

1. *The Keepers*—A race of powerful wizards, believed to be long dead, who ruled over Ethoria during the Ancient Times. The first known inhabitants of Ethoria, they used powerful forces, called Magic, in their daily lives. After a devastating civil war, their civilization declined and then disappeared. Not a single Keeper has been reported since, and few descriptions have survived to tell about the ancient race.

    a. *Fallen Ones*—the rebel Keepers, who followed the belief that Magic was to be used to create a perfect world. Their leader was known as the Master of the Old.

    b. *Spirits*—after the demise, some Keepers chose to continue to live on by bounding their spirits to the waters of lakes and ponds, thus prolonging their lives for as long as the lakes existed.

2. *A'als*—An ancient race that repopulated Ethoria after the Keepers disappeared. Although no one knows for sure when the A'als first came to the world or why they settled in Ethoria, they have been a part of the region for thousands of years. In earlier times the A'als ruled vast empires and even tried to conquer the Northern Wastes beyond the Land's Edge. But since then their influence was reduced considerably, mostly due to a civil war among their kin. Now they are believed to be living within the Great Forest realm, not concerning themselves much with the troubles of the rest of the world. The A'als look very much like the humans, but much taller than an average man, slender, and graceful. They have pale, almost white skin, blue eyes, and golden hair. While no one knows for sure, it is thought to be true for the A'als to posses powerful magic. It is also believed that the A'als live much longer than men, and have often been considered immortals among humankind.

3. *D'ars*—Once a part of the A'als race, the D'ars split from the A'als after the war with the Master of the Old. Although physically identical to the A'als, the D'ars always thought of themselves as unique. It is unclear why, but the D'ars always hated the A'als, which caused many wars between the two. For years one conflict followed another. In the end the D'ars were defeated and the few survivors fled into the mountains, not to be seen again. Since the birth of the first human nation, nothing has been uncovered to explain the ways of the D'ars. The A'als have been willing to share this knowledge, binding themselves never to speak about their former kin.

4. *Humans*—By far the most numerous of all peoples of Ethoria. The human nations occupy much of the world with the exception of the Great Forest, which has always belonged to the A'als. Among the human race several groups should be mentioned:

   a. *Ethorians*—People who dwell in Ethoria's mainland and the isles of the Seven Seas. By far the largest of the groups, it counts dozens of nations.

   b. *Grass Folks*—Dwellers of the Great Plains with primitive tribal culture and no single ruler.

   c. *Wild Men of the North, or the Nords*—Dwellers of the Northern Wastes, located beyond the Land's Edge. At least ten tribes are known, but many suspect there are more.

   d. *Desert Riders*—Sons and daughters of the Horde warriors who invaded Ethoria during the First Age, now inhabiting the kingdom of Bahagor. Appearing only seldom to raid some of the border villages of the Amber Empire, they live in the depths of the desert, rarely showing themselves to outsiders.

5. *The Dark Ones*—Creatures from the Ancient Times. The legends say the Keepers created the Dark Ones after the completion of the Land's Edge to guard its mountains from the Fallen Ones. Half-human, half-beast in appearance, the Dark Ones are believed to be living in the caves of the Land's Edge, though this is often considered to be untrue, as not one has ever been seen by any human.

6. *Trolliers*—Tall, green-skinned creatures that live in the Northern Wastes. During the human history of Ethoria the Trolliers have existed only since the Great War, when along with the rest of the Horde, they stormed the Barrier Wall.

Map 1: Ethoria

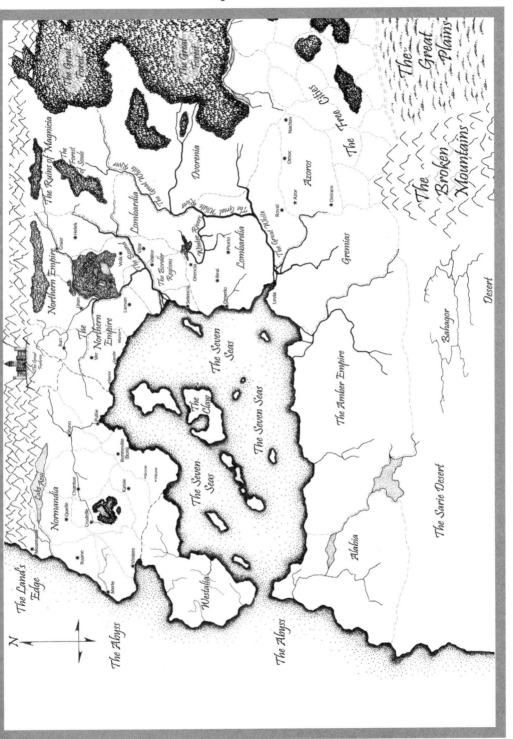

The Land's
Edge

N

Mountanie

Norman

Queile

Ruane

Crudelle

The Abyss

Merie

Viniere

Westalia

T

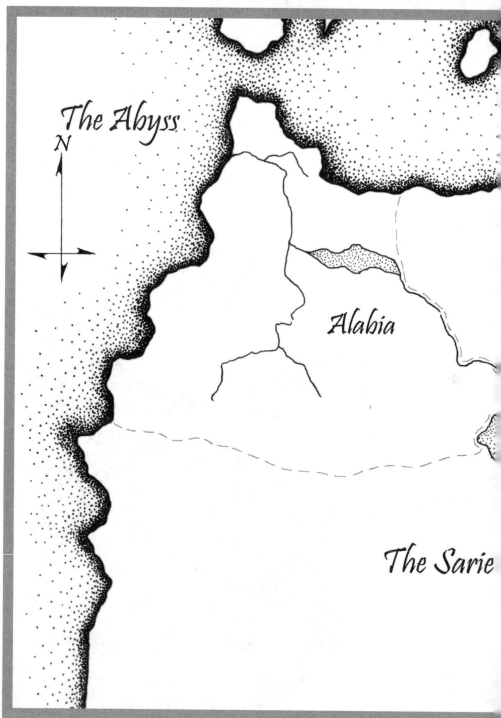

The Abyss

N

Alabia

The Sarie

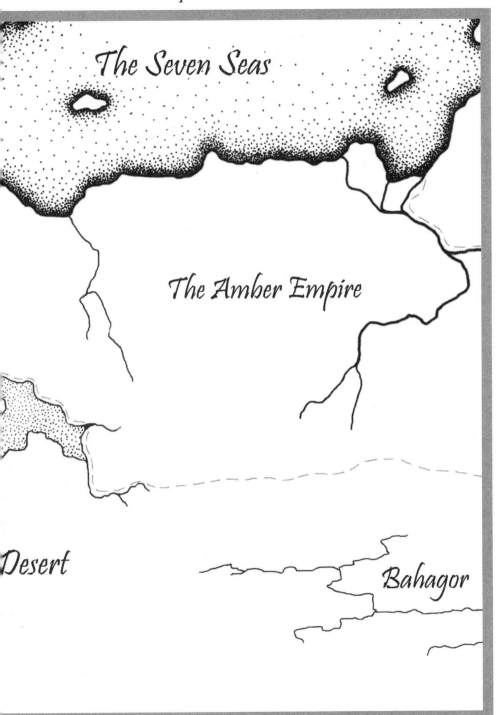

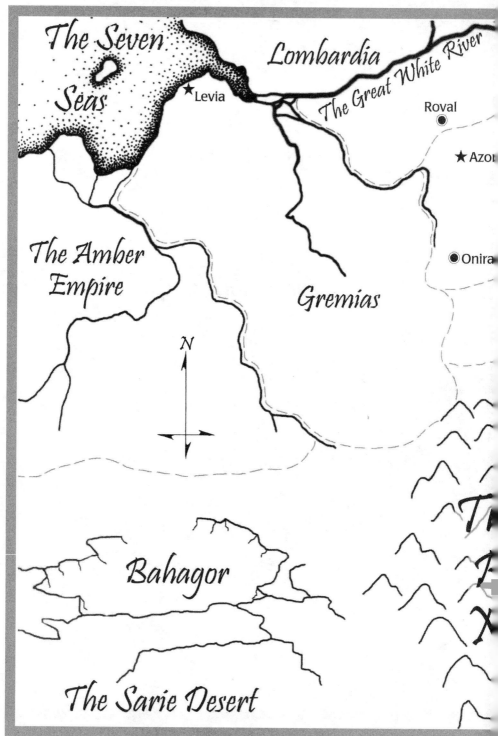

Map 6: Normandia

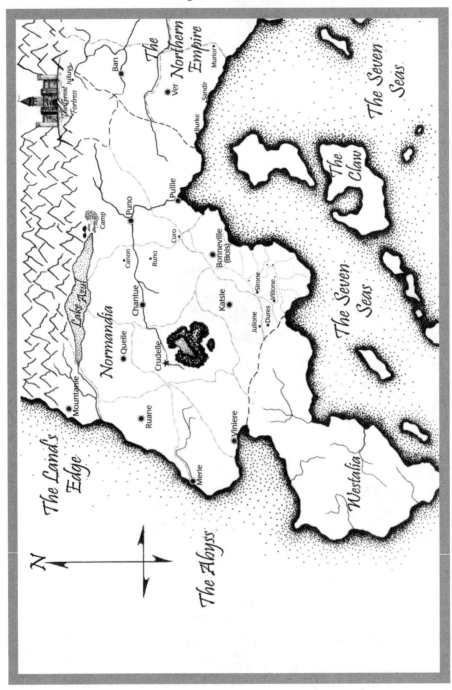

Map 7: Normandia

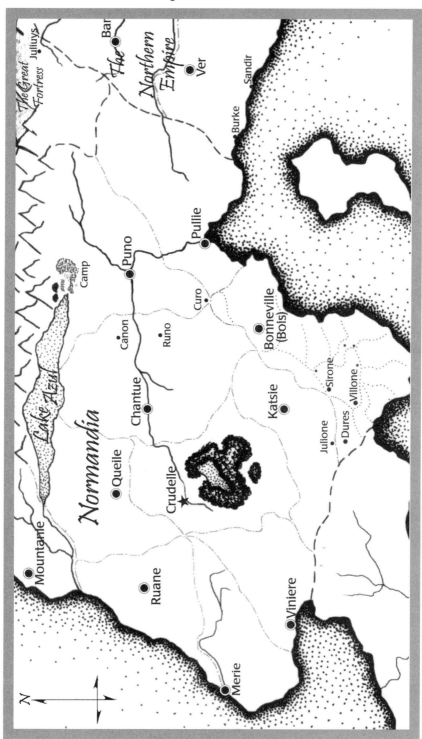

Map 8: Orencia

Map 9: Azoros

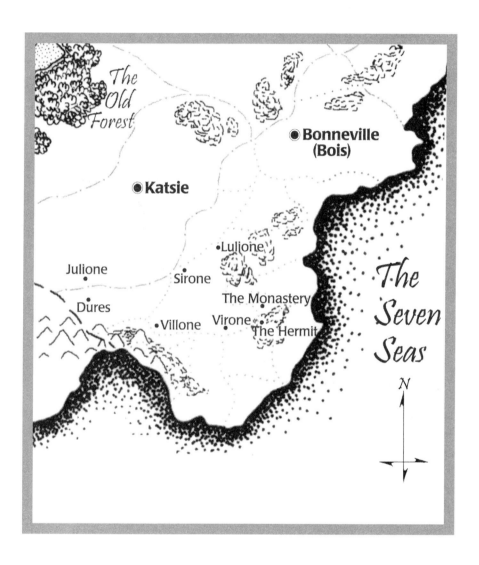

Part I

Ethoria's Chronicles

The Shadows of the Past

Chapter 1

APPROACHING FOOTSTEPS resounded in the air, resonating in an empty city street. Although the night was young, it was hard to see anything in the dark, as an invisible cloud shielded the night sky, robbing the city of what little moonlight there was. Illumination came only from a few lanterns and seldom-unveiled windows, which cast thin yellow strips of light onto the wet, slippery pavement. The city, so rowdy and busy just hours ago, seemed to have died out. But such a dearth of people and noise did not bother a lonesome figure that appeared from shadows at the far end of an alley and swiftly crossed the street, displaying a distinctive gentlemanlike stride.

As the stranger came out into the open, it was revealed that he was a tall man, dressed in black. A long silk cape was wrapped around his shoulders. He moved quickly and stayed close to the houses, gliding past closed doors. After another quick leap the man skirted a large muddy puddle of stale rainwater that overspread in the center of the street and came up to a two-storied house, distinguished from the rest of the dwellings by large clay ornaments placed around its thick wooden frames. The stranger stared at the unusual decor for a moment, then examined the closed windows, the entryway, and the lane behind him. There was no one in sight. The street was empty, as were the alleys that ran away from it. Certain he was alone, he walked up the high stairwell and knocked on the door.

The sound of his tap seemed loud, and so he stopped almost immediately, hiding his bony fist under the cape. He stood still at the entrance, his eyes focused on the small hatch in the middle of the door. Suddenly some noises came from the inside. A small yellow line of light appeared under the front door, and a heavy lock clicked several times. The hatch opened, and a pair of black eyes peered at the late-night visitor. The man behind the door studied the stranger for a moment, then nodded slightly and slid the door opened. More yellow light streamed onto the wooden stairs and the host's figure appeared in the opening. The two glared at each other, then the host gave another nod and took a step back, allowing the stranger to come in. The guest slipped past him and the door slammed shut. The darkness fell onto the steps and the street was quiet again.

The modest setting of the house's living hall told little of its owner. Simply furnished, it contained the usual set of items common to any Normandian house. In the very center stood a large square table, surrounded by several roughly crafted stools. Behind them, occupying almost the entire back wall, rested a stone fireplace. At its sides rose two tall bookcases, filled with many things of little importance. Next to them, taking the space around four curtained windows, hung shelves and all sorts of tapestries, the latter being suspended from the carved ceiling by long copper strings.

Throwing a passive glance around, the visitor pulled down the large hood and sat on one of the stools, easing into the leather cushions. The owner hurried after his guest and settled across the table. A single tall candle stood between them, its dim light illuminating both faces. The guest's was thin and covered with a black scarf. The owner's was red, with a vivid scar across the left cheek that he rubbed fearfully. When it began to hurt, he put his hand down and started to speak, keeping his voice low, almost at a whisper: "You have come early. Is something wrong?" The owner smiled, though there was little joy in his grin.

The stranger leaned further back and gave the other a hard glare. Instantly the bold host got even more nervous. His cheeks began to sweat and the scar started to twitch. He rubbed it again. The visitor smirked. "Is everything done?" he asked, ignoring the owner's question completely.

"Yes, yes. Everything is done," the host replied quickly. "It is all arranged, just as we promised." The owner swallowed hard. His guest remained unmoved, only tapping his fingers on the table.

"Do we have a deal then?" the visitor continued. His own voice was deep and carried a touch of a Southern accent, unusual for the northern parts of Ethoria. The owner nodded several more times, then reached under the table and pulled out a large rolled leather sheet. He hastily laid it on the table and let the visitor study a rough picture, which appeared to be a hand-drawn map. As the visitor's eyes ran through the lines burned into the thin yellowish hide, the owner hurried to explain: "Just as agreed, my partner will be waiting for you here." The owner reached over and pressed his finger into the leather. "And I will be waiting for you here. As I said, everything is done as promised, so it is a deal then, right?"

"Are you sure this thing is accurate?" the stranger inquired, still looking at the map.

"Oh, yes, yes. It is very accurate. My partner, the merchant, says you will have no problem in finding the rendezvous point. He says he will be there with his caravan in two days' time. It is a perfect spot—far enough from any villages or outposts. Woods surround it completely; there are plenty of good hiding places. Nobody will see you—that you may be sure of." The owner pointed at the map again, smiling slightly. "All you have to do is meet him there and then come back here to take my share. There is one thing, though. My partner, the merchant, asks you to make it all look like an ambush, so others do not suspect anything. He says we do not need too many questions."

"We do not," the guest agreed, then thought for a moment and added, "If he wishes for it to look like an ambush, I see no problem in it." The visitor paused again. This time he let the silence linger in the air for a while and only when the owner started to shift in his seat, did he resume: "How much resistance can I expect from the rest of the caravan's crew?"

"Not much. There will be no more than a dozen men, all locals, no hired swords, no trained guards. Those lads will be so scared of you that they will forget how to fight."

"What about patrols? Any army men around there?"

"Oh, no. There are no patrols in those parts. Barely anyone travels through those lands, so there is no need for patrols."

"Good. Because I do not feel like meeting with any regulars or, even worse, some stinking knight. It is already too much work for the money they pay me." The stranger rolled up the map and put it under his cape. When it was done, he suddenly leaned over the table. His face came within a spit of the candle; sharp gray eyes converged on the owner's face. "Will the merchandise be there?" he asked slowly.

"Yes. Yes. As I said, my partner and I will deliver everything as asked. I just hope your master will hold onto his part of the bargain and make that little debt of ours go away." The owner's lips stretched in another fake smile. The guest was about to grin back, but thought otherwise, and instead got up, kicking back the chair, knocking it on the floor.

"Do not worry. You deliver the goods, and we will erase your debt….Oh just one more thing…should you two play a trick on me I will be very disappointed. And I assure you, you do not want to disappoint me, or my master for that matter. Are we clear?"

"Yes, of course. You can trust me." The owner was quick to restore his guest's confidence.

"Trust you," the visitor laughed. "I stopped trusting your kind long ago. All I trust now is money. Since I have been already paid half of the money for this job, I want to make sure that it goes well. I just hope you are better in keeping your word, than keeping your money." The man laughed and walked out of the room. The owner trotted after the guest, carrying the candle in his hand.

Almost at the door the visitor halted and turned around. "My men will be at the location on time. We will be waiting. Should you or your friend decide to change your mind, I will know where to find you both. And let that little scar of yours remind you who you are dealing with. So let's make everything right the first time, and nobody has to get hurt." Those were the stranger's last words. Before the owner could reply, he slipped back onto the street and vanished into the darkness. Sounds of his footsteps faded along with him, and soon the owner was alone, standing motionless in the doorway. For a while he stared at the spot where he last saw his guest, then gave out a loud sigh and closed the door, locking it from the inside.

Unhurriedly he returned to his chair; drops of sweat were still running down his face. He did not lie to himself. The visitor scared him; all hired swords did, especially the ones from the South. But there was little he could do. The debt to the merchant's guild of Azoros was too big, and he had only one month to come up with the money. A thousand golden plates—it was an impossible task. The only option left was to accept the guild's offer, even though it involved one of the most vicious gangs of cutthroats in all of Ethoria. Like his treacherous addictions, making a deal with the foreign traders was a gamble. But it was the only chance he had to save his life and the lives of his family. He needed the plan to work. Another long sigh graced the living hall. Then he blew out the candle and walked upstairs, where his wife and four children had been sound asleep. Silence and darkness returned to the room. The next day promised to be better. At least that was what he hoped for.

Chapter 2

THE DARKNESS did not last for long. Bright colors soon returned and fell into a spiral, bringing nothing but a haze. Different shades of blue, red, and green spun like snowflakes in the morning sun until everything stopped and the picture cleared again. It was a new scene. Where I last had seen the chubby bold man was now a flaming red orb that suddenly splashed onto a nearby mirrored wall and instantly transformed into the new shape of a human-like figure. Dazzling flames touched the ground and a tall silhouette emerged out of the light, radiating evil scent, oozing through its dark contour. My sword and round shield were all but melted, consumed by the intense heat of the glowing blaze. Unable to use them any longer, I cast them off, my skin ripped on the spots where my firm grip had once been. I was left only with a short dagger and a small pocket knife, still attached to my leather belt. As far as I knew I had little chance to survive the upcoming battle. The enemy seemed too great.

While I tried to find a way to protect myself, the creature rushed forth with an overwhelming speed. Soon its figure came into the light and showed me a gruesome vision of a beast, foul in form and nature. A large brown body was covered with tangled brown fur; its long black talons twisted and sharp. Its big dark teeth were swathed in gray foam, large jaws snapping at me like two hideous grates, unclean breath reeking with an unbearable stench of decay. And those bloodshot eyes—two circles of red, full of fury and hate. They were locked on me, measuring me, focusing on my every move. It was a monster like no other; a creation of someone's wicked imagination. Before it I was defenseless, standing with one knee down, calling to the mercy of the Spirit.

A strike of luck came unexpected. Just as the beast was ready to thrust its fangs into my chest, my friend Ike lashed out of a dark corner, his thin but muscular figure blocking the creature's path. Quickly raising his long ornamented bow, he loaded the first arrow, tipped with a sharp metal edge of pure silver. Then came the shot, quickly followed by another, and another. Elegant shafts flew promptly, piercing stuffy, sour air. The first few arrows hit the beast's hardened chest, but its fur was too thick for them to penetrate and they bounced off, dropping onto the marble floor. So the next missile hit the target's forehead, sinking deep into the brown flesh. Immediately the monster stopped and stumbled. Uttering a horrifying roar, it grabbed the arrow and snapped it, breaking the wooden shaft at the tip. Then it hurled the cracked dart back at my friend and charged at him, only to be stopped again by another arrow.

That time the skilled shot struck the beast in the neck. Though the dart itself broke on impact, it brought the creature to its knees. When the fiend tried to get up, two more darts bored into it. One pierced the beast's thigh and the other punctured its red eye, sending specks of thick purple blood onto the floor tiles. The creature twisted in agony. Its roar was deafening; its movement was of confusion and anger. One more time it tried to lift itself from the ground, but it was not fated to be. The final missile went straight through the creature's open maw, and a ray of bright white light came out of it. A vivid flash then lit the hall. When it receded the beast was gone. There were just Ike and me, left in the large dark chamber. We were alive.

I slowly rose to my feet, breathing hard and fast. Ike was at my side, still holding his bow as vanguard. His tranquil face hid a sign of deep concentration as if he were awaiting another attack. But no more monsters came. It was the end of our troubles. We won…but I did not feel safe…

"Mishuk, wake up! You had a nightmare again, did you not?" I heard Ric's voice in my ears.

"Ah? What?" I mumbled and opened my eyes, still thinking I was inside the grand black hall. Instead I was in a small room, which resembled nothing more than my own bedroom: no beasts or battles, just my older brother and a morning breeze that started to make me shiver.

There did my story begin, in the year 1215 of the Second Age of the New Epoch. Back then my name was Mishuk Loyde, and I was a young blood of sixteen, who lived in the small town of Villone in the southern province of Bois, in the eastern part of Normandia, which was one of three kingdoms in the northern part of the world, called Ethoria. There I had spent my toddler years and childhood, always under the tutelage of my parents, and in the company of two older brothers and two younger sisters, who all tried to make sure I went through life with at least some sense of discipline and order.

Back in my room, I remained in bed, my eyes focused on my brother, who sat next to me on a small wooden chair pushed against an open window. I stared at him for a while, then slowly rose up.

"You were screaming in your sleep again," said Ric. "It is the third time this week. What is going on with you? I am really starting to worry, little brother."

"I had a bad dream again. You know, the one where Ike and I fight an ugly thing inside an abandoned tower. Only this time it was a little different."

"How different?" My brother's eyes narrowed.

"More real, I guess," I replied after some thought.

It was the truth. My nightmares were changing. I had started seeing unusual dreams some months back. I did not know why the odd visions came to me or what they meant. All I knew was they were strange and getting more frequent with every passing week. At first I blamed the old tales Ike and I were so fond of. For several seasons the two of us had been sneaking into a local chapel and reciting books of long forgotten adventures. We stayed there for hours, enthralled with stories of the past. And so, I thought those accounts of old battles, journeys, and quests were the cause of my troubles. But soon enough I realized my visions had little to do with stories. In fact the nightmares were of a completely different nature. They did not feel like regular dreams. Instead they felt more like episodes from a real life, more existent, more precise—a bizarre combination of unknown places, people, and events, filled with dangers, beasts, and iniquity.

It had not been long before I realized something was amiss. My condition was far from normal, and I had no idea what caused it. All my attempts to find an answer failed miserably. Finally after a few more sleepless nights I decided to consult my most trusted friend, Ike Aunders, a fellow in whose company I had spent almost all of my years in Villone, taking on numerous adventures, which often got us in much trouble. When I finally confided my secret to him, a surprise awaited me, as Ike rebutted my tale with a story of his own. Using many words and jests, as he usually did, he informed me he had been bothered by the same weird experience. Nightmares hunted him in his sleep too, and the images he saw were the same as mine, also locked in some strange mystery neither of us could understand.

While we tried to learn something about our unusual torment, the strange visions continued. Amongst them, there was one particular recurring dream. In it Ike and I were transported to a deserted street of some unknown murky city, a foreign place, cold and treacherous. The dream started when we walked down a wide dirt lane through large stone opened gates, to a massive tower made of unusual rock. Its black surface was smooth and flawless—no windows, no lights, no ramparts, just polished walls that stretched high into the sky, its top hidden in a mantle of thick gray clouds. At the bottom of the structure was a single iron door left wide-open and unattended.

Unaware of what lay ahead, Ike and I went straight through the tall black archway and into an ample passageway, which then took us deep into the heart of the tower. Where the corridor came to an end, another door awaited us. Great in size, it was made of black iron, its frame cast out of silver bars, trimmed at the edges with lines of gold. Despite its bulkiness, the door gave in easily, moving inward after a light push and revealing a view of a grand dark hall.

Indeed it was a sight to see. Made almost entirely out of black marble, the hall stretched for several hundred cubits in all directions. Its tiled floor was laid with mosaics of grotesque creatures; its ornamented cathedral ceiling was very high and supported by large square columns. In the very center, above our heads, surrounded by two rows of wide round mirrored pillars, an opening was cut. Round in shape, it was very large and displayed a view of a gray sky that offered little light, except for a single dull white streak along the lines of the glossy floor. Burned torches were left forgotten everywhere, and at the far end of the hall, covered in darkness, stood a massive old grate, a toothless mouth of some unknown beast. The layout alone made me very uncomfortable, and the silence that rested there was even more frightening. All for good reason, because a moment after our arrival, a glowing orb appeared in the ceiling's opening and rushed to the ground. Halfway down it slammed into one of the mirrored pillars and transformed into a flash, out of which appeared the foul monster. Then came the brutal fight, and after it a rude awakening.

Although the vision had the same plot, its details became more precise every time I saw it. It was not long until Ike and I started to wonder if the pictures we had been seeing were trying to tell us something. Perhaps it was a warning or a message of some sort, but we did not get it, not once. Of course there were other less horrid visions that bothered us too. Some told a story of journeys Ike and I took to foreign lands, others showed us interacting with strange folks, some human and some of unknown alien races, but always it was Ike and I, together. All that changed though when one night we were unexpectedly joined by two other characters, our good friends, Rob Ard and Ark Aclendo.

With their advent, the visions became even more comprehensive, our feats more genuine and vibrant. The four of us were then a group, a band of travelers on some unknown, lengthy journey. In real life though, Rob and Ark knew nothing of our secret. But one day Ike and I decided that we could not conceal our tribulations any longer. After much thought we invited the two to a local pond that lay just outside the town and told them everything. Our revelation did not startle our friends. Quite the opposite, actually, for they knew exactly what we were talking about—strange visions troubled them too. Although they had witnessed only some of the visions Ike and I had, the fact remained—it was the same situation, and now there were four of us, who shared these mysterious conditions, connected by a conundrum, which persisted to engulf us. The day when Ric brought me back from my restless sleep, the reality of the dream was particularly strong. My mind was battered and my senses dulled. Slowly I tried to come out of the daze, and once I did, I realized that I had slept far too long. It was almost ten and I had to get out of bed, before my dear parents caught me idling.

"Hey, Ric." I called to my brother, trying to beat my dreadful morning mood. "Where is Mother? Were you not supposed to be helping her this morning?" I rolled to one side and lifted myself up so that I could see the front gates of our house out of the window.

"I was, but as I was waiting for her outside, I heard you scream. So I came up to check on you." Ric smiled and rubbed his hands. It was a bit chilly that morning, and a light breeze streamed into the room and made the temperature drop.

"Sure enough, when I got to your room I found you rolling and shaking like a little baby." Ric laughed and gave me a light shove. I wanted to growl in protest of such a resemblance, but an unexpected yawn came over me. My jaws pushed apart, and a sudden sharp pain rushed across my face. My mouth opened too much, and I quickly grabbed my chin, rubbing it until the tension eased. When the hurting receded enough for me to speak again, I resumed. "Sorry about dragging you up here. I hope it was not too much trouble for you."

"Nah, do not worry about it." Ric waved his hand. "So, another bad dream?" He was quick to follow with a question.

"Yeah. I just do not know what to think of it anymore."

"How about a glass of cold water to clear your mind? I brought two buckets from the well just half an hour ago."

Ric's offer sounded tempting, but I suddenly felt too lazy to get up. As if reading my thoughts Ric waved his hand again. "Do not worry; I picked up some on the way here." He then pulled out a large clay jar from under the chair and poured a glass of crystal clear water, spilling over the edges in abundance. He let the water drip to the floor and then gave me the glass, which I downed in one sip. The refreshment was lovely, and made the heavy daze leave my head completely. My mind cleared, and I could think again.

"Why do you think you see these dreams?" Ric's inquiries continued.

"I do not know. Perhaps it has to do with a sickness of some kind, or magic, or…"

"Magic?" Ric interrupted me. His tone changed from concern to surprise. "I thought magic was dead."

"Maybe it is, or maybe it is not."

"But everyone says that it does exists no more. People say tales about magic are for little children and crazy old men."

"They sure do, but what if they are all wrong? What if magic does really exist? Personally I think it is alive. Remember those stories about Magnicia, before it was destroyed by the war in the middle of the Second Age? Those men, who lived there—they were wizards, real wizards, and not like the ones you see at fairs and tourneys. Back then there were a lot of wizards, and they all used magic. What if some of them survived the war? Many times already I have heard passing folks and rovers, who stop at the local inns, talk about wizards, who live amidst Magnician ruins. And I think it is true."

"I sure hope you are right, little brother. I would give anything to see real magic," Ric said slowly.

"If magic does exist, I bet you we will see it one day," I agreed. "I really think we will—" I wanted to say something else, but was cut short by a loud noise from outside. First came a squeaking of the front door and then two voices, which belonged to my other brother, Ave, and Mother. They had to be standing directly below us, because I could hear their every word.

"Where is he?" Mother sounded angry. "I told that half-witted brother of yours to wait for me right here in the yard. Sure enough he disappears the moment I turn way. Where is that boy? Ric! I swear my patience will run out one day, and then…watch out…it will not be pretty."

"We should check the barn," I heard Ave answer.

"Barn? What would he be doing in the barn? That boy!" Mother raised her voice some more so everyone could hear her. "If he is there, I do not know what I will do to him."

"Do not worry, Mother, I will find him. Just give me a moment," Ave replied and set out on a search for the missing sibling. His footsteps soon faded around the corner. Mother went somewhere too, talking to herself as she walked.

When her voice was gone, Ric peered out of the window, quickly drawing back, saying, "I think I should get downstairs. Mother and I were supposed to go to the market today. I promised to help her carry some of the baskets." Without any more words, Ric jumped and leapt out of the room, leaving me alone.

After lingering in my bed a little longer, I got up and started to put on my clothes, but then realized that with Mother gone I had at least another hour or so to waste. So instead of following my brother to the yard, I lay back again and stretched my limbs, preparing for another day of useless chores, which my parents were sure to entrust me with as usual.

When I finally decided to get up for good it was almost noon. The fresh air got warmer and streamed in and out of the room, bringing the pleasant scent of awakened nature. Gathering all my will, I left the comfort of my bed and made a few short steps to the window, where a glamorous view of the clear sky grasped my attention. I could have stayed there for hours, but the bright sunlight hurt my eyes and I turned away, switching my glance to my room, which was small but comfortable. A heavy oak desk and three stools stood near my single bed; next to them, pushed against the wall, were two sets of shelves, made of fine polished pine. Further away, across the room, was a small fireplace, and near it was a door, welded from a set of black iron bars, which held several wide treated boards of brown wood. And in the center, covering yellow parquet stretched a plain-looking woolen carpet of brown color, which, though not too attractive, was quite warm and soft.

After my latest nightmare I felt jaded, so I stood still for a while, my back to the window. Then I fixed my clothes—blue tunic, green trousers, and leather sandals—and headed for the door. But as I was about to open it, I heard my father's voice from the hallway.

"Mishuk, are you there?" he asked with an irritated voice. Somehow I had a feeling I was in trouble. Sure enough, before I could utter a reply the door opened, and my father stormed in, his large figure blocking in the entrance.

It was unusual to see my father come to my room. There had to be something very wrong for him to do so. What? I was going to find out.

"Are you forgetting something?" were Father's first words as he greeted me with a chilly glance that pierced me from under his thick dark brown brows.

Right away I tried to recall what I had to do that day or the day before, but nothing came to me. My mind was blank, and with no answers I resorted to the next best plan, which was to keep quiet and listen.

"I told you last night that I was going away on a trip to the capital. I told you to prepare my horses, did I not? I have just stopped at the stables and guess what? The horses are not ready. Not only that, there is so much litter in there that I could not even see the horses. Can you tell me why?" He raised one eyebrow and tapped a finger on the side of his vest.

I knew I had to say something. "Oh, the stables. I was just thinking about starting them," I said, pushing the words slowly out of me.

"Well, it is past noon and I do not see you anywhere near the horses."

"You will," I replied quickly and slipped out of the room.

"I better," I heard Father's voice, but it died out as I ran down the stairs and into the yard.

Stupid stables. I cleaned them almost every day, spending hours moving heaps of animal waste out of there. That day was no exception. Armed with a shovel and two buckets I rolled up my sleeves and marched inside, covering my nose with a cloth that barely helped me fight the overwhelming odor. Throughout my labor I heard my sisters, Agie and Ulie, giggling at me; Ric laughed too as he passed by, and even Ave, who was as serious as Father, dropped a quick smile when he noticed me scooping the muck with my hands. To see Ave smile was unusual, considering that he rarely smiled in the last season. His mind was preoccupied with upcoming trials for a spot at the provincial academy of woods and crafts, which he had been hoping to attend.

Founded by the first of the Dukes of Bois, the woods and crafts academy of Lorus was one of the best wood-crafting schools in the entire kingdom. Very hard to get into, it gave its students the best education there was, yielding considerable prestige for the graduates, providing them with very lucrative jobs throughout the entire Northern Ethoria. Since the academy was maintained solely from the Duke's treasury, its doors were also opened to the commoners, regardless of their social status and family's wealth. To be accepted though, one had to go through a set of two trials. As the school allowed only one try, the trials were considered to be the hardest in Normandia and almost impossible to pass.

During the first trial the applicants had to duplicate an item given to them by judges. To pass, they had to complete the work within a certain period of time, and a very short period of time at that. Those who were successful went on to the second trial, where they had to finish an already started piece. Again there was a time limit, but also an element of improvisation. Needless to say, only very few ever succeeded in finishing the second trial, making them the ones admitted to the academy, where throughout the next five years they could master the art of woods and crafts. Upon graduation, each student received an official mark of a craftsman, which allowed him to open his own shop.

In prospect of a good job Ave wanted to take his chances with the trials, and to make sure that he passed them he had spent several seasons carving, smoothing, and refurbishing all kinds of wood. His hard work paid off, as gradually he turned himself into a skilled apprentice-carpenter, gaining the respect of his master and fellow trainees. Word of his talent spread all around neighboring towns, and many folks came to Villone to ask for Ave's services.

As for me, my predestination laid elsewhere and involved the stench and dirt of our family's barn, which I grew to despise. Time spent there always went slow, and that day was no exception. Even so, some hours later the stables were finally cleaned, the horses fed, donkeys rinsed with fresh water, and I was free to leave the house and meet up with my friends, who were waiting for me in the park. After washing off all the grime, I changed clothes and headed for the park.

By the front gates I saw my father making last arrangements before another of his trips, which he often said were full of adventure and suspense. After each journey he told us tales and rumors that he had picked up along the way—accounts of distant lands, magnificent cities, and strange peoples. It all sounded very interesting and captivating, and I always hoped that one day he would take me along. But he never did. Instead he sometimes took Ave, and that morning I saw my brother working on the caravan too. Right away I realized why Ave was in such a good mood—he was going with my father to the capital. It was not fair. Ave had already gone four times these past three years, and I had not gone once, not once. Suddenly I felt jealous of my brother; I was also mad at Father, so angry I did not want to talk to either of them. So leaving them to their preparations, I yelled my farewells and ran off to the park. When I returned a little after dusk, the caravan was gone.

Chapter 3

IT WAS a silent night. The sky was dark, but clear, no clouds, just a bright moon and countless stars. Beneath, a wispy cool breeze moved through a dozen silhouettes huddled around a campfire, set amidst a small clearing and surrounded from all sides by thick old woods. The men had just finished their supper and were about to retire to their grass-made beds, when a sudden loud snap of a broken tree-branch came crashing from the shadows of the forest. There was almost no time to think. The campers jumped to their feet and grabbed whatever weapons they could find. Forming a tight circle they stared at the dark around them. Their weapons were ready to repel any attack, but clubs and shovels and short swords were useless against a stream of metal tips that poured from all sides, small metal blades, reflecting sparks of bouncing fire. One after another arrows hissed cross the clearing and struck the defenders, sending a few of them to ground, some dead, some dying.

Everything was over before a fight even began. Several campers were dead, and the rest were standing by the fire, their eyes full of fear and confusion. Surrounded on all sides the few remaining defenders prepared for another attack from enemies they could not even see. But no more arrows came. An uneasy silence settled over the clearing, broken a moment later by another loud snap. The noise came from afar and grew louder, until it was sounding from just a few cubits away. The defenders stressed their eyes to see through the dark veil of the night, their ranks tautened. For a while they saw nothing, but then noticed several vague shapes appear out of the shadows and move slowly toward them. A dozen strange figures surrounded the group and halted. The wordless standoff lasted for sometime until one of the figures stepped forth and walked into the light of the fire. The silhouette was a tall man, dressed all in black; a long silk cape flowed slowly behind him. There was something odd about his perturbed shape; only nobody could say quite exactly what, because the man's true features remained hidden from the light, shielded by his

16

cape, his scarf, and a large hood. The man stood at the edge of the lit circle, then crossed his hands and strode further toward the defenders. His moves radiated a disturbing aura, which made the defenders shiver. The common men were scared.

"I must apologize for such an unexpected visit, gentlemen." The dark stranger spoke in a deep soft voice, calm and defiant. "Excuse us for such a rude introduction. I am short on time and cannot waste any of it on useless overtures. I hope you understand." The man paused; his gray eyes, fixed on the victims, were the only detail of his face uncovered by the scarf.

"What do you want from us?" asked one of the defenders, an older gentleman, his head thick with brown hair. He raised his sword and pointed it toward the dark silhouette. "If you intend to rob us, you will have to go throw my sharp blade, and I can promise you we will not give up that easy."

"Ah, of course, the little game of ambush. How could I have forgotten? Oh well, let's play it then." The dark man chuckled and continued. "No, I am not here to rob you. Your goods are of no interest to me. I am here to meet with two gentlemen, who have an urgent appointment with my employer."

"Then you have come to a wrong place!" yelled another defender, a short stocky man. "Nobody here has any appointments with anyone."

"Beg to differ, but I think that I am right where I am supposed to be and those two gentlemen are standing right in front of me. But let us not be so general. I am looking for Brune and Ave Loyde. Unless my instincts are completely wrong, both of you are present here...." The stranger sighed and locked his gloved hands on his chest. After studying the defenders a little longer he added, "I will make it very simple for you all. If Brune and Ave step out and surrender, the rest of you can go. So what do you say?"

There came no answer. None of the defenders moved, and the small clearing remained silent. The tall dark figure waited patiently for a while, but when nothing happened, resumed. "Since I consider myself a man of reason, I will give you another chance and will invite Brune and Ave to identify themselves. Oh, if you do not, my men will start killing, one at a time. I know it sounds terrible, but you leave me no choice."

The pause that followed was brief this time. When the dark stranger was about to give an order to the other attackers, the same older defender stepped out of the circle and declared, glancing straight at his opponent. "If you are looking for Brune Loyde, you have found him. I am that man. Now, what do you intend to do with me?"

"I am not sure that you are in a position to ask any questions. Yet I will satisfy your inquiry, but only after I have gotten to meet your son. Ave, come out." The man grinned, his eyes sparking with an uneasy glow. "Huh. Perhaps you may be dead?" The stranger noted, when no one answered. "I hope not. My men tried to be very careful with their arrows. It is a shame if one of their darts hit you by mistake. Why do we not check?"

The stranger lifted his right hand and two of the attackers ran up and examined the bodies of the fallen defenders, scattered around the fire. After inspecting the last corpse, one of the men, also dressed in black, rose up and yelled, "No young bloods here!"

"Oh. Good, I guess this solves our little problem. Now, Ave, I suggest you join your father, or...." The dark stranger was about to move his hand again, when a young man with blonde hair lowered his weapon and walked up to join the older defender, keeping his eyes on the foe. "I am Ave," he said firmly.

"How wonderful. This is much better. With this task completed, we must depart. The two of you will have to travel with me. I know that you might have some other plans, but I am afraid you have no choice, unless, of course, you want to die in this miserable place. My advice to you is not to resist. Give up your weapons, and I promise to let the rest of your men go. I think it is a fair deal."

The rest of the defenders stared at each other in dismay. Fear grew in their eyes. The enemy was all around them and they were outnumbered at least three to one. It would have been an unfair fight, a sure death. No words were spoken though, just sighs and heavy breathing. Brune thought short and released the sword, dropping it at the stranger's feet. Ave followed, so did the others. With all the weapon on the ground, more attackers appeared from the shadows and quickly crossed the glade, seizing the trembling defenders. As hands of his comrades were being tied, Brune looked at the stranger. "I expect you to be a man of your word. We have surrendered to you. Now it is your turn to fulfill your part of the bargain."

"Oh, yes, which one?" The dark figure asked. His eyes narrowed and it was apparent that he was smiling. "Ah, yes, to let your men go, and so I shall." He turned and addressed the other captives. "Brune and Ave will travel with us. The rest of you are free to go, just as I have promised."

A sound of relief rolled through the defenders' shattered ranks. The restraints were removed and they were allowed to go. But as the men started walking toward the woods, a wicked giggle halted them. The dark stranger whistled and said: "There is only one thing that I have forgotten to mention. I cannot leave any witnesses behind. Sorry, lads, I have my orders." He sighed loudly and commanded, "Kill these poor souls. We do not need them anymore."

Before the words of the order died, the first of the prisoners fell onto the ground, cut down by a hail of arrows. The victims did not even have a chance to run, their cries for help incised by sharp metal needles. In a trice Brune and Ave were the only survivors; the others from the caravan were dead, their bodies carried away by the killers.

Soon after, everything became quiet again. The grass clearing was empty—no camp, no fire, no human.

This picture of a mute gale terrified me, because it was my father and Ave, who I had seen being taken away by those strange black-clothed men. I wanted to help them, but I could not. Suddenly the images dispersed, and I jumped up, calling to them, but everyone was gone. I was no longer amidst the clearing, but in my room. Drops of sweat covered my face; my breathing was fast, and my hands shaking. I gulped some water, but it did not help. I was still trembling from the nightmare. Slowly I looked out the window. Villone was quiet—it was yet too early for it to awake.

Chapter 4

ALMOST A month had passed since my father's caravan had left Villone on a journey to the provincial capital of Bois and after it, to the nearby province of Chantue, a usual route, which Father traveled several times each year. On the average a round trip like that took up no more than two weeks, and rarely did my father spend more than three weeks before coming back home. This time, though, his absence was longer than usual, and there was still no news of him.

Since the last war, which had ended almost forty years ago, roads within Normandia were safe for traveling. Certainly, there were troubles that lonely rovers could encounter during their journeys through the wilderness of the realm—loose bands of thugs and robbers, wolves, and other wild beasts—but those were isolated incidents quickly handled by the local lords. My father had little to fear. He was an experienced merchant, who had been traveling for years and knew every route like no one else. Besides, he hired guards to escort his caravan, and with a dozen men equipped with swords and clubs, he had little to be concerned about. Why he was late for his homecoming I did not know, and it worried me. Ever after the strange dream, where I had seen Father and Ave being taken prisoners by some strangers, I found myself thinking more and more about troubles they might had encountered while away. I hated myself for such dark thoughts, but could do nothing to avoid them. The harder I tried to get away from the gloomy considerations, the faster they found their way back into my mind, pestering me day after day.

My good conviction of Father's soon return began to weaken even further, when I noticed that despite absence of good reason, scores of Normandian knights began to frequent our town. Riding alone or in groups, they galloped through the dusty streets of Villone, displaying their heavy steel-plated armor, decorated with pictures and trimmed with gold and silver. Always mounted on large barded warhorses, clothed in long thick drapes, all lords flew under elegant banners and were followed by clusters of devoted squires and servants, whose many numbers made up lengthy processions full of colors, noise, and bustle.

Although such pageants were common for capitals and big cities, to see so many of the highborn Normandians in the vicinity of Villone was very unusual. Since most of the knights lived their lives consumed with wars, tournaments and lavish festivals, they rarely visited small towns like Villone, where nothing but a few fairs and summer dances ever happened. Several weeks earlier the noble vivid poise would have sent me running into the streets to gasp at their marvelous parades, but with Father and Ave still missing, the pictures of the lords left me much more troubled. There had to be something very important or something very wrong in our province for all those proud men of steel and honor to venture so far south into the pastured lands of Villone. Myself, I had a feeling that something was indeed amiss. What—I did not know, nor did I want to.

The evening was closing. Trying to battle my sour mood, I stood by the window of my room, watching the red disk of the spring sun slowly vanish beyond low grassy hills. Soon its last rays sneaked away and darker skies crept from the distant east, letting the first bright stars form elegant lines of constellations, sending soft greenish light onto the shingled rooftops of the still busy town. Consumed with thoughts of my father's caravan I turned to leave my room, but a loud knock made me stop. I did not answer, but the door opened revealing Ark, Ike, and Rob, crowding the entryway.

Unlike me they were in a much better mood. Joking and laughing, they stumbled inside, taking their favorite places. Ike climbed onto the nightstand under the window; Ark took a small chair next to the desk, and Rob sat in an old rocking armchair by the fireplace, already burning with a few large logs of dried pine. While Rob and Ike continued to talk to each other, Ark stretched his legs and turned to me. "So what do you think about our very last dream?" He smiled and then asked everyone, "I assume we all had the same dream again, did we not?"

Rob and Ike became quiet and nodded.

"If you are talking about a large ugly thing that tried to eat me last night, then yes I did," noted Ike and sipped from a wooden mug, making a long chuckling sound.

The dream that my friend described was yet another vision, the scene of a battle with a horrific creature. The beast was hideous at best, as it resembled a cruel mixture of a wild wolf and a human being. If it stood, the creature would top three cubits, long greasy strings of black fur covering most of its grotesque body. Armed with clawed hands and a menacing set of yellow sharp teeth, the monster leapt out of the trees that surrounded a narrow path and charged our company.

Giving out a raging roar, the fiend scurried forth, springing over fallen trunks of once towering trees. We drew our weapons and moved back, carefully, so as not to fall onto a slippery rough terrain. Our retreat seemed to enthuse the beast even more. As it sped up, its heavy breathing exhumed puffs of thick white steam. Watching the ugly figure grow before us, I prepared myself for the battle. My grip tightened and my feet dug deeper into the wet soil. Ike was to my left, and Rob to my right. Some distance away Ark stood still, but then started to chant something in a low deep voice. His humming got louder, and suddenly he threw his hands up, moving them in a circular motion. Once his fingers came together, a small blue sphere appeared in the air. For a moment the orb stayed suspended, moving up and down, but then disappeared, letting the darkness reclaim the space around us. By then the beast was upon us. Teeth snapping, its claws ripped through the ground, sending lumps of mire, flying over our heads.

With almost no time to spare, I jumped forward, charging the enemy full force. Rob and Ike followed promptly, swinging swords straight from the shoulder. Rob was the first to land a blow. His sword came down like lighting and sank deep into the creature's flesh. The beast gave out an agonizing scream and snapped its huge wide jaws, but missed. In turn its side became exposed and I was quick to thrust my weapon there. The fiend jerked back and stumbled only to find Ike at the other side. My friend's slashing attack penetrated the creature's thick fur coat and left a deep gash in its right thigh. Our attacks hurt the beast; yet it showed little sign of fear. Pain seemed to stir up its rage further, and it spun around to launch another attack.

At that time, Ark, who continued to chant something, raised his hands again and produced another blue sphere. The glowing ball hung in the air for a moment and then started to float away from Ark's fingers. It moved slowly but, past several cubits, suddenly dashed forth and flew across the lane, slamming into the creature's chest. A flash of bright blue light dazzled me, and when I could see again, I found monster's breathless body on the ground. The foul thing was dead.

Afterwards, Rob, Ike, and I stared blindly at the corpse and at Ark. We were shocked. Ark had used some incredible force, a kind of a mysterious power. It had to be…Magic.

"It all seemed so real," said Ark as he studied his hands with a puzzled look. "Only I have no idea, how I made that blue ball appear in my hands. Back in the dream I knew exactly what I was doing. I knew the words, the songs, the gestures. But, once I woke up I could not remember a thing." Ark put his palms together. "Can you believe it? Not a single thing." He thought for a moment, and then added, "I must agree with Mishuk. The dreams do seem to have a meaning of some sort."

"Yes, yes," joined Ike, "I sensed it too. Only I cannot figure out what it is."

"But if the dreams are telling us a story, what is it about? What is its purpose?" I asked my friends.

"Personally, I do not know," replied Rob, rocking back and forth in his chair. "Maybe we will find it out soon enough."

"But how?" Ike voiced the question. "We seem to be unable to learn anything about the visions."

"It is not entirely true, Ike," noted Ark, "We know that they come to the four of us. We also know that they are not of a normal nature. Personally I sense that there is something much more complicated to our dreams than simple nightmares. I have heard of stories that people tell about the Lake of Wonders. They say that if at full moon you drink its water and then sleep on its shores you will see strange apparitions, some of which can show the future."

"Do not be a fool, Ark," interrupted Ike. "I know tens of people who have gone to the Lake, and none of them have seen any visions. Those stories you hear are just that—stories."

Ark looked at Ike for a moment, and said, "Maybe there is another explanation; maybe it has something to do with magic."

"*Magic!*" The word sent Ike out of his seat. "Magic has been dead for hundreds of years. Have you not read about it in your little books?"

"Yes. I have learned much about magic from the books I have read," agreed Ark.

"Then you should have noticed that since the fall of Magnicia all magic has been lost," Ike stated firmly.

"Ignorance is the first sign of foolishness, my friend," parried Ark duly. "If you cannot see something, it does not mean that it is gone. Magic is alive. I am sure of it. Of course it is very rare these days, but it does exist. There have been many rumors of wizards who still live in Magnicia. Some folks even speak of secret schools of wizardry and magic somewhere in the Forest of the Souls."

"I am telling you, this is just silly talk, nothing more. You are not supposed to believe everything you hear. Like, this week, I have heard a tale about a dragon that lives in the mountains near the Lake of Azul. And what of that? Do you think I believed a word of it? NO! Just so, it is none other than a good legend."

"As they say, there is some truth to every story," insisted Ark.

"Do you have any proof? Anything that can tell me that magic is still here in Ethoria? I do not think so." Ike was starting to get angry, and his voice sounded very loud.

"No, I cannot produce any proof to you," said Ark. "But there are signs that support my theory. I, for one, think there are books, which you tend to ignore too often. As a matter of fact, I have just finished one very interesting piece. It is a copy of an old historical note, written by some sage about five hundred years ago, shortly before the first of the Wars of Towers, which destroyed the realm. It says there that in those days magic was as common as water we drink or air we breath or food we eat. It was everywhere, and many used it. Back then hundreds, no, thousands of wizards lived in Ethoria. Around shrines of radiance, they built their great cities and spell towers, where they perfected their skills and wisdom. All that was just a few hundred years ago. Of course, after the war, the knowledge of the magic lore has been lost, but it does not mean that magic itself has vanished. Do you really think that anything so ancient and so grand as powers of magic could have just evaporated because one small kingdom tumbled down? Such things can never happen. Magician cities did fall, but magic did not. Perhaps it is still there amongst the ruins."

"I hate to break it to you, but since the collapse of Magnicia, there has been no more magic. And Magnicia itself is a barren land cursed and abandoned. No one goes there, not to mention lives in that place."

"Even if magic is alive, how does it help us?" I asked next, tired of my friends' bickering.

Ark turned to me. "What the four of us are experiencing is not normal. No matter how hard we try to find any solution, we cannot explain anything. We have read through dozens of books, asked a thousand questions to everyone we know, from sages to clerics. No one seems to have any clue as to our ordeal. So maybe it is time to explore other possibilities, and one of these possibilities is the presence of magic. What if we have been affected by some enchantment?"

"You are sure right about one thing though. Our visions are not normal," noted Rob after listening to the discussion for a while. "I wonder if we are ever going to get used to them."

"How do you get used to something like that?" exclaimed Ike. "I am afraid to close my eyes at night. I do not want to get used to it, I want it to stop, and I will spare nothing to do so."

Ike's words had much truth to them. We all wanted for the visions to cease, though none of us knew how to put an end to them. For a while no one said anything. The four of us stared at each other, thinking of our own. Before we could resume though, a light tap on the door distracted us. The knock repeated several times, then the doorknob turned and Ric walked into the room, lowering his head as he passed through the entrance. Standing almost two cubits tall he glanced at us, unusually reserved. For the space of all the years I had known my brother, he had never been short of words, but that evening he was completely silent and grim. He greeted my friends with a brief nod and turned to me. Before he even began to speak I knew that something was wrong.

"What is going on, Ric?" I asked him. He did not answer, just turned and went back into the hallway. I followed, and then to the stairs, where halfway down he looked at me and said, "I do not know what it is. But it is not good." He did not say anything else.

Outside, near the opened front gates to our house, illuminated by dull lights of freshly lit torches, was a small crowd of locals. Amongst them I immediately spotted my two sisters, who stood timidly by the gatepost, tears rolling down their reddish cheeks, and further away I saw Mother near a large open wagon, holding onto the side of a wheel. The cart looked very familiar, and once closer I realized it belonged to Father. A glimpse of happiness overfilled my heart, and frantically I ran up to the gates, searching the crowd for Ave and Father. But even with so many torches lighting the street and the yard, I could not find them. Instead I noticed two horsemen, who stood near Mother, their heavily armored figures towering over her. Displaying an array of colors on their cloaks and large triangular shields, the two riders rested motionless in their saddles, mounted on big black stallions, dressed in thick barding typical only of Normandian warhorses. The two men were knights, their entourage, about ten men-at-arms and squires, lingering just on the street.

One of the lords was broad in the shoulders and wore a red cloth over his steel suit. On his right arm, thrown back, hung a long fur cape, which came down to shining stirrups, almost concealing a well-decorated sheath of a great sword. His helm, shaped like a wolf's head, with metal jaws as visor, was opened and revealed a rough gloomy face. At once I recognized the man as Sire Rone of Sirone, the faithful Lord of Normandia, and a sworn man of the Duke of Bois. His domain counted several villages and towns in the southern part of the province, including our hometown of Villone and all the lands that surrounded it.

The other knight was much younger, probably my age. He wore a uniform similar to Sire Rone's. His armor, made of typical Northern steel, was trimmed with golden chains and lines of colored gems, some blue, some red and yellow. The tunic thrown over it, was red and white and adorned with symbols of three racing wolves. At the lord's one side hung a kite shield and at the other, extending high into the air, rested a large black lance, a proof of power and glory, held by Normandian knighthood. And then the helm—crafted of polished steel and gold, it was round in shape and resembled a bull's head, with two large red stones as eyes, and black horns connected at the top with a golden sphere, locked between the tips. From the splendor of his attire and the youth of his face, I concluded that he was Sire Rone's elder son, young Lord Rollan of Sirone.

To see the two lords outside their keep at such a late hour was too strange indeed, and only meant one thing—bad news. Somehow I was convinced that the bad news had to do with Father and his caravan. My fears were correct. As I got up to Mother's side, I caught the start of Sire Rone's hope-breaking tale. His harsh words felt like razors, causing my heart to sink; the last remains of my decent mood shattered in an instance.

Under the clear evening sky, speaking in a low tone Sire Rone explained that Father's convoy had gone missing several days after its departure from Villone. When the convoy did not arrive to the provincial capital on time, its absence did not raise too much suspicion. Nobody, not even Father's partners, paid too much attention to the delay, thinking that the caravan made extra stops along the way. But when another week passed and there was still no sign of Father, people started to suspect something. Finally, after waiting a few more days, one of the partners sounded the alarm, notifying the local chief of guards about the disappearance.

At first the chief took little interest in the request. Only a week later did he finally decide to send out a patrol to look for the vanished convoy. The search party spent four days in the countryside looking for Father, but found nothing. It had been a while since an entire group had disappeared in the province, and so additional brigades were dispatched to broaden the search. After much questioning, chief's investigator established that Father's caravan had been seen only once since it had left Villone, and that was a day's worth of travel from the city near a small village of Lulione. After that there were no more sightings.

Assuming that some bandits had ambushed Father's party, several young Bois lords took on the task of finding the missing people. For some days they roamed the woods and fields of the province, but found no signs of the caravan. It was as if the entire group of a dozen men, some ten carts, horses, and loads of cargo had evaporated in thin air. Then a report came from one of the local taverns that some lonesome farmer had stumbled upon an abandoned wagon in the nearby woods. Too scared to examine the cart on his own, the peasant ran to the nearest village and told the innkeeper of his find. In his turn the owner sent a word to Sire Rone. Aware of the ongoing search, the lord relayed the message to the provincial capital, and himself rode out to investigate the rumor. Once at the village of Lulione he was led to the nearby forest, where under cover of thick leaves, his men found one of Father's carts. Right away the knight ordered to scout the surroundings for any signs of the convoy, those who accompanied it or ambushed it. But there was nothing. Sire Rone then concluded the search and escorted the lonely cart back to Villone, where now he stood, talking to Mother.

Such was the story, and once it was over, the two lords and the other men were gone, their farewells absorbed by the noise of the astounded crowd. While the view of the noblemen's steeled suits was taken by the evening haze, we remained still by Father's wagon. Everything was like a bad dream, one of the visions that disturbed my sleep. Suddenly images from my nightmare came back. Could it be true? Did I witness Father's kidnapping? Was it what had really happened to him and Ave? Torrents of infinite questions were rushing through my mind. My head was getting heavy, just like my heart overflowed with the feelings of grief, regret, and fear.

To ease the tension I closed my eyes and took a long deep breath. It did not help. My head was still spinning, my legs were giving way under me. To keep myself from falling I grabbed the side of the wagon and looked up to the sky. The distant green dots soothed my mind somewhat and slowly I regained my balance. Although the strength returned to me, I continued to hold onto the railing. Only when Mother asked me to help her shut the front gates, did I move. Quietly I pushed the large wooden doors to a close, leaving dozens of curious faces, and then followed everyone back to the house, where the whole family settled around a large dining table, waiting for Mother to say something. But she sat in silence, her eyes focused on the burning fireplace. Occasionally she sighed, frequently closing her eyes as if trying to find the right words for her sermon. At last she spoke, addressing us in her usual soft voice.

"All of you have heard the lord. Your father's caravan has gone missing. So far they do not know what has happened to it, and until they do we should not worry about it. Everything is going to be fine. As far as we know, your father has decided to change his route and instead of going to Bonneville, went to Chantue or Pullie. I am sure he has sent us a note. It has not just arrived yet. But mark my words, we will hear from him soon enough.

"In the meantime I do not want you to get upset over it. There is nothing wrong, and if I hear any of you say otherwise, I will be very disappointed. But most of all I do not want you to think that there will be any changes around the house. Rules and duties are the same as they have always been. Is this understood?"

Mother looked at us. We nodded.

"Good," she continued. Her voice sounded very sad. No matter how many times she told us that everything was fine, the reality remained—Father and Ave were gone, lost somewhere in Bois, maybe even kidnapped and taken to some unknown place. No words could ever change that. Cheerless, I glanced at Mother and saw she was looking straight at me.

"...And if anybody, I mean any of you, Mishuk, decides to do something stupid, like setting out on a search for the convoy—there will be severe consequences." Mother frowned, trying to make her words sound more decisive. It was unfair to single me out like this, even though I did tend to cause most of the troubles around the house. I wanted to protest, but suddenly my own thought halted me.

"Did she say a search?" I asked myself and quickly answered. "Of course she did. Oh, Spirit! How could I be so stupid? The dream! Now I know why I saw it. Father and Ave are indeed in danger, and I am to help them. I must try to persuade Sire Rone to resume the search, and if he refuses I should do it myself. Providence it is....But first I must tell Ike. Maybe he will join me."

My mind went on working frantically. Considering idea after idea, pondering plan after plan, I sat at the dining table until Mother let us go, and then hurried to my room, where, armed with a quill and a piece of paper, I began to write down a list of things I had to do before the start of my journey.

The very next morning, before the sun was up, I slipped from the house and sprinted to Ike's place, just two corners away. As I had suspected Ike was asleep. It took me a while to get him out of bed and to the window. When his sleepy face finally appeared in the opening, I shouted for him to come down. "Get over here. I must to tell you something."

"What do you want?" Ike muttered and rubbed his cheeks. He seemed unhappy about such an early awakening, and stared at me blindly, squinting his eyes away from the morning light.

"Do you know what time it is?...I do. It is too early. The only night I do not have any stupid visions, you wake me up at the crack of dawn." He yelled again, making an angry face. I did not know why, but the fury, which Ike tried to master, made him look comical, and I could not help laughing.

"Oh, you think it is funny, you idiot; I will show you what's funny," Ike exclaimed as he jumped out of his first floor window onto the street, ready to wrestle me to the ground. I dodged him quickly and raised my hands in front of me.

"Will you wait and listen for a moment?" I yelled. "I must talk to you. It is important."

"It better be or I will beat you senseless." Ike straightened up, breathing hard.

"Fine, just calm down." I sat down on the ground and asked, "Have you heard the news about my Father ?"

"No. Last night the three of us left your house right after you, through the back door. But what happened? Did he come back?"

"No. Sire Rone came, though, and brought one of Father's wagons. The lord then said that the convoy had gone missing and nobody in the province could find it."

"What? Your father? It cannot be. Please tell me all about it." Ike sat next to me. And I told him everything I had heard the evening before.

"They will continue looking for them, right?" asked Ike when I was through.

"I do not think so. Sire Rone said that they had quitted the search."

"They cannot do that. They must keep on looking."

"I know, but I do not think they will."

"Someone has to do it. Mishuk? Someone must find your father and Ave and all those other men."

"I know, Ike. I know…But there is more."

"Well, what are you waiting for? Tell me quick."

"Some time ago I had another dream. In that vision I was standing amidst some dark gale, watching as strangers ambushed Father's caravan. They took Father and Ave prisoners and killed the others. Ike, I saw them kill everyone— the hired guards, and old Tam, and little Ickis, and Ran. I did not think it was true, not until last night. Now I am afraid all I have seen
really happened."

Ike remained quiet for a moment, then scratched his head and uttered, "So, are we going to do anything about it?"

"As a matter of fact I have an idea of a sort." I looked at my friend and proceeded to describe the basics of my plan.

"This is…the best idea I have ever heard from you!" Ike exclaimed and jumped to his feet. "You and I on a quest to find your missing Father and Ave—and the caravan. It has been my dream since I was a kid." Ike was getting very excited, much more than me. In fact my friend did not just join me in my plan; he immediately became its most essential part, generating loads of ideas about equipment, supplies, and possible routes of escaping Villone. Before the morning was over the two of us were working hard to plot our journey. We had much to do and not much time to do it.

Chapter 5

A WEEK passed since the news of Father's disappearance, and my family was growing restless. Mother kept to herself and spent most of her time in the kitchen, attending to her daily duties. She tried to act as if nothing had happened, but in her eyes I saw much fear and concern. My sisters helped her as much they could, and when they got some free time, they spent it outside the house, on the bank of the pond, talking to each other and their friends. Their pretty faces were always grim, their giggles rare, and their glances full of sadness, the same sadness that filled Ric, who had become less loquacious since Sire Rone's visit. He spent much of his time alone, often taking long walks along the town streets, away from others, even me. But their behavior did not affront me, for I was busy, preparing for my trip.

Enthused by prospects of leaving Villone, my days went quickly. In the mornings Ike and I met near a local pub with the sound name of White Wolf. There we discussed new ideas of our plan, and once everything was devised, we were off to collect supplies—traveling gear, and equipment, some of which was hard to get. In the evenings we met up again to share our finds, and talk some more about our journey. Soon enough, after much activity, we gathered everything we needed, and with our travel bags packed, were prepared to leave Villone. There was only one thing left for us to do—that was to talk to Rob and Ark, who we had decided to invite along.

The morning before our departure from Villone, we met our friends near the White Wolf Inn to disclose our intentions.

"There is something very important we want to tell you," I said to Rob and Ark, when they settled next to me on a pile of freshly cut logs. "It is an offer and..."

"Let me guess, you two have decided to go off in search of your caravan. Am I right?" Ark interrupted me in his adamant tone, proving once again that he was one of the smartest people I'd ever met.

"How did you know? It was supposed to be a secret." steamed Ike, a hint of disappointment in his voice. "Mishuk! Did you tell them about our plan?" he looked angrily in my direction.

I shook my head in denial.

"Do not worry," Ark calmed Ike down. "Nobody told us anything. We figured it all out on our own. Do you think we have not noticed how the two of you have been acting lately? Those evening meetings in the park, huge backpacks you have been carrying around for no good reason, and of course, some petty thefts that have stricken our town in the past few days. While everyone blames a band of rovers for the stealing, I suspect that they are not the guilty ones. You see, there are only two individuals in all of Villone who could have any reason or skill to pocket two rusted swords, a blanket, and a handful of traveling gear, most of which was going to the rubbish anyway. Those individuals are you, and why would you want to take all of this stuff? The answer is simple, you are thinking about setting on a search for the missing convoy. Right?" Ark finished, smiling, satisfied with his insightful explanation.

"Almost," I answered. "First we want to talk to Sire Rone and ask him to resume the search. If he declines, then we will look for the convoy ourselves. At least this is the plan for now."

"Not a bad plan," noted Ark. Ike gave him a light nod and asked, "Does anyone else know about this?"

"No. Rob and I are the only ones," Ark replied, and placed his right hand over his heart. "I swear."

"Good, because we do not want anyone else to know." Ike breathed with relief and wanted to say something, when Ark cut him short. "By the way, our answer is yes."

"Yes? Yes to what?" probed Ike, trying to assume an innocent look.

"The answer to your next question. Rob and I will come with you," Ark clarified. "But we must put off the departure. We need some more time to prepare, besides we will want some real gear if we are to spend more than a few days in the wild."

"Sorry friends, but we are set to leave tomorrow," said Ike firmly. "If we wait any longer, someone will find out, and then we will never be able to leave, not me at least."

"Do not worry Ike. No one will learn about it. Rob and I will be ready soon enough." Ark sounded reassuring. Still Ike thought for a moment, then waved off his hand and stated, "All right, just a couple of days though." He looked at me, and I nodded in agreement, so the matter was resolved.

To make the final preparations go faster we divided our efforts. While Ike and I collected smaller things like leather flasks, a rope, two hunting knives, a fishing line with several hooks on it, and a bag of firestones, Ark gathered food, ale, and water, and Rob managed to get a decent sword, some maps, four pairs of woolen gloves, and traveler's cloaks, which we so desperately lacked. One week later we were finally ready to take our leave.

The night before the departure I could not sleep, thinking of the journey, waiting patiently for the morning light. When the first rays of the sun finally peered over the horizon I put on my bag and sneaked through the backdoor, quickly making my way to the deserted steps of the White Wolf Inn. Although I was the first to come, my friends arrived soon, and after a few brief words, we were off to the empty streets, heading steadily for the outer gates of the city. We did not run, yet kept a swift pace. The big leather backpacks pressed hard into our shoulders, and the dark green cloaks swayed in the light spring wind, revealing glimpses of crude steel blades. Composed and silent, we focused on the outline of the high wooden archway, distracted only once by a sudden squeak that came from an old abandoned house. In short we reached the last cottage at the edge of the town and stepped out through Villone's gates. There was nobody to take any notice of us, and our company of four young lads was quick to move down the road as fast as possible. The sight of the houses soon disappeared behind a crown of trees, and only boundless fields surrounded us. Our destination was Sirone, where we intended to seek an audience with Sire Rone.

Thus began the first day of our journey, Day One of the third week, of the first month of the Spring Season, in the year 1215 of the Second Age of the New Epoch, two weeks after Sire Rone's unexpected visit to our house, and more than a month since I had last seen Father and Ave.

Chapter 6

IKE AND I had been best friends ever since I could remember. A young fellow of sixteen, Ike had a sharp intellect and a pair of quick fists that made his living an easy task, and he enjoyed it, often taking on pursuits of fun roaming the streets of our hometown. The son of a local caretaker, Ike was a talented lad. Agile and fit, he enjoyed every kind of sport there was; he also liked music and had a taste for solving puzzles, some of which made even the wisest of the town folks rub their foreheads. And yet, despite all his skills, he struggled to decide on how to make his life.

Throughout his years he had imagined himself doing almost everything. At times he wanted to become a scholar, then a cleric, and a brother of the Order of the Spirit; after that he was to be a royal huntsman, a lonely ranger, and a wise councilor to the King himself. But none of those affections ever lasted for more than a couple of weeks, and before long Ike was pondering over a new craft or lore, to which he wished then to devote his manhood. In reality, Ike had no idea what he wanted from life and spent most of his time doing nothing. Eventually the tedium of his ways got to him, and driven by boredom, he began to assist his old man at the shop, soon finding himself absorbed by work there. The more time he spent at the shop, the more liking in his father's craft he acquired. And what started as a seasonal job, after a while became a full-time service, to which Ike devoted more and more of his time, helping his father, attending funerals and looking after the burial ground, located east of the town.

Yet, in spite of his busy timetable, Ike never lost his sense of adventure. His latest inspiration was one of a knighthood, which came to him after seeing the plated riders pass through Villone. Somehow Ike assured himself that it was his destiny to become one of the nobles. Although hard for a commoner to gain the title of knight, it was not an impossible task. There were three ways a common man could join the knightly ranks: one—through marriage to a noble family, another—by King's personal order, and the third—by serving as a squire. It was the last option that attracted Ike. Dreaming that one day he would become a true squire, and then a knight, he decided to begin training himself in the skill of sword fighting, which he thought necessary for any squire to possess. After trying to do it on his own, he then retained the services of an old retired soldier, who lived in a small hut on the outskirts of the town. Although the old man spent most of his time away from other folks, Ike persuaded the former warrior to teach him some basic moves with bladed weapons.

Keen on swords, and clubs, and bows, my friend tended to ignore his schooling completely. His urge toward history, recite, and scripture skimmed quickly, and that resulted in an unexpected visit of a local tutor to his house. Needless to say Ike's parents were not too pleased to hear that their son had been skipping lessons to practice sword fights; so afterwards Ike had to give up his pursuit of arms as books and quills became his daily weapons.

Even so, he did not abandon the training entirely. Stealing away into the woods, he went on practicing where no one could see him. When he got tired exercising alone, he recruited me as his sparring partner. I was excited to join my friend and once acquainted with the basics of sword handling, clashed my timber weapon with Ike's. It was fun, indeed. Frequently we amused our friends by running around and smacking each other with persistence and enjoyment. Feeling confident enough with sticks, we then switched to rusted iron bars, and then to half-broken swords, which Ike had borrowed from the old soldier. Eventually our efforts started to pay off. Our movements became smoother, and our grips tighter. Of course such progress gave us an irresistible urge to try ourselves against somebody else. For a couple of coppers we talked two other boys into sparring with us. The idea seemed fine at the time, but it turned ugly when one of our opponents got himself a bloody nose and ran home crying. Soon everyone in town, including my parents, knew about the accident. So after a long and painful conversation with Mother I had to promise that I would stay away from any sort of weapon for as long as I lived in her house. I swore to do that, but in secret continued to practice, hiding with Ike under the covers of fruit orchards, so plentiful in Villone.

The other persons who were sharing the road and the quest with me were Rob and Ark. Rob was the son of a small shopkeeper from the north side of the town. He was the youngest of five siblings, all boys, all tough competitors, who never gave up anything without a fight. For years Rob's life was one big stream of contests, which ranged from sports to fistfights. It was the constant rivalry within his household that eventually turned my friend into an unmatched contender. Anything he did was good. Not just good, but excellent. He jumped, ran, threw, and shot everything better than anyone else in Villone. Whatever physical skill there was to master, Rob did it, often putting little effort into it. At times I felt jealous of my friend's success. But as time passed, I got used to Rob's talents, and soon we became friends, very good friends indeed.

And then there was Ark, Grand Pa as we often called him for his striking wisdom and a thinning hair. He was a man of fascinating mind and character. Bestowed with the gift of acumen, natural to the elderly and shrewd, Ark, in his seventeen years, knew almost all about everything. If there was a question or a problem Ark had his own solution, which often gave him a chance to put most of us down with his surprising insight. But he never did. Polite and well mannered, he always accorded everybody much respect, thus making his company desirable and interesting.

Together, the four of us composed a distinctive and vibrant group, each bringing something distinctive to the medley. Best friends, we were at the start of our journey, the future of which was yet uncertain. After departing from Villone we took a course northeast, walking down a sandy path that winded through numerous gardens and growing green fields of Bois countryside. It was just high noon and our party—several leagues away from home. The sky was clear. The bright sun radiated the soothing warmth of an early spring season. Past a narrow patch of young trees, we reached a crossroad with a high pole in the middle, three of its arrows pointing in different directions. Although burned onto the wood, the letters were worn and hard to read. To make sure we had taken the right route, we decided to consult the map.

While the rest of us shared a flask of warm water, Rob studied the leather drawing, saying afterwards, "We should follow the smaller road until we come to another crossing. Then we will turn north and continue in that direction until nightfall. Not far from the second crossing there should be a small forest near the road. We can camp there."

"I thought the castle was just one day away from Villone," proclaimed Ike, disappointed that he had to wait another day to see Sire Rone's fortified keep.

"Yes, it takes only one day to get to Sirone if you have a horse," explained Rob, "But if you travel on foot it will take twice that much. Sadly we do not have any horses; that is why we will have to camp out tonight and get to the castle tomorrow."

"Fine. You do not have to treat me like a child," protested Ike, somewhat offended. "I was just asking. I have no problem camping out in the wild."

"Good, if no one else has any comments let's get back to our journey," concluded Rob, and he put the map away.

To resume our march, we took the road, marked by two wide brown ruts, evidence of some passing wagons. Looking at the tracks under my feet I could not but wonder if they belonged to Father's convoy. Familiar sadness returned to me, and I sighed deeply. The dark thoughts started to pester me again, and for a while I could do little to chase them away. Only when we reached the next intersection did my mind ease. By then the sun was already over the remote hills in the west, and evening colors came into the view. As Rob had suggested, at the second crossing we turned north and continued until a grove appeared in the distance. Slowly, the stretch of deep green got wider, and after some time, turned into a forest that almost came up to the road. High over our heads the moon made its nightly journey, and darkness was covering the countryside. Unable to see much, the four of us had to cease the advance and leave the path, moving toward the edge of the woods, where, past the first row of thick oaks, we found a small clearing, perfect for a camp.

Feeling a bit tired we dropped our heavy backpacks and sat down on the grassy floor, sparking a blithe chat, which was soon broken off by Ark, who made us all get up and gather firewood. After a large heap of it lay in the center, we settled around and watched Ark working his firestones. As small gray rocks produced a spray of tiny white sparks, recollections of hunting trips with Father came to me. Glimmers of the past filled my mind and I began to drift away with the pleasant thoughts. When my attention returned to the clearing, the fire was already alive, defusing a warm red glow around the camp.

"Well done," called Ike, as the flames stared to eat dry branches and leaves.

"Where did you learn how to do that?" I added.

"From one of the books," replied Ark, throwing more sticks into the fire.

"Ah, so when are we going to have our meal?" asked Ike, rubbing his hands.

"Patience, my friends, is a great virtue," said Ark courteously. "Give me some time and you will get your food."

"Whatever you say. Just hurry. I am starving." Ike rose to his feet and disappeared amongst the nearby trees for reasons known to him only. Meanwhile Ark started on a meal. Out of his bag appeared several rags with various foodstuffs. It was not much, but good enough for the occasion. A clay bottle of apple cider, four wooden plates, a large flask filled with water, some red onions, several slices of hearty wheat bread, and soft cream goat cheese. Ark arranged everything over a wide cloth, and strips of dried-up beef he threw into a small pot of boiling water, simmering the meat with some potatoes and onions. When the thin soup was ready, we started our supper.

"Hey, where is the real meat?" Ike exclaimed loudly. He had already returned from his short trip and was examining the food lying before him. "Do not tell me you forgot the meat. How are we supposed to survive in the wild without it?"

"Ike, stop complaining. There is plenty of food here," said Rob, filling his plate with the steaming soup.

"I do not know about you, but I think that dinner is the most important meal of the day," insisted Ike.

"Then start eating." Rob's voice acquired a note of annoyance.

"But, in every single story, adventurers have stews, and roasted boars, and rabbits," Ike mumbled, but began to fill his plate.

"I think you read too many stories," Rob commented. "Just remember that tales and real world differ a lot. We simply could not take too many things with us. It was a matter of lighter packs or better meals—"

"All right, all right. I get it; I will not utter another word," said Ike after a pause, realizing that his childish persistence was getting irksome to the rest of the company. "I just thought it would be nice to have a piece of cooked meat before we went to bed, that's all." He shrugged his shoulders and shoved a handful of crumbling cheese into his mouth.

Despite Ike's objections, the meal was savory and filling, and made us all tired. Finishing the last bits of the food, I began to feel drowsy and so stretched out on top of my cloak, thrown over a heap of pine branches. My friends settled around the fire too and talked. But I did not join them, turning away instead, and sinking into a pleasant drowsiness. Soon I only heard a playful fire cracking, and peaceful dreams came to me, dreams of home, Father, Ric, and Ave.

The next morning began with my friends' talking.

"Ark, what do you think?" I heard Rob's voice through my sleep.

"I think it is all very strange—the dreams, Mishuk's father gone, and us traveling to Sirone," replied Ark.

"Do you think our dreams meant to warn us about any of this?"

"I do not know. It is hard to say, the things the visions brought us were so odd."

Continuing to listen to my friends' conversation I slowly opened my eyes. The sun peered through a crown of leaves, throwing countless shadows on the grassy floor below, and I was lazing in a bower made of my own cloak, a heavy blanket, and branches, which gave my cradle the fresh scent of a forest. Ark and Rob sat a few cubits away.

"Hello, Rob; hello, Ark," I said, raising myself a little.

"Well hello there, sleepyhead. I see you have been enjoying your outdoors rest," replied Rob, smiling.

"We did not want to wake you up; you seemed to be very comfortable so we let you sleep," Ark added, then climbed to his feet and walked up to a big broken tree. There he ripped out a long dry bough and used it to shuffle left-over coals from the burnt campfire.

"Where is Ike?" I asked curiously, throwing a glance over the clearing that appeared much wider by daylight.

"Oh, he went to pick up some —" started Ark, but Rob interrupted him. "There he is."

I looked over my shoulder and immediately spotted the familiar figure that emerged out of the woods. In a cheerful mood, Ike walked across, jumping over low bumps and puddles, whistling. In his hands he held two small leafed cones, filled with something. Reaching us, he raised them and yelled, "Look what I found—Red Eyes." He then noticed me, sitting on the ground, awake and yawning. His face widened in a smile. "Hah, our friend is finally up." Ike quickly came over, sat down by my side, and extended his hand offering me his juicy finds.

Feeling hungry I took one of the cones and saw that it was in fact full of Red Eyes, tiny red berries, a little sour to the taste. Though in most parts of Normandia they came out at the end of springtime, in Bois these small fruits could be found as early as late winter season. One of the first treats of the year, they were always a great favorite amongst local folks, who flocked into nearby forests, armed with wicker baskets and traveler's sashes, hoping to collect as many of the dainty berries as possible. My friends and I were no exception, and with the promise of warm weather, I relished the little red fruits, chewing slowly so as to save the flavor. When I was done I passed the cone to Rob and Ark, who were also pleased to try Red Eyes.

Afterwards we gathered our belongings and left. Back on the path Rob checked the map again and then announced that we should be in Sirone before evening.

"Do you think visiting the castle is a good idea?" Ark asked me as our company headed down the main road. In truth I had been pondering over the same idea ever since we had left Villone. I knew that Father had supplied Sire Rone's castle with spices and wines. Once in a while he even took some per-sonal orders from the lord, especially when he was going to bigger markets in the neighboring provinces. Yet I was unsure that Sire Rone would remember Father, or care to assist me in my inquiries. After all, he was a lord and Father was but a trader. And I—I was a young commoner with no name or status. Still I had to try. Even if the knight refused to see me, I could ask someone from his garrison to help me with information, or, at the very least, get directions to the place where Father cart had been found.

"It is as good an idea as any," I replied. "It is the only idea I have." Nobody said anything. There was little to say.

Chapter 7

THE SPRING sun hung over thin clouds, filling the land below with bright colors and dry warm air that promised little rain. The wide dirt road continued to run north, presenting us with scenes identical to those of our hometown. Stretches of wheat fields, straw roofs of distant cottages, scents of early blossoms, and sounds of living countryside—everything was just like in Villone, and yet different—more real, more alive. At last we were on our own, away from the patronage of our parents, our nestled houses, our routine daily lives.

Set on getting to Sirone as quickly as possible, we kept a good pace. After some time, watching everything around me, I noticed a strange thing. The route we traveled was deserted, with us as its only guests. I remembered very well Father's stories about his trips, where Normandian roads were always filled with traders, carriages, and cargo. But for some reason the path from Villone to Sirone was empty, with no caravans to pass or people to meet. Instead of crowds of men and heaps of wagons, there were just the wind and rare gray rabbits that vanished into tall growing corn as soon as they spotted our presence. Why it was so I did not know and pondered on that question for some time. Meanwhile just as the sun began to take on a reddish tint, the first thin spurts of black smoke appeared in the distance, transforming then into larger shapes of shingled houses that seeded the landscape ahead. Around us the cultivated fields receded, too, and gave way to many smaller plots of gardens and orchards, which came up to the road from both sides, adding luscious green color to the whole picture.

Enthused by being just a few leagues away from our destination, we hastened our steps, and crossing a timber bridge thrown over a shallow ringing creek, came up to the edge of a small valley, where in the center rose a dominating silhouette of Sire Rone's castle. Guided by the high parapets of its four square towers we followed the path into the dale and up to a tall wooden arch, placed in the middle of a low fence. On it hung a large sign, which read,

"Sirone, Rim of Lios Hill. Est. 956 S.A.N.E." Bearing some resemblance to a city gate, the arch had no guards or cordons, and allowed our company—together with a few travelers, who had eventually joined us for the space of the last league—to stroll freely into the town, composed of two dozen small houses that crept near the base of a low, almost flat mound, with the lord's citadel at its top.

A small parish, Sirone sparked little interest from a passing folk. Yet it was not the municipality itself that attracted those who came there; it was the citadel, which made Sirone different from other neighboring communities of Sire Rone's domain. Stoutly built, it consisted of the keep itself and two rows of walls, the first of which was constructed entirely of tall wooden beams, planted deep into the rocky soil. Thick logs ran around the base of the hill and served as the first line of defense. Though not designed to be an absolute guard against a real enemy, in the absence of a moat, the picketed wall functioned as an obstacle that could delay a foe long enough for the defenders to scramble for safer ground inside the second barrier, which was made of large heavy stones, glued together with a dried mixture of clay and sand. Massive and wide it loped amongst four tall towers, and shielded the keep, providing much protection from all sides.

In the center of the southern side of each wall stood a gate. The first access was carved out of the logged barrier—just a single large wooden door that, in time of need, locked from inside using a giant beam. Then followed a one-track road, paved with flat white stones, that ran up to the second gate—a stone arch, equipped with two heavy steel-plated doors and a spiked grate, pulled up and down by three thick iron chains. Both passages were guarded by half a dozen soldiers, who stood leisurely observing the thin traffic below, most of which ran around the castle and to a small bazaar, located at the western part of Sirone. Although not sure if the cordons were free to pass, we headed there anyway, clearing through the town streets, which remained deserted and quiet.

By then the sun was already gone, and even though it was not yet dark, the soldiers started to light their torches, illuminating the area around the gates with a gentle yellow glow that cast small shadows onto the road. Prepared to be halted we slowed down, but to our surprise nobody said anything to us and we walked freely through the opened doors, past several standing guards, who took no interest in our company, preoccupied with their own conversation. At the top of the slope another group of soldiers met us. But they did not seem to care about our presence either, and throwing only a few dull glances, let us march straight into the inner grounds of the castle, filled with dust and white puffs of steam, which came down from several long iron pipes located at the far end of the court.

Although the yard was at least two hundred cubits wide, it looked small as it was packed with many different structures, spreading along the stone wall. To the right of us stood a row of wooden one-storied buildings, five or six of them in all, and before them was an open space, surrounded by a tall wicker fence, which encompassed an array of horses. Graceful animals walked calmly along the high hurdle, chewing on fresh grass fetched to them by a stable boy. At the front of the first house hung a wooden plaque, which said, "Lord's Stables. Keep out." A similar sign—"Lord's Barracks. Do Not Enter"—was nailed to a building on the left, which stretched for at least a hundred cubits along the inner wall, eventually turning into a two-storied, wooden tower-house. Next to it, directly before us, stood the keep itself. Made entirely out of large boulders, the structure was Sire Rone's personal fort, some fifty cubits wide and twenty cubits tall, lower only to the guard towers that surrounded it. At the top, its flat stone roof was adorned with six turrets and two metal standards that carried colorful banners of Sire Rone's house—a leaping wolf in the rays of the descending sun. Beneath the flags, running down the keep's smooth walls, which showed little sign of ageing, were rows of narrow slots, and further down, above a wide stairwell of white and red granite, stood a large door of heavy iron, decorated with imprints of warriors, dressed in ancient Normandian armor. It was the door we walked to.

Although we did not notice any guards around the keep, a loud yell halted us when we reached the stairs. A young soldier, armed with a long sword, appeared from the corner and hurried toward us, his shining chain mail ringing stridently as he walked.

"Stop where you are." The guard repeated his command from a few cubits away. "This is Sire Rone's private residence. No one is allowed to go in without permission."

The young guard came to the stairs and blocked our path with his chest. "Who are you? And what is your business here?" He asked, studying us thoroughly with his large brown eyes.

"My name is Mishuk Loyde, the youngest son of Brune Loyde, and these are my companions. We have come from the southern city of Villone to seek an audience with our lord and protector, Sire Rone of Sirone," I replied quickly, trying to give my words an official tone.

"What is the reason for you to meet with his Lordship?" asked the guard, unimpressed by my introduction.

"Father's convoy disappeared somewhere between Villone and Bonneville over a month ago. Sire Rone helped with the search effort, and then conveyed the news to my family. Unfortunately as of today the search for Father and his caravan has been suspended, and nobody knows where they are. I was hoping to talk to Sire Rone about it, maybe ask some questions, if he allows," I answered.

"Have you submitted your request to one of the captains of the guard?" the soldier asked next.

"No, Sire, we have never been to the castle before and do not know the rules," I replied frankly.

"Ordinarily you are supposed to see a captain first, and only then, if he allows it, you can meet with the lord....But under the circumstances...," the soldier paused. "Hold here. I will be right back." He turned and ran up the stairs. At the door he yelled something, and when it opened, disappeared inside, returning soon after to signal for us to come up. We did as told, and taking several steps at a time, entered the keep, where three more men, all dressed in chain mail, took away our gear and locked the door. They left us in the company of the young soldier, who promptly took us through a dim wide hallway, up the stairs to the third floor, and to another large heavy iron door, attended by several sentries. There he exchanged a few words with one of the soldiers, after which the door moved inward and we were allowed in, our figures watched closely by the weary eyes from inside full steel helms.

Leaving the soldiers and the corridor, we walked into a spacious chamber, crowned with a lofty ceiling, which stretched the entire length of the room, painted with many pictures of knights, castles, and animals. Along the sides stood two rows of polished round columns, which ran parallel to marble walls, adorned with many decorations—colored shields, glittering suits of armor, weapons of all shapes, and long tapestries, made of fine treated wool. In the very center of the hall, rose a large carpeted pedestal with an armchair placed upon it. Lit up by two huge iron lamps, the high seat, made of brown oak, looked rich in splendor. As armrests it had two figures of seated cats with large rubies for eyes; the paws and teeth were laced with gold and ivory. Carved in the back of the chair was the body of an ascending bird, rushing into the sky with its wooden wings wide apart. Beneath the bird, resting amongst many velvet cushions, sat the familiar man, Sire Rone of Sirone. Dressed in a robe of deep regal color, with lines of gold along his sleeves, the lord differed much in appearance from his visit to Villone. His tall, broad-shouldered figure now appeared ample in belly and showed extra weight on the sides too. His long, clean-shaved face was weary and showed signs of many bygone years, augmented with streaks of white in his long brown hair.

As we entered, Sire Rone was busy talking to a gentleman, standing next to the throne, holding a large leather book in his hands. The two were discussing something and did not seem to hear us come in. But as our steps resonated through the open space of the hall, they fell silent and looked at us. At once, the young soldier gave a salute and bowed.

"Your Lordship, I have here young commoners from Villone, who are seeking your counsel," the soldier declared and bowed again. For some time Sire Rone did not answer and just explored us, his face showing a hint of reflection. Then he said something to his companion, who nodded and moved down from the pedestal, but did not leave. Instead, he remained behind the throne, occasionally glancing out from under the wooden wings.

At last Sire Rone leaned over one of cats' heads and spoke. "Greetings to you, strangers." The lord's voice echoed through the chamber. "May I inquire as to what sort of advice you are seeking?"

Unaware of how to behave in front of a noble kind, I tried to remember everything my parents had taught me about manners, courtesy, and respect. But as often my memory went blank, making me very nervous. My hands started to shake a little and my throat went dry. Yet mustering all my courage I managed to constrain myself to speak, making the best effort to sound as courteous as possible. "Your Lordship, my name is Mishuk Loyde and these are my friends, Ike, Ark, and Rob. We have traveled here from the southern town of Villone, hoping to seek an audience with you, my lord." I forced the words out of me, my hands still shaking. "The reason for this unexpected visit is my father, Brune Loyde by name, a seasonal trader from Villone, your Lordship. His caravan went missing somewhere in your lands weeks ago, and until this day nothing has been known of his whereabouts."

"So you are one of Brune's sons," said Sire Rone abruptly. "I know your father very well, a good man and an honest merchant; I am also aware of the bad luck that has stricken your family. When the disturbing news of his convoy had reached me I joined other lords in a search. Regrettably all of the efforts were in vain. I am truly sorry."

"Thank you my lord, thank you very much. These are sad times for my family indeed, and this is why I wanted to speak to you. I was hoping you could tell me more about my father's disappearance," I replied, trying to keep my voice steady.

"A fair request, young man." Sire Rone raised his eyebrow. "I would be more than glad to assist you. But I am afraid I cannot offer you much help. Your father's disappearance is as mysterious to me as it is to you."

Sire Rone paused for a moment, thinking, then shook his head and resumed. His tone was the same as it had been when he had visited Villone.

"Over six weeks ago I called your father to Sirone to place an order for his upcoming voyage to Chantue. He came as summoned, and then left for home to prepare for his trip. The next time I heard about him was from Sire Ouis, the lord who holds neighboring lands north of here. He sent me a dispatch he had received earlier from Bonneville, where the Duke's chief of guards was urging fellow knights to give assistance in searching for the missing convoy, your father's convoy. As it was an appalling accident—a whole caravan vanished in Bois—many noblemen from across the province took on the Duke's call and sent their men to join the raid; so did I, ordering my own men to scout the surrounding woods. Yet it was not until a few weeks passed that I received the first report—a rumor out of the small Village of Lulione, a day's worth of travel from here. The story said that a certain farmer had found an abandoned wagon, hidden in the woods northeast of the parish. As the cart appeared to be looted, I suspected that it could have been a part of your father's party and immediately set out to investigate the case further. When I arrived to Lulione, local folks escorted me to the forest, where the lost cart awaited me. Once I examined the symbols drawn on the wagon, I understood that it belonged to your father. Hoping to find more clues, I instructed my men to search the entire area, but to my dismay they found nothing. The clearing, near which the cart had been discovered, the woods surrounding it, and the nearby roads were spotless—no signs of a struggle, no footprints, not even remnants of a campfire. It was as if your father's caravan had never been there; that, or somebody had tried very hard to conceal the fact that it had. One way or another, it all seemed very strange.

I spent the whole day in the environs of Lulione, but my stay was useless. Many hours later, frustrated and tired, I abandoned the effort and sent my men to the castle, while I myself rode to Villone to bring the cart to your mother."

Sire Rone stopped and took a deep breath.

"My lord, do you have any idea as to what might have happened to my father? Did he get lost? Was he attacked or possibly kidnapped?" I asked then.

"People do not get lost in Bois," he replied sharply. "Even if a lonesome traveler loses his way in our province, he always reappears somewhere, and if he does not, someone else finds him, him or his body. What happened to your father is not a simple case of going astray. An experienced trader, he knew all the roads very well. I doubt that he took a wrong turn, especially near his hometown. I fear that there may be something else at play here. An attack, or a kidnapping you say—maybe, or maybe something else. Strange it all is, very strange."

The lord closed his eyes for an instant, his right hand under his chin.

"My lord. Do you think it will be possible to resume the search effort any time soon?" I asked, when no more telling followed.

"Resume the search?" Sire Rone repeated, his eyes now focused on the floor. "How do you resume a search when you do not know where to start?"

The knight moved his glance to me. "I ask you, young son of Loyde, how do you search for your father if you do not have a single clue to his providence? Where do you begin? Where do you go? If something new comes to light, a rumor, or clue, another wagon, or a dead body perhaps, then I will begin the search again. Until then I cannot do anything." He thought for a moment and added, "I hope you understand."

But I did not understand. I simply could not. The lord's words made me angry, but there was little I could do. Sire Rone was the lord, and I was nobody. Yet, what I could do was to start my own search, but to do so required more information. Wasting no time, I asked my next question, caring much less for the manner of my discourse that time. "If you are not going to resume the effort, could you tell me a little bit about the place where my father's cart was uncovered? I would like to visit it."

Sire Rone stared at me. But then a light smile softened his face. "You deserve that much, at least. As I said, the wagon was found in the woods near Lulione. If you need directions, my captain will instruct you once we are finished here." The lord leaned back, his shoulders touching the wooden design of the chair.

"Thank you, my lord." I bowed, as did my friends. "We are very grateful for all your help. We will bother you no more."

When Sire Rone waved his hand dismissing us, we straightened up and were about to leave, but his voice halted us once again.

"Ah. I almost forgot. There is one more thing you probably want to know. The fellow who discovered the wagon said he had seen another man, a monk of some sort, wandering around the clearing, looking for something. I do not know how much truth there is to this story or how relevant it is to your father's disappearance, but it may be worth checking into. There is a small compound that belongs to the Order of the Spirit east of Lulione. If you are to expand your investigation, I suggest you stop there. Who knows, perhaps you will find a member-brother there who has seen or heard something about your father's convoy.

"In any case, I wish you best of luck, young son of Loyde. The captain will meet you outside. Oh, if you find out anything new about your father, I want you to inform me right away. Is that clear?"

The lord gave me a tough glare. I nodded quickly.

"Good. Now, you must depart." Sire Rone got up and started for a small door at the other end of the hall, concealed behind long dark blue drapes. The gentleman who had been standing by the throne all that time, joined the lord heading for the exit, speaking with him as they went. Meanwhile the soldier told our company to leave as well and took us out of the reception-chamber, downstairs, and back into the courtyard.

Outside the sky was almost dark, and lots of torches lit the inner grounds of the castle, by then crammed with scores of servants of all ages, who walked everywhere, carrying barrels, mops, buckets, and rags of various colors. Amongst them, seemingly unattended, also wandered many different living things— dogs, chickens, pigs, and geese, some of which were so huge passing men and women had to move around them. They all made such noise that it was hard for us to hear anything our guide tried to say. All I caught from his words was that he wanted us to stay where we were. Realizing that we were not going to leave, he walked away. As he did, another armed man came—a hard-faced, yet young fellow, who was clearly a lord, not of a big house, but a nobleman none-theless. His chest was embraced in thick leather armor and carried the sigil of Sire Rone's house, burned deep into its brown aged skin.

"Greetings," the man declared, wiping drops of sweat from his forehead. "Are you Mishuk Loyde?"

"Yes, Sire, that is I," I replied.

"I am Sire Ohn, the first captain with Sire Rone's garrison. I understand you need directions to Lulione." The officer nodded as if to reply to his own question and opened a small bag that hung from his girdle. "Can any of you read a map or should I explain it to you myself?"

"I can," said Rob, and he took a step forward.

"Good. It will save us a lot of time." The captain produced a small parch-ment and unwrapped it quickly, presenting us with a detailed map of the northern region of Bois.

"Here, look closely." Sire Ohn pointed to the leather sheet. "Do you see this large dot? This is where we are. Up here is Lulione and here is where we found the cart. I marked it with red ink in case you forget. If you use the main road, it will take you a day or two on foot to get to Lulione and half a day more to get to the clearing. But if you want to save some time I suggest you use a shortcut, which I indicated with this dotted line. I also took the liberty of marking the monastery. Right here, you see the blue cross? This is the compound. It is not too far from the village, but there are no roads that can take you there, so you will have to follow the trail through the woods. Once you are clear of the forest, you should be able to see the monastery. You might want to pack some extra food and water, because the only tavern anywhere around those lands is in Lulione itself. As soon as you are out of the village you will have to camp in the wild. So be prepared and watch out for anything unusual. After what happened to the caravan, I would be careful traveling at night."

With these words of caution, the captain handed the map to Rob. "Any questions? Well then, good luck to you and may the Spirit guide your way."

The officer then gave us a brief salute and left. After his figure disappeared in the shadow, cast by the back wall of the keep, Rob tucked the leather parchment away and we headed out of the castle, through the main gates, and to a tavern we had seen just outside the logged wall.

"At least we got some new information," I said to my friends as we walked down the hill.

"Yes, we did. We now have a place to examine and persons to talk to," agreed Ark.

But Ike rebutted, "It is not much though. I kind of hoped to get some straight answers from Sire Rone."

"I am a little disappointed myself," I concurred. "I thought Sire Rone had something more to share. He says he has spent so much time searching for my father, but he has come up with nothing. I find it very unlikely. Do you not?"

Rob and Ark nodded in response, but said nothing. Only Ike voiced his opinion: "Although the lord seems very concerned for your father, he has offered us no clues to his fate. I wonder why." Ike whispered the last words several more times, then stopped. Afterwards there were no more discussions. We walked down the town's main street in silence and soon reached a small house with a large wooden sign that read "Petite Pupon Inn."

The sound name was written in big letters and was accompanied by the date the inn had originally been constructed. Because Petite Pupon was one of few hostelries in the town, we proceeded straight through its swinging doors and to a spacious dining hall, filled with smoke and noise. Illuminated with many candles that allotted a murky low light, the place was packed with patrons, who sat at many tables, consuming food and drink of their choice. Scores of serving girls and boys ran back and forth, attending the guests, carrying steaming plates of the day's specials and large wooden mugs of thick brown ale.

The instant we walked in, Ike noticed a few vacant seats at the far corner of the room and led us to them, picking his way through the dense crowd. Although the round table was away from the kitchen and the bar, it was close to the fireplace, which promised heat and comfort to our tired company. Even though the past few days were unusually warm, at night the early spring season brought in cold air to open lands. The sight of a cozy fire was very welcoming. We quickly settled on squeaking chipped stools next to it and called the serving girls, who took their time getting to our table. When one of them finally did manage to see our raised hands, we ordered the evening meal and drinks.

Soon after, a generous supper was laid out in front of us. Four large plates of roasted pork, mixed with chunks of onions and carrots, were complemented with a large tray of cold meat-cuts, together with a warm loaf of wheat bread and fresh apples, some of which were of bright yellow color, unusual so early in the year. After two days spent outdoors, the food before us was a real treat, and we devoured it with astonishing speed, which only increased as we ate.

When our plates and trays were empty, we called the serving girls again, and then again, and again, until we could not eat any more. At last our hunger was gone, but in its place came weariness, which made us leave the table and walk up to the counter at the front wall of the dining hall, where the hardy hostess nestled firmly on a massive timber chair. After paying for the meal, which cost us two coppers each, we rented a room for a fair price of only five coppers a night. We went upstairs to the end of a long narrow hallway, where a small chamber with four straw beds awaited us. Feeling the weight of the earlier travels, we did not linger for long and soon were sound asleep, comforted by clean sheets and fluffy pillows, stuffed with heaps of white goose feathers. It was a nice rest, quiet and peaceful, just normal dreams, and no visions.

Chapter 8

ALTHOUGH WE did not have too much money with us, we had enough to
get us through a few weeks on the road. For the trip I saved six silvers and
twelve coppers, mostly from playing wall-throw with other boys in Villone. I
also borrowed ten coppers from Ric, which I added to Ike's three silvers, ten
coppers, and one gold plate he had accidentally pocketed from his old man.
And with Ark and Rob donating eight more silvers and twenty-three coppers
between them, our traveling purse was brought to the total of one gold plate,
seventeen silvers, and fifty-five coppers, a small fortune for the four teenaged
lads, who had no jobs or crafts to earn their pay. After settling the bill with the
owner of the tavern the day before, we still had plenty of money to spend, so
after vacating our room, we returned to the dining hall and ordered a light
breakfast, which consisted of fresh apples, bread, four hard-boiled eggs, and a
jar of milk.

As we ate our morning meal, cheerful streaks of early sunlight rushed
through glass square windows and transformed into white trails that played
along the freshly mopped wooden floor, still wet and slippery. Back at the table
Ike was working on a large slice of warm bread, which he finished in three
bites, rinsing it with sips of cold milk. Once in a while he threw quick glances
at a couple of patrons, who had stumbled into the hall half-awake from their
night's rest. Finding little interest in the strangers, he let them be and turned
his attention to his belongings, reshuffling the contents of his pockets, filled
with all sorts of things. Right away various objects that appeared before him
quickly turned into a small pile—a short steel dagger, its blade half-broken, a
pocket knife, some copper coins, pieces of carved wood, some narrow iron
bars, and a handful of tiny crystal balls that bounced on the flat surface and
rolled athwart, almost falling on the floor, stopped only by Ark's opened palms,
which he pressed hard against the table's edge. For a while Ike examined every
single article, flipping and turning it in his fingers. Then, satisfied with the

inspection, he gathered everything and shoved it all back into his pockets, rendering his work completely pointless.

At the other side, Rob and Ark were busy too. Using two aged greenish blade sharpeners, they labored hard on the two rusted swords, trying to give the weapons a decent look. Alas, the blades were too old to regain their previous splendor, and no matter how hard my friends toiled over them, the blades remained unchanged and only set off a lot of reddish dust, which flew everywhere, eventually settling on the floor a quarter of a cubit away. When all the groundwork was done, we finished the last bits of food, rechecked our bloated backpacks, and headed for the door, saying our farewells to the hostess, who seemed to be glued to her chair.

Keen on getting to the village of Lulione as quickly as possible, we squandered little time and marched out of Sirone. Soon the route became deserted again, and only familiar green gardens and orchards accompanied us. But they ceased too, surrendering to stretches of cultivated fields that ran along both sides of the road, occupying most of the landscape, with the lord's stronghold still posing dominantly over them. The view of Sire Rone's castle remained visible for a while longer, until it eventually disappeared behind some hills, leaving our company amidst the scenes of southern wilderness. For several leagues all that surrounded us were grass and low bushes, but then the outline of a distant forest loomed in sight.

In single file, we traveled north until the path began to slant slightly, forcing us to turn east and follow that direction for several more leagues. The woods to our right grew bigger and soon patches of trees were rising almost at the edge of the road, when suddenly our journey came to a standstill.

"Look. Did you see that?" Ark's abrupt exclamation made us halt and turn. Ark stood a few cubits behind, pointing west, at heavy bushes that peered over tall grass.

"See what?" I asked, following Ark's hand, stressing to find anything in the green lines of far-away leaves.

"I do not see anything," said Ike.

"Me neither," agreed Rob.

"This is strange." Ark continued to gaze into the vastness of the fields. But there was nothing unusual, just low shrubs and grass.

"I thought I saw something moving in those bushes," explained Ark, with some uncertainty in his voice. "It almost looked like someone was following us," he added, sighing shaking his head.

"I told you not to drink too much of that cider last night," joked Ike, tapping Ark on his shoulder.

"Hah. You might be right. It was probably my own imagination, or a reflection from the sun," reckoned Ark. The rest of us looked around a few more times, but saw nothing and resumed our travel.

Later in the day, as the sun started to head toward the west, we noticed that the trees around us thickened and turned into a denser forest, which spread along the path, taking on a ruddy color, cast down by the setting sun. When the soft dusk permeated the sky completely, we set up camp, settling near a small clear pond some distance away from the road. Surrounded by young trees, the place was ideal for a night's rest, as fresh water allowed us to refill empty flasks, cook hearty soup, and wash off all that dust from our faces.

That was just what we did. Piling our packs under a big tree, where its strong brown roots ran curling through thick grass carpet, we cleaned the dirt from our skin and prepared for the night. After Ike had collected enough firewood, Ark and Rob busied themselves with making a fire; as for me, I unrolled the blankets, placing them in a circle around the forthcoming blaze. When flames grew big enough to survive a mild wind, Ark unwrapped some of his little bags and bundles, and started sorting through his stocks of herbs and spices, ready to adorn our evening meal. Not longer after that, the food was ready. That night we had freshly made vegetable soup, a round soft rye bread, and a bottle of milk that we had picked up at the Petite Pupon. As the night before, we ate quickly, urged by the hunger that always came to us by the end of a day, and afterwards, retired to bed, feeling weary and sleepy. For a few moments I listened to my friends' chat, but unable to keep wakeful, closed my eyes and drifted away. Alas, that time I was not destined for a restful night.

Countless stars dimly lit the dark sky, and a refreshing warm breeze felt comforting and relaxing. My cape thrown aside, I lay over the blanket, shocked by the images that had come to me. Since we departed from Villone none of us had seen a single odd apparition, and I assumed that those troubles had left us be, but I was wrong. Under the cover of the open sky, the visions I hoped were gone returned.

Chapter 9

AT FIRST, my sleep recalled peaceful scenes of home and long passed childhood. But then it changed and I found myself in a strange place, at a time that differed from the present.

Once more, I was not alone. My three friends were there with me. We stood at the edge of an opaque forest, facing a long open field. A misty haze covered our feet, rolling further down tall wet grass. The gray sky pressed hard over us, offering only some faint pale light. Cold bitter air swept across dry soil, spreading an uneasy feeling. At each side of us stood a host of armed men. Noises of ringing metal, anxious horses, strained timber, and movement of thousands of feet were everywhere, constantly interplaying with the shouts of soldiers and their commanders.

Most of the armed men near our company were footed and wore thick ring mails, closed glistening helms, and woolen cloaks that waved from side to side, picked up by wisp of strong freezing wind. In their hands, they held long wooden spears, topped with sharp steel points, and massive oval-shaped shields, fastened tight to their arms. The sign of a burning chalice was engraved on their chests. Amongst the lines, which the footed soldiers held, moved groups of riders. Some of the mounted men were lightly armored with bows and short swords hanging at their sides. Others looked like knights, though they were not Normandians. Instead they wore the same suits of white metal and rode tall barded warhorses, their shields, capes, and banners also decorated with the symbol of a golden chalice burning inside a light blue circle. Most of the clad horsemen were armed with thick lances, long swords, and morning stars, some weapons decorated with numerous symbols and incrustations of colored stones.

The knights were a sight to see, but my attention was soon drawn away from them, across the grassland, and to a massive dark column that peered over the horizon. I studied a great wall of shields and spears, formed by thousands of men and horses, that stood firmly on the other side of the open field, awaiting their orders, which came quickly, announced by distant sounds of battle horns. Any confusion around us stopped, and soldiers quickly tightened their ranks, ready to advance toward the enemy ahead. More battle horns came to life. That time they sounded from our side, immediately followed by a monotonous rhythm of countless drums. As one the human lines rippled and started toward the center of the field. On the opposite side of the field, the other column set out as well, descending slowly toward us. A battle was about to begin, and we were right in the middle of it, walking along with others, our faces grim and focused. Yet as we marched on, the picture shifted and turned pale. The images became vague and everything blurred.

While scenes of battle smeared, new images slowly emerged. When the picture reappeared, soldiers, knights, and the noise of bouncing steel were all gone; in their place was a dark nighttime forest. Our lonely party was moving down a narrow barely visible path. Near us everything seemed asleep and only remote sounds of an owl accompanied our steps. We proceeded along the trail until we came upon an open clearing. The small circle of an open ground made us cautious, so we sped up trying to get to the cover of the trees at the other side as quickly as possible.

Suddenly a distinctive whistling sound pierced the air. One after another a dozen arrows filled the sky, making their way swiftly in our direction. Even though it was impossible to see where the deadly shots were coming from or where they were landing, I threw myself forward and rolled on the ground toward an island of short shrubs. An arrow hit the ground missing my foot by half a cubit. Another came over my head and crushed through branches, cutting several leaves with its sharp tip. Struggling to avoid the menacing darts, I scrambled to the bushes, and quickly realized that their thin greenery offered little cover. Hastily I studied the clearing some more, and noticed a large tree that stood alone several cubits away. Its thick trunk offered enough protection from three sides, and having little choice, I dashed there. Several more arrows flew my way, but they were aimed too high. Unhurt I reached the safety of the branches and dropped to the ground, spinning around to look back at the open glade, trying to find my friends.

Although the moonlight was bright, it was hard to see much. Still I managed to pick out three figures pressed against the cold soil, waiting for another attack. Assured that none of them was wounded, I turned my attention to the darkness of the woods, studying it carefully in hopes of finding where the deadly arrows had been coming from. For a while all I could see were frozen silhouettes of trees that surrounded the opening. But as I focused more, I detected four or five murky figures, creeping vigilant near the far edge of the clearing. Little by little the shadowy shapes moved out of the shadows and advanced toward my friends, who were still on the ground. A few more moments and the enemy would be upon them. Cautiously I turned to my friends again and gave them a signal, pointing in the direction where the dark figures made their approach. My companions looked toward the attackers then and started to crawl toward me. Yet they did not have enough time. The enemy was too close.

What I needed then was a plan; all I could come up with was to attack first. So gathering all my courage I drew my sword and placed it on the ground next to me, concealing the steel blade in the grass. The few brief moments seemed like hours as I waited for a chance to launch my assault. When the enemy was just a few cubits away, I hoisted my weapon and moved to their flank. As I did, I realized the hostile shapes were four well-built men, dressed in dark clothes. Two of them held broad swords; the others carried heavy crossbows, with bolts loaded in the slots.

Still unaware of my presence, the attackers were busy scouting the clearing before them. Having a chance to strike a first blow undetected, I closed the remaining distance swiftly and sank my long thin blade into the closest of the unsuspecting foes. By the time the stranger's eyes found me, my steel weapon was already drawing a thin stream of blood that dripped rapidly from the side of the blade. The man did not utter a sound, and just stared at me, struggling to keep his balance. Then his eyes rolled up and he fell to the ground, still baring my weapon inside. Although I was not sure if the man was dead, I yanked my sword out, immediately finding the three other foes glaring at me, their weapons drawn and almost ready. But not ready enough for the attack from my friends, who came from the other side, rushing to my aid, their weapons unsheathed, moonlight reflecting off the blades. When Ike and Rob slammed into their enemies full force, I too darted forth, choosing another swordsman for my target.

After several strikes, I managed to separate my opponent from the rest of the battle and made him move closer to the large tree, opening more ground to maneuver. For a while my thrusts brought no results. The foe dodged my blows, then counterattacked himself. Throwing his body at me, he held his long rapier pointed directly at my neck. With only a moment to react I leapt aside and hit his blade with my own sword. My strike was so strong, the enemy lost his grip and the weapon flew out of his hands. The man immediately jumped to pick it up, but before he could do so I grabbed him by the cloak and yanked down. His attempt to stay on foot failed. He dropped to the ground like a bag of stones, followed by my weapon that landed across his spine, extracting a thumping hollow sound. The man jerked violently and screamed in agony, but when my second blow hit him in the neck, he twitched and froze. He was dead, but I did not want to take any chance and hit his lifeless body one more time. Then I turned back and rejoined my friends, who had already won over their opponents and stood some cubits away, breathing heavily. They seemed tired and worried, their blades wet with blood.

When their breathing stabilized Ike signaled for us to remain quiet and pointed to the far end of the clearing, where Ark stood alone and still. He had no weapon or shield. Yet, two cloaked corpses lay next to him, petrified in their last moments of anguish. The fight was over and with it the vision that depicted it. Blackness filled the scene and I woke up, finding myself staring at the dark sky.

The night was coming to an end, and the fire had turned into a pile of red flickering coals, which still radiated pleasant warmth across the camp. I raised my head and looked curiously at my friends, who rested close by. They were awake, looking at each other in silence. A moment later Ike's voice broke the stillness.

"That was some fight," he said and rolled to one side so as to see everyone.

"It sure was," agreed Rob. "How many of them were there, five? Six?"

"There were six of them," replied Ark. "The four came from the left side of the clearing and attacked you, or should I say, were ambushed by Mishuk, and two more remained in the woods and tried to shoot their arrows at you. Being occupied with hand-to-hand combat, you did not see them; so I went off to deal with them myself."

"Oh, that reminds me!" exclaimed Ike. "How, in the world, did you do that? How did you kill those two men? I do not recall seeing any weapons on you."

"You are right, Ike. I did not have any weapons with me," Ark replied, and paused for a moment. When he resumed, his tone was serious. "As you have probably noticed, we do not have any control over our visions. We simply watch them, just like a stage performance, put on by street doers who often pass through Villone in the summer seasons. And just like in a street play, we have no say in what or how events are going to unfold. Only instead of viewing some players do the act, we see ourselves perform, and as a spectator like yourselves I can only tell you what I have seen and not how I have done it."

"Then tell us what you have seen," persisted Ike.

"If you insist." Ark rubbed his hands together and coughed. "I saw myself moving quickly toward the two men. Once I was about thirty cubits away from them, I walked around their positions, and undetected, hid in the shadows. As soon as they began to stress their bows, I stepped out and began to chant, just like that other time with the monster in the woods. Anyway, I was chanting until my hands produced a bright red line. I wish I knew how I did it, but I do not.

"All I did was watch as the line grew thicker and thicker, until it became as thick as a staff. Then it separated from my fingers and raced toward the enemies. When it was almost above them it split in two and smashed into each of the men, piercing them like lighting. There were no screams, no noises, just a brush of wind and a splash of light, which vanished in an instance. Before I knew, the two dead bodies lay in front of me. It was an unpleasant sight by far. You should have seen their faces—so cold, so pale."

Ark grew quiet, rubbing his hands.

"Wow. I wish I was there to see it," uttered Ike, fascinated with Ark's tale.

"I am sure you will have another chance. I have a feeling this was not our last vision," replied Ark with a barely visible smile on his face.

"So what do you think about it all?" asked Rob.

"Now as I think about it, as long as we keep winning I do not mind seeing them too much," said Ike.

"But what about the first part, the battle?" I interjected.

"It was indeed very strange," noted Ark. "If these pictures have anything to do with our future, I am not looking forward to seeing it in a real life. Mishuk, you really think these visions are somehow connected to our future?" Ark looked at me.

"I still cannot say for sure. Maybe it is something completely different," I answered, uncertainty in my voice.

"I have been thinking too," continued Ark. "About two weeks ago I found an old scroll in the back rooms of Villone's library. As I was helping the old guru with his history assignment, I stumbled upon a text of just a few pages. Written sometime during the Second Age, it recited an abstract from an even older book, which was written by some wizard from before the Great War, who was explaining the workings of several magic spells. Although the writing contained no details as to how to cast the spells, it did say a little about what the enchantments did, and amongst them, was one special enchantment, called the Fortune, that interested me more than any other.

"It appeared that when cast, the Fortune allowed a person to see images of his own future. It said that the foretelling often took the form of visions that came to a caster in dreams. In them the spell delivered brief messages about the future life, which a caster then interpreted with the help of special books. When

I first read about this enchantment, I immediately thought it was similar to our condition. But then as I examined the text further, such contention left me. Although the spell's effect did resemble what has been going on with us, it was not the same."

"Not the same?" Ike almost cried out as he jumped from his grass bed. "Let me get this straight. You learned about a spell that caused visions and did not tell us?"

"It did not seem relevant," replied Ark calmly. "According to the description, the spell only affects the caster and nobody else. Because none of us has any idea how to cast spells, it has nothing to do with our strange condition, not to mention the fact that we all have been seeing the same dreams."

"Whatever," started Ike, but I interrupted.

" Is there another spell, like the Fortune, that affects someone other than a caster?"

"I do not know," answered Ark wistfully. "I would think so. Of course I could not find any allusions of such enchantment. But I only had access to a handful of text. I am sure if I had more books to research, I would find something about it. Until then though, all I can do is guess."

Ark's words made us think again. Our company was back on the ground. There was no more banter that night. Soon my friends were asleep, and I too drifted back to sleep, grabbing a few more hours of rest before the day's coming.

Chapter 10

JUST AFTER dawn pale gray colors settled across the morning blue, blocking any hint of a sunny morning. Amongst the vale of grayness, a few darker clouds floated lazily over our heads, marking the only difference between the shades of the sky. A small red tip of the rising sun that had been visible earlier disappeared completely into the grimness, signaling the beginning of yet another day. I was awake and yawning. My friends were too, stumbling around the camp, picking up their blankets and packing their bags. After observing them for a bit, I climbed to my feet and walked up to the pond a few cubits away. With delight, I dipped my hands into the cold sheer water and splashed it on my face, shivering from the refreshing chill. I rubbed my cheeks thoroughly and splattered some more of the reviving liquid on my neck and arms. When the last remnants of my sleep had vanished, I dried myself with my own tunic and went back to the camp, rejoining my friends, who already stood with the backpacks over their shoulders.

By the time we resumed our journey a strong wind had picked up from the west and the gray mantle gradually dispersed, exposing parts of a clear blue sky. An hour later the drab colors were gone, with only small clouds remaining hanging over some distant hills. With the brightness of the day restored, we kept a good speed, coming over a low hill and to a wide-open wild valley, which accompanied us for several leagues, until we reached the first cared fields that surrounded Lulione. By then the road had become much wider and busier, with several farmers and other folks, joining us on our way to the village. Up the lane, in a company of unfamiliar faces, we went, with rising spirit, and anticipation, for we could see the first rooftops of the parish straight ahead, and with it a chance to find new clues to our quest.

Soon enough we stood at the outskirts of Lulione, which was a small, but neat and peaceful place. Twenty or so cottages stood in a row on one side of the road, and on the other, outlined by a short woven fence, ran orchards and gardens that stretched deep into the back, filling the landscape with the many colors of awakening nature. As Bois was at the most southern part of Normandia, the early spring brought a vivid blooming season to its parishes, and in Lulione countless fruit trees and shrubs were bursting with flowers, emitting the fresh scent of honey that melted quickly, leaving a sweet savor on the lips. Near some of the buildings, bundles of hay lolled unattended, serving no other visible purpose, but as resting spots for fat local cats that had climbed out of their hideouts in numbers and slept peacefully, bathing in the rays of warm sun, wasting little time on anything that transpired around them. The same could have been said about the villagers, some of whom strolled causally along the unpaved street, caring little for our presence.

We headed straight for the only large building in the village, which turned out to be a tavern and trading post all in one. Constructed of dark treated logs, it was two stories high, with many small round windows placed evenly along its walls. A large sign dangled loosely over two massive board doors that were opened and revealed a spacious hall, filled with a half dozen long tables, all of which were deserted. The only visible people inside were two men at the far end of the hall. One of them, a chubby older man, sat behind a narrow low counter, talking to another much younger fellow with more hair and less flab.

The strangers looked preoccupied with their chat and did not see us enter the hall. When they finally noticed us, their voices sank into a murmur and then stopped, as their eyes studied us carefully, probably trying to figure out the purpose of our visit. But even before we reached the counter, the bold man, who looked like the owner of the place, waved his hand several times and yelled his greeting. "Greetings, travelers. My name is Eter of Niore, but most here call me Old Eter. I am the owner of this humble establishment." The man's face widened in a fake joyful smile and he lowered his head. "How can I be of assistance to you?"

"Greetings to you too, Old Eter. My name is Mishuk Loyde, and these are my companions. We have come from Sirone to investigate a late incident that had occurred here not too long ago." I finished with my introduction and moved right to the subject of our visit. "We have heard that some of the locals found a lost wagon not too far away from this village. So we were wondering if you knew anything about it. We will appreciate any help you can give us."

Before I was even done, the owner's face lit up with a spark of interest. His small eyes narrowed and he began to shift in his chair. Then he frowned and composed a serious face.

"Ah ha, so you are looking for the missing caravan, are not you boys? I do not know how much help I can be to you. I have heard some rumors here and there. A couple weeks ago Sire Rone himself came down here with his men. He talked to people, asked questions, and then left. Since then I have not heard anything about this matter."

Eter gave us an illusive look, which made me dislike him even more.

Yet I kept my aversion at bay and asked the next question. "Are you sure there is nothing you can tell me about the incident, anything at all?"

"Uhm, you see, I am an old man and my memory is not as good as it used to be. Sometimes I forget things," replied Old Eter, while casting a quick glance at a small pouch that hung on my belt. I immediately realized what he wanted and slowly opened the pouch, taking out a handful of coppers. I casually placed the money on the counter, enclosing them with my hand and waited for another response. At first the owner remained unruffled. He tried to keep an indifferent look on his face, but the glitter of coins that came through my finger finally took over him and he started to nod. I then lifted my hand and let Old Eter grab the money, which he tossed quickly under the counter.

"I think I recall something now," he said joyfully and scratched his sweaty bold forehead. "One of our local peasants claimed to have found an abandoned cart in the woods and called the soldiers to investigate. Then the lord came and searched the whole place. But all he found was the wagon. I think he took it with him when he left. I personally never saw the cart or the place it was found at, but I know a person who did. His name is Aul. He lives two leagues east of Lulione. If you take the next turn down the road you have come into the village, you will be on your way. He has a small shack and an apple orchard right next to the trail. You will not miss it. When you see him, make sure you tell him that Old Eter has sent you. He is a little strange and does not like visitors. I guess years of living alone will do it to you. But do not worry. He is a good fellow. He may sound crazy at first, but his wits are fine. He will tell you everything you need to know."

"Well, I guess your memory is not so bad after all," I whispered and then said barely politely. "Thank you, we will not disturb you any longer. Farewell, Eter of Noire."

"No problem, young men. I wish I could help you more. It is always sad when something bad happens to good people," Old Eter replied, then immediately resumed his earlier talk with the young fellow, who had been keeping quiet throughout the conversation.

We did not spend any more time with them but came back outside, deserting Eter and our money along with him. Not wanting to think about the sleazy trader anymore than I had to, I concentrated on Aul, the local farmer who, I hoped, had more answers for us.

A couple of leagues was a short trip and with the day still in its prime, we swiftly left Lulione and headed to the peasant's home.

Chapter 11

THE AIR was hot. The road dipped and climbed, as we hurried eastward, delighted to meet someone who had actually found Father's wagon. Surmounting one low hill after another, we left the last glimpses of the village and soon came to a small house that stood lonesome by the side of the road. It was a tiny wooden structure, made of large logs, put together so as to form an almost perfect square. It was well built, but through the years, had fallen into complete disarray, seeing little or no repairs. Although the walls and the base of the building remained intact, many of its parts had collapsed and lay on the ground, scattered pieces of wood and iron. Several windows and doors seemed to be equally wrecked, and those that looked at the road were shut, with wide, dried-out patches of wood and leather pressed against the frames. A high fence surrounding a small apple orchard came up to the left side of the house, where there was a small gate, barred from the inside by a large curved tree branch.

At first the house looked abandoned, but soon we noticed several things that indicated someone was actually living there. A pile of freshly cut firewood lay on the ground by the fence, and behind it, where the road went past the gate, was a trail of footsteps, imprinted in the short-cut grass. Convinced the home was occupied, we came up to the twigged crooked door and banged on it several times. When we got no answer, we tried again, at the same time calling loudly for the host.

While Rob, Ark, and I continued to shout, Ike pulled out his sword and slid it through a gap between the gate and the fence. He wiggled his weapon several times, then lifted it up, along with the tree branch on the other side. The stick did not budge at first, but as Ike shook it several times, it moved up and fell on the ground. The door then opened up and we walked into the yard that was packed with all sort of useless junk. Through it we made our way to an undersized porch and knocked again, pounding our fists on a flimsy front door that started to move in and out, barely hanging onto a couple of rusted hinges, nailed to an old cracked frame.

We knocked and called Aul's name, but there was no answer. Disappointed we headed back to the road, when suddenly the door opened and a head peered through a narrow slit. The stranger stared at us for a moment, then vanished into the darkness and shut the door, locking it from inside. Frustrated I ran back to the porch and started to hammer on the boarded flap, putting all my strength and diligence into it. At the same time, Ike, who was standing behind me, shouted with irritation, "Hey! Quit your stupid games. We all saw you. Open up. We just want to ask you a few questions."

While the man said nothing in response, I could hear sounds of hustle and movement inside. Whoever the hairy fellow was, he was not too anxious to talk to us. But frankly I did not care. He knew something, and I was going to get it out of him one way or another. Taking a deep breath, I made my last polite attempt to lure the man out of his hideout.

"Listen," I said calmly, picking the words so not to scare the man too much, "Do not be afraid. We do not mean you any harm. We just want to talk to you, that is all. We have already spoken with Old Eter. He is the one who sent us over here."

I finished and listened.

A brief moment passed, then I heard the lock click and the door opened a little. A pair of small murky eyes gazed at me out of the dark opening.

"Did you say Old Eter?" The man said curiously, continuing to study Ike and me.

"Yes. We talked to him just this morning in Lulione. He told us you could help," I replied immediately, putting my hand on the edge of the door, afraid the odd-looking fellow would disappear again.

"He did?" the man asked as if he was deaf.

"Yes, yes. Do you have some time to spare? We really want to talk to you."

"Time? Maybe. Maybe not."

"At least may I ask of your name?"

"My name? What for?"

"Well, we are looking for a fellow, named Aul. If you are not Aul, we will leave at once."

"What if I am Aul, what then?"

"In that case we would like to talk to you."

I was getting tired of repeating my every question. Luckily the man slid back into the dark and opened the door wider. Immediately light streamed into the room, illuminating its simple layout and the short shaggy man, about one and a half cubits tall, half naked and dirty. The stranger seemed no older than forty, although it was impossible to tell for sure because his face was covered with long hair and a beard. No matter how hard I tried to depict his features, all I could see were a round short nose and two gray eyes that ran back and forth, examining our company, and all the gear we had with us.

"Did you say Old Eter sent you?" asked Aul, done studying us.

"Yes he did. We just have some questions, and we want to—"

"Questions? What kind of questions?" interrupted Aul. "If you came here to talk about those old pots I do not know nothing about them. They were broken before I got there. I did not touch them and I will not pay a single copper. You hear me? Not a copper."

The man shook his small fists in the air.

"Oh no, we are not here to ask about any pots, we are interested in something else."

"You say, you are not here for the pots?"

"No."

"Are you sure? Because I—"

"We do not care about your pots," I exclaimed, my patience running out.

"Then what do you want to ask me?"

"We are looking for the missing caravan that disappeared several weeks ago somewhere around this area. Some days ago we learned that someone from around here had come upon an abandoned wagon. When we finally came to Lulione, Old Eter told us about you."

"A wagon, you say? Yes I did find a cart some time ago. It was very strange. I never found anything like this before, not in these woods at least. But it is not here anymore. They took it away...the lord and his men."

"Can you tell us how and where you found it?"

"Let's see...Oh yes, I remember. That day I went to get some wood. The nights had been very cold and I needed more firewood to keep me warm. I did not want to go to Lulione. It is too far and they always charge me for it—two coppers for one load of dry wood! Can you imagine, two coppers, for wood? It is robbery in broad daylight. There were times when I could—"

"How awful, we completely understand. But what about the cart?"

"Oh, yes, yes, I needed some wood, so I decided to get it myself. There are plenty of dried-out broken trees in the forest nearby. I know, I know—you need a lord's permit to cut the wood on his land but I did not cut any trees. I only took what I found on the ground. If you do not believe me, you can go and check yourself, all the trees are there, I did not break the law. No, not me. I like the law, it makes things right. You can tell the lord I said so. I like him too, you know. I am not lying. I—"

"We believe you, we really do. Can you continue with your story, please?"

"Of course. Where was I? Ah, yes. I took my axe and headed out sometime in midafternoon. I think it was midafternoon. It could have been earlier afternoon, or later morning. I remember the sun was high. At first I thought to go north. I knew a spot there that had good dried-out pines. But then I changed my mind. Frankly, I just did not want to drag any heavy loads all the way back to the house. So I decided to go east. The wood there is not as good, but it was just a league or so away."

"I spent almost three hours looking for good stumps, when suddenly I noticed something sitting in the bushes. I did not know what it was so I went over to get a better look. That's how I found the wagon. It was a nice wagon, broken a little on one wheel, but still well made. I never saw such a good wagon, not even in Lulione. And there was a big symbol painted over its sides too. I do not remember what it looked like, but it was pretty, with some letters and pictures. I did not think anyone would have left such a good wagon in the woods by itself, so I left quickly, before its owners could see me.

"The rest of the day I carried the loads back to the house. On my last trip to the forest I decided to check on the wagon again. I went back and found that the cart was still there. I thought it was strange, so I figured if I wandered around for a bit longer, someone would show up, but no one did. And after waiting for three hours, I finally decided to examine the wagon again. This time I took a look inside. But I found nothing. The cart was almost empty, except for one big box, which I did not touch. I stayed at that clearing for another hour, and when nobody came, I decided to leave, but then..."

Aul leaned forward and his voice was a soft whisper. "I saw someone walking out of the woods. I hid in the bushes behind the cart and watched as a man dressed in a robe, kind of the one that monks wear, walk around the clearing, poking everywhere with his long stick. Since I had never seen that man before, I stayed in the bushes while he searched the glade, and when he was gone, I ran to Lulione."

"Where did the man go?" I asked quickly.

"He did not go to the road. No. He went the other way, south...yes, south...I am sure of it. So...I ran home. No...I ran to the village. Yes. To the village—to tell Old Eter about the wagon. He promised to tell the others of my find. I guess he did, because some days later, soldiers came, then the lord himself. They stopped by my place and asked me questions. When I told them everything they went to the clearing and took the cart. I know, because I went there the next day and the cart was gone."

"Is that all that happened?" I asked Aul.

"Oh, yes, yes…that is everything…. If I knew anything else, I would have told you," replied Aul timidly.

"Was there anyone else who had seen the wagon before the lord picked it up," I inquired, remembering what we had learned from Sire Rone.

"No, Sir, I was alone…yes…alone…I am sure about it. Except for that monk, there was no one else, but me."

"Are you sure?"

"Yes. Yes. I did not see anyone there. And I was the one to report about the wagon. Nobody else did, just me."

"Many people live around here?" I asked then.

"No, just me. Most folks do not like the wild too much and prefer to live in Lulione. Travelers do not come here often either. They take the roads west of here, where there are fewer woods and more cities. And I do not blame them. There is really nothing around here to look at—some trees, a few small villages, and farm fields," replied Aul with a slight note of sadness in his voice.

He sounded sincere and I had no reason to distrust him. Yet his recollections did not satisfy our inquires. Whatever the case, it was clear that we had to pay a visit to the monastery, which we decided to do right after examining the place where Father's cart had been found.

I asked the lonesome farmer a couple more questions, but got few lucid answers. He did not know much else about the matter, but he did have a lot to say about other things, continuing with his own fables—long tales about his life, his house, and his apple orchard, which as he claimed was one of best in the entire province. Very soon my friends and I had learned that Aul lived most of his life alone, without family or friends. Yet he was a good and hard-working fellow, who spent his years looking after a small plot of apple trees that grew neatly behind his house. In the spring seasons he prepared the soil and treated the roots, and in the fall gathered apples and sold them to Old Eter, who happened to be the only vendor in Lulione. When the winter came he traveled to the village and stayed at the tavern for many days, listening to stories from the few passing voyagers. When his money ran out, he returned home, and everything started all over again. Such was his simple life, and Aul liked it, though probably in his heart he dreamt of something better.

When Aul was done with his tales, he invited us for a late lunch. Although we tried to decline his offer, he continued to insist until we gave in and sat down on dusty timber chairs, squeaky and wobbling. While we waited, Aul ran behind a long drape, where he remained hidden for some time, his absence complemented by occasional sounds of dropped pots, splashing water, and chopping knife that indicated an intense cooking. When Aul finally reemerged from the kitchen, in his hands he had a tray, full of various food and drink.

That day, the farmer treated us to a flavorsome stew, thick with steaming chunks of juicy meat, a jar of murky apple cider, and a handful of baked apple cakes, all of which exuded a scent of freshly cooked food and made the fare so tasty that it vanished almost instantaneously into the depths of our bellies. Alas we could not spend too much time enjoying Aul's cooking as we had more pressing matters to attend; so after finishing the last of the apple cakes we said our goodbyes and went back to the road. Our departure upset Aul very much, and he tried to make us stay for a bit longer. Only when we promised to stop by on our way back, did he set us free, allowing us to leave his small dwelling.

Chapter 12

AROUND US the trees became bigger and more frequent and soon transfigured into a dense forest, which consumed the road from both sides. A bit later we stepped away from the main road and to a smaller path, which took us deeper into the depths of woods. At first the route was rather wide and allowed the four of us to travel abreast if needed. But then it got thinner and eventually turned into a narrow trail that winded constantly amongst the trunks and shrubs of the underforest, carrying us further and further away from the more traveled route and to an edge of a clearing that, according to the map, was the place near which Father's cart had first been found.

Resembling a small island of grassland in a sea of trees, the glade was shaped as an almost perfect circle about fifty cubits in diameter. Straight ahead lay a flat grass floor that hosted scores of young spring flowers, all different in color. To the left, a range of short, but bulky bushes enveloped almost half of the forest line, and to the right, a squat mound rose from behind two fallen tree trunks that rested flat on the ground, making the site perfect for a late-night stop.

At first a sense of peace and solace imbued me, but as I studied the layout of the glade I realized that it looked very familiar. It was as if I had seen it before—but when and how? Then suddenly I recalled—my dream, that awful dream about Father and Ave and the strange dark man, who spoke with a Southern accent. The disturbing images sprang out of my memory, engulfing me with a disturbing, chilling feeling. It was there the caravan had been ambushed, and it was there the mysterious assailants kidnapped Father and Ave. A sense of fear came over me, but I did not know what scared me more—the fact that my vision had come true, or that I might know what happened to Father's convoy. I shook my head, trying to make my wits work straight. Slowly my thoughts settled and I could hear my friends' voices again, who stood several cubits away, talking to each other.

"Are you sure, Rob?" I heard Ike inquire as he walked around the glade, looking up into the sky.

"According to the map this is the place," replied Rob, stuffing the map back into his pocket.

"It is," I said as sadness overwhelmed me. "I saw it my dream. It is the place." My friends all looked at me.

"So…this is the spot," commented Ike. He moved to the center of the opening, spinning slowly to observe the woods around him.

"If this is it, we should start looking. The sun is going to set soon, and we might not have enough time. Maybe we will find something useful here," said Ark as he joined Ike in the midpoint.

"I agree, let's search this place," noted Rob.

"And afterwards, when we are done, we can have a nice hot meal," Ike added, coming back to the edge of the forest, sliding his backpack from his shoulders.

"Ike, you just ate a couple of hours ago. Is it all you think about, food?" retorted Rob angrily but then smiled. "I say we split up. Ike and Mishuk— check those bushes. Ark, you can take the mound over there and I will look under the two trunks next to it."

"That is fine with me," I replied slowly.

"Just do not venture too far into the woods; we do not want anyone to get lost," warned Ark finally, and we all split up.

Quickly Ike and I walked up to the line of bushes, studying every speck of the ground. We decided to work together. Initially, Ike went first and I followed. When we got to the end of the ridge, we switched and searched the shrubs again, often getting to our knees to look underneath the leaves. Yet we found nothing. The ground was undisturbed. Not ready to give up, we turned to make another pass, but Rob's voice distracted us.

"Hey, fellows, I think I found something!" he yelled, signaling with both arms for the rest of us to come over.

"What is it?" called Ark back from behind the mound.

"Come here and look for yourself," answered Rob.

"We are coming," I blared and rushed toward the center, hoping to see something, anything that could help me solve the mystery behind Father's disappearance.

In a few long leaps Ike and I reached Rob, who stood between the logs, looking down at something. Once at his side, I followed his glance and spotted a purple pouch, sewn with thin golden stitches, on the ground just under one of the logs, covered in dry brown leaves. Promptly I kneeled down and reached for it. Right away my fingers found the soft velvety fabric, and I brought the find into the light, studying it as I climbed back up. Barely the size of a grown pear, the container was very light to the touch and had no letters or symbols anywhere on its whiskered surface. After flipping the pouch in my hands I drew on two thin golden strings and emptied its content, which consisted of two gold plates, five silver coins, and a ring.

While the money looked ordinary enough, the ring did not. A thin elegant brass circle embraced three reddish stones, oval in shape with elegant figures of elks engraved on their surface. A detailed design, in which the animals were carved, pointed to exclusive craftsmanship, which, in turn, suggested that the ring was an expensive piece of jewelry, too expensive to leave in the woods to be found by some strangers like ourselves.

"How did you stumble on it?" I asked Rob as I inspected the ring from all angles.

"It was stuck in that small opening down there," replied Rob, pointing at a hole on one side of the log. "I was checking the ground underneath the trunk when I noticed something glittering, I looked closer and saw a purple cloth sticking out, so I shook the log, and when the bag fell out, called you."

"I think I know this ring." Suddenly Ike's words made everyone turn to him, eyes full of surprise.

"What do you mean you know this ring?" I asked him impatiently.

"I mean that I have seen a similar-looking ring before," replied Ike. "My mother had a ring just like this. She got it from her mother, and her mother had gotten it from her mother. A few months ago my mother gave the ring to my older sister as a gift for her eighteenth birthday. Unfortunately my sister has very thin fingers and the ring did not fit her, so my father had arranged for someone to have its width adjusted."

"Is this your sister's ring?" I asked my friend, anxious to hear more.

"I do not know if it is her ring or not. I am just saying that I have seen one similar."

"Can it be that your father has given this ring to Mishuk's father to get it altered in a big city?" asked Ark.

"That may be. As I said, it was too big for her." Ike looked at the ring again. "Now as I think about it, it may very well be my sister's ring. Yes. I think it is. I am almost positive. It had three red gems with elks in them, just like this one."

"Huh, three red gems with figures of elks carved into them." Ark noted thoughtfully, "This is too much of a coincidence. I think Ike may be right."

Ark paused for a moment, and then added, "Now everything fits, the wagon, the ring. Fellows, we may have found our first clue to the missing caravan."

Ark took the ring from Ike and lifted it up to examine it closer in the light of the descending sun.

"What do you mean?" I asked, confused.

"If it is your father's pouch and this is your sister's ring, it can mean only two things," answered Ark, true to his sharp sense of reason. "First, your father might have lost this bag here, while camping at the clearing. Since his cart has also been found close by, I am almost positive that his caravan passed through this glade. What happened then remains a question. The caravan could have moved on, after camping here, or….

"Of course it is possible that the convoy has never been here. Instead the cart was either lost or stolen someplace else, and then brought here for looting. The pouch was amongst the stolen goods and was later misplaced by robbers. Although it may be so, I find this line of reasoning very unlikely, because people rarely lose something so valuable as this ring once they have acquired it. So it brings us back to my first suggestion.

"It hurts to say, but I suspect that your father's caravan stopped here, and…never left. Something must have happened at this clearing. Again I do not know what. All I can think of is that it has been something out of the ordinary, a robbery perhaps. This also collates to Mishuk's strange dream. It is a dark thought, but what if there was an ambush waiting for the caravan here? And then some days later Aul found the remains of the convoy and reported his find to that old fat trader in Lulione. The pouch probably slid off your father's belt during the ambush; that or he could have put it in here intentionally, perhaps as a hint, or a sign, to tell others what had happened to his caravan.

"And as for the wagon, it could have been your father who hid it; or maybe the bandits, who had their hands full and could not take the cart with them, left it here. Whatever the real cause may be, we will not be able to understand it until we find more clues. Perhaps a trip to the monastery can get us further answers."

"Let's say my father and his men did come here, and someone did kidnap them. Then, where did they take them?" I asked Ark, who, I hoped, had more answers than me.

"That is what we have to find out, and I have a feeling we will. Look, we have already found the pouch, something that Sire Rone and all of his men could not do, and we have a sighting of a brother of the Order to explore. I say that so far we have gotten more answers than anyone else. I think it is a good start, do not you?"

He was right again. We faced more questions, but we had things to look into. With this in mind we decided to seize our search and march to the next destination, the hospice of the Order of the Spirit, a widely known religious group responsible for spreading the words of the Spirit through the many realms of Ethoria. Since a trip there was worth one whole day of walking, after a quick break we gathered our things and finding a small trail at the eastern edge of the clearing, started cautiously down yet another path, reforming our single file. Several hundred cubits into the woods the route became steep and eventually brought us to the base of a large bare hill, which towered over the adjacent forest. Discreetly we climbed to the summit, where we halted for a moment, studying the view of a vast field of treetops, which surrounded us on all sides. Unable to detect anything unusual, we continued with the journey. Once back in the forest, the trail turned sharply south and continued in that direction for several leagues, passing through some shallow streams of clear cold water that pierced the forest grounds like little veins on an invisible body.

In time the dusk came and then moved west, giving way to the evening cool dark shades of deep blue. Trying to cover as much ground as possible before the darkness we stayed on the course until the stars came to life, then settled at the first small glade we spotted. It was a narrow stretch of open ground, clinched within lines of old oaks. There we started a small fire, and made a simple meal. By then it was completely dark. A big moon shone a yellowish light onto the grass and the soft glow of the timid fire illuminated portions of the woods. That evening we felt particularly tired and soon after finishing our dinner went to sleep, quickly taken into another realm of visions, dreams, and nightmares.

Chapter 13

I RODE a stunning tall steed, enveloped in an elegant white cloth, stitched with strings of gold. With a long gleaming sword that swayed freely at my side, I wore large plates of shining steel, covered by a red and white robe, which bore a familiar symbol of a burning golden goblet on a blue circle. Traveling swiftly through streets of some unknown city I led my friends toward tall white walls of a magnificent fortress, carved out of a mountainside that bathed affably in a bright blue summer sky. As we came closer, we took a sharp turn and entered a wide avenue, paved with black stones that dazzled brightly in the light of the day, reflecting it back to the sun.

It was filled with people on both sides. Old and young, tall and short, they crowded the lanes, displaying an astonishing palette of colors that streamed from thousands of vivid banners, plentiful clothes, and countless gemstones of every shade. Cheerful tunes, noises, and endless talking were everywhere, giving the human lines the unique trait of a living being, with its own personality and manners. Through all the folks we jaunted onward, finally coming to the edge of a spacious plaza, also pressed with many men, who all stared anxiously toward the center, awaiting something or someone to appear at an elevated podium some several dozen cubits away. Suddenly shouts of joy and admiration unfolded through the ranks of spectators and quickly transformed into an incessant loud hum.

Trying to trace the source of the excitement I lifted myself high off the saddle and looked ahead. At first all I could see were people, people, and more people everywhere. But as the crowd began to shift, pushing closer toward the stage, I spotted a column of knights that emerged from another street across the square and moved slowly toward the podium, scattering the observers to the sidewalks. There were at least fifty clad horsemen, and at the front of their column traversed a tall man, who held a massive standard of the burning chalice at his side. His movement was graceful and his posture unfaltering. Directing his huge pitch-black stallion he proceeded toward the platform, exuding flashes of sunlight reflecting off his golden armor. Once there he handed the banner to another horseman, then sprang from his mount and disappeared amongst the men below, re-emerging at the top of the vacant stage.

He did not raise his hand or say anything. Yet when the people saw him, they went crazy and started another wave of cheers, clapping, and shouts that erupted in one deafening roar. The knight observed the men before him, then threw aside his stunning vibrant mantle and drew a long dazzling sword out of its sheath, lifting it high over his head. The sight of the beautiful weapon made the frenzy louder. Shouting and applause continued even when the man lowered the sword and hid it back into the bind. The knight observed the crowd some more, then slowly took off his luminous polished helm, revealing his true appearance.

Although I was only a hundred cubits away I could not catch the man's features. Hoping to get a better look up, I grabbed the straps and moved my horse closer to the stage. While I fought my way through the dense crowd, the knight walked to the very edge of the podium, and then finally I saw his face. What a surprise it was to find the tall man in the golden armor to be no other than my own brother Ric. I wanted to yell something to him, but I could not. I opened my eyes and realized that it was all a dream.

"Mishuk, Mishuk." Suddenly I heard Ike's voice whispering at my side.

"Ah, what? Oh, Ike," I replied, rubbing my eyes.

"Did you see it? I mean, did you see Ric just now, amongst all those people?"

"Uh…yes, yes…I did. Was it another vision?"

"Of course it was."

I raised myself off the ground and sat down, pushing Ike aside. Then I turned to my friend and whispered, trying not to awaken Ark and Rob, who were lying quietly nearby. "I thought it was just a normal dream."

"Me too," agreed Ike. "It did not feel anything like the other visions."

"Did you see his armor and that sword? That was something, ah?" continued my friend. "Is it the first time your brother came to us in a dream?"

"I think it is," I replied, then thought some and added, "Yes. It surely is."

"I wonder if he has seen it too. You know like we do."

"I will remember to ask," I said pensively, then paused. "If we go back to Villone."

"Villone! I am not going back home. Not any time soon. Not for a year, or two." Ike was clearly still distressed by the slightest idea of facing his parents again and refused to even talk about it.

"Do not worry, Ike; nobody is going home yet." I tried to calm him down, smiling a little. "There is much we need to do out here."

For a while the two of us talked about the latest images. Then we got quiet and soon after Ike fell asleep. I, however, did not feel like sleeping and instead sat by the fire, listening to its soft soothing whisper. Careworn I stared at the flames, thinking. Alas the promising respite of peace and silence did not last for long, as a loud sound of breaking branches sent me up to my feet. Ike was up too, with his short sword in one hand and a dagger in the other. Pressing a finger against his lips, he tossed me the short sword and went over to Ark and Rob to wake them. Soon the four of us were standing around the fire, listening to the silence that filled the air.

We remained still, carefully picking through the surrounding shadows, but everything was quiet. By then the morning mist began to spread a thick blanket across the ground, floating calmly over the grass. An uneasy mixture of feelings filled me—anticipation and a sense of fear. As we continued to wait, a barely visible motion came across the northern edge of the glade and I jumped, startled by the sudden movement.

"What can it be ?" whispered Rob.

"I think we have some unwelcome guests," replied Ike, peering into the outline of the forest.

"Someone is coming from the northern corner," I interrupted and aimed my sword at the spot where I had seen some movement.

At that moment another loud burst of splintered wood echoed athwart the clearing. I shook off drops of morning dew from my hand and squeezed the hilt harder, pushing my fingers deep into its leather padding. It was no mistake. Something or someone was out there. I peered harder into the haze and soon detected a vague shape that emerged out of the shadows and started slowly in our direction. The silhouette then transformed into the figure of a short man, who walked peacefully, leading a shady brown horse behind him.

"Greetings to you, travelers," the young man said calmly as he stopped within a cubit from the tips of our swords. "My name is Minia Emile and I am looking for a party of four young voyagers from Villone who have left Sirone two days ago. I was wondering if you have seen them anywhere around here?"

"What do you want with those men?" I asked, holding my weapon pointed at the intruder.

"It is a fair question. I am a squire in service of Sire Rone, who is the lord of these lands. My lord has sent me to assist a fellow by the name of Mishuk Loyde, who, along with his friends, is searching for a missing caravan. Mishuk has visited Sire Rone at his castle, and then left north. The lord has ordered me to find him and offer my services as a token of his Grace's goodwill."

"How do we know that you are telling the truth? Maybe you just want to rob us or trick us into doing something we do not want to do?" I asked still holding my short sword up.

The man who had called himself Minia, smiled slightly and nodded as if it was his question that was answered, and not mine. "From your questions I can guess that I have found the right men. As to your distrust of my words, I suspect you have all rights to doubt me. Yet, let me say that you are obviously very new to traveling through the wilderness." Minia paused for a moment, and closed his right eye. "Do you think I would have made all that noise back there if I wanted to rob you? Or would I have stood here and talked to you if my intentions were hostile? I will let you figure out those answers on your own. In the meantime, I am a bit tired from a fast dash from Sirone and would like to get some rest before the morning comes. To resolve your doubts I have a letter here from Sire Rone that will prove the truth of my declaration."

With those words Minia reached into his vest and extracted a thin tube, which he unrolled and handed to me.

"This is the dispatch, signed by Sir Rone himself. If any of you can read you will find that it states my name and rank and purpose of being here. Surely you will recognize the lord's crest and the stamp at the bottom of the page."

A little hesitant I grabbed the parchment from the stranger's hand. It looked genuine. At the top a bleached yellow paper was decorated with a large silver family crest and held rows of carefully traced lines, written in rich blue ink. And at the bottom, I noticed Sir Rone's name, sealed with an imprint of his personal ring, which depicted the familiar figure of a racing wolf. Bringing the scroll closer to the light I cleared my throat and started to read loud enough so that my friends could hear everything I said.

Mishuk Loyde,

> *Please forgive my scrupulous knowledge of the matter, which involves your father's convoy. But there is little I can add to my earlier statements. By now you know as much, if not more, about your father's disappearance, as I do. Yet, I cannot, in good conscience, let your father's mystery continue, knowing that I could have done more to help you and your family in the time of need. For this reason I have decided to send one of my men to aid you in your honorable quest.*

The name of my servant, who will accompany you, is Minia Emile. He is one of my personal squires and knows a great deal about traveling in Normandian countryside. I have instructed him to track your party and join you. I think you will find his services very useful. Accept him and his skills as a small token of my help. Once you complete your journey, successfully or not, Minia will escort you back to my castle where I will await you with my inquiries.

This letter serves as a proof of my intentions, and will be given to you by Minia himself. In the meantime, farewell and safe journey.

May the Spirit guide your way.

Sire Rone of Sirone. The lord of Purone region of Bois. The knight of the realm of Normandia. The sworn man of the Duke of Bois, and the faithful servant to King Philip the First.

Indeed the letter stated exactly what Minia had just told us. Although still cautious, I did not have an uneasy feeling about the stranger, nor did I sense any fetid play in his words. Finished with the letter, I handed it to Rob, who studied it thoroughly and passed it to Ark and then Ike. When my friends were done, I lowered my weapon, pushing the blade under my belt.

"I am sorry for such an icy salutation," I said. "Now as I am assured that you are telling the truth, Minia Emile, I kindly accept Sire Rone's offer of assistance and welcome you into our camp and into our party." With these words I stepped aside and extended my hand showing the new companion into the camp. Minia accepted my invitation with a nod and after tying his horse to a low branch of a nearby tree, strode to the fire where the last remaining pieces of timber were giving up to the heat of the blaze. My friends and I followed the squire, and after he had sat down, settled next to him, staring at the newest member of our band with unconcealed interest.

From what I could tell, Minia was older than the rest of us; nineteen or twenty, maybe older. Although still young, his face showed traces of a sturdy life and some experience, unknown to most young bloods in Bois. A simple man, he looked like any other traveler we had met along the way. His short and stocky figure showed signs of a preference for tasty foods, and was enveloped in dark plain clothes with little ornaments of splendor. A black cotton shirt was accompanied by a dark green vest very similar to the one Rob had, except for rows of large round metal buttons on its sides. His long brown trousers were tucked carefully into hard leather knee-high boots, and at the waist a thick black belt held several of the usual items retained by a typical rover that included a hunting knife, a small pouch, and a sheathe. The outfit was completed with a long dark cloak, topped with a large hood, and a small hat, which had a little black feather stuck to its side. In all, if it were not for the letter, I would have never guessed Minia was Sire Rone's servant. Yet again he was just that, and a squire too.

Squires—a dream to many common boys. Every Normandian knight, young and old, always had several squires at his service. Young commoners, chosen from the fittest and the bravest of their retinue, the squires served their lords with honor and devotion, always at their master's side, sharing all their perils and dangers. Although often ridiculed by the other soldiery for their seemingly easy life, the squires were by far the most skilled fighters of all the lord's men, entrusted with the utmost important task of protecting their master.

Amongst all the tradition that inhabited the Normandia populace, the notion of becoming a squire had always appealed to the common folks of the kingdom, for if a squire managed to complete a valiant duty, he could be raised to the rank of a lord, which implied a title, wealth, and lands. The prospect of a knighthood was a dream of all commoners, and every year scores of young men from all over the kingdom left their parents' homes and traveled to the lords' castles, in hopes of becoming squires and later knights. Yet to most, knighthood remained as far away as stars in a nighttime sky, as only very few of the squires ever succeeded in gaining a noble status. For the rest, there was a simple soldier's life—some decent gear, food, and a few coppers as a pension to ease their passing days.

Yet, there was one other benefit to being a squire that made it worth the work—a horse. Aside from regular cavalry, squires were the only other troops to have horses. Although mares and steeds were as common in Ethoria as men themselves, they were expansive to acquire and maintain. While lords and traders had scores of the animals, far greater population of Normandia and Ethoria could not afford such luxury and resorted to traveling on foot, regardless of distances and time. Back in Villone I thought about getting some horses for the journey, but there was no way I could have acquired even one. Although my family was amongst the lucky few, having several animals, Father had always taken them all on his trip, leaving only a couple of donkeys and a goat, useless things in any travels.

Certainly Minia was fortunate. He had his own mount, a creature of average size, brown in color, with only some splashes of white on its legs and forehead. Its long black hair fell randomly down its neck and side. The equally black tail was cut short and waved constantly from side to side, chasing away whatever parasites the Normandian woods had to offer in the early spring. A regular buckskin seat was placed over the animal and was stacked with various things— a sword, a round shield, and a few hefty bags. While the horse quietly chewed on wet grass a few cubits away, sitting around the fire, we listened to the newcomer with interest.

After a slow start our bond with Minia began to form. The young squire seemed a nice cheerful fellow who had some good stories for an evening tete-à-tete. After a few questions we learned that Minia was in fact nineteen years old. He had a wife and a small boy of two years, who lived inside the castle. Before becoming a squire, Minia lived with his parents and five younger sisters in a small house on the outskirts of Sirone. His father had been a servant for Sire Rone's long deceased father, and though he was a hardworking man, he often struggled to support his large family, as there were many days when Minia's household went by without a decent meal or a warm fire. When Minia reached his fourteenth birthday, his father decided to give him away as a squire to Sir Rone to ease the burden on the other children, most of whom were still toddlers. Since then, Minia had lived his life as a faithful servant to his lord, training himself in many arts, required by his line of duty. Soon he became a decent fighter and tracker, and earned respect from his liege, who started to take the young squire everywhere he went. Hunts and tournaments became a part of Minia's existence. He carried his lord's weapons, cleaned his armor, strapped his horses, and cooked occasional meals, always following Sire Rone, always at his side.

Retaining a handful of useful skills, Minia could have easily earned himself a good coin if he had chosen to leave the service. But he could not do so, not until Sire Rone himself allowed it, which he did not. So Minia remained a soldier, a hunter, and a servant to his lord, ensuring the well-being of his lord. He did not mind such living and enjoyed being a squire, a military man in service of a knight-lord. His position brought him good coin, a nice home, and a few favors from the lord, something many common men could only dream of. And of course there were stories. Tales, rumors, gossip, songs, and odes, which Minia learned along the way, gathering them on his many trips from various folks, nobles and not.

Each of the tales was different, interesting, and exciting. Captivated, my friends and I could not get enough of them. When Minia was done with a legend, we showered him with questions until he started another. Afterwards we requested more and more, until the sun was already up and a warm breeze rolled freely through the glade, spreading the scent of the awakening forest. It was too late to catch any sleep. So, finished with the last tale, we got up and helped Ark make an early meal for the whole party, including Minia.

Chapter 14

THE SQUIRE waited on his horse, while the rest of us rolled our blankets and packed them into the bags. Without delay we departed from the small clearing and paced down the same path, which continued to lead us through the woods. A thick wall of hanging branches pressed hard against the narrow lane and pushed us back into single file, also forcing Minia to dismount and let his horse trot passively after him. In time the morning wore off and the heat grew stronger. Even the shadows did not help, leaving us prey to the hot dry air and hardly visible sun. Relief came only when we reached a narrow fold that ran across our way, quickly disappearing into the nearby lines of shrubs.

A thin stream of fresh water flowed joyfully at the bottom of a creek, making a ringing splashing noise. The sight of the clear water made me very thirsty, and with the backpack on my shoulders I scrambled down the bank and dipped my head into the light torrent, enjoying its icy feel. While I cooled myself, my friends came down too and refilled their flasks.

"Does anyone know where we are?" asked Ike as his container gulped the water.

"I think so," replied Rob. "According to this map we should be out of the forest and into the valley in no time. Once in the open we should be able to see a road that will eventually take us to the monastery."

Rob pointed at the map and then showed it to Minia, who looked at it inquisitively and nodded in agreement. "That is right. I have been in these woods before and it is exactly the way we should go."

All the flagons full, we returned to traveling, only to find out that the creek itself presented us with a challenge. Although it was shallow and thin, its banks were rather high and made it hard for us to get to the other side with heavy loads on our shoulders. Yet, we had little choice, and after finding no better spot to cross, attacked the stream straight on, going through the running watercourse, which came up to our knees in places.

First to get across, I climbed up on the other bank and helped the others, who were not too far behind. Ark came up next, then Rob, and Minia, and finally Ike, who, unlike the rest of us, managed to lose his footing on the soft ground of the verge and fell backwards, splashing water all around him. Soaked to the last stitch, he lay on his backpack and half sank in the water, casting and swearing at his bad luck. When we finally stopped laughing, he clambered back up and crawled to the higher ground, brushing off the cold water that was dripping from him.

Reunited, we fed Ike a few more laughs and then went on with the journey, walking first east, then south, and then east again. After the last turn the lines of trees retreated a little, and soon a small opening appeared out of the woods ahead. The gap grew wider and eventually divulged a portion of rolling grassland lit with the afternoon sun. A bit tired of the timberland we hurried forth, and after another league reached the edge of the forest, stepping into a valley of tall wild weeds. As Rob had said, almost at the edge of the woods the road we had been traveling on joined a larger trail, which then ran along the rim of trees, coming from the north and then veering southeast away from the forest, gradually disappearing into the field.

Once we were off the trail and on the main road, we decided to make a brief stop, settling near a pile of large boulders that lay on the ground, half grown with dump moss. A bit weary from the walk, we removed our backpacks and rested on the lawn, relishing the view of the open sky. For a while I stared blindly at the clouds above me, then rolled to my side and observed my friends.

Across from me Rob checked his gear, meticulously inspecting each of the items, first the weapons, then the maps, the cloak, and his boots, plastered with chunks of dried mud from the creek. Further away, standing behind the stones, Minia attended to his horse, and Ike helped him.

While the squire fed the animal some grains from a large brown sack, Ike asked him questions, often pointing at different objects strapped to the saddle and the bags. And next to them, sitting on one of the rocks, Ark worked on the midafternoon meal. He had already retrieved several of the small cloth bundles from his back and was arranging them on top of the boulder. Once done, he opened the packs and distributed some of the provisions, which consisted of red onions sliced in half and seasoned with a mix of salt and red curry, strips of beef jerky, hard wheat bread, and a bottle of apple cider. We ate the food with delight, hungry after the long jaunt, and as we did Minia treated us to some more of his tales. He told us about tournaments and duels that he had seen as a servant to Sire Rone.

The squire's accounts were so interesting that we did not notice how hours passed, and the afternoon turned into its final stage. When we finally noted that the sun was reaching the far west corner of the sky, we scrambled to our feet, but it was too late. Our intermission at the edge of the forest had been far longer than expected, an unplanned delay, which meant that we would have to spend another night in the open before coming to the Monastery's grounds.

Still we tried to salvage whatever time we had left. We quickly resumed our stride, speeding down a widened road, eager to put several more leagues behind us before breaking for the night. In the open Minia was finally able to get back on his horse and rode happy next to us, occasionally galloping onward to check the view ahead. A few more hours passed promptly and the sunset finally went past the fields, letting the night into the world. The vast and empty landscape around us was dreary, and welcomed a hidden tiredness to overpower our weary minds. Slowly we grew bored of the walk and began to look for a suitable place to spend the night. To make the matter worse, Ark began to sing some of the old Normandian songs. He seemed to enjoy himself and let his voice ring across the road, bellowing the well-known rhymes to all who wished to listen. But none of us wanted to hear him sing—Ark was tone-deaf, and no matter how hard he wanted to bring joy to the rest of our company, his singing sounded more like the crooning of a lonely cat in springtime. Sadly Ark did not know that and, persuaded that he had all talent to become a bard, harassed our tired file with outbursts of earsplitting noises that had nothing in common with actual songs. Chased by Ark's terrible intoning, we veered off the road and after walking several hundred cubits into the field, broke camp amidst the open vale.

Soon a small fire sent burning sparks up the wind, and the cracking of the wood sounded soothing. Weary of the heat and walking, I wrapped myself in my cloak and drifted leisurely away into the world of dreams. The night was just like any other, a quiet breeze, soft sounds of moving grass, and lonely stars above. None of us heard a thing. Luckily our only horse had sharper senses. Picking up something unusual, the animal started to yank the straps and wail, beating its hooves on the ground. The sounds of the fretted animal made me open my eyes and peer into the darkness, trying to find the source of its irritation. Not surprisingly Minia was awake too. He was already on his feet, standing next to the mount, patting it gently on the back.

I stared at the squire, and then back at the bewilderment around me. Suddenly I heard something. A strange noise came from somewhere near and brushed off any relic of my sleep. Cautious, I listened harder. When the noise recurred, it sounded even closer. In one jump I climbed to my feet, glancing at Minia, in hopes of getting any clue to what was going on in the dark grass. The squire remained still, one hand on the horse, and the other on the hilt of his sword. When the strange noise came for the third time, he drew the blade and moved away from the fire, vanishing into the shadows. Nervous, I followed Minia's example, and grabbing the short sword that rested at my side, scrambled cautiously away from the camp. Once I was out of the illuminated area, my eyes could see much better through the darkness, allowing me to pick out vague outlines of the surrounds. Vigilantly, I slid slowly around the campsite, inspecting every shape and silhouette I could spot. But I could not find anything out of the ordinary. It all seemed normal, peaceful, and undisturbed.

I did not trust my eyes, though, and after taking another look, headed back to the camp, to the spot where Ike lounged serenely, enfolded in his cape. Quietly I tapped my friend on the shoulder and woke him up. With his eyes gazing bluntly at me, I pressed a finger against my lips, then pointed at my weapon and at the blackness of the field. It did not take long for Ike to grasp what I was trying to say, and after a lengthy yawn, he pulled out his long dagger and got up. Together we sneaked back into the dark and, circling around the illuminated portion of campground, headed for Rob and Ark. We got halfway, when suddenly a strange figure leapt out of the grass and charged us from the right flank.

At once I found myself lost. My blood raced through my veins; my mind refused to ponder logic. Although I had seen many fights in my sleep, in real life I found myself stunned and confused in the face of a living, breathing threat. In dreams I watched myself dispense enemies of every kind. I was agile and strong, and knew exactly what to do. But that was all unreal. The man in front of me was real, and from what I could tell, his intentions were far from affable. Desperate, I tried to regain control over myself, but could not. My hands were shaking, my mind went blank, and my knees were bulging as if made of soft clay. All I could do was tighten the grip on my sword, holding it with both hands. A cubit away Ike stood frozen too. His dagger was trembling a little, his eyes staring blindly at the intruder, who did not waste any time. Speedily closing the gap between us, he lowered his sword edge so it pointed straight at me. All of a sudden I wished that Rob and Ark were awake; they would have known what to do. But they were too far away to help us, and

Minia, he was nowhere to be seen. Ike and I were alone, with the enemy in front of us.

A slim long sword resting in the stranger's hand caught a flicker of light and flashed before me, posing an immediate threat. I had to do something, and quickly. Gathering all my will and strength I lifted my sword and spread my feet far apart so to give myself more balance. Then I moved backwards a little and pointed the weapon at the dark figure of a tall man who, undeterred, finally reached Ike and me. He leapt forth to throw his long thin blade at my chest. His action was so fast that I barely escaped a sure death. Jumping away I avoided the sharp edge that whistled over me and bounced to one side only to find the enemy in front of me again. Dodging another incoming blow I could not strike even once and continued my frenetic dance instead, my heart racing, drops of sweat streaming down my face, hands, and body.

Consumed with staying alive I did not notice how Ike danced along with me. For every attack the intruder launched at me, he sent another at my friend, making him bounce and dodge just like me. Yet, somehow, after one of the attacks, Ike managed to counterstrike, thrusting his dagger at our opponent, aiming for his exposed ribs. But my friend's attempt fell short of the target and he was forced to retreat quickly so to avoid being hit by the passing steel edge.

When the man switched his attention to Ike, I got a moment to catch my breath. My heartbeat eased a little and my mind cleared. At last I could reason again. The days that Ike and I had spent training swords in Villone came back to me, and I circled around the enemy, planning my attack, looking for an opening in his defense. Then as my friend dodged yet another blow, I charged. Unexpectedly I did not miss. My blade hit the thick hard surface of the man's vest and slipped down, leaving a wide streak of shredded leather. Although the strike did not wound the attacker, it made him pause for a moment as he stumbled back, staring at me in disbelief.

The enemy did not panic. Instead he shifted his weight from one leg to the other and dashed forth again, choosing me as his prey. His movement became sharper, and I did not notice how he slipped around me and emerged at the other side, ready to strike a devastating blow. But before he could do so, Minia's stocky silhouette sprang out of nowhere behind the intruder. The squire's weapon came down with great speed, sinking deep into the stranger's back. Stunned the stranger yelled in pain and stumbled, his knees buckling underneath him. Yet, despite a gaping wound that sent streams of dark red blood down his cloak, the enemy kept his balance. He pulled up his blade and spun around to face Minia. It was at that moment that Ike and I suddenly knew exactly what to do. Blades blazing, we attacked the enemy from both sides. My sword hit the man first and sliced his arm by the elbow, sending his sword to the ground. Then Ike drilled his blade into the foe's shoulder, making him scream again. Taken by our assault, the enemy became disoriented and stopped, leaning slightly to the left. But when Minia put his cold steel deep into his stomach, the intruder fell. The last deafening cry of anguish pierced the night air, waking both Rob and Ark, who were still sleeping, unaware of the raging battle near them. As they scrambled to their feet, the stranger rolled to one side in his last effort to get up, but the life force left him, and he froze in an unnatural pose, murmuring something to himself. I could not catch the words he uttered, but it sounded almost like a prayer. A moment later he was dead.

Baffled Ike and I stood next to Minia, towering over the half-lit figure of a young man average in build and pale in skin. Never before had either my friend or I been in a fight, or killed someone. Seeing a lifeless body at our feet was truly a shock. For a moment I sensed my stomach turn, but I held, instead turning my attention to the ground, where, lying on his back, the stranger stretched petrified as if he was simply resting before a long tiresome day. A black cape wrapped around his neck, spread across the stumped grass; the large hood slipped from his head and exposed a slender, clean-shaved visage with two glassy ice-blue eyes, staring sightlessly at the sky, hiding the last thoughts that had raced through the man's mind as he took his final breath. The stranger did not look anything like the local folk. Maybe it was his light skin, or the blue of his large eyes, but I could tell right away that he was an outlander.

His clothing, well made, yet simple was black in color. Sewn of fine fabrics, some cotton and some silk, it bore no symbols that could tell us of his name, profession, or social status. A leather vest, ripped in places from the fighting, covered an elegant long-sleeved shirt, which was clasped with a wide belt, decorated with rows of small metal spikes. Wide black cotton pants were pleated neatly into long travel boots and concealed two sharp throwing knives that peered through open pockets, reminding us of the danger the man had wielded. A long cape, and an empty sheathe completed the costume, and proved once more that the man was a native of a foreign realm, which I found rather strange, because our home province had never been frequented by people from abroad.

While there were plenty of foreigners who had visited the kingdom every year, only a handful of them ever traveled through Bois. Any time an outlander came through the province, he was looked upon as something unusual and often stirred much talk amongst the locals. And to be attacked by one of them— that was worth ten stories if not more.

While I pondered the dead man's identity, Ark and Rob finally joined us at the edge of the camp, their faces puzzled by the scene that met their eyes.

"What in the Spirit's name is going on here?" asked Rob, scratching the back of his head, staring at the body just a cubit away.

"Is he dead?" Ark followed with another question. We nodded. "Who was he?"

"I have no idea who he is, but you have just missed your first sword fight," replied Minia as he stooped down to get a better look at the attacker.

"You sure have," added Ike, showing everyone his dagger, bloodied from the encounter. His voice had lost the usual cheer and concern came in its place.

"How did it happen? Where did he come from?" Rob and Ark barraged us with one question after another. Ike and I tried to answer what we could, but in reality we did not know much ourselves. Everything had happened so fast that only after the stranger's death could we reflect on the incident. Meanwhile, Minia retrieved the intruder's blade and lifted it up, holding it closer to the light of the campfire.

"This is odd," pronounced the squire, flipping the weapon several times.

"What do you mean?" I asked, staring at the rapier with its curved wide blade, which looked no different from any other sword.

"This attack might not have been a simple robbery after all," clarified Minia quickly. "You see this blade? This is a good weapon—well made and very expensive. I have seen a good handful of thieves and robbers in my years. I even hunted some of them with Sire Rone. But I have never seen any of those thugs carry blades like this one. I am not even sure if you can buy this weapon anywhere in Normandia. To find something like this, you would probably have to travel to Azoros or the Free Cities." Minia put the sword away and continued. "And look at his clothes. His outfit seems ordinary to an untrained eye, but it is a trick. Look over here."

Minia directed our attention to the inside padding of the man's cloak. "Do you see it?"

Following the squire's finger I traced the smooth silk lining of the cape and when the glossy fabric caught a glimpse of the light, spotted a strange symbol, drawn in dark red ink—a thin circle sketched over a pair of widespread wings. The picture was unlike anything I had seen, and so I turned back to Minia with questions in my eyes.

The squire then lifted one of the corners of the cape with his own sword. "This drawing is not just a simple diagram. It is the symbol of a very well-known band of mercenaries, who tend to make their money by performing not so highly appreciated jobs across Ethoria. Amongst other things they often hire themselves as assassins, renting their services to anyone who is willing to pay their price."

"Assassins?" Ike put down the dagger and kneeled to get a better look at the drawing.

"Yes. Assassins. The Snake Bites is their name. If you look closer you will notice that the circle is actually a snake, drawn over a bat with its wings spread out. The snake represents their order, and the bat—their association with the underworld."

"Underworld? What is that?" I asked curiously, not knowing what the word meant.

"This is the name people gave to various criminal kinships in bigger cities."

"Do cities in Normandia have underworlds?" asked Ike, at last taking his eyes off the dead body.

"Of course, every big city does, no matter if it is in Normandia, or Azoros, or the Amber Empire. Where there is crime, there is an underworld."

"What about Villone, does it have an underworld?" Ike continued.

"Yes it does," replied Ark. "You, Ike, and probably Mishuk, for that matter."

Under any other circumstances I would have found the joke offensive, but still recovering from a life threatening experience, I found it funny, and started to laugh, loud and sincere. It was a laugh of relief and happiness that I was still alive.

"But why would an assassin try to kill us?" I turned the discussion back to the subject afterwards.

"That I cannot tell you. Only that I am sure that this is a Snake Bite," replied Minia.

"So you mean to tell us that someone hired this fellow to kill us?" Ike spoke slowly, his tone more serious now.

"That is precisely what I am trying to say. Sadly we will not be able to find out who the employer or the target were, but one thing is obvious: This man came here to kill someone, and that someone is standing amongst us. What I can also tell you is that he did not come cheap, and whoever hired him paid a hefty sum. This will probably not be the last visitor we will have. So I suggest we better be careful from now on. We should keep our eyes and ears sharp during the day and take turns guarding the camp at night."

"An assassin," repeated Ike, even more slowly. "Why would anyone want us dead? We did not do anything, did we?"

"Can it be that this attack is somehow connected to our quest?" I asked, ignoring Ike's murmur.

"It may very well be so," replied Ark. "We have been asking many questions. Someone might not have liked it."

Rob and Minia agreed.

They were right. There were a lot of strange things that suddenly started to unfold once Father went missing. Were they all connected? I did not know, but I hoped to find out sooner or later.

While Rob, Ark, and I continued to talk about the incident, Minia resumed his search of the lifeless body. Except for Ike, who was accustomed to dealing with the dead, none of us wanted to touch the chilled corpse and so we let the two of them recover whatever items they had found on the assassin's body, which included one rapier, one dagger, four throwing knives, a pouch full of some dried herbs, a blank parchment, and a leather flask containing some liquid of a terrible odor. There was nothing useful—no money, maps, written notes, or anything that could have explained something about the mysterious intruder. When all the items had been removed and stored safely in Minia's traveling bags, we threw the cape over the man's frozen face and buried his poor soul in a shallow grave at the far side of the camp.

At the camp the talk about the attack continued on. One question stirred another, and another, taking our discussion deep into the night. Listening to my friends, I finally had a chance to reflect on everything that had happened to me. I had to admit, the sense of victory was somewhat pleasant, even though it was mixed with perplexity and fear. It was my first battle and I managed to survive it. That in itself was incredible and I had yet to understand it fully. Until then I took note of what my friends had to say about it. Soon the conversation died out and I felt very tired. Pulling my cloak from underneath me I lay down and closed my eyes. My thoughts and dreams slowly came together, intertwining and mixing, and somewhere through them I heard Ike's whisper.

"Mishuk, how does it feel to kill someone?" he murmured in the darkness, which settled after we had put out the fire, so not to attract any more attention.

"Not good, not good at all," I answered after a long pause.

"Same here. It feels almost dreamlike, and I do not mean just the fight, the visions too, and Sire Rone, and our trip....All of it. Frankly, I had no idea that it would turn out like this. When we left Villone I thought we would spend a few days on the road, go to Sirone, and come back. But this..." Ike grew quiet for a moment. "It is mind-boggling. Mishuk, do you hear me? Mind-boggling."

I did not say anything—what could I say? My friend was right. For a while we lay in silence, and I was starting to fall asleep when I heard Ike's voice again. "And still, you know…I could have taken that assassin all by myself."

Sure, Ike, sure, I thought to myself, closing my eyes. Images returned and soon I was asleep.

Chapter 15

NEXT MORNING the dawn was especially cold. I awoke with the realization I did not have some horrible dream. A vicious fight was not a mere plot of my imagination, but the reality of last night. One thing was certain: Someone had taken a very personal interest in seeking my death or the death of my companions. Why—I did not know, but my search for answers took yet another turn, inflating the journey with more complexity and danger than ever before. With any luck I hoped to find some clues at the hospice of the Order of the Spirit.

It was midmorning when I rolled up my blanket, fixed my cloak, and cleaned my hands of some dried bloody speckles, reminders of my first victory. The sun was up too; lively birds sang in the distance, and the moist grass waved leisurely in a light wind. Right over me a handful of sparrows fought vigorously over something in the air, and under them my friends were getting ready for departure. As always Rob was studying his maps. Ark adjusted his high boots; Minia huddled around his mount, fastening the saddle straps, and Ike did absolutely nothing, sitting on the ground and whistling a cheerful melody. Though I felt well rested, my body still ached a little, my right arm sore from all the swinging and thrusting I had done the night before.

Finished with my bag, I put it aside and walked up to the spot where the battle had taken place. Surprisingly, the site did not look that much different from the rest of the camping grounds. Signs of furious fighting that I had imaged to be there, were almost all gone. Pools of sticky blood that had covered the grass only several hours before, soaked into the soft soil, leaving little trace of redness on the turf, and circles of footprints that marked my maneuvers were melted into the milieu, leveled by the walking we had done after the fight. And then the attacker himself, he was gone too, buried a short distance away under a low mound of fresh dirt that rose slightly over the weeds, denoting the outlander's resting place.

With little to look at, I concluded my observations and went back to the camp. I stopped by the remnants of the fire, near which a couple of slices of bread lay unattended on top of a cotton rag, probably left there by Ark, who had already fixed the early morning meal. Thinking little about the food, I put the hardened pieces into my mouth and washed them down with cold tasteless water from the flask. Then I was ready to go.

The mood amongst us was bleak. Since the morning everyone spoke little, each reluctant to share any thoughts. So quiet and gloomy, we continued through the southern vales of Bois, moving in a single line, with Minia riding ahead to scout the upcoming route.

By midday we reached another intersection, which marked our final approach to the compound. A long time ago there were signs that pointed to places the two roads led. But the wooden marks had long been gone and passing travelers either had to consult a map or guess as to which way went where. Of course we had our maps and Minia. While the squire helped Rob read the map, the rest of us sat down, glad of the chance to rest our strained limbs.

"This is where we need to turn east," announced Rob finally, looking at Minia as he spoke. The squire looked at the map and then glanced in the direction Rob had suggested. I looked there too; the same dull picture sparked little excitement.

"Are you sure we should turn here?" inquired Ike, relaxing comfortably on the grass. He did not want to resume the walk and tried to stall our departure for as long as he could.

"Yes, we are sure," Minia replied and sprang back on his horse, "This is the route to the monastery." The squire pointed east and yanked the bridle, sending his mount into a fast trot.

"The map seems to agree with him," added Rob. He started after Minia, sticking the map under his vest.

"If you say so, *Sire,*" Ike uttered mockingly and rose to his feet, groaning loudly. "I trust, you two will not get us lost." He shrugged his shoulders to adjust the backpack and headed out, following the rest of the company.

Keeping to Rob's instructions we turned east and moved down yet another unfamiliar course, which was a bit narrower than the previous route, yet flat and even. Slowly the junction behind us disappeared, and the sea of weeds restored its domination. I did not bother to look back. Rather I concerned myself with things ahead, hoping to spot the first glimpses of the monastery. Soon I noticed changes to the adjacent landscape. Grass that ran along the edges of the road became shorter, as if it had been cut not long ago, and the roadway itself broadened and started to show signs of broken pavement, which then turned into a well-tended lane of flat large rocks that I found particularly unusual, considering how few people actually visited these parts of the province.

The stone thoroughfare extended in the eastern direction for a league or so, but then circled south and came up to a small, steep mound, which blocked the view ahead. Resolute, we climbed the hill at speed, and at the top for the first time in almost two days saw rooftops surrounded by a logged wall, situated several hundred cubits into the valley below. At last, the monastery's compound was before us, and with it, answers to our many questions. Excited and somewhat troubled we scrambled down and to the front gates, which were composed of two huge barred oak doors. Though looking small from the summit of the hill, the monastery turned out to be a sizable stronghold. Comprised of several large structures, it was hidden behind a tall line of thick sheared tree trunks, planted to form a massive wall that shot up into the sky some five cubits over our heads.

After studying the base of the wooden barrier, we strolled up to the gates in hopes of finding someone who would at least talk to me. Of course, we did not know a single thing about monasteries, nor about brothers of the Order who dwelled in them. Our scarce knowledge came from short tales and thick boring history books, and we had no idea as to how to act around the followers of the Spirit. We also did not know if the suspicious fellow seen snooping near Father's wagon was actually a member-brother himself. Even if he was, he could have been from any other monastery in Normandia, or even worse, from any other monastery in Ethoria. But we had little choice. We needed all the answers we could get

Standing on the doorstep to the remote compound of the followers of the Spirit, I wished for one thing, and one thing only—a chance to ask a couple of questions and maybe have some answers in return so I could carry on with my search for Father, Ave, and all the other missing men. Determined to do just that, I banged on the large doors, my friends just a cubit behind. When I did not hear any answer, I knocked again, that time a bit harder and more persistent. Yet no one seemed to hear my call.

Hitting the door a few more times, I started along the gates, examining their wide oak boards and thick rough iron plates. At first thin black lines of wood gave out nothing, but then I detected a vague outline, barely visible in the reflection of the sun. Immediately I walked up to it and traced the fine fault with my fingers. Indeed it was a small hatch, neatly placed in the larger door. The smaller gate looked closed, so I took a step back and kicked it, making as much noise as possible. At once, a clanking sound came from the other side and the panel slid inward. Somewhat surprised I put my right hand on the timber and pushed. The small door gave way easily and making a prolonged squeaking noise, invited in a stream of light that pierced a lengthy shadow. After staying still for a moment I stepped through, and halfway into the monastery's grounds, I tapped on a door again. As before no response came. So I went forth, soon finding myself inside the compound, strangely quiet and deserted.

Everything around me looked blank and filled with a yellowish shade from hay and sand that covered the ground, making the place look flat and unpaved. Three large buildings dwelled inside the enclosure. To the left stood a broad one-story structure. Pressed to the inner wall, it was made of thick brown logs, which ran the entire length of the house, barring no windows or doors, except for one large opening, impeded by a wide door, left ajar, inviting strangers like ourselves to a peek inside. An almost identical building stood across from it to the right, as if one was a mirror image of the other.

The third building looked much different though. Located straight across from the gates, it resembled a chapel of some sort. Unlike the other two, it was slender and tall, and had a triangular roof that stretched far into the sky, finished at the top with a large crystal sphere. Although the building was also made of logs, they were much better refined and were pushed together so tight that not a single crack could be seen even at a very close range.

The craftsmanship of its decorators was equally alluring. The entire facade of the building was highlighted with various designs. The very base of the chapel was painted white and hosted rows of unique adornments of wood-carved frescos, devoted to various motifs. Further up, around the front doors, another set of carved pictures presented viewers with scenes from ancient history, many of which I did not recognize. In between the colorful murals, tinted mosaics of glass and metal decorated several narrow windows, which ran across the front and the sides. Their slender long frames were made of elegant brass bars and imprints of fantastic creatures. At the lower part of the facade, rising in a prolonged arch, stood the grand entrance, comprised of three swinging doors, opened so as to present us with the view of a spacious inner chamber.

Yet, it was not the striking architecture of the buildings around me that caught my attention. It was the complete absence of any living things that halted me once I was inside the monastery's courtyard. As if spellbound, the compound was empty and silent. No matter where I looked, I could not see a single soul. There was no sign of people, animals, or even birds, just gusts of wind that picked up dust and straw from the floor and threw them from side to side, often halting abruptly, only to resume a moment later with more force. Immediately the image of the glade where Father once had passed, returned to me. Somehow the deserted monastery looked similar. It was just as deserted, and just as spotless. And just like the clearing near Lulione, the serenity of the place felt unnatural, as if there was something sly about it, something suspicious.

"Greetings to all!" I yelled out as loud as I could. "We are simple travelers; we mean no harm." I became quiet and waited for a reply that never came. Those who had dwelled there had long been gone.

Saddened, I sighed in regret and moved into the center of compound; my friends had made their way inside and were following me in a slow stride. Only Minia was still missing, but he appeared shortly after, leaving his horse wandering outside, at the base of a wall where there was plenty of succulent fresh grass. The squire joined the rest of us in the middle of the yard and stared keenly around, the same question in his eyes.

Faced with another setback there was little else for us to do, but to explore the vacant grounds in hopes of discovering something useful for our quest. To save some time, we decided to split into two groups. Ike and I were to search through the house to the left; while Rob, Ark, and Minia were to look in the building across from it. The chapel we chose to leave for last and explore it together, as it seemed to bear some significance to the entire stronghold.

Through the open doorway Ike and I entered a long wide hall, its inner walls coated with dark blue sheets of thick but rich cloth, with rows of brass candleholders protruding, some of which still held half-melted sticks of yellowish aged wax. Further in, three gigantic wooden tables stretched across the entire length of the chamber, accompanied by several low benches. A large fireplace, constructed of gray river stones, rested at the far end of the hall, and along its sides ascended two standards that pictured images of a golden chalice encircled by a bright blue ring.

It was a familiar picture. I recalled seeing a similar symbol in my dream. Only the chalice was not burning and was placed inside a ring and not a disk. For a moment I wondered if it was of any importance, but soon returned my attention to the fireplace, next to which stood a long stone counter covered with a drape of deep red fine silk, trimmed at the corners with golden strings in the images of weaving flowers. Over the dais, suspended from the beams of the ceiling hung four swinging lamps. Once lit, the rough iron lanterns provided enough light to illuminate the entire compound. But their oils had dried out and their filters were plastered with layers of dust, which suggested that no one had ignited them for days if not weeks.

Ike, who was kneeling down by the grate of the fireplace, supported my theory. "There has not been a fire here for some time."

"How do you know?" I asked curiously, peering at the sooty coals.

"You see. The ashes are black and small. No logs, no half-burned wood." Ike pointed at the back of the hearth that composed the bottom portion of the fireplace.

"How long?"

"I say this grate has been cold for at least a week or two," stated Ike.

"Two weeks."

"Maybe more, it is hard to tell."

I glanced down the hall again. The occupants had not left the place in a hurry. Everything remained as it probably always had been. The place was abandoned willingly. I had no doubt about it. But why? It was another question I had to answer.

Finding nothing else of interest, Ike and I made another pass through the hall, then headed into the courtyard, finding our three companions already there, shaking their heads as a sign of their equally poor progress.

"So you did not find anything either, huh?" inquired Minia as Ike and I joined them in the center.

"No, nothing interesting, just tables, benches, and other useless junk," replied Ike.

"What do we do now?" I asked.

"Let's check that chapel, see if there is anything there. Then we can scout the inner grounds again, in case one of us has missed something" replied Minia, who then proceeded toward the only unexplored building in the compound. Feeling discouraged, Ark, Rob, and Ike walked after him, while I trailed slightly behind, peering into every shadow there was.

"What do you think happened here?" I heard Ike a few steps ahead.

"The gates were left unlocked, the place emptied, and all the doors opened. Besides, there are no signs of violence, no hints of fighting, or broken gear. As far as I can tell those brothers just picked up their things and left. Does it look strange? Sure it does. One day someone, who looks like a member-brother noses around Lulione, and the next the whole monastery disappears," deduced Ark in his usual manner.

"Any ideas as to how long the monks have been gone?" asked Rob, when Ark was finished.

"Ike says two weeks ago," I said, recalling my friend's earlier assessment.

"I did not say two weeks; I said around two weeks, it can be more or less. I was just guessing," protested Ike, then he turned around and gave me an angry look.

"It does not matter really. It has been more than a day, and that is enough. They can be as far away from here as the border," declared the squire, making Ike turn back again.

There was a short pause, then I asked wistfully, "I wonder why they left?"

"Who knows? Maybe they got tired of this place. Or maybe they had something to do with the missing caravan. Whatever it is we will not know until we find them." Minia's response had much seriousness to it.

"I hope we do," I said quietly. "But where?" Although I whispered the question to myself, Minia heard me nonetheless.

"Somewhere we will, one way or another. Someone will see them someplace; there will be rumors. One thing I have learned in my years as a squire is that it is not all too hard to track someone, not in Normandia, at least."

Those words spoken, we came up to the entrance to the chapel. The doors were open, but we were hesitant to go in. We stood in front of the building and listened to a whistling of the wind, our eyes focused on the shaded hall. Inside we saw tall walls covered with long polished boards that climbed all the way to the ceiling, made of brown wooden beams and supported by two rows of large square columns, which ran parallel to each other along the entire length of the room. On the floor, lines of benches stretched from one side to another and occupied most of the space, leaving only a narrow passage in between that stretched to the far end of the chamber, where a massive decorated pedestal stood towering in the center. Behind the carved altar, three white silky drapes came down from the top, displaying the same picture of a chalice and a blue ring, this time also coated with rich gold paint.

Minia was the first to break the silence. He pulled up his loose belt and sauntered nonchalantly through the doorway, past rows of timber benches, and up to the podium. There he stopped and turned, inspecting the far end of the room. Overcoming a disquieting uneasiness, the rest of us followed, and motivated by the squire's example, spread out, each covering a part of the chamber, all hoping to find something of any worth. Ike and I searched the left-hand side, while Rob and Ark took the right. Meanwhile Minia remained up front, persistent in his examination of the altar, the long drapes, and everything hidden underneath. Together we explored every cubit of the place, but all to no result. Just like the other two buildings, the chapel was empty and spotless. No matter how hard we looked, we found absolutely nothing that could explain what might have happened in that remote abandoned compound.

After wasting more time to the exhausting hunt, we left the chapel, along with its stuffed air and long, springing shadows that had started to make me feel dizzy. Outside a fresh breeze of warm spring air met us again, and enjoying the wind's soft touch, I stood motionless at the top of the stairs, breathing deeply with my eyes closed. Many thoughts pressed hard on my mind. The monastery had been abandoned weeks before. But why? Why had the followers of the Spirit left? And where did they go?

Suddenly Ike's lurid yell snapped me out of my state of turmoil. I opened my eyes, shook off my gloomy thoughts, and realized that I was alone on the steps of the deserted chapel. My friends had already gone somewhere; to locate them I had to stop and listen. Before long, I heard Ike's voice again, coming from around the corner. Too far to make out the words, I hurried there, soon finding my companions around the building, huddling near low bushes, looking at something concealed in Ike's hands.

"What is it?" I asked, trying to see what it was that startled them.

"Hey, get over here," Ike replied and turned to face me, holding something brownish in his hands.

"What is it?" I inquired again, making my way past Rob, Ark, and Minia, who kindly let me through.

"I found this thing down there behind that bush," explained Ike as he handed me a small square-like object, wrapped in dirty brown cloth. I carefully took the item and tentatively removed the rag. As the hard fabric slid down it revealed a small book, about quarter of a cubit long and a tenth of a cubit wide. Light in weight and hard to the touch, it was enveloped in a thick leather casing that carried a pattern of engraved symbols depicting two strange figures, one a man, dressed in a long robe, and the other a large leafless tree, its branches spread wide apart. The corners of the book were sealed with metal and in the center the cover's edge was bound by a heavy iron catch; its implied lock missing. Carefully I slid the metal hook out of the pivots and lifted the front lid, divulging thin white pages filled with handwritten lines of deep blue ink.

Everyone stood still, full of anticipation. Tying to keep my hands from shaking, I turned the first page, then the second, and the third, each time revealing more script and pictures. At first I thought the symbols that composed the paragraphs looked familiar, but after a closer look I realized that I did not recognize the language in which the book had been written. Indeed it was a foreign tongue, something I had never seen before.

"What in the world is this?" I asked aloud, staring blindly at the rows of unfamiliar lettering.

"I have no idea. I told you I just found it there. I did not even know it was a book," replied Ike, shrugging his shoulders. In turn I glanced at Ark, looking for his lucid explanation. "No, I mean the language. These symbols…I do not know what they are. Ark, do you have any idea?"

"I do not," replied Ark in short. It was very unusual for my friend not to know, and that was not good.

"Me neither," added Rob. He passed the book to Minia, who started to examine the tome, flipping through pages, several at a time.

Everyone stared at the squire, who kept examining the book. Then Minia closed the front cover and nodded, as if agreeing with himself. "This, my friends, is Uru, one of the dead languages of Ethoria. Back in the days, before Normandia even existed, the world had been divided amongst several great empires that had long since perished a little after the Great War. Each of those realms had its own language. What we now know as Normandia, had once been a part of the empire, called Titul, which meant a human parish in the old tongue. The kingdom was huge and covered lands from the western shores of the Abyss to the eastern rim of the Great Forest. Little now is known about those who lived in that realm, but that they spoke a language called Uru. Alas, Titul was destroyed during the War and so was Uru. Although some scholars continued to speak it years after the war, it was never meant to reach the common people and so it died. Ever since Uru has been considered a dead language, a relic of a long gone past."

Minia took a long breath and skipped a few more pages.

"I learned all this back at the castle. Sire Rone had all his squires, including me, take some schooling with local wise men. One of those scholars was an historian. Before coming to Sirone he had traveled around the Northern regions, collecting books and writings from the old days, and once he started teaching us he spoke a great deal about the world's history; alas I did not always listen. Now I wish I had."

"How do you know this is Uru?" I asked the squire, taking the book from him.

"The sage showed us several books written in Uru, and I remembered some of the symbols, which I see here too, like these crosses and half circles."

"Can you read any of it?"

"Unfortunately not. As I said, all I know is a bit of history, but this is it." Minia gave out a loud sigh, gloomy in his expression.

"Oh, great, so what are we going to do with it now?" said Ike, waving off his hands and rolling his eyes.

"We can always try to find someone who knows Uru," suggested Ark. "Minia; did you say there was a wise man in Sirone who knew the language? If he is still there, we can take the book to the castle and translate it there."

"Sadly, it will not be possible," replied Minia. "The sage I have just told you about left Sire Rone's service many years ago, and I have no idea where he is now."

"Ah, more good news, it gets better and better." Ike's remark was full of irony, and I could not blame him, as similar thoughts pestered me too.

"Yet...I think I have a solution to our little problem." Minia went on calmly, "There is an old hermit who lives two days south of here. He is a strange fellow, but he knows more about the world than anyone else I have ever met. If you want, we can visit him."

"Are you sure?" I asked the squire, making certain that the two extra days of traveling would not go in vain.

"I am pretty sure. Remember...I am the lord's squire after all," replied Minia with a particularly firm smile, which none of us dared to doubt.

"Then, let's visit that hermit," I concluded, and turned around to examine the spot where the book had been found.

"What about the monastery? Should we tell anyone about it?" asked Ark.

"Of course we should," affirmed Minia, and immediately added, "But only after we learn something about this book; when we know what it says we will go back to Sirone and report the whole thing to Sire Rone."

Chapter 16

IT WAS already midafternoon. We ate and rested in the safety of the monastery. As there was still plenty of time left before dusk, we decided not to waste any of it and resumed our journey, leaving the deserted compound, heading south along a narrow almost invisible path that winded left and right through hilly fields of grass and flowers. Since Minia was the only one who knew the way to the hermit's place, we let the squire guide us through the unfamiliar landscape. With him riding on the horse way ahead, our group followed the new route quickly and orderly, Rob walking first, then Ark, Ike, and me.

By the time the sun came down, we had already covered a distance of several leagues and were closing in on a pair of mounds, which peered dominantly over the horizon. Without the warm sunlight, the air became cold, and cool evening winds rolled from the west, reminding us once more that it was still an early spring. With the growing darkness our march became more difficult and we halted, finding refuge on higher grounds of the grassland. After assembling our camp, we fixed ourselves a neat small fire, a meal, and five hard grass beds. Although the view was calm and peaceful, we knew that was deceptive. With the memory of the recent ambush fresh in our minds, we took Minia's advice and set up turns to watch the camp, splitting into three groups. Ike and I were first; then Rob and Ark, and finally Minia, who volunteered to keep watch alone, or should I say, in the company of his horse. In that order we went through the night, extinguishing the fire first.

Once relived of my duty, I took a resting spot near Ike and closed my eyes. Flashes of the distant past engulfed me with sad, but warm reflections of those I loved and left behind. The pictures I saw were pleasing to my heart and I enjoyed their serenity. Although I was asleep I knew it was a dream. I also knew that it would not last for long. Sure enough before long I came out of my sleep, awakened by a loud and monotonous snore. Annoyed, I lifted myself up, searching for the source of the disturbance. Across from me, sitting by the fire, Rob and Ark talked to each other, swathed in their capes. Further away Minia slept quietly by his horse, which could not be said about Ike, who, lying next to me, snored like a wild boar, groaning and turning as he shifted in his sleep. I stared at him for a moment, debating whether I should throw something at my noisy comrade. But before I could decide, Ike rolled again and suddenly the noise stopped, allowing peace and silence to return to the camp. Afraid that it might not be for long, I closed my eyes and made myself slip into another dream, less pleasing and uneventful.

Next morning I was last to get up again. Overwhelmed by the bright light of the rising sun, I rubbed my face with my hands and climbed up, still half a sleep and not well rested. Ark, Minia, and Rob were sitting in a circle by the long-dead fire, and Ike was moving about, whistling another of his favorite tunes. When he heard me stir, he clapped his hands several times and hauled out a cheerful greeting. Satisfied that I was, in fact, awake, he then sat down next to me and handed over some leftovers from breakfast, along with a flask of water. I quickly ate the offered meal, then splashed water on my face, packed my belongings, and strapped the heavy backpack to my shoulder. By the time I was done, everyone else was on the feet, and soon we left.

As we marched on, the morning came to an end, and a particularly strong wind descended into the valley, bringing larger clouds along with it. The blue sky swiftly turned gray and signs of an inevitable rain appeared in the air. Throwing our hoods over our heads, we kept walking, looking further ahead, where shades of dark gray swathed the sky like a heavy mantle and imposed a dreary feeling over our progress. The weather grew less favorable with every step and shortly after we had passed over the two mounds, the clouds began to sprinkle. The light drizzle lasted for some time, but then intensified, maturing into a heavy rain that poured streams of water on the land below with all the vengeance it could muster.

The raging storm persisted through the day, leaving us at the mercy of the cold shower, the wind, and lighting that sprang up often in the displeasing sky. In due course the falling water transformed the roadway into thick mud, which made our progress even more tedious, forcing us to step away from the slush, and onto the grass that provided some relief to our battered boots, much laden with heavy chunks of brownish mire. But soon even the wet lawn could not offer us enough support and we slipped back into the mud of the road, which had retained only a hint of its usual solidity thanks to a flood of water that seemed to come from everywhere at once. If that was not enough, the view turned even duller around us, with lines of weeds as our only company. The only thing that illustrated any excitement was a pile of rocks we encountered somewhere along the way. Weathered stones were old and broken and vaguely outlined the foundation of a house that once had stood there. But time and winds had done their job; long before we passed by, the stone-built walls had turned to rubble, revealing little of their past. And since the ruins could not grant us any refuge from the increasing rainfall, we skipped the wrecked site and continued forth, trying to find harder ground along the weaving lane.

For several leagues we kept moving east until the road rolled southward, and continued in that direction for the rest of the day without deviations or turns. In time the day came to a close, and prevailing darkness shrouded the panorama ahead, compelling us to break for camp again. Wet, hungry, and tired we leapt over puddles and small torrents of muddy water until we spotted a small island of trees just a few cubits off the route, which promised at least some shelter from the never-ending rain.

Under the thick crown of young leaves, which covered thick branches of aged oaks, we dropped our bags and settled down, all at once, each enjoying a long-awaited break from a dull journey. Except for Minia, who did not express any visible signs of fatigue, our party was stock-still. For my part, I was so tired I could barely move, so I lay on the wet grass, indifferent to the raindrops and the chilly wind that beat against my soaked clothes. That night we had no fire and no hot meal, just a few slices of hard bread, a handful of dry cheese that Ark had managed to extract from his seemingly bottomless pack, and plain water from the flask. The hard food was tasteless, but no one cared. Once our stomachs were full, we skipped the evening chat and retired to our soggy beds, keeping the same watch arrangement as the night before. I did not remember how my shift went, but when it was done, I enfolded myself in my drenched cloak, pulled the hood over my face, and fell asleep, thinking little of the bad weather that persisted to harass the countryside.

This time I slept, hunted by another vision that conveyed me to a mysterious place, which I had never seen before. It started with me walking along a blackened passage, which streamed away toward a distant pale light. Alone, but unafraid, I moved unhurriedly through it, peering into the distance, trying to see what was ahead. Suddenly the strange light grew brighter and engulfed me from all sides, erupting a moment later in a dazzling, blinding flash. Sightless, I fell as the ground moved from underneath me, and I started to float in the air, drifting somewhere I could not see. Then, as if following someone's silent command the whiteness faded, and a picture of a marvelous green glade appeared before my eyes. The clearing was small and full of sunshine. Encircled by a mass of tall olden trees that reached far into the sky, spreading their long thick branches around the meadow, the clearing reminded me of a supple gentle carpet of short green grass, soft to the touch and showered with count-less little flowers of random colors. The little blossoms emitted a flavorsome sweet scent that floated through the air, making it particularly easy to breathe. Unwillingly I took a long pleasing gasp, and at that time heard a woman's voice that filled my ears with the soothing sound of many tiny ringing bells.

Although I heard the voice clearly in my head, I could not understand what it was saying. Curiosity overwhelmed me, and I turned around, hoping to see the one who was talking to me. But no matter how hard I peered into the leaves, I could not find anyone. Then as I turned around several more times, a dizzy feeling came over me. When the lightheadedness grew fainter, an invis-ible wall lifted from my ears. Suddenly I could understand every word the strange voice uttered.

"Mishuk Loyde," the voice said gently. "Follow a line of purple flowers to the edge of the forest. There you will find a passage that will lead you into the forest and to my quarters."

Immediately I looked down. Under my feet ran a narrow lane of flowers, which stretched to the edge of the clearing and disappeared amongst the wide greenish trunks. Strange, I thought to myself. I did not remember seeing the blossoms earlier, and I was sure that I had examined the clearing very carefully. But the purple path was there, and somehow it did not surprise me all that much. For a moment I hesitated to move, and as I did the voice spoke again. "Do not be alarmed. There will be no harm done to you here. This is a safe place, free of dangers and worries."

Although I did not know if I should trust such a declaration, I took the trail as instructed and walked up to the edge of the forest, where unseen from afar, a small opening emerged out of the live wall, inviting me in. Not even bothering to check what prowled ahead, I stepped through the gap and found myself at the start of yet another path, covered with many fallen leaves, which retained their original green color. Further into the forest I went, only it was not really a forest anymore. What seemed to be the woodland at first glance was in fact a grand hall, with living trees and vines clasped together in one complex mosaic that formed the inner workings of the spacious atrium. Thick tangles of deep green foliage created velvet drapes that came down from the high ceiling, composed of massive tree branches, beneath which lay an even flat floor of short soft grass.

Puzzled by such an unusual setting, I halted mid-step, startled by the view. Although the hall had no visible windows, splits, or gaps within the growing walls or ceiling, the place was filled with light that seemed to stream down from nowhere in particular, and everywhere at once. Although the glow was even throughout the chamber, it felt brighter at the far end, where a young beautiful lady sat in a towering elegant armchair. The woman's face was slim and pale, its gaunt features stunning and mesmerizing. Her long golden hair came down to her shoulders and then dropped freely onto her breast, covered with a silky green gown that looked weightless and was embellished with countless fresh flowers as ornaments of incomparable splendor. On top she wore a glittering thin silver band of a crown adorned with ruby gems and golden drops, crafted as tiny crystals that reflected gentle sparkles of light onto the woman's pallid skin, giving it an appealing velvety tone. Although the stranger looked like a young maiden, something told me that it was an illusion, and she was much older, for in her ice-blue eyes I saw such wisdom and depth as I had only seen amongst the elders.

I did not know how long I had stood still, staring directly at the beautiful visage, but I could have done so forever if it were not for the lady herself, who raised her hand gracefully and gestured for me to come forth. I complied instantly and strolled spellbind across the hall, and as I walked, the lady spoke.

"Do not be afraid, Mishuk," she said again and gifted me with a warm smile. Right away I knew that it was her voice I had been hearing ever since I had emerged out of the light.

"Come, sit with me, I have some things to tell you." The woman raised her other hand and pointed at a spot beside her, where, a living chair grew out of the ground. Saying nothing, I sat down, not for a moment taking my eyes off her captivating visage.

"My name is A'tie-Fray-Mour'ter'itea, but you can call me A'tie. I have come to you tonight from the far depths of the Great Forest, where I dwell amongst my people in the serenity of the ancient stalks, shielded from the chaos of your world. As you have probably already guessed, I am not a human, but an A'al. You can soothe your disbelief though. The old tales tell the truth. We, the A'als, do exist, even though some may doubt such a fact. And I cannot blame them, for it has been long since my people had called Ethoria their home. Rarely we leave our green home to meet your kin, as most humans have long forgotten our kind, and those who have not, often shun our company, fearful of our different ways. Yet, despite our seeming isolation, we do not ignore your world, for everything that transpires within the human realms affects us too.

"It was not too long ago that we saw a hint of trouble born within your world. So far we can see only the shadows of the danger, but soon the menace will become more apparent and if not stopped in time, will grow to become a catastrophe for Ethoria and all who dwell there. And it is because of this yet small threat, I have brought you here to my home."

The mysterious woman paused and I tried to reflect on her strange tale. An A'al, I wondered. How did I know that she was an A'al? I had never seen an A'al. I knew very little about any races besides the humans that inhabited Ethoria in the many years of its existence. And what little I did know came from small talk around taverns and scarce old history books that I never cared to read scrupulously. Even so, ever since I could remember there were always rumors of strange peoples who lived hidden within the immensity of the Great Forest, of magical powers they wielded, and of great wisdom they possessed. But I always deemed those tales fables, nothing more. Could it be the A'als actually existed? I looked at the pale stranger before me. Indeed at a closer look the woman did not seem exactly human. Her features were more alien, her deep blue eyes almost mystical. And yet her warm smile and kind glance looked very human. But what if this was just a dream?

"You are right," the woman replied to my silent question. "It is a dream, and yet it is not."

Struck by disbelief, I stared at the woman, who smiled again and leaned forward just a little, her voice becoming even softer. "Yes, I can read your mind. But do not worry. Whatever your thoughts may be I understand them completely and do not take them personally. As to your question, what you see now before you is a dream, a vision, as you call it. But it is not a normal dream, because it is also real, as real as the rain that beats against rooftops or the sun that dries them later. Right now you are asleep, and yet your mind is awake, and it has traveled many leagues here to this hall. But I am getting ahead of myself." The A'al woman paused and studied me while I remained motionless in my chair.

"Do you know what a Fore Sight is?" she asked me, and I shook my head. "I do not mean your eyes or ears, but something hidden within your mind, something known only to you. For a while now you have been seeing strange visions. They have invaded your life and distorted your dreams with pictures of things you often could not substantiate. You have not been alone in such encounters either. Several others, all your close friends, have also witnessed strange apparitions. Puzzled, you have searched for answers together, but found nothing. Even now, as you are listening to me, you are still looking for explanations, and I am willing to give them to you.

"As I said, right at this moment you are in the land of clad horsemen, you call Normandia, and I am in the far reaches of the Great Forest; yet we are talking to each other as if we were together in the same room. It sounds impossible, but it is not. Nor is it a joke or a ruse. Instead what you are experiencing is a marvel of a Fore Sight, a sense just like your eyesight, which enables you to expand your mind, reaching out far beyond the known boundaries of your consciousness. Altering your perception, it allows you travel distant places, without taking a single step, to hear and see things that are leagues away; it can even show you the future, giving you clues and warnings that otherwise would have eluded you. The Fore Sight is all of these things and more, since it is also a channel through which you gain an ability to reach out to others who share the same gift. Thousands of leagues apart you can call upon them, and through your mind commune with them, just as we do this very moment.

"Many years back, before the Blood Wars, the Fore Sight was very common to Ethoria. Humans, A'als, D'ars and others exploited its many traits in their daily lives, using them along with other powers that you call magic. Alas that time ended long ago. Some of the races, such as D'ars, have died out, and others, like the humans, have lost the knowledge of this sense. Today the A'als are the only ones who have retained the gift, and even we toil hard to preserve it amongst our kin.

"Yet, the Fore Sight is not lost entirely to humans. Although your people have forgotten all about the Fore Sight, the sense still dwells within their unsuspecting minds. Like any other sense, it cannot vanish but can be suppressed, and there comes a time when it is pushed so deep into the cellars of the consciousness, that it is impossible to bring it back. I regret to say it, but the majority of your race has done just that. For them it is too late. Their minds are too stale and weak to accept such a great power as the Fore Sight, and to impose it on them would be to destroy their frigid wits. Even so, there are still men amongst you who can evoke their Fore Sight, though it requires much guidance and help from the outside.

"You, Mishuk, are one of these men. Your mind welcomes new things and allows it to explore the depths of the unknown, free of tainted predilections of your world. Your intuition is also very strong, and thus is what is needed for the Fore Sight to spring back to life. Since I first saw you, I knew that you had the gift. Now it is time to extend it, to let it grow so you can master all of its many sundry traits. And to do that you need help, which I am willing to grant you if you wish."

Abruptly the woman who called herself A'tie waved her hand. Several silver sparks that looked very much like snowflakes appeared from under her sleeve and slowly descended onto the grassy floor, disappearing in the deep green carpet, leaving behind beautiful silvery trails. Mesmerized by the display I stared at the floor, and then back at the woman, who smiled again and leaned forward a little. "Do you believe in magic?" she asked me in her soft voice. Unable to say anything, I nodded stupidly in response.

"While everyone likes to tell tales about magic, nobody really believes in it anymore. You, however, are not like the rest of your kind. Where most Ethorians have forgotten about the ways of lore, you still hope to find it, to prove that magic still exists. Let me assure you that magic is very much alive, and as always is amongst us, near us, and inside us.

"The visions you often see have been induced by my enchantment. Do not be afraid. The spell will not harm you. It is designed to help you find your Fore Sight, to teach you how to drawn on its vast powers. Evoking the forces of magic I opened a channel between our minds. As our thoughts linked I called upon your hidden gift. It did not answer me at first. Your young and fragile mind was struggling to cope with the intrusion. Nightmares stalked your dreams, robbing you of a peaceful sleep, keeping you awake for hours. It hurt me to see you suffer, but I had to let the spell run its course. To help you cope with your experience I placed the same enchantment on your friends, for I knew well how much their support meant to you. My plan worked. Sharing the encounters with your comrades made your mind stronger, and soon your Fore Sight started to awaken. Although nightmares did not stop, they gradually subsided, and new visions came in their place. These were more settled, more real, more truthful in their meaning, the sign that your mind has accepted the Fore Sight.

"You are probably asking yourself why I have enchanted you without first asking your permission. I will answer. There was no other way. As with any other human, you could not stir the Fore Sight on your own. You needed help and I was ready to aid you. Unfortunately I could not contact you with your senses still asleep. I had to wake them up before I could open a channel to talk to you. To spark the Fore Sight within you I used my powers. Although I feared that my spell would fail, it did not. Your Fore Sight awoke from its long sleep, and now you can use it, though more often than not, you will not know that you do.

"As for the enchantment, it did its job and brought out the gift in you. Now there is nothing else for it to do. Soon the spell will wear off, leaving your new sense to evolve on its own. In time you will understand how to control it. But beware—the Fore Sight is a delicate thing. If you ignore it, it will slip away and leave; if you abuse it, it will turn against you—your mind will be overrun, and you will go insane. And if you apply it too cautiously it will stop evolving, locking you out of its many powers. The challenge is to find the perfect balance, a way to use it for the best, so it can flourish, opening a new world, a world that only the chosen ones can see. With my help, you will learn how to do so, that is, if you wish to learn it of course.

"Regrettably your friends' fortune lies elsewhere. My spell could not stir up their senses, as they were too deadened and too afraid to accept the gift. Although they may still have some visions, once my magic goes away, their lives will return to normal. They will be free from weird dreams, sleeping well again. You, however, will be the only one who will continue to experience the apparitions, though they will be apparitions of a different kind. At times they will be visions from your present life, or the lives of others you know. Occasionally they will be scenes from the future or from the past, yours and of strangers. And sometimes they will be images of a symbolic nature, with warnings, clues, and answers hidden in their images. Whatever their nature is, the visions will be brought to you by the Fore Sight, and will always have a meaning, good, bad, or simply different. The question is whether you are ready to accept your new acumen. And if you are, will you be keen to go forth with it, to use it wisely, and strive to understand its traits? Think hard, for your answer will change your life forever."

I did not think for long. Suddenly everything about my weird visions made sense. It was the Fore Sight. I could feel it stirring within me, and knowing that it was alive I was eager to explore it, to understand its true nature, its powers and its effects. I was ready. I looked straight at the A'al woman and gave my answer, my words echoing through the hall. I was not nervous nor was I afraid, though I knew in the morning I would wake up a different person. But it did not bother me. I knew the Fore Sight had always been a part of me…helping me, guiding me through life.

"I am glad to see I was not mistaken in you. Indeed, you are the one I have been looking for," said A'tie, a little afterwards. "Now, as you know about the Fore Sight, there are several things I need to tell you about. Although much of what I will say will sound bizarre, I can assure you that all is true."

A'tie moved back in her high-back armchair and continued. "The quest you have undertaken is dangerous, but also righteous and very important. It has been so designed that your father's disappearance was not an accident. It was a part of an elaborate plan, which set in motion events of great proportions, foretold a thousand years ago. No matter what you might have wanted in your life, your lineage has predetermined your fate: to play a part in a great conflict that will decide the future of Ethoria and will affect the balance of power, which has become so fragile in the past thousand years.

"It was also a part of that plan for you to come to the abandoned monastery and find the strange book written in an ancient language. Indeed, the book is very important. Not only does it hold a piece of the puzzle of your father's disappearance, but it also holds much worth for a far greater question, the question of the safety of the world itself. So guard it with your life and try to learn of its contents as much as possible. For that you should follow the squire to the hermit, who will decipher the foreign words for you. Make your way hastily, for time is of the essence. I must warn you, though. Once you translate the book it will bring you closer to the perils, which until now did not concern you. So be prepared to face new obstacles, and do not let anything stir you off the chosen course.

"This brings me to my final counsel, which worriers me much. A great danger is lurking around your brother. I cannot say much about what this danger is, but I can tell you that it is not too late for you to help him. Return home once you are done with the book and seek your brother out. Once you find him, take him with you, because, if you do not, he will be dead before the first summer day. While he is in your company, watch over him, because he will need your protection and help until he is ready to venture on his own. Do not question this task, for I cannot tell you more than I have already done. Remember—find your brother, take him as far away from Villone as possible or the enemy will destroy him. Hurry. Translate the book. Take Ric. Protect him."

I moved my lips to ask the A'al woman a question when her image began to melt. Her features became vague, and gradually faded away, leaving me alone within the blackness of my mind. Then I awoke, somehow sure of my cause and of what had to be done. Blinking repeatedly I lifted myself up and looked around. It was still dark, but I could see the sky above. The rain had stopped and clouds receded, showing parts of the moon and stars that sparked a hope the next day would be less wet and more pleasant than the previous one. Not far away Rob and Ark continued with their watch, which meant that there was still plenty of time before dawn. Cold from the nighttime chill I rubbed my hands together and lay back, pulling the cape over my shoulders, shivering and shifting. For a long time I could not fall back to sleep, struggling with thoughts about what I had just seen. Although the vision's true meaning continued to elude me, one thing was certain—something very serious was happening around me, something I could not comprehend yet, something that connected all into one long chain. With any luck, the strange book from the monastery would give some clues.

I gave in to the fatigue shortly before sunrise, only to get up a few hours later predictably unrested. As I scrambled to my feet, I saw Minia and Ike, working on the morning fire, talking and joking as they threw short branches into the rising flames. A few cubits away Rob and Ark were still lounging on the grass. Soon they too came to their senses and joined the rest of us, stretching their numb limbs closer to a still young blaze. When the fire was big enough, Minia boiled some water, and after throwing a handful of dried herbs into the pot, fixed us a morning meal, which was neither hot nor tasty. Gulping the food with no appetite, I debated if I should tell my friends about my last apparition. Since none of my companions had mentioned anything about the strange A'al woman, I gathered that they did not see the same dream, which made my decision even harder. For once I had some answers, but did not know if they were to be believed. Yet, I could not keep such information from the rest of the company, and as we were getting ready to depart I called my friends and told them all about the vision, trying to recapture everything I could.

Under the warming sun, seated on the ample grass I described my encounter with the A'al sorceress, her tale of our predicament, and her instructions regarding the book and Ric. As I divulged what I beheld, my friends listened in silence, and when my story drew to a close, asked their questions, all-serious in their stance.

"Are you sure it was not just a dream?" Ark asked first, rubbing his knuckles against his still-damp coat.

"Frankly, I am not sure of anything," I said, almost inaudibly. "It did not feel like an ordinary dream, more like…," I hesitated for a moment, realizing that I really did not have too many words to describe it.

"Like the other visions we have seen?" Rob tried to complete my thought.

"Not really," I replied, after thinking about it for some time. "It felt more like I was actually there, within the hall of trees."

"So you mean to tell us that an A'al sorceress, or whoever she is, has summoned you across the world through some sort of magical channel to tell you all about the visions, the book, and Ric," Rob recollected, looking at me with a taint of mistrust in his glance.

"Yes, it is exactly what I am trying to tell you," I insisted, true to my own conviction. "Hold on here," I heard Minia's voice from a distance. "What in the Spirit's name are you four talking about?"

Instantly everyone grew quiet. My friends and I completely forgot that our new companion was unaware of our experiences. Although we had no intention of letting the squire in on our secret, after what he had heard that morning, we had no other choice but to tell him everything about our unusual condition, starting from the point when we had seen the first shared vision back in Villone. While Minia probably expected a concise account, he got a bizarre tale of weird dreams, nightmares, and speculations. Yet he listened carefully, looking at each of us, constantly shaking his head. I was not sure if he believed our story or not, but he said nothing, except for a few short questions, practical in nature. Then he swore to keep our secret safe, and did not talk about it again, not that he could, because Ike returned to the subject of my latest dream the moment we had finished describing everything to the squire.

"To go back to Villone! Are you crazy?" Ike said almost shouting. "I cannot go back home, my father will kill me."

"I know, Ike, I do not want to go back home either, but my brother's life may be in danger." I tried to calm my friend down.

"What if it is just a dream?" Ike persisted. "And why did not the rest of us see it too?"

"I am not really sure. Maybe because it was not meant for all of us; or maybe because I was the only one who could see it," I replied, though my answer was not entirely true. One thing I did not mention to my friends was the Fore Sight. I kept such wisdom to myself, afraid that my companions would not have understood. A'tie's tale was unbelievable enough; to tell the others about the gift meant to confuse them even more, which I could not afford to do. I felt guilty for hiding the truth from my companions, but I could not do otherwise. I had to wait.

"How sure are you about the vision though? I mean, I do not mind its message, but can we trust it?" asked Ark.

"I do not know. All I can say is that it felt real, so real that it convinced me. Besides, A'tie's words carried a warning about my brother. True or not, I cannot ignore it. If Ric is indeed in danger, I must help him, vision or no vision," I replied firmly and glanced at each of my companions one at a time.

"Huh. I do not see why we cannot trust Mishuk," said Ark at last. "Although we do not know how true the vision's message is, it did explain a lot about our ordeal. We cannot ignore the fact that the story about the spell makes sense. As for the warnings, I suggest we take them one step at a time. First we see about the book, and since we have been going to take it to the hermit anyway, it won't cause us any problems. If A'al's predictions are correct and the book does hold some answers to our quest, we then can consider thinking about retrieving Ric from Villone. Otherwise, we head straight for Sirone and report our finds to Sire Rone before moving any further."

As always Ark's suggestion made sense. Everyone agreed that it was the best course of action, to try to translate the book first, and then see what to do next. Soon we left the camp for the morning winds and went back to the road, adding yet another day to our journey.

Chapter 17

GLAD THE dreadful weather had left us in the night, we walked along the fields, on the path that carried us south. Occasionally hills sent our party up and down gentle slopes, exposing nothing new. Little by little the remnants of the heavy clouds moved away, taking the misery of the last day along with them. In their place came a lighter cloak of thin white haze, which let the shafts of bright sun rays fall onto the ground that was still wet and slushy. Although I was getting hot and thirsty, I welcomed the dry day with all my heart. Sensing pleasing warmth in the air, my wretched disposition shifted for the better, and the heavy thoughts that had taken me over that morning moved aside. And later, as if to soothe my mind further, a nice cool breeze came from across the wild pasture, bringing relief to my sweating body, making the journey swifter and easier.

Walking in a column, our party came upon another mound, which was somewhat higher, then the ones we had encountered so far that day. As we climbed to the top, a native landscape appeared before us, stretching deep into the immensity of the green fields. Straight ahead the familiar grassland extended south and west, and in the east a distinct line of distant forest emerged from over the horizon and some leagues later descended into the valley, creeping close to the road that continued on in the southern direction, running along the wooded rim. Drawn by the view of the faraway trees, we hurried down the hillside and toward the trees, soon coming within several cubits from the wall of trunks that was so thick that it was impossible to see anything past them. After an hour of following the verge of the forest, we reached a small dell in the woods and halted. There Minia dismounted from his horse and waved for us to gather around him.

"Well, fellows, we are almost there," said the squire as he pointed to a small lane that ran into the trees, announcing yet another alteration to our course.

"This is the way to the hermit's place. It will probably take us some time to get there, so I suggest we eat here before going into that green maze."

"Sounds like a good idea," exclaimed Ike, glad of a chance to throw his bag off his shoulders.

"I am kind of hungry too," agreed Rob. Ark and I did not waver and together we sat down on the ground, finding drier spots amongst heaps of long-dead branches and stumps dispersed around the opening, a few cubits off the road.

Working quickly, Ark and Minia readied the food and shortly after we gobbled the midday meal in a few quick bites, paying little attention to its taste. When lunch was gone, warm bitter cider rinsed our throats, and our backpacks returned to our shoulders, pressing hard with their leather straps. Anon we were inside the forest realm, guided by a barely noticeable thin trail that floated into the depths of the olden woods. As we advanced, shafts of muted, golden sunlight shot through with sparkling motes of breeze-born pollen, and pierced the thick canopy of leaves and branches, bringing an almost magical luminescence to the all-pervading twilight of the forest. A colder, damper air spread between the endless legions of trees and shrubs saturated with the sweet piquant flavor of the living plants. The singing of birds and the calls of unknown creatures echoed from a distance and reminded us that we were but guests in that very different and hidden world.

After several hours or so, spent in the milieu of the wild, we cleared another stretch of thick undergrowth and past it, emerged at a gate-like opening, where a hint of a small glade could be seen. Pushing the last of the branches away from our faces, we sauntered through the gap and into the lesser island of an open plot of land wrapped in sunlight and prolonged shadows, cast down by the tall live branches. The meadow that lay before us was no more than fifty cubits long and some twenty cubits wide. Shaped as an uneven circle, the glade was plastered with a carpet of short succulent grass, encircled by a dense wall of leaves, twigs, and limbs. At the far side of the glade stood a humble little structure, an earth-house, half buried in the soil.

At the front of it, a low entryway, impeded by a windswept, kindling door, peered over the ground, and at the loamy walls, covered with greenish turf, I noted two little round windows, coated with a layer of hardened dirt that had been sitting there for months if not years. A small metal pipe, which probably played the role of a chimney, came out of the curved roof and exhaled wisps of white smoke that moved playfully up the wind, eventually disappearing into thin air.

Judging by the rate at which the bulbous curls left the tube, the hermit was home. Although each of us wanted very much to hurry to the hut, we let the squire handle the introductions and once our company reached the center of the gale, we stayed back, while Minia went up to the door and knocked. When the sound of his light tapping ceased, the door opened, and Minia slipped inside. For a while he remained unseen, swathed in the darkness that stood in the opening, but then came back out, escorted by a tall skinny figure that belonged to an old gray-haired man. "The hermit—it has to be him," I thought to myself as the stranger started toward us, following the squire, telling him something as he walked.

Although I had never seen any hermits before, the stranger before me looked like one. His face was worn by the passage of time, and his long locks, white as snow, came down to his shoulders, blending perfectly with an equally white beard that covered his bony cheeks, streaming further down to the waistline in a gentle cascade.

Standing two cubits tall, the man towered over Minia by at least three heads, and despite his age, which had to be ancient, looked lively and brisk. His skinny stature was clothed in a long brown robe, supported by twine, made out of strings of vines woven carefully into a thick hard braid. The gown hung slackly from his shoulders and dropped to the ground, concealing his feet, creating an illusion that the man did not walk, but glided across the floor. In his right hand he held a small grain sack, and in the left a lengthy wooden pole, which was nothing more than a well polished twisted tree-branch, with weird symbols carved along its length.

Unhurriedly the old man approached our group, studying everyone with his dark brown eyes. When he was almost upon us, he smacked his lips and sighed loudly, displaying his unpleasant disposition, probably caused by our unexpected visit. In silence we stared back at the elder, letting the hiatus continue for several minutes. But our silence seemed to irritate the hermit, and after releasing a loud groan, he shook his gray head and spoke in a deep clear voice.

"What do we have here?" said the gray-haired man, and he coiled his eyebrows.

"These are my friends," replied Minia, and he introduced each of us.

"Ah ha…young peasant boys, who try to play adventurers …I see…. But what do they want with me?" the hermit grunted, clearly unimpressed by our appearance.

"In our travels we have stumbled upon a very interesting piece of writing," continued Minia. "It is a strange text, written entirely in Uru. As the book may be very important to our present quest, we need to know what it says. Unfortunately none of us can read Uru, so we have come to you, to ask you to translate the book for us."

"Mmmm. A quest, you say? What sort of quest?" the hermit asked, frowning again.

"The quest is for a convoy that went astray several weeks ago somewhere within Sire Rone's domain," replied Minia, "So far we have found few clues; this book is one of them."

"And you want me to translate it for you?" interrupted the old man, "You little brats are lazy. Do they not teach you anything these days? The answers to all your questions are always right at your fingertips, and all you need is a bit of patience and persistence, nothing more. But, no. You want the old man to do it for you instead. What makes you think I will do it, huh?"

"Because we really need your help, because lives may be at stake here, because you are the only one for leagues who knows Uru, or maybe because Sire Rone himself has taken a personal interest in this matter," Minia answered bluntly, yet politely.

"Oh, and you think that these are reasons enough to bother me? Why did you not come back to your lord's keep and study some of the books he keeps there? I will tell you. You are just too lazy," the old man grumbled on, clearly irritated by Minia's words.

Looking at the hermit and the squire made me think of Villone. The hermit sounded exactly like the local tutor, Master Auck, who was infamous for riding every young lad in town about any little thing he thought was wrong. Come to think of it, Master Auck even looked like the hermit—old, bitter, and skinny. The squire, however, reminded me of our town crier, Big Adi, a little man, who had a unique talent for persuading others by talking to them for hours, always cool and polite in his words. Just like Adi, Minia continued to demur the hermit, conferring with the old man in a calm, yet firm tone.

"I understand all this," the squire persisted, "I am sorry for our intrusion, but we really need your help. As I said, it is not for us. There is a caravan that is missing, several dozen men are gone, and nobody knows where they are. This book may hold the key to solving the mystery behind their disappearance."

Minia gave the hermit a harsh glance, although I was not sure the old man even noticed it, since his eyes were focused on my friends and me.

For a moment the hermit did not speak. Mumbling something to himself, he groaned and smacked his lips, often lifting his staff off the ground. Then he turned to the squire and said, "Lucky for you, I have some free time today;

otherwise I would have sent you away like so much bad news." He spun around and walked back to the hut, saying nothing else.

Unsure about what we should do, we stayed where we were, watching as the old man vanished behind the opened door, leaving our company in the center of the clearing. When the door closed, Minia leaned toward me and whispered, keeping his voice down, making sure the hermit did not hear him, of which I was not too sure.

"Do not take him too seriously; he is actually a decent man. It is just that he does not like to be disturbed." Minia looked at the door one more time, "I think we should follow him."

"Are you sure?" asked Ike, voicing my concern as well.

"Yes, I am telling you he will help us. Trust me on this. I have seen him do this before; he grunted and complained, but then he helped. "

"I guess he thinks that the book is important then," noted Ike, smiling.

"Maybe he does, or maybe he likes you," replied Minia with the same grin on his face.

"I do not know about you, but I did not seem to catch too much fondness from the man," commented Rob. The rest of us agreed, though no one cared to laugh.

"I guess we will find out soon enough. In the meantime, let's get to the hut. One thing the hermit dislikes more than visitors is waiting." Minia threw off his bag, leaving it on the ground, and strolled to the den. The rest of us had little choice but to follow him, somewhat confused about the hermit's odd ways. At the door Minia stopped us again, pointed at the hut, and murmured softly, "Oh, there is one more thing. His name is Irk the Wise, so you know. But do not say it until he introduces himself. And by all means do not ever call him Sire. He hates it."

Ark, Rob, Ike, and I concurred with nods, and Minia opened the door, allowing us to slip inside.

Even before I made my way into the chamber, a heavy thick air hit my nostrils. The scent of old rugged clothes, dried herbs, burned-out wood, wet turf, and smoky pipe filled up the little space there was and made it hard to breath. As I struggled not to choke, my eyes watered, and tears rolled down my cheeks, forcing me to wipe them off several times so nobody could see me snivel. When I was finally able to get used to the unusual aroma, I followed my companions inside, where, sitting beside a round table, I saw the hermit's lanky figure. The old man was leaning back in a crooked chair, his arms crossed over his chest. His staff rested next to him, and in his right hand he held a long smoking pipe, which he repeatedly lit with his boney finger.

As for the hermit's dwelling, very little could have been said about it. It was but a simple round room, dug in the ground and covered with a logged roof, plastered with dark-brownish clay. On the inside the ceiling was supported by several long wooden beams, placed so low that we barely missed them with our head as we walked in. The walls, also covered with dry clay, ran in a small circle about ten cubits in diameter. Their surface was very uneven and in places showed glimpses of the black turf and pieces of large round rocks that sometimes stuck out, revealing their smoky rough surface. In the center of the room, surrounded by a row of flat river stones, pressed into the floor, stood a miniature hearth. Made of something that resembled clusters of mud, it was attached to a metal pipe that climbed straight up to the ceiling and through the roof. Within, it held an iron grate, where a small fire made a cracking noise, bursting from time to time with light ashes that drifted across the bare floor, covering it with a grayish, feathered veneer. Besides the fireplace few other items of little splendor decorated the place. A worn square table, two chairs, a sort of cradle, and three heavy barred chests were shoved to the sides in disarray, pointing to the fact that their owner did not concern himself with neatness and order.

After watching us walk in, the hermit cleared his throat and gestured for us to take seats around him, which we did, Minia taking the chair across from the man, and the rest of us settling on top of the big chests around the hearth. With everyone in places, the hermit lit his carved pipe one more time and, making a chuckling sound, began to blow tepid puffs of smoke out the corner of his mouth.

"So you want me to translate something written in Uru," said the old man and shifted in his chair so that his right elbow was on the table. "Okay, let me take a look at this thing." With these words, the hermit put down his pipe and reached into his robe. After searching there for a while, he extracted two round pieces of glass attached to a metal string. After cleaning the odd instrument with the corner of his gown, he lifted the thing and put it on his nose.

"How long do I have to wait for it?" exclaimed the hermit once the glass disks were sitting firmly on the rib of his nose. "Are you going to show me anything, or should I go to bed and wait until tomorrow?" The old man sighed loudly, knocking on the table several times with the pipe. At the same time, Minia hurried to get the book out of the bag. Once the tome was unraveled, he passed it to the elder, who continued to tap the pipe impatiently with an expression of annoyance on his face. But when he got the book, his look changed to curiosity as he studied the manuscript for some time, slowly flipping through the pages, whispering something to himself.

"I see. I am surprised to say it, but you are correct. This is indeed Uru. Remarkable. Just remarkable," said the hermit, as he turned more pages, immersed in the study of the tome. "I must admit…It is a very impressive sample. You, you better find a place to wait, young brats. It will take a while for me to examine it. Perhaps tomorrow morning or afternoon. Or…." The old man mumbled something else, but none of us could hear him. Afterwards, the hermit did not pay us any more attention.

Absent of any other instructions, we continued to wait inside the den. After a while I got tired of sitting on the hard surface of the chest. My legs started to feel numb and my bottom sore. Rubbing my different body parts did not relieve me of the discomfort and I had to get up so I could move around, bring some life back into my deadened limbs. When the pain receded, I went to return to my seat, but thought otherwise. The rigid wooden shell was just too unwelcoming, and having no desire to sit on it again, I looked for another spot, which turned out to be a rather difficult task. Since there were no more empty chairs in the room, and I definitely did not want to touch the old man's bed, I was left with the option of standing, which I did, leaning backwards against the wall, planting my feet into the soil floor for balance.

The noise that I had made distracted the hermit from the book, and he raised his head, looking at me from over the glass disks. Irritation was written all over his face, which became even thinner once he began to speak. "I told you it would take a while." The hermit's voice grew louder. "Do you not understand? Or are you deaf? I will not have anything for you until the next morning. Is it clear enough?…And I do not need any distractions here either. So take your follies outside." Irk the Wise grunted some more and added, "Get out and wait there. If it rains you may go into the forest, and if wolves come to the clearing, fight them, or let them eat you. Whatever you do, just do not bother me. When I am done with the book, I will let you know. Until then, farewell."

"Sire, but how long will it take to—" Ike uttered from the far side of the room.

"I said. I should be done by tomorrow. What else do you want?" snapped the hermit, "and *stop* calling me 'Sire.' Those titles are for fools and snobs and nobles. My name is Irk the Wise. So next time you want to ask me something, call me by my name, and do not use some idiotic designation."

The old man dropped his glance back to the book, not bothering to look at us again; yet it was fine with me, because I had no intention of disturbing him any longer; nor did I want to spend any more time in his stinky den. So right after the hermit's discourse, I reached for the door and left the place, joined by the rest of the company.

Outside, the sun was not yet down but had already submerged behind the massive treetops, leaving just a glimpse of yellowish tan in the clear sky. Not long after, the blonde color of the sky grew fainter and soon turned to red, and then to a cooler evening palette of blue, announcing the closing of the day. A creamy pale crescent came over the clearing, its weak glow falling in one long wide streak onto the cairn of the grass below. Although around us was only darkness, I did not have worried feelings. For some reason the hermit's glade did not look hostile. On the contrary, even at night it brought a warm feeling of peace and safety that chased away my fears of the past night.

As shadows of the forest transformed into a pitch-black pall, we huddled near Irk's den and started a small fire. In an instant, the glade illumined and a sheer column of smoke rose slowly from the flames, mingling with the wisps from the hermit's chimney, gradually fading away into the cool dark sky. Along with warmth, the fire gave us a chance to make a hot meal, which Ark and Minia gladly fetched from their depleted supplies. The taste of searing onions and beef jerky was pleasing and once everything was ready I guzzled away tender slices, finishing them off with long sips of cold clear water from my flask, which still tasted fresh, unsullied by several days of travel. When my hunger was satisfied, I said my nighttime salutations to the others and rolled onto my blankets, covering myself with my cape. My friends' voices gave me a calming background din; which, paired with the chilled breeze and sounds of the wind, helped me drift away into the refuge of my sleep.

Chapter 18

THERE WERE no visions that night. My dreams were clam, no battles to be fought, no trails to explore, and no A'al sorceresses to listen to. Next morning I woke up feeling rested and replenished, ready for another day. My companions were still asleep, except for Minia who was up, cleaning his horse with a patch of grass wet from the early dew. The squire did not see me and I let him be, instead, stretching on a soft spring carpet, observing the squire from afar. Satisfying feelings spread softly through my entire body, letting me enjoy the serenity of the glade and the woods that surrounded it. I remained still for a while, then yawned and lifted myself up, deciding to bother Minia, who was still scrubbing dirt off his mount, unsuspecting of my presence. As I walked across, I thought of how well he had fit into our small questing party. In just few days he managed to become friends with everyone in the group, and as we spent more time together, my friends and I grew fonder of our new companion, always eager to hear more of his tales, each more fascinating than the previous one.

In several long steps I reached Minia, greeting him with a loud whistle. Seeing me standing next to him, his face lit in a wide smile that showed rows of snow-white teeth, uncommon for Normandian folk, and waved.

"Greetings, Mishuk," called Minia, returning back to work.

"Greetings to you too," I said cheerfully and looked around. The place was quiet and calm. It was a truly perfect morning, and I wished for it to last a little longer. "This glade—it is so nice. I do not know what it is, but I have not felt so rested in days."

"There is something placid about this place, is not there?" noted Minia. "I think it is why Irk the Wise has chosen this glade for his home." Minia stopped scrubbing the horse and inhaled the morning sweet air. I took a deep breath too.

"So who is he exactly?" I asked and sat on the ground, leaning back on my elbows.

"You heard him yesterday; he is Irk the Wise, the hermit of Bois, an old man…" Minia paused for a moment. "And supposedly the greatest scholar in the entire kingdom. But I do not know too much about him."

The squire let go of the fastenings and allowed his mare to wander off, then took a seat next to me near a large dried stump.

"I first met him two years ago when I accompanied my lord on his trip to the southern regions of Bois. We did not stay here long and I only saw the old man for a few brief moments. Sire Rone was the one to talk to him, in that den over there. The two of them spent several hours together, and once the lord returned, he ordered us to depart. On the way back, I asked Sire Rone about the hermit—who he was and what he did. It was then I learned a few things about Irk the Wise."

Minia shifted to get a better seat, then resumed. "According to Sire Rone, Irk the Wise was once a well-known and respected sage. He lived in many places and served many masters. It is said that he was born into a wealthy and very influential family in the eastern portion of the Great Amber Empire. The youngest son of a border baron, he lived his childhood on his family's estate, knowing nothing but luxury and brilliance.

"While his older brothers had been arguing over their father's domain with all its subjects, wealth, and armies, Irk the Wise turned to scholarly things. Uninterested in the art of war, intrigues, and politics, he was drawn to the fruits of knowledge and wisdom concealed in books and manuscripts. Studying constantly, he did not miss a single chance to learn more, often passing hour after hour reading, searching, and writing. Soon constellations, figures, letters, and mechanics became his true love and passion, as he spent days, weeks, and years secluded in many libraries, revising everything he could lay his eyes on.

"By the time he reached the age of twenty he was already renowned around his father's lands as an exceptional scholar and a gifted tutor. Noble families from all over the Empire came to his father with lucrative offers of marriage and engagement, eager to reserve Irk's captivating mind for their own opulence. Soon enough, his father realized his son's aptitude as a great bargain and did not waste any time exploiting it to his own benefit. Talks with numerous counts, lords, and merchants from other parts of the Empire and neighboring kingdoms persevered, until Irk's father chose the best of the proposals and quickly arranged for a rewarding matrimony between his son and one of the daughters of a rival baron, who paid plenty for the young sage. When all was agreed, the couple were wed, Irk's mind exchanged for land and several chests of hard gold plates. But it did not bother the young scholar. Irk was unconcerned with such minor matters as his wedding and gladly agreed to leave his parents' domain, striving to enlarge his pursuit for enlightenment.

"Settling in one of the vacant mansions to the east of the Imperial capital, Vahu, Irk continued to polish his knowledge of the world. But soon the capital's collections of books and scrolls were not enough. The young sage needed more, and very quickly began to dream of higher wisdom secreted in other cities across the Empire. As he grew more restless, the binds of his new home and his responsibilities as a family man weighed heavily on his mind, and after several long years of fighting his own desire, he finally departed from his estate, leaving behind his wife and children, setting out on a long journey across the vast Imperial domain in search of many sparks of learning.

"Particularly interested in the history of ancient civilizations, the hermit ventured through the Empire, acquiring as many rare texts and writings as his could. Of course such things were often very pricey, and to afford them Irk started to hire himself out to greedy nobles, who were willing to pay well for the services of the infamous scholar. In return he received gold and jewelry and lands, which afforded him a careless and rich life. But money did not interest Irk. To him his wealth was nothing more than a way to more enlightenment, so desperately desired.

"As time passed, Irk became more and more obsessed with science, taking little notice of the world outside his study room, high in the towers of patrons' castles. Mixing poisons, designing catapults, and upgrading Dvorenian crossbows was no different to him from constructing a windmill or finding a cure for a vile disease. He took on any job that paid, and as he did, he moved from one city to another, learning languages, studying olden manuscripts, examining long-forgotten cultures, and building machines of both destruction and creation; along the way he wrote books, cured sicknesses, and drained the hefty purses of those who hired him. It was many years later when Irk was forced to change his ways.

"Although the hermit cared little for his wife or children, he thought of himself as a man of honor, someone who always respected endorsed agreements. His marriage was one such agreement. Though the arrangement was imposed on Irk by his father, the scholar nonetheless appreciated it and supported his family, sending his wife considerable sums of money, which he had meticulously collected every month. Along with money he included letters in which he described his travels and his thoughts. Though the notes were not too personal, Irk enjoyed writing them as they gave him a chance to tell some-one else of his progress. But one day his early dispatch was returned.

"When Irk was working for one of the princes from the Free cities, south of Azoros, a servant who had been instructed to deliver the money and the note, came back to him and conveyed a terrible news that Irk's wife and chil-dren had been killed during an unexpected raid on the home castle that belonged to Irk's father. Although feeling little remorse for such a tragic loss, Irk decided to travel back to see everything for himself. When he finally arrived at the father's estate, where his wife and children had been guests for some seasons, he found it burned to the ground, the ruins of the once imposing mansion greet-ing him with blackened shapes. Everything—the fortress, the small parish around it, and nearby farm fields were gone; most of the locals were killed; Irk's wife, all of his children, his three older brothers, and his late father were amongst the dead. The few survivors who had come back to bury the dead, told the scholar that the castle had been attacked by a horde of marauding bandits who had come from across the border, burning and killing everything on their path.

"More interested than horrified, the hermit examined the aftermath of the destruction with his usual precision and quickly realized that such devastation had not been caused by swords or arrows, but by a massive power of war en-gines, which true bandits rarely possessed. As Irk looked more closely, studying the trails, the ashes, and shattered stones, he understood that the machine that had killed his family was his own creation, something he had designed and sold to one of the neighboring barons many years back.

"The more he looked at the carnage around him, the more he recognized the fruits of his own work. It was then, Irk the Wise began to comprehend what evil his mind had brought into the world. The revelation ravaged him. Suddenly he despised himself for his ignorance, for his selfish ways and hollow aspirations. Unable to endure the view of the scorched land any longer, Irk left the estate and never returned, scared to face his fears again. But demons did not leave and persisted to hunt him everywhere he went, letting the pain and sorrow engulf his once unmoved heart. Dark thoughts attacked his mind like a pack of hungry hounds, spreading like a wild fire, hurting more and more with every passing day. Irk could not think or work anymore. All he saw were the black ashes and the vague faces of his family. At last, he understood that prod-ucts of his wisdom were not neutral, but often malevolent, used by others to kill, destroy, and pillage. And for that Irk hated himself, his work, and his life.

"Unable to escape his most fearsome enemy, his conscience, Irk gave up all of his possessions and disappeared. Some barons tried desperately to find him in their jealous desires to use his wisdom once again, but they never did. He simply vanished. Some say that he went to settle scores with his family's killers; others that he ventured to the Great Plains, roaming the vast realms of uncharted lands, trying to isolate himself from the world, or the world from himself. Whatever he did, nobody saw him for many years, until ten seasons ago he unexpectedly reappeared in Bois and after meeting with the local lords, settled at this glade, starting a new life as a hermit, living in the solitude of the aged forest. Since then, amongst the locals he has been known as the Hermit of Bois, the wise man of the south, who shuns the others, but always comes to aid if needed."

Minia drank some water from the flask and concluded, "I am not sure how true this tale is, but that is what I have heard. Myself, I do not want to ask the hermit to verify it, and I recommend you do the same."

No sooner than Minia's last words had left him, a squeaking sound came from the hermit's den as the small door opened and Irk the Wise appeared in the doorway, coughing and groaning loudly. The hermit looked the same as the day before with the exception of a broad pointy straw hat worn over his gray hair. For a moment Irk looked around him, and once he spotted us sitting some cubits away, he gave a light nod and motioned for us to come over. Minia and I climbed up and hurried across the glade, while the hermit continued to gaze at us, rubbing his bearded chin. When we were standing next to him, he pointed at me with his staff and walked back inside, without a single word. Unsure about what I had to do, I turned to Minia for explanation, but the squire only shrugged his shoulders. With a sigh I shrugged back and followed Irk inside. Minia went after me, but the old man's voice halted him in the doorway.

"You, boy! You stay outside. I will talk to you later. Right now I need this one with me." The hermit pointed at me again. The squire concurred silently and turned back. A second later, the door slammed behind me, and I was left alone with the hermit, who was already back in his chair, lighting the crooked pipe with a firestone. He took off his droll hat, and reached into his robe, from which appeared the familiar cover of the strange tome found at the monastery, along with several pages, which Irk quickly stacked at the edge of the table, pressing them with a good-size round stone.

Chapter 19

"SIT DOWN," said the hermit after checking something in the book, I did as told and settled on the chair across from him.

"I am done with the book," he then declared, and opened the tome, running his fingers through the lines of the text, coughing.

"What did you find, Sire?" I blurted out without even thinking.

"I told you not to call me Sire," snapped the hermit. "It is Irk the Wise. Irk the Wise. Do you understand?"

"Yes, yes. Irk the Wise. My apologies." I hurried to correct my mistake and was about to add, "Sire," when I caught myself and took a gulp of stuffy air instead.

"Good. Now, I have a question for you, young man. Where exactly did you find this book?"

"As you already know, my friends and I are on a quest to find the missing convoy, my father's convoy. When we began our search a week ago, the only report we had was of my father's wagon, discovered near Lulione. And since Sire Rone was the one to bring the cart and the news of my father's disappearance back to Villone, we decided to go to Sirone first and seek an audience with the lord, who was kind enough to listen to us and tell us things he knew about the search for the convoy and strange things that surrounded it, amongst which was a sighting of a monk, who had been seen lingering around the clearing where my father's wagon was found. Once our audience with Sire Rone was over, we set out further north, to the village of Lulione. After talking to the locals, who verified the story of a strange man dressed as a monk, we headed to the glade. But there we found nothing and so decided to investigate the story of a monk. Conveniently enough there was a monastery that belonged to the Order of the Spirit just a few days away; so wasting little time we went there to seek answers.

"When we finally reached the compound we found it deserted. There was no one there. Although the place looked abandoned and strange, we examined it anyway. There we found this book, lying behind a chapel, hidden in the bushes and covered with a brown dirty cloth."

"Uh-huh," the hermit interrupted me, mumbling to himself. "The Order of the Spirit you say. It makes little sense. Even so..." The old man stopped whispering and glared at me. "I must say you have brought me a very interesting piece of writing."

He turned a page and read a short passage, loud enough so I could hear. Yet the words sounded unfamiliar, and I did not understand a thing.

"Do you know what it is?" inquired Irk afterwards.

"No," I answered truthfully.

"It is Uru, one of the ancient languages from the First Age. When our predecessors settled these lands, they were not the only dwellers in Ethoria. There were others, antediluvian races from the old days. Those folks were not like us. Their appearance, their language, their culture and traditions were very different from ours. But those peoples did not survive the passage of time. Legends say that some of them died during the many wars fought across the world; some left across the Abyss to explore the lands beyond the seas, and some simply vanished, gone with the wind as one may say. You probably have already heard such names as A'als and D'ars. It is from those old folks that our ancestors got their knowledge, and it was they who passed Uru to the human kin.

"Nobody knows where the language was born and who spoke it first. Until this very day it is a mystery, and even I cannot tell you much about its history. There are scholars though, who believe that Uru came from the north, across the Barrier Walls, brought in the beginning of the New Epoch by the wild tribes who found their way into Ethoria through the mountains of the Land's Edge. Yet others say that it was the A'als, who gave Uru to the humans so that they could teach the young and primitive men the marvels of the world. Whatever the reason, Uru became the first known language of our race and for many years sounded across Ethoria, reaching as far as the Great Plains and beyond.

"Only when the first human nation began to split did Uru changed. As more realms formed, each adopted new dialects, gradually transforming the language into many different tongues. Yet, at the footsteps of the Land's Edge, where now the Kingdom of Normandia stands, Uru remained prevalent, spoken within the borders of the most powerful of the old realms, the vast empire of Titul. Alas the great nation was destroyed by the Northern Hordes during the Great War, and with it went Uru, gone along with mighty cities and brave armies of the empire. Imagine…"

The hermit stared at me with heavy gray eyebrows hanging over his eyes.

"What was a potent language then, now is just a glimpse of history. I suppose, after a while, everything fades. Sadly it is so. Uru has descended deep into the ancient times along with thousands of precious pieces of wisdom that were written in that language."

Irk the Wise took a deep breath of air and leaned back in his chair, resting his old limbs on the side of the table. "But enough of my mumbling. What I want to talk to you about is not a thing of the past, but of the present. What I have here…" The hermit lifted the book in front of me, "…is something very different from what I have encountered in my years of studying the ancient languages. For one, this is not an old text. Although its pages look aged, the book is a work of our time, written not too long ago. Until now I have known only a handful of those who could read Uru, not to mention speak it or write in it. Whoever inscribed this text possessed a phenomenal knowledge of Uru, something I have never seen before. But it is not the only thing that concerns me…"

The hermit then turned another page, examining it from over his disks of glass. "The passage I have just cited….It starts with the words—Alavantar Dus Muros Gri. Do you know what it means? Ah, Of course you do not. Loosely translated it means Glory to the Final Reign of the Old Master or the Master of the Old, depending on how you put it. It is a motto of a devout order, a sect if you wish, secret and, as it seems, fanatical. Those who make up its ranks call themselves the Alavantars or the Bringers of the Glory. In their dedication they strive to bring the new age, the time when armies from beyond the Land's Edge invade Ethoria again and conquer it once and for all.

"This book that you have uncovered within the walls of the deserted monastery is not a simple piece of writing. It is a guide, a handbook for the members of this sect. My guess is that this tome is given out to the initiated members who decide to join the cause of the sect. It contains rules, descriptions, rituals, and fragments of prophecies, and, as far as I can tell, lays out the foundation for their beliefs."

The hermit read another passage and then explained, "Here it says that there will come a day when the glorious forces of the North, led by the Master of the Old, will rise from the depths of the ice-clinched wastes and descend upon the New World, bringing an end to its existence once and for all. Strange, is it? Well, not really, if you know a little history you will know exactly what it means."

The old man licked his dry lips and then his fingers. "How well do you know your history, young man?" he asked afterwards.

"I studied it a little at the local seminary back in Villone, but I am afraid I do not know nearly as much as I think I ought to."

"Just as I thought. Oh well, it is too late to wish for learning now. I guess I will have to give you some insight about days long past myself."

Irk the Wise sighed. "Ethoria was not always like this. Just a few hundred years ago it was a different place. The earliest descriptions tell a story of a land where magic forces formed the essence of all life. Although nobody knows where magic came from, it is known that the first people to use it were the Keepers. If you never heard of them, they were the ancient race that first inhabited Ethoria before the humans, the A'als, the D'ars, and other races. Believed to possess a secret to everlasting life, the Keepers moved through time, using magic to keep the essence of life flowing through their bodies. Yet immortals they were not, and their reign came to an end.

"Although for thousands and thousands of years they enjoyed order, peace, and prosperity, standing unchallenged in their rule, one day they found themselves on the verge of a great conflict, their enemy emerging from within. It started with an argument of a serene nature. While most of the Keepers believed that their magic powers ought to be used to nurture and protect all forms of life, some were convinced that they were meant for a far greater task, the task of creating a perfect world where there was no sorrow, no suffering or anguish. At first the debates had gone without any threat to the Keepers' harmony, but then took a menacing turn when a young Keeper by the name of Alin joined the opposition's ranks and quickly rose to become its sole and undeniable leader.

"Devoting his life to the works of magic, Alin dreamt of changing the world to his own design, and once his support amongst the challengers had reached its peak he took matters into his hands. Induced by his ideas, he persuaded many of his followers to rise against the popular views. Taking control over several large cities, Alin declared a new regime with him as its absolute ruler. While traditionalists tried to decide what to do, he and his disciples exploited their powers, keen to reshape the world according to the vision of a so-called ideal world. Streams of most eloquent magic flooded the lands, drying out seas, erasing mountains, and altering the very foundation of nature. The changes were so grave that the entire look of Ethoria began to change, forcing death upon many living things that fell victim to Alin's doings.

"Shocked and angered the other Keepers moved to stop the crazy rebels. But by then the mutineers had grown very strong and so a devastating civil war tore the once mighty nation in half. For years and years arms and magic clashed throughout Ethoria, raging in the sky, fields, cities, and forests, killing and destroying much of the Keepers' own creations. In the end the rebels were defeated, their strongholds destroyed, and their sources of magic drained. Alin and some of his followers, who had survived the last battles, were captured one by one and as punishment for their deeds, were sentenced to exile, cast away into the Northern wastes where ice and gusty winds held little hope for an easy living.

"Afraid of Alin and his followers, the Keepers did everything to prevent the rebels from ever coming back. To seal the captives in their natural prison, they built one of the greatest wonders of Ethoria, a massive range of high gray mountains, known to this day as the Land's Edge. Using magic, out of the ground the Keepers raised rows of snow-capped peaks that stretched from the waters of the Abyss in the west to the deep unwelcoming forests in the east, cutting off the snowy regions from the rest of the world. But before the marvelous formation could be completed, the Keepers' powers weakened, and a narrow passage was left, unlocked and free for anyone to pass. The Keepers could no longer raise mountains to close the gap, instead they had to build a smaller edifice, a grand wall of polished black stone, which ascended several hundred cubits from the ground as one massive shield against the troubles of the north. That wall has since been known as the First Barrier.

"Alas, without magic the Keepers could not live forever. Their numbers slowly shrank as they died from age and injuries and sickness, and soon enough their nation disappeared altogether. Nobody knows exactly when the last of the Keepers left this world, but some old writings suggest that many of the ancient people did not die. Instead they used their final drops of magic to transform themselves into an astral state. The ones who managed to become spirits regained a prolonged life, but in return were bound to depend on the waters of the lakes as it was there their life force was concealed. Drawing upon the energies of tarns, the Keepers continued to live in their new form, and for as long as the lakes were there to sustain their existence, they went through ages, watching as their world fell to the hands of other races that started to rebuild it all anew.

"It is not known how many Keepers chose such a destiny. But as most of the olden lakes dried out long before our ancestors came to Ethoria, this mystery dried up along with them. Yet people say that one of the ancient lakes cheated time and witnessed the coming of the Second Age. If that is true, the last Keeper of Ethoria might have survived until our days. The lake the people speak of is here in Normandia, hidden amongst thick trunks of the Old Forest.

Some call it the Lake of the Spirit, others, the Lake of Marvels, and you probably know it as the Lake of Wonders.

"Whatever the name may be, it bears the same meaning, which derives from the very old legend that every three hundred years a Keeper's Spirit emerges from the calm dark waters of the lake and wanders the lands in search of his missing kin. When he does not find them, he returns to the lake; but before he submerges into the waters, he grants one woman a gift, the gift of a child who is not an ordinary child, but a Keeper by blood, rewarded with the powers and wisdom of the ancient race. But there is also a more recent legend that tells of the Lake's power to tell the future. The belief is that if someone wants to see what lies ahead, he should come to the Lake at full moon, drink three cups from its waters, praise the Spirit, and go to sleep. When the dreams come, they will bring apparitions, images of what is yet to come. Both stories have been so intriguing that for hundreds of years pilgrims from across Ethoria have traveled to the shores of the Lake in hopes of finding out their future or receiving the precious gift of the Keeper's blood. Regrettably, I know of not a single person who has succeeded in getting either one."

The hermit shrugged his boney shoulders and paused to coughed a few times. Then he continued: "As for those who remained jailed at the other side of the Land's Edge, their fate had been unheard of for many years, until a strange dark force began to lurk unchecked behind the battlements of the Barrier's wall. At first there were few troubles, but as time passed they became more frequent, and then one day, vast hordes of Trolliers and wild men and foul creatures stormed the fortifications of the First Barrier in an attempt to find their way into Ethoria and the realms it harbored. Back then the world belonged to the A'als and D'ars, who unlike humans were prepared for such invasion. Meeting the aggression in full force, they fought hard and brave, defending their kingdoms, standing firm against a seemingly unending flow of foes. It was the time of many wars, each furious and brutal, and when the last of the battles was over the races of Ethoria emerged victorious, pushing the enemy back beyond the mountains. Yet with victory in hand the A'als and D'ars knew well that the threat was not over and so they continued to protect their lands, guarding the great walls and towers of the First Barrier, ready to defend it at the first sign of danger.

"But A'als and D'ars went away too, and in their place came humans who had no knowledge of the menace from beyond the Land's Edge. With no concern for the desolate lands of the north the men cared little for what lay at the other side of the Barrier, leaving its walls and towers abandoned. What a mistake it was, though our ancestors did not realize it until it was too late. While myriad kingdoms and empires occupied themselves with trivial quarrels, the darkness crept unnoticed in the north and in the summer season of the year 2521 of the First Age of the New Epoch, the evil emerged again, streaming over the unguarded battlements of the Barrier, with a stream of savage warriors and beasts pouring into Ethoria, destroying everything along its way.

"Like thousands of years before that, the Northern armies numbered many thousands—wild men, and Trolliers, and wild creatures, dogs, and wolves, and giant human-like fiends, with bodies covered in dirty white fur. Seeding fear amongst confused and outnumbered defenders, the bloodthirsty hordes moved with great speed, annihilating any resistance they met. And in command of such an awesome, terrifying force, stood a distinguished massive figure, a single fighter of great size, who towered over his minions, always riding a black stallion with an immense broad sword in hand. None in Ethoria knew his name or his title, and none ever learned it, as even captured enemies were ready to die before divulging it to their captors. So the dark figure remained nameless and those Ethorians who had to face his mighty army created their own designations. In those dark days, they called him Alin, for to them it was the symbol of the greatest and the mightiest of evils that once was powerful enough to destroy the Keepers, the strongest of all races.

"In several years of the War the forces of the North destroyed most of the old kingdoms and reached the southern edge of the Sarie Desert. For some reason they did not stop there, but continued to push forth, moving deeper into hot white sands. It was one mistake, which cost the invaders everything. Unprepared for harsh conditions of the arid southern lands, the Northerners fell prey to the desert sun and dry scorching winds that attacked them without mercy. Casualties mounting, Alin lost half of his army and eventually had to turn back. But as he led his soldiers to the coast of the Seven Seas, the Ethorians, those who had survived the many battles, gathered their forces for the one last fight, forming the greatest and largest of the armies, like none before. Thousands and thousands of men answered the call and came to the Amber River raising their arms and shields to face the invaders one last time.

"There on the banks of the mighty river, the final battle was fought. It was indeed the utmost of clashes. Accounts of those days tell of fighting that lasted for several weeks, with front lines on both sides extending for leagues across the open fields. Although Alin expected nothing but victory, the Desert weakened his army, and in the end his forces were defeated. Alin himself was slain during the final day, his huge body chopped to pieces by the soldiers of Ethoria. With their commander dead, the Northern army broke and fled, chased from the field of battle by the triumphant forces of men.

"For months bands of Ethorian warriors hunted the invaders, killing them without remorse. Yet some invaders escaped and took flight back into the desert, disappearing there amongst the sands. Too weak to fight again, Ethorians could not pursue the enemy any further and had to abandon their revenge. Instead they returned to their world, devastated by the years of war. The horrifying aftermath of the years of ravaged fighting was everywhere, cities and entire kingdoms destroyed, cultures annihilated, thousands and thousands dead. It was then the survivors saw the sorrowful effect of their misstep, and to remember what the ignorance had done to their world, they named the gorge across the Land's Edge, the Shadow Pass, so as to remind future generations of the price our people had to pay.

"Ascertaining well the dangers that prowled beyond the mountains' rim, the battered kingdoms pulled together their scattered resources and began to rebuild the Barrier Wall, pledging to never again leave its battlements unguarded. In the next decades the men of Ethoria restored the First Barrier and some leagues south, at the other end of the Shadow Pass, they built another wall—the Second Barrier they called it. As big as the first blockade it was fifty cubits thick and stretched for ten leagues across the corridor, like a snake of shiny black granite. In between the two walls, to watch over the safety of the region, the stonemasons raised a grand stronghold; the Great Fortress was its name. Divided into many sections, the citadel had seven towers, each as big as a normal castle, each manned with hundreds of men, and linked together with tall wide walls, as big as the Barriers themselves.

"For years to come, the Great Fortress guarded the Shadow Pass, supported by all kingdoms across Ethoria that sent their men money, and stocks of food and weapons, necessary to sustain the large garrison that counted over five thousand men. But as it always happens with our kin, some generations after, the people began to forget the lessons of the past. As old nations died and new ones came to be, the men befell to troubles of their own, pushing aside the horrors of the ruthless Northern hordes, great sorrow, bloody battles and destruction. All those painful memories became just that, and soon turned to legends, told to children at bedtime.

"You think that we, the humans, who pride ourselves to be so wise and able, would have remembered what our ancestors had gone through. But no. Foolishly, today, we ignore the history and all that it has given us. The Barriers still block the Shadow Pass, but they are unguarded once again. The many kings and queens do not care for the safety of the walls. Their false sense of protection they find in politics and small armies, seeing foes amongst their rival kin. But in all their bustle they forget about the true enemy—the cold and brutal north. While our proud nobles concern themselves with little squabbles, the Barriers stand empty, just like they did thousands of years ago, and just like then it may be our vital mistake."

"But I thought there are still those who serve at the wall." I remembered my father saying something about our lord sending folks to the Great Fortress as barrier guards. He even showed me one of the caravans that headed to the Shadow Pass. I did not see it up close, but I could swear there were many men amongst the travelers.

"Ah, yes, Normandian traditions. I am afraid I have to disappoint you young man. Those men who you have seen departing for the Wall are not guards; they are criminals, thieves, bandits, and murderers who have been sentenced to serve their time at the Barrier's mines. And that title that you hear—Barrier guards, is but a hollow name."

"You see," the hermit looked up and closed the book. "By the middle of the Second Age, many of Ethorian kingdoms ceased to contribute to the Barriers. The only nation that continued to supply the dwindling garrison of the Great Fortress was Normandia and even it stopped its aid once your kings had found little use for the region. But several cycles ago, something unexpected happened. Within the mountains that ran between the two walls, old mines were discovered and with them deposits of gold and silver, and a rare red ore that was twice as tough as normal ore. With no other means to support themselves, the men of the Great Fortress began to mine the precious metals and sell them to the neighboring kingdoms. Soon everyone understood how valuable the mines were and local nobles did not waste any time trying to reclaim their ties to the region. One after another they sent their emissaries to the Great Fortress in hopes of resuming relations with the garrison.

"For most of them it was too late. By that time the Great Fortress had become an independent realm, with its own rulers, laws, and customs. With mines under their control the commanders of the Barriers refused to grant the other kingdoms access to the precious resources, seizing their value for themselves. Only Normandian kings were successful in striking a deal with the commanders. The agreement was that several of the mines would come under Normandian control, in exchange for a supply of workers that your kingdom pledged to send to the Barriers to work in the mines. And so it became that the Barrier guards turned into workers, miners, whose titles were the only reminder that once they were people who defended the walls. And the proud officers of the Great Fortress, they became the supervisors, the men who watched over the miners, making sure that the work is done and no criminals escape without serving their time first. The soldiers they have once been, but now they are traders, wardens, and overseers who know little of the Northern Wastes that lay beyond the Walls or the dangers they possess.

"As for the Barriers' defenses, they were left to be. Sentries still guard the walls, but that is done to keep the wild men from stealing stocks of gold and ore. Those few defenders are all that is left of the once mighty army that was there before, and even they cannot be called the true Barriers' guards."

Irk the Wise grew quiet again. He sat with the book closed for some time, then smacked his lips and opened the tome, moving his palm, slowly across the page. "Sad it is, very, very sad. Those who supposed to remember do not, and those who should not, do. The Alavantars are the ones who are aware of the past. They know it well, and they do everything in their power to make sure that nothing changes, that people continue to waste the time, as they prepare for the new age, the age when the North returns to Ethoria.

"The Alavantars believe that beyond the Land's Edge, a great figure has been born again, a true conqueror who will rise to unite all of the dwellers of the Northern wastes, and lead them across the mountains of the Land's Edge into Ethoria, avenging the defeat of their forefathers. They truly consider this personage to be their master, their future sovereign, and the ruler of the world. It is he they await and it is in his name they live and work.

"The origin of such belief has come from ancient prophecies, written accounts from the past that date more than seven hundred years back, to the times when Magnicia was still a mighty nation. Sometime in the fifth cycle of the Second Age a group of seamen from Lombardia brought back an ancient artifact found amongst the untamed wilds of the Isle of the Claw, located in the middle of the Seven Seas. The common sailors knew little of the object's purpose and quickly sold it to a merchant for a profit. The trader also did not understand anything about the relic and when the chance presented itself re-sold it to a wizard, from Humar, an ancient city in Magnicia. The sorcerer's name was Arac Cron, a renowned scholar in the arts of magic and alchemy. He brought the artifact home and began to study it, searching for a key to unlock the mystery hidden within. With help from his many apprentices, Arac spent days laboring on the problem. He used all his knowledge, but the puzzle did not give. Then, one night, he decided to try an old A'als' spell he had learned years back. When at first the foreign magic covered the strange item nothing happened, but then magic took its course and the object blossomed from its shell. Something happened then: Arac lost consciousness and once he awoke strange visions engulfed his mind. The images were not dreams, but something else.

"Confused and scared, Arac did not understand the things he saw. His mind hurled into a spiral spin, and there came a time when he decided to kill himself. But as he stood at the ledge of his high tower, ready to plunge into the depths of the moat beneath, a sudden revelation came to him. The apparitions he had seen were not a wicked curse of A'al magic, but pictures of the things that were yet to come. It was then Arac understood that he was witnessing the future.

"Immediately excitement overwhelmed the wizard's mind. Clarity returned, and he resumed his work. No longer afraid of his state, Arac recorded everything he had perceived in his many journals, which later came to be known as Arac's Verses. Unfortunately before the wizard could complete his work, he died of a mysterious cause. A strange death it was. One moment he was seen writing in his journals, and the next he threw himself into the fire, burning to ashes so that not a single speck of him remained. Until this day there are many theories as to what exactly made the prophet kill himself. Personally I believe that the visions destroyed the wizard. But it was not Arac's death that set off much of the upheaval; it was his work, his journals that made everyone utter Arac's name. The problem was that Arac was a strange man. After he had started to record his visions, he became very afraid that someone would steal his work. To protect his opus, he used a code to inscribe his passages. The words and phrases he employed were known only to him, and only he could have provided the key to their understanding. And after his death his work became a mystery to all, its meaning locked in a tangle of strange symbols.

"For cycles, sages and wizards of Magnicia kept those verses hidden in their libraries, trying to solve their riddle. They studied the journal's every line, every word, and then, after years of hard labor, they succeeded in deciphering the texts. At last the verses opened up to them and gave out the true content of Arac's labor. Predictions of the future came to life again. Although not everything was translated, the parts that were decoded foretold the coming of a dark lord, a rise of a warrior of virtue, and a Great War, which promised to bring much sorrow and devastation to the world.

"In his passages Arac revealed that some cycles after the fall of Magnicia, a great evil would be born deep within the frozen lands of the North. Its only goal, its only desire would be for power and domination over every living thing. Feeding its ever-growing appetites on destruction and chaos, the evil would take on the form of a man, a figure, called the Master of the Old, who will lead immense armies from the North across the Land's Edge and into Ethoria, conquering every kingdom and every city, not stopping until the whole world lay at his feet. It will be a time of war, the Great War, with seas of soldiers fighting on each side.

" Arac also said though that, '...the evil will not be born alone....' Somewhere in the world, another man will come to life, who will carry an uncorrupted force of goodness in his heart. That man will work his way across the lands and come to stand against the resurrected Master of the Old. Unaware of each other at first, the two will follow their paths and when they start to draw near each other the world will know many battles that will scar the lands, soaking it in blood and tears. And once they finally meet face-to-face, there will be the greatest of all battles, the clash of forces that cannot be described by words. It will be then, the fate of the world will be determined.

"Unfortunately Arac's verses said nothing about the outcome of the conflict, since the wizard died before he could complete his work. So, auspiciously, the outcome remains uncertain."

Irk changed his tone slightly, sounding even more serious. "Although I could not find the exact date, I took the liberty of doing some estimates as to the time frame of these cataclysmic events." The hermit chuckled. "It appears we may be living on the verge of this conflict. To be precise, a vague mark that I have found in this tome refers to a time period between 1215 and 1245. As you can see, it is today.

"If the legend is true, in the few coming years, we will witness the beginning of some unsettling events. And as I found just last night in this book, I am not the only one who thinks so. The Alavantars agree with me, assured that their Northern master will rise in the near future. They anxiously await the dark lord, and prepare themselves so they can help him to conquer Ethoria. In return they are hoping for great powers, which will allow them to rule the lands as his faithful disciples. Their leaders have gone even further, and claim to be connected to the Master of the Old themselves. For that they have sacrificed their humanity, and used their empty souls to open a link between themselves and their lord. It appears that the members of the sect truly believe that they are the ones who must stop their master's rightful adversary, the protector of Ethoria, the Chosen One, as Arac calls him. Again they find their guidance from the verses, which say that the Chosen One will come from the west, from the realm of Wonders. Born into a family of good he will be surrounded by love and care. One of many he will follow in the steps of his ancestors and will rise to stand against the evil, as it is his destiny and his choice.

"Do you see? This clearly explains why you have found the book in Bois. The Alavantars are looking for the Chosen One here in Normandia. They want to kill him before he gets stronger, before he realizes his true fate. Yet, it surprises me much that you have found this book inside the monastery of the Order of the Spirit. The religious path, which the brothers of the Spirit follow, is exactly the opposite of that the Alavantars have taken. The whole purpose of the Order's existence is the protection of Ethoria from the Northern threat. Guided by the Great Spirit of the Keepers, the brothers of the Order watch over Ethoria, protecting its people, fighting anyone, who fends for the evil North. Why have the brothers of the Spirit had this book of the Alavantars inside their compound is beyond my understanding. One things is ceratin though. Something is very odd here, very, very odd."

Irk grew quiet, while I reflected on his last words. Living in Bois, I had heard much about the Order of the Spirit, and those, who called themselves its faithful brothers. Since most Normandian folk followed the Ways of the Spirit, the Order had always been popular in our kingdom. The King and the Dukes, all, employed members of the Order as their advisors; and many lesser nobles often invited the brothers to live in their domains, either for good luck or spiritual protection. Across the kingdom, monasteries were constructed in numbers, and almost every city had a temple where the brothers performed their services, devoting their prayers and acts to the Great Spirit of the Keepers, the divine being that watched over everyone and everything in Ethoria. Villone too had a temple, and a brother, Uncle Alior, who lived inside a small chapel and conducted daily ceremonies, inviting all town-folks to take part. Once in awhile he asked my friends and I to come too, but we rarely did. Hearing about 'the Ways of the Spirit' over and over was just too boring. Besides none of us cared much about religious matters, or the Order. As a result my knowledge on the subjects of the church and the Great Spirit was inadequate at best. The hermits speech made me regret my ignorance, but only for a brief moment, for there were other things in the old man's tale that I found far more important at a time.

"But how will they know who the Chosen One is?" I asked after a pause.

"I cannot answer this question, child. Only the Alavantars can. But as you have already found out, they are not that easy to locate."

"Can it be that my father's disappearance has something to do with these Alavantars and the prophecies?"

"Huh, that is an interesting thought. Did you say your brother was traveling along with the caravan?"

"Yes, he was heading to Bonneville; he was going to sell his bow at the markets there."

"Huh. If those mad Alavantars are looking for someone, they are probably looking for young men like your brother. Maybe they have sought to find your brother and kidnap him, as he does fit the description of the Chosen One, but so does almost every youngster of a fair age. Oh, Spirit. If it is so, then nobody is safe in the entire kingdom; not when these insane evil worshipers are running loose, trying to get rid of anyone who even remotely resembles their acclaimed foe. I wish I had more insight into this matter. I wish I knew more."

Another long sigh followed. He read several more passage quietly, then frowned and raised his voice: "Maybe this will help. The Alavantars have one leader, Agraz, who is the supreme servant to the Master of the Old. As opposed to most of the ordinary members, he does not concern himself with petty matters of daily life. Instead he upholds a link with his dark lord, in which he receives the guidance from the master and passes it to those he thinks fit.

"While Agraz gives out the directives, their implementation is entrusted to his acolytes, the faithful members, who compose the second link in the unyielding chain of command referred to in the book as the council of Jeg Aazes, loosely translated as servants to the one. It says that the Jeg Aazes is made up of seven most trusted Alavantars, each of whom leads a separate chapter, located somewhere in Ethoria. Leagues apart, the members of the Jeg Aazes are united with each other through a link to Agraz, always following their leader's orders, never questioning his choice or reason. But the reach of Agraz and his devoted sect goes even further, as besides the chapters there are many smaller groups, placed throughout the kingdoms, clandestine from the eyes of the local lords. I wouldn't be surprised if such fraternities exist somewhere within Normandia. The book you have found serves as a proof to it, and that compound that you have come across might not had been a monastery of the Order of the Spirit, but the Alavantars' stronghold here in Bois."

I wanted to ask a question, but the hermit halted me. "I know you have your inquiries. It all probably sounds very bizarre to you. Do not worry, I feel the same way. It is all a mystery to me too. So hold your questions, let me finish first."

Contentedly, I sat back and listened. The hermit adjusted his glass disks, licked two of his fingers, and said: "Something made those so-called monks depart from their compound. I do not know if it has had something to do with your father's caravan, or your search for it, but I have a weird feeling that it all is connected somehow. Your brother is especially worrisome, as his abduction would have fit perfectly into the sect's workings. If it is so, and the Alavantars are responsible for the convoy's disappearance, Normandia may face a handful of problems in the very near future. Probably there will be many cases of kidnappings all throughout the kingdom. Several young lads here, a few more there—it will probably look accidental, often blamed on bandits and the treacherous woods. Most folks won't ever notice it, and will continue to put the fault elsewhere, and rightfully so, they are not aware of the Alavantars and their wicked design. Yet, we are—you and me.

"That is why we should act and act quickly. My feet may be old, but I am not dead yet. I will start my research of this matter immediately. As for you, I cannot force you to do anything. You should decide for yourself. Think hard and make your decision wisely. If you choose to get involved, you may find yourself caught in a conflict that hides a far greater danger than you think. It may be that you will no longer search for your father and his caravan, but will be entrusted to investigate the Alavantars or maybe even help stop them. Yet, if you are not ready for the perils of the quest, tell me now and I will seek help elsewhere. Do not think that I will judge you for your choice. Whatever it is, it will remain between you and me. So the choice is yours, but you have to make it today."

Thoughts, thoughts, and more thoughts. "What should I do? What should I choose? Was I ready to face the Alavantars, whoever they were?" I did not know answers to any of those questions. I was not sure if I would ever know. But I was sure about one thing—if, to find Father, Ave, and the other men, I had to look into workings of some secret mad sect, so be it. I would do what was needed, and more. Despite what others might say, I had to take the challenge and assist the hermit in his inquiry into the deeds of the Alavantars. I repeated the words in my mind several times. They felt right; I knew what I had to do and I made my choice—I was going to get involved. I informed the hermit of my choice. In return, Irk nodded slowly with a hint of approval in his eyes.

"I am glad to hear these words," the hermit said. "Since we both know what we are dealing with, we should not waste any time. Your first task will be to take this book and my letter to Sire Rone, tell him about the dangers that may be plaguing his domain; ask him to check if there were any disappearances of young men in recent months; explain what I have told you, and do not forget to mention the monastery—it is very, very important.

"Another thing I should mention is that the Alavantars may have many powerful allies amongst those who I would not usually suspect of being evil followers. It may be that some of our very own knights have been corrupted by the sect. With that, I warn you to be wary of everyone you meet on your way. Be careful who you talk to, especially if you have to venture outside Bois and into more distant lands. The matter that you have uncovered is of grand importance. I am not quite sure if what the prophecies foretell is true, but the Alavantars surely think so. There may still be time to find out more about them before it is too late. Be careful though. This book and my letter are the only evidence we have about the Alavantars. If they are gone, we have no proof. Also think carefully of what is about to unfold before you, and do not forget to warn your friends, they deserve a choice, just like you."

With these last words, the hermit closed the book and placed it in the center of the table along with the letter, which consisted of some yellow pages that hid rows of handwritten lines. Then he got up, took his staff and strolled passed me, walking straight onto the glade. I was alone in the room. I was about to go after him, but then stopped and sat back, thinking of the strange tale. Alavantars, Arac, the Master of the Old, those words were ringing in my head. It was so hard to comprehend the complexity of the affairs that had unraveled before me. Suddenly my temples started to hurt. "Am I, a youngster from a small rural town, to play a part in events of such great magnitude?" I wondered. All I wanted was to find Father and Ave, bring them home, and return to what I liked to do, run around Villone and get in trouble.

An awful headache made its way to the back of my head, threatening to split my wits in two. The air around me became thicker and a sour aftertaste made me shiver. It became hard to breath and I dashed for the door. A burst of fresh air hit me in the face. Slowly I began to recapture my consciousness. Feeling better, I looked up to the sky and took a deep breath. After standing still for a moment I lowered my head and glanced at the camp. Everyone was up. My companions had already fixed a quick breakfast and were sitting in a tight circle, talking joyfully to each other.

Alas the jokes and smiles of my friends did not draw me; I stood in silence at a distance, thinking of a way to tell them of what I had just learned myself. Slowly I crossed the glade, still wet from the morning dew, and picked a spot next to Ike, dropping down onto my backpack that lay undisturbed from the night. After a gulp of air and a sip of cold water I started with the news, once buried in the pages of the book we had brought a day before. As I told my companions everything, their smiles faded, and soon the last traces of their cheerful mood dissolved into grim serious faces, all focused on me. Even though I felt awful about subjecting my comrades to these taunting, I had no choice. It was their decision as much as mine. I chose my way, and it was time for them to do the same.

The camp was silent. My companions sat unmoving, seldom looking at each other and me. Uneasy, I waited, with a forced thin smile on my face.

Ike's voice came first, alerting the rest of the group. As he spoke, everyone lifted their heads and turned to hear what he had to say.

"To tell you the truth, I did not exactly expect to hear such a lovely legend so early in the day," announced Ike, then gloominess left him, and his cheerful state returned. "Mishuk, if you think you can catch all that fame and glory saving the world from the wrath of evil, while I am sitting bored at home, you are dead wrong. This whole journey was as much my idea as it was yours, and I am not going anywhere. What if you find some hefty treasure, or a lost relic that holds some secret magic power, do you think I will let you keep it and not share it with me. Not a chance. We either go together, or we do not go at all."

Ike smiled and Rob picked up the banter.

"As much as I would like to get back home someday, I just cannot let you two halfwits run around Ethoria frightening innocent, unsuspecting folks. Who will guide you, who will help you?...," Rob smirked, thought a bit, and added, "And how can I be sure you get home in one piece? There is no question. I am coming with you."

He leaned forward and slapped Ike on the back.

"I will help you too," sounded Minia next. "I am a man of arms, a servant to the lord. I was sent here to assist you in any way I could. Those were my exact orders, and until I hear otherwise from Sire Rone, I will do as told. If there is another task for me, I will learn of it once we get to Sirone; until then, I am at your service."

He bobbed his head and gave me his squire's salute.

"Huh, another trial of our character, I like it. Count me in," said Ark. He stared at me seriously, then smiled. "Besides if I do not tag along with all my supplies, you will starve to death. I did not see any of you making your suppers lately."

We all laughed.

So there it was. That sunny spring morning we made up our minds and took on yet another quest, the quest that promised to lead us further away from home and deeper into the wilds of our kingdom. Sitting in the middle of the sunlit glade, we accepted the hermit's offer and prepared to investigate the doings of some surreptitious sect of false believers. From then on, our simple lives changed forever. Of course back then we did not know it. All we wanted was new experience and adventure, and we got both.

Chapter 20

IT WAS early when we were done. The sun was already up, and we were finishing with the morning meal, feasting on Arc's delicious cookery, when abruptly branches of the nearby trees moved to one side and someone walked into the glade. Not recognizing the man at first, I was about to lurch to my weapon, but seeing that it was Irk the Wise who had walked out of the woods, I slid back into my seat and gave him a wave of my hand. The hermit nodded in response, either greeting me or moving his hair, and then walked up to us, carrying two small pouches of hard dark leather, tied with ribbons of blue and red.

"I see you all have made your choice," said Irk, towering over our band and staring, his eyes focused on me. It was strange. I did not remember seeing the hermit anywhere near the glade since I had left his den. Yet somehow he was aware of my friends' decision.

"I should say I am very pleased with your devotion to each other, but I hope you understand that by taking on this quest you may subject yourselves to dangers that otherwise would have escaped you. Oh well, your choice is your choice. So let's not waste any more time on flaunting words; there is much to be done."

The old man, pointed at the pouches that he had placed on the ground beside him.

"Here is something I have gathered for you. The bag with the small blue ribbon holds the book from the monastery and my letter to Sir Rone. Be very watchful of these items, get them safe to Sirone, and do not let anyone see them, not until you show them to your lord first. The pouch with the red ribbon contains some useful things I have collected for your journey. Amongst them you will find herbs and salves and potions, each marked with a label that will tell you what it is for."

The hermit paused and, overlooking the entire group, leisurely shook his gray head.

"Also…within your backpacks, you will find extra stocks of provisions. It is not much, but it will help you get to the castle without scavenging for food or drink. Be careful not to waste it all at once."

As the old man spoke, we instinctively opened our bags and looked inside. Indeed amongst our possessions we found a dozen strips of smoked meat, several small sacks of dried wild berries, and wooden jugs of some drink with a decent taste to it. It was a pleasant surprise and we appreciated such help, especially since we had already begun to run low on provisions, left only with a quarter of a slab of cheese, two onions, and half a loaf of hard bread.

Excited with the gifts, we whirled over our backpacks. The hermit turned around and headed for his den, but halfway across stopped and without turning uttered:

"Take care of yourselves, young brats. I wish you luck and Spirit's guidance. Do not forget, wits are often better than the most powerful blades. Be wise, and if you ever come back to these forgotten woods, do me a favor, stop by the old hermit's hut. I would be very interested to hear those tales of yours," Irk thought for a moment. "Bring me good tales, young brats." Those words spoken, the old man resumed his stride and quickly disappeared inside his dwelling.

Afterwards I wanted to come to the burrow to say my farewell, but Minia stopped me, suggesting otherwise, and so I did not; instead I gathered my belongings and followed my friends back to the open fields, leaving the hermit and his glade to the morning sunshine. Our next destination was Sirone, and to get there we had to choose between two routes. One lay straight across the valley, past the small village of Gurion, and down the western trade way, which ran straight to Sire Rone's castle. The other went along the southern border of the province, through the village of Vierone, and then north along the same road we had taken when we first marched to Sirone a week ago. Although both routes were equal in time, the second one promised to take us directly through Villone, making such a course a cause for heated debate, a carryover from our earlier discussion about my latest vision and the strange woman's warnings.

As much as my friends and I wanted to avoid our place of birth and childhood, we could not disregard the message of the vision, especially since the first part of A'tie's sermon turned out to be correct. The pages of the monastery's book did bare some answers and provided us with another clue that promised to shed some light on the mystery of Father's convoy. And though the part about Ric was yet to come, there was a chance it would be true as well. Of course, to go back to Villone was very risky, with chances of our being caught high. We also were not sure if we could find Ric that very night. But we had to try; at least I did, as it could have been my brother's life in jeopardy. So after much dispute, which lasted until we reached the edge of the forest, we decided to trust the advice of the alien woman from the dream and take the route through Villone, where we hoped to find Ric and persuade him to come with us.

As the narrow track that led us out of the dim green cover of the forest and onto a side of open grassy stretch, came to an end, we returned to the main road and went south. Afraid to spend too much time in the open at night, still remembering the recent attack from two days ago, we picked up the pace so we could make it to the nearest parish before dark. Behind us sounds of the woodland sequestered in a distance, and I glanced back at the wall of branches, thinking of the hermit. Although I did not expect to see anyone there, I still hoped to find Irk's slim figure, strolling after us. Yet there was no sign of the old man, his crooked staff, or his straw hat with its small twisted top sticking in the air. Looking at the trees and blue sky that capped over them, I suddenly felt a little sadness in my heart, as there was something very alluring about the strange sage, which made me become fond of him despite his growling and cursing. Slowly I gave out a soft sigh and peered one more time at the forest, sending it a silent farewell; then I turned back to the road and rejoined my friends, even though my thoughts were of Irk's tale, A'tie's warnings, and the mysterious Alavantars.

Pondering, I did not notice how time passed; the sun disappeared beyond a faint line of faraway trees, and greenish stars took its place, filling the dark void of the night sky. A shroud of darkness came onto the walking lane too, and after several leagues we could not see much ahead. Yet we carried on, swiftly passing through the shadows of black shapes until we saw a spray of yellow dots that sputtered at a distance in front of us. Guided only by the lights, we sped up and a couple of leagues later entered the small village of Vierone, a community that lay on the banks of a shallow stream called Sister's Hair. No different than any other place in Bois, the parish was a peaceful haven for local farmers and passing travelers, who happened to venture far off the main trade ways and into the farm-dotted countryside of southern Normandia.

That night the plain-looking village was quiet and deserted. Encircled by low-laced fences that hid numerous well-cared orchards and gardens, two rows of houses stretched along the only unpaved street no more than five cubits wide. Most of buildings were one or two stories high, sturdy, and in fairly good condition, which showed that the village had been blessed with some good fortune of plentiful harvests in the past few years. Some of the structures were a little bigger than others, and the ones that were really big looked like barns, with wide gates and shutters closed from the inside. Since it was already late, many of the windows were lit. Most of the dwellers had already departed to their homes, chased away by evening hours, and only a handful of young lads argued passionately at the doorsteps of a stone-walled building, some cubits off the road. The men were taken completely by their quarrel and paid us little notice, which we found fitting, as we let them be and continued on, heading for a local tavern that stood discernible past the village's center, surrounded by a dozen cottages of pale gray color.

Carefully dodging a few murky dens and puddles, half-dried but still mucky, we walked up to the entrance of a wide, two-level wooden house, built of solid logs of aged brown color and patched at the front with long wide boards. The place had no visible decorations, no ornaments, or any fancy signs. The only thing that gave out its purpose was a small wooden plaque nailed over the front door that welcomed patrons, announcing that they were about to enter the Golden Duck Inn of Sister's Hills.

Finding little meaning in such a name, we strolled through the large doorway and immediately found ourselves inside a narrow corridor that served the purpose of a foyer, beyond which lay an open dining hall that took up almost the entire bottom floor. There was just a small section left for a kitchen and a counter, where several large barrels were fit into the wall, providing thirsty guests with a constant supply of fresh cold drinks. At the far end of the big room, where three long tables were pushed together, rose a wide stairwell that led to the second floor. The upstairs was allocated to sleeping quarters, rented out to weary journeymen for two coppers a night, a fair price that included not only a stay, but also a generous morning meal and a bucket of hot water to get rid of road dust.

To our surprise the Golden Duck turned out to be a popular watering burrow for the villagers, farmers, and all those wishing to hear fresh rumors and new tales of exotic places, beasts, and daring adventures. Although Vierone itself was a simple village, its crowd of patrons was a colorful bunch. Dim lights struggled through a thick smoky haze that came streaming from the kitchen, the fireplace, and numerous pipes, favored by many of the noisy guests, some of whom played a card game at the end of the counter, yelling and screaming every time one of them threw a card on the table. Across from the players, sitting at the three long tables, a group of locals enjoyed the taste of many mugs of ale, talking loudly amongst themselves, occasionally bursting into laughter and often pounding their fists on the boards. And near closed windows that ran along the left-hand side of the hall, sat men of rover's kind. Most of them wore rugged travel clothes, gray, and dark blue, and brown, none of which looked either rich or sturdy. Yet their tables were full of various food and drink, suggesting that they had at least some money to spend.

For a while we stood in the foyer, watching the host, searching for a suitable place to sit. To our luck, soon after our arrival three older men got up from a round table by the stairs, and after slapping some of the other patrons on the back, strolled past us onto the street. Immediately two serving girls raced to the empty table and cleaned it with wet rags, leaving thick watermarks on its surface. Seeing that no one else had taken the vacant spots, we seized our chance and hurried past the barricades of men, chairs, and benches, soon finding ourselves sitting on top of high stools, with our bags stored underneath them.

Before we even raised our hands, a short thickset girl of about ten years came out of the heavy mist. She wore a white cotton short-sleeved shirt, stained in places with drops of some red liquid, and a simple linen green skirt that dropped straight down from her waist, covering a pair of bare ankles. On her head she had a band of wide green lace that held back dark short hair, outlining her girlish wide face that appeared to be red in color, victim of countless freckles sprinkled across her nose and cheeks. Holding a large round tray in her hands, she greeted us with a cheerful smile, showing rows of young white teeth, and bowed.

"Welcome to the Golden Duck, good Sires! My name is Janie!" she yelled, as it was impossible to hear otherwise through the noise that filled the hall. "What can I do for you this lovely evening?"

"Hello to you too," replied Minia merrily. "We would like some food that will fill the five of us, a room for the night, and a dry place in your stables for my horse."

The squire then smiled at the girl and winked, making her blush so her ears and cheeks turned even redder.

"Yes, Sire. Right away, Sire. We have plenty of vacant rooms with comfortable beds and clean sheets. For the five of you, I suggest two large rooms at the far end of the northern hallway. They have three beds each, big trunks to store your heavy bags, and fireplaces," explained Janie still red of face.

"I do not think we will need two rooms, young lady. But we will take one," said Minia, and the rest of us nodded in agreement that it was better to save money for other occasions.

"Very well, Sire, I will see that the room is ready when you are done with your meal. Would you like me to arrange for your bags to be moved upstairs?" the girl pointed at our loads, and once she noticed the expressions on our faces added reassuringly, "Do not worry, Sires, nobody is going to take anything. All your things are safe in the Golden Duck. We have not had a single theft in years." When we nodded in consent, she gestured for another youngster, a boy of ten or eleven, to come over. The lad quickly ran up to our table and picked our bags, which turned out to be too heavy for him so he had to drag them across the floor and up the stairs.

"And for your horse, I will make sure it gets the best stall in our stables. If you want, for an extra copper, I can also feed it and scrub its back," the girl continued.

"That will be good," agreed Minia and rubbed his hands together. "Now, what can you bring us to eat? We are starving."

"Oh, this evening we have fresh chicken soup, cold cuts of beef, some leftovers from yesterday's stew, wheat bread, slabs of butter, goat cheese, and berry cakes for dessert. You can order everything for two coppers a person, or you can choose whatever items you desire for half a copper each."

Hearing all the foods that Janie described I suddenly felt hungry, so hungry that without any second thoughts I picked the full course, skipping only the goat cheese, of which I was starting to get very tired.

"Will you care for anything to drink with your food?" asked Janie when I was done listing my order. "We have wild berries' ale, cold water from the well, jars of apple cider, and warm fresh milk."

"I think I will have some of your ale," I replied.

Minia added, "A jar will be better. I will have some of the brew too."

"Well, make it two jars," interjected Ike, grinning. "I think we will all have a taste."

"Two jars it is, Sires. I will bring them right away." The girl bowed again, and once all of our orders were completed, disappeared back into the crowd.

Meanwhile, more folks came into the hall. Although most men immediately blended with the mob, two of the newcomers stood out, seizing my attention as they made their way across the room to a half-empty table by windows. While the men's gear looked ordinary, their faces did not. From just one glance I could tell that the strangers were not locals, nor were they from Bois, of that I was certain. Their features were too angular and too thin for Northern Ethoria; instead they reminded me of the man who had attacked us in the night, the hired sword from the south. Broad eyebrows and hair were thick and black, and their beards, trimmed at the chin, had two streaks of white, each line straight as if drawn with a brush. The men's clothes were also odd. Although they appeared common in design, dark brown cloaks, leather leggings, pants, and simple vests, their quality was perfect, and made me doubt that the two were simple rovers like the others at their long table.

As I watched the men closely, the strangers sat down at the corner of a bench and studied the throng around them. For a while their attention was on a group of noisy farmers who were consumed with a game of bones, attracting most of the idlers who had flocked from all sides, trying to take a pick at the action near them. Then they turned to another table, where an out-of-towner was telling a story of his latest adventures, which he had encountered along the way from the distant Kingdom of Lombardia. But they did not stay on him for long; all of a sudden their heads turned, their gaze focused solely on me. Startled I shifted my eyes elsewhere, somewhat embarrassed to be caught red-handed. For awhile I observed my friends, who were consumed with a light chat, and then returned my glance to the strangers, just for a moment. But as I did, I found the two staring directly at me. Suspicious, I looked away again and was about to alert my friends, when the serving girl reappeared with the same large tray in hand, full of mugs and plates.

She quickly slammed the servings on the table, spilling some of the ale on to her petite hands, unloaded everything, and immediately ran back into the kitchen to retrieve the rest of our food. My appetite demanded satisfaction, and so, forgetting about the strangers for a moment, I grabbed a juicy piece of cold cut beef jerky and threw it in my mouth, chewing it appetizingly and rinsing its savor with sips of tasty sweet ale. After several more mugs, the tension eased within me, and a good mood engulfed my mind.

Soon jokes and laughter sprang amongst our ranks and began to attract a small group of locals, who quickly persuaded Minia to tell them a few of his stories. At first the squire denied such a request, but after another mug of wild berries' ale, answered the plea and bestowed the men around him with several tales from his arsenal, devoting much of the telling to Sire Rone's adventures, reluctantly avoiding any mentioning of Irk the Wise, the Alavantars, the visions, or Father's caravan.

While Minia went on with his accounts, more and more people huddled around the table. Some of them asked questions, and some commented on what they had heard, but all listened with interest, which made me think that it was not often they had been treated to storytelling of any sort. Almost all of the men who encircled us were farmers, some rovers, and a few villagers. Observing them I listened to the squire for a while. Then I remembered the two strangers who had been eyeing me ever since they sat down, and peered through the wall of people. For some time, though, I could not see past the listeners, and when I finally caught a glimpse of the far tables, I found its corner deserted and the strangers gone. A feeling of relief came, and relaxed I turned to the table. But as I glanced across at Minia, amongst the men behind him, standing in the back of the crowd I noticed the familiar brown cloaks; the two men were amongst the listeners. Although they tried hard to conceal themselves from my sight, I saw them nonetheless, and once one of them spotted my glance on him, their figures disappeared again, leaving me with a sense of danger and caution growing swiftly within me. In a flash I found little comfort inside the dining hall, and trying to be as discreet as possible grabbed Minia by his sleeve, yanking him closer toward me to whisper, "Let's get upstairs. It may not be safe to stay here."

For an instant Minia gave me an inquisitive look, then nodded and finished his tale, all to the great disappointment of the onlookers, who started to yell out demands for the story to continue. But the squire was firm. Despite the crowd's protests he paid Janie for the food and stay, picked up one more slice of bread, and took us to the staircase.

Following my companions to the second level of the inn, I halted halfway up and gazed at the room below, and again I saw the two strangers, standing amongst the patrons, watching me. My uneasy feeling intensified, and once we were inside the long corridor I halted everyone with a loud hiss.

"Listen up," I exclaimed, keeping my voice down so no one else could hear. "I think we might be in some sort of trouble. I do not know if you have noticed, but there were two strange men down in the dining hall, who were staring at us."

"Mishuk, calm down," replied Ike. "Half the inn was staring at us. Did you see how many people gathered around our table?"

"No Ike, those two were different. It was as if they knew who we were."

Immediately Minia grabbed me by the forearm. He pressed a finger to his lips and nodded toward the end of the hallway.

"Get inside," he whispered and walked fast toward the last door in the hallway. There he pulled out a key that was attached to a large metal ring and slid it into the narrow slit, turning it several times. With ease the door opened and we staggered inside a spacious room, simple and yet useful in its layout. To our left three spacious wooden beds stood pushed close to each other, with small chests attached to their sides. Further away, a large desk was placed between two windows; three chairs tacked under it. Across from them, more trunks sat in a row next to a tall fireplace, unlit, but stacked with firewood. And on the floor of polished boards lay a thick woolen rug that stretched from one end to the other, unveiling a crude scene from some love story with pictures of young couples captured in a moment of passion. The mat was of poor quality, but fulfilled its purpose and made the room quite suitable for a good night's stay.

The door closed, I turned to the squire, who spoke softly, his eyes studying the room. "Now, Mishuk, tell us exactly what you have seen." The squire was very serious, and such seriousness made me more nervous.

"As I said, there were two strangers in the dining hall. They walked into the tavern later into the evening, and ever since they sat down they watched us. It was as if they knew exactly who we were and what we were doing here."

"Can you describe them?" asked Minia once he had locked the door from the inside.

"Both wore simple clothes, brown cloaks, and leather vests. Oh yes, they also had very strange beards with two white streaks painted on them."

"Two white streaks," Minia repeated my words and thought for a moment, then sat down on one of the beds and said, "I do not like it. I do not like it a single bit." He shook his head, while the rest of us stood and waited.

"What do you mean?" I asked, becoming more anxious.

"Streaks of white—I do not know what they mean, but only the people from the South wear them. I think it is sign enough for us." Minia became silent in thought.

"What shall we do then?" I asked of the squire.

As if to answer my question, a sudden light tap came from the corridor. Someone was at the door. Quickly we grabbed whatever weapons we had and stared at the brown frame. No one made a sound. When the tap came again, Minia got up from the bed and walked to the door, pressing his hand on it.

"Who is there?" he asked.

"Good Sire. It is me, Janie," the familiar girlish voice replied. "You had forgotten your change downstairs, so the hostess ordered me to bring it to you."

"Change?" I whispered, looking at Minia, clearly remembering that we gave exactly fourteen coppers, four for the room, and ten for our meal. There should not be any change left. Probably thinking the same, Minia lifted his hand and said, "Are you sure Janie, because I do not remember leaving extra coins."

"No, Sire. You did, you gave sixteen coppers instead of fourteen."

"Well, keep them, girl. You deserve the two coppers for your good service."

"No, Sire. I cannot. Unless you give the coins to the hostess yourself, she will not let us keep them," the girl replied. "Sire, please, I need to talk to you. It is very important."

For a moment we all stood frozen in our spots. Was it a trick? Or was the girl really trying to tell us something? The answer was unknown. Yet after some forethought, Minia motioned for us to move away from the door and once we did, turned the key. The lock clicked, and the door opened. Preparing for the worst, we half drew our weapons, but finding only the red-faced girl in the hallway, sheathed them back.

With the gap big enough, Janie immediately leapt in and Minia closed the door after her. Finding herself surrounded by our grim faces, Janie smiled widely and assured that we did not mean her any harm, spoke out fast, her voice ringing loudly, "Good Sires, I must warn you. Downstairs there are two men, two outlanders, who have been talking about you. Bad things they said, very bad things."

"What did they say, girl?" asked Minia as he patted Janie on a shoulder to calm her down.

"Once you had left the hall they started talking about you. Only they did not speak our tongue. No, they spoke the Southern way. No one here knows the Southern way, except for me. My mother was from the south, Free Cities she said. She came here when she was a girl herself and married my father. Ever since I was a little girl, she had been teaching me the Southern way. She died some years back though, and I forgot how to speak the language, but I can still understand much of it."

She paused for a moment to catch her breath. "It was the Southern way the two strangers spoke. At first they discussed our village and our province, but then one of them said that it was luck that they had found you in the Golden Duck. I knew that they were talking about you because they mentioned some of your stories, the ones about the knight and the hunt. They also said that one of their friends had been tracking you, but he had disappeared some days back and that it was their turn to hunt you now. Yes, yes. That was exactly what they said—hunt you and kill you. They said they needed to kill you to get the prize. I do not know what prize they spoke of, but I think they want to kill you tonight. They did not say it, but I could feel it in their words. Good Sires, why do those men want to kill you?"

"I do not know, Janie. I truly do not," replied Minia, thinking.

"They are so angry and so mean. I do not like them, but I like you, and I do not want anything to happen to you. That is why I think you should leave. I already took the liberty of preparing your horse; it is waiting for you behind the stable yard."

"How nice of you, Janie," said Minia when the girl finished. "Is there another way out of the inn besides the front door?"

"Yes, there is a back exit, but it is downstairs and you will have to cross the dining hall to get there. I do not think you want to go downstairs; I would not if I were you. I suggest you take the window here. Your room is not too far off the ground, and there is a pipe that runs on the side of the building, you can use it to get down. But hurry, I think those two men will try to do something soon, something very bad."

"Very well, Janie, we will do as you ask. Now I think it is best if you go, we do not want you to get in trouble because of us."

"Oh, no Sire, I will not get in trouble. And while you are leaving, I will alert the hostess, she may be able to do something about those two; although I am not sure that she will; she does not believe me much. She says that I do not know the Southern way. She thinks that I made it all up to impress the others, but I did not. Just because others do not know the Southern way, does not mean I do not know it. Does it?"

"Of course not," Minia appeased the girl and after giving her another pat, opened the door. Janie quickly bowed and stepped into the hallway. But as Minia was about to let her go, she halted him.

"Here, good Sire, take your four coppers back. You will not be staying here tonight so there is no need to pay for the room." Janie smiled and ran off before the squire could answer anything. With her gone, Minia locked the door and faced the rest of us, his face very grim.

"So, what shall we do?" He asked.

"I say we leave as soon as possible," said Ike and he stared at the window.

Rob halted him with a question. "Can we trust her? What if she has made everything up?"

"I do not think she did," I replied. "I saw those men and I did not like them either."

"What if those two paid her to tell us all those things? What if in truth they are waiting for us to get out of the inn and into the open where we will have less chance of defending ourselves?" insisted Rob.

"That may be," uttered Minia. "But I do not know if common folks in Bois connive with strangers all too often, not to mention the ones who speak the Southern way. And Janie, she looks too young to be lured by money. I think she tells the truth."

The squire's words had reason in them, but so did Rob's. What should we choose? This question was tough and for a moment I pondered the answer. But after recalling Janie's innocent freckles and gentle smile I had to side with the squire. The girl was too gullible to conspire with the outlanders. Besides she sounded so sincere.

"I think we should leave," I said afterwards. Ike and Ark agreed, and so did Rob, though he said nothing.

Quickly we blew out the lanterns inside the room, and in the dark opened one of the windows, then climbed onto the ledge and down a large metal drainpipe to the grass carpet that surrounded the inn. From there we crept along the back wall to the stable yard, where, just as Janie had promised, Minia's horse was waiting for us. As quietly as possible the squire drew his mare after him, leading our group across the open grounds, along a row of dark cottages, and to a side of the street, a good distance away. Safe from the lights of the few streetlamps that were placed mostly around the tavern's main entrance, we stopped and looked back. The dark road and the inn next to it looked calm and deserted. At first we noted nothing odd about the two windows in the corner, through which we had fled. But as we began to fasten the bags, a sudden brief movement of a single light brushed across one of the screens. For a moment I thought it was just an illusion, but as I peered harder I saw it again, a little yellow dot that moved quickly inside the room, like a light bug in the night sky.

"Thief's lantern," said Minia, as he walked up to me and looked into the distant shape of the inn, holding his horse by the bridle. "I guess we should thank Janie for the early warning."

"We surely do," I agreed, and was about to say something else when Rob cut me off.

"We should go. Those men will be after us soon." My friend jerked his backpack onto his shoulders and made a move down the road, but did not get far, as Minia's stillness made him stop. The squire did not move. Instead he studied the bouncing light some more, and when it was gone, turned to us, looking very serious.

"We cannot leave now," he said and pulled the horse away from the street. "Come. We will hide behind these houses." He pointed at the two broad buildings in the back of the row. Once behind them he closed his hands around the horse's mouth and continued, "If those two men are really after us, they have already found out we are gone, and will most definitely give us chase. Should they be hired swords like the one we faced two nights ago, and I suspect they are, they will have horses, and how far do you think we will get on foot before they catch us? I say we let them leave the village first and then move out, unseen and safe."

Minia's words made sense again, and even Rob, who had some doubts, agreed.

In silence we remained behind the unlit houses, waiting, often peering around the corner to see the street. Soon we heard a thumping sound coming from the direction of the inn. Right away we huddled at the edge of the house, looking out onto the road. By then the noise got closer, and we saw two dark shapes of horsemen rush past us, galloping along the deserted avenue toward the outskirts of the village, heading in a western direction.

"Just as I thought," said Minia afterwards. "They think we are heading west to Sirone. I guess they have heard my stories about Sire Rone. I think we should wait a bit more. I want them to move away as far a possible." The squire let us linger in the shadows some more, and afterwards leapt on his horse. "Let's get out of here before they come back."

He snapped the bridle and let his horse trot to the road; we walked after him, not really sure what we were doing.

Striding out of Vierone, we left behind the Golden Duck with its comfortable rooms and Janie, whose funny freckles and warm smile settled in my memory, reminding me of the pleasant moments in our trip. At the outer edge of the village, we turned away from the well-traveled route that ran west and stepped into an open field, following a barely visible trail south, staying on it for sometime, barely finding our way in the dark, fighting through bumps and caverns that harassed the land. When the lights of Vierone had vanished we turned, walking west, and after several more leagues, reached the side of a hill, enclosed on one side by a half-broken old wall.

"We will rest here," the squire said after he had checked the ruins.

"Should not we keep on walking?" asked Rob. "Those men, they…"

"I do not think they will be here any time soon," replied Minia in a dry tone. "They have no idea where we have gone. Besides once they realize that we are not on the main route, they will come back, and most probably search the village, after that they will run east toward the hermit's forest, looking for us there. Only when they realize that we have slipped past them will they think about coming west again."

"Huh. And if they do not?" insisted Rob.

"Even so, as a squire with some years of service under my belt I may assure you that they will not find us here," said Minia as he dismounted and tied his horse to a bush nearby. "This is just too remote of a place for any outlander to know, and these walls at night, they blend with the sky, and with no light to outline them they will serve us as a perfect cover. We will be safe here until the morning, and then there will be people out and around, so no one will attack us then. And once we get to Sirone we will tell Sire Rone about our ordeal.

Until then, let's keep it simple. First we sleep, and then we go to Villone, and then Sirone."

"But I must agree with Rob," Ark differed. "We will be safer further away from Vierone."

"Believe me. This is the safest we will ever be. What's more, we need rest. Without it you won't be able to walk tomorrow, and we need to cross some leagues." Minia sighed loudly and unrolled his blanket. "We will keep the same watch. No fires, no sounds, just rest."

Minia spat on the grass and lay down. He closed his eyes and did not say anything else. The rest of us did the same, though Ike and I did it a little later, once we were done with our shift.

Chapter 21

I SLEPT through the night, seeing nothing but dreams that made little sense. Yet I took pleasure in them, thinking little of the real world. But my refuge did not last and before I knew it, a soft touch of cold fingers awoke me. Uneasy, I opened my eyes and saw Ike standing over me, his face greeting me with a smile. "Good morning, Sire. Are you ready for breakfast?" He laughed and let me move up. I rubbed my face, then grinned back, yawing a few times, and replied, "Thank you, Sire Ike. I will be out in a moment."

Laughing Ike turned around, but I stopped him in mid-swing. "What time is it?"

"It is still early in the morning, and it promises to be another beautiful spring day. There are hardly any clouds and it is already warm."

As if to prove my friend's words a fresh tepid breeze brushed against my skin, and a succulent scent of blooming flowers filled my nostrils. The sky was still dark, but the lighter shades were visible at the horizon. Taking several deep breaths, I lay back, my eyes opened, and enjoyed the tingling sensation.

The next few moments I spent idling, but then sat up and after sorting through my traveling gear, climbed to my feet, joining my companions several cubits away. Preoccupied with their pastime, they did notice my approach, and only when I sat next to them, did they acknowledge my presence with loud whistles and a few sharp comments, which I was quick to wave off, turning my attention to the food—Irk's jar of liquid, a bit sour but pleasant to the taste, and a half-gone loaf of still-hard bread, covered at the top with dried-out crumbs of goat cheese. Despite the poor look of the morning meal, I ate it without any reservations, trying to replenish my strength, so needed for another day of the journey. But before I could finish the first slice Minia made everyone rise to their feet. We had to leave, that was all he said, and we did not argue. The strange pursuers could have been somewhere nearby, and before anything bad happened we had to get to a more populated part of the province. Yet, before we could do so, we had more wilderness to cover. Only on the morning of the second day, after traveling along the untamed field, we finally came onto a well-traveled road that promised to take us straight to Villone. Unlike the other routes we had passed in the last week, the way to our hometown seemed much busier. Every few leagues we met different folks, who came alone or in groups, often accompanied by trails of carts and wagons pulled by horses and ponies and horned cattle. From time to time a horseman or a well-built coach rushed by and disappeared in the distance, leaving us covered in clouds of dust. Yet, except for some occasional glances, most folks paid us little notice and in turn we ignored them too, remembering the hermit's cautious advice. Throughout we kept our eyes and ears sharp, but saw no sign of the strangers from the Golden Duck. It looked that Minia was right—after losing us, the outlanders probably returned to Vierone and then rode out east, letting us escape unnoticed. Be as it might, their absence did not soothe my worries, as I knew well that the calmness of the road was often illusive, with dangers prowling just a short distance away.

When we reached Villone the afternoon was coming to a close. The sun rolled quietly from the east and vanished behind the western edge, leaving the land to the mercy of the night that promised to make its way into the realm without a prolonged delay. While most of the farmers had already retreated into the comfort of their homes, done with another day of hard labor, town folks were still out and about, wandering the streets well into the hours of the evening, either meeting up with some friends or chatting with neighbors, or simply enjoying a pleasant coolness after sundown. Although I had favored such habit just two weeks ago, that time I found it to be an obstacle to our daring plan. Having the entire town out of their dwellings meant that we had to wait until the very late hours, hiding at a distance in the thick shrubs of the orchards that surrounded Villone from all sides. It also meant that we had to leave the main road some two leagues from the town and go around it, seeking shelter in a mass of fruit trees and the dimmer lights. Doing just that, we retreated from the lane and sneaked into the nearby line of trees, taking a narrow path to the center of the grove, where we settled under green branches, waiting for a moment to go forth.

As I sat down on the fresh grass a recognizable sugary air so heartening to my senses, came to me, and inhaling it with pleasure I studied the view of the town's many patched roofs that peered through the leaves. Although I could not see my house or my street, I knew they were there, behind the cherry shrubs, just as they had always been. At last I was home, but not for long. In several short hours I had to crawl into my house, find my brother, and leave again, without as much as saying "so long" to my beloved mother and two little sisters, whom I truly missed. It was hard, but it had to be that way, my quest demanded so.

In a cheerless state I let the time pass, and when Ike's low voice distracted me from my deliberations it was already after dark. As I looked up at my friend, I noted a merry expression on his face. Only, I knew that it was false. Ike was tense, and it showed in the slight twitching of his lips, something only I could spot. To lift his spirits I climbed up and gave him a shove, grinning. In return Ike smirked too. "I think it is safe to go in." I nodded.

"Mishuk and Ike…. I have heard that you two know this place better than anyone," sounded Minia as he came over, along with Ark and Rob, who gathered around us. "I think it is best if you go in, and we wait here. It is of no use for all of us to venture into town. Too many men means a greater risk to be discovered."

"Huh. It does seem right," agreed Ike. I added, "It is safer that way. Should anything happen we will have a better chance of getting out, just the two of us."

"Then it is done. You will go in, find Ric, and come back here," reaffirmed Minia, Ike and I acquiescing.

"You might want to think about taking a shortcut through the baker's grounds. That way you can skip the streets completely and get to Mishuk's house from the east side," suggested Rob right away.

"It is a good idea. Only I am afraid it will not work. At the start of the season the old man fixed all the holes in his fence. If we go there, we will get stuck at a wall that is two cubits high and so will have to go around it, down to the western side of the central square. And there are always people, no matter how late it is. So we better think of something else," explained Ike, with me agreeing.

It had been long known that Ike and I were the utmost experts on ways in and out of Villone. In many years of our search for adventures, we had inspected every corner, every street, every hole, and every shortcut there was. Nobody could match our proficiency, even though nobody really wanted to. It was our domain, and we excelled in it. That evening, all the experience was to be put to the test.

"My thought is that it is safer to go behind the chapel, then run across the main street and hide in the alley next to my house. It is chancy, especially so early in the night, but it will save us a lot of time, and we do not have to stay in the open for too long." I suggested what I thought to be the best course of action. Ike weighed the idea for a moment and then consented. I continued,

"Once in the alley I will sneak into my house and try to get Ric. His window is just above the yard. If anyone sees me I will run back through the chapel's grounds and into the gardens."

Again, Ike agreed, and I was about to resume, when Minia asked me his question. "Are you sure Ric will be at home?"

"I cannot promise you anything," I replied honestly. "As far as I know he can be anywhere. I just hope he is in his room. If not, I can check the barn, the pond, and a little getaway on the eastside; I know he likes to spend time there. But if he is not in any of these places, I will not be able to find him at all and we will have to leave without him."

I scratched the back of my head, not sure if I should say anything else, then added nonetheless, "At least we will find out soon enough if the A'al's words hold the truth."

"I guess we will," replied Ike, lifting his arms, stretching. "Let's get it over with."

Without hesitating, my friend removed some of the gear that hung on his belt and strutted through the young trees toward the nearby lights of the first houses. I hurried a step or so after him.

To our surprise our hometown was deserted as if all of its inhabitants had gone to sleep a bit earlier. Charily we slipped into Villone, our two figures lurking from shadow to shadow. After a short dash through several private plots, we came up to the fenced backyards of the long common houses. We skidded across, jumping over the low railings at the other side, and emerging behind the town's chapel, a narrow tall building, which cast a perfect shade that covered much of the space around it. There we halted, looking about. The chapel's court was empty, just like the street that ran along its front. Assured that no one was in sight, we darted athwart the lane and quickly vanished in the darkness at the other side, running down the narrow alley that took us past a row of houses and to the wall of my own backyard.

Standing under the familiar fence, gasping for air, I immediately started to look for two loose boards that so often had let me in through the high picket barrier. While I was moving the planks, Ike stepped back several cubits and took position halfway down the passage so he could observe the street for any signs of trouble without any risk of being detected. At last all of the boards were removed, and I squeezed through a thin opening, staggering into the familiar quad, lit by the windows and a large crescent moon that allowed me to see perfectly in the dark. Cautiously I examined the soft bare sandy ground, and then hid behind a pile of logs a few cubits away from the back door.

Tracing the lights that streamed through the windows, behind draped slots I could see two silhouettes moving around the dining hall, and one more standing in my sister' rooms on the second floor. Without a doubt the outlines were of Mother, Ulie, and Agie, as always, busy with their many chores and duties. Regrettably, there was no sign of my brother. His room's single large window was opened and well lit, but I could not pick out any movement inside. Maybe he is downstairs, I thought to myself and looked for a way to get closer to the house. Although the back door remained in shadow, a bright yellow light from the kitchen window illuminated the ground around it and left little chance for me to sneak up to it. So instead I moved along the fence and to the rear wall of the barn, burying myself in a stack of hay that had been dumped at the far end even before my departure.

Quietly I peered at the open windows on the first floor. By then all the movement inside stopped, and I saw nothing but the yellow light. Maybe Ric is in his room after all, I thought again. Then an idea came to me, and I picked up a handful of stones, weighing them in my palm. Finding the rocks light enough I tossed the first pebble in the air and then threw it into my brother's window. To my own surprise the little stone fell short of the target and bounced off the boarded wall, making all sorts of noise. Afraid that someone besides Ric would hear the clacking, I hid back behind the stack and waited, peeking out of my hideout through a little hole in the hay. When no one came I took another stone and measuring the distance for my next pitch, took a step back. But when I raised my hand someone's light whistle startled me. As I spun around, several cubits away, standing in a narrow gap of the opened barn gate, I found my brother.

"Ric, what in the Spirit's name are you doing here?" I almost yelled, but held back, and kept my voice down.

"Me? What are you doing here?" he asked in return, then shook his head. "Though you do not have to tell me. I think I know the answer already."

"What do you mean you know the answer?" Surprised even more, I tried to comprehend his words.

"You came back for me, did you not?"

"Yes…but how? How did you know?"

"It is all very strange. To tell you the truth, I am not sure if you will believe me. I am not sure if I believe myself."

"Ric." I cut him off. "In the past week I have seen so much, I will believe almost anything you say, so do not fear any ridicule from me."

"All right then," Ric whispered and stepped out of the yard, taking a spot next to me behind the haystack. "It all happened two nights ago, when my dream turned into something very strange. It did not feel like a normal dream, but like a..."

"Vision?"

"Yes, a vision," agreed Ric and went on to tell me his story. It appeared that before my arrival to Villone, my brother had a strange guest, who visited him in his sleep. It was A'tie, the A'al sorceress, the same woman, who had come to me some nights before, and just like me, she invited Ric to a great live hall, where amidst the green vines she told him a long and memorable tale of dark times and lurking dangers and magic and Great Wars. She also revealed to him that his life was in jeopardy, and that to save himself, he had to get ready for an unexpected journey, which was soon to come. She told him that I, his younger brother, would return to Villone and take him away on a voyage that would determine his true destiny. Such were A'tie's words, and neither Ric nor I could grasp there true meaning.

"So I guess the sorceress was correct," Ric concluded and after a short pause added, "Now, can you tell me what is really going on, because I am completely lost?" My brother shrugged his shoulders.

"All you have to know for now is that the strange visitor of yours is real. At least I think she is. Several nights ago she came to me too. But I will tell you about it later. Right now we have to go, others are waiting in the eastern copses." I bobbed my head toward the alley. "Are you ready?"

"I am set," replied Ric and lifted his traveling bag, a satchel that went around his neck.

"What about Mother, I mean will she be all right with you gone too?"

"When you left she was not angry. She told us that we should not worry about you, and that you had to leave on business, and would be back whenever you were done with all your duties. That was all she said, so I think it will be the same for me. Personally, I think she already knows that I will leave; she just does not say anything. Yet, if I were you, I would not show my face to her tonight. I do not think she will let you leave again that easily."

"As much as I want to see her, I cannot afford to stay here," I said with some sadness in my tone. "There are some things that must be done first."

I thought for a moment, and then motioned for my brother to follow. "Let's go."

After throwing our final glances at the familiar windows, Ric and I slid back into the alley and met up with Ike, who had been creeping in the shadows overlooking the street. Together we retraced our steps back to the outskirts of Villone and swiftly slipped unnoticed into the covers of the orchard. There we changed the pace and strolled unhurriedly through the dark foliage, at last announcing our arrival with a loud cracking of disturbed branches.

"We are back," I said cheerfully as the three of us stumbled into the clear.

"Any problems?" asked Rob, and once he saw Ric, waved his question off.

"Everything went fine. We did not see anyone, and nobody saw us," replied Ike, and he picked up his bag. He put his arms through the straps and placed it on his shoulders, jerking it a few times.

"I think it is best if we move on, we cannot spend the night here," said Ike. "If we follow the same path we have come on, we will circle around town and return to the road way up north."

There were no objections, and after reforming our single file, we moved out, stepping one after another, making sure that no one fell behind.

Guided by the cold moon that crept across the sky, we soon left Villone and headed north. When the last of the lights vanished from our sight, we stepped into the fields, away from the road, and set our camp, hiding amongst a small pocket of trees far enough from wary eyes. Swathed in darkness we spent the night. Since we had only a few hours before the country folks were drawn out of their beds by another working day, we decided not to sleep, but only rest, sitting on the grass, keeping our eyes on the shadows that lurked in the distance. Yet, despite everyone's effort, one by one my companions fell prey to the darkness and fatigue, and soon only my brother and I remained conscious as we had much to talk about.

"You said you had been waiting for me?" I asked quietly, so as not to wake anyone.

"Yes. The woman told me you would come and she was right—you did. How did she know? Was it magic?"

"It is all very complicated, but I will do my best to explain. There are many things that I must tell you, brother."

I took a brief recess, picking out a good place to begin my odd tale.

"Where should I start?" I asked myself aloud. "Well, I guess I will begin from the time I left Villone."

Then I looked at the sky and went on to tell Ric all the accounts of my journey. It was indeed a long fable, but my brother did not seem to mind. He listened carefully and when I was done asked questions, many questions, about the book, A'tie, the Great War, and Father's convoy. I answered every inquiry as well as I could, and once Ric had no more queries, we both fell quiet, thinking or dreaming—I could not really tell the difference by then.

As I sank deeper into a hazy state, I caught myself on the thought my journey had come full circle. Having left Villone I returned there, incited by the A'al sorceress, who had asked me to find and save my brother from the clutches of an unknown enemy. I wished the circumstances of my visit were different, but they were not. So far, the sorceress was right in her predictions. The book revealed a whole new stance on the past and the present and gave answers that kept my quest alive. My brother—I found him too. Yet, A'tie's true presence remained unexplained. What did she want with me? And what did she want with my brother? In truth it bothered me that Ric had seen her too. But why did not she tell me that she had placed the same spell on my brother? She knew I would find out sooner or later. There had to be a reason, but I could not see it yet.

Indeed, there was just too much arcane. The queries weighed heavy on my mind. Father, Ave, and the caravan were still missing, and the only lead I had was tied to the puzzling inhabitants of the deserted monastery, the so-called Alavantars, Irk had told me about. Maybe the further investigation into the existence of the sect would cast some light on the matter. Until I could discover more clues my quest continued to be quite a challenge. I had to find Father and Ave and learn more about the Fore Sight, and the mysterious alien woman, and the Alavantars and their prophecies. How could I do all this? Again I did not know.

Chapter 22

SUNRISE FOUND me awake, getting ready to resume the journey, encouraged by the pale morning sky. Determined to avoid any unsought attention, we set out at the crack of dawn, leaving the sanctuary of the camp, moving away from Villone, none of us too fond of such an early departure. Trailing after my friends, I rambled unmindfully through the repeating countryside, pushing off a returning repose of lurking sleep, with my abdomen distressed by a piercing ache in my stomach, caused by the simple fact of a missed morning meal. Although the pain and drowsiness were growing I did everything not to complain, not even to myself, trying to stay firm on the uneven tracks of the beaten route.

For a while the landscape and the road around us remained empty, with the exception of a lonely farmer who happened to pass our company, riding on top of his squeaking flimsy cart, pulled by a shaggy grayish mare. But the man went by quickly, granting us a mere glance, and with the serenity of our march restored, we kept on walking, though our advance was soon hampered by a scorching heat that settled in the air, making the hours drag on forever. After a few more leagues, it got so hot that we had to take off our cloaks, roll up our sleeves, and unbutton our shirts, letting the light breeze cool our sweating bodies. Alas the wind was brief and brought us little relief, and only when the cool evening colors descended onto the land did we find refuge from the heat.

When darkness halted our march, we broke camp, and sheltered by a single thin oak tree, slept until the next morning. Although we rested a little longer after dawn, it was not enough to make up for the missed hours of respite from the previous day, so I awoke worn-out, drained of strength. After washing my face with water from the flask, and catching a hasty bite of hard cheese, I followed my companions back to the road, only to start dozing off some leagues later. Striving to keep my head up, I tried to entertain my mind with the view around me. But it proved to be useless and several times I stumbled over some rocks that lay unattended along the way, every time making my friends laugh. I cared little for their comments and silently kept to myself, hauling after the rest of the company, paying closer attention to the lanes of yellow dust under my feet.

By midday it became clear that we had made good time and would get to Sirone long before the end of the day. The news was cheering, which made my mood shift for the better as I rejoined my friends in their talk about magic spells and A'als. My disposition continued to improve, but as the road slanted eastward, and a small blur appeared farther ahead, the uncomfortable feeling of distress came back. Making an effort to peer into the vague haze of the heated air, I stressed my eyes but could not pick out any detail. Blaming the high temperature and sunshine, I rubbed my face several time, and when it did not help, splashed some water on it, hoping to sharpen my dull senses. Yet, for a while, only a smeared image met my eyes, which then began to clear and slowly turned into a thin silhouette of a coming horseman, closing swiftly on our company. When my friends noticed the stranger too, they stopped abruptly at the side of the road and grabbed onto their weapons, watching the rider closely, each getting ready for a possible fight. But the man stayed to his course and, seemingly unconcerned with our presence, galloped by without stopping, soon vanishing in a cloud of dust, letting our nerves unwind a little.

Although the rider had long been gone, we remained still, and only when the last of the distant dust clouds settled back onto the road, did we resume our journey, gazing cautiously at the horizon. But for the rest of the day we traveled undisturbed, crossing an all too familiar view of the local scenery, which was calm and lonesome. Chasing after the sun, we plodded until we saw the first hints of the castle's lofty towers, rising dominantly over the settled surrounding parish. It was the second time in a week we walked into the shadows of Sire Rone's keep, which looked unchanged from the previous visit.

After stopping briefly to refill our flasks at a local well, we made our way toward the main gates, where the same guards rested contentedly, leaning on their long spears, throwing occasional lazy looks onto the vacant street. The doors behind them were open again and we proceeded through, Minia taking charge as we walked. But when we were about to step onto the path that ran up the slope to the second gate, one of the soldiers lifted his spear off the ground and moved a bit closer, blocking our path with his body. Although his face was solid in expression, his look did not show any sign of concern, and after we came up to him, he smiled and lifted his free hand in a gesture of greeting.

"Hey, little man," the soldier yelled and pointed at Minia with a gloved finger. "How are you? I have not seen you in ages."

"I am fine, and you, Ken? I see the captain put you at the gate's house again." Minia waved his hand too, letting the straps fall onto the horse's neck.

"Fourth time this season," complained the guard. "I do not even know what I have done to deserve such peril."

The squire gave the man a quick smirk. "Are you sure you have not visited Three Cats Inn lately?"

"Just a few times, and I did not drink anything there. You know me," replied the guard. "I only stopped there to catch up on some rumors, nothing else. I swear."

"Huh, not even a sip?"

"Oh, heck, it might had been a sip, but only one little gulp." The guard chuckled and added, "Anyway, who are you friends here? They look like country folk." The fellow turned and gave my friends and me a passive look.

"Sire Rone has asked me to bring them here. There is a matter they need to discuss with the lord. It is kind of urgent."

"It must be something very important then for the lord to ask for them. If Sire Rone wants to hear what these fellows have to say, you better go inside. He does not like waiting."

The soldier moved to one side and pulled up the spear. Minia waved in response and let his mare carry him past the wooden gate up to the second gate and through. Inside the stone wall Minia dismounted, and handing over his horse to a young servant who had emerged out of the stables to assist the squire, took us to the keep's brass door.

Complemented by the loud sounds of our heels we walked up the stairs, where Minia knocked on the door several times. As his pounding still resonated inside the citadel, the door opened, and an unfamiliar hard-faced soldier appeared in the slit. "Halt there," the man barked loudly. "State your name and purpose." The guard glared steadfastly, but when he noticed Minia amongst us, his face lightened and his icy look turned into a wide grin.

"Minia. Good to see you again," he exclaimed. "Where in the world did you disappear? I started to worry if you decided to leave this place for good. How are your wife and son? I hope they are all right."

"Everyone is fine, Faru. Thanks for the concern. As for my absence, I have been away in the countryside. Our lord gave me an assignment to help these folks." Minia gestured at my fiends and me.

"Oh, I see," replied the guard and studied our company carefully.

"Do you mind if we pass through? We have important news to report to Sire Rone."

"If you say so. Go ahead. I just need to collect all your weapons."

"Of course," replied Minia and handed over his short sword and two daggers. We all did the same.

When the last of our blades had been stored away, the guard moved aside and let us in. One after another we entered the same dark corridor, and trailing after the squire, marched straight up the stairs, through another familiar hallway, and to the double doors guarded by five soldiers. Halfway down the passage, Minia made us wait and went on to talk to the sentries. After a brief exchange of words and laughter the squire slid inside the meeting hall, leaving us alone with the guards. Several minutes later one of the doors opened again, and the squire's head peeked through the gap, signaling for us to go in.

Inside the grand hall, where we had once spoken to the lord, everything looked just as it did the first time—the paintings, the fake weaponry on the walls, and even the streaks of light that brushed against the marble floor. Although the lord himself was absent, three more men stood by the empty throne, looking straight at us. When we came over, they talked to Minia and went away, leaving us surrounded by the splendor of the decorations and the low sound of a wind, which came down from above. But we did not stay there for long. A moment after the guards' departure another man came in; tall and skinny, the stranger was dressed in deep red robes, his head clean-shaved, and his face carved with deep wrinkles. Giving us a dry short salutation, he told us to follow him and escorted us through a concealed back door into a smaller chamber, a fraction of the size of the spacious meeting hall.

The room's layout was peculiar in its purpose and designation, looking more like a foyer or a waiting room. Maybe twenty cubits wide and ten cubits long, it had no windows, no fireplace, and just one large armchair, carved out of a solid piece of wood, painted in black and gold. Two tall lamps, stacked with burning candles, were placed behind it and made up the only other fixtures, across from which stood another entryway, impeded by a heavy door and shielded by two silk curtains that hung down from the top of the frame, dropping over it in a gentle cascade.

Convinced that everyone was inside, the man in the red robes gave us another dry gaze and headed out the same way we had just come in. And once the door closed after him, the noise of looming footsteps sounded from behind the other entrance. Then several locks opened and curtains moved to a side, revealing three figures—Sire Rone, and two younger gentlemen dressed as nobles, their glittering chain mail and swords' sheaths adorned with much luxury. The three greeted us briefly and strolled to the chair, Sire Rone taking the seat and his two companions towering at his sides. The lord studied us with his wary eyes, then leaned back and raised his voice, calling for our full consideration.

"I have just received notice that you have brought me urgent news from Irk the Wise," announced the knight, skipping all formalities, his tone plain, his speech free of grand expressions. He tilted slightly on his elbow, his cool, but friendly face affixed on Minia. "Let me hear what the old hermit has to say."

"Of course, Sire." Minia hurried to reply. "Irk the Wise has asked us to deliver a dispatch for you."

The squire motioned for Rob to get the hermit's blue-ribboned pouch. He then opened the bag and extracted the two articles—the book and the letter—passing them over to the lord. Sire Rone quickly unwrapped Irk's letter and started to read it, occasionally lifting his head to look at the other men, who came closer so they could also read the note. Once done he set aside the yellowish papers filled with handwritten lines, and opened the book.

While the lord examined the strange text, Minia continued with his report. "Just as you had instructed, I caught up with Mishuk's party in the forests of Luro. They were camping several leagues from the valley, near Bendor Creek. Once I told them of my orders and showed your dispatch, they gladly accepted my services, and together, we marched to the monastery of the Order of the Spirit, which you had mentioned. A day later we reached the front gates of the place of worship. But the sanctuary of the Spirit's followers was deserted, abandoned days before our advent. Amongst the empty houses we spent several hours, searching for any clues that might have been left behind. It was there we came across this strange book. As soon as we opened it, we knew we could not understand a single word. Fortuitously I recognized the language to be Uru, the ancient tongue of our ancestors, and since none of us could read its unfamiliar idioms, I suggested taking the book to Irk the Wise, the only man I knew could help us. So we went to see the hermit, who was kind enough to agree to translate the book. Once done, he uncovered many troubling things, of which he told us in due course, concerned and ill at ease."

What followed next was Minia's detailed account of everything we had learned from the hermit, about strange and mysterious Alavantars, the prophecies of Arac, the Great Wars, the old one and the new, the coming of the Master of the Old, and the rising of the Chosen One, along with many other strange things, which were probably mentioned in Irk's letter. Throughout, the lord listened carefully, often lowering his eyes to look at the opened book.

"Is it so?" Sire Rone asked once the squire was done. He put down the book and lifted himself from his chair, but then thought otherwise and sat back, his eyes fixed on our faces.

"The news you bring me is disturbing. In any other time I would have questioned the validity of your story, but tonight I am afraid you speak the truth, which troubles me even more. What you have told me is the same Irk has mentioned in his letter and suggests that we may have a new strife in our realm."

The lord finally rose and walked up to one of the younger gentlemen who stood to his right, dressed in a silver mail that came down almost to his knees.

"Sire Uri, take this book to the master counselor. Make sure he takes a good look at it. I want to know everything there is to know about this transcript."

"Sire Enville." The lord addressed the other man, who wore a white shirt of rings with a bright red symbol of a flower drawn over it. "Take four or five of your squires, along with a brigade of my men-at-arms, and march to the monastery. Search that place and the surrounding woods. I want to know who lived there, what they did, and where they have gone. Ask the locals, talk to traders, question anyone who might have seen anything strange lately. And do not forget to check the northern outpost; maybe someone there has spotted too many people on the move. Also, send a word to the House of the Spirit in Bonneville. Since this matter may involve some of its brothers, I want to make sure that the Order knows everything. By all means, we do not want to put a strain on its relationship with the Duke. We have enough problems as it is."

"My lord...there is something else, you may find important," the squire said courteously, when Sire Rone paused.

"Yes?"

"On our way to the monastery a stranger attacked us," Minia continued. "It was just one man, but he was no ordinary bandit. He was a mercenary from the south, a member of the brotherhood of Snake Bites, its symbol we found on his cloak once we disposed of him. And then there were two more strange men, whom we met in Vierone, while staying there at the Golden Duck Inn. They were also outlanders, and the local servant told us that they spoke the Southern way. She also said they were talking about hunting and killing us."

"Are you sure?" asked the lord again.

"Sure as I will ever be. The serving girl said the two men were hired swords. Although I am not sure how accurate the accounts of a ten year-old can be, but someone was in our room shortly after our hasty departure from the Golden Duck, and then we saw someone else ride off in the western direction. My thought is that the girl had told the truth. Those men were probably hired swords too; Snake Bites would be my guess."

"Huh. If what you say is true, the situation may be far worse than I have expected," the lord thought for a moment and then motioned for the fellow in the white mail to come closer. "Sire Enville, when you leave, keep your eyes open for any suspicious outlanders who do not belong to any caravan. If you find any, bring them here; maybe they will know something about Snake Bites roaming around my lands."

Sire Rone then switched his attention back to Minia. "Come, my squire, there is much I should ask you. As for you, Mishuk Loyde—" the lord looked at me, "you and your friends are free to go. I would like to speak with you again tomorrow so do not wander too far from the town. Until then, you are excused. My servant will escort you to the guest's quarters, where you may rest and eat and wash up."

The lord did not say anything else. He simply turned around and left, his two peers and Minia following half a step behind. At the door the squire halted and with a brief gesture of goodbye, said, "Go ahead and get some rest. I will see you tomorrow."

Then he disappeared behind the curtains. We stayed where we were and waited until the same bold man came back in and took us to the lower reaches of the keep, where the servants' area was.

The guest quarters the lord spoke of were located in the bottom level of the basement, along with the kitchen and a dining hall for the serving staff. Most of the living chambers were taken, and only a few of them were vacant, left for common visitors like ourselves, often servants of noble guests who came to the castle while visiting Sire Rone's domain. Except for constant noises and the distinctive heavy scent of cooking that were coming from the kitchen, the two rooms prepared for us were suitable for dwelling. Despite their diminutive size, each of the chambers was fully furnished and clean. Although there were no windows, no mirrors, and no fireplaces, it included a handful of candles, placed on top of four brass lamps that spread a dim light, casting shadows on the floor made of large rough boards, covered in places with woven rugs of plain brown color. The four naked walls also free of any decent color, were decorated with occasional narrow strips of tapestry, which came down from the ceiling, presenting guests with poorly drawn images of some large flying creatures, the lines of which had long ago faded away, giving way to many rips and holes. Three heavy beds were feebly made and fit with thick mattresses stuffed with straw, each covered with dark blue sheets of rough cotton. In between the cradles stood woven chairs and nightstands that were barely big enough to stow a few pieces of clothing and some not too bulky gear. Yet such simplicity did not repel me. In truth I could not have expected more, as the lord's generosity toward us had already surpassed all our expectations, considering that all the accommodations were free of charge.

Once we split the rooms—Ike, Ric, I taking one, and Rob and Ark choosing to stay in the other—we washed, changed, and killed time until the evening meal, which proved to be a tiresome task. So when a quick knock on the door announced that it was time for supper, we did not wait for a second invitation but ran into the hallway, our feet carrying us to the kitchen where an array of delicious foods had been prepared, all to our great satisfaction. A whole grilled rooster stuffed with apples and buckwheat, jars of sweet honey and milk, loaves of bread, boiled apples, and a steaming warm cherry pie—we ate everything with appetite, and by the time the last piece found its way into my mouth, I was beginning to struggle with the sleep. My eyelids grew heavy and I caught myself falling asleep at the table, drained of my last bits of vigor. A few more abortive attempts to keep my head up failed, and surrendering to the fatigue, I stumbled back to the room, where a hard, but clean bed received me into its hold, in which I slept undisturbed until the next day.

In morning loud noises that came from the corridor woke me up. I tried to force myself back into sleep, as it was just too warm and restful under the blankets, but it was not meant to happen. All I heard around me were sounds of my friends' awakening, their constant moaning and yawning robbing me of my peace. It was useless to resist any further, so I made myself get up and leaving behind the relative solace of the straw mattress, approached the bucket of cold water. Slowly ambling, I lifted the lid and splashed some liquid over my face. It felt good, and I did it several more times. Refreshed I dried myself with a towel and threw on some clothes, at which time the front doors opened and the bold servant from the day before, dressed in his usual red robe, walked in accompanied by two soldiers who carried short spears and iron-cast round shields.

"You men," he yelled loudly. "Sire Rone awaits you in the councilor's chamber. Get ready and meet me outside."

The man did not say anything else, but turned around, closing the doors behind him. In the next moment I heard his voice again, this time sounding in the other room, giving Rob and Ark the same orders.

When Ric, Ike, and I finally came out, the bold man and the guards were still standing by the door, talking quietly amongst themselves. They paid us little attention and continued with their chat until Rob and Ark appeared, after which they escorted us up the staircase and back into the familiar windowless room next to the meeting hall. When we entered, Sir Rone was already there. He sat in his tall chair, holding the book and the letter in his hands. Next to him stood a very old man. Just like the fellow in red robes, he lacked all of his hair, and many wrinkles that covered his round head pointed to his ancient age.

"Here you are. Good," the lord said and pointed at two long benches, pressed against the far walls. Built of heavy brown half-cut logs, the benches were swathed with glittering shine, and covered with rows of maroon pillows for extra comfort.

"Yesterday I told you that I have some matters to discuss with you. Now it is time to do so. I will ask you to listen carefully, because my utterance is an important one. As you probably already know, there is something very strange happening in our province. We all know what Irk has found in the book of the Alavantars. You may also have heard tales that have become quite widespread in the past seasons—stories of missing people, unexplained kidnappings, and mysterious robberies. Most folks think of them as simple rumors, and for a while I have done too, but not anymore.

In the recent weeks certain things have been happening in Bois that do not seem normal. Taken alone, each of the incidents is nothing more than an ordinary occurrence, but put together they reveal a disturbing picture."

Sire Rone paused and shifted in his seat, coughing several times as he moved.

"I began to hear odd things from the local populace in the fall season of last year, gossip for the most part, spoken of during social gatherings, tourneys, and banquets; usual things—someone got lost in the woods, cattle went missing, a few hunters never came home. The first real report came to me in the beginning of the winter season from Sire Illow, whose family held a plot of land northeast from here. According to his note, a group of farmers had not returned from their ordinary trip to the forest. The men vanished without a trace, along with their gear and a horse. The incident would not have been deemed so somber, if it were not for the children who were a part of the missing party, five of them to be exact. Such a number stirred a concern amongst the villagers; panic was not far behind. To calm his subjects, Sire Illow sent out his soldiers to search the woods, but the men returned empty-handed. The poor souls were simply gone, and so their disappearance was blamed on the treacherous swamps that had already claimed many lives before them.

"With Sire Illow's subjects still in mourning, I got another dispatch, that time from Sire Anton, a young lord who lives across Bois' border in the neighboring province of Kantsie. His father, an aged noble, paralyzed below his waist, asked him to investigate the disappearance of a wealthy shopkeeper and his entire family from the small town of Juilion. At first everyone thought the merchant simply set on one of his long trips, but after two weeks of absence suspicions rose. People started to talk and again, the lord had to do something to calm the common folks. Sire Anton himself set out to look for the missing merchant. He searched for several weeks, but found nothing. Just like in the case of Sire Illow's farmers, there was no sign of the trader or his family; who vanished in thin air. Again, the loss was labeled to be an accident, and soon forgotten as other troubles took its place.

"Although more reports continued to come in, the problem of the missing men did not spill over to concern the Duke, until he received a personal note from the Lech family. Sire Even Lech was a good friend of his. The two knights had spent many years together, serving the King and the realm. The noble's aged wife sent an epistle, in which she pleaded for the Duke's help. Her husband and two of her sons did not return from their hunting trip. While they were expected to be off for several hours, they went missing for days. And that was not all. Along with the noblemen, a dozen of their squires and men-at-arms had ventured astray too.

"Deeply worried for the well-being of the Lechs, the Duke dispatched three of his captains, who immediately traveled to the missing knight's castle. With no news of Sire Lech, afraid that he might have been ambushed by some bandits, the captains hurried to assemble a fighting force, and taking two regiments of squires and three dozen local guards, explored the nearby lands, checking every patch of trees, every glade, and every creek there was. Alas, there were no signs of the knight or his party. Just like in the other incidents, the men disappeared, leaving not a single trace as to their whereabouts. But unlike the other occurrences Sire Lech and his escort were not common folks. They were renowned soldiers, well armed, and versed in the art of fighting, ready to repel any ambush. To topple them one needed to have a lot of men, men who knew the ways of battle. Such thought alone made the Duke's captains very alarmed, and dubious, they headed back to Bonneville, where in due course they conveyed the tragic news to their lord, who, I must say, took the matter very personally. Without delay he launched an inquiry and sent out pressing messages to all of the lords in the province, urging every knight to mount a search for Sire Lech and his sons. Many answered the call, including me, and for several weeks roamed the countryside, but all for nothing. The noblemen were nowhere to be found.

"Empty-handed, I returned to my castle, still troubled by the bizarre quandary, only to receive one more disturbing report, this time from the southern border of my own domain where, near the town of Ghuleo, somebody attacked a small mining camp. The bandits worked fast and brutally. They launched an assault in the middle of the night and butchered as many miners as they could. Very few of the men managed to escape into the nearby woods, and when they returned to the camp, they found all their comrades dead, silent witnesses to a senseless slaughter. Unknown were the reasons behind the attack, but it was a strange assault at best, as during it all of the young miners, boys, green lads, and toddlers had gone missing, not a single one of them found amidst the dead or the survivors.

"Troubling was such a peril, but it was not the last, as a few weeks later more distressing news arrived. Brune Loyde's convoy had gone astray too, its fate surrounded by strange circumstances, a single cart as the only clue. Until last night I could not spot a connection between all the occurrences. Now, after reading the hermit's letter and hearing the accounts of your journey, I am convinced that there is a linkage, which I suspect has something to do with the mysterious Alavantars. This book…," continued Sire Rone, lifting the tome, "…serves as the standing proof, possibly holding the key to the puzzle of the recent disappearances; for those foul believers who dwelled right under my nose were not some harmless preachers of the Spirit's Ways, but probably disciples of the clandestine sect, devoted to the works of evil. I would not be surprised if they had been using the monastery grounds as their asylum from us, the knights of Normandia, concealing their dark deeds under a veil of virtuousness.

"I must say that for a while their plan has worked, but now you and I have become aware of their purpose and so they have left, moved elsewhere, escaping my inquiries, as if they knew their secret was no longer safe. But I do not intend to let them go so easily. I am keen to see justice and order prevail and to do so I will investigate the matter of the Alavantars personally. Yet, before I can proceed with my inquiries, I need to know why and where they have gone, but most importantly, I want to find out what threat they pose to this kingdom and to this province. It is here you can be of service to me. You can help me learn more about the sect, its ways and habits.

"There is a reason why I have chosen you for such a task. Unlike most people under my tutelage, you are already aware of the sect and its filthy endeavors. You have also been toiling with the quest, which may have some connection to the matter of the Alavantars. To find someone else equally prepared to take on the mission will require time, and it is time I do not have. I need to act fast, before it is too late. Accordingly, I am presenting you with this chore of great importance. But since you are not in my service I cannot order you to do so. You can either accept the duty, which may very well take you on a long and dangerous journey, or you can decline it and leave it for others. Should you choose to take the assignment, you will become my servants, which means that following our sacred rules of knighthood, I will have to raise you to the status of squires."

Sire Rone paused and glanced at us more keenly

"Are you ready to give up your normal lives and serve the Kingdom of Normandia as have done many brave and righteous men before you?"

A serious question it was. Somewhat startled, I looked at my friends. Frankly, I was uncertain about what I should do. I had heard of squires and their duties. I had seen them far and wide And then there was Minia, my new companion, who had become a good friend to all of us. But at the same time I did not have the slightest idea as to what it really meant to be a soldier, and if I was cut out to be one. Aside from our earlier victory near the monastery, I never considered myself to be a fighter. I also did not know a single thing about tracking, cooking, or hunting, and could not even read maps. Yet, I also knew that I did not have much choice. Sire Rone was right—there was a connection between the Alavantars and the disappearance of Father's convoy. Although I could not see it, I sensed it, and if to find Father, Ave, and the others I had to serve Sire Rone as his squire, then so be it. I would become one.

After some forethought I was ready to find out what lay in a store for me as Sire Rone's faithful servant. But before I could voice my choice I saw Ark rising from his seat. My friend took a step forward and looking straight at the knight, his tone full of vigor and certainty, stated, "I think I can speak for us all, and say that we have already made a promise to Irk the Wise. When we pledged to deliver the book and the letter to you, my lord, each of us assured the hermit of our complete commitment to prevent the men who call themselves Alavantars, from ever succeeding in their malevolent plans. Our answer to you, Sire, is the same as it has been to Irk the Wise. We will take on your assignment and serve you in a just cause."

"We are ready to become your squires, my lord." Rob stood up next.

"Me too," said Ike.

"And me," added Ric.

Suspense and excitement were evident on their faces. I was the last to leave the comfort of the bench pillows, and standing in the middle of the counselor's room at the lord's castle, signed on to continue the journey, as the squire to Sire Rone, together with my three most trusted friends and Ric.

"I am glad to hear that you have fighters' hearts," said Sir Rone, and a light smile crossed his face. "You have made a fine choice. Now I must swear you in as my squires....Step forward, one at a time."

The lord pulled out a long sword from the sheathe that hung at his side and holding it firmly in his right hand got up and pointed it at me, his left hand gesturing to get on my knee before him. As I knelt, the old scribe suddenly woke up from his sleep and extracted a large, seemingly heavy book, which he held open while writing something in it. Sire Rone waited for the man to finish, and then resumed his speech. The lord's deep voice resonated through the room, and the scribe began to work his quill again, not looking even once at what was going on around him.

In all my years as a boy I always thought becoming a squire involved a complex and colorful ritual, with lots of lights, big words, and sounds. But the ceremony that followed was anything but glamorous. It began with the announcement of my name and age, which were quickly recorded by the old man. When the scribe finished, the lord came up to me with his sword raised and lowered it slowly on my shoulder, tapping it several times. As the shiny blade bounced off my tunic, Sire Rone said something in a strange tongue, then declared a sacred pledge, a collection of oaths I had to repeat after him, trying to sound clear and precise. Afterwards, the lord moved his weapon onto my other shoulder and patted it too, at the same time making me place my right hand on my chest and swear the fealty again, this time adding a few more lines that stated that from the moment on Sire Rone of Bois was to be my sole lord and commander, to whom I would become a swordsman and a faithful servant. And once the words were spoken, I was sent back to my seat, giving way to Ike, who was next in line.

In less than half an hour we were done with the formal part of the ceremony and went over to the old scribe to register ourselves in his large book, which turned out to be the journal of the castle, a tome in which all of the names of Sire Rone's fighting men were put into for records. After leaving little crosses beneath short passages of freshly written texts, we placed our thumb prints, as proof of our accord, and were declared squires to the house of Sire Rone. When the old man checked our signatures and closed the book, the knight nodded his head, tacked back the sword and sat down, his body sinking into the cushions of the seat.

"From this point on, you are my soldiers." The lord's voice sounded forcefully. "You will learn more of your duties later. For now, remember that as squires you must obey orders given to you. And my first order is such—tomorrow you will set out on a trip to the provincial capital of Bonneville and deliver my personal message to Sire Tem, the honorable Duke of Bois, who holds his seat there. Once you convey my dispatch to the Duke, proceed with your original quest and try to find out what has happened to Loyde's caravan; also learn as much as you can about the Alavantars, who they are, what they do, and where they hide. When you discover anything, come back to Sirone at once, as I will be expecting a full report."

Sire Rone then got up and walked up to the scribe, who whispered something and bowed. The lord gave the old man a reply, which I did not hear, and returned to us. "It is essential that you set out as soon as possible, so I have instructed my chief guard, Ao, to assist you with your gear and weapons. Seek him out near the armory and follow his instructions. To help you further, I have ordered Minia to take command over your company, making sure that you will get to the provincial capital without any complications. Now…Go and get your gear. You are dismissed."

The lord concluded and then left, the scribe trotting after him.

Chapter 23

THROUGH A crowd of servants, town folks, soldiers, horses, livestock, and dogs, we picked our way across the castle grounds. We walked toward the far side of the keep, where we were to meet the chief guard. He was already waiting for us, standing near a small shed attached to the side of the citadel and a small door that was the entrance to the lord's armory.

"New recruits, are not you?" the wide-faced, red-haired soldier asked, studying us with a hard glare. "If you do not know yet, I am Ao, the chief guard here in Sirone, the man responsible for the safekeeping of this castle. Since you are new to this garrison, I will give you a few tips. So listen carefully and remember. First and foremost you obey all commands of your superiors. You do not question your orders, and never doubt your assignments.

"You are not here to think—thinking is for lords and their officers. The common soldiers like yourselves do as told. Second, as the lord's squires you will receive your gear from his armory. You do not sell it or bargain it or lend it to anyone. It is not yours to give. The same goes for the horse and supplies. The only thing you can give is your salary.

"Of course, if you are smart you will save every copper you get, but if you are not you are free to waste them as you please. Third, you do something stupid around here, you answer to me. You try to steal anything, or hurt someone, or bother Sire Rone or anyone of his household, you answer to me. You break something of value within the castle grounds, again you answer to me. And the way I deal with all the troublemakers is prison time and Barrier Walls. Understood?"

Ao gave us another look and resumed when we did not answer. "Finally, from the moment you have placed you finger in that book, your utmost task as the lord's fighting men has become the protection of Sire Rone. You see or hear or smell anything that might threaten his well-being, you do everything to eliminate it. If you cannot do it yourselves, find others to help, but never ever put your lives before the lord's. Remember, courage is what earns you disposition here, not cowardice."

Ao paused, examining us some more, then spat on the ground and continued. "Now, Sire Rone has instructed me to prepare you for a journey to Bonneville. Although if it had been my choice I would not have let you anywhere near the armory, but lord's orders are lord's orders."

Uttering those words, the chief guard pulled out several keys from his pocket and started to open the locks on the door, one at a time. After the last catch was removed, he pushed the door inward and was about to walk in, when Minia showed up from behind the shed and greeted everyone with a high salute. "Hey fellows. It is good to see you again," he said cheerily and walked up to the chief. The two shook hands.

"Did they give you any trouble?" The squire asked in the same spirited tone, and immediately added, "Ah, I see you have already opened the armory. Let me take them down there. Sire Rone wants you in his quarters."

Minia padded the chief guard on the shoulder and took the keys from him. Ao gave up the metal ring without question, and after nodding once, took off, hurrying along the Keep's wall, disappearing quickly amongst the crowd.

Meanwhile Minia gave a pull on a heavy thick iron handle and opened the door further, disclosing a narrow stairway that ran down, circling around a cold stone column. "Come on in," he said, as he waved and stepped inside. "If you want to be real squires, you need real weapons and armor. Let's see if we can find some decent items for you here."

The squire picked up a lantern from the wall and lit it with the firestones. As the darkness retreated down the steps, he gave us another wave and ran after the light, taking a few steps at a time.

The spiral staircase led us several floors down and into a round chamber, some forty cubits in diameter. It was illuminated by three oil lanterns, wide metal cones hanging from chains, attached to the moist stones of the ceiling. Their glow was not too bright, but did not hamper our eyesight, allowing us to make out a small black-oak door to one side, marking the only visible way out, besides the stairs. After lingering at the door for a little bit, Minia halted and removed a large iron deadlock that protected the way into the armory. Freed from restraints the door slid inward and a piercing screeching sound of rusted hinges made me shiver. I closed my eyes and when I opened them again, the squire had already disappeared in the darkness beyond the entryway, his dark silhouette outlined by the flickering light of his lantern, also reflected off the sodden walls and strange objects.

For a while Minia's distant lamp was the only source of illumination within the chamber, but soon a row of other lights began to spring up along the walls, revealing a view of a large wide hall that stretched over a hundred cubits, its arching walls crammed with various battle gear of every form, size, and shape. Suits of plated armor, chain mail, shields, and weapons of all sorts were stored on long wide racks, their wooden frames pressed against the sides. While many items were in excellent shape and bore no sign of rusting, some were clearly old and dented, and the ones that were particularly damaged, either by a splash of corrosion, or by prolonged use, were thrown into a large pile at the far end, separated from the rest of the tackle by a low metal rail.

My eyes fixed on the lines of equipment, I stepped through the doorway and slowly made my way toward the squire, who was standing in the center of the hall, working a large rusted lamp. As I walked I first passed swords and battle-axes, placed closest to the exit, occupying two large three-shelved racks. After these I went along a lengthy stand of bows, crossbows, and arrows, neatly stored inside special slits so as not to damage fine taut strings and delicate feathered ends, and then a row of spears, a good five-dozen spikes, lined up perfectly one after another, forming one impressive fence of wood and iron.

Once at Minia's side, I halted across from the javelins, and studied the rest of the hall, filled with armor suits; chains, plates, and leathers, which rested on tall hangers, supported by thick wooden beams that ensured that no outfit would fall, dragged down by a heavy weight.

"Ho, ho, look at it all," exclaimed Ike. By then he was also standing in the center, his face glowing with surprise and an inevitable desire to get his hands on all the things around him.

"Are we here to choose anything we want?" I then asked the squire, who was still busy fixing one of the lanterns that mulishly refused to work.

"Tentatively, you can pick anything from the arsenal." Minia answered without letting go of the lamp; when the rest of our group gathered around him, he continued. "But there are a few things I must mention before I let you run wild in here. There are many weapons and armors that are used in the world these days. Most of them have different attributes and require certain skills. Some are heavy; others are light. Many can be used single-handed, while a few require two hands to wield. There are also those that work best for a horseman, and the ones that are best suited for a man on foot.

Generally, the best way to go about choosing your weapons is to consider how, where, and when you will be using them. If, let's say, you have a lot of traveling ahead, you probably want to keep to lighter armor and more flexible weapons. Of course, if you are a knight, you do not have to worry too much about it, since squires and men-at-arms will carry all your gear. Then there is also a question of knowing how to use your weapon. If you have never shot a bow in your life, it will be unwise for you to equip it, even if it is the best bow in the world. Similarly, if you have never balanced a spear, do not even think of taking it with you into battle. It will not do you any good, as you will probably injure yourself before you can even get to the enemy. So my advice to you is to be resourceful in your choice. Find a good weapon and try it. If it feels right, take it, because it is probably the one that will be best for you. Do not go simply with size or looks. Don't pick the easiest or most destructive. Remember your life may depend on it. Walk around, check different things, handle them.

As for the armor, your choice is limited. Squires in Sirone are only allowed to wear leather or chain. In your case, you are to check chain mail only, so do not bother with any other kind. You can find them at the far end of the armory. Pick your size and bring the suits to me. I will see if they need to be fitted."

Minia stopped his sermon and motioned toward the racks.

"Your pick, squires." He stepped aside and let us wander off.

The more I looked, the more I felt like a child surrounded by toys. Bows, maces, swords, and shields; everything was just what I had always dreamt about. The only problem was that I had to choose one, maybe two things. At first I set my eyes on a massive, threatening morning star, which rested at the bottom rack, reserved for the maces. But as I lifted the awesome weapon, I remembered that I had no idea how to use it, and acting on Minia's advice, let the bludgeon be, instead turning to swords.

After trying several of the edged weapons I came to the conclusion that my choice was with them. But I needed a light weapon with a strong blade that could withstand the heat of battle. It also had to be of a good size, yet not too long, as I wanted to be able to maneuver with it in any setting, indoors or outdoors. Prudently, I burrowed through the medley, and after casting aside several less suitable blades, spotted a stylish thin handle peering from beneath a stack of heavy broad swords. Intrigued by its elegance, I moved the other weapons aside and reached for the grip. For a while it did not budge, and I had to muster all my strength to pull on it. But once I did, in my hands I found an exquisite narrow-bladed sword of a perfect make that reflected sparkles off the burning lanterns.

One of the most beautiful pieces of weaponry I had ever held, the sword was a cubit long, its blade a straight line of glittering steel, along which an unusual figure of a tree, encircled by a single vine, was etched. The weapon's handle was also made of steel, and was encased in fine soft leather, decorated at the top with a large red stone pressed into the metal, and framed with thin streaks of golden dust.

My hands were shaking a little as I lifted the beautiful piece of weaponry and thrust it several times. Surprisingly it felt natural and easy to handle. Feathery and yet solid it was well balanced, its grip—comfortable and soft. Pleased with my find, I set the sword aside and started to look for a suitable sheathe, when Minia's question made me turn.

"Where did you find it?" he asked with a hint of wonder in his voice, inspecting the blade carefully, slowly tracing his finger along its cold steel lines.

"Right there, under all those swords." I pointed to a disturbed heap of weapons.

"I have not seen such blade in many years. I did not even know that Sire Rone had something like this." Minia's words were full of wonder, which made me very curious.

"What is so unusual about this sword? It looks very much like any other weapon here," I said, trying to understand what it was that made Minia so interested.

"This is no ordinary sword," replied the squire. "This is an A'al shadow dagger. You see this symbol of a tree on its blade? Only A'als put such carvings on their weapons."

The squire flipped the sword. "After the A'als and D'ars departed from Ethoria a lot of their weaponry was left behind. Those weapons passed to our ancestors who considered them to be the best in the world. And it was true— the foreign blades never rusted, never chipped or broke. They were perfect in their marksmanship and none of the human masters could duplicate their traits, not even with red ore. But soon the men noticed there was something wrong with those arms. The tales say that humans could not wield the foreign pieces for long as those who did eventually came to strange and unexpected ends. Since none could ever explain such predicaments, people deemed the weapons of the old races as cursed and cast them aside, locking them deep within many armories and vaults all across Ethoria. After some years people forgot about the foreign armaments and now only very few can be found still in use."

Minia stared at the blade some more and noted, "I guess Sire Rone had one of those weapons too."

"Do you think it is true, about the curse I mean?" I asked, looking at the strange sword.

"I would not trust those rumors too much," answered Minia. "But super-stitions are terrible things. Though you do not really believe in them you still do not want to test your luck. Personally, I would not own a shadow dagger, but it is my choice, and I do not see a reason why you cannot have it if you want. I do not think anyone will miss it. I bet nobody even remembers it is still here."

Minia swung the sword once and gave it back to me. "A word of caution if I may. People do not often appreciate foreign things; they become wary and uneasy around them. Although there are a lot of A'al and D'ar items in Ethoria, trophies of long-forgotten wars, many folks tend to think of them as wicked or corrupted. If I were you I would keep this thing sheathed as much as possible; that is of course if you do not want to cause trouble."

Listening to the squire, I examined the sword one more time, debating if I should take it or not. Minia's warning was a serious one, but there was just something about the blade that drew me to it. I had a feeling that I needed it, that it would help me somehow in the future. After turning the blade in my hand for a little longer, I sheathed the sword into a plain leather case and said, "I think I will take it anyway."

"As I said, the choice is yours," replied Minia, who motioned for me to leave the weapon with him and go to the armor sets to find my suit.

While I pondered with my pick of the chain mail, the rest of the company continued to search through the weapons, each trying many different things. For some time Ike lingered by a rack that held pieces of archery. He rampaged through the stacks of curved bows and sturdy crossbows, turning and tossing them as he looked. Finding nothing of interest, he let them be and moved down the hall to maces, then axes, and finally swords. There his eyes lit up with even more excitement and he began to snatch one hilt after another, pushing aside unwanted blades, not even bothering to place them back into their slots. Complementing his inspection with a loud jingling of his newly acquired chain mail, Ike went through the first rack and then the second, but by the third, he got tired and was soon forced to make up his mind, appearing before Minia with a broad sword and a long thick woolen hat with long flaps, in his hands.

Rob, Ark, and Ric were much more settled in their selections. At first they walked together, slowly moving around the armory, trying only a few items, often huddling together to discuss their choices. Then they split. Ark went over to a pile of old damaged weapons and began to look for something there. Although I had no idea what he was hoping to discover in that heap, I did not want to question my friend as he had his own ways and probably knew precisely what he was doing. Soon he extracted a short-sleeved mail and an impressive mace, made of a round metal spiked ball attached to a thick wooden handle. While the armor was dented and had traces of rust on it, the weapon looked like it was in good shape, and despite its average size yielded a great deal of respect; as from just looking at the thing, it was clear that its wielder was quite serious about his ways of combat, which always served as a good warning for any overzealous tough.

Not too far away from Ark, Rob and Ric were working on their choices, standing next to a selection of battleaxes. The two seemed to share the same affection for the massive destructiveness the axes possessed and were eager to find a piece that could match their large fit. After some deliberation, each chose a serious heavy weapon, furnished with double blades and spikes. Satisfied, they took the axes with them and went over to the armor stands, where Rob found a set of chain mail of a slightly bluish color and a round shield, a sizable disk that required a good grip and a strong hand to hold. My brother chose similar-looking armor and shield, and also picked a helm, a large metal cap, sealed by a rind of polished steel, which resembled a silver bend.

Soon my friends and Ric finished with their choosing and came over to Minia to show him their finds. But I was still struggling with my selection, strolling slowly along a row of hangers that held different metal suits. There was plenty to choose from. Although all ringed costumes looked similar, they varied in size and form, designed to accommodate a wide range of likely torsos. At last after another failed attempts to find something that fit me, I called to Minia for aid. "What am I looking for?" I asked the squire, nodding toward the hangers.

"No problem," replied Minia and came over, immediately beginning to leaf through the pieces of armor himself.

"Whatever armor you choose, it cannot be too short or too long. You also want to have as much freedom in your movement as possible. Therefore, you should get something that is light in weight and strongly made so it can protect your torso from an average blow."

Minia ruffled through another set of hangers, and after rejecting several of the armors that sat on them, pulled out a plain-looking suit of woven steel rings.

"Try this one," he said and handed me the piece. "It is not as bulky as the others, but is well made and will hold well against the perils of travel."

Curiously I looked at the thing. Interlocking rings were bounded together to form a coat of metal that covered chest, arms, and midsection, but fell far short of shielding the thighs, stopping just below the waistline, caught there by a spiked leather belt, made of three separate laces. Shaking the suit a couple of times, I put it on and tried to move. At first it felt heavy and cold, and somewhat uneasy, but, as I twisted my body in different directions, bending and twisting in between, I began to appreciate its flexibility, and despite some awk-wardness, decided to keep it, taking it away with me to the stairs, thus concluding my first trip ever to an armory.

With our hands full, we returned to the courtyard, where the next stop awaited us—the lord's stables. To get my own horse was one of my sacred dreams, and I could hardly hold my excitement, hurrying after Minia, breath-ing fast and heavy. Outside the sun shined brightly, and the castle grounds seemed even more crowded, with people everywhere. A few servants passed in front of us, carrying water buckets in and out of the large buildings, spilling some in long wet trails. Some distance away several more men dragged carts of dirt and stones across the sandy floor, and at the far side a group of young bare-chested lads were rearranging a stack of hay, throwing it over their heads and onto a large platform that was then lifted up to the wall, where two more men carried it away down the parapet.

Trying to keep up with the rest of the company, I marched to the set of houses, which were the lord's stables, walking up to the large entrance that was supported by a series of wooden planks. The wooden gates were open, and a strong animal odor was coursing out of it. Inside were many horses, each stand-ing tied to long poles of rough untreated wood. Most of the animals were in good shape, and some were even of a high breed, Westalian steeds—the pride of any noble who had the money to pay for them. Sire Rone had four of the foreign mounts, graceful beasts that stood in their stalls, occasionally wriggling restraints of heavy leather straps.

"Usually the squires are allowed to pick their own mounts, but we have been short on horses lately, so the animals have been chosen for you," said Minia as he stepped inside the stables. "You can find your animals at the far end. Each will have a marker with your name on it. Pick your animal and meet me outside."

Smiling, Minia moved aside and allowed us in, himself staying in the yard.

All at once we strolled into the stables, trying to find the creatures with our names written on their labels. Patiently I went from one booth to another and finally in one of the corner stalls, found a young steed, which bore a large leather slice with my name burned into it. My heart racing, I walked up to my new companion and studied it. The beast that stood calmly in his booth was a fair animal of an average size, with its velvety toned body looking well nour-ished and fit. Its dark brown hide was speckled with splashes of white on its legs, chest, and forehead. Although quite short, its hair came down one side and covered part of its neckline, giving it a slender, elegant look, which suited me fine.

Knowing a few things about handling horses, I approached the steed carefully, trying not to make any sudden movements, extending my right hand so that my fingers touched its rough brown hide. The animal did not seem to mind my company, and continued to stay still while I traced my palm along its side, until I reached the bridle. Whispering softly, I untied the straps and slowly led the mount into the courtyard. There I let it walk alone, while I went over to the side of the building and picked up a large saddle. For a moment I stood motionless with the saddle in one hand, and stroking the mount down his large neck with the other, and then I slowly slid the saddle onto the horse's back. To my surprise, the mount continued to be calm, allowing me to strap the saddle and climb into it, its surface hard and slick.

After several quick spins, I let the steed pace leisurely across the yard, where I carefully turned it around, pulling on the straps, and strode back, concentrating on keeping my balance and posture. In the same way I made several more circles, soon realizing that I liked the ride. Pleased, I dismounted and returned the horse back to the stables. There I fastened the leather belt to the pole, patted the beast again, and walked out into the yard, joining Minia, who sat on top of a wooden fence, observing the others from our company.

"Do you know my horse's name?" I asked the squire, when he looked at me with a grin.

"Soft Wind," replied Minia. "He is a good horse, young and well trained. I think you won't be disappointed."

Minia wanted to say something else, but Ike had emerged in the courtyard, leading his mount after him. Struggling a little, he pulled a black stallion of average size into the open and after throwing a large bulky saddle over the animal's back, climbed it. Once he got used to the uncomfortable leather cushion, he galloped back and forth across the stable yard's sandy floor, clearly enjoying the ride and the cool light breeze hitting his face.

With Ike striding along the walls, Rob and Ric appeared too, each with their own vigorous mount—Rob's gray, and Ric's brown. Since both were the tallest members of our party, they got the two largest mounts that towered over the rest of the horses, like their riders over many folks in the yard. And just like their riders, the horses were very calm, standing passively as their new owners saddled and mounted them, making them then trot back and forth, pulling on the straps, and jerking the bridles.

Ark was the last to emerge. He came out unhurriedly, bringing with him a skinny grayish creature that was the smallest of the entire lot and looked more like a pony than a horse. Its appearance alone made everyone smile, which could not be said about Ark, who was clearly not all too pleased with such a gift. But there was little he could do, and having a choice between riding the pony or walking on foot, my friend chose the first and worked with his mare, saddling it, and fixing it for the ride, which was a short one.

By the time we finished with the horses, the day crawled to its midpoint. Each of us stood near the fence, awaiting further instructions, which were to come from the chief guard, who had come out from the keep a bit earlier and sat down near the squire and me, observing the others, often commenting on what he saw. When Ao was done talking, he signaled to follow him and guided us to a large building across the yard, which as Ao explained was the garrison's dining hall. There, on top of several long tables rested an assortment of food and drink, which made up our afternoon meal—free of charge, another benefit to becoming squires to the lord. There Ao left us, and free of his tough glare we ate.

"Our departure is set at six in the morning," Minia said when he finished the last bit of food on his plate. "It will be an early rise and a long day after it, so you better get some sleep." The squire got up, adjusted his belt, freeing some space for his extended belly, and turned to leave.

"Are we to do anything else today? I mean, we are squires now, and all…" I chased Minia with the question.

"You are done for today and free to do what ever you want; just do not leave the castle's grounds. As a part of the garrison you can go outside only if you get permission papers from your superiors, who will be the chief guard, Ao, his two deputy chiefs, Sire Rone's three captains, or the lord himself. In your place, I would not bother any of them yet," explained Minia as he resumed his walk. But then he halted again and added, "Dinner is served at seven. Do not be late, or you will go hungry until the next morning."

The squire nodded in conclusion and departed, leaving us alone at the table. We did not sit there for long but soon after returned to our quarters, escorted by another young guard, who was kind enough to help us find the way.

Inside my room, I spent the remainder of the day, worrying myself with few deep thoughts of any kind. After talking to my friends for some time, I turned to the newly acquired equipment, spending a good hour or so, fitting it, trying it on, and just looking at it. Content again with the quality of the pieces I had chosen, I put everything away and rejoined in my friends' chat, devoted solely to the events of that very morning. Amidst all the talking we did not notice how the afternoon turned into evening, and the time of supper came.

At exactly seven o'clock, we were summoned up to the soldiers' dining hall. Most of the garrison's men, those who were not on duty or on leave, were already sitting on the benches, every one with a wooden glass and a plate in front of him. Consumed with their own sermons they paid us little notice, and undisturbed we walked to the far end of the room, where five seats were left vacant at a table full of young fellows—squires and young recruits, who had come to the castle to serve their lord. Since most of them had already known each other for some time, they talked amongst themselves and ignored our company, granting us brief comments and jokes, none of which were loud enough to be heard. But such brusque disposition of the other youngsters bothered us little, as we knew very well that we would not spend much time with them. In the morning we would depart to Bonneville, entrusted with a very important mission, something those boys could only dream of. Besides, our reasons for becoming squires were different too. While most of the boys joined Sire Rone's garrison because they wanted to, or because their parents made them, we were there because of our quest, the quest that involved much mystery and danger. So reserving to our own company, we sat down and ate our meal, which consisted of a bowl of warm stew, made of carrots and lamb, a fresh onion, and a slice of corn bread, complemented by a sweaty mug of honeyed brew that had a sour-sweet flavor to it.

When the food was gone, many of the soldiers and squires left, and soon we found ourselves alone again, sitting at the table until the sound of a distant horn announced the start of the night, making us pick up ourselves and return to our rooms, eager to catch some sleep before the early morrow. Once in the comfort of the bed I let the weariness overwhelm me and surrendered to the drowsiness, swiftly falling into a dreamless sleep.

Chapter 24

IN THE middle of the night a medley of loud noises—the sound of dozens of running feet, shouts, clattering, and ringing of distant bells—woke me up. Trying to grasp what was going on, I crawled out of bed and fighting a deep desire to return to sleep, staggered to the door, but before I could open it, a hard knocking rocked the wooden frame. Letting go of the brass knob, I stepped back and saw the door move inward, revealing Minia's fully dressed figure. A torch in one hand and a naked sword in the other, the squire studied me for a moment and then waved the burning tip before my face.

"Come! Sire Rone wants to see you!" Minia yelled and stepped away from the breach. For a moment I glanced at the squire in confusion, not really comprehending his words, but when he shouted again, I ran back to my bed, got dressed, and walked out into the hallway, along with Ike and Ric, who had gotten up too, and were fastening their gear as they walked, often stumbling and dropping something to the floor. Outside the sounds of the bustle were louder. We remained in there until Rob and Ark appeared from there room, and then, hurried by the ringing of some distant bell, followed Minia in a quick dash to the stairs and the courtyard above.

Although the sky was very dark, the castle grounds were alive and lit, yellow lights flowing from dozens of lamps and torches, most of which were carried by men, soldiers, servants, and commoners, who moved everywhere in disarray, often bumping into each other, tripping, and cursing. While several scores of men were suited for battle, wearing their metal suits and holding round shields, most looked hastily dressed, some of them without out any armor or even tunics, running across the sandy floor barefoot and bare-chested. But almost everyone I saw had weapons—swords, axes, spears, forks, and shovels, their faces very grim, and their eyes focused on the stone walls around them.

"What is going on?" I managed to ask Minia, as we ran across the stretch of the yard, heading for the northern wall, where a group of men, including Sire Rone, and Ao, stood huddling around something that lay on the ground.

"There was a break in," replied the squire without turning back. "Someone tried to get into the castle not long ago. They were spotted by the guards, and gave fight. Some of our men died."

Before Minia could finish with his answer, we had reached the far side of the castle grounds and joined the other soldiers, who immediately stepped aside, freeing a narrow passage so we could get to the front, where Sire Rone and Ao were standing. Seeing us come in, the lord raised his hand and gestured for us to hurry. In several long leaps we passed the remaining guards and soon found ourselves at the lord's side, halting cubits away from the wall, next to two mounds covered with gray stretches of cloth, their outlines resembling human forms.

"Do you recognize these men?" Sire Rone asked and raised his hand. Right away one of the soldiers from the crowd kneeled down and yanked the covers, exposing two unmoving figures. I was correct in my assumption—before me lay two men, two dead men. At the first, their cold pale faces appeared unfamiliar, their features twisted in a moment of pain. But as I looked closer, I quickly realized that the men at my feet were the same ones I had seen at the Golden Duck Inn just two nights ago.

"Yes, I have seen them before," I said firmly, alerting the lord and the other men. "These are the men we told you about, the outlanders from the Golden Duck Inn."

"Are you sure, young man?" asked Ao, his expression grim as a winter night. At first his tough stare made me doubt my words, but as I looked at the cold faces again, I knew I was not mistaken. "Yes. I am sure. I will never forget them," I stated firmly, looking back at the chief guard. Then, I turned to Sire Rone. "My lord, may I ask as to what has happened here?"

"These two were caught sneaking into the castle," replied Ao instead and ordered the same soldier to pull the covers back over the corpses. "They had almost managed to get over the wall when the inner patrol spotted them. Once they realized they had been uncovered, they tried to fight their way to the outer gates. Those fools—they did not have chance."

"Be as it may," interrupted Sire Rone. "But four of your men are dead and two more are wounded. Had there been more of them tonight, who knows, maybe they would have succeeded in getting out of here."

"That would not have happened, not ever, not while I am the chief guard here," protested Ao, then quickly realized his mistake and quieted, lowering his head.

"No need for any grievance," Sire Rone said after a short pause. "I do not doubt your ability to keep this castle safe. What I am trying to say is that these intruders are no simple robbers, and so deserve serious consideration."

"Who are they, do you know?" I let out the question, not really noticing that I had done so.

"As you have said earlier, they are hired swords, Snake Bites to be exact," Ao replied and to clarify his words, ordered another guard to lift a corner of a cloak sticking out from underneath one of the covers. As the light from several torches fell onto the inner lining of the intruder's cape, I noted the familiar symbol, drawn in red ink on black silk—a Snaked Ring and the Bat sealed in it.

"There is more," continued the chief guard. "One of the men had a letter on him. It was of—"

"Enough," Sire Rone cut him off. "We will discuss it inside. Sire Ohn, Minia, Mishuk, and your friends, come with me." The lord turned and strode to the castle's door, followed by a dozen guards and our company, leaving the rest of the soldiers and Ao by the corpses.

Inside the meeting hall, lit only with torches carried by the men, Sire Rone lowered himself into the chair, pulled out the letter, and gave it to his captain.

"Sire Ohn, tell me what you make of this," he asked the younger lord when the last had finished reading the note.

"It looks like someone has taken a very personal interest in seeking destruction of Mishuk and his company," Sire Ohn replied without any forethought.

"I think so too," the lord agreed. "I am afraid the matter is more serious than I expected. We cannot waste any time.

Sire Ohn, as my first captain, take all of your squires and organize them in patrols around Sirone. I want every cubit of this town covered. Also, check all the local inns and eateries. Find out if the intruders stayed in one of them, or if anyone in town saw them. I want to know if there are other outlanders in Sirone, and if there are, bring them to me, I want to have a word with them; maybe one of them knows something about this night's incursion."

The lord then turned to my friends and me. "Mishuk Loyde, the letter we found on one of the intruders, holds a very detailed description of your company, and having a band of hired swords with a sketch of you on them means only one thing—someone wants you dead. Although I do not know why he seeks your demise, I know he is serious about it, hiring mercenaries from the South to do the job. Lucky for you, so far you have been able to avoid your mysterious foe's clutches. You dispatched one of the hired swords near the monastery, and the other two found their end here inside my castle. Still, we do not know if there are more of them out there looking for you. So, I think it is best if you leave for Bonneville immediately, before anyone else tries to kill you."

The lord drew out a large yellow envelope, sealed by a waxed stamp that showed his family's crest and held it in his hand. "This is the message you are to take to the Duke of Bois. Should he have questions, and I am sure he will, answer them like you have answered mine. And if he asks you to perform a duty, do as ordered, and do not forget, time is of the essence." The lord gave the letter to Minia, as the commander of our company, and then dismissed us, returning his attention to Sire Ohn.

Giving out brief salutes, we followed Minia's example and left the meeting hall. Once in the hallway we talked to the squire about our departure, and then hurried back to our rooms where we gathered our gear, fixed our bags, and put on our new suits of armor. Though the iron-shirt was a little constraining, I felt comfortable enough in it, able to move and turn without too much effort. Satisfied with the fit, I wrapped the metal chemise with a thick black leather belt and fastened my new sword, unsheathing it once to get another look at its beautiful blade. Over the mail I threw a cotton vest, which came with the armor and bore the colors of Sire Rone's house, my designation as a squire. After studying myself with the new colors of the lord, I hid them beneath my old cape, which I tied around my neck, and with a pair of leather gloves strapped to my belt, walked out of the room.

Hastily our company returned to the courtyard, still busy and noisy, and illuminated by the flickering lights. We headed for the stables, where Minia had been already fixing a saddle on his mare. Our horses were out too, all saddled and ready for the journey. After checking the leather seats, we strapped our bags onto them and turned to listen to Ao's final orders.

"Men!" yelled the chief guard. "Sire Rone has given you a task, which is of utmost importance. As you know, you are to travel to Bonneville and deliver our lord's personal dispatch to the Duke."

Ao paused and gave us another hard stare. "Are you ready to take on such a task?" he yelled again.

"Yes, Sire!" we roared in one voice.

"Not Sire, you dumb wits, chief guard," exclaimed Ao.

"Yes, chief guard!" we repeated as loudly as we could.

"Good. When you deliver the letter, wait for any instructions from the Duke or one of his captains. If they do not have any duties for you, you are to continue your search for the missing caravan. Once you leave this castle, Minia will assume the command of your company. You are to obey his orders and follow his instruction. There will be no mutiny and no disobedience. Understand that as soldiers you are subject to the military justice of the lord, which implies severe punishment—lashing, imprisonment, and even death. I can promise you, neither one is pleasant."

The chief took a deep breath and added, "Good luck to you, men." He gave us a salute and walked away.

By the time we were finally ready to set out, the sky had already begun to brighten as the first glimpse of the morning colors peeked over the horizon. Before the morning came, we rode out of the castle in a column of three pairs and headed in the northern direction, first circling around Sire Rone's castle, and then taking the road past the still sleeping town. Soon the last of the rooftops disappeared in the early morning mist, and we were off on another journey, which promised to take us all the way to Bonneville, the capital city of Bois—the biggest parish in the entire province and the place where the Duke held his court.

Chapter 25

SEVERAL LEAGUES outside Sirone, our path turned east and for a while carried us toward the coastal province of Pullie, eventually slanting back north and staying on that course until the end of the day, taking us directly to Bonneville. Entrusted with the letter and cautioned by the latest incident back at the castle, we did not want to take any risks and chose to take the main road, which was the safest and the fastest route north, well-traveled and often patrolled by local men-at-arms. Around us fields and gardens that had accompanied us from the outskirts of the town slowly faded and left the ground to low bushes and stunted trees that became more frequent further into the voyage. In time the cultivated lands disappeared completely, and scenes of wilderness took their place, making the landscape quiet and seemingly peaceful. In such serenity we rode until dusk and then veered off the road, stopping several hundred cubits into a field protected from one side by a rim of old pines.

Although I had enjoyed the ride at first, after many leagues in the hard awkward saddle the pain began to consume my body, and as my feet touched the ground, I finally understood how sore my every limb was. Walking alone made me screech, and after using all my will to secure my horse and unroll the heavy blanket, I dropped to the grass, refusing to move again. Except for Minia, everyone suffered too, our swears and moaning sounding through the evening, turning our mood so sour that after eating a quick dinner, we lay in our beds in silence, surrendering to the pain and fatigue.

The morning that came was as uneventful as the evening before it, and was followed by a whole day of a monotonous ride, which was concluded by another night in the open field. Next day, still stuck long way from our destination, we continued on, our ride tainted by the worsening weather. Although it did not rain, the air turned cold and the piercing wind picked up from the west, keeping us company until dusk, becoming even stronger as we entered a wide shallow valley. When darkness eventually fell onto the land, we sought cover in nearby trees, which we spotted a short distance away, and shielded by the crowns of young green foliage, went to sleep, once done with a quick supper and some light talk.

Swathed in gloom, four shapes crawled cautiously toward the flickers of a distant campfire. Sounds of their steps melted unanswered in the surrounding darkness. Unseen, they drew closer to sleeping men, who lay near a burning fire, wrapped in their thick blankets. Rutcker peered hard as he moved, but was still too far away to see his target. Although he had been given a detailed description of the poor fellow he had to slay, he did not bother picking him from the group of six, as it was easier to kill the entire party; that way he did not have to worry about losing his pay.

Counting on the surprise of his forthcoming strike and his experience of many years as a hired sword, he was confident that the task was an easy one. Picking his steps through a thick line of low bushes, he inspected the ground before him and then took his men closer to the camp, soon bringing them to the very edge of the lit circle that ran around the fire. Throughout there were no useless movements or pointless sounds that could have disturbed the resting company, which made Rutcker pleased.

Indeed, that night he was in a particularly good mood. A seemingly easy assignment that fell into his lap promised to yield a hefty payoff. Only two weeks ago he had been sitting in Bonneville's Lion Heart Tavern, trying to find something to do; when two strangers came to him and offered an opportunity that was hard to pass. In exchange for killing some farm kid from the southern town of Villone, who had been traveling in a company of equally young pals, the mysterious men promised four hundred silver coins—four hundred silvers—a truly good trade, which would give him enough money to pay off all of his debts and then enjoy his life as he pleased for at least a year.

Although Rutcker did not have a committed crew, he agreed to take the job anyway, and once the advance payment was in his pocket, he went on to recruit some cutthroats to carry out the task. After checking several local taverns he quickly built up a band of fifteen men, composed of twelve local thugs, whom he split into three groups, and three hired swords from the south, who belonged to the renowned order of Snake Bites. After giving each of the men the description of the target and paying them small installments, he sent the groups out into different directions, so they could cover as much ground as possible, paying particularly close attention to the three main trade routes south of Bonneville.

His plan was simple. One of his teams would find the country boy, kill him, and return with the victim's head to the capital. Then Rutcker would take the trophy from his men and present it to the employers, who would surely pay him the rest of the reward. Since he was the only one in contact with the employer there was no need for him to worry about his associates double-crossing him on the deal. It was a perfect strategy. On one hand it was an effective way to track the target in the unfamiliar lands, and on the other, it ensured him that he would get the prize no matter which of the men completed the assignment.

Rutcker himself took on the main southern route, which ran across the province to the border of Westalia, and along with a team of three local thugs set out on a hunt, trying to be as discreet as possible. As if luck had not given him enough, on the eighth day of his search he spotted a band of youths on their way to Bonneville. Although not completely certain, Rutcker's intuition told him that he had found his man. And since none of the other groups had reported any finds yet, he followed the young rovers, observing them from afar, keeping away from their unsuspecting sights in the covers of distant hills and forests. Still, to make sure that he was tracking the right men, Rutcker decided to postpone his assault and trailed after the youngsters for another day, concealing his every move. By the time the second night rolled in, Rutcker was convinced he had his target, and then it was just a matter of time before he could finish the job and get back to Bonneville to collect the reward.

A little after midnight Rutcker made his men move out toward the distant camp. As he walked down the field, his face lit up in a smile and he murmured, "Four hundred silvers. I should definitely start spending more time in this kingdom. If I can get requests like this twice a year, I will be set for life."

That pleasant thought soaked comfortably into his mind. He grinned even wider and drew his long dagger. Although to get to the camp he was forced to leave the shelter of the woods and venture into the open, fortune smiled on him again, as that night the sky was particularly dark, with clouds enveloping the moon and stars, giving him and his men a perfect cover to mask their every move.

From afar a strong wind started to pick up, hitting Rutcker in the back. For a moment he worried that the breeze would carry his scent across the camp and alert the horses that stood by the sleeping men, chewing on grass. But the animals did not seem to notice them. He only needed a few moments, Rutcker thought. It would be over soon enough. A soft whistle, which mocked a nighttime birdcall, sounded across the valley, and his three men advanced forth, creeping through the last line of vegetation.

"Easy…. Easy. A few more cubits, and…"

A loud snap of something breaking ripped through the air like a razorblade. Rutcker immediately looked back, peering into the dark, thinking that it was one of his men who broke the silence. But he was mistaken. The noise did not come from behind. No. It came from the camp. He turned back toward the camp and quickly realized that something was amiss. The men at the camp were no longer asleep. They were yelling and moving, swords in hands; one of them charging straight at him.

Desperately Rutcker tried to recoup, but it was too late…

The piercing sound of a splintered wood echoed through the valley. It felt that the snap came from somewhere close. I opened my eyes. Was it a vision or did I hear something? I thought to myself and listened. When no more strange noises drew near, I flipped to the other side and jerked back, as leaning close to me was Minia. He stood with his sword drawn, his left foot stamping a broken twig, which I suspected was the source of the disturbance. His eyes were focused on the darkness ahead, one hand closed on the hilt, and the other on my shoulder.

"I think we have company," Minia said aloud, and nodded toward the black grass field behind me.

"What company?" I muttered, tracing the squire's glance.

"There is someone out in the field," explained the squire and moved away from me, peering ahead. Meanwhile the others in the camp woke up too, voicing their questions as they climbed to their feet. Next to me, Ric and Ike stumbled toward the edge of the lit circle, their weapons drawn. And across from the camp, Rob and Ark picked up their gear, quickly realizing that they had fallen asleep during their watch.

"Cursed fire, I was dead asleep," exclaimed Ark, looking around, his eyes still half closed.

All of a sudden another shuffling noise came, this time from somewhere outside the camp. Alarmed we all jumped up, but as the light from the fire made a sharp contrast with the rest of the landscape, creating an invisible wall of blackness around us, we could not pick out much from further than five cubits away and had to step out of the lit circle, moving after Minia, who had started swiftly toward something or someone concealed by the night. Once our eyes got used to the murky shadows, we too spotted four creeping shapes in the grass some distance away. Instantly, I felt a light jolt. Rutcker! My vision—it was real. My Fore Sight, it was trying to warn me. A sense of clear danger punctured through my wits—Rutcker, the name belonged to the man, who wanted to kill me, the man, who I knew was out there in the dark, just a few cubits away. Without delay I unsheathed my shadow dagger and shouted, "Watch out! It is an ambush!"

"I see them! Me too. There. There are three of them. No, four."

My friends' shouts filled the air; our blades reflecting the fire and our eyes fixed on our targets, four creeping shapes a couple of leaps away.

Just like a few nights before, confusion filled my mind. Unable to think straight I stood frozen on the spot. But when I saw Minia charge the nearest opponent, clarity returned and I rushed after him, my alien sword raised high. By the time I reached the squire, he was already swinging his weapon, throwing himself at the intruder, who managed to dodge the squire's blow and jumped back, defending the ground with his own long dagger. Three other enemies were on their feet too. Their swords unsheathed, they darted to assist their comrade and rolled into our ranks, dispersing us across the field, sending a hail of blows at our newly acquired armor.

Ike and I were pushed aside by one of the assailants, who pressed us hard with two short swords. Another foe was fighting Ark and Rob, circling around them, trying to take their left flank, and next to him the fourth fellow with a thin rapier harassed my brother, forcing Ric to retreat toward the fire, warding off persistent strikes with his massive axe, its blade almost glowing in the dark. At one moment it looked like my brother would not last. As his right foot caught a small turf knoll, he stumbled back and almost fell, barely keeping his balance and completely lowering his guard. Seizing the moment his opponent launched at him, but his own foot slipped and the enemy skidded across, dangerously close to Ric, who immediately used the opportunity to strike. He threw himself forth and swung at the man who had been besieging him just moment before. Unable to react in time, the enemy caught the heavy blow right in his rib cage, which instantly cracked open and let out a heart-breaking low thump, engulfing the soil with a stream of maroon blood. Although the man was still alive, he could not fight anymore. Holding on to the gashing wound, he staggered several times and then dropped to his knees, moaning loudly, calling for the Spirit's help. But his pleas remained unanswered as my brother's axe came flying from above one more time, crushing the man's unprotected skull, sending the villain to the grass, face first.

Meanwhile Ike and I were still trying desperately to win our bout. Even though it was two on one, our opponent was well versed in the art of fighting. Then again our numbers took their toll. As I continued to hack from my shoulder with full force, Ike moved further left and found a perfect moment to drive his blade deep into the man's torso, making him jerk backwards, allowing me to land my own sword at the attacker's neck. That time I did not miss. My sword hit the man's soft flesh, and a huge bleeding slit appeared above his shoulder. The strike was clearly the final one. The intruder went down like a bag of stones and stayed there, his weapon frozen in his hand. I did not even check if the enemy was dead, because I was already running to assist Rob and Ark, whose fight was not yet over.

By the time Ike and I made it to our friends' position, Ric was there too, making our chances of winning even higher. With odds of five on one, it was our victory. Even so, wary of the danger posed by the foe, we encircled the intruder without striking. The man did not attack either, but waved his sword in front of him, moving as we did, watching us, his hands shaking slightly. At last Rob dared a quick leap, which made the man jolt backwards. Yet, instead of safer ground further away, the foe found Ike's cold steel, which drilled swiftly into the man's back, making him squeal in pain. His knees buckled, and he slid to the ground dead, leaving us with only one more attacker, who had been battling Minia at the other side of the camp, retreating from the rest of the melee toward the old dry broken logs.

Unlike the other enemies, Minia's opponent was a skillful fighter, demonstrated by his almost perfect moves and posture. He had already knocked off one of the squire's weapons and was pushing hard to nail our companion to the rough surface of the trunk, robbing him of any means of escape. The plan would have worked if it were not for our hasty arrival. As the foe was about to launch his final assault, our five figures rose behind him and made him turn. Yet he was not surprised. Before we could attack he retreated into the field and took up a defensive position several cubits away from the light of the fire, robbing us of a clear sight. Unable to see the enemy well, we took caution pursuing him. While Ike and I followed after the attacker, the others circled around him, taking the flanks. For several moments we continued to dance around the enemy. Then Ike's quick swing distracted him, and Rob's hurled axe fell onto the man's back. An all too familiar thumbing sound came out of him, and another lifeless body plunged before us.

As quick as it had begun the fight was over. The enemy was vanquished; still we continued to keep our defensive positions, waiting for more enemies to spring out of the darkness. But none came, and as the silence settled in the air, our senses slowly calmed. My breathing soothed, and once my hands stopped shaking, I glanced around me. Amidst the darkness, four motionless figures lay in the grass, trampled by several pairs of feet, fear and pain still discernible in their last expressions. One of the slain, the man who had fought Minia, was slouched just at my feet, his face cool, his eyes opened—pupils staring at the sky. Indeed it was the face from my dream. Rutcker—I pronounced the name in my mind, and as I did, a sudden stream of images came over me, taking me away, back in time to the moment when my vision ended with the hired sword glaring at our camp.

Rutcker jumped out of his hideout, struggling to keep his balance. The element of surprise he had been counting on vanished in a trice, and a seemingly well-planned operation turned into a disaster. Hastily he took up the defensive position and got ready for the first of the enemies to arrive, regretting things that had brought him to that place—his greed, his impatience, his poor choice of companions, and his light-headiness. Alas it was too late for such remorse. The time came to stand his ground.

When the closest of the six men came with his swords drawn, Rutcker sprang forward and pulled out his second blade, hoping his men did not abandon him. If those thugs of his were half as good as they had claimed to be, the four of them had a good chance against the youths' greater numbers. A few fast moves, some dodging, and the fight would be theirs, and also the grand prize of four hundred silvers. Rutcker moved forth to meet his opponent.

As his description said, the fellows he was facing were ordinary peasant boys, country folks who did not know a single thing about swords. He, on the other hand was a fair swordsman who had had his share number of duels and skirmishes, in which he had always come on top. The man in front of him was nothing much to look at—a simple stable boy of average size, a little short and not too fast. Rutcker smiled to himself and confident in his strengths tightened his grip. But as his first blow landed astray, he realized that his rival was also a decent fighter who knew his ways with the blades. Yet he was no master, and so Rutcker continued to press on, slowly gaining ground, eventually managing to knock away one of his opponent's daggers. His intuition told him that he was close to winning. Another charge and he would triumph. He only needed a little bit of time.

Alas it was time he did not have. As he was preparing for his final attack, enemies suddenly swarmed him like bees about their hive. The situation was quickly turning grim. Desperately Rutcker tried to find his men, but could not see them anywhere. Where are those stupid halfwits? he thought. Why do not they come to my aid? Then he realized—his companions were either dead or gone, and he was just one man. He also understood there was nothing he could do but surrender. His enemy did not look like a ruthless type. Maybe he could strike a deal with them; he still had plenty of silver coins, stashed away under his vest. He was ready to offer it all. Heck, he was even willing to go to the Barrier Wall and serve his twenty years there. He just did not want to die in that cold backward place they called Bois.

Raising his sword up, Rutcker opened his mouth, wanting to cry out words of submission, but they never left his lips as a thin line of steel flashed before his eyes. He backed up to avoid the swing, but as he stepped away, a sudden overwhelming pain pierced through his spine and quickly filled his entire body, sending him toward the ground screaming. An uneasy sense of fear consumed his mind, and he could feel his life streaming away. A moment later everything went dark and quiet. There was no more pain, no sounds of battle, and no worries; there was nothing…

The images suddenly seized. I shook my head, somewhat confused by what I had just seen. The lifeless body of the hired sword was still at my feet. Nearby, trying to control their emotions, my friends walked around the campsite, gesturing, shouting, and breathing hard. Although there were no more enemies hiding in the grass, they were still watching the dark pasture, weapons drawn and blood stirring.

"Who in the world are these guys?" Ike asked then.

Not waiting for an answer, he kneeled down to examine one of the dead that lay at the other side of the lit clearing, and opened the stranger's cloak so to expose his leathered torso. At the same time my brother came over too and poking the motionless foe with the tip of his axe, asked, "Where did they all come from?"

"They were hiding along the west side," replied Minia, who went over to pick up the weapon he had lost during the fight.

"How many were there?" asked Ike, still crouching, his hands on his knees.

"I counted four bodies," replied Minia. "If there were more, they have already fled. I do not think they will be coming back."

The squire deliberated for a moment and then added, "This attack worries me greatly. Last time there was one man, then two, and now—four. Such a tendency does not leave me with a good feeling. Like the other attacks, this ambush was no simple incident. Someone is after us, and I suspect the further we get, the more desperate our hidden enemy will become. Let's hope we will get to Bonneville before that someone succeeds in his malevolent plan, whatever it is."

"Should we expect another ambush?" Ike's tone was tainted with a hint of fear.

"Though I do not think anyone will attack us tonight, it is best if we find another campsite. Just in case…," Minia said thoughtfully. He leaned over the slain man, and opening several pockets on the bloodied vest, added, "Before we go, let's check the bodies for any clues and then bury them. They may be our enemies but they are in the Spirit's realm now, we should not deny them their trials in the afterlife."

With those words, Minia searched through the body, motioning for us to inspect the other three, which we did, though with little pleasure.

Within half an hour we were done. Then Minia ordered us to gather around the fire that was still burning with small flames and pulled out a sizable pouch of dark green velvet, emptying its contents in his hands—a small folded letter and many silver coins all with the sigil of Lombardian Royal Treasury.

"Another band of mercenaries," Minia finally announced, and lifted his hands up so everyone could see the silvers.

"How much is it?" I asked, startled by sight of so much wealth.

"There must be at least fifty coins," noted Ric, looking over my shoulder.

"Sixty-two, to be exact," conveyed Minia, then put the coins back into the pouch and unfolded the letter. He paused for a while and once the silence was crisp, continued, his voice low and grim. "This note holds numbers, calculations of some sort. Although it does not say what purpose the figures serve, my guess is that these are the amounts promised and spent. Knowing as much I do about hired swords I think that the coins make up an initial deposit of a total sum of four hundred silvers."

"Four hundred?" we all exclaimed at once.

"It is a hefty sum," agreed Minia, "which means that whoever is after you is not poverty-stricken and does not hesitate to put a good price on your heads."

"But who is he? Who is the one wishing our deaths?" I exclaimed, my nerves so tense that I was ready to burst from anger and frustration.

"I did not find any clues as to who their employer was, but I can tell you a little about the men themselves. Three of the fellows were locals, probably from Bonneville, regular dwellers of the underworld, nothing special. Most likely, they were hired on the spot, lured by decent pay. I would not be surprised if they had never even seen their true employer. As for the fourth fellow, it looks like he was another hired sword, definitely not from Bois, possibly a Snake Bite, but most probably a freelancer, someone who traveled the world in search of work and easy money. Many come from Azoros, others from Lombardia and the Free Cities. It is hard to tell where this lad is from exactly. But it does not really matter, because he is just the weapon and not the wielder.

"He did not care who we were, or why he had to kill us. All he wanted was money. If my assumptions are correct he met his employer somewhere in a big city, not too far from here, Bonneville, Pullie, or maybe Nori'l. After accepting the offer he put together a team and set out on a hunt, looking for us or someone very akin. Whatever the case, we won't get any answers from him now. Instead we must go to Bonneville. Perhaps someone there has heard or seen something. Besides we can always ask the city watch or the castle guards, or maybe one of the Duke's captains for help. I am sure they will assist us."

As I listened to the squire, unsettling thoughts hounded me. After the latest assault, there was no doubt in my mind that somebody was trying to kill us. Who—remained a mystery. But I had a feeling I would find out more soon enough.

After wandering the campgrounds for a little longer, we gathered our things and saddled up, soon leaving the cursed fields along with four shallow graves as reminders of the recent fight. Back on the road, the darkness was thick, but we stayed on our course for several hours, until we realized that we needed rest. Too tired to continue, we veered off again, that time paying close attention to the seemingly serene landscape, and halted for the second time. There was no fire, no talk, and no blankets. We slept on the bare ground, keeping watch two at a time.

In the morning we woke up to find out that the night had passed without any complications. Dawn was near, yet the sky above was grim, swathed in large gray clouds, which hid the sun and the warmth behind their thick veil. It was cold and windy, and my body ached from the hard bedding, which seemed to have drained most of my vigor as if it was rainwater. Slowly I rubbed my numb limbs and climbed to my feet, picking up my weapon, kept unsheathed through the night. Nearby, Minia was working on breakfast, and the rest of the company were preparing their horses. It was a dull start—chilly wind, a tasteless meal, hard saddles, and the memory of the brutal fight.

Chapter 26

THE REST of that day we spent on the grimy road. Well into our journey, I started to notice some changes in the landscape, and soon the flat grassy pastures that had followed us for a while gradually became shallow hills. Later, lines of wheat fields and orchards began to spring up ahead, marking our final approach to the city of Bonneville. By midday, we arrived at an open junction where we turned east and traveled in that direction until we came up to a stumpy hill that blocked our view. Over it we went and at the summit found ourselves before a stretch of long wide valley, covered with many houses of various shapes, colors, and sizes.

If just several leagues away there were hardly any voyagers, from up top, I could see the outskirts of Bonneville were filled with rows of little buildings, lines of wooden fences, gardens, and hundreds of stirring dots, that were people, wagons, and livestock, all moving in long noisy and seemingly unorganized streams of traffic. Minia later explained that the reason our route was empty was because the road we had taken was not a commercial one, and for the most part was used by local folks, who rarely left their nested homes. Unless there was some business to conduct, merchants and travelers who happened to voyage to southern Normandia usually took different roads. Those loped around wild pastures of Bois, running along the province's western borders, and were more suitable for trade and leisure.

While Villone was considered to be a place of decent size, it was no match for the provincial capital with its crowded streets, lavish shops, mansions, colorful gardens, and the huge castle of the Duke, located in the very heart of the city and now vaguely visible through a thick gray haze that hung over the big parish. The sight of the city was so grand our company halted and for a while remained still, gazing ahead, down the slope, and into a vivid crowd, where other journeymen joined together on their way to the city. Only when Minia's loud whistle snapped us out of our amazement, did we start to move again, picking our way through the heavy flow of traffic and toward the outer rim of Bonneville.

As it was already too late to see the Duke—or so Minia said—once we had passed under a tall brick gatehouse and entered one of the streets, we started on a search for a suitable place to spend the night. Of course to me it sounded a little strange that we had to wait until the next morning to deliver the message, especially since the hermit and the lord, both, told us how important it was to deliver the dispatch as quickly as possible. But Minia promptly explained that the Duke was a busy man and had specific times assigned for people like us, some hours in the morning and then a few more in early afternoon. And since the rules were the rules, we had to postpone our visit for another day. Instead we rode after Minia through the city's narrow alleys, soon reaching a large three-storied green building with a wooden sign hanging high from its side, that read, "The Valiant Knight Inn—always here to ease your tired souls."

At the front door, which was made of thick logs, we stopped and Minia jumped from his horse. "We will stay here for tonight. It is a decent place, good meals and fair prices." The squire gave the straps of his horse to Rob and ran inside, reemerging a little after, accompanied by a group of stable boys, who grabbed our horses, and once we had dismounted and picked up our bags, took the animals around the corner. Meanwhile we piled into an anteroom that was nothing more than a small square foyer with four large archways carved in each of the walls. Straight ahead a short corridor led up to a wide staircase that ran up to sleeping quarters on the upper levels. To our left, another arcade was blocked by a grate of solid iron bars, behind which peered a sizable storage room, probably used by guests to stow some of their bulkier gear. And to the right, a wider opening displayed a view of a spacious dining hall—a long rectangular room with a dozen long timber tables set in two rows, seating at least ten people each. Along one side ran a high counter that served as a reception stand for new patrons to pay for their rooms and as a divider that separated an open kitchen, which unlike most other places, was not situated in a detached room, but rather was a part of the dining area. There several cooks and servants labored hard to fix countless meals, accompanying their preparations with noise and clatter. Amongst them, sitting contentedly in a large padded armchair, observing his staff and guests, towered a tall blonde man, who was the owner of the establishment.

As there were very few people, most of the tables and benches were empty and clean. We quickly picked up a vacant table, across the kitchen near a plastered wall, with a closed round window. Hard wooden benches felt awkward, but it was still better then the hard leather saddle, which made my lower body sore and blistered.

"I have already arranged three rooms, hot baths, and some food for us," said Minia, when all of us were at the table, pushing our bags under it so nobody could get to them without our noticing. The squire raised his hand and gave a signal to one of the cooks, who quickly nodded and ordered some of the servants to pick up their trays. While the food was being delivered, Minia went to explain our plans for the next day. "Tomorrow we will go to the Duke. The visiting hours start at ten. But we should come there earlier so we can get in line before the others. You never know how many people decide to see the High Lord. I think it is best if tomorrow we meet here in the morning. I am sure you all will appreciate a couple of extra hours of rest, which, by the way, does not mean you can waste the night at some local pub."

Minia observed us with an unyielding glance. "For those of you who do decide to seek some adventures, there are plenty of spots in the vicinity of the Valiant Knight. If you are in the mood to lose some of your money, there is a coin toss game here at the inn at nine. For more exotic amusement, there is also a large fair, where country folk, like yourselves, can find plenty to look at—cockfights, flame throwers, street performers, and spectacles, money games of all sorts, and foreign dancers. Some entertainments are free of charge, others are pricey, but it should be interesting nonetheless. Should you decide to go there, take the main street toward the Duke's castle. When you come to the first plaza with the fountain, turn left and follow the avenue until you reach the fairgrounds. Be careful though, this is a big city. There are plenty of shady characters lurking around the streets, and it is easy to get into some unneeded troubles, especially with so much strangeness going on."

Minia gave us another serious look. "Any questions?"

"Ah, do we have to pay for anything here?" asked Ike curiously as he saw the food arrive to the table.

"Since you are here on the lord's official business, his estate will take on all your expenses for lodging and provisions, which means you do not have to pay for your rooms, meals, or gear while on duty. Anything else will come out of your own pockets."

"I kind a think that if we drink some ale here it will be a legitimate expense, will it not?" said Ike, grinning. But Minia's response was unexpectedly firm. "No, it will not, drinking ale until you pass out does not relate to your duties. If there are no *more* questions, Ike, I suggest we start with our meal."

There were no more questions. Instead we turned to the food, the main course composed of large chunks of roasted pig, served with fried apples, onions and seasoned carrots, two big plates of sliced fresh rye, soft moist goat cheese, strips of smoked veal, three jars of cider, and some sweet mixture of warm honey and herbs to bring out a better mood. Although I did not feel hungry during the trip, when I smelled the cooking spreading across the room, my belly sang a starving tune. To my good fortune, the many flavorsome things on our table were just an arm's reach away and I was quick to send everything into my mouth, several pieces at a time.

When the dinner was over, Minia left us downstairs and went up to his room to prepare for the upcoming audience with the Duke. The rest of us did not feel like resting and thought about things to do with our free evening. As it was still too early we decided to unwind for an hour or so upstairs and then venture onto the unfamiliar streets of the big city. Agreeing to meet downstairs two hours later, we retired to our two rooms—Ike, Ric, and I sharing a larger chamber with a fireplace, while Rob and Ark took a smaller, but cozier place.

Stripped of the tiring chain mail, heavy boots, and weapons, my body could finally relax. After wandering around the room in my tunic and trousers, I then took them off and, wrapping a soft white towel around my waist, went to the end of the hallway, where several large tubs of warm water and scrubs were prepared to help our company to rid of the sweat and dirt, gathered during our days in the countryside. Enjoying a feeling of freshness, I soaked myself until the water got cold, and then return to the room, where a new set of clothes awaited me. I gladly put them on, leaving the dirty attire by the door for the servants to launder before the next morning. Then I lay on the bed, chatting with my brother and Ike, who also had washed up and changed. Unlike me though, they did not want to spend too much time in the room and quickly went downstairs to grab a couple more mugs of local ale. I, on other hand, remained in the room and enjoyed the quiet of the solitude. Only when I felt rested enough, did I slide back into my boots, throw the belt over my waist, with a long dagger attached to it, just in case, and go to the dining hall to join my friends, all of whom were already there, drinking brew and talking to the local girls, most of them servers at the inn. Although the girls did not say much in return, they enjoyed the attention and tossed quick frequent glances back at the table every time they passed nearby.

I drank a glass of cold cider and returned to the discussion of our pastime. Although a coin toss game was an attractive venture, we did not have the money to play it. The silvers we had found on the dead mercenary were promptly surrendered to our commander Minia for the benefit of Sire Rone. So our funds, although enhanced by the lord's will, were moderate at best, and we had only a few coins to spare, which we wanted to save for later times. Watching others play did not sound too appealing either, so we decide to see the fair instead. Although back in Villone fairs came several times during the year, they only lasted for a day or two and were comprised of little festivities, with only a handful of street dancers and performers to put on shows. And even those festivals were often boring, as most of the better performing teams preferred the bigger cities, such as Bonneville, where larger crowds could be drawn. To see a real fair was a treat, and once the first of the coin toss games started in the inn, we hurried onto the street, taking our first nighttime tour of the provincial capital.

The sound of our own cheers escorted us as we strolled along the paved lane, observing the commotion around us, noting all the marvels of city life. Following Minia's directions we reached the first plaza with the fountain and turned, taking a wide avenue to a large open arena packed with all sorts of tents and tables. People of every sort and age crowded the place, laughing, talking, and just watching as countless men and women performed many different acts. At one tent, painted blue and yellow, stood a small pack of several dozen spectators, before whom a fellow dressed in wide red robes was telling some story, accompanying his telling with sliding pictures that came out of a square slit in the tent's wall. When a new image slid into the slot, the crowd applauded, and some even tried to climb up to the low podium to see the picture better. But the man in red robes kindly kept the spectators where they were and continued with his tales, waving his hands and raising his voice.

Further away, on top of a large open wagon, two performers who wore large paper masks and long white capes that dragged after them in long streaks were playing a scene of some love story. The men were jumping and running across the cart, pretending to be a couple in love. People seemed to like their act and cheered loudly, often clapping and whistling. And across from them, occupying another stage, three skinny fellows with bare chests were trying to attract bystanders by tossing long thin torches into the air. Immediately I recognized them as flame-throwers, the men who ate fire. I remembered the first time Father told me about the men who ate fire, describing their show that rivaled even the best of the festivals in Villone, and ever since I always wanted to see those strange men, who made the fire their slave. But since Villone was too small for such entertainers to visit, I never did, not until that evening in Bonneville.

Mesmerized, my friends and I watched as the men before us played with fire, throwing it, eating it, making it spring to life and die. Alas too soon the show was over, and the three men vanished behind a large curtain. For a while a large crowd of spectators remained at the stage, waiting; but then most of them lost patience and walked away. We did too, moving further into the array of tents, spinning our heads like children, following the sandy lanes, often stopping to look at something new. So interesting was the experience at the fair that the hours we spent there went unnoticed. Before long closing time came and as the tents began to shut down, we went back onto the city streets. But we were not ready to hit the hay, and on the way to the inn stopped by several pubs, each time downing more ales and ciders. At last the big city proved overwhelming, and as our vision began to cloud we stopped drinking and retraced our steps back to the large plaza with the fountain and then our street.

By then most of the town folks had already departed for the night, and only a few souls wandered the sidewalks, minding their own business. We were almost at the doorstep of the Valiant Knight when we heard a shoveling noise, coming from an alley that ran off the street along the side of the inn. Paying it little attention at first, we proceeded to the front door, but the sound came again. Finding it odd, we stopped and listened. Hearing nothing, we started up the stairs, but a loud scream for help that erupted through the air made us stop once more. Immediately we sprang back to the pavement and ran along the tavern's facade toward the alley, drawn by the desperate cry, which pointed to some troubles unfolding nearby. As we turned the corner, we quickly saw three murky shapes further in the dark narrow passage. As it was impossible to make out what the men were doing or who they were, we stepped off the lit street and proceeded toward the strangers, keeping our hands on our weapons—just daggers we had taken with us for the stroll around the city. Meanwhile the strangers, who did not seem to notice us, continued with their affairs that did not look like the ordinary course of business. But as we covered half the distance, one of the figures suddenly turned and spotted our approach.

"Hey, what is going on there?" my brother yelled out, alerting the men before they could do anything.

The strangers froze, yet did not answer.

"Is everything all right there? We heard some screaming," continued Rob. The figures continued to keep silent, which made the situation very tense, so tense that I could sense the prospect of a fight.

"We do not want any trouble," my friend added, probably sensing the altercation too. "We just want to check if everyone is all right here."

By the time Rob finished we were almost at the scene, and were about to meet the three men, when two of them suddenly broke off and sprinted into the blackness of the alley, leaving their comrade behind. For a moment the third man stood still in front of us, then stumbled forward and collapsed onto the hard brick pavement. Though it was dark, I could see a small pool of blood oozing from underneath his slouching body. It was clear—the man was hurt.

"Good Spirit, is he dead?" exclaimed Ike. He had tried to give chase, but after several cubits lost his target and came back to check on the remaining stranger.

"I do not know. He does not look alive to me," said Ric, towering over the body.

I knelt down next to Rob, who was already holding the man's hand by the wrist. To our surprise he found a weak, but steady beat under the skin, a hopeful sign of life still lurking in the slouching body.

"He is alive!" exclaimed Rob right away, a note of relief in his voice.

"Come on, help me out; we must get him to the tavern. I am sure there is someone who can help him." Rob climbed back up and grabbed the bleeding man by his shoulders. Ric and I took the stranger's legs, and aided by Ark and Ike, carried him out of the alley and into the inn, where only a few of the late-night patrons were still sipping their ales. Seeing a motionless bloody man in our hands, they dispersed to free a wide passage for us to bring in the body. We placed it on top of one of the tables, packed with half-empty plates.

"Do we have a healer?" shouted Rob through the almost empty room. "We have a wounded man here."

"What is all this noise? What is going on?" The owner appeared from under the counter and came down, escorted by a score of serving boys and girls.

"We have an injured man here," Rob repeated quickly. "Can you help him?"

"What happened?" The owner came over and studied the unconscious fellow, who lay still on the table.

"We heard some screaming outside in the alley next to the tavern. When we got there we found three men, standing in the dark. Two of them ran away once they saw us and this one fell down," explained my friend, rubbing the dried blood from his hands.

"Ah ha. Did you check if he is still alive?"

"Yes, his pulse is weak, but stable."

"Ugh hmm, I suppose none of you have any knowledge of curing. Am I right?"

"Whatever we know will not help him."

"Then step aside, let me see." The owner made us move and leaned over the body. After some mumbling and probing, he raised his head and yelled out.

"Quick, Lori, I need a bucket of warm water, some clean rags, and a couple of dry towels. Simy, you run upstairs and bring me two large green jars from the medicine cabinet. Make sure you take the green bottles and not the blue ones. Susy, go outside and find Master Az; tell him to come over here as soon as he can; tell him it is important. Also if you see a city watch patrol, tell them that we have had another robbery behind my tavern and they should check the alley by the tavern. Now, all of you—hurry."

The three youngsters ran in all directions, tripping over their own feet. Meanwhile the proprietor stripped the wounded man of his cloak, along with the leather vest, and ripped the tunic to examine the wound, which represented a long thin bloody gash across his lower torso. The owner probed the cut with his fingers, then raised his head and yelled again, hurrying the girl he had sent to the kitchen. As his voice echoed through the hall, the serving girl sprinted back into the dining hall, carrying a tall bucket of steaming water, white rags thrown over her shoulder. The owner hastily took one of the towels and proceeded to clean up some of the blood that covered most of the man's chest. Soon came Simy, the serving boy, with two green jars in his hands. He gave the containers to the vendor, who opened one of the bottles and spread a thick creamy substance over the gash, leaving greasy stains on the stranger's clothes and on the table.

While he continued with the procedure, the front door opened and a middle-aged skinny fellow walked into the hall, dragging a small leather case behind him. Poised, the man walked silently to the table and gave the owner a quick nod.

"Oh, Master Az, how kind of you to come over here on such short notice." The owner greeted his new guest and wiped his hands on the side of his tunic.

"What do we have this time, L'iote of Ellis?" asked the visitor.

"Well, the young fellows over here have brought this poor soul with a stomach slashed from side to side. They say they found him in the alley, right around the corner, in the company of two others, who fled the scene as soon as they were seen."

"Ah, another robbery, huh," noted the man by the name of Az. He leaned forward to inspect the wounded stranger.

"The second one this week," complained L'iote. "I am going to lose all my customers if it continues to go this way."

"I do not know what to say, my friend. This is a big problem for all of us. People are afraid to come out at night; some are even scared to stay in there homes. Hopefully the Duke will do something about it, and do something quick."

"You're absolutely right, Master Az. I am sure our lord is working hard to solve this problem, why else would he bring more soldiers into the city?"

The owner looked over at the visitor, who straightened up and rolled up his sleeves, rubbed his palms together, and said, "Let's not waste time, my friend. How far did you get with this man?"

"I cleaned the wound, put on some of your elixir and was about to wrap him up with dry bandages; but now since you are here, I will let you handle the rest."

"Huh, let's see." Az leaned further. "It looks like you did a good job. There is little else I can do. Just soak the cloth strips in my mix before applying them." Az pulled out a small wooden box from his case and opened it. Inside were rows of potions—red, green, blue, and white. After looking at the selection for a moment, Az picked a small red bottle and handed it to the owner.

"Mix it with water."

L'iote immediately poured some of the reddish liquid into a bowl of warm water, and stirred it gently with a wooden spoon. Then he handed the bowl to Az, who placed several strips of white clean cloth in it and let them soak for a little bit. When the laces turned red, he pulled them out and placed them on the open wound, pressing hard with his palms.

"Here. This should prevent it from rotting," said Master Az once done.

"Do you think he will live?" asked L'iote as he took away the bowl and the remaining strips.

"It is hard to say right now, but if he can last until tomorrow, he should be fine," replied the visitor, while examining the man's pupils. Afterwards he wrapped a dry towel over the wound and covered the man's chest with a blanket, which one of the serving girls had also brought from upstairs. "That is all I can do for now," said Az. He stepped back from the table, sighed, and added, "You know, this man is very lucky these lads found him soon enough. A bit longer and there would be no one left to save."

"I just cannot believe this is happening again," repeated the owner, shaking his head, clearly upset.

"And there have been three more attacks by the northern gates too," replied the visitor in a grim tone.

"I just do not know what is going on around here. Our city is getting more dangerous every day. I know we always have had our share of problems in Bonneville, but six murders in just three weeks—this is too much."

"You are right; there has never been so much blood until now. I wonder if it has something to do with the problems in the Border Regions of the Northern Empire. I have heard that some bandits killed a lot of people there. Maybe some of that scum has found their way to our province."

Master Az shook his head and sat down on a chair, stretching his legs, massaging his knees with his hands.

"Well, if they did, I hope our fine lords will do everything to drive them back to where they came from. As I said, they have increased a number of night watchers and there are more guards patrolling the streets too, though it does not seem to help."

L'iote took a seat next to his guest, and leaned on one arm, holding the other at the side of the chair. "I will tell you what the problem is. The Duke allows too many outlanders to stay within the city. Why does he not send them out to the hills? There is plenty of room there. If they want they can live there, for all I care. I just do not want them anywhere near my inn."

"Count yourself lucky, my friend. It is worse in other cities. The capital is swarming with southern kin. Some even say there is not a single inn with a vacant room." Master Az smacked his lips and lit up a long pipe, which immediately began to smolder, exhuming puffs of gray smoke into the air.

For a while the two men talked about their worries and unpleasant changes that plagued the provincial capital in the past few months. Although we had many questions about what we were hearing, we did not ask any of them, and instead listened to the owner and his guest. But before they could cover all the things that troubled them, the front door opened and three heavily armed fellows staggered into the dining hall. The three appeared to be local city watchers, who duly displayed their uniforms, red in color with symbols of the city gates painted on the front. Their tunics were thrown over long ring mails that fell down almost to the men's knees; at their sides long swords hung off thick belts with the same imprints of the city gates on their buckles.

There was no exchange of greeting. Standing in the entryway, the guards studied everyone with distrust, their glances running across our faces and to the wounded man. Then they strolled to the table and one of them took off his iron-cast helm, revealing the face of an aged man, rugged and sharp. His eyes, gray, almost colorless, were fixed on the wounded.

"We have received news that someone was attacked in here," said the guard abruptly and turned to Master Az, who got up slowly and bowed.

"Not here, in the alley around the corner," corrected L'iote, who also rose to his feet and leaned forth in a slight bow.

"Huh, and who might you be?" asked the soldier addressing the vendor.

"Me, I am the owner of this establishment. L'iote of Ellis is my name."

"I see. Go on then, tell me about this attack."

"There is really nothing much to tell. Someone tried to kill this man, but failed," explained the proprietor, and he pointed at the man. "There were two robbers or whoever they were. When caught, they ran away, leaving their victim lying in the alley."

"You say that all this happened in the alley. Then what is he doing in here on this table?"

"These young men brought him." L'iote pointed to us and added, "They are the ones who saw the whole thing."

The guards turned toward us and smirked. "So, you have seen everything, have you not?"

"We did," I replied hastily and started to recount the same story we had told L'iote and Master Az. But almost immediately I had to stop as the soldier cut me off. "Hold on, lad. First state your names and purpose of being in Bonneville."

"My name is Mishuk Loyde and these are my fellow companions. We are squires in the service of our lord, Sire Rone from the town of Sirone. We have come here on orders to deliver a personal message to the Duke. If you need to know more ask our commander, Minia of Emil, who is upstairs at the moment. He will tell you everything you want to know." To prove my words I moved aside my cape and displayed the colored tunic that adorned my chest.

"Squires, you say," said the soldier, quickly noting my uniform. "It is nice to see someone from a soldiery handling this." The guard paused for a moment. When he continued, his disposition changed. "Aerie of Lak, Sergeant at Arms with the second regiment of the city watch." The man gave a salute. I replied in the same manner, after which the guard returned to the subject of the recent incident in the alley, "Now, tell me what happened out there."

I resumed my story, telling Aerie everything I remembered. Throughout he listened carefully, and once I was done, said, "Indeed, it sounds like a robbery. We will search the nearby streets and see if we can find anything. In the meantime, you should stay here; our chief may want to ask you some questions once he is finished with other duties."

"As you say, Sergeant. We will remain here until your superior arrives," I assured the guard, after which Aerie waved his hand and together with the other two soldiers left the hall. When the city watchers were gone, Master Az and L'iote sat back in their seats, both looking at us.

"Squires, huh," the owner said slowly, and Master Az added, "I must say you have done a fine job today. If everything goes well, you may have saved this fellow's life tonight. I am sure he will appreciate it once he gets his sense back."

"He will live then, will he not?" asked Ike. The healer let out a long sigh. "Perhaps....It is up to him. Let's just say that if he is strong enough he will pull through, otherwise there is nothing else we can do for him. Do not feel too bad though. You have done everything you could, and so did I."

When the pause settled in the hall again, I suddenly felt tired. My back started to hurt and I wanted to sleep. Unable to hold off the fatigue for long, I politely excused myself and departed to the room, leaving my friends and our new acquaintances downstairs, who were busy preparing the injured man to be carried into one of the empty rooms in the back of the kitchen.

Lying in bed, I shut my eyes, worrying less and less about the wounded stranger and other perils of the day. Yet the rest I desired so much did not last for long. In its place came another vision, the Fore Sight came to life again.

Traveling through the familiar dark tunnel, I floated toward the light, and once there, found myself standing at one end of a large assembly hall, surrounded by high clear polished walls and crowned with an arched painted ceiling, embellished with pictures of some epic battle from the past. The place was so ample and empty that only the sound of my own footsteps echoed over the floor tiles. Alone, I wandered down the hall, heading toward the other end, where I could see a large throne and a row of long low benches placed before it. Almost at the center, I suddenly heard some noises from behind and stopped. Quickly turning I saw a group of five men walking toward me, their pace steady and fast.

At first I wanted to hide, but the men were too close for me to escape their attention. I knew they had seen me already. But then I realized that it was not so. The strangers did not seem to notice my presence. I was invisible to them and they passed me by without even dropping a glance. Relieved, I started after the men, trying to listen to what they were saying. A few more steps and I was close enough to hear—the five men, who clearly were Normandian nobles, were talking of troubles that had been brewing between the kingdoms of the Northern Empire and Lombardia.

The two nations were never friends. In truth they had a long and violent history, filled with countless wars and border disputes, which brought sorrow to many generations of men. Once a part of Lombardia, the Northern Empire had come to exist as a result of a war between Lombardia and Normandia, which took place five hundred years back. A bitter dispute that started off as a simple feud between bordering lords lasted for over fifty years and ended with a complete Normandian victory at the battle of White Water Lakes. As the aftermath of the triumph, the Normandian king had annexed a part of the Lombardia territory that he later split into two parts. The lands that bordered Normandia the king granted to his sworn men, the knights of the kingdom, who had fought so bravely for their realm. And in the areas that lay closer to Lombardia he created a buffer, creating a new nation, called the Northern Empire, that separated the rival sides and insured a safe passage through the land.

At first the Northern Empire lived under the tutelage of the Normandian kings, but as time passed the new nation claimed its sovereignty and became free of its creator. Although the new rulers swore to uphold a neutral state, not taking arms against either Lombardia or Normandia, their promise was short-lived. As it so often happens, twenty years after its founding the Northern Empire allied itself with distant Amber Empire, located in the Southern part of Ethoria, and launched a war campaign against one of its neighbor, Lombardia, from which it was eager to seize more land and wealth. After four years of bloody battles, Lombardia was defeated again and forced into another humili-ating treaty. And ever since these two nations have been on the worst of terms, their kings and common folks alike have hated each other with passion.

That night, standing unnoticed in the unknown grand hall, I learned that the war may have returned to the Border Regions, the troubled area of the Northern Empire that shared a frontier with Lombardia in the south and in the north was cut off from the rest of the empire by the mighty river of Great Bound. The men before me were discussing alarming reports delivered from abroad, that described disturbing incidents, which had been taking place along the border between the two nations—numerous attacks on passing caravans and villages, each assault swift and brutal, with no survivors or witnesses that could have helped to solve the crimes.

Despite all the efforts to protect the vital trade routes, the local Imperial nobility found itself fighting a losing battle. With no assailants ever caught, attacks persisted, upsetting the normal course of trade throughout the north-eastern regions of Ethoria, making many of the traders and rovers scared and concerned. It was no surprise that after several weeks of disturbance some in the Northern Empire started to point fingers at the neighboring Lombardia—which of course denied any ties to the unsettling events. Yet, despite all refutations, the tension escalated and had reached the point where the court of the Northern King, Uiris Fromnask, began to talk about a probable drive against their wicked neighbor, retaliation for the problems sent to their realm.

If a war was to break out again, the whole northern part of Ethoria would fall into disorder as most of the inland trade routes would be cut off, making the flow of trade cease. Such a prospect was not very welcome to the Normandian lords, whose many treasuries depended on foreign trade. And so the men inside the hall were worried about the future and wanted to send someone to the stressed borderlands, so they could learn more about the unsettling events.

As for me, at that time I cared little for troubles in some distant land. Instead I was concerned with another question. What did it all have to do with me? I wished the vision had been clearer. I wished I knew how to interpret what I saw. But my Fore Sight remained elusive. For how long, I did not know— but did I ever…?

Part II

Ethoria's Chronicles

The Shadows of the Past

Chapter 27

MINIA AND I were the only people left in the room; everyone else who had been waiting for an audience with the Duke had either spoken with the lord or gone home, hoping to come back some other day. We had our orders and had to sit in the long wide foyer until closing time, which was a little after midday break. Although I considered our matter to be of the highest importance, the Duke's councilors, in charge of the visitations, decided otherwise. As we waited for our turn to speak with Sire Tem, the anticipation and excitement that had filled me earlier in the morning left me. After long hours of sitting, I did not care much for the Duke or his entourage, composed of numerous pages, servants, guards, and nobles, who squabbled in the long hallways of the meeting quarters of the castle.

It was my first lesson in the local bureaucracy, and I could not say I was too pleased with it. First, the guards downstairs refused to let everyone from our company through the main gates, insisting that there were just too many of us and we had to pick two representatives to go inside. So Minia and I went, while the rest headed back to the inn, where they passed time amongst traveling folks of all kinds, awaiting our return. Then, Minia and I had to stand in a long line and watch almost everyone else go before us. As Minia explained later, it was because all visitors who came to see the Duke were sorted according to the their wealth and place on the social ladder. The most distinguished of the lords were always granted audiences first; then came the younger and less decorated knights, followed by other members of nobility—wives, widows, children. Once all the upper class had gone through, merchants, traders, and collectors were allowed to proceed with their cases, forming a long, noisy line before the large oak doors, guarded by four sets of well-armed guards. After the men of coin came squires and messengers, like us, each with orders to convey some sort of dispatch or news to the Duke. Hosts of townsmen and commoners concluded the procession. The simple folks were not allowed to sit with the others and had to pass their time in separate waiting quarters, located several floors down and guarded by more men-at-arms. Needless to say, not too many of them got their chances to see the lord on any given day and had to spend several days, hoping for the audience with the Duke.

In that exact order, we stayed in line until our turn came. At the very end of the visitation hours the two doors opened up and a figure of young boy, no older than twelve, appeared in the entryway. The lad was one of the Duke's pages and was responsible for announcing and escorting visitors in and out of the meeting hall. After reading something from his long white scroll, he observed the crowd before him and cried out several names, including ours. At first we did not notice the announcement, but when the page repeated his call, we climbed to our feet and walked up to the boy, who met us with a disinterested glance and a fake dry smile. After waiting for the others on the list, he checked our names and rank one more time, and led everyone through the doorway and into a spacious hall, the main audience chamber. The place was grand in design; at least a hundred cubits long and fifty cubits wide, crowded and full of noise.

Without delay we strolled across the polished marble floor and toward a massive throne-chair that towered assertively in the center, situated firmly on top of a large podium that was covered in thick carpet of red and gold. In it sat a man, observing all things below. It was Sire Tem, the Duke of Bois, the High Lord of the province. In all my years I had imagined him to be a man of grand stature, great in size and valor. Yet before me I found a skinny short gentleman whose youth had long left him, peppering his short receding hair and trimmed mustache with streaks of white. Still, in his dark green eyes, which peered from under sweeping thick brows, I saw a true lord, a strong soldier, and a confident ruler, with the province well under his control.

Earlier on, when Sire Tem was a young knight, he served in the king's army; first as a regular knight of the realm, and later as the commander of king's vanguard. Eager to test his worthiness to the king, he took part in several campaigns, which ranged from hunting outlaws to putting down uprisings in the northern province of Puno. It was during those days that the younger Duke proved himself as a fearless soldier and a skilled leader, who, after many good years of service, was promoted to the rank of King's captain and bestowed with the title of Duke, thereby entrusted with the protection of the entire province.

First Sire Tem oversaw matters in Chantue, and then he moved southeast to Bois, where he continued to serve the kingdom, winning respect from common folks and minor lords alike. After all—he kept the province safe, trade flowing, and levies reasonably low, especially in times of drought and flood, quite frequent in the southern regions of Normandia.

Almost at the throne, the page halted and announced our approach in a loud clear voice that carried a high-pitched girlish tone. "Milord. The squires of Sire Rone are here to see you. They are carrying a personal message from their distinguished lord, Sire Rone of Sirone, son of Sire Limo, your sworn man, and the servant to our King."

The young servant bowed and stepped forth, taking Sire Rone's letter from Minia and passing it over to one of the guards, who examined the rolled scroll and, satisfied that it hid no dangers, handed it to the Duke.

The High Lord of Bois quickly opened the dispatch and read through it, occasionally bringing his hand up to his chin, rubbing it a few times with his long fingers, adorned with many rings of fine metal and jewels. Afterwards he whispered something to one of his councilors, who was standing next to the throne, and then gestured for another young man, dressed in silk blue robes, to come over. Instantly the fellow ran up to the podium, and after listening carefully to the Duke's instructions, which were hard to pick out amongst all the noise, disappeared back into the crowd. The Duke then leaned back in his chair, returning his glance to the letter and at us.

"So…," announced the lord in a deep low voice. "You are Sire Rone's squires…"

"Yes, Milord," replied Minia and bowed. I did the same.

"The message you have brought me is…How should I put it?…interesting, and I would like to learn more of the matter it describes. But I do not think this place is the appropriate venue to do so. There are too many eyes and ears that I do not know well."

The Duke looked over the hall, as if proving his point, and said, "I want to move the discussion to a quieter, less crowded place. My servant tells me that you are staying here in town, and I am sure you would not mind coming back here at a later hour. When I am done with other matters, I will send for you; then you will tell me everything about Sire Rone's worries. For now, you are dismissed."

The High Lord raised his hand at which point the same page emerged before us and escorted us back to the foyer. From there we returned to the courtyard and after receiving our weapons back, left the castle grounds, heading for the Valiant Knight.

Back in the inn, the rest of our company was entertaining themselves with a game of wall-throw and a jar of chilled cider, which I suspected was not their first. Once they noticed our late arrival, they overwhelmed us with countless questions, which took some time to respond to, as Minia and I went on to tell all about our visit to the castle.

"Tell us…Did the Duke see you? What did he say? Did he take the letter?" my friends asked as one, bringing much noise into the empty dining hall.

"We saw him all right," I said, lowering myself onto a stool, with still lingering displeasure regarding our treatment at the castle. "We waited for hours, then spoke for a moment, and then were back off into the waiting room."

"Easy, Mishuk," Minia stopped me quickly. "He is a busy man; he has the whole province to worry about. Do you know how many squires he has to see each day? So just let it go."

Minia paused and after the silence was restored proceeded with his report. "Now…We have given the Duke the letter, and he wants to talk to us later today. I do not know how long it will take for him to call for us, but I suggest we do not leave this place, not until we hear something from him. This is not a request; it is an order. If you do not want to stay downstairs, stay in your rooms. Just do not wander outside, not today."

Minia gave us a hard glance. "So, how about some lunch? I assume you did not eat yet, did you?"

"Ah,…No,…just some cider, that's it," answered Rob, trying to sound honest, though his face, as well as the faces of the others, turned instantly from excitement to innocence. I grinned, Minia did too, then leaned back and said, "In that case, let's eat."

Time passed, the afternoon was coming to a close, and there was still no word from the castle. Waiting anxiously we remained downstairs, talking amongst ourselves; our chat interrupted when the back door opened and L'iote walked into the hall, carrying two baskets filled with freshly baked loaves. Noticing our party he put down his load and greeted us with a wave of his hand after which he picked up the baskets again and disappeared behind the counter.

That was the first time I had seen the owner since the previous night. The city watch never came back, and in the morning we were off to the castle. Seeing L'iote brought me back to the incident of the night before.

"How is our wounded? Is he all right?" I asked, sure that my friends had already found out what had happened to that poor fellow we had dragged into the inn.

"I completely forgot!" exclaimed Ike loudly as he slapped himself on the forehead. "He is alive. L'iote says that he has survived the night and now it is only time before he can walk again. He stayed here through the night, but in the morning some people came and took him away. I presume they were servants of some sort."

"Servants?" I sounded more surprised, than interested.

"L'iote said the wounded was some rich kid from Lombardia. Apparently he had come to our kingdom to see the Lake of Wonders and stopped in Bonneville for the night. Of course only Spirit knows what he was doing in that alley at such a late hour. Good thing luck was on his side." Ike shook his head and poured himself another glass of cider, leaning backwards, rocking in his chair, occasionally grabbing onto the edge of the table to keep himself from falling.

"This certainly is good news," said Minia with a sigh of relief. Though he did not witness the incident and only found out about it in the morning, he was concerned for the well-being of the stranger, whom he had not even seen, and was pleased to know that the wounds were not fatal.

"Did anyone happen to catch his name?" he asked then.

"Ah...I think one of the servants mentioned something. What was it? Marey? No. Harey? No," Ike struggled, looking for the answer in his always crowded mind.

"Was it Marley?" Rob tried to help.

"No..." Ike scratched the back of his head.

"I think it was Arley," said Ark next.

"Arley. Yes, Arley. That was his name," announced Ike, proudly and clapped his hands once.

"Arley," repeated Minia. "It does not sound too noble. Oh, well, the important thing is that he is alive."

A little after dusk, with us still in the dining hall, the front door opened again and a younger slender gentleman walked in, shaking off dust from his sleeves. He did not look like a regular of the Valiant Knight, or an outlander traveling from other kingdoms. Dressed in a fine cotton tunic of dark green color, he wore a long black cape, a pair of sturdy leather boots, green trousers, and a velvety beret. His hat was adorned with a round metal pin in the shape of the Duke's family crest and a large white feather that stuck straight up, waving as he moved.

Hesitant, the young man looked around the room, carefully observing each of the patrons, slowly moving his focus through the crowd and to our table. He studied us for a while and then set out in our direction, showing his graceful manners to all who bothered to look. Past several empty benches he came up to Minia and, giving him an all too familiar fake smile, asked, "Hey you. I am looking for a company of squires who are staying here at the inn. Is there any chance you have seen them around?"

The young man threw a quick glance over his shoulder and back at us.

"As a matter of fact, there is such a chance. The party you are looking for is sitting right in front of you," replied Minia, and he lit his face with a similar fake grin. "We are the squires of Sire Rone. My name is Minia Emile, and I am the commander of this band. Can I ask you why you seek us?"

Although Minia knew perfectly well why the youngster had come to the Valiant Knight, the fellow acted so snobby that my commander could not help but give the pampered white-skinned fellow a hard time.

"I am the personal page of Sire Tem, the Duke of Bois," replied the boy firmly. "He has sent me to find you and escort you back to the castle for a private audience."

"How do we know you are telling the truth?" persisted Minia.

"Oh, well, I…," the youngster suddenly began to mumble, clearly startled by the question, "…Everyone knows I am the page, and I have a pin, look." The youngster took off his beret and showed the pin to us.

"Ah, the pin. Of course, how could I miss it? So, what do we have to do?"

"We should leave for the castle. The lord wants to see you as soon as possible."

"We cannot make the Duke wait. Lead the way." Minia rose and we all followed the page onto the street.

Outside the evening breeze was soothing and the sky was clear, with the stars and moon casting soft light onto the paved lane. In short time we made our way to the castle and soon stood before the front gates of the citadel that stretched some fifty cubits over our heads, equipped at the top with many parapets and watchtowers, heavily guarded by scores of armored soldiers, whose bright torches paced back and forth along the walls. At the doors stood more guards, ten of them in all. Though their faces showed distrust they let us pass without any complications, and after surrendering our weapons, we quickly crossed the inner grounds and traced our way back into the main keep, where we were brought into the same waiting room. The chamber was empty and quiet, and we had to remain there until the doors to the meeting hall opened and a tall soldier with long whiskers invited us in. Just as in the foyer, the grand room was deserted. The crowds that had filled the place just hours before were gone, taking along with them all the colors, noises, and squabble, restoring complete silence, disturbed only by the sounds of our own footsteps that resonated loudly, like battle drums before a fight.

Across the hall we went. Once at the western wall we came up to a smaller door and stopped. The soldier and the page then quickly disappeared behind the drapes, while we remained at the clothed doorway, whispering amongst ourselves, intimidated by the echo that inhabited the place. Soon though, the heavy satin curtain moved aside again and we walked in, finding ourselves at the start of a short well-lit corridor, which stretched for about thirty cubits. At the other end the page opened yet another door and revealed a view of a room filled with bright light that fell down from countless candles affixed on top of a large chandelier, composed of three receding wooden rings and iron-cast chains that held the whole thing tightly together. The chamber was rather small, its high ceiling and the tiled floor painted with light blue color; its walls covered with lavish fabric of green and gold, the far wall occupied by a large fireplace that cradled a heated blaze, which emitted pleasant warmth and the sweet smell of burning wood. Next to it, arranged in a half circle stood a handful of tall timber chairs with a large armchair placed in the center, comprising the only fixtures in the room.

Although we expected the Duke to be late, Sire Tem walked in almost right after us and once inside, strolled hastily for the largest of the seats, clearly prepared for him beforehand. To my surprise the lord did not have any escort, no servants, councilors, or guards. Granting us a quick nod, he lowered himself in a chair, at which moment the page bowed and declared, keeping his head down, "As you have requested, Milord. The squires of Sire Rone and their commander Minia Emile are here at your service."

"Good," replied the Duke in short, then threw a brushing glance at the page and the soldier. "You two can leave now. I will speak to these men alone."

The two men complied without question and retreated to the exit.

"If you need anything, we will be just outside," said the page already in the hallway, and he closed the door.

The Duke did not reply, and simply nodded, either greeting us, or acknowledging the page's words.

When the servants were gone, and the sounds of their voices ceased, the High Lord raised his hand indicating the chairs next to him, and said, "Now, as we have our privacy, I would like to talk to you about the matters that concern your lord so much. In his dispatch, Sire Rone has voiced concerns about an unusually high number of kidnappings and unexplained attacks that have been plundering our province for the past season. He suggests that all the incidents are in fact not isolated, but connected through some secret brotherhood, or sect, whose members may be responsible for the mischief. I will not mislead you, everything sounds very strange to me, and I would like you, as his servants, to bring some light into all this."

"Milord, I will be honored to fill you in on all the details known to us," stated Minia and then he proceeded to tell the High Lord everything about the secret order of the Alavantars, Arac's prophecies, and a possible threat from beyond the Land's Edge. With all due diligence Minia described the accounts of our journey, the encounters with the assassins, the abandoned monastery, and the strange book.

"So what you are saying is that some band of so-called Alavantars is the source of all the troubles?" the High Lord asked when Minia had finished and sat back in his chair.

"Truth to be told, we cannot even prove that the Alavantars actually exist. All we know is that people are disappearing throughout Bois and there is some strange connection that ties it all together. Although we are not certain if the Alavantars are responsible for all the attacks, we have a feeling they know something about them."

"Huh. It is a strange tale you tell, young man. If it had not been for Sire Rone's letter, I would have doubted your words. But your master is a fair knight, who is my sworn man, and I have no reason not to believe him. And if he thinks that the matter of those Alavantars is important, then so do I."

The Duke leaned back and took a long breath, filling his chest with the light warm air. His eyes closed, he thought for sometime, and then resumed, his tone more narrative than commanding. "I have heard all kinds of rumors in the past two seasons. Some came from my sworn men, knights of the province and men-at-arms; others were brought in from common folks, traders and such. As always, most of the stories held little truth and told of adventures, money, love, and betrayals. But starting with the fall season, the tales grew stranger, more disturbing, with sings of something darker and unsettling hidden in their plots. Throughout people spoke of missing men, unexplained attacks on travelers and convoys. On land, bandits began to reclaim parts of isolated lands, harassing common folks and lords alike; at sea, pirates grew more daring in their strikes and chased the safety from the Seven Seas. And right here in Bonneville robberies and assaults on the townsmen and visitors have jumped threefold. Although I put more soldiers and more patrols out on the streets, the crime continues to spread, scaring people, some of whom have left the city, trying to find a safer place further west, closer to the kingdom's capital."

The Duke ran his fingers across the chair's handle. "Until today I had only suspicions, but now, with Sire Rone's letter and your accounts, I begin to think that there is a sound reason for what has been happening in my province, and the Alavantars or who ever they are may be the answer."

"We do think so too, Milord."

"Then I should learn as much as I can about that strange sect of yours. Tell me—What orders do you have from Sire Rone?"

"We were instructed to deliver the dispatch and wait for further orders from you or one of your captains. If none came, we were to resume our original quest, which was to find the missing convoy."

The Duke thought for a moment and then said, "In such case, I will entrust you with another duty. As I said, I want to find out more about the Alavantars, and you will assist me in that. Start here in Bonneville, walk around, ask people, collect as many clues as you can. Also speak with my second captain, Sire Jim. He knows a great deal about the underworld of this city, and since you have had a couple of skirmishes with hired swords, he will be able to help you find out more about the men who had attacked you. Once you have something more than a hunch, come back and seek another audience with me. I will be more than interested to hear your report. In the meantime, Bois thanks you for your service, squires. Sire Rone has, indeed, chosen fine men to serve him. Remember, if you uncover anything about the Alavantars, return at once. Now, go. Do your job well, and you will be rewarded, if not by me, then by the people. You are dismissed."

Without any further reservations the Duke rose to his feet and left. We did not stay in the room for long either. The door soon opened again. The page walked in and after giving us a few moments to absorb what we had heard, took us past the meeting quarters and to the stairs, where, instead of going down, we went up several floors and entered a large room, which oversaw the courtyard below and rewarded us with a view of countless rooftops of the provincial capital.

Chapter 28

BEHIND A large oak desk, lit by three massive brass lamps, which were filled with a dozen yellow candles dropping murky shapes onto the walls and the floor, sat a middle-aged man. He was broad in the shoulders, his sturdy neck adorned with a thick gold chain that dropped down onto his chest and revealed a large metal disk with the Duke's family crest engraved on it. Ignoring our arrival, the man kept his eyes on the table and wrote something with a long white quill. He did so for a while and once done, picked up the piece of paper and read it to himself. Satisfied he slid the note into a large envelope and immediately sealed its corners with wax stamps. Then he hid everything inside his desk and turned his attention to our company, slowly rubbing his fingers across a shortly trimmed black beard, and studying us closely with his dark brown eyes.

"I assume you are those squires the High Lord has told me about," announced the man as he got up and stepped away from his desk.

"We are the squires in Sire Rone's service. His Lordship, the Duke, has directed us to speak with his second captain, Sire Jim," said Minia, bowing slightly.

"Then you have come to the right place. I am Sire Jim of Ogar, the second captain with the Duke's garrison, and the commander of the city watch, responsible for assigning the watch patrols, administering the safety of the streets, and supervising the capital's reformatories. Being put in charge of safety in the environs of Bonneville makes one know a lot about what goes on within this city. You can say that I deal with all sorts of shady characters, and believe me, in six years as captain. I have come to learn a great deal about the underworld. So if you are looking for those who may know something about shifty deals and bargains, you have come to the right man."

"Sire Jim of Ogar"—I had heard that name before, from Father, who happened to supply the knight's family's lands with spices and herbs. The youngest of three brothers, Sire Jim was the son of Sire Rimdor, the elder lord, who had possessed a domain south of Bonneville. Since his family's wealth and lands were split between the two older siblings, Sire Jim had left his father's castle many years before and set out on a search for things denied to him by birth. After years of wandering around the kingdom, he had finally come back to Bois and found himself admitted to the Duke's garrison, pledging his arms and valor to Sire Tem. Because of his noble heritage, Sire Jim was granted a position of the deputy second captain, serving under the older knight, Sire Druis of Ron. After two years of faithful service, when the old lord passed away, Sire Jim was promoted to the position of second captain, taking over command of Bonneville's city watch, entrusted with protecting the capital from the pests of the underworld.

"Now, as we are done with the introductions, state your need and purpose for being here," continued Sire Jim, who stood straight.

"Well Sire," said Minia, "for the last several weeks we have been investigating the source of troubles that have been plundering Bois. In our quest, we have come upon a secret order, whose followers call themselves the Alavantars. We believe that the sect has adopted as their faith some ancient prophecies that foretold a return of the Northern horde from across the Land's Edge. No matter how odd those predictions sound, the Alavantars seem to deem them true. Worse is that they have also chosen the so-called ruler of the lands beyond the mountains as their sole and ultimate master, pledging themselves to the task of helping him to bring an end to Ethoria and establish a new rule, where they would serve as his disciples.

"From what we have gathered so far, it appears that the way they are trying to aid their cause is by kidnapping and killing young men from Normandia and other Northern kingdoms, thinking that one of those poor souls can be the foretold adversary of their master. At this point, we cannot prove any of this; as everything we know comes from rumors, tales, and our conjectures. Yet, there is one thing we are certain of—the Alavantars are real and are somewhere amongst us.

"What is more, in our search some strangers have coincidently attacked us three times in the past two weeks." Minia paused for a moment and gasped for air. When his breathing slowed, he continued, telling Sire Jim about the ambushes, the strange nighttime foes, and the symbol of the mercenaries' brotherhood of Snake Bites.

Minia told as much as he could about the accounts of our journey. When he was done, the second captain shook his head. Then he massaged his right temple, clearly thinking hard, and after some thought spoke out, with his voice unchallenged and as steady as before.

"Your story is undoubtedly very interesting. In fact, I have heard some rumors that do not sound all that much different from your accounts. Travelers and locals alike have come to me with reports of attacks on their persons and cargo. Some told me of strange assailants who came at night, when people were asleep, and killed the poor souls, most of whom were young men, boys, and even toddlers. All this worries me greatly, and although I do not know who is behind such disturbance, I will do everything to find out, and so I will aid you in your investigation."

"Whatever help you can give, Sire, will be greatly appreciated. Thank you," Noted Minia and he gave a salute.

"Huh, let's see…," the captain thought some more. "Since you have mentioned hired swords in your accounts, I suggest we start there. And the place to do so is the main jailhouse here at the castle. With crime on the rise, most of the cells are full of deceitful individuals, many of who have come here from other parts of Ethoria. Maybe some of them have heard a thing or two about less honest hired swords from the south, and those who have been trying to reserve their services. Surely, I will be able to persuade a few of those thugs to divulge some information, particularly with the Duke being so reluctant to grant death warrants instead of Barrier duties."

Sire Jim walked up to the door and opened it. "Shall we?" He nodded and stepped into the hallway, taking us prudently back to the stairs and then into yard. Although it was already dark, the castle grounds were thriving with commotion that washed over the sandy floor, filling the air with loud noise. With the barking of dogs, the squeaking of passing carts, and many voices mingled together in one medley of sound, we covered a distance of several hundred cubits and reached a sturdy one-storied stone building that was attached to the inner wall of the fortress, its doorway blocked by thick iron grates and two large-framed men, their chests clad in plated suits of shiny steel. Seeing Sire Jim the soldiers gave a salute and pushed the door inward, letting all of us into a wide hallway, illuminated by a row of torches placed along the sides, dropping flickering light onto the surrounding polished stones. Following the second captain we went through the dim corridor and then descended down a wide staircase, emerging several floors below inside a spacious round chamber, with three sets of iron doors situated on one side, and a group of guards who sat behind a simple boarded table, on the other. The soldiers had been busy with a game of dice and did not see us come in; each of the rolls was accompanied by yells and laughter. But when they finally saw us standing next to them, they immediately stopped their contest and jumped to their feet, kicking back their chairs, dropping them soundly to the floor.

"How are things here in the dungeon?" asked Sire Jim, before the soldiers could say anything, stepping forth and inspecting the mess that covered the table.

"Everything is in order, Sire. No problems so far. All birds are in their cages—quiet and happy," one of the guards declared in a loud voice; but Sire Jim stopped him quickly.

"Did they bring anyone else since my last visit? I have not checked the list yet."

"No, the most recent arrivals came this morning; the ones who tried to kill a young noble from Lombardia a day before," replied the guard with the same enthusiasm.

"A young man from Lombardia." I recalled the soldier's words in my head. The description sounded awfully familiar. I quickly glanced at my companions—their faces too showed a sign of surprise. "Could it be that the guard was talking about the same poor fellow we had found in the alley the night before?" To find out I had to ask.

"Sire, can you tell us some more about that young Lombardian lord? Your man said that someone tried to kill him. Do you know where the attack took place?"

"Why does it interest you?" inquired the captain, staring straight at me.

"The thing is that we have witnessed a robbery too. A young man was stabbed last night near the tavern we had been staying at."

"What do you say the name of your tavern is?"

"The Valiant Knight, Sire."

The second captain thought for a moment, and giving me an inquisitive look, continued. "Then you must be those squires who have saved the noble's life?"

"I would not say we saved his life, Sire. All we did was carry him inside; that is it. L'iote and Master Az did the rest," I replied.

"Master Az insists otherwise. He tends to think that if it had not been for your actions, the son of a Lombardian count would be dead by now. Oh, you did not know already?…The man who almost lost his life last night was Arley Erbeis, the only son of Rolle Erbeis, one of the counts in the northern region of Lombardia."

Sire Jim smiled at us and added, "You did a fine job out there."

"Thank you, Sire," Minia replied.

But the second captain broke him off. "You do not have to thank me; it is me who should thank you. I cannot even begin to imagine what sorts of problems would have come if that nobleman died here in Bonneville. Luckily for us, he survived. His servants took him back to Lombardia, which reminds me—Before they left, one of them passed a note to me, which Arley had dictated for his saviors. I have it here with me."

The second captain searched inside his vest and then pulled out a thin leather tube. "Do you care to read the letter?"

Sire Jim extended his hand and passed the cylinder to Minia, who opened it and extracted a white piece of paper that held the handwritten text. Minia unrolled the letter and began to read it aloud:

Dear Sires:

I thank you deeply for your brave actions. Last night you have saved my life, and I am forever in debt to you for such a courageous act, worthy only of the best servants of Normandia. Of course, these words cannot possibly express my fullest gratitude, not that there are any words to do so. Nevertheless, I can only pray that you get this note, so that you know how grateful I am for what you have done.

Unfortunately, my condition does not allow me to proceed with my original plans and I have to return home. Yet I would like to extend my courtesy and express my appreciation in the future. Remember, from now on I am at your service and if you need anything, seek me out, for I will be always ready to help you. My name is Arley Erbeis, the son of Rolle Erbeis, the honorable Count of Lombardia and the most precious ruler of Orencia, located in the northern region of our great kingdom.

Once again thank you and I hope to meet you some day in person.

The stamp and the official title were engraved at the bottom, along with a curved signature, which was clearly the work of a nobleman.

Minia finished and put down the letter, but before he could say anything, Sire Jim proceeded with the business at hand without even giving us a moment to reflect.

"About those thugs who almost killed him—we caught them this morning when they tried to sell some of the nobleman's things to a local shop. Good thing, the vendor was an honest man and immediately alerted one of the patrols. The thugs were captured and brought here for questioning. I personally led the interrogation, and it did not take long for them to confess to their dirty deed. Now I have to decide what to do with them. Although they may deserve death, I am not too quick to dispatch executions. As our Duke says—there is always an alternative to every action. Besides, those two are regulars at many shady watering holes around Bonneville's underworld. Maybe they will be willing to trade their useless lives for some information."

The second captain chuckled, drew his sword out a bit, just to prove that he was serious about his words, and at the same time addressed the guards. "Men, bring me the new prisoners."

While two of the soldiers immediately rushed for one of the doors, the third sentry came up to another gate and opened it.

"Let's see what we can get out of them," Sire Jim said again and stepped into a plain looking chamber, which was the main interrogation room of the Duke's jail. A perfect square of stone, the place was simple, gloomy, and cold. Along the sides, two long wooden benches stretched from one corner to another, and in the center, placed before a wide desk, were three metal chairs, screwed tightly to the bare floor, each equipped with chains and shackles, which ensured that those who sat in them did not have anywhere to move.

I felt uncomfortable, although the place was neither scary nor dirty. At first I tried to manage my discomfort, but the uneasy feeling persisted, and with my heart racing a little, I quietly picked a seat on one of the benches, closer to the exit and away from the awful-looking chairs. My companions settled next to me, while Sire Jim strolled straight to the desk, where he remained until the heavy door opened and the guards pushed in two scrawny little figures, whose hands and feet were bound by bulky iron chains. The prisoners did not look threatening at all—their thin bodies were swathed in simple clothes, dirty with mud and straw; their faces full of fear and confusion. It was hard to believe that just a day ago they had almost killed a man. Indeed, the sight of the two was pitiful. But I had little pity for them. They were criminals, and I had little mercy for such kind.

"Tie them up to the chairs," ordered the captain as the guards pushed the captives across the room and threw them down onto the metal seats. Not standing upon any ceremony, the soldiers slid the hands of the prisoners into the round constraints and locked them up with heavy rings, confining the two firmly to the metal frames. Done, the guards then excused themselves and walked back out, leaving the prisoners in the company of Sire Jim and us.

The second captain took only a brief pause before strolling to the men, studying them with his inquisitive glance. When he was at their side, he spun around and returned to the table. There he turned again, smacking his lips loudly, and addressed the prisoners. "I suppose you have had a good time here," started the second captain, facing the alleged robbers. "I do not know if you have heard yet, but you have gotten yourself a nobleman this time. I am sure you are familiar with the punishment for such a crime."

Sire Jim emphasized his every word; he moved slowly around the prisoners and halted behind them, placing his heavy hands on to the chairs' rails, close to men's trembling shoulders. At first he remained still, saying nothing; but then he leaned forward so that his lips were next to the men's ears, and with his voice becoming very cold and indifferent, whispered, "Did you think you could avoid justice? Not today, and not on my watch. Death will be your sentence, and hard cold steel will be your judge."

"Good Sire, but you said yourself that the nobleman did not die. We did not kill him. Does it not count for something?" sounded both men at once, a clear note of fear high in their trembling voices. The second captain straightened up and not justifying the plea with any answer, walked back to the desk.

"It does not matter if the poor man is alive or not. The fact remains—you tried to kill him, and this is all that matters. Death is what will be of you. But since the man actually survived, I will be merciful and allow you to decide how you want to die. You have my word on it; you will have your choice."

"No…Please…Good Sire, no. Have mercy on us…We did not want to kill him; we just wanted to steal some of his jewels. We thought we could scare him and get the gold, but he did not want to yield. He started to fight back and accidentally stumbled onto our blades. But we did not mean to hurt him. No, Sire, we did not."

The two men were pleading desperately for their lives. Tears rolled down their unshaved rough cheeks, and their once-firm voices turned into lengthy sounds of weeping. Yet, Sire Jim was obstinate. He let the crying go on for a little longer, and then cut the men off with a sharp gesture. When silence was restored, the second captain said, "Frankly, I do not know if I should believe you. I have all the proof I need to execute you."

"No, no, you have to believe us, please. We did not mean to…," the two men resumed with the whimper. Sire Jim continued to show no sign of care. When the men eventually fell still again, probably tired of their effort, he placed his hands on the edge of the desk and leaned forward.

"There is one thing that may change my mind though," uttered Sire Jim and paused, at which time the prisoners jumped up and cried, "Oh, Sire, anything. We will do anything you ask; just spare our lives. Please."

The second captain nodded, not as much to them as to us. "There have been reports that someone has been seeking services of hired swords to do some dirty work in the countryside. I do not suppose you have heard anything about it, have you?"

"Oh, yes, Sire. We know a little bit about it. We do," the men exclaimed, almost as quickly as the question had sounded.

"Then let's hear your story. If I like it I may consider switching your sentence to Barrier guard's duty; or to fifty years in quarries of Puno, should you prefer hard labor."

"Yes, yes," one of the men hurried to explain. "Last year two men came to Bonneville at the start of the fall season. We have no idea who they were, or where they had come from. But once they got here, they stayed for a while in several of the local inns, spending all their time recruiting people who were willing to attend to a couple of jobs, mostly in the countryside.

"Although there was always someone in Bonneville looking for shady deals, those two were very different in their desires. Their requests were always secret and their purse—hefty, as they offered very good coin for the services they required. One of our friends, who is dead now, took on one job with them, and got three hundred silvers. Three hundred silvers! Most so-called employers will not pay a half of that for any job, and that is on a good day. In a rainy season, the quote is fifty coppers for one mission.

"Needless to say, word about the strange paymasters spread quickly. Soon they were very popular in town and characters of all sorts flocked to the city trying to get their hands on easy money. We heard about the offers too. After asking around, we got ourselves an audience with the unusual employers at the Dirty Cat pub at the eastern edge of Bonneville. Though the place itself was a refuse pile, the men who met us were no low lives—slick, well dressed, with expensive blades, and very nice entourage, and I mean, women of high caliber, too expensive for most city dwellers, including the lords."

"How did they look?" Sire Jim interrupted the story.

"Who? The men?"

"Of course, the men, who do you think?"

"Ah, one was tall, about two cubits; another shorter—one and three quarters, maybe less. Both looked like foreigners—Southerners from Azoros, the Amber Empire, or Free Cities. The taller man was skinny, long faced, and dark haired; his friend—round faced, bold, and a bit chubbier, yet not fat. They did not appear to be of a noble kind, nor were they merchants of any sort, more like wealthy rovers, hired swords, or freelanced swordsmen, with similar outfits—long capes, dark trousers, green tunics, and fine leather vests."

"What sort of job did they offer you?" asked Sire Jim next.

"The night we saw them, they were recruiting crews to hunt down some youngsters from lesser towns of Bois. They said it was an easy job. Kill poor lads, cut of their heads, and bring them back as proof. For each of the assignment the foreign paymasters offered four hundred silvers—fifty coins up front, and the rest afterwards. Big prize they were, but not for us. We are no murderers. As for last night—it was an accident. We swear."

"Let's talk about it later; for now, go forth with your story."

"As we said we do not kill people, not to mention youngsters. So we refused and left. Later we heard people say they had found some hired swords from the Free Cities to do the job. Though, we do not know how true that gossip is."

"Is that all?"

"Yes, that is it. We swear."

"You better…"

"We do, we do…Ask the others; talk to the crowd at the Dirty Cat, they have heard about those two, they also saw us leave. If you do not learn anything there, check the Flying Bird, a tavern by the fairgrounds. People said they had seen those two there a few times too."

"Oh, I will. You can count on it," the captain said, pacing across the room, with hands behind his back. "If you tell the truth, I will act on my word and spare your pitiful little lives. In the meantime, you return to your cells and hope that someone else verifies what you have told me."

With those words the captain walked up to the door and pounded on it several times. A moment later, the lock clicked and the same guards appeared in the entrance.

"Take them back," ordered the captain. "I will deal with them again later."

The soldiers quickly picked up the criminals from their metal seats and took them away, the ringing of the iron constraints resonating as they moved. When the door closed again, Sire Jim sat down on top of the desk and spoke, after blowing out a deep loud sigh.

"What do you think, squires? Does it sound familiar to you?"

"It sure does, Sire," replied Minia.

"It appears we are in luck. Your story may have a carryover after all." The second captain thought some more, then added, "I think we should start with the Dirty Cat Inn first. Who knows, maybe those two vile persons were telling the truth."

Sitting inside the interrogation room of the Duke's jail, I felt my mind working hard. Too many things had happened since we had departed Villone, and the latest confession was yet another turn in a complicated plot that was slowly unwinding before us. Knowing nothing in the beginning, we left the cold chamber, finding ourselves a step closer to understanding a confused and obscure scheme of unseen dangers and mysterious foes. There were two strangers—the secret foreign employers, who were interested in killing young men in Bois—and we had to find them.

Chapter 29

SINCE IT was already too late to start the search, everything was postponed until the next morning. A little after sunrise my companions and I gathered in the dining hall of the Valiant Knight Inn and then headed out to the Duke's castle, where inside the empty yard we found Sire Jim already giving orders to a group of guardsmen, who stood in two rows of five, their round shields and short wooden spears placed before them. When the second captain was finished with the instructions, his hand went up and the armed column started to move, first through the open castle gates and then toward the local watering holes that lay at the outskirts of Bonneville. Having little choice, we joined the procession and hurried after the guards, keeping close to Sire Jim, somewhat afraid to lose our way amongst unfamiliar surroundings and the many spectators, who had flocked to the streets to stare at the city watch march across their part of town.

As we cleared one street after another, the sun ruled over the sky, making the air hot and dry again. At last, our large company came to a round market square, where behind lines of empty vendors' tents—most of which were empty—we spotted a small, dirty-looking structure with the words "The Dirty Cat Inn" painted over its front door. The place itself was nothing to look at, yet it was there we hoped to uncover at least some clues as to the whereabouts of the mysterious paymasters. But our search was fruitless, as no one inside had any information that could aid us. Although the owner vaguely remembered the two men who resembled the description, he did not know anything about their identities or their whereabouts, and so unable to find even the slightest hint amongst the blur of talking from the proprietor and few patrons, we left the hostelry and moved to the next stop, the Flying Bird Inn, the establishment situated at the far side of Bonneville's fairgrounds.

To get there, we had to leave the wider streets and pick our way through narrow alleys filled with garbage, a terrible odor, and strange people, most of whom quickly gave way once noticing the city watch appear from around the corner. Wandering the filthy browning lanes of dried-up mire and sand for some time, we eventually arrived at another unpaved deserted clearing, surrounded by several similar-looking houses, one of which, a shaggy two storied building, was adorned with a large swaying green wooden sign that read "The Flying Bird—Peace to all who enter." Surrounded by a low wooden fence that had fallen backwards in places, the abode was by far one of the least lavish spots in the city, and those who had an extra coin avoided it, preferring better, cleaner places, closer to the castle and the city watch patrols. This in turn made the Flying Bird into a site that attracted a colorful cast of shady characters, many of whom preferred to stay away from the attentive eyes of the law, hiding themselves in the dumps of the poorer parts of Bonneville.

At the entrance that was made of a simple brown frame and a loose door, Sire Jim stopped and gave further instructions to the guards, dispatching three of them to cover the back exit, three more to position themselves up front, and the remaining four to follow him inside. As for us, we entered the inn too, finding ourselves within the walls of a deserted hall, silent except for a conversation between two men who sat leisurely at a high counter at the far side, sipping on some brew poured into tall wooden cups.

Seeing us come in, the men stopped talking and lifted themselves off their stools, their eyes focused on Sire Jim, who proceeded forth, his metal gear clanking loudly as he stepped firmly over the dusty rough floorboards. Before the second captain even reached the counter, one of the men, who had clearly recognized Sire Jim, produced a fake smile and bowed his head, speaking in a soft voice, "How are you this fine springy day, Captain?" The man's tone was polite, yet spurious.

"Quite well, Nton, thanks for asking," replied Sire Jim, his own intonation full of pretense.

"It is truly a treat to have you in my humble establishment, Captain. What brings you here? I hope nothing serious. Because if you have come to check for troubles, I can assure you that you will not find them here."

"Is it so, Nton?…How long have we known each other? Huh?"

"Oh, far too long Captain, far too long."

The man, Nton, who was obviously the owner of the place, bowed again, his grin drawing even wider.

Although there was an obvious tension between the two, their conversation was surprisingly civil. Both knew each other well and both knew what they had to say once the two met. As one had been always trying to avoid being caught, while the other did the opposite, this perpetrated a game of cat and mouse, which seemed to have been going on for quite some time.

Yet, for that visit, the shifty owner and his little schemes did not concern the second captain. Sire Jim was interested in the other matter and so said, tapping his naked sword on the side of his boot. "Relax, Nton; I am not here to raid your 'humble establishment.' I am looking for a couple of men, travelers from afar, who might have been staying here for some time. They would have been usual rovers, if it were not for their dealings here in the city. It has come to my attention that they had been offering particularly generous prizes for seemingly easy jobs that involved the disposal of some youngsters from Bois. With the last words Sire Jim's tone changed and became plainly serious."

"Oh, I am afraid I won't be of much assistance to you," replied Nton quickly. "There have been so many travelers these past two seasons that I could not possibly remember any of them."

"Maybe I can help you narrow it down," snapped the second captain. "These two have been hiring local thugs and mercenaries to kill young men from our province. Does that help?"

"I am afraid not. I have not heard anything like this. Maybe you got the wrong place."

"Or maybe, I got the right place, and you are just trying to hide something from me. If so I must assume that you are in business with those criminals; which means that you are in the business of kidnapping and murder, and I am sure you are familiar with the consequences of such an association, are you not?"

"Even so, you cannot prove anything. The Duke's court will never let you get away with such accusations; not without solid proof, which you do not have." Nton sounded very firm but such determination vanished once Sire Jim interrupted him again.

"I do not really have to prove anything. With the recent surge of crime, my authority has been extended. All I need to do now is to find a couple of 'honest' men who will be willing to spill some useful information about your little place here. And once they do, I will come back with half the Duke's garrison and turn your place upside down. Should I find even a hint of lawbreaking, I will arrest you on sight and deliver you to the court. Although, with your prudence, you will probably win back your freedom, I can assure you that it will take many days if not weeks; all the while your tavern will remain vacant and unlocked. I am sure you can imagine what will happen to it during your absence…..

"So, I will ask again—what will it be, a quick tip that no one has to know about, or my personal interest in your dirty deals?"

Nton kept calm, but his eyes told a different story. He debated within himself for a moment, and after weighing all the possibilities, slowly pushed out a reply, shaking his head and wiping drops of sweat from his forehead, nervously and uneasy.

"Now, as I think about it, I do remember someone who matches your description. There were two men who came to the tavern some weeks ago. They took my biggest room and paid for it in advance. I do not know what they do or why they have come here, only almost every evening they have been sitting at a table over by the fireplace, talking to different folk—locals, outsiders, and mercenaries of all sorts. Though I did not speak to them much myself, I heard them offering good jobs and generous pay for removing some 'candidates' from Bois. I did not know that those candidates were actually young men and that removing them meant killing. I swear, should I have known, I would have come to you. I would have—"

"Please, spare me your explanations." Sire Jim raised his hand and Nton stopped, while the second captain continued. "You said they paid in advance—for how long?"

"Until the end of this season."

"Have they left?"

"Not that I know of. They were here three nights ago. Of course they often use the back door to get in and out of the inn, so I can not be sure if they are in their room or not."

"And you said the rooms were…"

"It is at the very end of the hallway, third door on your left. You cannot miss it. If you want I can show you."

"No," rejected Sire Jim abruptly. "I want you to stay here…Trust me, you do not need to get involved."

As Nton sat back down, the second captain turned around and gave a quick nod to one of the guards, who immediately ran out onto the street and returned a moment later with the three men posted outside. After throwing a glance at the city watchers, Sire Jim turned to us and said, "This is what you will do. My men and I will go in and check the room. If those strangers are there, we will have a little chat with them. In the meantime, I want you to remain here in the hall and keep watch. Make sure nobody leaves this place, not even Nton, but most importantly do not leave this room unless you hear from me otherwise. If something happens I do not want you to get slashed out there. The Duke will have my head fed to an executioner's axe if I let anything happen to you. So stay put and keep your eyes sharp. That is an order."

"Yes, Sire," we replied as one. The second captain nodded again and turned his attention to the guards. "It is time, let's go."

With those words, he raised his sword and led the seven men into the shadows of a wide corridor that started at the end of the counter.

Left alone with Nton and another stranger, we stayed within the empty dining hall. For a long while we could not hear anything. Time passed slowly, and when there was still no sign of Sire Jim or any of his men, an uneasy thought started to crawl into my mind. The hot stuffy air of the inn made me feel uncomfortable too, and to ease some tension I shifted my focus away to an open window, where rejoiced by sunlight I could see a group of children, chasing each other in circles. The game seemed to be very interesting and the youngsters laughed loudly as they ran. Listening to the light jingle of their voices I smiled too, but not for long as my attention was soon returned to the corridor, from where came a sudden burst of sounds—splintered wood and clanging metal, intermingled with shouts of several men and Sire Jim's strident commands, all of which indicated that something was amiss. A fight was taking place, and I was not a part of it. Instead I had to stand on the side, amongst my companions, listening to the combat.

The noise from the battle kept everyone on their toes. Eager to help the second captain, my friends, Ric, and I looked at Minia, hoping that he would let us go. But our commander was unyielding and remained still, though his eyes were focused on the corridor and his fingers played along the hilt of his sword. The fighting inside the hallway lasted for some time, and ended as abruptly as it had begun. The uneasy silence returned, but was soon disturbed by the beat of several feet that sounded inside the corridor, all moving away from the dining hall. Anxiously, we continued to wait, until a silhouette appeared from the dark opening of the corridor. Instinctively we grabbed our weapons, but immediately eased our grips, as it was Sire Jim who walked into the light, his elegant blade covered in blood all the way up to the hilt. Silently he reached us at the counter and then threw a glance back at the hallway just as several guards rushed across and vanished behind the front door, slamming it so hard that it bounced off several times.

The second captain appeared to be very tired. His breathing was hard, and his right hand was shaking a little. The fine silk tunic was dirty with splashes of blood and was ripped in places, showing glimpses of a well-made chain mail under it. After keeping the pause for bit longer, Sire Jim ran his hand along the side of his face and uttered, "We found those foreign paymasters, only they were not too pleased to see us."

The second captain took a deep breath. When my men and I got to the door we heard some voices and burst in, but as soon as we were inside, we realized that we were up for a fight.

As Sire Jim spoke, the front door opened again, and the same soldiers returned, dragging two long stretchers along with them. Saying nothing they rushed passed us and vanished in the hallway. The second captain followed them with his glance again and then continued, shaking his head as he spoke:

"I must admit—they put up a good fight. If it was not for our superior numbers, I might not be talking to you right now. One thing is certain—they were no ordinary thugs, nor were they simple men of coin. They were exceptional fighters, professionals. Frankly I have not seen such skill and agility since I hired a trainer for the Duke's garrison. He was an old mercenary from Azoros, who had come to Normandia to teach the lords and their men of swordsmanship. He was a swordsman like no other, and the two in that room, they were just as good.

A tough match it was. Before I could react, two of my men were dead and two others barely escaped the same fate, getting nasty wounds instead. There were then four of us remaining against the two of them. But fortunately by then the guards I had posted in the back heard the noise and came to assist. Still, the enemy managed to hold us off, wounding two more men and slicing my tunic on one side. Only when we wounded one of them, did they try to run. We succeeded in stopping one foe, killing him as he tried to get to the door, but the other one dove through the window and jumped out into the alley. He did it so fast that none of us could react in time. When we scrambled outside through the back door, he was already gone."

Sire Jim stopped and when his breathing finally returned to normal, threw another glance at the hallway, from where more noise came. He stared into the shadows for a while, then turned back and said, with a hint of disappointment in his voice, "Let's get back into the room. Maybe we will find something amongst the things the enemy has left behind."

Trailing after Sire Jim we went down the corridor to its far end, where a group of soldiers bustled around their fallen comrades, picking their way amongst the splintered wood and dropped weaponry. The sight was an unpleasant one and reminded me of our scuffles in the countryside, just days ago. And though we did not have to fight that time, the aftermath was still displeasing and brought up the same feelings of uneasy tension and sadness.

The view of the room was no different. The place was thrown into complete disarray, crowded with armed men, broken pieces of furniture and shattered glass. Four of the Duke's guards lay on the floor: two still alive on stretchers, and two dead, their motionless figures covered with white cloths, exposing only the worn-out heels of their leather boots. The sight of the soldiers' cold bodies made me turn away, yet as my eyes traced the room's grim floorboards I came upon another body that lay several cubits away.

Unlike the guards' bodies, the man remained uncovered, his dark brown eyes opened and focused on the ceiling. It was one of the foreigners we had been looking I had no doubt. Strangely there was nothing unusual about him. His features looked ordinary—short black hair, long sideburns, and finely trimmed beard that outlined the square rough-skinned face, his muscular jaws still locked, showing the intensity of the recent fight. His clothes appeared equally common—thick vest of boiled leather, green tunic, tucked inside brown cotton pants; short boots, and a small cape of a plain brown color. Yet, there was one distinctive detail in the stranger's outfit that made me wonder—his belt.

At first glance it seemed ordinary, but at closer inspection it became obvious that it was not. Its making was exceptional and its buckle—very unique. Made of a large square polished plate, it held the imprint of a racing wild dog that was carefully painted gold, incrustations of silver and red gems decorating its eyes and paws. Underneath the fresco was a line of unfamiliar symbols that I could not read. Did it have a particular meaning, or was it simply an exquisite item from the southern parts of Ethoria? I did not know, nor did anyone else, including Sire Jim, who was well versed in the ways of hired swords and mercenaries. Still the symbol made we wary and I memorized it, hoping to ask someone about its purpose. Meanwhile, my friends had followed the captain to the other end of the chamber, stopping at a high, carved desk, on top of which lay heaps of books, ripped pages, ink pots, and quills, some broken and some covered in ink.

"Hey, Mishuk, quit meandering around. Come here, I think we got something." I looked up and saw Ike waving for me to get to the desk. Everyone else was staring at a piece of paper that the second captain held in his hand.

"Huh, it seems the two were busy writing a report," said Sire Jim as I made my way toward him. He studied the yellow page in the light that streamed from the broken window and then began to read.

> *Be it known to you, Azmal, our arrangement is working*
> *fine. Although we are only in the second season of the opera-*

tion, already most of those on the list have been taken care of. I am sure you will be glad to know that at this point we have paid out over twenty bounties. If all goes well we will expect to finish off with all the candidates by the end of springtime and then will return to Pullie to present you with our final report. With this in mind, we kindly ask you to prepare our reward and place it with the settler, as agreed.

Alas, three of the names from your list have escaped our efforts. We have hired several men for the job, but they failed miserably. It is just too hard to find any specialists in this backward kingdom. But we consider it to be a minor setback. Besides, if we cannot find anyone suited for the job, we will follow up on it ourselves. One way or another the problem will be corrected.

There is also another matter that requires your attention. Some of our sources within the Duke's castle tell us that one of the local lords has become unusually suspicious about our operations in Bois. There is rumor that he has sent some of his servants to investigate our late activities. Without revealing our presence we cannot examine these reports more thoroughly. Therefore, we suggest that you hire additional assistance from our friends in Pullie. Should you decide to do so, we will forward you their names and where you can meet them.

In the meantime we will continue to work as scheduled and…

"I do not know if they were the same men who hired your attackers, but similarities are striking," noted Sire Jim after finishing the broken last sentence of the letter.

"Do you think they are responsible for the attacks?" asked Ike, peering over Ark's shoulder so he could get a better look at the letter.

"It looks like it, does it not? And the letter matches what those two jail mates told us yesterday. Too bad we did not get them both. Although my best men are searching the city as we speak, I have a feeling they will not find anyone, not in Bonneville at least."

Sire Jim shook his head once.

"So what now?" I asked, unable to see through the next step myself.

"For one, thanks to this unfinished letter, we know a little more about those strangers," replied the second captain, "My guess—they were high-paid dogs, working for a man, whose name could be Azmal. They had been instructed to hire others like themselves to eliminate some men, whose names are on some mysterious list. We also know that those two came to Bonneville in the fall season and had immediately proceeded to recruit extras for their plot. And finally, it appears their employer, Azmal, has found refuge in Pullie. The problem is that he may not be there for long. With the second paymaster on the loose, we must expect that Azmal will find out about our inquiries soon enough. He will definitely move someplace else, where we cannot find him."

"Then we do not have much time, do we? We must get to Pullie before Azmal learns about our investigation," I exclaimed, as suddenly I had a clear idea of what had to be done next.

"You speak right thoughts, squire," agreed Sire Jim. "You should depart Bonneville as soon as possible. And while you travel to Pullie, I will continue to search for the missing paymaster and any other who might have known him. Come, let's get back to the castle; we need to arrange for your leave and report everything to the Duke."

It was decided then, in the middle of a roach-infested room of the Dirty Cat Inn that we were to get on the road again. That time it was off to Pullie, the coastal province east of Bois, four days' trip from Bonneville by horse. Time was of the essence, and preparations for our departure had to commence at once. After spending the remainder of the day at the castle, we returned to the Valiant Knight, where we quickly packed all our gear, ate a simple meal, and fixed our horses, preparing them for the lengthy journey ahead. Leaving our farewells for L'iote, who was absent for our leave, we returned to the castle and reconvened with Sire Jim, inside a large three-storied building with flat roof and narrow windows, guarded by several younger soldiers.

Within a large room, next to a burning fireplace, the second captain stood motionless, rocking back and forth on his heels. With his eyes focused on the fire, as he noticed us come in, he waved his hand and mused, "It is good to see that you did not waste any time." He then turned and granted us a brief smile. "I assume you have everything you need, as far as the provisions are concerned?"

"Yes, Sire. We got enough food and drink from the Valiant Knight to last for a week," reported Minia.

"Good. Then you are set." The second captain thought for some time, then spoke. "A journey to Pullie is not a difficult one, but under the circumstances I think it is best to exercise extreme caution. The advice I can give you is to cover the distance with haste. Do not stay in any taverns for a night.

Instead break camp in the open, keeping watch at all times. Once in Pullie, do not let your guard down. It is the biggest harbor in the kingdom, and as a result its streets are packed with all sorts of crooks and criminals, some of whom may very well be working for Azmal. As you will probably have to spend more than a day there, I suggest you settle at the Five Stars Inn. To get there simply follow one of the streets to the harbor, then across the bazaar, and to the first alley that runs up the hill. Past the second plaza, you will see a three-storied building with shutters painted green. It will be the Five Stars Inn. Go in there and find Master Lik. He is the owner of the place and is a good friend of my family. Tell him that I have sent you and he will take care of you. I cannot promise you that the place will be the best you have ever seen, but at least it will be safe."

Sire Jim walked up to a desk and picked up an envelope, which he then handed to Minia, who immediately stashed it under his vest.

"This letter is for the High Lord of Pullie. It tells everything that we know about the Alavantars and the disappearances within our province. Take it with you and show it to the Duke of Pullie or one of his captains; with it you will have their cooperation. But hurry. You need to get to Azmal before anyone else does. Remember, the matter is very important to our province, and Sire Tem himself is following it closely."

The second captain paused again, and after studying us with his eyes, concluded, "May the Spirit guide you. You are dismissed."

We replied with a salute and left, returning to the yard, where, back on our horses, we strode out of the castle's main gate and down a busy street, heading east toward the coastal province of Pullie, a completely new world for everyone within our little group.

Chapter 30

AT LAST, the busy day was coming to a close. The red disk of the sun crawled to the west, and pockets of white clouds that occasionally floated across the sky finally dissolved beyond the horizon, letting the red color reign over the land. Soft western winds streamed across the valley and seethed into the thick stretches of fruit orchards on both sides of the road. With little room to move, we slowly picked our way through the traffic, heading for the open crossroad some distance away. At the junction, we made a right turn and started down a new route, riding east to the capital city of Pullie, located on the banks of the Loman River, the mighty watercourse that ran all the way from the mountains of the Land's Edge to the waters of the Seven Seas.

Driven by the urgency of the situation, we tried to speed up through the stream of men and wagons, but for a while all we could do was let our mounts saunter along. Only several leagues later, when the crowds began to thin down, we switched our pace to a gallop and rode forth without stop, quickly leaving the tended orchards behind and entering an undisturbed part of the countryside, covered by untamed grass fields that drew out for many leagues in all directions. After a while other travelers disappeared completely and we traversed alone, enjoying the serenity of the surrounding landscape. But soon enough the daylight left us too, and as darkness fell, we moved a couple hundred cubits into the pasture and set up camp.

Next morning it was an early rise. Awakened by Minia's firm commands, I lifted myself from underneath the warm blanket and stared blindly at the scenery. It was nice, just like the day before. The sun was not yet up, but the night had already retreated, and the blue sky had settled over our heads. There was no movement in the air, and the warmth was soothing to my skin. Again, our quest demanded a speedy departure. After just a short breakfast that consisted of cold strips of meat and hard bread, we mounted our horses and returned to the route.

The midday break time came and went unnoticed, while we continued on. Once in a while we met some lonely travelers, farmers, traders, and others. One time we passed a nicely decorated carriage, accompanied by two mercenary guards. And then a few leagues afterwards, a group of horsemen standing on the side of the road, talking loudly amongst themselves. Cautious of possible dangers, we rushed by them, our weapons ready. But the men ignored us, and so we left their figures covered in puffs of dust, lifted from underneath the hooves of our mounts.

In the evening we stopped in the open again. As before, we set up camp off the road and remained there through the night. Alas, even after a whole day of riding, I could not fall asleep. Although I kept my eyes closed and turned away from the flames, I failed to make myself surrender to the drowsiness. Deep thoughts persisted, one thing transforming into another—my family and friends, Sire Jim and the Duke, the sneaky Alavantars and mysterious Azmal.

At some point, my head started to hurt, and I remembered then what Father used to say about such times, that there were moments when before you fall asleep, you ventured into "the hour of the wolves"—the point where your fears, regrets, and worries come back to your consciousness and rip it apart, like packs of hungry wolves. In the last few seasons Father mentioned such hours often, and to ease his troubles sipped on harsh "white water," a strong brew made of grain and sugar. I did not understand him then, but in my nineteenth day of the journey, lying under the night sky, I started to grasp the meaning of his words. It was the hour of wolves for me now, and I was struggling to cope with it.

I did not notice when reality faded and dreams began. It was as if a magic spell came over me and took me into another world, where dark thoughts changed to pleasant images and lovely sounds. But I was not truly asleep. Through the colorful blur, the familiar voice reached me. It was A'tie. The mysterious A'al woman was back.

"Mishuk, it is time to meet again," she said slowly. "Come, join me and we will talk."

Suddenly the haze disappeared and I found myself standing amidst the recognizable meadow, full of sunlight and flowers. A natural path, this time, made of yellow blossoms ran under my feet and to the forest, where behind the wall of trees, inside the grand live hall, A'tie sat gracefully on top of a high chair of vines and branches. As I walked closer she welcomed me with a light warm smile and nodded as a sign of greeting. I bowed in return and settled beside her on the chair, listening.

"I welcome you back, my young warrior." The A'al woman continued with her muse. "Much has happened since our last visit. In that time you have learned a lot—about the Alavantars, the prophecies of Arac, and the evil plots that had come from them. You have also uncovered clues that are guiding you across your kingdom to the city of Pullie. It is of these clues I want to tell you.

"It so happens that we both are facing the same enemies. Alavantars pose much danger not only to you and your kingdom, but to my kin as well. While they are not the true source of the evil, they are a part of it, instruments of a much greater foe, whose identity is still unknown. Soon though, very soon the time will come when you will learn who is the true enemy, and when you do, you will be faced with an even bigger challenge—to rid the land of his foul presence. But before you can do so, you must eliminate his aids, his disciples— the Alavantars—because if you do not, they will come for you, rendering all of your efforts useless.

"To defeat the Alavantars is not an easy task either, as they are not alone in their doings; many others favor them, lured by coin, fame, or alliance with some magic powers. No matter who they are or what title they hold, they serve the sect's dark purpose and must be stopped as well. In your investigation you have already stumbled upon a name that is guiding you to the city of Pullie. Follow it, as it will lead you to the answers you so desperately seek. Alas, I cannot tell you what will happen when you arrive to the port city, but I can warn you of one danger that you will face."

A'tie paused, and once she was convinced that my entire focus was on her, resumed:

"Watch out for the slippery one. He will hide behind a friendly face; he will promise his help and tell you that he is on your side. But do not trust him, as he stands with the enemy and will do everything to seek your demise. You will recognize that man by a golden bird he possesses. It will not be an ordinary bird, as its eyes will be of different colors—blue and green. Should you see such a bird, be as careful as possible, and remember that he will want your death, just as the Alavantars, whom he serves."

Silence fell upon the grand hall again. It lasted for some time, and I began to suspect that the vision was drawing to a close when…A'tie's voice caught my attention.

"We have a little time left before I have to leave you; enough for one question…Ask if you want, and I will try to answer…"

Suddenly my mind went blank. All those questions that bothered me ever since I had left Villone vanished, and I had to think hard to come up with just one.

"My lady," I said, struggling with my forethought. "Why did not you tell me that you have visited Ric too?"

"Because you did not need to know it then. Besides, I came to him after our meeting. He needed my guidance, just like you did, and I gave it to him."

A'tie gave me an inquisitive look, then concluded, "You had your question, now you shall leave."

I did not know if it was magic again, but as soon as her words died in the lengths of the hall, all of the important questions came back to me. My voice still sounding loud, the images blurred and in their place sailed green stars that seeded the black sky over me. I was back in Bois, awake and confused. My Fore Sight had brought me another vision and with it a warning. But was I to trust it? Probably. A'tie had been correct twice before, and I had no doubt she was right this time. I just hoped that I could spot the danger from all the vague clues she had given me.

Thinking, I closed my eyes again and listening to the rhythmic sound of the fire, and drifted back to sleep, a normal sleep.

When the time to rise finally came I woke up with a slight headache that settled uncomfortably at my temples. During the night the weather had changed yet again; the wind had switched its direction, bringing a burst of cold air, and once innocent white clouds turned into gray monsters that floated slowly across the sky, making the prospect of rain very high.

Shivering from the chilly breeze, I dislodged my bed and throwing the hood over my head, collected my belongings. I placed them back into the saddlebags, then ate a little breakfast, and once Minia gave the order to move out, mounted my horse, directing it back onto the road, along with the rest of our party. In time the cold dawn moved into an even colder day, and the pale line of the horizon that had been visible earlier, vanished from sight, consumed by ever-growing clouds, which by then were rolling like chariots from the south. Soon though, the dreary weather amended for the worse, as drops of rain started to drip from above and quickly transformed into a serious downpour that made the journey much more unpleasant for everyone who was unfortunate enough to be caught wandering outside.

Through the wall of water, the surroundings looked dull. Infinite grass fields stretched for leagues, seldom giving way to patches of distant trees and shallow creeks that crossed the valleys, carrying fast streams of water toward the coast. By midafternoon the path began to slant northward, and came upon a shallow stream running across, bringing a sound of moving water along with it. Although the brook was no more than two cubits wide, a small wooden bridge was built over it. While on a dry day it offered travelers an easy crossing, under the pounding of the rain, the thick timber boards became slippery and our mounts struggled not to skid into the water as they made their way to the other side. Luckily nothing bad happened, and we were back on the not-so-firm soil, pressing forth toward a vague outline of some structures peering shyly through the heavy shower. As we got closer the shapes became more defined, and slowly I began to distinguish the silhouettes of some two dozens houses that stood on both sides of the road, making up a small parish.

At the sight of the angular roofs, patched with rounds of hay and straw, Minia, who had continued to ride up front, turned around, pointed at the dwellings ahead, and yelled through the rain, "This is Pione, the last village in Bois. Past it is Pullie." The squire shook off water from his hands and added, "I suggest we stop here for lunch. This way we will have a hot meal and will save ourselves some time."

Nobody disagreed. Nobody wanted to. We were soaked, cold and hungry, and the idea of hot food and a dry place was very welcome. So we followed our commander and after a quick dash through a coarse door-less gate, arrived at a wide, one-storied building adorned with a wide wooden plaque that announced that we were about to enter the halls of "The Sparrow's Hill Inn."

Eager to leave the outdoors we led our horses into the open stable yard, and after tying them up at low poles, ran up to a porch, seeking shelter under its extended roof.

Past the heavy front door, a gust of hot stuffy air and the view of a wide square hall forty cubits long, greeted us. Throwing back our wet hoods, we gave the room a quick look and, finding a vacant table by a long counter that ran along the entire length of the wall, ending at one side with a stairwell and a large grate at the other, we settled in, ordering a fixed meal that consisted of hot plates of local stew, some soft wheat bread, and a jar of milk.

While the meal was getting ready, we had some time to talk...

"We are doing quite well so far," said Minia as he stretched his legs under the table.

"What do you mean?" asked Ike, curious.

"We are making good time," replied Minia. "We have already reached the provincial border and it is not yet evening. After tonight, we will have less than a full day of travel left. By tomorrow afternoon we should be in Pullie, which means that we will beat the fugitive by two days at least."

"How do you know?" I asked, not all too sure how Minia had come up with such an estimate.

"Assuming that the mercenary left Bonneville before us and is heading to Pullie, it will be hard for him to take any of the main roads, not with Sire Jim and his city watch after him. If I were him, I would have had to find some other route out of Bois, a back road or a hunter's trail perhaps, and that would surely add two extra days to the journey, that is if he has a horse of course. Should he take the voyage on foot, we will have to spend even more time on the road."

"How long until we reach the border?" my brother then asked once Minia had finished.

" Five or so leagues from here. I saw two large mounds marking the borderline between the provinces—one hill is located in Bois and the other in Pullie."

"I did not see any mounds," Ike was quick to complain.

"It was hard to spot them in the rain, but I can assure you that they are there." Minia was about to add something else, but the food had arrived and everyone turned to the steaming thick soup. Done with the chowder, we finished the bread and the milk, and then returned outside, where the floods of water continued to harass the land below. Wrapping ourselves in our damp capes, we departed from the small parish parish and, moving along vague muddy tracks left on the ground by some recent wagon or a coach, resumed our stride.

Somewhat bored, I let my horse take me after the others, while I stared blindly at my cold, wet hands that held tight to the straps of the bridle. When I finally decided to look up, to my surprise, I realized that the two mounds of which Minia had spoken, were behind me. If I were to believe Minia's words, I had left my province without even noticing it. Never before had I traveled so far from home, not to mention come to another province. People in Villone would have been so jealous to learn of my luck. I could just imagine their faces, when I told them about it. Such thought made my mood improve. A smile graced my face, and even the misery of the bad weather that had accompanied us through the remainder of the day, did not seem so dreadful anymore. Whistling a wordless tune I watched as dusk slowly hid the vale of grayness in the darker shades, and late hours announced a halt to our advance.

While we could still discern objects around us, we scouted the nearby fields, and after locating a shallow hollow shrouded in large maples, we settled at its edge, avoiding a muddy pool at the bottom. Our attempts to light a fire failed and we had to resort to a cold dry dinner, which was tasteless and hard to swallow. Still the food was filling and eased our hunger, allowing us to lie down on the wet grass, not even bothering to take out our blankets as they were soaked and made no difference on the bare ground.

At dawn, following the same routine, we recommenced the voyage. Fortunately the rain had stopped and the gray shroud dwindled, with patches of blue sky peering sporadically over us, sending out glimpses of long-awaited improvement in the weather. Encouraged by a dry morning and guided by the sightings of the occasional farms that began to appear in the distance, we sent our steed into a gallop. Some time later, we struck a well-cared path that took us up a gentle rise and to the edge of a low valley, where a strong warm wind brought in a distinctive scent that I had never smelled before.

"A very strange smell, what is it?" I asked, breathing in and out several times.

"That, my friend, is the aroma of the sea," replied Minia and as if to demonstrate took a deep long breath himself, releasing the air slowly through his nose.

"We must be getting very close to the city of Pullie then; it sits right on the coast," noted Ark, and he too inhaled.

"A coast? I have never seen a real coast before. I have never seen a real sea either. What does it look like? Is it big? What color are its waters?" Ike went on with his questions, the same questions that had come to me as well.

Although Bois held a long stretch of Normandian coastline, our hometown was too far west from the shores of the Seven Seas and with the folks in Villone not all to keen to travel, almost none, including us, had ever come far enough to see the open waters, reserving to learning about the seas from tales and various pictures. Unlike us though, Minia had been to the sea before— once, when he was a little boy—and though much time had passed since then, he remembered everything and described it to us in detail.

"Oh, the sea is dazzling, my friend." Our company's leader spoke with a note of excitement in his voice. "It has a deep blue color and stretches as far as your eyes can see. Sounds of the coming waves are like music, and the waves are graceful when they move."

Heartened by Minia's sketches, our pace increased. Before we knew it, our mounts were galloping down the open lane, soon bringing us up another mound, where at the summit we had to stop, startled by a view of the open waters that stretched in a long line before us. It was my first glimpse of the Seven Seas and I had no words to describe it. Though I had heard stories and had seen pictures of the vast seas and ocean of Ethoria, they were nothing compared to what was ahead. As far as I could see there was the color blue. Calm and clean as a blank parchment, the waters caressed the coastline, rippled by the reflecting light of the high afternoon sun. While, further off the shore the azure surface was undisturbed, closer to the land the water was seeded with numerous tiny dark dots that reminded me of ants. But they were not ants; they were ships, vessels of different makes and sizes that streamed in and out of Pullie's harbor, situated on the banks of a large bay, shaped in a half circle. The Bay of Winds it was called and it was considered to be the busiest inlet in all Northern Ethoria.

After spending a few more moments at the top, we followed the road down for some time, enjoying the freedom of the open land. But after several more leagues, our advance was slowed to a trot, as other people, on foot and on horseback, began to join us from numerous side lanes, all heading in the direction of the port. The route became much busier and soon its entire width was filled with travelers, horses, and wagons, some dragged by men and others by packs of mules, horses, bulls and ponies, accompanied with much noise and constant squeaking of dozens of spinning wheels. At a snail's pace we fought our way through the dense traffic along the coast, eventually sighting a large hill, which stood bordering the blue of the Sea, its slopes and the land before it seeded with points of rooftops, battlements, and flagpoles.

Before us lay the city of Pullie that was much bigger and very different from any inland municipality like Bonneville. Situated in the lower part of the bay, it started out at the very top of the massive mountain-like rise, its peak dominated by the high battlements of the Duke's immense castle—a massive structure of white stone. Further down, settled along the slopes, grew equally impressive mansions and keeps, which belonged to local nobles who had claimed the higher grounds for themselves so to be close to the main citadel and the High Lord. The richer part descended all the way to the bottom of the hill, where it gave way to the common grounds that composed the bulk of the city and spread for several leagues along the waters, lengthy threads of houses and wide town streets, full of the life suited to the largest seaport in the entire kingdom.

Even though there was still some distance to the first rows of wooden shacks, stone cottages, and logged barracks that marked the outskirts of the city, the traffic about our company grew heavier. On foot and on horseback, alone and in groups, people cramped the wide lane of the road, most moving into the city, later splitting into smaller human streams, filling the many colorful boulevards, wide avenues, and narrow alleys, and merging back a little later at numerous market squares, plazas, and parks, some of which were swathed in a haze of white smoke and dust. Slowing our mounts even more we navigated through the human torrent past the first houses and into a broad street that promised to take us straight to the harbor, where we hoped to find the Five Stars Inn and master Lik along with it.

Convinced that it would take us hours to get through to the sea, I was surprised to find that as we rode further into the city, the crowd dispersed; its movement took on an orderly fashion and allowed us to travel unreservedly in a column of three pairs. Spinning in our saddles and turning our head, we cleared several plazas and reached a tall stone wall that ran athwart the road, blocking it with a large open arch. The road there was guarded by a group of young soldiers, who stood leaned against the barrier, holding onto their long pikes, talking. Although the arcade did not have doors, at the top hung a row of thick metal rods that peeked dauntingly over the path, a hint of a heavy grid, hidden under the large gray plates, ready to be released to impede the way further in.

At first we stopped before the gates, thinking that we had to say something, but as the guards continued to ignore us, we proceeded forth and passed through the archway, throwing our heads up, studying the masonry of the structure. Ten cubits of stone passed quickly and we were back in the open, descending down a gentle slope. Free of another plaza, we eventually came up to a large open bridge, thrown across the grand river that split the city of Pullie in two. The stream was very wide and ran toward the Sea, carrying along its waters numerous boats and fishing scrubs that composed the traffic almost as thick as in the streets above. Constructed of white stone, the bridge was equipped with low iron chain railings and several well-crafted statues of soldiers, which stood at the both ends, each towering some three cubits over the passing folks. Studying the stone figures with interest, we went across and once at the other side, made a quick turn, catching a better view of the harbor tucked between the lines of buildings that ran along the sides. Excitement overwhelmed us, and we hurried our horses, passing the occasional person or cart. Almost at the end of the street the crowd around us became dense again, and for the last several cubits we had to struggle through the course, at long last emerging at the side of the harbor, which was divided into three distinctive areas.

Straight before us, lined up against the stone seacoast stretched wide wooden docks. Wooden wharfs several hundred cubits long, shot into the sea, supported underneath by thick square logged columns that disappeared into the water. Some of them were empty, and others hosted different vessels, which varied in construction and shape. And past them, further to the right, a spacious loading area was set up, its sandy court packed with crates, sacks, and barrels that were placed in long rows, attended by a score of bare-chested dirty men, who moved hastily amongst the loads, always carrying, lifting, and pulling something.

At the other side of the piers, outlined by a low metal railing, was the big market square. Tents of every colors and form, booths, and simple canvas-covered tables made up an intricate maze through which moved vendors, customers, and idlers, a motley crowd that bought and sold everything there was to buy and sell in Ethoria, making much noise and bustle, which at times even overlapped sounds from the docks.

Following Sire Jim's instructions we headed toward the bazaar and circled around it, riding close to the coastline, which was delineated by a tall stone barrier that prevented anyone from falling into the water just several cubits below. Though the distance was a short one, it took us some time to get to the other side of the market grounds, where without stopping we pranced into the first adjacent street that ran straight up to the side of the hill, and we hurried up the slant. Eventually we reached another plaza and a large wooden building with a metal sign attached to it, which read "The Five Stars Inn—All Good men are welcomed."

The building was ordinary in construction. Three stories high, the outside of the house was painted white and the windows, doors, and shutters were coated with a layer of green. Several men stood at the front entrance, but as we came up they left right away, giving us tough glares that hid a glimpse of curiosity and concern. We ignored them and after dismounting, stayed outside, while Minia disappeared through the door, returning a few moments later accompanied by three stable boys. The youngsters quickly took our horses around the corner, and we followed our commander into a small busy dining hall, where several dozen men passed their time, eating, drinking, and playing different card games. Although we did not have the description of the owner, he was not hard to pick—a short, bald man, who sat near large barrels, counting copper coins that he had just received from one of the patrons. We walked straight up to him and after introducing ourselves, explained the situation that had brought us to his place. While we spoke, Master Lik stared at us with suspicion, but after hearing Sire Jim's name, he warmed up and quickly arranged for the aspects of our stay. He allowed us to rent one room for just two coppers a night, and gave us free lunch, which we ate with pleasure. Afterwards we returned to the street, picking our way further up the hill toward the High Lord's castle, keen to seek an audience with the Duke or one of his trusted captains.

Chapter 31

THE CITY lanes took us through the common part and into a more upscale district, which was far less populous, with wider streets and fewer houses. High walls surrounded most of the buildings and elegant metal fences hid lavish gardens and parks, with sounds of music coming from behind some of them. Occasionally two or more avenues came together at large plazas, each decorated with clay tiles and water fountains carved out of solid blocks of white glittering stone. Although there were fewer people on the streets, the number of guards was high. Armed men stood on almost every corner, observing the many gates and open entryways, keeping track of all that went around them. Yet none of the soldiers talked to us, and undisturbed, we continued our climb.

Soon we emerged at a covered bridge built over the deep moat running along the base of the impressive marble barrier that surrounded the mighty fortress of the Duke of Pullie—a formidable structure, different from any other castle we had seen so far. Larger and more complex, the main stronghold of Pullie province sat at the very top of the hill and was composed of three different levels stacked on top of one another, all guarded by their own walls, towers, gates, and bridges. Designed to withstand any siege for months and maybe years, each of the bastion's ranks served both as a separate self-sufficient fort and as an integrated part of the larger defenses, allowing easy access for troops and supplies as circumstances dictated.

Back at the outer bridge, our way was blocked by a well-built gatehouse, which served as the first line of defense, equipped with two heavy metal doors and guarded by a host of heavily armed men. As we came up to the entrance, one of the guards halted us. Lowering his spear and preventing further passage, he moved his glance through each of us and raised his voice, which carried a slightly different accent from what we were used to in Bois.

"Lads, do you have any business being near these gates?" he asked, scratching his nose with his free hand.

"Yes, we do. We are the squires of Sire Rone, the sworn man of the Duke of Bois. We have been sent here by Sire Jim, the second captain with the Duke of Bois, to seek an audience with your High Lord, or one of his captains," replied Minia, unhesitatingly.

"Do you have anything that can prove your words, lad?" the soldier asked.

"Yes, we do." Minia presented Sire Jim's envelope. "This is a letter from the second captain, addressed to the proper authorities. I am sure you will have no trouble detecting his seal on the reverse side."

Minia handed the dispatch to the soldier, who studied it with curiosity. It did not look like the man could read any of the words, but he did recognize the stamp, imprinted in the hardened red wax.

"It looks good enough," he noted in a disinterested tone and lifted his spear, letting us through to the bridge. Underneath a high stone archway, we passed onto the viaduct and hurried across to where another group of armed men stopped us again. They asked the same questions and after inspecting the letter, allowed us through another set of metal doors of the main gates. Past a wide tunnel that stretched beneath the thick outer wall, we entered the inner grounds of the castle's lower level, allocated primarily to living quarters for soldiers and commoners, who manned the many towers and bastions that surrounded the place. Locked in between two rows of stone, the open courtyard made up a wide lane of two hundred cubits and hosted a dozen large stone one-story buildings, placed in two lines, separated by a broad pathway of black bricks, which ran up a gentle slope to the next gatehouse on the upper level.

That day the inner grounds of the lower part of the castle were cramped with people who moved along, minding their own affairs, ignoring our group as we stood at the verge of the tunnel, looking around. For a moment I even thought our arrival went unnoticed, but then as we were about to step forth, a tall older man, dressed in chain mail with a bright red tunic thrown loosely over it, appeared from behind one of the buildings and headed straight toward us, followed by three other fellows, also clad in mails and red tunics.

"Greetings, strangers," the tall soldier addressed us. "I am the sergeant at arms with the guards here at the lower circle. What brings you here tonight?"

To answer, Minia repeated everything he had said twice before at the bridge and showed the letter, which the sergeant studied briefly. Once done, he asked us to dismount and while the other three men attended to our horses, escorted our company to the nearest buildings, keeping the letter to himself. There he took us inside and then across a large hall without any walls to where behind a small elegant desk, covered in red silky cloth, sat a man dressed in the uniform of chain and red tunic. Yet, he did not look like the other guards in the room.

His features were too elegant, his manners—too graceful, and around his neck hung a thick chain with a steel disk attached to it. Without a doubt, he was a nobleman who held some rank.

The man seemed busy with papers that were scattered around the table, but as we walked up, announcing our presence with a loud clank of steel, he raised his head and leaned back in the chair, looking curiously at the sergeant and then at our group.

"Vick, what is it?" The man at the desk said, crossing his arms over his chest.

"My apologies, Sire Van, but I have a group of squires from Bois, who are here to ask for an audience with our High Lord."

"What is the reason that entitles them for such request to be granted?"

"They have a dispatch from Bonneville, addressed to the Duke."

"Uh-huh, do you have it?"

"Yes, Sire, I do." The sergeant handed the envelope to the officer and took a couple of steps back, joining us several cubits away. Sire Van examined the letter and noted, "The seal seems to be authentic, and the names on the front are correct. I do not see why they cannot speak with someone at the second circle. Vick," the lord turned to his man, "escort them to Sire Matt Atefield. He will know what to do next. Before you do though, collect their weapons. We do not need any trouble out there."

Sire Van threw another glance at our company and without ever addressing us, waved his hand off, quickly returning to his paperwork.

Outside we surrendered our weapons and headed up the slope, trailing after our guide. Making several stops along the way, we passed three more sets of guards and arrived at the second level, or the second circle as it was called. Different from the lower part, the higher grounds appeared was much more colorful, with a lot of green coming from many trees and patches of grass covering most of the space between buildings, many of which were two or three stories high, and made of large logs, coated with white clay. At least three stable yards and several more holding pens were there too and held a handful of animals, horse, cows, and goats that were attended by scores of servants, mostly boys and young men, who used buckets to fill in long wooden trays with yellowish fodder.

Past them, we looped around the base of the inner wall and came up to one of the few stone structures, whose doors and windows were braised with thick steel rods. At the entrance three soldiers of fair build were sitting on the steps, two more were resting by a far corner, and another group of four men huddled by an open mud pen, where several lazy hogs leisurely lay on top of the dried-out mire. As we arrived, the men at the front door got up and lifted their spears, blocking the way. But after talking to the sergeant, they stepped aside and we went into a dark corridor, then up the stairs to another hallway on the upper level, whose clay walls were covered with large red banners, decorative weapons, and low-hanging lanterns that radiated a soft glow.

At the other end of the passage was a round doorway attended by two more men. Vick talked to them too, and once we were inspected for weapons, we proceeded through the cast-iron door and into a larger round room, where a heavyset, middle-aged man stood near an opened window, staring blindly at the court below. He wore the same red tunic as the rest of the men inside the castle, which covered his shiny mail, bound by a thick silver belt with a long sword attached to it.

The man by the window was clearly an officer, a nobleman of a high class. He remained unmoving for a while, then took a deep breath and turned to us, granting us a strict, examining glance. We remained quiet and let our guide greet the officer with a well-trained salute, straightening up and pushing his skinny chest further out. In that pose the sergeant froze. In response the officer nodded, accepting the salutation, and turned back to the window, sighing loudly before beginning to speak, his voice soft, his speech genteel.

"I assume you have something important for me," said the man slowly.

"Yes, Sire. These are the messengers from Bois. They were sent here to deliver a personal dispatch to our High Lord or one of his captains," replied the sergeant hastily.

"Do you have the dispatch?"

"Yes, I have it right here."

"Then give it to me." Apparently irritated, the officer extended his hand still looking through the window and waited as the sergeant hurried to get the envelope out of his pocket and into the hands of his superior. The nobleman then flipped the letter several times and was about to open it, when Minia's objection broke the silence.

"Sire, before you do anything with this dispatch, may I have the privilege of inquiring about your rank?"

"Why should I tell you? I do not assume you hold a rank of any kind, do you?"

"No, Sire. I am but a squire in the service of Sire Rone, but I have my orders."

"Huh, squires. That is a waste of resources; to send six men to deliver one little letter. How inappropriate…"

"Be as it may, I still have to ask you to reveal your rank with this garrison, Sire," insisted Minia. It was rather strange to see my commander acting with such boldness. Clearly the man in front of us was no ordinary soldier; he probably was not even an ordinary officer either. But it did not seem to bother Minia as he refused to give.

"Why is my rank so important to you? I can assure you I am entitled to see the content of this letter. You have done your duty; you have delivered the message. Now leave…"

"I cannot do so. Sire Jim, the second captain of the guards with the Duke of Bois, has instructed us to give the dispatch to the High Lord or one of his captains. Unless you hold such rank, I must insist that you escort us to someone who does, so I can personally deliver the letter."

"Huh, you say you were instructed to do so…How odd…"

"If you do not trust my word, look at the writing on the envelope. It will prove everything I have just said."

The nobleman flipped the letter again, then brought it up to the light and ran his eyes through the few short lines inscribed in the left-hand corner of the envelope. A brief smile graced his face, and he added, "Indeed, it does say that. I guess you know how to read after all. Oh well, my apologies." The officer handed the letter back to Minia and stepped away, adjusting his tunic around the waist. "Since you have asked, I am the second captain here at the second circle. Sire Matt Atefield is my name; of course you did not know that, did you? You are but a squire."

The man returned his glance to the window and continued. "As you can see, I have all the rights to read this dispatch…but I will not do so, because I respect the request of the honorable Lord of Bois. Therefore, I will personally escort you to see one of the captains. That way you will be able to deliver the message, just as you have been told to do, and I will make sure that you do so properly, squire…"

Emphasizing the very last word, the second captain walked toward the other end of the room and picked up a pair of light leather gloves. After he tugged them under his belt, he gave out another loud sigh of irritation, and nodded for the sergeant to open the door. Vick complied immediately, but Sire Matt did not follow. Instead he walked back to his desk and opened one of the drawers, looking for something. He brushed away some of the papers and feathered pens, and extracted a long necklace and put it on. It was a golden chain with a large round medallion affixed to it. Although I only saw the necklace briefly, there was something familiar about it, something that gave an uneasy feeling. But I brushed my worries aside and trailed after the second captain.

In the yard, Sire Matt turned left and followed a sandy lane for several hundred cubits, soon reaching another building, similar to the one we had left a moment before. Two stories high, it was also laid in stone and heavily guarded by at least ten men. Seeing the second captain and the sergeant draw near, the men gave out salutes and stepped aside, letting us proceed through a series of short hallways, eventually coming to a large room occupied by four men, one of whom was another officer, his outfit much brighter, and more luxurious than the others. Before us stood Sire Signum, the captain of the second circle, an older gentleman, his hair and short beard touched by long streaks of gray. A bright red vest covered his armor and displayed a fiery picture of a sailing ship, coming across the waves. And though he did not wear any weapons, I could see a large sword hanging on a wall behind him, a splendid blade, which showed that this man was the captain.

Just past an iron-framed door, my companions and I halted while Sire Matt walked forth and accompanying his speech with a graceful bow, went on to explain the aspects of the visit, pointing at us now and then. I stressed my ears, trying to catch the words, but as the second captain turned again, I was suddenly startled by what I saw. Incised onto the polished surface of the golden medallion that swung on Sire Matt's chest, was a symbol a bird, its eyes adorned with two different stones, one green and one red. "A man with a strange golden bird." I recalled A'tie's warning. She had said be wary of a man who owns such bird, as he is the enemy. Was she trying to tell me of Sire Matt? If so then the second captain was the foe. But how could it be? How could a lord, an officer with the Duke's garrison, be a traitor? The questions were hard and I had no answers. My eyes focused on the golden bird's almost perfect image.

The day after the visions of A'tie had come to me, I told my friends about the warning. They seemed to take its meaning seriously, but some hours later forgot about it. I did too. But standing before the image of the golden bird, inside the second circle of Pullie's grand citadel, everything came back to me— the vision, the A'al's words, and the warning. Unfortunately my friends did not seem to notice the disturbing image, and I had no way of letting them onto my find. All I could do was hope that none of them would reveal anything important about our quest in front of Sire Matt, not until we could be sure that he was not one with the enemy.

Hearing little what transpired a few cubits away, I remained absent until a loud deep voice restored my awareness.

"…This is a very interesting manuscript you bring me today." I caught the speech in its midst. "I can see why there has been such a need for you to deliver this dispatch to me directly." The captain, whose name was Sire Sigmun, walked to a chair placed in a corner, in the shade, and climbed into it, dropping down on a soft saffron pillow that covered the seat.

"Leave us," he said, when he felt comfortable enough. "I need to speak with these squires alone."

While some men in the room obeyed the order without question, several of them, including Sire Matt, stared at their commander in confusion. But when the lord repeated his command they left too, except for Sire Matt, who remained unmoving. The silence filled the space. We did not dare to speak, nor did we have to. The pause lasted only for a moment as the captain was quick to raise his voice again, addressing Sire Matt directly.

"I said. I want to speak with these men alone, officer. Is there anything you do not understand about the order?"

"No Sire, but I do not think it is wise to be left alone with six of them. We do not know for sure if what they claim is true. I think it is a question of your safety," started the second captain. But his explanation was cut short.

"Thank you for your concern, but it is up to me to decide on questions of my own safety. So…," the captain gave the officer a tough stare and nodded toward the door.

"But, Sire…"

"You have heard me."

"As you wish, your Lordship, as you wish." The second captain waved off a brushing salute and walked out, shutting the door from the other side. When his footsteps finally died out, Sire Sigmun relaxed in the chair and said, "Now, I need you tell me all that the letter does not say."

"Yes, Sire. What would you like to know?" asked Minia without hesitation.

"Everything, squire. Everything."

The captain's request was fulfilled to the highest extent. Minia told him everything, from our first meeting in the woods of Bois to the arrival at Pullie, nothing escaping his story. While Minia spoke, the captain listened. Occasionally he threw a quick glance at the letter and often moved his head, as if verifying the authenticity of the account.

"Do you think those Alavantars are responsible for all of the mischief in our kingdom?" he asked when Minia was done.

"We are not certain, but the only way to find out is to catch the one called Azmal. Judging from the letter we found in the inn back in Bois, he is hiding somewhere in this city."

"Huh…that can be somewhat of a challenge," said the captain. "I know Bonneville is a big city, but Pullie is twice its size. There are more people around these walls than in the entire province of Bois. Merchants, strangers, pilgrims, sailors, and common folks, all of them come here for one reason or another. Although we manage to keep track of those who dwell within the castle grounds, beyond the outer walls—it is nearly an impossible task. Only Spirit knows how many people are wandering there.

"But since this matter is indeed very serious, I will do as Sire Tem has requested and help you look for that Azmal. Besides I owe your High Lord a favor. You probably do not know, but he was the one to recommend me for this job. Yes, yes. I served under his command back in the old days, when knighthood and chivalry meant something. Not like today, when any halfwit with a noble name can claim himself a knight. Those young fools who flock to the kingdom's capital, can barely handle their spoons; how can they use swords or lances?

"I ask you, where are those brave men, the fierce warriors who put down the uprising in Puno, or fought in the border wars against Westalia, paying dearly with their own sweat and blood? I will tell you—they are all gone— many have died and those who are still alive waste time within their castles, too old or too drunk to raise their arms again. Common soldiers are no better. Look around. Only a handful of the men here at the castle have seen combat. Most of them have never been face-to-face with an enemy. They may look and act tough, but anyone can do it against street drunks and petty thugs. When it comes down to a real battle, I am afraid not too many of them will retain their valor.

"Sad, is it not?…It is…" The captain continued to talk but his voice got softer and softer, turning into a mumble which none of us could understand. For a while the old lord whispered to himself, but then shook his head, and as if remembering that we were still in the room, returned his glance to us.

"In any case, you have a job to do, and you can count on my assistance." The captain got up and walked across the room, where, hung on the wall, was a broad tapestry with a picture of the city drawn on it.

"This is Pullie. Impressive, is it not?" the captain said thoughtfully, pointing at the thick black lines woven into the colored cloth. "There are four major districts to it. The castle, the upper side, which is right below us, the common quarters, which make up the majority of the city, and the harbor. I do not think you will find your perpetrator anywhere within the castle. No stranger goes unnoticed here, no deal is done without approval from an officer. The upper side is an unlikely site for such activity either. There are no taverns, no inns in the district, and the local nobility are too busy with their petty intrigues, love affairs, and lavish parties, having no time or brains for such conspiracies. Besides, it is not even worth trying; a few leagues from the hill you can do almost anything you like and nobody will care. The harbor slums are heaven for the underworld—dozens of taverns, and hundreds of pubs, where thugs and outlaws find their refuge. It is my guess that the one you seek is there, sitting in some watering hole, scheming his new strike against our kingdoms.

"Alas, I will not be able to help you much when it comes to the lower parts of the city. While the Duke's garrison takes care of the castle and the upper slopes, the city watch handles the rest, and though the city watchers are considered to be military men, in truth they are simple commoners picked from amongst the city folks, having little knowledge or skill when it comes to martial duties. Still, there are a few of them who know their job and do it well. Master Huck is one. For the past five years he was Pullie's chief of the city watch and since it takes much experience to know about what goes on within the poorer areas and the harbor, it is him you should consult. If he knows anything he will tell you, and if he does not he will offer his help to narrow down the search. Should his effort be useless too, come back to me and we will try our luck in the upper parts. But I am afraid that by that time it will probably be too late."

The captain walked over to a desk that stood several cubits away from his chair and picked up a piece of paper, on which he quickly wrote several lines of black ink. Then he sprinkled some white powder over the writing and folded the letter, sealing its edges with hot wax, marking it with an imprint from his ring.

"Give this to the chief of the watch," the captain said and handed the scroll to Minia, who tucked it away under his leather vest. "One of my men will escort you to the city watch headquarters down at the harbor. You are dismissed. Now go."

Sire Sigmun grabbed a small brass bell that hung unnoticed at his arm's reach and rang it several times. The door opened and the same familiar faces appeared in the doorway, quickly refilling the place, resuming their duties, and bringing the noise back inside. The only two who did not return were Sire Matt and Vick. I found it strange, but did not give it much thought, as we were already heading to the yard.

Back outside a young fellow, short and skinny, met us with a loud yell. "Hello! My name is Iko and I am the squire to Sire Sigmun. He tells me you need some help getting to Chief Huck. If there is nothing else you want to do here, I am ready to take you to the harbor."

The young soldier grimaced and once we nodded in assent headed toward the main gates. After leaving the castle and the outer bridge, the squire led us through one narrow street after another. It was a different way, not the one we had taken up the hill. But the man knew his way around the city, and soon the first glimpses of the harbor, began to linger amongst the rooftops of the houses ahead. By then we had left the last of the lavish manors, and entered the much busier streets of the common area, halting half a league later at the entrance to a wide bulky-looking house that stretched for at least a hundred cubits along the paved lane. Except for its size, the structure looked ordinary, plain carvings around many of the windows, thick brown boards, and simple gray masonry at the base.

Unlike the castle, the city watch headquarters' front doors were left unattended, with people of all sorts walking in and out of the building, paying little notice to a large wooden sign that served as the only reminder that it was, in fact, a military post charged with the duty of protecting streets and alleys from troubles, booze, and larceny, all too common for the bigger cities like Pullie.

Following Iko, we went inside and immediately proceeded up the stairs, coming to a big open hall, packed with many desks and chairs set up in several long rows. Behind each desk sat a man dressed in black clothing, and opposite him stood groups of people, commoners for the most part, who formed numerous intertwining lines that created an image of complete disorder. Yet somehow everything and everybody moved amenably, as if knowing exactly where they had to go. Unlike them, I felt completely lost and kept close to the squire, who, maintaining the same fast pace, took us to the door at the other end of the hall. Stopping there, Iko knocked several times. Right away the large timber flap opened and another young fellow, also dressed in a black tunic, appeared before us. He and our guide exchanged a few words and then stepped in, inviting us along with them.

The room we had entered was ordinary in its layout—a desk, a couple of chairs, two windows, some tapestries, and stacks of paper, placed randomly, attended by several more men; all young and all dressed in the same black uniforms. Each of them looked very busy, writing or reading or moving something, and remained silent, paying us just quick disinterested stares. The only one who did not was a heavyset man who sat behind the largest desk and followed us curiously as we made our approach. After Iko presented him with a report, the man shifted in his seat and addressed us.

"Greetings to you, squires," he said, sounding strict. "My name is Master Huck, Huck Enric, and I am the chief commander of the city watch in Pullie. Can I have the note from Sire Sigmun?"

"Here it is," Minia was quick to respond, handing over the letter, which the chief began to read slowly, massaging his temples as his eyes moved across the page. While he did, I took a moment to get a better look at the him.

Master Huck was a man in his forties, not young, and not yet old. Wide in the shoulders, he was not tall, and his once-fit body had long since lost its shape to food and ale, which took away most of the man's athletic looks, leaving him with a large belly and wide cheeks that had a slightly red tan to them. Unlike the others in the room or in the building, Master Huck did not wear black. Instead his clothes were of a dark blue color and on his chest, just under a broad pocket, hung a large silver badge with the symbol of a flying bird, similar to the one I had seen on Sire Matt, only more plain and without any incrustations.

"It says here you need some help with a case of yours…"

"Yes chief, we need to find a man. We do not know who he is, but we think his name is Azmal and he is here in Pullie."

"Why do you seek him?"

"We believe that he is connected to a series of murders in our province."

Hearing that, Master Huck thought for a moment, scratching his chin with his large fingers, then said, "It is a serious business. But I can tell you that it will not be easy. There are plenty of places where characters like your Azmal can hide and it can take weeks before we find him.

"Mmmm. Let's see. We are most probably looking for someone with a lot of cash, who prefers to stay away from the law and closer to places favored by thugs for hire." The chief thought some more then said, sighing, "He could be anywhere…." He clapped his hands. "I will tell you what we will do; I ask one of my men to take you on a little tour around the less favored part of the city. Even if your character is not there, someone may know something about him. In the meantime I will check with some of my sources in the city and try to find some leads. With luck we will come up with something by the end of the day."

"Hey, Pete," Master Huck addressed one of the men next to him. "Set aside your work and take these boys to see Lark. Tell him they need an outing around the strip. Also, tell him to take a couple of his lads along just in case. You never know what you will find in those holes. Any questions?"

"No, chief," roared the man and took off for the door.

"Well, fellows, follow Pete to one of my deputies. His name is Lark and he will help you with your search. Before you go, just a piece of advice—be careful out there. Most of the patrons in those establishments you will visit are not too friendly. Make sure you have your weapons ready. You may encounter a scuffle or two. Try not to kill anyone though…Save me some paper work."

We promised the chief to be gentle with any opponents we met and after thanking him for his assistance, hurried after Pete, who was already at the other end, waiting for us near the staircase. When we caught up with him, he resumed walking and, pushing aside some of the visitors, descended down to the first floor. At the base of the stairs, he made a turn and, past a long wide hallway, brought us to another room, where a group of several men sat around a table—deputy Lark and his guards. All of them were cheerful young lads who did not mind helping us, though I suspected that they were just too bored to sit idle and were glad to catch some fresh air. Since it was already past sunset, we decided to postpone the tour until the next morning, when some hours before midday break our company was to meet Lark and his men at the city watch building and then set on a prowl through the worst parts of the seaport.

Chapter 32

ONE AFTER another, we visited local watering spots dispersed around the city's lower districts. While there were a few decent places on our route, most of the so-called establishments were too small and filthy to even have names.

Gathering holes for some of the worst characters the seaport had to offer, there was little civility or order. While the majority of the hostelries were deserted, the people we did find yielded little sympathy, as they were either too drunk or too quick to remove themselves from the eyes of the city watch, disappearing into the many shadows of the surrounding houses. The only people who did talk to us were a few bartenders and tavern owners. We heard the same things—nobody knew anyone who resembled Azmal's description and nobody noticed anything suspicious going on. That diminished our chances of ever finding the mysterious paymaster, and coupled with the hot temperatures that settled over the city, made our search even more difficult.

By midafternoon we had gone through several dozen spots that gave us nothing we could use in our quest. Then, an hour or so later, we came up to a small, plain-looking cottage that sat amongst other equally boring structures of simple design and construction. Once painted white, its walls carried a grayish tint, and at the base were splashed with muddy brown streaks that had dried out and crumbled in places. Composed of two levels, the building seemed to be very old and slanted heavily to one side. Yet it remained intact and even hosted several complex additions, affixed at the sides that hung over the street like olden branches on a dead tree. Several large windows looked just as crooked, some of them covered with aged boards, nailed to the frames from the inside. Two doors, low steps, a railing that separated half-ruined stables, and scores of insects of all colors concluded the picture and served as the only indication that it was in fact a tavern we were looking at.

Although the place looked no different from other sites, I noted a few oddities about it. Weary from all the walking in the sun, nobody but I observed, in a brief moment, as a couple of strangers who had been sitting on a low bench in front of the building, slid back inside once they spotted us. Nor did anyone notice how at the same time two other fellows took off running down one of the side alleys, taking with them their lengthy dark capes that concealed something resembling long swords. Concerned, I wanted to alert the others, but by then most of city watchers and my companions had already entered the untidy house, led by the deputy chief, who seemed to enjoy the tour a little more than the others. I hurried after them and went into a murky hall that stretched for twenty some cubits, its walls covered with cheap old rags that once had been colored draperies. At both ends two separate corridors were placed at either side of a low counter, behind which peered many barrels and crates, stacked in one large heap. A rather repulsive ceiling, made of straw bundles and pine boards, had largely been damaged by the recent rains, displaying large yellowing stains. And under our feet, wide, unpolished boards composed a tilted floor, occupied in places by rows of square tables and benches, all of which exuded the odor of filth and sweat that only added to the distaste that ruled the tavern.

A small crowd of ten men sat in different places, chatting away about something that concerned us little. Our arrival made them raise their heads. But as soon as they noticed the city watch amongst us, their eyes darted away and remained elsewhere, pretending not to hear us come in. Reluctant to stay there for too long, my companions and I remained at the door and waited as the deputy and his men went on with the questioning, which usually lasted for a brief time and included some yelling and shoving of those not too enthusiastic to answer the inquiries.

The first to be questioned was a small man behind one of the tables. Although I could not hear much, I saw as the stranger shook his head several times and pointed toward the counter, where a well-built tall fellow was sitting pensively on a high stool, flipping some silverware in his hands. I did not know if he was the owner of the eatery or simply worked there, but he seemed to be the one in charge of the hall. As Lark went over to him with his questions, the man answered with short phrases, and the two engaged in a prolonged discussion, which again evaded my ears since the other city watchers decided to busy themselves with commenting aloud on a couple of young serving girls, who happened to pass by, letting loud remarks and bursts of laughter eat away the peace.

With the interrogation well on the way, bored and hot I skid my eyes across the room. Though there was little to look at, I found it somewhat interesting to observe three drunks who were debating over whose turn it was to pay for their next drinks. None of them had any money, but their thirst for more ale was overwhelming, and so they argued violently amongst themselves, shoving and accusing each other of every possible wrongdoing. Tension grew and I was about to witness a brawl, when the entertaining scene was interrupted by Lark's voice.

The deputy had returned from the counter and was standing next to us, tapping his gloved fingers on the hilt of the sword.

"I think we may have some luck today," he said quickly. "The owner was kind enough to indulge me with a small piece of information that may be useful."

Lark chuckled and turned his head as if worried that someone else was listening. Assured otherwise, he returned his focus on us, grinning. Then, he nodded toward the man at the counter, who was still standing several cubits away, pretending to be busy cleaning clay plates, and added, "If that fool is not lying, a group of strange foreigners have been seen in here for the past several weeks."

"What do you mean by foreigners?" Minia followed with a question.

"They looked like typical hired swords from the south. Several of them came here last season, and reserved two rooms, for which they paid handsomely. Weeks later some more of the men arrived and once they did, strange dealings started to take place. Although the owner claims he does not know what the Southerners have been doing in his tavern, he says that almost every day they received scores of visitors. As you can probably guess those guests of theirs were not exactly the cream of the crop; I mean; they were people you would never share a cup of ale with—some of the worst cutthroats you can find here."

"It sounds very fishy," agreed Minia, following the deputy's telling closely.

"You are right, it does. Look at this hovel. Even the least respected rovers have to be persuaded to come here, not to mention do any business. It is either that those foreigners are plain stupid, or they have something they really do not want the authorities to see. I would bet you my whole month's pay it is the second one, and I am intending to find out what exactly they do not want us to know."

What I had heard from the deputy sounded that we were on a right track, and though I did not think that Azmal was amongst the strangers who had been spotted there, I hoped that someone would know something about him.

In any case, we had to try the new lead. While everyone huddled together at the front door, Minia and Lark discussed the next step. The two spoke for some time, and afterwards presented the rest with a plan, which was quite simple. Since the owner claimed to have seen some of the Southerners departing from their quarters a while back, we were to start with their room. If no one was there, we would wait for them in the dining hall, while several of the city watchers would remain inside the chambers, in case the Southerners used the back door.

Soon all the preparations were over and we were ready to begin. The deputy and five of the city watchers led the way into one of the hallways and positioned themselves around a small timber door. We kept several steps behind, weapons ready and tension rising, waiting for the city watch to make their move. Since nobody was sure what to expect on the other side, the deputy suggested utilizing the element of surprise and ordered his men to break through, which they did, planting their shoulders into the boards, splintering them into many little pieces. With debris flying everywhere—some of the chips even hitting me in the face—the men of the city watch charged through the broken entryway, Lark taking charge, his sword raised before him. We dashed forth too, but had to wait as the opening was crammed with the deputy's men. The backs of those in front of us blocked our view, but I could hear shouts and commands that soon changed to sounds of an ongoing fight, joined a moment later by cries of the wounded.

Finally the entry was free and we moved in, emerging at the edge of a large room full of commotion. The scene was chaotic. The spacious chamber looked small, as at least twenty men came together in a clash, leaving no room even for the full swing of a short sword. Thick damp stuffy air made it hard to breath, and heartbreaking screams of the injured and dying were deafening. With craziness all around me everything blended together, and I struggled to separate friend from foe. Confused, I paused, but not for long, for my dilemma was soon resolved when a sudden blade almost took my head off.

Luckily for me, my brother was next to me, ready to parry the attack. As a thin line of steel bounced off Ric's axe, I spun around in one motion and came face-to-face with the source of the aggression—a tall slender man dressed in short-sleeved chain mail, covered with a light leather vest. His long blonde hair was strapped into a ponytail, and a pair of gray eyes hid little mercy for my soul. Granting the foe but a glance, I launched my own attack, giving in to the frenzy of the moment current. Dodging another blow, I slid to one side and threw myself forward, but the attempt failed as my sword sliced the air just a tenth of a cubit away from the enemy's neck.

I tried the same move several more times, but all my efforts failed, and I had to change my tactics. Relying on my brother, who was about to thrust his huge axe at the opponent, I slid behind the man. To my surprise, the enemy did not notice my maneuver and so had to accept his fate, which was decided with just a single strike of my weapon. The A'al shadow dagger sliced through leather and metal with ease and sank deep into the man's flesh, stopping him from ever letting out a single shriek. His body froze, his weapon left his hand, and he fell down onto the floor, already sticky with blood. As his last breath of life breezed through the air, I was busy with another fight.

Without even a glance at the motionless man, I hurried to Ark, Rob, and Ike who were with another enemy. Their foe was very effective in keeping my friends from scoring a single blow, parrying their every hit, still having time to counterattack. One of such counter strikes barely missed Ike's chest, and another sliced off a piece of tunic from Rob's sleeve. Yet nobody got injured and the fight continued, four men moving sporadically around a broken chair that lay on the ground. But it did not last, as with my arrival the foe's concentration broke. Focusing on my movement, he missed Ike's lethal blow that struck the man's rib cage. Fatally wounded, the enemy still did not die. His face twisted in agony, he stepped back; but unable to fight anymore, he grabbed onto his side and slid down, moaning loudly. With him no longer posing any threat, we switched our attention elsewhere.

Hastily overlooking the room, I spotted the deputy, who was pushed against a wall, battling two opponents at once. Lark was struggling, so I rushed to help, crushing into the enemies' ranks, sending them flying in opposite directions. As they stumbled, one of them lost his balance and fell to one knee, dropping his sword in a process. Unluckily for him, before he could pick it up, Rob's double-edged axe crushed his spine. The heavy metal razor slashed through man's neck and shoulder and almost split his body in half. The gory image was too violent to look at, and I could feel my guts spinning inside me. But there was no room for sickness; the other enemy had rejoined the fight, assisted by one other man, who had disposed of a young city watcher a little earlier.

"Who are these people?" I let the words form a question, struggling to keep my breath steady.

"I have no idea," replied the deputy. "I can tell you one thing though…" The deputy parried another blow and leapt forth to counterattack. A quick strike, then another, and he was back to the same spot. "They do not like the city watch."

I ducked and let a sword pass over my head.

"Was it something you said?" I asked, hoping to bring a little spark of humor into the ordeal.

"I am sure that is the reason," the deputy replied as he lodged back, avoiding the tip of a rapier, which disappeared as swiftly as it sprang out. "Why else would they be so upset with us?" We smiled.

Around us more men fell, some still alive, some dead. Bodies of guards and their foes were scattered everywhere. Besides our company, out of some twenty men who clashed that day, half were on the floor and the rest were trying desperately not to meet the same end. And though there were fewer fighters, the battle continued with everlasting fury. Soon it became visible though that we were winning. Still the remaining enemies were still unwilling to surrender. They persisted in holding their ground and presented us with the challenge of getting out of that luck-forgotten place alive. But when one more of the foes collapsed, their ranks broke and those who could move, scurried for the doorway and the windows. Three managed to escape; two others were cut down trying. Several of the city watchers dashed after the fleeing men, yelling as they ran. Soon though the sounds of pursuit were gone, and where once I had heard the clanking of metal and screams of the wounded, now were soft shuffling noises from many feet and heavy breathing. The fight was finally over.

Chapter 33

WHEN THE dust settled, I took a look around. Puddles of blood turned the floor red. Stools, desks, and trunks were strewn everywhere, scattered across the chamber, some tipped over, others completely smashed by the fight. By the shattered windows, where several bodies lay uncovered, the deputy chief was arranging his men, discharging a couple of them to pursue the fleeing foes, and one of the others to bring help from headquarters. The remaining watchers were grouped around two other doors placed on one of the side walls, which had remained closed throughout the fight.

"Three, two, one…" The deputy counted silently, waving his hand, and in a chorus two groups, city watchers and us, burst through, sending the doors inward with full force. Minia rushed first, then Ric, Ike, Rob, and Ark, with me last. Our blades were ready to swing at anyone who might be hiding inside, but there was no one to confront. The room was empty. Only a half burnt candle showed some movement, and even it died out, swallowed by the gust of wind that entered along with us.

Plain walls of oak boards bound a little square space that greeted us. A small window was left open at one end, and at the other—a single desk stood pushed up to a half-round stone structure that towered two quarters of a cubit off the floor and served as a fireplace, exposing a heap of blackened ashes stored inside a small cavity.

Relived that we did not have to fight again, we lowered our weapons and slowly walked up to the table, studying cautiously the items that occupied it— books, parchments, and fragile piece of yellow paper. But as we were about to examine the first text, the deputy's voice reached us from the other room.

"Hey, squires…Come over here, I think you need to see this."

Words still ringing through, we hurried into the next chamber where the group of city watchers huddled around something to the left of the door. Keen to find out what it was, I crossed the empty chamber with no windows or fixtures and, shaking an unpleasant odor, made my way through the ranks of men, halting at last, startled by what I had uncovered. Less than a cubit away, almost touching the tips of Lark's boots, sat a man. He was covered in dirt, and his hair was long and dirty, oily streaks giving it a greasy vile look. Black stains spotted most of his bare skin and his clothes were nothing more than a pile of rags, which retained only a fraction of their form, suggesting that the man had spent more than a day or two behind those dark walls. Such suspicion was reaffirmed when I noticed that one of the stranger's ankles was bound by a large crude iron ring, which was attached to a thick chain screwed into the floor and reinforced by four metal bars that ran diagonally along the edges of the link.

While everyone stared at the stranger quietly, the deputy questioned him. But the man did not answer and only sat on the floor, glancing straight at Lark, composed and somewhat relaxed.

"I will repeat myself," said the deputy angrily. "What is your name and why are you here?"

The man remained silent for a little longer, then spat on the floor and climbed to his feet. He stood over two cubits tall, towering over most of the men before him.

"Who is asking?" his voice finally rang out calmly as he faced his questioner. While his shaggy outfit yielded pity, his manners and posture showed confidence and strength. The poor condition of the holding cell and a thick chain at his ankle did not seem to bother him much, nor did our numbers and weapons, some still drawn and ready to strike. Whoever the stranger was, he did not look scared.

"I am the deputy with the city watch of Pullie," replied Lark. "Now how about some answers? We do not have all day, and frankly, I do not have much patience either."

"Huh, the city watch you say…Where were you four weeks ago, when they dragged me in here?" the stranger replied in a cool tone. This time I could pick out a distinctive accent, common to people from the south of Ethoria.

"That can be discussed later. What I need right now is a correct response, or should we escort you to a less comfortable setting? There are always some extra rooms in our jail. Maybe a couple of nights in one of them will clear your mind. What do you say?"

The deputy was clearly irritated and I could not blame him. After hours of tiresome search through the worst spots of the city, and the brutal fight, there was little room left for patience.

"Does it really make any difference?" The stranger leaned against the wall. "Still I would rather enjoy a nice warm bed and a hot meal. So if you must know, my name is Elson and I have come here from the southern realm of Azoros."

"Azoros! Would you, by any chance, be one of those southern hired swords Azoros is so famous for?" The deputy asked, with a hint of interest.

"Indeed I am," replied the prisoner. "Elson Rian of the Amber River, a swordsman for hire at your service."

"I knew it. Another mercenary, huh?" the deputy's reply was quick. "Do you have anything that can verify your words?"

"I did, but as you can see, I ran into some troubles, and subsequently lost most of my possessions. I do not know what exactly they did with my things, but I would not be surprised if most of them have found new owners at one of the local markets. Yet, something tells me that this explanation is not good enough, is it?"

"No, it is not. I will need to see some real proof."

"I figured so." The man knelt down and searched through a stack of hay next to him. Shortly after, he came back up and showed a small metal object, attached to a thin chain. It was a medallion, a silver disk with the symbol of a sword splitting the sun, drawn in it.

"The Southern Circle," uttered Lark, staring at the unusual emblem.

"I see you are familiar with my kind. I am flattered; I did not realize that anyone would recognize it so far north."

"What does it mean?" asked one of the younger city watchers, who stood next to the deputy. I had the same question.

"The Southern Circle," repeated the deputy. "It is a well-known mercenary band from Azoros, notorious for completing every mission it has ever been hired for. It is said that they are some of the best fighters in the world, and each nominee has to go through years of training and initiations before becoming a member. This mark—the sword breaking the sun—is their insignia, given only to the initiated associates of the band."

The deputy looked at the amulet one more time, then Elson picked it up. "You are correct so far. The Southern Circle is a group of men, like myself, who provide assistance to those who can afford us. We do not deal with assassinations, nor do we kill without consent from the local authorities. Our main duties are mostly private investigations, protection of property, retrieval of stolen goods, and search of missing persons. While other mercenaries take jobs from any employer, we work only with those who are in good standing with the law. And though our prices are high, we always finish assignments, even if it means scarifying our own lives."

Elson smiled and pointed to the medallion. "Do not worry; this is as authentic as it can be. I was lucky my attackers did not find it when they took away all my belongings."

"Assuming that you tell the truth, what business do you have in Pullie?"

"Actually my business is, well was, in Chantue. A client of the Southern Circle, a famed merchant from the House of Glory, which rules of the city of Nacitav in Azoros, requested to investigate the dealings of two traders from Normandia, who, as he believes, had stolen from him a considerable sum of gold. Those merchants live in Chantue and it was there I was heading. But before I could reach my destination, I stopped in Pullie to purchase some supplies. Alas, my plans were obviously disturbed. One night, when I was coming back from the harbor with a load of grain sacks a group of thugs ambushed me. They descended from the shadows and caught me by surprise. I managed to fight them off for a while, but their numbers were too great. Before I knew it, someone hit me over the head, and when I came back to my senses I was in this cell, with shackles on my ankle, tied up like a dog."

"Would you care to tell me, exactly, who put you here and why?"

"The answers to both questions are simple," replied Elson as he ran his hand down an unshaved greasy cheek. "I do not know. The only thing I am sure about is that they did not intend to kill me, as they could have done so back in the alley. I assume they knew who I was and probably wanted to ransom me back to the Southern Circle—or even better, sell me off to one of its enemies."

Elson gave the deputy another look and added, "Since you are asking me these questions, I assume none of my captors has survived the skirmish."

"I am afraid so. A few managed to escape; my men are looking for them as we speak. But I would not be surprised if we never see them again."

"Too bad, too bad," commented Elson. "But, what can you do…?"

The Southerner thought some more and asked again, "Can I inquire as to your plans for me—am I under arrest? Because if I am, I want you to know that I have not done anything illegal, nor do I intend to do so in the future. All I want right now is a hot bath, a sharp razor, and a soft bed—those haystacks are very uncomfortable, you know."

"Although I do not see any reasons to arrest you, I still have to check your story. So while I will not put you in jail, I instruct you to stick around for a day or two, so I can clear up all my questions with headquarters and the castle. If nothing comes up, you will be free to leave Pullie without reservations. Until then, my men will keep you company. I do not think it will be too much of a burden, will it?"

"You are the deputy. Besides, I have nothing to hide." Elson grinned again and shook his shackles. "Will you?"

"Trod," commanded Lark to one of his men. "Take these things off our friend. I am sure he will be better off without them."

The city watcher immediately stooped and removed the restraints, allowing Elson to take a short stride across the room. The mercenary did so with pleasure, moving slowly, stopping several times to rub his ankle, still sore from the rough metal edges.

"Ah…This is much better. Thank you," he said afterwards and nodded.

"My men will escort you to the dining hall. Wait there, until I am done with other matters. As you can see, there is still a lot for me to do here."

The deputy finished and waved his hand. Three men from the city watch cleared the way and led Elson out of the room.

When they were gone, Lark turned to us. "What eatery are you staying in?"

"Five Stars Inn. Sire Jim recommended it," Minia replied, and the deputy thought for a moment.

"It is a decent place, clean and honest. I will instruct to bring that mercenary there. I trust my men will be fine, guarding him, but I do not want to take any chances. And since you are already staying there, I will not have to worry about Elson slipping away unnoticed. Who knows who he really is?"

Lark paused, but soon his attention went elsewhere, as more city watchers showed up, bringing healing potions and stretchers along with them. The wounded were carried to a local nursery, while the dead were placed on a large wide cart and wheeled away. Just as the deputy had predicted none of the enemy survived the fight. I was not sure if they died from their wounds or with help from Lark's men, some of whom remained in the large room while the rest of us had been talking to Elson. Whatever it was, it made me very upset, for we had lost a good chance to get some clues about out quest and had to resort to a search through heaps of paper and books scattered everywhere.

"Huh, look what I found." Minia's voice halted everyone, sometime after we had started to burrow through a stack of paperwork in the smaller room with the open window.

"What do you have over there?" the deputy responded immediately. Although he was not in the room, he seemed to hear all and was quick to walk into the chamber, joining us by the desk.

"This looks like some sort of a note. See...," Minia pointed at something written on the scroll.

"Um. This is interesting," Lark studied the note.

"What does it say?" Ike and I asked at once.

"It is a list, or something....listen." Minia began to read. "Chantue...23:15 delivered...5 lost...3 escaped. Eight thousand twenty-nine paid.'...It goes the same for Puno, Pullie—oh and here is Bois. 'Bois—25: 20 delivered...3 lost...2 escaped... Seven thousand forty-three paid. One thousand to be paid on delivery.'"

"What does it all mean?" I asked confused.

"It is a list," replied Minia.

"I know it is a list, but what is it for?"

"That is what we have to find out," replied Lark as he grabbed the paper from Minia. "I will take it to the chief. He will know what to do with it. In the meantime, keep looking, maybe we will find something else."

The deputy hid the note inside his vest and walked back out into the large room, while we recommenced our dig, somewhat confused by his actions. But in the end, we did not find anything else, just old books, receipts for something unknown to us, and useless notes that revealed nothing of importance.

At last, disappointed and tired, we concluded our search and, at the deputy's orders, departed from the tavern and headed back to the city watch headquarters. Outside the sun was still up, but evening was near and dusk was ready to settle over the city's uneven skyline. Elson and three city watchers were gone, and only a couple of locals stared at us stupidly, scratching their heads. Amongst us, a deep silence ruled. But it was not the weariness that caused the stillness. It was the poor results of the raid. By the end of the day, managing to survive a brutal encounter with some strangers, we failed to acquire any information that could lead us to Azmal. The enemies we fought so hard were either gone or dead, and the strange prisoner we had found in one of the rooms, was too suspicious to trust. And though there was the odd list that could have helped our quest, we did not have it anymore. For some reason, the deputy had taken it away from us and refused all our requests to see it again. Why? I wished I knew.

Dispirited and angry with the present circumstances our company trailed along the empty streets that led us back to the harbor and then to the city watch building that remained unguarded even after dusk. At the front door we stopped and Lark ordered us to return to our tavern, where we were to await further instructions from the chief. Of course we protested, but the deputy insisted, and soon after, we found ourselves walking back to the Five Stars Inn, by then thinking only of soft beds and hot meals. But that evening I had no appetite. The food seemed tasteless, and the cider bitter. We ate quietly and once the food was gone, went upstairs to our rooms, except for Minia, who stayed behind to exchange a few words with the owner.

Saved from the heat and filth of the outdoors, I took off my street clothes and after washing my face with cold clean water, slipped into a fresh tunic, which felt weightless compared to the heavy burden of my chain mail. Letting my limbs relax, I lay down on the made bed, staring through an invisible visor of my own deliberations. Before I knew it, I was on my feet again, for a light knock snapped me out of my daze. The door opened and Minia stumbled inside, looking very concerned. Saying nothing, he locked the door behind him and settled on a high stool next to me. Minia then pulled out a small bundle from underneath his tunic and unwrapped a loosely tightened lace that held together a stack of white pages.

"Listen, fellows," he announced seriously, holding the papers in his hand. "I may be wrong, but something is not right here."

"What do you mean?" I asked. In reply Minia motioned for everyone to be quieter, and dropped his voice to a whisper, barely loud enough to be picked up from across the room. "This raid today, did it not look strange to you?"

"Now that you have mentioned it, it did," I replied almost immediately, my own concerns fresh in my mind.

"I noticed it too…," added Ark.

"Did it not appear odd to you that not a single enemy was caught? There had to be at least one wounded foe, do you not think? And what about the list I found after the fight? Was not Lark's reaction peculiar?"

"What do you mean?" I inquired.

"Before any of us could grasp its meaning, he took it away without even looking at it once. Later on, when we reached headquarters, I asked to see the list again, but he refused, saying that he had already surrendered it to some other deputy. Strange thing is that I did not let him out of my sight even for a moment, and I did not see him give anything to anyone once we left the tavern.

"There is more…Master Lik has told me that Lark has a shady reputation, having been suspected of a series of crimes, none of which has ever been proved. Although there is no real proof of the deputy's untrustworthiness, I am starting to believe that it is so. Still, not everything is bad. That list Lark confiscated— well it was not the only piece of writing I stumbled upon. There were two more notes, which I failed to mention to anyone. I think you will like what I found."

Minia smiled and started to read, keeping his voice as low as possible: "Azmal,—"

A gasp of surprise ran through our ranks. Everyone, including me, jumped from our seats. But as we were about to launch into a frenzy of questions, Minia halted us with a quick gesture. When we settled back down, he resumed reading:

Azmal,

> *I am quite satisfied with your progress regarding our matters in the southern parts of the Kingdom. The numbers you have sent us show a lot of promise, and with such a pace our task will be complete before the set date. Your job is well done, but there are rumors that some of the candidates have managed to elude your attention. That we cannot tolerate, not when time is working against us. Be sure to correct whatever mistakes you have made, as we expect nothing, but good news in your next report. As to your request for additional funds, we will send you the money with the next shipment. But do not be too generous. The cost is already high, and if it continues to rise, our plans may suffer a setback, which, as you understand is unacceptable—we cannot fail—not when we are so close.*

Tasar-Or-Rac

"Azmal!" I exclaimed, unable to hold it any longer. "But is it the same one?"

"How many Azmals do you know?" Ark replied, with a bit of sarcasm in his voice.

I made a puffing sound, a bit offended by the comment, but said nothing. Minia started to read the next note:

Azmal,

> *I believe you have received the desired funds. I expect it to cover any future expense you may incur. At the same time I would like to express my satisfaction with our current situation in Pullie and Bois. If your reports are correct, we are all but done with that part of the Kingdom, which comes as good news, especially since we have had some troubles in the other provinces. As you probably already know, our man in Crudelle has*

been exposed, and many of our followers had to flee to avoid detection. Now, we must start all over again, and we have chosen you to lead the overhaul. When you are finished with your duties in Bois and Pullie, wait for our instructions. Until then, keep up a good work.

Tasar-Or-Rac

Minia turned another page. "There is more. Listen."

The circumstances are such that you should leave Pullie as soon as possible, as we require your assistance elsewhere. Before your travels though, I want to speak to you in person. Our man in Pullie will give you directions to our compound in the north. I hope your memory is as good as your sword, for you will not be allowed to write down the routes. We cannot afford to be uncovered, especially since the suspicions are rising with every day.

Do as told, and come as fast as you can.

Farewell and may the Master of the Old guide you safely.

Tasar-Or-Rac

Minia put down the last page.

"Master of the Old? That sounds oddly familiar." Ike spoke first.

"Master of the Old, the Chosen One, the Alavantars," listed Ark. "It all comes from that book we found at the monastery."

"The question now is who is that Tasar-Or-Rac, and where does he want Azmal to go?" Minia stared at the pages, as did everyone else. Questions followed questions, but one thing was certain—At last we were on the right track in our quest.

Chapter 34

ALTHOUGH OUR fatigue was overwhelming, Ike and I headed downstairs so we wouldn't bother our sleeping comrades. At such a late hour the dining hall was deserted, and only a stable boy slept on a long bench by the front door. When we walked in, he woke up and half-asleep, hurried to our table to ask us of our needs. To our surprise, we found out the kitchen was still open and quickly ordered a few items from the late menu, choosing two plates of meat stew and a jar of ale. Once the youngster had memorized our request, he bowed deeply and with his strap sandals in hands, ran off into the kitchen, emerging a moment later in the company of an older woman, who waved at us with a wet brown towel and yelled, "It will take some time for the stew to get ready. Do you care for any snacks before that?"

"No, ma'am, just the ale and some bread," replied Ike cheerfully. The woman nodded and disappeared behind a swinging door.

Unlike a few hours before, when the food finally arrived, Ike and I ate with gusto, washing bits of steaming hearty soup with warm flat ale. Suddenly, when we were almost done with the meal, the stairs gave a shrill sound, and a tall man stepped into the hall, wearing nothing but a sleeveless shirt, tucked into long black trousers. I recognized him at once: Elson Rian, the former captive we had freed earlier that day. Put at the Five Stars Inn by Lark's order, the Southerner was staying several rooms down the corridor from us, and though we did not see him until now, we already knew it was him because of a young city watcher, who had been posted at his door. Elson's appearance changed much since our last encounter. His long dirty beard was gone, his hair was cut short, and his skin was free of oily brown stains. After examining the room, the Southerner ordered a mug of ale from the same stable boy and proceeded straight to our table, starting a conversation from halfway across the room. "Cannot sleep either, huh? Mind if I join you?" He pointed at an empty stool next to me and added, "It turns out, resting on a hay bed grows on you after a while."

Not even waiting for our reply, he sat himself down, took a long sip from a tall wooden cup, and relaxed his limbs.

"How are you feeling, free and all?" inquired Ike, a bit unsure where he should start.

"Hey, I cannot complain. Four weeks in that hole was a bit too much. But there were some benefits: I got to spend a lot of time with myself. Sometimes it is not such a bad thing." The man smiled and took another long sip.

"And where is the guard? He did not come down here with you?" I asked.

"No, he is here all right." Elson nodded toward the stairs, where at the top stood the familiar figure. The young city watcher looked bored, but continued to perform his duty, overlooking the hall below with precision. Elson waved at him, but the man paid him no notice. His face remained composed, his eyes focused on our table.

"What was it like to be stuck there for so long?" Ike asked, turning away from the guard's glance.

"Not that much different from a common prison cell—dark, cold, and stinky."

"Have you been in a real jail too?" Ike and I exclaimed at the same time.

"A few times. Back when I was young and stupid. But it is all in the past; I do not trouble the law anymore."

Elson smiled and added, "May I ask of your names, young men? You seem to know mine, and I would like to return the favor."

"Yes, of course. I am Mishuk and this is my friend Ike, we are from Villone," I blurted out, then quickly realized the potential danger of my words and grew silent.

"You are not with the city watch, are you? Because, you do not look much like those city dwellers who patrol the streets here."

"Oh no, we are squires in service of Sire Rone, a lord from Bois. We were sent to Pullie to attend to some of his matters."

It was now Ike who did the talking. To stop him I hit my friend under the table. Ike understood everything quickly and bit his tongue. Yet, our conversation with the new acquaintance did not stop. Probably sensing our distrust, the Southerner asked us general questions about the city, the things we had done back at Villone, and of our plans for the near future. We answered what we could and in return inquired of his living. Strangely enough, as we spent more and more time with the mercenary, our suspicion eased, and we did not notice how the night chased away its second hour. By then though the long difficult day took its toll, and we found ourselves dozing off, drifting away from the conversation. Unable to keep our heads up any longer, Ike and I excused ourselves and returned to the room, leaving Elson downstairs with his mug of ale, the stable boy, and the old woman.

I thought I was dreaming when I heard strange sounds from somewhere nearby. Slowly I opened my eyes and listened. Intermingled with heavy breathing and the soft monotonous snoring of my comrades, I could detect a soft shuffling of feet coming from behind the door. My sleep was gone in an instant. Grabbing my sword, I jumped to my feet and slipped to the door. Quietly I pressed my ear to the boards and listened, quickly distinguishing low voices, at least three of them, that sounded from several cubits away. Suddenly the memory of our past attacks came back to me, and I immediately moved through the room, alerting my companions. Meanwhile the voices got louder, the noise became more frequent, and was joined by the clanging of metal. There was no doubt in my mind—something was going on out there.

"What should we do?" I whispered to my brother and Ike, who stood closest.

They shrugged their shoulders. At that time, Minia found his way to the door and stressing his senses asked, "What do you hear there?"

"I do not know. Maybe they are other patrons, like us, returning to their rooms," I replied, though my words sounded more like a question.

"Oh heck, what if they are not guests, but the assassins, like those Snake Bites we met in Bois. Good Spirit! We need to do something," Ike whispered fast.

"Do not panic, Ike," said Ark in a calm tone. "There is a city watcher in the hallway. If there was trouble, he would have alerted us by now."

"If he had time," interjected Ike quickly. My friend's comment made sense and we all tightened our grips.

"Before we do anything, let's try to see what is really going on out there," said Minia. He motioned for everyone to step back a little and himself pulled on a brass handle, producing a narrow gap, big enough to reveal a view of the corridor ahead. As a thin line of light streamed into our room, he peered into the hallway. I did too, looking over Minia's shoulder, and immediately spotted several figures lingering by Elson's door. The men wore the uniforms of the city watch.

Cautiously, I described the scene to the others. "One, two, three…four; there are four city watchers out there. No wait, someone else is coming. It is…Lark."

"What is he doing here?" Minia raised his voice a little.

"I have no idea. But…Something is going on. They have their weapons drawn. It looks like they are about to go inside Elson's room. Oh wait, no, Lark is going in alone, the others remain outside."

"Maybe it has something to do with our earlier raid? Maybe they have found out something about the mercenary?" asked Ike, unable to see anything.

"Why do we not ask?" noted Rob, but suddenly sounds of broken timber and fighting rushed through the hall, making us turn our focus back to the hallway.

At the door the four men stared at each other, confused and disoriented, clearly not expecting such a turn of events. Their short swords were out of their sheaths, yet they did not move. Sensing that something was amiss, Minia threw open the door and, followed by rest of us, walked straight for them. The city watchers were quick to spot us, but did not do anything as their faces showed more surprise than caution.

"What is going on here?" Minia called as we approached. The men looked at each other and then at him. By then I recognized the three of them. They were in that ill-fated tavern by the harbor's slums, along with us, when the fight broke out.

"We are not sure," one of the guards replied, shrugging his shoulders. "Deputy Lark is in there with the Southerner. He said he needed to talk to him."

"But what about that noise?" Minia pointed to the door, where sounds of struggle could be heard.

"Deputy Lark specifically told us not to leave this post. He said that he did not want anyone escaping this time. As for the noise, sometimes the deputy gets rough on crooks. Although he is not supposed to do so, it is often the only way to get that scum to talk."

The city watcher wanted to say something else, but Minia pushed him aside. "I do not know about you, but I do not like what I am hearing. So if you do not care to check, then we will. Come on lads, let's move." And with that, he shoved the door inward.

We slid through the opening and entered the quarters, which were composed of two separate rooms. The first chamber, which probably served as a foyer, was very dark and empty. The only light came from the hallway and a small crack under a closed door that blocked the way into the second section. We moved quietly. To our surprise the entry was unlocked and opened easily, the thick oak sheet of wood swinging inward, exposing a view of a dully lit, furnished square chamber.

Inside we also found two men—Lark and Elson. The deputy was standing by the window, his sword in one hand and a dagger in the other. Across from him, holding a half-broken chair was Elson, with whom Ike and I had so cheerfully chatted just hours before. His tunic and breeches were splattered with blood and his face held an expression of pain. Facing each other, the two looked very tense and in the dim light of three single candles, did not see us standing in the doorway.

"What in the world are you doing?" Minia yelled out as soon as the scene met his eyes. His question came unexpected to Lark and the Southerner. They both jumped up and gazed in our direction. Spotting the six of us, Elson quickly moved aside and lowered the chair, placing his now free hands onto his ribs red from a recent cut. At the same time the deputy stepped further back toward the window. His eyes ran back and forth, and it was obvious that he was startled and at a loss for words. A short pause only added to the suspicion. Then the Southerner let out a slight sigh and spoke. "This mad man tried to kill me." Elson let the words out of his mouth slowly, studying his palms, covered with blood.

"Do not listen to him. I came here on a personal order from the chief," protested the deputy. "As I suspected, he lied to us back at the tavern. He is not who he claims to be. The chief and I found out he was wanted in Chantue for a string of murders. His description was sent to us last season. I have it back at headquarters. It is a perfect match. I should have detained him last night; I guess this is the price you pay for being so trusting. It is one of my vices, I suppose."

"Do you care to explain then, why did you not call for help, four of your men were outside, waiting?" asked Minia, looking straight at the deputy.

A sign of worry wiped out any relic of good mood from Lark's face.

"What?" The deputy's voice was turning into a shout. "This man is a criminal. He attacked me. You cannot possibly believe what he says."

"I would not trust those words," announced the Southerner from his end. "What I know is that when I opened my eyes, this man was about to sink his blade into my belly. Luckily I managed to jump to one side before it was too late. But he managed to slice me a bit anyway. Look."

Elson opened his hands again and showed us a gash on his side, fresh but not too serious.

"This is a lie, it was he who attacked; I only defended myself," said Lark.

My companions and I moved our eyes from Lark to Elson. The standoff was taking a very dangerous turn, and someone had to give. But it was Minia who spoke first:

"That is a serious accusation you are making, Deputy Lark. I am sure here in Pullie you have the same laws as we have in Bois, and assaulting a member of the city watch is a crime punished by death. Although I did not see the start of your confrontation, I cannot disregard the facts. Elson is the one who is wounded, and all the weapons I see are in your hands."

"I am the deputy," Lark interrupted, "...I...I...Guards!" The deputy's raging scream rang through the room.

In an instant the four guards, who had been standing in the hallway, rushed into the room.

"Deputy Lark, what is it?" one of the city watchers exclaimed, as the men halted in the doorway, looking even more confused than before.

"That hired sword over here assaulted me." Lark pointed at Elson, who remained calm, just a leap away. "And these six tried to help."

At first, the men made a step toward us, but when we raised our weapons, they stopped and stared at Lark. But before the deputy could say anything, Minia came forth and said, "I do not think we need any more violence. This matter should be resolved peacefully. The deputy claims that he has been following the chief's orders. He also says that there is evidence that Elson is a wanted man. Why do we not go back to headquarters and see if such statements are true? Should we find proof of the deputy's words, we will gladly surrender the foreigner and pay whatever price we must for doubting the officer of the watch. But should we find otherwise, we could ask Master Huck about a further course of action. I am sure he will know what to do."

"Fine by me," noted Elson. "I know I am innocent and have no problem going to the station. I only have one request, we all go together. I do not want my throat slashed on the way there." The Southerner raised his hands and smiled. Lark, though, refused to give.

"You are but a squire, lad," he continued to yell. "I do not need to take orders from you. This man is a killer and I will serve the punishment to him. Men—seize him. Do it now."

The deputy snapped his jaws and raised up the sword. But nobody moved. The four city watchers stood still with weapons lowered, staring at the deputy and at Minia. The deputy screamed again, and again. Yet the guards ignored him. Then they took a step back and one of them said, "I think you are right. We should talk to the chief before we do anything. I do not want to go to the wall."

"You coward, where is your loyalty? Spirit knows you will never serve on the city watch again. It is a promise." With those words, Lark taunted him and raised the hand that held the dagger. It looked as if he was about launch an attack, but instead he threw his weapons at us and leapt out of the window. Startled, we rushed to the ledge, hoping to see the direction of Lark's escape. But before we could look out, a heartbreaking scream of pain came from below.

Lying on the pavement of the deserted dark street, awakening unsuspected townsmen from their sleep, the deputy rolled on the ground, holding onto his legs. As it turned out, Lark had a dreadful landing and broke both of his ankles, which disabled him all much to our satisfaction. Not having to chase the crooked city watcher, we headed downstairs. When we got outside, the earsplitting screaming stopped, and I began to worry that the deputy had run off. But he had not. Unable to handle the pain anymore, he had fainted and lay silent on the stones of the pavement, his feet severely deformed and twisted.

There was little else for us to do but to carry the senseless officer back to the station. With the remaining city watchers still in confusion, and Elson under suspicion, Minia took charge and split our company into two groups. The men from the city watch were to carry the deputy and the six of us were to look after the Southerner, making sure he did not slip into one of the darker alleys along the way. In one column, we moved through the street, led by the dull light of the lanterns and occasional windows. Around us, the city was calm and silent. A few drunks stumbled near some corners, an unattended dog trotted along the dirty sidewalk, and rats dashed across the street every now and again, keen to get to their next feeding hole as quickly as possible.

When we finally reached headquarters, it was quiet and deserted. The front gate was shut and we had to bang on it for some time before one of the guards finally let us in. His half-closed eyes showed little interest. Seeing the city watchers among us, he waved our company off, and hurried to get back to his long chair, eager to retreat into a sleep. Unfortunately for him, we had other plans. Grabbing the man by his sleeve, Minia explained the reason for our need to see the chief at such a late hour.

Although the man did not know Minia, he obeyed instantly and ran off, vanishing in the darkness of the upper level. While we waited, the four guards put down the deputy, who was still unconscious, and settled on the floor, exhausted from the hasty trip. Rob, Ark, and Ike joined them, talking to Elson, who showed no sign of worry. Then came a loud call from above, and everyone was up again.

At the top of the stairs a different man, another deputy, met us and after asking a few questions, took us to the chief's chamber at the other end of the hall. Master Huck was already there, sitting behind a desk, leaning slightly forward, supporting his body with his arms. He wore only light clothes and his red face suggested that he was got up a few moments ago.

Once our company of six squires, four guards, a former prisoner from the south, and the crippled deputy were inside, the chief nodded as if counting us, and raised his voice. "You better have a good reason to wake me up at this hour."

"Our apologies, Master Huck, but the matter that brings us before you is far too important to set aside until morning."

"Then...I am listening," said the chief and Minia went on to describe the events of the night. During the story the chief's face grew dark; his eyebrows slid down and he began to mumble something, barely moving his lips. When Minia was done, he stopped whispering and raised his head.

"These are very serious accusations, squire. To blame an officer of the city watch for a criminal act, you better have some good reasons." Master Huck sounded very serious, and maybe even angry. But Minia was unmoving.

"I am aware of this, Chief, and this is why I have brought the matter to you. There are certain things that can support or disprove any charge I have made. First of all, the deputy has claimed that he was following your orders to arrest the Southerner. He has also said you had proof that Elson was the man sought in Chantue for a series of murders."

"My orders?" The chief exclaimed, interrupting Minia, looking very awake by then.

"Yes, those were the deputy's exact words, if you do not believe me, ask the others."

"Did you hear the same thing?" The chief switched to the four city watchers, who stood timidly by the door.

"The deputy told us that we needed to apprehend the mercenary from Azoros for some crimes he had committed in some other province. The deputy also said that a large force would spook him and so he took only just four of us instead," replied the young guard, who had been guarding Elson ever since he was freed from his cell.

"I do not remember giving any orders to arrest any mercenary. I do not even know who that mercenary is. What is his name again?" The chief was almost shouting now.

"Elson, Rian Elson, the man of the Southern Circle. Your men freed me last afternoon." The Southerner raised his voice.

"Huh, so you are the prisoner everyone is talking about?"

"Apparently I am, but I cannot tell you why your men want to arrest me. All I know is that I am accused of something that I have not done, and that I do not like."

"We will sort it all out very soon…Elson Rian. Where are you from?"

"Azoros, southern Azoros to be exact. I have come here to investigate a matter very dear to my employer, Fruhji Olero, a well-respected trader and a member of the House of Glory."

"And what matter would that be?"

"If you insist,…I have been sent here to see if a couple of traders from Chantue would be interested in returning their debt to my employer." The Southerner smiled. "Alas, I do not have anything that can prove my words. The problem is that four weeks ago I was attacked by some thugs while here in Pullie. Those men imprisoned me and took all of my possessions, including the letter that could have explained my purpose and intentions. Yet, I can assure you that all of my actions were legal and civilized."

"As long as none got hurt and nothing was stolen, I do not care."

"None such things have ever taken place."

"Good. I must say I do not recognize your name, nor do you fit any description sent to us from elsewhere. Whatever Lark was after, he must have done it on his own, which, frankly, bothers me a great deal."

The chief paused and looked at the deputy, who was still lying still on the floor. "Will someone pour water on that man?" Master Huck yelled firmly. Instantly a bucket of water appeared in the hands of the city watchers, and a splash of cold water soaked the deputy's pale face, sending him back out of his unconscious state. Letting out a loud moan, Lark tried to get up, but unsuccessfully. He fell down and settled on the floor, and looked about the room. Once realizing where he was, his face changed; he took on the expression of a confused and frightened animal backed into a corner.

"Deputy," started the chief, "These men claim that you have tried to kill an innocent man tonight. Do you have anything to say to that?"

"It is all a lie. I did not want to kill anyone. It was the mercenary who tried to kill me. And these so-called squires—they wanted to kill me too, but I escaped. I jumped out of the window—"

"How interesting. You say they wanted to kill you. But why did they bring you here instead? I presume you did not venture halfway across the city on your own, did you?"

"Do not listen to them, they have tricked you; they want to blame me, but I did not do anything. I was just trying to do my job."

"And what would that job be…?"

"I was trying to bring this foreigner here for some questioning. He looked suspicious to me and I wanted to know a little bit more about his business in Pullie."

"In the middle of the night? Why such urgency?"

"Because I was afraid that he would skip town before the morning."

"How would that be possible, since your men have not taken their eyes off me ever since you met me?" Elson rebutted, but the deputy cut him off.

"Do not listen to him; his is a mercenary, a cutthroat."

"But is he a murder, as you claim?"

"Me? No, I did not say he was a murder, though he probably is. All I said was that he fit one of the descriptions we have received from Chantue. I thought I saw some resemblance."

"But these men here tend to think differently."

"They are all a bunch of criminals, including those four." The deputy pointed at the city watchers. "These men are not worthy of their status. They got so scared that they betrayed me. I think they were bribed….yes, yes, bribed…"

"Everyone is guilty but you?"

"Yes, yes. I swear. Who would you listen to? They are commoners, squires, and a hired sword; I am the officer of the city watch. I have served you for three years. I took the oath."

"An oath is not a free ticket to do as you please…It is something you prove every day to yourself and your fellow city watchmen. So do not talk to me about oaths. Instead try to explain why your story sounds so false."

"No, no, Master Huck. I tell the truth."

"Do you take me for a fool? I did not become chief for nothing. It took me ten years to get where I am now. And my experience tells me that you are lying. Will you prove me wrong?"

"You do not understand they—"

"Enough." It was not a yell, it was roar. The chief put an end to the whining of the deputy, who bit his tongue and lowered his eyes so to avoid the devastating stare of his superior.

"Men, you can leave now, you have done your job well. Go get some rest, I will speak with you tomorrow." Master Huck dismissed the city watchers and then turned to us. "As for you, squires, stay a little longer. Let's see if we can find out more from our friend, here."

When the door closed, the chief addressed Lark again. "Deputy, in the last two seasons I have heard much about you. There were reports from all sorts of people who accuse you of much mischief. Although none of them had any solid proof, I tended to think that they were right, and that one day someone would bring you down. When it happens I will make sure that you get death as your punishment. But, you can try to save your life now. Give me your confession and I will arrange something less unpleasant for you—a duty at the Wall, perhaps. You do like the Northern weather, do you not?"

The deputy thought for a moment, weighing his options, then shook his head and said, "I am sure you will find me useful. In return I will accept your offer to take up a guard's duty at the Barrier. But I must ask that I am not sent there for life. Ten years will do just fine, and not as a common guard, a blue scarf is suitable enough."

"I do not think you are in any position to bargain."

"Oh, Master Huck, but I am. Believe me, what I can tell you will earn you a lot of points with the lords up at the castle."

"Then we shall see…"

"Unfortunately I must insist on your word first. Promise me that I will get ten years and I will tell you all you want to know."

"Fine, but if you are fooling me, I will deliver you to the execution chamber myself."

"As you wish Chief Master Huck." Lark licked his lips and began to speak. "I am not the man you should be looking for. I am just a servant, a simple soldier. The one you want to talk to is an officer with the second circle. Oh yes, the honorable lord, the nobleman, the pride and joy of Pullie. His name is Sire Matt and he is the second captain there. It is him you need to arrest.

"So happened that several years ago, when I was just starting as the deputy, he came to me to ask a small favor—to deliver a message to a crook in the slums. For that he paid me a silver coin, which was fine by me. I needed money and it was an easy job. I did as told. Sometime after the lord came to me again, and then again. His requests were simple—to let some folks into the city, or unload small ships away from the docks, or send out a patrol on a different route. Every time Sire Matt paid well and once even promised to take me into the castle one day as his trusted sergeant. But all that was nothing, compared to the jobs he had in store for me starting last season. Sometime in late winter he called me to an inn by the harbor and ordered me to remove a local noble, a rival of his. I refused at first, but when he threatened to turn me in I had no choice. That very evening I killed the poor soul and for that received ten golden plates. A good price—but I would rather have had it burned in the deepest fires of the Land's Edge, as very soon the second captain made me do more of his bloody errands. In all, I killed seven men—a nobleman, three foreigners, a commoner from the slums, and two local traders."

The deputy paused and looked at the chief, who was grim and unmoving. Lark took a hard swallow, sighed, and resumed. "Except for the noble, who I had to kill on the street, I used the same method. I would declare that I had found a suspect and go to arrest him, taking three or four city watchers with me, just in case. While I made my arrests, the men remained outside. As you can guess, all my detentions failed. The suspects refused to surrender and attacked me, forcing me to kill them, all in self-defense. A good plan it was. It would have worked today too, but for this colorful company of peasant boys who spoiled my intentions."

"Why did you want to kill the Southerner?" asked the chief.

"After getting the assignment from you to raid the slums, I reported it to Sire Matt, who told me what to do. Did you think luck brought me to that tavern? No, the second captain pointed out the place. He instructed me to go in there and kill any mercenary I found. I do not know why he wanted them dead; nor did I care. They were all hired swords from abroad and nobody would miss them. Unfortunately, Sire Matt did not say anything about prisoners. When we found this Southerner, I did not know what to do with him. I could not kill him, not without raising questions. Nor could I arrest him in front of all my men and these squires. So I let him go, though I kept tabs on him. Only, when Sire Matt found out about what I had done, he got really mad. He said that I had spoiled his entire plan and if I wanted to live I had to kill the Southerner. As you can see, I had to act quickly, which I did.

"As before, taking a few of the men with me, I went over to the Five Stars Inn to make my so-called arrest. Without any problem I left the others in the hallway and myself went in to finish the job. But the opponent proved to be good fighter. Before I could land my blow, he dodged my blade and managed to hold me off long enough for the so-called squires to arrive. And this is pretty much it."

The deputy finished and gazed blindly at the chief. He did not say another word, nor did anyone else, as none of us, including Master Huck, could have expected to hear such tale.

Chapter 35

BY THE time we had left the city watch headquarters, after getting everything we could out of the crooked deputy, it was already early morning. In silence we stood at the gates to the second circle, overlooking the outline of Pullie that came up to the blue waters of the sea, touched with streaks of white that rolled over the rocky coast in great numbers. Above us the sky was clear, and the streets below were beginning to fill up with traffic, sounds of the awakening city mingling with noise from the harbor.

At long last Master Huck and two of his deputies who had accompanied us to the castle returned, and we headed around the second circle's inner wall, to a large stone building that, unlike other structures in sight, was not only well built, but also well defended. Three-stories high, it looked similar to Sire Rone's keep, only a little smaller and thinner, its flat roof attached to the outer wall by a wooden stairwell.

Four towers sat at each of its corners, along with the concealed figures of several guards who watched over a stretch of the open sandy lane, paying close attention to our arrival. More soldiers stood at the massive iron door, each holding a short spear and a round shield, blocking the way with their unmoving figures. The men clearly expected us, and greeting the chief with quick nods, stepped aside. Since we had already surrendered all our weapons back at the lower level, we were allowed in—with questions—quickening after Master Huck to the top of the stone stairs. There inside a round foyer, the chief exchanged some words with another guard and then took our company into another much larger square chamber, dwelt in by a group of four men, all lords, all dressed in their colors and armored suits.

Amongst the unfamiliar figures, I recognized Sire Sigmun, the captain of the second circle, whose bright crest of a sailing ship stood out amongst less decorative symbols, pictured on the tunics of the other nobles. He was sitting behind a round table, his hand placed before him. When we walked in, the captain greeted us with a hard glance and announced, "We meet again, squires. These are my fellow officers here at the second circle. They will attend to this meeting, for the subject we are about to discuss is of the utmost importance." Sire Signum raised his chin up so he could scratch his throat. "I am informed that you have uncovered a villain amongst us. Is it so?"

"We believe we have, your Lordship," replied Master Huck. "As much as it hurts to admit,…but Lark of Juilous, my former deputy, has confessed to committing a series of illicit acts. He also revealed that the person who has been giving him orders is no other than Sire Matt Atefield, the second captain here at the second circle."

"Indeed…a Pullie knight—a traitor? Do you understand what sort of allegation this is?" Sire Sigmun let a pause linger in the air. When nobody dared to speak, he continued. "If it was anyone but Master Huck who brought me this news, I would have ordered him executed on the spot. But hearing it from the chief himself makes me cautious that maybe there is some truth to such accusations. I think that it will not hurt to ask Sire Matt about it. An honest man has nothing to fear, and I am sure the second captain will disprove any charges thrown at him."

With those words Sire Sigmun rose from his seat and saying nothing else, walked out of the door, followed by his entourage, the clanging of their armored suits resonating off the stone walls.

Outside, a regiment of some twenty soldiers joined the captain, and everyone headed back toward the gates, soon reaching the steps of the familiar house, which was Sire Matt's headquarters. Nothing seemed to differ from the other day. The same chipped paint covered the base of the building, the same guards camped leisurely by the open front door, and the same old fat cat slept on a barrel, bathing in the warm rays of the still rising sun. Seeing our procession approach, the sentries sprang to their feet; pushing their mailed chests far up to flatten their bellies, they saluted the lords. But the noblemen ignored the commotion and, trailed by their armed escort including the six of us, walked straight inside. They soon arrived at Sire Matt's spacious quarters, where two young men, probably some squires, were busy tossing stacks of paper into the flames of the fireplace.

"Where is your lord?" Sire Sigmun declared, not only his presence, but also his rank and authority unchallenged by anyone within the walls of the second circle.

"Your Lordship." The men dropped their loads and immediately saluted the captain. "Sire Matt has left some half an hour ago. He said he was going to check on the sentries."

"Did he tell you when he was coming back?"

"No, Sire, but it takes him about an hour to do a round."

"And what are you doing here?"

"We were just about to burn these scrolls. Sire Matt has asked us to get rid off all these useless papers. He said he wanted to have the room cleaned before his return. Is there anything wrong?"

"It is not for you to know, squires. Leave everything where it is and get out."

"Yes, Sire." The youngsters bowed and made their exist, barely visible to even a wary eye. Meanwhile the captain strolled up to the desk and picked up a piece of paper from the floor, reading it carefully.

"Looks like junk to me." He turned toward the other officers. "What I want to know is where is Sire Matt? Sire Lex, take your men and find the knight. I want him here and I want him now. Go."

The young clean-shaved lord gave out a salute and vanished behind the door along with three other soldiers. I could hear their footsteps pounding on the wooden floor and then their shouts outside. Soon though the noise moved down the lane, and eventually ceased. With the search for the missing officer on the way, everyone waited in the room. Some half hour later Sire Lex returned, bursting into the room, gasping for air. When his breathing returned a little, he bowed and dropped down to one knee.

"My lord, we have found Sire Matt." The young noble took another deep breath before continuing with the report. "We spotted the second captain at the first circle's gates, trying to leave the castle. My men tried to stop him, but he ignored our orders. Instead he dashed for the bridge, his mount breaking through the gate guards. We gave him chase, but it was not until we reached the bazaar that we finally caught up with him."

The officer paused again, still panting. "My lord, I urged him to surrender. I told him that we only needed to ask questions. But he refused and in response started to swing his sword. Two of my men were injured, another one is dead, so are three city watchers. I am truly sorry. But I had no choice. I am afraid Sire Matt is dead."

An uneasy silence settled in the air. Although the captain's face did not even twitch, his eyes showed much strain. I did not know if he was angry or upset, but one thing was certain, he was not happy.

"Where is the body?" Sire Sigmun said at last as he rose up from his seat.

"Inside one of the first circle's barracks," replied the young lord.

"Take me there. Master Huck, you should come too." He walked away from the desk and out of the room, but in the doorway halted and said to one of his officers, "Sire Drew, you stay here and take a look through these papers. I have a feeling there is a reason why Sire Matt wanted to burn them. You can use these squires from Bois to help your men."

Then the captain departed, along with the chief, his deputies, and the other nobles, leaving Sire Matt's quarters to the tall, long-haired knight, three soldiers, and the six of us.

"Men, you have heard the captain. Start digging and try not to miss anything," Sire Drew said in a commanding tone, then walked out too, settling in another room two doors down the hallway.

For hours we continued to burrow through stacks of notes, slips, parchments, books, and scrolls. Yet, all we found were bills of sale, conviction slips, official reports of all sorts, and the confessions of some poor fellows. But there was nothing that could help our quest. At long last more soldiers arrived and took up our duties, letting us walk back outside, where we settled on top of dry logs across the lane.

Everyone was tired and the mood soured. Again it all looked pointless, but not for long, as some time after, a guard who had been helping us with the inspection appeared in the entry and ran to us, shouting cheerfully, "Hey fellows, did not you say you were looking for some maps or something?"

"Why?"

"Well, I have found something, but I cannot read. I tried to show this to Sire Drew, but he sent me off, saying not to bother him. So I figured I would ask you. You can read, right?"

When we all nodded, he displayed a letter of some sort and gave it to Minia. "So, can you tell me, what does it say?"

To answer the guards and everyone else, Minia carefully unfolded the piece of paper, revealing a drawing of some lands with a passage inscribed at the bottom.

"Indeed this looks like a map." The guard smirked and asked, "What do those words mean?"

Minia moved the man's finger away and began to read aloud.

Our faithful son,

I am glad to see that our plans are going well. Yet we are not too happy with the progress of some of your recruits and so decided to terminate our dealings with one of them. Our friend Azmal proved to be too stupid, recruiting hired swords and paying out huge bounties, thus attracting all sorts of attention to our operations in the eastern regions. And though we do not blame you for his foolishness, we must remove him, and you will help us do so.

We have come up with a plan to get rid of Azmal and his men without them ever suspecting anything. Along with the last shipment we sent him a letter, whereby we requested his assistance in another part of the Kingdom, asking him to come to our compound as soon as possible. Since Azmal does not know the location of our camp, I suggest you give him these directions. You probably understand that after his departure nobody will ever see him again.

We also want his men dead, all of them. When you get rid of their souls use their money to hire new cutthroats, those who will be smart enough to complete the assignment. We cannot tolerate any more setbacks.

You know what to do, do it.

I will contact you soon.

"Huh. It does not sound too good, whoever that fellow is," commented the soldier afterwards. He looked at the map and the writing one more time, then sighed and added, "Do you still want it?"

"We sure do, thank you."

"All right then, I am off to finish the sweeping. See you around." The man turned and ran back inside, leaving us alone with the new piece of evidence.

"So much for loyalty," Ike said when the man was gone. "Poor Azmal thought he was getting a promotion. Instead he got a piece of cold steel in his back."

"That is what you get for working for scum like the Alavantars," added Rob.

"Well, at least we know who our true enemy is," Ike added.

"But that does not explain what we need to do next." Minia looked at the map.

"With Azmal and his men probably all dead, and Sire Matt killed at the bazaar, there is no one to warn them of our progress and this can buy some time to figure everything out," said Ark, thinking.

"Oh I am sure they will find out soon enough—" Ike began.

"Not before we get to them first," I broke in. "We have the map, what else do we need?"

"I am afraid this it not the map we need. This is where Azmal was to go and we know it is not the compound," Ark rebutted.

"Still we can use it, can we not? We can go there and see what we can find. Maybe there will be more clues." I refused to give.

"You may be right, Mishuk. But before we go there, we must return to Bonneville and report all to Sire Jim," Minia said firmly.

"We do not have time for this. We must get there as soon as possible." Ike joined me.

"I think you two are forgetting something. You are no farm boys anymore. You are squires and so must obey orders—my orders—and they are for us to go back to Bois and report to the Duke. Then if the High Lord approves we can use this map. Any questions?" Minia gave Ike and me such a sharp gaze that we did not say anything else.

"Good, let's settle things here, and go back to the Five Stars Inn."

Chapter 36

THE SUN had already set, the sky was turning dark, and the wind that streamed through the open window became much colder. In silence we lay on our beds, pressed hard by Minia's obstinacy. Only when a light knock repeated itself several times did we rose and turned our attention to the door, which then opened. Standing in the hall we saw Elson. He stayed in the doorway for a moment, leaning on the flimsy frame, then spat out a large chunk of brownish substance that he had been chewing on, and cleared his throat. "May I?" he asked loudly. Minia nodded and the Southerner walked in, closing the door behind him.

"I have heard you got that knight, back at the castle," he said after a brief pause. "Too bad he did not live to tell all of his secrets. It seems to be the usual thing around here—to kill all the suspects."

For a moment the Southerner paused and looked at us, checking out our reaction. "I have also heard you are leaving soon."

"Where did you learn that?" Minia asked, irritably. "We have not told anyone about it."

"Are you sure? Because half of the tavern is talking about it." Elson smiled and put another patch of brown stuff into his mouth, placing it under his lower lip and pushing it back and forth with his tongue. "Hey do you have a cup or a bucket?" he asked, completely off the subject.

"Yes, right under the table." I pointed to the desk. Elson waved to Ike to pass him the small can. Then, he moved his chew some more and spat into the canister, resuming his talk afterwards.

"Anyway, there is something that I want to talk to you about. Since I kind of owe you one from last night, I thought I would return the favor. As you all know I have been chained down in a cell for a few weeks. And though it was a dreadful experience, I cannot say it was completely worthless. A couple of times I heard my jailors tell some interesting stories.

"From what I gathered, they were working for some crazy guy named Azmal, who wanted to kill all the young men from your kingdom. Horrible—maybe…Strange—absolutely. It appeared that they had problems with a pair of so-called candidates. Some were young lordlings, who lived inside their family's castles and were hard to catch. But those they did not worry about too much. Instead they were all nettled about a group of young lads from some farmlands west of here. Not only did those farm boys manage to evade their grasp, they also killed several of the men Azmal had hired."

Elson paused and again studied us. When none of us said anything, he smirked lightly and asked his question. "So I was wondering if you know anything about that sort of thing?"

"Us? Why?" asked Minia, choosing his words carefully.

"I will be honest with you. Ever since I saw you in that roach-infested place back in the slums, I could not help but think as how odd you six looked. You do not appear to be from Pullie, or any other city for that matter. You took part in a raid along with the city watchers, and yet you hold no rank amongst them. Then, you call yourselves squires, but have little of the real men-at-arms in you. But most of all, for some reason, I always find you mixed up in some strange things—freeing me from my jailors would be one, exposing a traitor lord amongst the local lords another. Something tells me that none of this is a coincidence. And so I wonder if you are in fact those young lads that Azmal and his men had been looking for all along."

I was stunned. All our efforts to keep the true goals of our quest as secretive as possible had failed miserably. A mercenary, a man we had met just a day before had figured everything out. What did it say about us as squires? But most importantly what would the Southerner do with that information? There was one positive thing, though. Elson was no friend of Sire Matt's or the Alavantars. Still my nerves were stressed.

"It is quite an assessment you have made," replied Minia in the meantime. "But I am not sure you have come to the right conclusion. We are merely squires…"

"I was not born yesterday, lad. How old are you? Sixteen, seventeen? All of you…I have a dozen years over you and as a grown man I have learned to detect when someone is trying to lie to me. So spare me your fake explanation."

The Southerner stared at us, then smiled and leaned back. "You do not have to worry about me telling anything to anyone. As I said I am in debt to you for saving my life and I have a proposal to make."

"A proposal? Huh, let's hear it then." Minia smiled too, though his smile was much tauter.

"What you know about me is not exactly accurate," the Southerner began. "Although I am someone, who is considered to be a mercenary, I am not a member of the Southern Circle. The medallion, the descriptions—all fake. It is a trick I learned back in Azoros. People seem to respect what they fear, and having a medallion from one of the toughest gangs in Azoros surely helps.

"Also my employer is not a merchant from the House of Glory. Instead I am working for a scholar, who has hired me to conduct an investigation regarding a certain secret devout sect, suspected of the recent disappearances in the Northern Parts of Ethoria. My assignment was to travel through the Northern Regions, collect information, find out how many people had gone missing and what had happened to them. Those men who were holding me worked for Azmal, and he in turn worked for that sect. Starting with last season I had been following them around. But no matter how hard I tried, I could not get too close to them. So one night I formed a daring plan. When Azmal and most of his men were inside their hideout, I sneaked into the tavern. Alas, I got too careless too soon, for they caught me as I was scaling the wall. Luckily for me, they did not kill me on the spot, only because they were trying to find out who I was working for. I do not know how long I would have lived, but your unexpected arrival helped me a lot."

"You spoke of some strange sect a little while ago. What was its name?" asked Minia.

"I think you already know the answer, but anyway, the Alavantars is the name for those who make its ranks. Do you know such a name?"

We hesitated for a while, looking at each other, then I slowly raised my voice. "Yes we do, and I cannot say we like it much."

"I am sure you do not; otherwise we would not be talking right now." Elson grinned again.

"So what about your proposal?" Minia followed quickly.

"My employer, Revor Eynol, a great sage from the city of Azor, knows much about the Alavantars, and he hates them greatly for they have brought much sorrow to him. Until today he was alone in his battle against that evil. But now as I have found you, he will be glad to know that he has allies. I am sure he would love to meet you and share his knowledge about the common enemy. If you are interested in learning more about the sect and its devious plans, I can introduce you to the sage. The only problem is that we will have to travel back to Azoros to see him. It is a long trip, but I can get you there in just a few weeks' time."

The proposal was unusual at best. I did not know what to think of it. It could have been a trick, or it could have been the break we needed all along. Of course, there was no way to tell.

"How do we know your intentions are true?" inquired Minia. "You ask us to trust you, to travel great distances, to abandon our current quest, but why? As far as I know you could plan an ambush somewhere along the way."

"It is a fair statement, but I will try to prove that you are wrong." The Southerner pulled out a rolled tube of parchments and gave it to Minia. The scrolls made up a journal, which contained dozens of dates, places, and names.

"These are the names of people kidnapped in Pullie and Bois, starting from two seasons ago and until the day of my capture, the ones I had managed to uncover in my search," explained Elson. "This is my work. Every single time I heard a story about a missing person I investigated it, finding and recording who, when, and where. At the very least this is proof that there is in fact a pattern and a reason behind all those vanishings."

"But what does it do for us?" I heard Ike from the back.

"With this you can finally prove that someone is deliberately targeting young men from your kingdom. Now all you need is some proof that ties the Alavantars to these disappearances. And with that I will help you too."

Elson extracted another set of papers and handed it to Minia.

"Ever since I started following Azmal, I recorded their every move. I also managed to seize some of their letters. Do not worry, the messengers still live, though they may not remember much. In any case, here you will find everything about Azmal's group and their activities. If you put the two accounts together, you will get a very good picture of who is responsible for the turmoil in your kingdom."

"He is right," noted Minia, reading through the pages.

"There is more," Elson continued and extracted another paper tube, laced with red strips. He quickly removed the cords and tossed the scroll to Minia. Once unwrapped, a small map lay before us. "This map I drew myself after following a trader who had been hired by some men to deliver four loads of wine to some distant place in the northern province of Puno. The reason I went after that merchant was because he had caught my eye—not him, but the coins he had paid with at some of the local shops. They were the same coins many of the mercenaries received from Azmal and his men. As I always say, if you want to track a man track his money. So I went after the trader, soon to find out that there was a strange encampment set up in a remote area near the Mountains of the Land's Edge. Although I did not know who those people were, I could tell you that most of them were mercenaries, bandits, and such;

nor were they interested in receiving any visitors either, with guards posted far away from the camp. If you asked me, those men wanted to keep their presence secret; something a secret sect would do, do you not think?"

Minia studied the map. "Would you be willing to come back with us and tell your story to the Duke of Bois?"

"I would like to, but my duties require me to return to Azoros. I have already been absent far too long. My employer is awaiting my report, which you can see is very grim. I will be more than glad to let you copy my journal and the map. That way you will not have to return home empty-handed. But what about my offer?"

"We cannot, orders are orders, and they require us to go back to Bonneville," said Minia.

"And we still have to find what has happened to Father's convoy," I added.

"As to that, I think you may be able to find such information in Azoros too. While I was a prisoner here in Pullie, one day I overheard Azmal and his men talk about some other mercenaries, who, as they said, had taken several Bois traders prisoners and prepared to escort them south some place. Azmal was considering intercepting the other band and seizing the captives for himself, so he could trade the poor men for ransom. I cannot say if your father was among the captured traders, or if Azmal in fact attacked those other hired swords. But I can assure you that if the mercenaries were involved in kidnapping local traders, someone in Azoros would know all about it. With Revor's help we will be able to learn more if you wish."

It was an unexpected turn of events. Could it be that Father and Ave were being taken to the southern regions of Ethoria by some strange mercenaries? If so, I had to learn more. "What if we split up?" I suggested after a pause, now eager to get on the road. "What if some of us go back to Bois and the others travel with Elson to Azoros."

"Spilt the group?" Minia asked thoughtfully.

"Yes. I am sure Sire Rone would not mind," added Ike, supporting my idea.

"It does sound like a decent plan," joined Rob. "If we do split, we will not waste any time, and at the same time, learn more about our enemies."

"But how should we do it?" Minia continued. "I must return, and I will need at least one of you to come with me. I am sure nothing will happen, but...," He thought some more and then added, "Let's see. Arc and Rob, you will travel with me. Mishuk and Ric, you will go with Elson, and Ike—you can choose, back to Bois or forward to Azoros."

"Azoros, of course. I would not miss it for the world. They say houses there are covered with gold, and gems hang from trees like apples." Ike wanted to say something else, but our laughter made him blush.

And so it was decided then and there that Ike, Ric, and I would travel south, in the company of our new cohort, Elson. In the meantime Minia, Ark, and Rob would return to Bois and deliver the journal, the map, and the tales to the Duke. Alas, nobody knew how long we would be apart. In truth we did not even know whether we would see each other again. But our fate was such that there were two routes, and we could not travel them both together. The lords of Bois needed to know all about the mischief that fell upon the land while we needed to know everything about the Alavantars, and the only way to accomplish it was to split up our company.

When the morning came we packed our bags, ate our last meal together, and led our horses out of the city, where, on the outskirts of the Normandian largest seaport, we shook hands, traded some last jokes, and headed in different directions, never looking back so not to change our minds. There were much more important things at play, and we were becoming a part of them.

Part III

Ethoria's Chronicles

The Shadows of the Past

Chapter 37

MY JOURNEY to Azoros began simply enough. In the company of Elson, Ric, Ike, and I left the city of Pullie and set out east, traveling along the ever beautiful coastline of Normandia, heading for the border of the Northern Empire, the nation, known for its plentiful markets and mistrustful barons, always fearful of possible intrusions from the neighboring realms. For several days our mounts trotted down a trodden road, through a landscape filled with fresh images of lively parishes, smaller towns, and tended fields, often nurtured by scores of farmers. Yet, despite the freshness of the forthcoming scenes, I did not feel too joyful, for I still remembered when Rob, Ark, and Minia rode alongside, warming the march with jokes and laughter, boosting morale and confidence, so needed and so missed. Alas they were not with the company anymore; they were heading in the opposite direction toward the city of Bonneville, driven by the urgency of our recent discoveries.

As for us, our company continued to travel one league after another, coming closer to the frontier, the splendid line of which so many tales spoke. Although to me it was always a thread on a weathered map, I expected the sight of the eastern border of Normandia to be spectacular at least, for in our kingdom alone so many lives were sacrificed for it. But, when on the third day of our flight from Pullie, we finally reached the boundary of the realm, I was disappointed to find that it was nothing I had thought it would be. There were no forts, no mighty gates, no guards or common crowds. In truth there was nothing that could distinguish that strip of land from any other we had visited so far. And where I envisioned high walls packed with unconquerable battlements, there were only rolling crests and rare trees, through which ran a lonesome empty lace of the road that quickly disappeared into a faraway mist. I did not mind when we crossed the bare land without stopping and continued on down the route, which persisted to lope the length of the shoreline, guiding us to the fair-sized town of Burk, a seafaring community abundant in cheap, affordable places where rovers like ourselves could catch some rest and quick hot meals.

Although for most of the trip the traffic we encountered was of a trickle, some half a league before the wooden city gates, the number of travelers on the roadway grew considerably; as one after another, men came from adjoining lanes and hurried toward the outline of the many houses that composed the view of the first foreign city I had ever seen. Being a seaport, Burk was situated at the foot of high rocky cliffs and was set up around a small harbor, with its ever-widening street coming down to a small opening by the water, from which five timber piers stuck out into the sea like the black fingers of some giant creature. Along each of the paved avenues ran rows of houses, all coated with dry clay that had been painted gray. While some of the larger structures stood by themselves, most of the buildings were connected by long sidewalks, crowned with wide boarded roofs, which allowed people to walk up and down the lanes without fear of rain or snow. At times the streets were broken into open round plazas that hosted small bazaars, crammed with vendors' tents and counters, around which locals and outsiders moved, usually in a disorganized manner, seemingly unaware of anyone or anything besides the goods displayed before them.

Amidst one of the plazas near the harbor, Elson found us a suitable hostelry, where, amongst a host of patrons, none of whom looked either rich or poor, we settled for the remainder of the day. While the evening hours went on, we stayed in the dining hall, sitting at a large table by the window, trying to catch conversations telling tales of foreign lands. But for some reason, nobody amongst the tavern's visitors cared to divulge any gossip. During the entire time we spent downstairs not a single story was told or a song sung. I asked Elson about it, and he replied that it was so because of the type of place he had chosen for our stay, much smaller than other inns in the city and located away form the center. "Being in a foreign realm was a serious escapade," insisted the mercenary, "and any outlander caught away from home had to be extra careful about his ways." The Southerner also said that since most noisy places in Burk were favored by less pleasant characters, many of whom came in with the vessels docked at the harbor, we had to stay away from them, so not to jeopardize our journey any more than we had to. The mercenary's answer made sense, and deciding not to bother him anymore, I departed to the room, where Ike and Ric were discussing new things encountered outside our kingdom.

The following morning the sky dawned bright. Cheered by the absence of clouds, the sunlight caressed shingled roofs below and a light breeze from the sea sent gusts of warm air through the open windows. After a quick meal, we left the nameless inn and rejoined the ever-motley mass of people, who had used the early rise to accompany us out of the city and into the open stretches of the Imperial countryside. Once we passed Burk's outskirts the human stream became even thicker and we had to guide our horses into the unfenced field, riding along the crowd's side, thudding on someone's prospective crops. Soon though another even-wider roadway joined our route from the north, and most of the traffic turned there, veering away from the coast and toward the outline of some distant hills. We remained on the same path and continued to trot east, leaving the people and the bustle that they had brought behind.

For the rest of the day we traveled alone, but as the sun began to set, the township of Sandir came into view. Like Burk it was a small community of fishermen and traders who had settled near the shore of the Seven Seas, at the base a leveled mound that overlooked the open blue waters. Not as busy as the previous town, Sandir nevertheless supported a small harbor and several inns, near one of which we soon stopped, encouraged by the smell of cooking streaming from the entryway that was left opened.

Silver Crow was a two-story, well-built clay-patched structure with a large stable, an open yard, and a spacious common room, inside which several dozen patrons sat behind long boarded tables, drinking strong cider and playing games of wall-throw, also a favorite pastime amongst the Imperial subjects. While Elson went on to talk to the owner about the details of our stay, Ike, Ric and I took seats by the fireplace, so we could finally get a good look at the people of the Northern Empire. Although a few of the guests wore clothes of fine fabrics, which distinguished them as traders, most of those in the Silver Crow that day were plainly dressed, rugged and rowdy. Their faces were unshaved and hands dirty with grease and grime—a true sign of a common man. Indeed many of the men were commoners, and as commoners they did not look any different from our countrymen, all speaking the same tongue—the Northern Way— and all sharing the same allure for gossip of some distant realms, adventures, wars, and local nobility.

Yet, despite the striking similarities, the new people were different and very interesting to us. So even after the food had been placed on our table, Ike, Ric and I could not help but mingle with the others, quickly finding ourselves befriended by a couple of older fellows on a nearby bench, who after some talk, began to insist on hearing accounts of our journey. We refused at first, but the men insisted and soon, unmindfully Ike and I began to recapture parts of our trip. What we were telling seemed to captivate the listeners, and before long more people joined the table, eager to hear what we had to say. And say we did—stupid it was, but we could not help ourselves. Until that evening we were always the ones listening, and now people were hanging onto our own words. We were the source of the excitement; we were the tale.

Bedazzled by all the attention, we failed to note how our stories became more detailed and our tongues began to describe events that none of the strangers should have known about. In a cheerful tone, Ike and I described how under cover of the night assassins tried to cut our throats amidst the open fields of Bois, how we escaped another attack in a remote tavern in the south, and how some of our foes dared to climb over the castle wall so they could kill us. It was a splendid tale, but it was very foolish of us to tell it. Of course none of us realized it, not until Elson arrived at the table and pierced my friend and me with a sharp glare from his gray eyes. It was too late for mending though. The attention of the entire tavern was on us. Scores of men chanted for us to continue; some shouted that we were making everything up; others asked questions, but no one ignored our presence. And though we tried to excuse ourselves, the crowd did not want to buy it, insisting that we go on, its mood slowly turning sour and angry.

Again it was the Southerner who came to our aid. After keeping quiet for a while, he suddenly kicked back a chair, slammed down a large wooden mug and raised his voice, rolling it into a loud tune—"A Story of Lost Seamen," a song known to almost every man and child in the Northern lands of Ethoria.

Composed hundreds of years back, during time of the First Age, the verses told a story of brave adventurers who took on the great task of crossing the Abyss, inspired by the call from the old Kings of Titul and promises of new worlds. Daredevils and fools, they set their sails toward the west, heading into the depths of the great ocean. For several years they were gone, and when they finally returned, there were only a few broken beaten vessels, a tiny fraction of the fleet that had set out. Those who survived had little sanity left and only recited stories of their flight in and out of the Abyss. Soon these tales were put to music, and ever since had been gracing the dining halls and fairgrounds of the many kingdoms, narrating accounts of days when bravery was a thing of fashion. In Sandir, amidst the smoky haze of the Silver Crow, Elson was telling the story again:

> *From those who left that rainy day,*
> *Few ever found their way,*
> *And those who did were grim as night,*
> *Afraid to speak of their flight,*
> *With fear deep in their hearts.*
> *Their tales were of evil's lust,*

Of raging winds,
Of icy waves,
Of sleepless nights and restless days,
Of tainted creatures of the deep,
And poor luck and restless grief,
Of scorching sun, of broken ships,
Of death, of madness, pain, and myth.
Oh luck, oh luck, oh we need you,
But have no time to wait for you.
Oh land, oh land, oh where is your sight?
For we may never see the light.

The first few verses the Southerner sang alone, but by the time he came to the middle of the song, others were humming along. When "A Story of Lost Seamen" ended, "The Golden Rain" began, and then another song, and another. A chorus rang out and hands rose, sending clay mugs and glasses into the air. Toasts sprung up everywhere, and the people's focus turned away from us, giving our company a chance to slip away unnoticed. With bustle, laughter, and singing at their peak, we hastily picked up our belongings and followed the mercenary out of the common room and to the second floor, where a small sleeping chamber with four straw mattresses was reserved for us. There, the Southerner locked the door and turned to the rest of us, his face showing signs of irritation and anger.

"Are you out of your minds, farm-grown, half-witted fools?" He snapped, keeping his voice as low as possible. "We are already in enough trouble as it is. Do you think we need some more? What were you thinking?"

"I do not know," started Ike. But Elson cut him off. "Of course you do not know. If you did, you would not have done such a stupid thing."

"But—"

"No Buts. Only the Spirit knows who might have been down there to hear your lovely stories. I would not be surprised to learn that word of where we are and where we are heading is already on its way to our enemies."

"But we did not tell them our names or where we came from," I said timidly, trying to persuade myself more than the Southerner. "We just told a story. How can they be sure that we did not pick up that tale from someone else? Spirit knows, we do not look like real adventurers, heck, we do not even look like squires. There were people who did not even believe us—you heard them, right?"

"You may be right about not looking like real squires," replied Elson, still angry. "But there a lot of things you do not understand, things that come from experience and years of training. Believe me, if someone out there has been trying to find us, after your telling that would not be a problem." Elson paused, thought for a moment, and then added, "Anyway. It is too late now. We cannot stay here anymore, not after your performance in the dining hall. While I take care of some things, get to the stables through the back door and wait for me there. When I come, we leave."

Elson did not say anything else, nor did he have to. We did as told without question, and wasting little time, sneaked out of the tavern and to our horses that still had saddles on their backs.

Outside darkness enveloped the deserted streets, and the only noise came from the dining hall of the Silver Crow, its many windows also casting strips of yellow light onto the sanded lane. After a short while, the Southerner emerged from the back door and, unseen by anyone, we took our leave, riding through the city gates and onto the open road, heading east. Traveling in the dark was not easy, but Elson seemed to know the way and guided us safely for several leagues until we reached a small wooded grove that cropped up by the side of the road. Finding a barely visible trail amidst the wall of thick trunks we turned left and trotted for another half a league into the depth of the forest, eventually halting at a small clearing, its outline consumed completely by the nighttime void.

That night, there was no fire; nor did we unroll our blankets either. Instead we lay down on the bare ground, our capes tucked under our heads. While Ike, Ric, and I tried to fall asleep, Elson remained awake, sitting by the horses, his legs crossed and his eyes fixed on the trees before him. I wanted to say something to him, to apologize for my mistake, but his grim expression deterred me from raising my voice. Giving the mercenary just a glance I turned away and closed my eyes, trying to find comfort in the grass bed, which was hard and bumpy. Yet, it was not the bedding that robbed me of my sleep. Another vision visited me.

Chapter 38

DEVOID OF any warning, I tumbled down a spiral tunnel until images of scorched earth emerged before my eyes. No longer was I in the woods some leagues away from Sandir. Instead I was standing at the edge of a blackened streak of land seeded with deformed shapes that peered from the ground, like ghosts amidst the sunless sky. A once living parish was now in ruins. Not a single house was standing. In their place only silhouettes of stone chimneys rose out of the rubble, still radiating columns of gray smoke and a terrible odor of burned wood and flesh. Yet, it was neither the odor nor the destroyed dwellings that grabbed my attention. Just cubits away, amidst the wreckage lay bodies of human beings, grotesquely twisted by the exhausted blaze.

At first, all I could distinguished, were corpses of soldiers, some still holding onto their weapons, swords, spears, and axes. Their uniforms were torn and dirty and I could not depict any of the symbols depicted on their shields and tunics. Picking my way among the dead men I staggered further toward the center where more bodies lay uncovered —women, children, even pets and cattle, all dead, dozens of corpses thrown in heaps, some as big as large mounds and some just a half cubit high. In all I counted some fifty piles, but I suspected there were more, hidden in the rubble around me.

Dismayed, I hastened my pace and reached the other edge of the ruined parish. With my back to the horrific scene, I prayed to the Spirit for the images to go away, but when I turned, the picture remained unchanged—the same dark shapes, the same blackened bodies, and the same stench, bitter and harsh. Finding little comfort, I was about to turn away again, when Ike's voice got my attention. My friend appeared at my side, walking slowly through the rubble, bouncing a long sword on his shoulder. His clothes, once finely made, were dirty with ashes, his face locked in an expression of concern.

"We are too late," I heard myself say aloud.

"Again." Ike added as he cleared the last few cubits and stopped next to me.

"How many have we lost so far?"

"Twenty-one villages and three towns...," Ike replied slowly as if counting in his head, his voice filled with sorrow.

"It is too many. Do you think we will find any survivors this time?"

"I am afraid not. They did not have a chance. Poor folks, they probably thought it was just another passing regiment of the Army."

"This is war for you." My words were the last I heard, because suddenly everything blurred and I found myself back in the woods, staring dully at the stars above.

The vision was a puzzling one. The image of the scorched village, the dead men, and the talk of war—all that made me feel very uneasy. Was it just another warning, or perhaps a glimpse into the future? I did not know, but I remembered A'tie saying something about the foretelling that the Fore Sight could bring. As I tried to sort through my own thoughts, a low whisper reached me from nearby. I turned and found Ike, staring straight at me.

"Mishuk?" He murmured so as not to wake the others. "Are you awake? I know you are." My friend lowered his voice even more. "Did you see it? Did you see the village, the corpses?"

I nodded silently.

"What do you think?" Ike raised up a little, and when I did not say anything, added, "Is it another one of your warnings?"

"I do not know. Maybe, or maybe it has to do with our future," I replied slowly.

"When is it all going to stop?" Ike uttered then, as if he did not hear me answer. "These nightmares; these stupid visions. I want them to stop. Mishuk, do you hear me? I want them gone."

He sounded sincere in his upset, and I could not blame him. He did not know anything about the Fore Sight. In truth he did not know a lot of things I knew about the visions, as I did not tell him, not him nor anyone else. It was not because I did not want my friends to know; I just needed to learn more about my condition before I could explain everything to the others. I realized it was unfair, and deep in my heart I felt regret for hiding things from Ike. But there was no other choice. I only wished that A'tie's words would come true and soon her spell would wear off, freeing my friends from the visions that had been haunting their dreams.

As for me, I had no other recourse but to continue to study the Fore Sight. Suddenly I felt exhausted. The view of the sky moved away and I fell asleep; it was a dreamless rest though, as yet another vision came over me. And this time the images were reserved just for me.

Chapter 39

SWATHED IN the colors of late evening a small group of horsemen swerved off the road and halted for the night, finding a perfect cover amongst a small patch of old crooked pines. They looked as if they had been riding for days, stopping only to water and feed their horses that seemed as weary as their masters. With darkness all around, a small campfire sprang lively amidst the trees, its tiny blaze chasing away the cold chill. When a simple meal of hot thin soup and dried apples was gone, the men huddled closer together.

For a while I observed the three figures from afar. But unable to see them clearly, moved up a dozen cubits. Afraid to make much noise, I looked down to watch the ground below, but as I did, my eyes failed to find my own feet. Shocked I raised my hands—but they were invisible too. A strange sensation filled me. I was there, and yet I was not. I was walking along a wet grassy stretch, and yet I did not feel the movement. Then it hit me. None of it was real. What I saw was another vision, and the images of the three figures—they were Minia, Rob, and Ark who sat before me. The sight of their worn-out faces startled me, and I stood still for a moment, until a sudden recollection came to me. In one of our meetings A'tie had warned me that there would come a time when my Fore Sight would begin to evolve, enabling me to witness things distant from my own reality, both in time and place. Could it be that the scene that met my eyes was of my friends' journey to Bonneville?

Eager to learn the answer, I stepped closer to the fire, and invisible to my comrades, joined them in the midst of their council.

"We have to take it easy tomorrow, or we will risk losing our mounts," said Minia, his eyes full of fatigue. "I suggest that in the morning we walk for a couple of hours before saddling them."

"Do you think we can afford it?" asked Rob, as he stretched his hands toward the flames.

"We will loose much more if we do not," replied Minia.

"It does make sense," noted Ark, and he rested his back against a half-dried trunk of a crooked tree, adding, "I wonder how Mishuk and the boys are doing. I hope they are all right. I am still not sure if they should have trusted that mercenary."

"It worries me too," agreed Minia, slowly shoveling the burning firewood with a long stick. "I have sensed some strangeness to him. But we cannot do anything about it now." Minia sighed. "Let's get some sleep. We have another tough day tomorrow."

At that, everyone fell quiet and suddenly the scene faded away, leaving me amidst a colorless void. For some time I saw nothing, but then the images returned, and I found myself back at the edge of the same clearing. Several hours had passed, and it was almost time for Ark to take his shift. Rob was sitting by the fire, counting the stars above, when a strange noise came from a distance. The soft crack of timber went almost unnoticed, consumed immediately by the howling of the wind, but Rob was already on his feet. Knowing to take any disruption seriously, he put out the blaze in one swift motion and woke the others.

"I think somebody is out there," he whispered, pointing in the general direction of the recent disturbance. "There were strange noises, as if someone has stepped on a fallen branch or something."

"Another ambush?" asked Ark as he climbed to his feet, seeking cover under low-hanging branches.

"Whatever it is, we cannot take any chances," said Minia quickly. "I think it is best we find another spot to rest, just in case."

Minia then gestured for Rob and Ark to get to their horses, and himself fixed the blanket behind the saddle. A moment later they were off, riding away from the camp, seeking shadows of barely visible clouds that floated high over their heads. Although they did not make the horses gallop, their pace remained swift, and in a short while they covered a distance of several leagues. Throughout the flight they did not notice any pursuit, and once assured that they were indeed alone, stopped at the verge of another patch of trees, choosing it for their new camping ground.

For their protection, they did not reignite the fire. The chill of the night was tolerable, and their blankets were enough to keep them warm. They also decided not to unload the horses, for, if something happened, they had to be ready for another hasty departure. Instead they let the animals walk nearby, and themselves took spots on the ground, soon falling asleep, except for Minia, who did not close his eyes, not once, and just hummed something quietly under his breath.

At some moment, the picture twitched again and changed, presenting me with a new image of the trees and my friends amongst them; only then it was a little after sunrise. The early birds were signing their usual tunes, and the warm wind brushed leisurely against young leaves. Minia stood some distance away, scouting the surroundings for any signs of trouble, and the others packed their belongings, also checking the straps of their saddles that might have gone astray during the night's dash. Then Minia returned, and the three took their horses by their bridles, ready to trace their way back to the road, when a group of dark shapes appeared at the far end of the lane. The figures of six horsemen came down a gentle slope and galloped down toward the trees, behind which my friends stood. Although the strangers' line of sight was blocked by rows of trunks and branches, Minia, Ark, and Rob still dropped to the ground, hiding under more foliage, observing the coming company with caution. Without a doubt, the men were no common farmers, nor did they look like passing traders either. With plenty of weapons—swords and bows—hanging at their sides, they appeared to be mercenaries, and they were looking for someone.

The horsemen hurtled a bit further and then stopped, all looking at the island of trees that hid my friends' camp. For some time they moved along the margin, yelling something to each other and to another fellow, a large tall man dressed in something very dark, who had appeared a little later and was riding toward the group on a large black steed. When he finally arrived, the others huddled around him, and he began to speak.

"They are looking for someone all right," uttered Minia at last, watching as the riders talked amongst themselves.

"I hope it is not us," noted Ark in response, squinting his eyes. "Because I do not think we will be able to take all seven of them."

Silently, Minia nodded in consent.

"Should we do something?" asked Rob next.

The question was followed by a long pause, during which Minia glanced around him and then at a larger mound at the other side of the trees.

"Rob, Ark, take the horses and get behind that hill," said Minia, "And make sure to go around and not over it, so those men cannot see you there."

While Rob and Ark looked over their shoulders, Minia opened a pouch that dangled on his belt and took out a leather case, which held the papers collected in Pullie. He checked the knots and laces on the package and then handed it over to Ark, saying, "If anything goes wrong, deliver these letters to Sire Jim."

"Why? Are not you going with us?" asked Ark, surprised.

"No. I will stay here and see what our guests want. If their intentions are hostile, I will stall them while you make your escape."

"Absolutely not," Rob protested. "We will stay with you."

"This is an order," replied Minia firmly. "You do as I tell you, understood?" When my friends did not reply, Minia added. "Should those strangers decide to attack us, most probably all three of us will die. And if we are dead, who will then tell the Duke and Sire Jim about the discoveries we have made in Pullie?"

"He is right," consented Ark, "Someone has to go to Bonneville, no matter what."

Meanwhile, back at the road, two of the riders separated from the rest and sent their mounts across the glade toward the edge of the grove. Seeing the men draw closer, my friends stopped debating, and Minia whispered, "Hurry, we do not have much time. Go, Leave."

"You heard the man," said Ark, patting Rob on the shoulder, and creeping back to the horses. At first Rob did not follow, but after some forethought, climbed to his feet and hurried after his friend. Together, they quickly made their way out of the trees and around the hill, leaving their third companion alone, his eyes focused on the approaching men.

As sounds of steeds' thumping hooves and riders' voices were drawing near, Minia retreated further away, squeezing the hilt of his weapon. His plan was simple—to remain in his hideout until the intruders left, and then join his friends behind the hill. But if the strangers were to discover him, he would give them a good fight—that was, of course, if their intentions were hostile, which he would found out soon enough.

Staying put, Minia observed alertly as the two men rode into the trees and then to the clearing. There, one of them leaned toward the ground and yelled, "Hey, Par. Look over here. Do these not look like footprints to you?" The rider spun his horse in a short circle, as he continued to study the dry turf.

"Yes, and there are some more over here too," the other said, pointing to the ground.

Making another tight circle, the first horseman straightened up and halted. "It looks like they have left not long ago," he said, and spat on the grass.

"They cannot be too far. The prints are still fresh," called Par.

"Do you think they are onto us?" asked the first fellow.

"I cannot say for sure, but it does appear strange that they left this place so early. Look, they did not even set up a fire to cook a morning meal," Par replied and dismounted, jumping into a puddle of mud concealed by tall grass, a remnant of the earlier rains.

"Oh, rat's tail! Brat, I got mud all over my boots."

His friend laughed.

"This is not funny. These boots cost me a fortune," the man uttered angrily, even though his anger sounded more like disappointment.

"How long since they took off?" asked the fellow named Brat, returning to the subject of the search.

Par kneeled down to inspect the prints, brushing the grass with his gloved fingers. "Not very long."

"I am telling you, they know we are after them. I told the captain last night not to get so close to their camp. It was too quiet. Every step we made sounded like a bang."

"I guess you are right." Par sighed and hit one boot against the other, trying to shake off some of the mire.

"I know I am right," reaffirmed his companion. "Why do you think they put out that fire so fast and took off in the middle of the night? If you ask me, they know that we are after them and probably are galloping to Bonneville as fast as they can, trying to outrun us."

"I do not think it would be possible. If they keep pushing their mounts too hard, they will soon lose them. Should that happen they will have to continue on foot, and how long do you think it will take for us to catch them then?"

"Whatever you say, Brat. Just do not tell the captain I have doubted his plan. He can get really crazy sometimes."

Par shook his head and walked back to his horse. Meanwhile his friend smiled again and added, "Do not worry, he will not find out anything. Let's go."

The danger was almost gone. Feeling some relief, Minia lowered his weapon and took a deep breath. But as he shifted the weight from one leg to another, he hit a small puddle of stale rainwater and his footing slipped. He tried to hold onto something, but all the branches were too flimsy to keep him from falling, and with a sound crash, he dropped to the ground. For an instant, Minia thought the two horsemen were already far enough away not to hear the noise. But he was wrong; before he could get back to his feet, the riders had already spun around and were rushing to the grove, tramping through the shrubs, their swords in hands.

There was little Minia could do. Lifting his weapon, he stepped out of the trees and yelled, "Hey, boys! Are you looking for me?" The riders ignored his comment and ran their horses even harder. But the branches around the spot where Minia made his stand were too thick, and the horses could not pass through them. The large animals jerked and whirled, denouncing their masters' orders. For a little while Minia was safe, but when another attempt failed, the men abandoned their steeds and dismounted.

Even before the enemies' feet could touch the ground, Minia leapt forth, his swift movement accompanied by the sharp whistling sound of a flying dagger. The narrow steel blade soared through the air and one of the riders, Par, thudded to the ground, gasping for air, his hands grabbing onto the hilt of the stiletto that stuck out of his chest. By the time Par stopped moving, Minia was already besieging the other foe, pushing him toward the center of the clearing. The enemy proved to be a poor opponent and very soon my friend's sword found its target, a tenth of a cubit off the man's heart. The man died quickly, but before he did, he let out a loud cry. Minia had no doubt the others at the road had heard the yell. He did not care though. He only hoped Ark and Rob did not disobey his orders, because he knew that he would make sure they had enough time to put a good distance between themselves and the mysterious attackers.

His intuition did not lie, and once his focus was back on the stretch of land between the trees and the roadway, he could see five more men galloping toward him. A real battle was about to begin, only I did not see it, as the picture suddenly shifted, and I was carried away behind the hill where Rob and Ark stood, waiting anxiously. They could not see anything, but could only hear the noise of the fight. Still, they did not make a move, but just shifted in the leather saddles, holding their weapons on their laps.

"Will we just sit here and wait until they kill him?" insisted Rob, as his consciousness refused to cope with Minia's orders.

"No, we will pick up the straps and ride as far away from here as we can. We need to get the reports to the Duke. Everything depends on it. If not us, then who?"

"But we must help him!" Rob exclaimed in response, waving his axe in the air.

"No, Rob. We have our orders," replied Ark calmly. "You know me, I would be the first one out there if it were not for this dispatch. The whole reason why those men are fighting Minia is because they want to stop us. So who do you think wins if all three of us die today?"

Rob did not answer. He frowned and snapped the bridle abruptly. "Heck, let's roll then," he said quickly and galloped off toward another mound, visible from afar. Ark trailed after him, leaving behind Minia's horse.

"Why?" asked Rob as two were moving further away from the fighting.

"The horse?" Ark looked back. "Minia needs his ride; we cannot let him run on foot, can we?"

"I guess not," Rob uttered, and hit his horse with his hand sending it into an even faster gallop.

Once more, the vision changed, taking me further in time, when the sky was completely dark, and my two friends were trotting slowly down a barely visible lane of naked turf. They did not hear the sounds of fighting anymore; nor were there any signs of pursuit. They were alone, tired, silent, and gloomy. Riding next to each other, they traveled until their horses stopped. Then they dismounted and dropped to the ground, falling asleep almost immediately. At last, in their dreams they found some peace; but it was not to last, because the morning came too soon, and it was time to ride again. Bonneville awaited them.

Chapter 40

SUDDEN BLACKNESS replaced the picture, but soon the colors returned, and though I lost touch with Minia, images of Ark and Rob remained with me, as I saw them riding toward Bonneville, determined, weary, and wistful. At times their thoughts blended with mine, and then I knew of their plans. Soon I observed my two friends arrive to the edge of a forest, through which they seemed to be trailing for several hours. Behind them remained the thick green wall of trees and in front, an open valley and a wide road that looked deserted. Convinced that it was safe to venture out, Ark and Rob climbed back up onto their horses and moved forth. Already in the field, they threw a glance back on a narrow track that peered through the green mass of the woods. They hoped to see Minia, but there was no one.

For a while, the wind was my friends' only companion; yet by late afternoon others began to join them, and soon the route was packed with different folk. Several smaller villages came and went, but it was not until the outskirts of Bonneville that the traffic became really thick. To my friends however, it was a welcome sign, for as long as they stayed amongst the stream of travelers they were safe from unexpected attack. And though their enemies were always cunning, none would dare to attack someone in the open, with so many witnesses and guards in sight. Still, my friends did not feel completely safe, not until they saw the outline of the battlements of the Duke's castle towering before them.

The capital of Bois met Ark and Rob with the same indifference and frenzy on the streets as it had during their first visit many days ago. It was the same place with the same people, and even the same odor, somewhat distinct and unpleasant, especially compared to the freshness of open fields and blooming forests. But my friends needed to skip all that bustle, noise, and frantic movement, and hurry to the Duke's massive citadel At the front gates they had to stop and answer a few brief questions from the stationed guards, and then proceeded straight to the barracks, where they hoped to catch Sire Jim before the evening meal.

The word of their arrival had to travel fast; because sooner than they could dismount from their horses, a soldier called to them from a distance. "Sire Jim will see you now," he yelled, and waved his hand several times. Ark and Rob complied immediately and, clearing the yard in several long leaps, followed the guard to the second captain's quarters, which were filled with people. Almost everyone in the group was a nobleman, with the exception of a few commoners who mingled with the guards at the far wall of the chamber. Sire Jim himself stood behind his desk, leaning over a large leather map laid out on the table. He did not see my friends come in and continued to talk to the other lords, pointing to different places on the yellowish sheet of skin as he spoke. Done with instructions, he straightened up and only then noticed Rob and Ark waiting at the door.

"Ah, my dispatchers. I have heard of your return," he said cheerfully and addressed the others in the room. "These are the squires of Sire Rone I have told you about. They have come back from Pullie to bring us news of their investigation into troubles that befell on our province."

The second captain then studied the squires for a moment, and added, "Where is the rest of your company? I remember there were six or seven of you. And where is your commander, Minia Emile?"

"I must inform you that we had to split our company in Pullie. The two of us and Minia were to return to Bois with the news of our finds, while the others were to travel to Azoros, to investigate the matter further. As for our commander, on the way back to Bonneville, a band of armed men, who we think were hired swords, ambushed our camp. While Rob and I managed to escape, Minia stayed behind so he could stall the enemy, giving us time to flee. We wanted to stay with him, but he insisted that we leave. Alas, it was the last time we saw him."

"Indeed, this is an alarming report," said Sire Jim. "If someone has sent a band of mercenaries after you, then your discoveries must be important ones. Everyone, let's all take a moment and listen to whatever these squires have to tell us, for it may be crucial to the safety of our province."

Sire Jim sat down and nodded to my friends. With everyone listening, Ark went on to reveal the whole tale of what our company had managed to uncover on our recent journeys to and from Pullie, also passing on the package that contained letters, maps, and journals. That evening, Sire Jim and the other lords learned about the Chosen One, the Master of the Old, the treachery of

Sire Matt, and the finds made by the imprisoned mercenary, named Elson. In all it was a long and dark story, and it was all true.

"Lord, Sire Jim," my friend said slowly, "what we have here is proof of the existence of a wicked plot, designed by a foul sect of false believers who call themselves the Alavantars, to hurt our people, our kingdom, and our king. After reading these papers, you will see that for a while the Alavantars have been trying to follow an ancient prophecy that had foretold the coming of the Second Great War, when another army from beyond the Land's Edge would descend upon Ethoria, driven by revenge and hatred for everything that our world is.

"In their efforts to help their Dark Master, the one who they see as the leader of the savage Northern armies, they have established many chapters across Ethoria, through which they burrow into the depths of every kingdom, polluting the minds of the populace, spreading their tainted words and lacing their treacherous web. Along the way they recruit more followers, those willing to join their cause. When they need more help they hire mercenaries by the hundreds, luring them with marvelous prizes and easy jobs. And though, right now, their strength is not yet great; they already possess an army of acolytes, connections within many noble courts and merchants' leagues, money, and wisdom. It is only time, before they rise from their hiding spots, challenging the peace and order of our kingdom and the entire world.

"From what we have gathered in our investigation, we are convinced that many of the recent disappearances in Bois are the direct result of their work."

Ark paused briefly and after clearing his throat, went on to reveal the whole tale of what our company had managed to uncover on our recent journey to and from Pullie. That evening, Sire Jim and the other lords learned about the Chosen One, the Master of the Old, the treachery of Sire Matt, and the finds made by the imprisoned mercenary named Elson. In all it was a long and dark story, and it was all true.

When Ark was finally finished, there was silence. No one spoke a word. The pause lasted for a long time, finally broken by Sire Jim.

"How could we have missed it?" he murmured more to himself than to the others. "The signs were everywhere, but we did not see them."

The second captain rose from his chair and addressed my friends. "Whatever the outcome of your investigation may be, you, squires, have done a fine job and so deserve a fair reward. Before that though you must repeat your story to the Duke. Our high lord should know everything at once."

Right after those words the vision ended.

Chapter 41

THE MORNING arrived along with loud noises from the surrounding landscape. Prolonged signing of birds intertwined with the barking of dogs from
far away and the constant tapping of hammers that came from the road. Slowly
I opened my eyes and stared at the green crown of leaves over my head, the
clear sky, and the sun—shining brightly. My companions were already awake.
Elson was nowhere to be seen, and Ric and Ike sat on the grass floor, hands on
their knees, playing a game of bones. Often bursting into a heated debate over
whose turn it was to roll two small white cubes, marked with black circles and
triangles, the two argued passionately, robbing me of any peace or quiet. Unable to ignore the sounds of their bickering, I pushed out a long yawn and
climbed to my feet. By then branches at the other end of the clearing moved
aside and Elson stepped into the opening, seemingly more cheerful than the
night before.

"A slight change in our plans," he said, as he strolled to his horse and
untied the reigns from a low-hanging branch of a nearby oak.

"What do you mean a change of plans?" I asked, rubbing my eyes, getting
rid of the remnants of my sleep.

"It appears that we have to take a detour. Last night the Imperial army set
up a roadblock a few leagues ahead. They say the coastal roadway east will be
allocated for the needs of the Imperial forces; so all the traffic has to move
north to another route. From what I could gather from the passing men, in the
past several weeks there has been much disturbance in the border regions of
the kingdom. A lot of villages are rumored to have been raided by some bandits. Only the local barons do not think those were regular bandits; they are
convinced that the attackers were Lombardian soldiers, who disguised themselves as bandits, sent in by the Lombardian counts to drive the Imperials from
the area and take the lands for themselves. Personally I do not believe a word of
it, but many people do, including the Imperial nobles."

"How long will it take us to go around the route?" asked Ric, putting the cubes away into a small pouch that he then dropped into his pocket.

"Another week, give or take a few days," replied Elson.

"A whole week!" exclaimed Ike, jumping to his feet. "This is already going to be a long voyage as it is. Besides, I really enjoy the view of the sea. Is there any way we can skip the roadblock? I am sure there are plenty of back roads we can take to clear through the sentry posts."

"I am afraid it will not be possible. The word is that a large Imperial force is on the move and is heading east to the Lombardian border. If it is so, there will be plenty of guards posted along the route, making sure it is free for the troops to pass. Should any of them see us anywhere near the roadway, we will find ourselves in a whole lot of trouble. So I suggest we do as told."

When the Southerner finished, Ike, Ric, and I did not say anything, but just nodded and went over to our horses to fix the saddles for the upcoming ride. With everything ready, we mounted our steeds and retraced our way back to the road, where, as the day before, people of all sorts were moving down the lane, paying little notice to anything but their loads and the beaten tracks ahead. Our late arrival did not seem to attract any more attention than the rattling of wheels from the passing wagons, as most folks kept their eyes on a distant hill where, raised high over the ground, swayed several flags of bright green color, split in the middle by a thin white stripe. These were the banners of the Northern Empire, displaying colors of the ruling family and King Urris Froumusk the Third, the sole ruler of the realm.

Next to the standards, overlooking the road below, a group of armed men moved leisurely around the summit. Two of them were mounted on large black stallions and clearly held some rank. Wearing shining plated armor and long green capes that waved in the wind, they studied the passing stream of men and carriages distractedly, sometimes giving orders to a dozen other footed soldiers, all clad in steel chain mail, sleeveless tunics of the same green color, and tall boots of dark boiled leather. Each of the soldiers had a long sword attached to a belt, and held a long spear tipped with a thin metal cone. Next to them, placed at a spot where the road began to curve around the base of the hill, a large wooden sign displayed a line of writing, which read, "All traffic turn North at the next Crossing."

The intersection of which the board spoke was visible several hundred cubits away, where a much narrow track of brown land joined the main road-way from the north, forming a T crossing, similar to the one we had seen near Burk. As the way east was indeed blocked by two huge unhorsed wagons at least three cubits high, and guarded by another host of foot soldiers, all the traffic had to turn left toward the view of some distant woods. Following the others we went north too and started down the unpaved flat path, which, due to the noticeable absence of rain in the past week, was easy to travel on.

Passing occasional hollows and large rocks that at times obstructed the way, we continued in the same direction through the day. After dusk we camped in the open in the company of several farmers, all of whom were going to the capital to buy some young cattle to replenish their depleted stock. Their company was pleasing and made the evening pass quickly, as stories and songs filled the hours before sleep. At dawn we resumed the journey and by late afternoon arrived to another junction, the point were everyone turned east and took the roadway that ran parallel to the coastline, left a day before.

Throughout the detour we met more folks, also forced to take the alternative way east. At times the stream of people was so dense that we were once again struggling to steer our horses amongst the scores of travelers who thronged the lane, trying to push themselves ahead of the others, eager to get to their destinations as soon as possible. For a long while, most of them moved in the same direction we did, but after the third day more people began to come at us, and soon two-thirds of roadway was crammed by those who traveled west.

So many people out and about made it extremely hard for our company to find a decent place to spend the nights. Although, since leaving Sandir we had passed several parishes, all of the inns and eateries there were always full, and we had to sleep outside in the fields and pastures by the road, often joined by others, who did not mind sharing a fire with a couple of Normandian squires and a mercenary from the south. Luck came to us only on the third evening, when we reached another small village of Murior. To our surprise, its only inn had some free rooms, one of which we gladly took, though I suspected that the owner overcharged us gravely.

With all the matters of our stay settled, we picked a corner table inside a small but noisy dining hall and, sipping on the local brew made of wild berries, busied ourselves with listening to rumors that other patrons told nearby. Across the room, the main theme was the unexpected maneuvers of the Imperial army. Although most of the guests spoke only of their speculations, at one table, located next to a large blackened grill, four men—clearly rovers in the Northern lands—were describing the accounts of their journeys, and keeping many of the patrons on their toes.

Looking very much like outlanders from the south, they wore fine silk of gray colors and fair tailoring, unavailable in smaller places, like Villone. Two of the fellows had silver bands on their forearms and another one—a thick golden chain, wrapped around his neck. The only people I had ever seen wearing such ornaments were traders or hired swords, and since the men did not look like merchants, I assumed they were of the second sort. All four were speaking the Northern Way, though I could hear an obvious accent, which made some of their words sound broken. Yet that was but a minor defect that did not ruin their speech, to which I found myself listening with great interest.

Missing the beginning, I caught on at the point when one of the outlanders, a red-haired man with long whiskers, described their voyage through the Border Regions of the Empire.

"As I said. It took us several days to get to the Border Regions, and once we did we found nothing but a wasteland. I mean burned grounds with not even a patch of grass left."

At that point a mug of chilled ale arrived from the bar and the teller switched to the drink, while one of his friends, a clean-shaved man with two rings in his left ear, picked up the story.

"Of course we had heard rumors of the disturbance in the region, but did not expect it to be so bad. Every village we visited showed signs of recent attack; a few were completely destroyed, all those who did not hide—killed or crippled. Then on the fourth day we arrived to one parish that was still intact, I think it was called Solier."

"Solier?" exclaimed one of the listeners. "My wife is from there. Please tell me, was everything all right there?"

The man with whiskers nodded, then took another gulp of the brew and took up the storytelling. "As Sale said, Solier was spared by the raids; though most of its folks were gone, fled over the River to safer ground. Yet, a few of the villagers remained; some shops were open, and so was the tavern. It is there we went, tired from the long ride north. The place was a bit deserted, clean, but not too quiet, with a dozen or so guests, mostly local militia, occupying a few tables. Everyone was talking about the raids.

From what we could gather, the toll of the attacks on the region was horrific—over fifty villages ransacked, a quarter of the pastures burned, and some two hundred people killed or missing. And while the raids were as frequent as spring season's rains, until then nobody had been able to catch those responsible for the evil deed; not even the Imperial forces, dispatched to tend to the trouble. Every time the mysterious attackers were gone before the troops arrived."

"It cannot be true!" yelled someone from the crowd. "Our King's armies are the best in Ethoria. How is it possible that our soldiery could not track some loose bands of roaming thugs?"

"That is what everyone else thought too, that simple criminals and lowlifes were to be blamed. We did too, until we witnessed what happened in Solier.

"Not an hour after our arrival to the village, a fellow ran into the room, screaming at the top of his lungs, 'Help! Help! They are coming! They are coming!' Everyone around us jumped from their seats and rushed outside. We followed, but before we could get to the exit, the owner and his servants barricaded the doors and windows, pulling up chairs, benches, tables, and whatever else they could get their hands on. When we tried to ask them what was going on, no lucid answer came."

"You said it right, Voril," agreed the bold fellow, by the name of Sale, whose arm's bands began to glitter in the flickering light of the many candles.

The whiskered man nodded and continued. "Time passed slowly while we were inside. But then we started to hear noise from the street—many feet running, horses galloping, and sounds of fighting, mingled with dozens of voices. Somewhere far away a woman cried for help. A bit closer several men yelled out swift commands, and someone else was pleading for his life. Eager to know what was happening, we peered though windows' heavy shutters to find many of the houses around the tavern on fire, and people—women, children, and the elderly—running out of them. Only the poor souls did not get too far; almost immediately they were cut down by groups of passing horsemen dressed in unmarked clothes, quick with blades and good with mounts. It was only time before the strange attackers came for the inn. Sure enough, before we knew it, the front door rattled and then broke. Tables split and timber flew everywhere, opening a large gap through which a stream of men poured into the dining hall. Most of them had their faces covered with long scarves and some wore bulky leather helms with round slits for their eyes.

"Some folks inside began to scream, others tried to fight. It was all so confusing—swords, torches, bodies soared every place, blood splattered the walls, and the sound of the clash was deafening. Forming a line of defense by the far side we watched as the foes cut their way toward us. And once they came their fury knew no limit. Yet, we stood our ground, parrying wave after wave of the attacks. While our opponents were decent fighters, their skills were still too rugged, as they acted more like brutes than swordsmen. But what they did not have in proficiency they gained with persistence. After much fighting, we finally began to get tired; our ranks loosened and we found ourselves pushed closer to the wall."

"Imagine this," interjected the bald man. "Corpses everywhere. A few cubits to the left several of the servants were being butchered; a step to the right the owner, overcome by the attackers, was losing his head. Enemy everywhere and no place to retreat."

Sale paused and all of the outlanders took several gulps of ale. When he lifted his hand to order more, before he could even say a word to a serving girl, several of the listeners had their coins out buying drinks for him.

"What happened next?" I heard one man ask from across the room. Other bystanders picked up the plea.

Voril curled his whiskers with two fingers and grinned. After enjoying the torment he was giving the listeners, he finally cleared his throat and his voice sounded again. "As I said, we were fighting hard, but there was no end to the enemies, who continued to come at us. Another wave of swords and we would not have lived to tell you the story, but something happened. A horn sounded from the outside, and suddenly the foes' ranks broke. Without a glance they dashed for the door, leaving us as if nothing had happened. Quickly we scrambled after them, and onto the street, finding the enemy fleeing to the forest, hundreds of cubits away from the village. For a moment we thought it was a trick, but when we saw the Imperial cavalry galloping from the other side, everything became clear.

While the soldiers pursued the enemy, we remained on the street, surveying the carnage, when some officer of the Imperial army came up to us. Assured that we were not the bandits, he thanked us for our service and offered a reward. Although we refused the pay, he gave it to us anyway. Fifty silvers each—it was a good prize for one battle."

A few in the crowd gasped in astonishment. As proof one of the outlanders extracted a pouch and showed a handful of silvers with symbols of Imperial talons imprinted on them.

"But that was not all," added Sale. "He also asked us if we wanted to join the Imperial forces. It was a tempting offer—full pay, good horses, plenty of food and lodging. But we are not a military kind—we are adventures, if you know what I mean."

Many of the listeners hummed in agreement.

"Did they find out who the attackers were?" a chubby fellow who stood closest to the tellers asked, when the noise settled.

"The officer told us that his regiment was on patrol, when they got word from a local farmer about a strange band of horsemen coming toward Solier. The troops immediately rode out to investigate, but alas, they were too late. By the time they got to the village, half of it was destroyed, with many villagers dead or wounded. I must admit though, the locals put up a good fight, keeping the enemy busy until the arrival of the soldiers."

"But who were the attackers?" another man repeated the question.

The four men looked at each other and at the crowd around them. When all eyes were on them, Voril took a deep breath and uttered, "Lombardians."

A sound of surprise and shock rolled through the hall. Some listeners gave out curses; others pounded their fists on the tables.

"Not only that. They were regulars with Lombardian royal legions. Of course they did not wear their uniforms that day, but the Imperial soldiers found tokens of Lombardian Guard on each of the dead attackers."

"Cursed Lombardians, rip it and clean it," interjected Sale and he spit.

"I knew it," the same chubby man shouted angrily, and shook his fist violently. "Shell eaters are trying to steal our lands again."

"They kill our men and our families, burn our villages, and our barons do nothing. How long will it last? How long do we have to suffer? Where is our army? Is the King paying heed?"

Angry shouts poured from the crowd. The mood was quickly getting bitter. The topic was now focused solely on the neighboring kingdom and its foul subjects. The men were fuming, their attitude turning violently angry; so angry that I felt lucky I was not of a Lombardian kin.

Fury brewing everywhere, I turned to my companions, saying, "Oh heck, this place is on the edge."

"A lot of anger here indeed," Elson noted in reply. "But it does not surprise me one little bit. There has been a sense of warring in the air for quite some time. And if stories like these continue to stir the commons, war will be inevitable."

"War?" Ike pronounced in surprise, putting down a slice of bread. "But why?"

"War is a profitable business. At least the Imperial barons tend to think so. They will do anything to persuade the King to start some military campaign so they can make money supplying his troops. Lombardia is not exactly the toughest opponent right now. If done properly, a war against it can bring a quick victory and a lot of profit."

"But do you think this story about Lombardians attacking the border regions is true?"

"Let's not discuss this subject here; as you can see the other guests may take offence to whatever I say." Elson nodded toward the nearest table and took a sip of ale, smacking his lips several times.

"Do you think we will be able to reach Azoros before the fighting starts?" I asked a seemingly neutral question, concerned of trouble that the conflict may have for our voyage.

"I would not worry about it now. By the time the generals decide to do anything half a season will pass."

"But they have closed the main rode already, have they not?" Ike raised his voice.

"This only means that they are starting to move the troops east. First they will spend weeks relocating the men and supplies, then another week setting up camp, and several more planning the offensive. So as you can see I would not worry about it if I were you."

I hoped that the Southerner was correct in his assumption and we would pass through the border long before the war began. Meanwhile, the dining hall was boiling with emotions, and when random brawls began to take place we had to leave, slipping upstairs into the room. But as soon as the lock clicked, I suddenly recalled leaving my saddlebags back at the stables. Though there was little of value in them, I still did not want to loose any of my gear, so I ran downstairs to the yard. The open court was empty; the fresh air cool, and the sky darkening. Shivering from the cold breeze I hurried across to the stables, which to my luck were left open and unattended, as all of the stable boys were inside, listening to the tales. After finding my mount in one of the far stalls, I checked the bags, which were untouched.

With the load on my shoulders I turned to head back, when I heard voices coming from the yard. Having learned to take everything with caution, I immediately lurked into one of the empty stalls and hid behind the wide boards, listening. Shielded by the shadows, I peered through a narrow gap, studying four figures that appeared a few cubits away from the stable's gate. The men talked about something, then two of them separated and walked inside, heading directly for me. When the men passed me, I caught a glimpse of their faces and right away recognized them—the talkative outlanders from the tavern. They seemed to be in a cheerful mood and chatted energetically as they picked up four steeds of gray color and led them into the yard. Intrigued, I crept after them, keeping myself in the shade.

"You did not have to worry, Rol. Those fools believed every word we said," the man with the shaved head by the name of Sale said as he yanked on the bridle of his horse.

"I never thought it would be that easy," rebutted his companion with a smirk.

"Why? You do not think the story of our adventures sounded true enough?" Sale placed his left foot into the stirrup and lifted himself up, settling firmly into the large leather saddle.

"These are dark people. All they need is a simple story to make them believe almost anything," noted Voril, the man with whiskers. He came up to the gates and took one of the horses. In one jump he settled in the saddle and turned his horse slightly to face the others. "Did you see the expressions on their faces? Even before we finished, they were ready to run to the next recruitment post and sign up for the Imperial army. Besides, others believed our words too. How many places have we visited?"

"A few dozen," replied Sale from his seat.

"That is right, and every time they ate everything up like small children, not a single question or a doubt in their eyes." The whiskered fellow grinned, and the others laughed.

"Right you are. If all continues to go as well, we should ask the barons for a raise."

"Of course we will, but let's finish with Sandir first. I have heard there were quite a few Lombardian sailors there, restocking their ships. If we are lucky we may even start a brawl that should earn us some extra silvers." Volir smiled again and turned to leave the yard. His three companions followed, and soon their figures disappeared into the dark. When the noise of their leave was gone, I finally left my refuge and walked outside, staring at the point were the outlander once had stood. Seeing nothing there but dust, I clutched the saddlebags and ran inside, eager to tell my companions about the things I had just heard.

Chapter 42

WHEN THE next night came, a new vision visited me, starting with a sensation of unbearable pain. It was not my pain, though—it was Minia's. His shoulder ached, as if pierced by a thousand needles, and his skin burned, leaving his flesh and mind battered and weak. I saw him riding his horse, holding tight to the loose reins, barely able to move. He tried to concentrate on the road, but his senses abandoned him and he began to faint. At first breathing deeply seemed to help, but soon even the cold air did not bring relief. A desire to escape the pain grew like a wildfire, and after much struggle Minia finally gave in to it. His eyes rolled back, and he dropped from the saddle, his left foot caught in the straps. His seemingly lifeless body hit the ground, making a soft clunking sound, and dangled after the mount, leaving a long wide trail on the sandy floor of the road. But Minia did not care. It was easier that way. Soon his thoughts drifted away, and a pleasant stillness came over him. He did not know if he was dead or alive. It was all black, black around him and black around me.

As Minia lost consciousness, the vision stopped, sending me back to my own reality. Awake, I found myself being overwhelmed with feelings of sadness, fear, and uncertainty for my friend, all mingled together, making me feel very worried. Right then, I wanted to know more about Minia's fate, what happened to him and if he was alive. Alas, my wishes went unanswered, as the vision did not return, not that night, or the next four nights. But as I began to suspect that Minia could be dead, on the fifth evening since I had last seen an apparition, I suddenly sensed my Fore Sight return.

The vision started with blackness, yet from afar I heard people talking, their voices sounding real, making me believe that it was not a simple dream. I tried to see who the men were, but could not; my eyelids were too heavy, as if filled with iron. I tried to speak too, but my lips did not move. My mouth was glued together, and my throat was dry and stiff. Pondering on the question why I could not do anything, I suddenly realized that it was not I who could not move, or see, or speak—it was Minia.

He was lying someplace, trying to gather his strength. After several more attempts, he finally managed to open his eyes, but all he saw was a blur. Only when the mist faded some moments later, did he distinguish the outline of an open window, and past it images of the blue sky and soft white curly clouds. By then the voices were gone, and Minia found himself alone, resting on a large bed, inside a small, clean, and simply-furnished chamber, its walls painted white. Next to him stood a round table that held a small jar and several towels of bright blue color. "Infirmary," Minia thought to himself, and he took a deep breath. It was a sigh of relief, his and mine. He was indeed alive. The memories of the battle that had almost killed him were vague. He remembered fighting several men; he remembered wounding and killing some of them and getting hurt himself. He also remembered the pain when their swords sliced his flash, sharp pain that made his eyes water. He did not remember though how the engagement ended, if he won, or how he escaped. He tried to recall any details, but could not. His mind was just too weak.

Dwelling in the pleasantness of fresh air and soft waft he wondered how long he had been asleep. He wanted to ask somebody, but there was no one to ask, not until a door opened behind him and someone walked in, making very little noise. Curious, yet unafraid, Minia tried to see who it was, but it hurt to turn his head that far, and so he remained still, waiting for the guest to come to him. For a while the visitor lingered in the back, but then moved closer and Minia saw a young servant, a girl in her teens, blonde, thin, and very pleasant to look at. She did not notice Minia staring at her at first and went on about her chores, changing water in the jar, and fixing long sheets around his bed. But then her eyes rose and she caught Minia's glance. Somewhat startled she quickly stepped back and bowed.

"Greetings, Sire. I am so glad to see you are getting better," she uttered slowly. "We were very worried about you for a while. You did not wake up for five days. We were afraid you would not make it, but the potions seemed to work. Uncle Srola makes great potions. They smell funny, but work very well. Look, they helped you."

Minia tried to say something, but only groaned. He was still very feeble.

"Oh, no, no. Do not say anything. You are not allowed to talk. How silly of me to bug you with my questions. You need your rest. I will leave you now and come back when the sun is setting. But if you need anything just ring this bell; someone will come to help you."

From one of her pockets she extracted a small brass bell and put it on the bed next to Minia's hand. He tried to grab it, but his fingers did not obey and he dropped the tiny metal cone onto the blanket where it remained. By then the girl had already left, and when the door closed, Minia dozed off again, even though he did not want to.

The next time he came to his senses it was already late evening. The window was closed and through its thick glass he could see the darkening sky. He liked the view at nighttime and stared past the wooden frame until his eyes got tired. Then he moved his glance away and shifted onto his side. Indeed the potions were working very well, and Minia was pleased to find the pain subside. Still he was very weak and it would take much more than a couple of potions to get him back on his feet. From what he could remember now, his wounds were very serious. In the fight amidst the grove, before he managed to retreat to his horse, one of the attackers had pierced his shoulder, and another hit him in the ribs. If it were not for an extra leather tunic Minia always wore underneath his armor, he would not have lived to see another day. But he did, and despite his injuries, felt elated that he had survived a serious battle against seven mercenaries, five of whom he had managed to dispose of. Such thought made him smile, and suddenly he felt hungry, so hungry he could have eaten anything, even a dried-out rotten apple.

Quickly finding the small bell, he rang it several times. For its size, the tiny metal cone was very loud, and a moment later the same girl appeared at the foot of Minia's bed, giving him a cheerful smile that made her red cheeks even redder.

"Do you need something, Sire?" announced the girl as she bounced up and down on her toes.

"Some food would be nice," replied Minia, his voice half its normal tone. "I do not suppose you will get me a nice cold mug of local brew?"

"You are funny, Sire. You cannot drink ale. Uncle Srola will not let you have it, not even a little sip."

"Huh, if you say so. I will take a glass of water then, can I have that?"

"No," said the girl firmly. "Uncle Srola says you can only have his medicine and warm milk, that is all. If you want to recover you better do as he says. He is very good you know, the best healer in the whole province."

"Then, I will have some milk." Minia sighed and grinned.

"Good," noted the girl and turned around to run back out, but Minia stopped her with his question. "Can I have your name before you go?"

"It is Sala, Sire. I am the daughter of the second maid here at the castle."

"The castle?"

"Yes, Sire Tem's castle in Bonneville. Oh, you do not remember how you got here, do you?" The girl playfully tossed her hair. "Some peasants found you near the main road several leagues away from here. Your foot was caught in a stirrup and your horse dragged you everywhere. I do not know how long you had been like that, but all your clothes were ripped up and your skin bloodied. When the men saw your wounds, they brought you to the local tavern. But then they found your squire's bandage and immediately carried you here, to the castle. It is the law you know that all the lords' fighting men must be brought to the infirmary."

The girl looked at Minia, and when he said nothing, lowered her eyes and asked, "Are you someone important, or maybe famous, a hero of some sort?"

"What makes you ask this?"

"It is just that the entire castle is talking about you. The Duke himself has asked to be informed about your progress, and several of his captains have come down to check on you. You must be very important, because in my fourteen years I have never seen lords visit common squires. My mother though, she says it happened once many years ago, when two local men had been brought in here from the forest. They were commoners just like you and they were hurt. My mother says that they saved a lord's life during a hunt and for that were declared heroes. And that was the only time when the lords came down to see the common men at the infirmary. So you see, you must be a hero. Are you?"

Minia laughed, at least he tried to. "No, girl. I am not a hero. I am just a squire. I got in some trouble, trying to get back to the city. I truly do not know why the Duke or his captains would be interested in me. But once I get some strength into my legs I will find out. To do so though, I will need some food. I am starving."

"Oh yes, yes. Of course. I will be right back." The girl ran out, and returned a moment later with a glass of warm milk in one hand and a hot plate, filled with some white pulp, in the other. The mush looked not too pleasing, and Minia immediately questioned its flavor. "Can I inquire as to what it is you have brought me?"

"It is my mother's porridge, good Sire. All the sick and injured must eat it. It will give you strength and help your wounds heal faster. Do not worry, it only looks strange, but actually it is very tasty."

Somehow Minia did not believe Sala; yet he was hungry enough to try anything. Pulling himself up off the pillow he took a spoonful of the porridge and stuck it quickly into his mouth. To his own surprise, the puree had a decent taste to it—a little sweet and tangy, but not at all revolting. After several swallows Minia started to enjoy its oozing texture and finished the whole plate in an instant, washing it down with the milk. The food felt warm in his stomach and he wanted to rest again. Before he could say his thanks to Sala he was asleep.

Sometime later more voices began to ring in his head once more. He heard them talking, but it was dark and he could not see anyone. "A strange dream," thought Minia to himself, but realized that it was not a dream. He was not asleep, and there were indeed people in his quarters. The voices sounded very familiar, and Minia quickly recognized them as Rob and Ark, who were standing nearby, talking about him. Glad that his friends were alive, he immediately opened his eyes and said, "I am sure happy to see you two safe and sound."

Hearing the words, Rob and Ark stopped their conversation and turned to Minia, smiling.

"We can say the same," replied Rob after a brief pause, his tone very spirited. "Frankly we were afraid we had lost you back at that ridge. You do not know how thankful we are to see you alive."

"Did you find out who those men were?" said Ark, "Because here we still do not know. Sire Jim sent out several scouting parties, but they found nothing."

"Some mercenaries, I guess," replied Minia, "Frankly that whole fight is a blur right now. But what about the message, did you deliver it?" Minia finally sat up straight and looked at his companions.

"As soon as we reached the castle," said Ark.

"Do not worry, everyone knows all about the Alavantars" said Rob. "The Duke, Sire Jim, and the other lords, they found our evidence very compelling, and have already called a war council to prepare for an expedition to the Land's Edge—that is where the Alavantars are supposed to hold their camp. The Duke has also sent out word to Sire Zuros, the High Lord of Puno, and to the capital, telling the King about his plans. Sire Zuros has already agreed to join the campaign, and once a reply from the royal court is received, we may see an expedition force depart to the shores of Lake Azul."

"There is more," Ark joined in. "Sire Jim said that we could come along if we wanted."

"Could it be? A real military expedition, maybe a real battle too?" The thought alone made Minia very excited. It had to be a marvelous sight to see an army of Sire Tem's march into a field of combat—straight columns of armored horsemen, riding as one, flying under many banners of the kingdom, bright, strange, and distinctive. Behind them, also moving in tight lines, came men-at-arms—rows of soldiers with shields and spears and steel helms, and of course, squires, faithful servants of the knights, who traversed alongside their masters, scouting the lands, always ready to fight for their honor. Ever since Minia was a little boy he had dreamt about taking part in a true war campaign. But it had been years since the knights of Normandia had taken up their arms. Of course there were minor incidents such as riots, bandits, and small skirmishes along the border with Westalia, but none could ever compare to a real crusade. All that was about to change though; the province of Bois was getting ready for a new military expedition, and Minia was invited to join.

Daydreaming, the squire could already see himself galloping next to the Duke and Sire Jim, when a sharp pain in his shoulder brought him back to reality. His bruised body still ached, and the bandages on his ribs restrained his movement. Before he could go anywhere; he had to heal first, and that could take some time.

"Did the Duke say when he plans to depart?" asked Minia, hoping that he would have enough time to recover.

"The courier from the royal court is yet to arrive, and many of the lords are still trying to get to the city as well. It will be at least a week before the expedition is assembled," replied Ark in an encouraging tone.

"A week. This is good. I should be up and ready by then." Minia let the air out of his lungs and wanted to say something else, but Sala walked in and quickly put an end to their meeting. Frowning and shaking her head, she set aside a large tray and pushed Rob and Ark out of the room, telling them to come back the next day. When they were gone, she moved the tray to the bed and swiftly departed, leaving Minia with another plate of white pulp, a glass of milk, and small pieces of warm homemade bread, which was his supper. The sight of food brought a sense of hunger back again, and Minia ate everything. He could swear there was something mixed into the food, because once he had finished it, he fell asleep and did not wake up until the next day.

Chapter 43

ALTHOUGH THE Fore Sight brought me joy with pictures of Minia, Rob, and Ark alive and well, my actual journey did not. Days passed slowly, dragging one after another. Chasing the same flat beaten road our company of four traversed east, leaving behind plain villages and towns of the foreign realm. Later on the view of the tended lands faded, as the route took us away from the cultivated meadows and closer to a line of trees that peered importunately in a distance. The sight of the forest accompanied us for some time, but then left too, as our company came up to the bank of a wide stream, the Bound, as it was called. The mightiest of the rivers in the upper parts of Ethoria, it took its beginning deep within the depths of the Forest of Souls in Magnicia and ran southward to the Seven Seas, splitting the Northern Empire in two: the mainland and the border regions.

The grand stream was so wide that it was impossible to see the other bank, and after staring at its dark blue water that moved in low waves toward the sea, I suddenly realized it presented us with a serious obstacle. We had to get across, but how? For answers I turned to the Southerner, who stood at the summit of a rise, overlooking the Bound. Yet, as I made my way to join Elson at the top, I noticed a distant township that sat at the southern slope of the hill. No bigger than a very small village of five or six large buildings, it circled around a tiny harbor, composed of several long piers that hosted an array of boats, some empty and some moving. Most of the vessels were fishing scrubs, and none looked strong enough to carry a large party across, none except for one. Resting next to one of the wharfs stood a larger ship, equipped with two thick masts and a wide deck, big enough to hold several dozen men and loads of cargo.

"It looks like we are lucky today," announced Elson, as if answering my silent question. "They are still loading the ferry. If we hurry, we may get ourselves a quick ticket to the other side."

"What about the horses? Will they fit on there too?" asked Ike as we started our descent toward the parish.

"I see you have never been on a ferry before, young man." The Southerner smirked. "They have enough room on that thing for people, horses, and cattle, all put together."

Elson snapped his mount's bridle and hastened its step. We did too, asking no more questions.

It was still early. The weather remained kind, and there was no sign of rain or clouds anywhere. The full light of the morning sun highlighted the brick pavement of the village's only street, which we took straight to the harbor. There a small crowd fussed around stocks of barrels, crates, and sacks, thrown in and around a large barrack that probably served the purpose of a storage place. Near the wharfs the Southerner stopped, dismounted, and motioning for us to stay where we were, vanished around the nearest corner, returning some time later with a smile on his face.

"Good news!" he exclaimed cheerfully and raised his hand, which held a long thin paper slip with some writing on it. "We are going across the river today. The ferry is scheduled to leave at midday. So I suggest we get to the boat before all the good spots are taken."

The prospect of traveling on water for the first time in our lives made Ike, Ric, and me very excited. Without the slightest hesitation we quickly jumped off our horses and taking them by the straps, headed up the pier toward the boat that floated at the other end, some half a hundred cubits away. After exchanging a few words with some of the sailors, we then crossed a large boarded ramp, placed in between the ship and the pier. We entered the spacious deck, where a young man, dressed in sleeveless tunic of blue color, greeted us with a salute and a thick southern accent.

"Welcome to the Maiden Pride," he said as soon as he completed his bow. "Please lead your horses to the lower deck. Your stalls are five through nine. You will find them at the far end of the second row. I will send someone to assist you when I get done here. Oh, and make sure you tie your animals to the fixing poles. Some of the beasts can get really anxious traveling on water; we do not want them kicking and biting anyone down there."

The lad then pointed at a large opening in the center of the floor and immediately switched his attention to another set of passengers, who had just gotten aboard and were waiting for us move out of the way.

Following instructions we led the horses to the gates, down a steep, but even, slant, and to the second deck below. An odor of livestock and stale hay was overwhelming, and I had to shield my nose with my cape so I could breath, trying to walk by several dozen stalls, some empty, and some occupied by cows, donkeys, horses, pigs, and even people, those who preferred to stay indoors, either afraid or tired of the water. Just as the young sailor had said, at the end of the second row we found our spots, four small cubicles, barely big enough to fit an average horse. Fastening the straps to thick wooden poles that ran along the inner wall, we secured the mounts, and after storing our saddles inside large iron chests, headed back to the upper deck, already thick with men and cargo.

While there were only several dozen men on the floor, bulky crates and wagons took up most of the space, and people, including ourselves, had to settle on top of barrels and sacks set in rows along the railings. When the commotion shifted completely from the pier to the ship, a large man with wide-flapped hat, who was the captain of the ferry, shouted quick orders, instructing the sailors, all dressed in blue sleeveless tunics, to remove the ramp and the ropes. Once everything was done, a loud cracking sound came from under the berth, and a forceful jolt made everyone on board stumble against each other. Curses and shouts ran through the crowd, but soon ceased as the boat rocked again and started to move away from the shore, heading for the open blue of the river.

Just as expected the trip across the Bound took all afternoon. Only at dusk, a line of land appeared in sight, quickly turning into a picture of a village, almost identical to the one left earlier that day. The small parish of several houses was situated at the base of another hill and surrounded a tiny harbor. The only difference was that a much larger crowd of people packed the riverbank, anxious to see the boat arrive. In fact, once they spotted the vessel in the distance, their ranks came to life and moved toward the piers, cramming the thin boarded lanes so tightly that not a single cubit of the docks remained empty. But that was nothing, compared to the craziness that began when the Maiden Pride finally reached the harbor. Scores of men, women, and children, pushed forcefully toward the boat, all eager to get on board, not even bothering to let any of the passengers out.

For a moment, it seemed that the ramp would break under the weight of so many bodies. But the wood held and the people continued to push forth until the gray-bearded captains took charge, and with a help of his sailors drove the crowd back to the pier, freeing a narrow passage for the passengers to leave the ferry. Afraid that we would not get another chance, our company hurried to the horses below, and then off the deck to an open market square, located at the edge of the harbor. Somewhere along the way I got separated from the rest of my companions and, unable to find them anyplace, had to fight through the human mass alone, away from the piers and to the street, where I was finally able to stop and glance back.

Before me, the crowd remained thick. The few wharfs were filled with people, and not a single man could turn without pushing someone else into the water. Those who had arrived with us were still trying to get out, and those who had been waiting for the ferry did everything to get onto the boat, pushing forth as hard as they could, shouting, cursing, and shoving each other aside. Yet, in such a scene of complete disorder I managed to catch a glimpse of Ike and Ric, making their way toward me. The only one missing was Elson, but he too appeared, his tall figure emerging out of the traffic, walking in front of his mount.

"Did we lose anyone?" he asked, clearing the last few cubits of the harbor's paved floor.

"Everyone is here," I answered and adjusted my cape that had shifted in the stampede.

"Why do all these people want to get on the boat?" asked Ike, still looking at the mass of men not too far away.

"They are refugees," replied Elson, jumping into the saddle and turning his horse to leave the village. "They are fleeing from the border regions. Do you not remember the stories we have heard?"

We did, and so it appeared that at least some of those tales were true. The Border Regions were indeed in turmoil, with many of its people trying to leave for safer ground across the Bound.

Once a part of Lombardia, the area known as the border regions had long belonged to the Northern Empire. Although some years back, the Imperial barons had tried hard to improve the stranded lands, such efforts were rendered useless, as the deep waters of the Bound proved to be too serious of an obstacle, stalling much of the travels in and out of the area. As time went on, people began to leave the Border regions, lured by much wealthier and bigger markets across the river. One after another cities disappeared and along with them trade, since with revenues declining, the merchant guilds of the South had ordered their caravans to pass by the hampered territory, saving the goods for the better bazaars of the west. In turn, the King and his barons, too, lost their interest in these lands and so dispatched just a fraction of the Imperial army to guard some of the main trade routes, three small garrisons that served only to protect the passing caravans and a few of the larger settlements. With such a poor military presence, it was only time before the border regions fell prey to scores of thugs and bandits, who started to pay frequent visits to the area, harassing smaller communities and stranded convoys with an increasing persistence. Still, those troubles were but pests, compared to what came to pass within the last several seasons, when a mysterious enemy emerged out of nowhere to devastate the lands, erasing one village after another, leaving many of the inhabitants dead or homeless. The day when my companions and I crossed the Bound, we witnessed the reality of dismay that had come to the Border Regions, with most of the scarce populace desperately fleeing to the mainland and the Imperial garrisons doing little to correct the situation. Indeed, those were disturbing times for the eastern part of the Northern Empire, and our company was about to travel through there.

Leaving behind the coastal parish, we took a new road east. As before, the route ran parallel to the coast, promising to get us to the border of the realm within the next several days. After that our course was straight south, through the Kingdom of Lombardia, across the Great White River, and to the city of Azor, the nominal capital of Azoros. Several leagues into the valley, the landscape around us began to take on a distinctive look. While the wilderness remained similar to that of the valleys across the Bound, signs of human presence became rare. There were but a handful of travelers, whom we had seen near the coastal village, but they had disappeared long before, leaving us alone in the unfamiliar lands, which hid no signs of any parishes or farms or tended fields. It was just grass and trees and clear sky with the disk of the sun hanging low over the site.

In solitude of our own company, we galloped forth until reaching a summit of a low hill that overlooked another dale below. A wide view of flat green fields stretched far before us and with the exception of a single track of road, we saw no traces of any human ever being there. Yet, after studying the land a little longer, I noticed several strange black spots, peering in a distance, some small, some big, some round and some of uneven odd shape. Initially they looked nothing more than shadows, cast by the clouds in the sky, but as I strained my eyes I realized that those were not plots of false illumination, but something else.

"What is that over there?" I lifted myself from the saddle and motioned at the strange sighting with my hand.

"A bunch of black circles, if you ask me," replied Ike quickly and turned around to look back.

"Judging from this far, it looks like a ruined village," said Elson. "A couple of houses, maybe more."

"What?" exclaimed Ike and turned back. "What village? Where?"

Ignoring Ike, I turned to Elson. "Are they recent?"

"My guess, two, three weeks old," said Elson and saying nothing else, gave his horse a forceful kick, hurrying it down the slope and toward the circles.

"What did he mean—two, three weeks old?" Ike asked me, following the Southerner with a worried expression on his face.

"The raids—Do you not remember?…We are in the Border Regions now." I snapped my own bridle too and galloped after the mercenary; Ric and Ike trailed not far behind.

By the time our company descended into the valley the day was at its very end. The night sky remained clear and the young moon promised to be bright. Without stopping we left the strange shapes of once sturdy houses behind and treaded for a while longer, then settling within an island of shrubs, some half a league away from the road. Aware of the possible dangers that hunted the region, we decided against a fire and instead, after finishing a plain supper, retired to bed, always keeping watch. When my turn passed, I did not feel too tired. Yet I was eager to return to the realm of dreams, for I knew that my Fore Sight would take me to my friends and their adventures back in Normandia.

Chapter 44

I SAW the visions of my friends almost every night. I watched them walk among the gathering host of the Duke's force, determined to cleanse the kingdom of the foul sect. It was exciting to know that they had become a part of something greater, something important for us all, and for our realm. Excited for them, I had a hard time concentrating on my own journey. In the days that came my company passed several burned down villages, ruined houses, and rows of freshly dug graves. With so much of the farmlands scorched and many villages destroyed, it was no surprise that often we were the only travelers on the road. It was unsettling at first, but then I came to think that it was for the best. Nobody knew where we were and that meant less trouble for us. After following the eastern route away from the coast for awhile, it was finally time for us to leave it and come back south. When the first crossing came into view we turned right. Like days before, we met no one, not even a bird or a squirrel. But as we veered from behind a patch of tall pines and to the edge of a sharp drop that overlooked a low valley, just off the southern route, we stumbled onto an unexpected find.

At a distance of several leagues an elongated dale that spread before us crawled with thousands of tiny dots. From afar they reminded me of ants, only they were human figures. Before us spread a large military camp, unfolded for a few leagues across the green fields. In several long lines stood hundreds of round tents, all of the same black color, interlinked by fences, stretched along worn-out earthen paths, which lay stripped of grass by thousands of feet and hooves. Soldiers, horsemen, and war wagons crowded the entire place, presenting the sight of an army readying for battle.

"What is this?" I heard Ike say and lifted myself off the seat.

"This is the Imperial army," replied Elson quickly, also staring at the camp. His face bore an expression of surprise. "What I want to know is why they are here, so close to the border. I thought they were seasons away from reaching the valley. They have just closed the main road, and I, myself, have seen their soldiers, leagues away, beyond the Northern Bound."

"I guess someone gave you a few wrong answers," I noted, though there was no sarcasm intended in my words.

"That it may be. Or else someone has been very good at keeping a big secret," replied Elson. He rose up again so he could get a better look at the men below.

"How can you hide so many people? How can you sneak the entire army out without anyone noticing it? This is impossible." Ike waved his hands off.

"Nothing is impossible. All it takes is a handful of good spies, some lies, and no witnesses," said Elson.

"Sill, someone must have seen something. There are thousands of them out there," insisted Ike.

"Huh. The southern road from here to the capital has been closed. People are not allowed even within a league of the route. And do not forget, even if there are witnesses, they can always disappear. We are in the Border Regions. Remember? The lands are empty, with bandits everywhere."

Elson shook a bridle in his hand looking blindly at the straps and added, "Whatever the reason may be, it tells me that we are not going to be welcome there. If we did not expect to find them here, they sure did not expect us to find them. It may be wise if we keep our distance from the camp. A war is brewing, and I do not want to be stuck in the middle of it."

Saying nothing else, the Southerner turned around and we all galloped back to the edge of the woods at the base of the hill. Once at a safe distance, we stopped and talked of our further plans.

"So what is going to happen now?" I asked as my mount searched through a heap of fresh grass.

"We have to travel east again until we are safe from the Imperial scouts," replied Elson.

Nobody had any objection to his proposal. Ric, Ike and I were strangers to these lands, and any route was good to us as long as it kept our company away from trouble and closer to Azoros. Still I did not understand why the Imperial soldiers would have any problems with us, especially since we were from Normandia, a neutral kingdom to the recent conflicts in the Border Regions. I wanted to ask Elson about it, but the Southerner had gone well ahead, and by the time I caught up there were other concerns, as a light rain picked up and I had to search for my cloak, so neatly stored in the side bag of my saddle.

The remainder of the day we spent riding nonstop through the rough terrain, getting further away from the Imperial encampment. When the sun set we stopped and rested, resuming the journey in the morning. As the day went on heavy rains persisted to pester us. Our clothes were completely drenched, and coldness froze our limbs. Around us everything looked wet and dreary. Peering through the shower I studied the rise, when suddenly a whistling sound rushed from above, making me look up at the sky. At first I did not see anything, but then another screech came. That time it sounded louder, closer to my ears. Although it took me a few moments to recognize the noise, soon I found myself seeking cover as arrows flew at us. Immediately yanking on the reins, breaking my mount's trot, I spun around, searching for the source of danger. But the rain was too thick and all I could see were vague silhouettes, which shifted back and forth, playing tricks with my vision. Suddenly another arrow came my way. The thin black shape soared through the air in a long elegant stride and dropped to the ground several cubits away. That time I noted the point on a hill, where the dart came from, and there spotted a group of uniformed archers moving at the summit.

Although I did not recognize the strangers' outfits, they had to be of a military kind, as all of them wore the same colors. The figures stayed still, and then vanished. Shortly afterwards they returned, and immediately the sound of the passing arrows came back with them. Only that time the shafts fell closer. One arrow fell just before my horse, and another passed within a cubit of Ike. Under the menacing shower of bolts we retreated away from the attackers, who stretched their bows again, letting arrows fly in our direction. But their shots fell short of our position, and they immediately disappeared behind the hill, yelling something to each other. Moments later they reemerged and descended the slope, mounted on shorthaired mares of a brown color.

"Who are they?" I shouted. Elson looked at me, then down the field.

"They look like Lombardians."

"Lombardians?" asked Ric from the back.

"Yes, Lombardians," reaffirmed Elson. "See their uniforms? These are Lombardian blue vests, which means that they are with Lombardi royal legions."

"Why are they attacking us then?" asked Ric. "We have not done anything."

"Maybe they think we are the Imperial scouts."

"Or maybe they just do not like strangers," added Ike.

"What do we do then? Can we flee or should we fight?" I asked, looking at the Southerner.

"I will tell you one thing. I am not sure if we should charge them right now. It is too risky. Even if we make it across, their numbers are twice ours. It will be a very tough fight." Elson thought a moment. "I say we take off and circle around them. There is a road further south. If we are lucky we will be able to put some distance between them and us."

"Are they not going to chase us?"

"They might. But as you can see, their horses are short-legged, cheap steeds that will not last for long. If we take off now we will have some time on them."

Nobody objected. The Southerner was right on one thing: We did not stand a chance in the open against the bows that our enemies had.

Following Elson we prepared to gallop away from the enemy, but suddenly noticed another group of riders appear from the east. Their host counted at least twenty men, and they hurried in our directions. When they got closer I realized that they were not coming our way; instead they galloped for the hill, where our attackers had also spotted the unexpected visitors and huddled together to form their own defenses. It was clear that the two sides were not friends, meaning that we had a chance to skip a bloody fight.

As the horsemen closed on the bowmen, arrows flew in numbers. Several of the riders fell down; a few horses stumbled, sending their masters to the ground. But the mounted group proceeded with the charge. Seeing that their shots were ineffective, our attackers tried to flee. But it was too late. Although the assailants' horses put all their strength into the dash, they could not outrun the much taller, better mounts of their pursuers. Very soon the swift assault of the riders caught up with the archers and broke through their ranks, sending them in all directions. By then it was evident that the unexpected company of horsemen had the upper hand. In moments they cut down half of the foes, and chased the rest away. Within moments everything was over. The fight was done, and many of those, who were so eager to kill us lay dead themselves.

Before we could decide if we should flee or stay, the victors, also dressed in bright blue vests, came over.

"Give up your swords, scum!" yelled one man, who wore a distinguished dark blue cape with white threads at the edges. Confused, I looked at Elson, whose composed face gave me some assurance.

"Hey, we are just travelers, nothing more," said the Southerner, as he raised both of his hands in the air. His sword remained on his lap.

"Of course you are. That is what they all say," the man in the cape answered and shook his head. Two more of the uniformed men rode in, bringing one of the curved bows. They gave the weapon to the man with the cape, who was inspecting our company with tough firm stares.

"Your Lordship, these are our bows," said one of the men, and he pointed at the weapon. "Probably from our eastern garrison. They had two patrols gone missing within the last ten days."

The man in the cape nodded and gave back the bow, switching his attention to our company. "Travelers you say. I say you are lying."

"No. We are not," replied Elson, still holding up his hands.

"Uh-huh. And those fellows were not your friends either? Eh?"

"Those men tried to kill us. Why do you think we were standing here. We tried to flee. Look around. See those shafts in the ground? Do you think it was a jolly shooting practice we had?"

"Why should I believe you, outlander? You look like a regular mercenary to me. Those were too. If you want to make me listen, get rid of your weapons first, then we will talk," said the man.

"Wait a moment." I found myself yelling from afar, as I set my steed next to Elson's. "We are squires from Normandia. We are traveling to Azoros on a personal mission from our lord, Sire Rone. We mean you no harm nor any trouble. All we ask is a free pass through these lands. You have my word, the Northern Empire has nothing to worry about from us."

"The Northern Empire?" exclaimed the officer. "I hate to break it to you, young man, but we are border guards with the Lombardian greater legions."

"Lombardians?" asked Ike. "Those men on the hill, they were Lombardians too, were they not?"

"Oh those. No they have nothing to do with the legions. Those are bandits who wear our uniforms." The man sighed. "They attack our patrols, steal our outfits and our weapons, and then they march across the border to raid villages in the Northern Empire. The likes of them are responsible for all the recent troubles in the border regions. For some seasons now their bands have been attacking parishes and caravans east of the Northern Bound, pillaging and killing everything in sight. And every time they launch their onslaught, they pretend to be us. For a while they hid their plan so well that we could not understand why so many common folks of the Empire blamed us for their misfortunes, but then we sent our scout party to investigate the matter and so got our answers—the thugs had our weapons and our colors. This season alone we managed to catch over a hundred thugs, who claim to be Lombardians at first but then tell a tale that is almost always the same: that they were paid to dress like us and pillage the border regions.

"We are a scouting party too. Our orders are to check the western routes for any signs of bandits. During our ride, we heard a report of a small caravan that had been ambushed some leagues from here. Two days ago we spotted them at the shallow creek. Unfortunately they managed to lose us in the hills afterwards, and only today have we been able to catch up with them. I guess you could have been their next target. That is, of course, if you speak the truth."

"We are truly grateful for you help," said Elson.

"Save your gratitude. I still have little reason to trust you."

"Why? We say the truth. We are the squires from Normandia," exclaimed Ike, before anyone else could say a word.

"I do not care if you have come from beyond the Barrier. We must have proof that you are no bandits."

"Bandits may be the least of your problems," said Elson then. "The Imperials seem to think you are responsible for their troubles. They are thinking of war."

"This is stupid. Why would they even consider doing something like this? The last thing they need is a war," replied the caped officer, shaking his head.

"You might want to prepare for worst. The Northerners are preparing for a fight, and it will be soon."

"What do you mean?"

"I mean, there is an army that sits just off your border, north of here."

"An army?" another man sprang to his feet. "Where?" Elson did not hesitate to answer his question either. He quickly told the soldiers about the location of the troops, their numbers, and the equipment that was visible to us.

"We have to get back to the post. We must tell the captain," exclaimed one of the Lombardians. A brief scuffle sent the men to their horses.

"You better come with us then; our superiors must check your story," said the officer. It was not a threat, but it was not a request either. We were not prisoners, but we were not free either. Shortly after meeting the Lombardian scouts, we were on our way to the nearest post, described by them to be hidden a few leagues away in the nearby woods.

Riding amongst the foreign men, the four of us entered the new Kingdom of Lombardia, the land famed for its ships and wool. The way we went, there was no road, nor any tracks. Yet our escort marched confidently, picking its way through the uneven grass and wild crops. Before long we made it to the edge of the forest and halted. Immediately a couple of men vanished amid the trees, while we remained in the open. When they returned we were asked to dismount and proceed into the trees. The path, barely visible from the outside, led us deep into the foliage. A couple of times we had to step from a narrow lane and fight through the low branches until we found another one, only to do the same a little later. Eventually the paths ended altogether, and we came out onto a wide clearing.

The glade was not natural. It was handmade, with stumps from freshly chopped trees standing around us. Where once stood mighty trunks we saw several one-story log huts, a few tents, and a tall tower that stretched up several dozen cubits leveling almost perfectly with the tops of the trees. A boarded box, with its sides covered in leaves, sat at the top, and in it—three small figures of armed men, who observed the land from above.

Our arrival was expected. About twenty armed men and women stood around the clearing, each looking at our group. It made me uneasy, but I did not show it, or at least I did not think I did. Two of the soldiers from our escort brought us to the center, and then took off, heading for the largest of the houses. Before they could reach it, three other men came out of the hut. Undeniably the three were officers. Their clothing was more elaborate and carried many distinguished military marks. One of the men even had a metal chain wrapped around his neck, which served as a mark of an army rank. Their quick talk with the soldiers indicated that we were the source of the huddle, and after finishing there, they came over to us. When they were close enough, one of them spoke, his voice deep and solid. He had a thick Lombardian accent. Nonetheless I understood him perfectly.

"What is it that I hear about an entire Imperial army, sitting at our doorstep?" he spoke and wiped a drop of spit from his long yellowish mustache.

"As I have reported to your men, we have stumbled onto a camp, some few leagues off the border. It was the Imperial army, in full battle gear, getting ready for something big," replied Elson.

"Why should I believe you? It is clear from your accent that you are not Lombardian," said the man, ending up coughing loudly into his fist. "Wicked rains," he said afterwards. "Gave me some nasty bug." He then spat onto the grass and cleared his throat several times.

"You are absolutely right. I am not Lombardian, nor is anyone from our company," spoke the Southerner, and he raised his hand. "Let me introduce my friends. These three men are my companions. They are honorable squires from the distant lands of Normandia, on their way to Azoros, entrusted with a personal quest from a Normandian lord." Elson turned and pressed his hand to his chest. "My name is Elson…I am a person of Azoros, and as you can probably already guess, I serve as a guide for these men, ensuring that they will not get lost in the foreign lands." Elson bowed slightly, barely leaning forward.

As Elson straightened up, the man resumed, "Three Normandian squires and one free soul from Azoros. It is an interesting band you have here. Since we have started with introductions. I am Sergeant Rosso with the Lombardian border legions, serving under the command of our honorable Count Erbeis, the ruler of his estate and the town of Orencia." The man was about to go further with the titles, when another burst of uncontrolled coughing stopped him.

"Count Erbeis?" I repeated, taking advantage of the interruption. "Sergeant Rosso...I believe I know a person by the name of Arley Erbeis. Is he the count's son?" My question remained unanswered, so I continued. "The count's son, or the man who claimed to be one, left us a letter, which I have here with me."

I searched through my bag and extracted the envelope, quickly handing it over to the sergeant. The officer inspected the dispatch with curiosity. "It says here that you are the people who saved the young count's life," he noted, suspicion in his voice.

"Actually there were six of us. We stopped a robbery in Bonneville. Back then we did not know the victim was of noble heritage."

As I repeated the whole story to the best of my recollection, the sergeant and his men listened.

"I do not know if I can believe you," said the sergeant afterwards. "As far as I know you could have robbed the real owner of the letter, and now are trying to get some favors from the count, maybe get a reward." He looked at me with even more suspicion.

"I can assure you this is not the case. We were not even supposed to come this way. Our original route lay along the west coast, leagues away from here. But the unexpected movements of the Imperial troops made us change our plans. I give you my word as a squire—we did not know these lands belonged to the Erbeis family."

The sergeant deliberated with his men, then looked at the letter and at me. "The unfortunate incident that Arley encountered in the north was disturbing news to all of us. People still talk about it. Some even say a rival count paid some hired swords to do the job. But I do not believe the rumors. The count Erbeis has few enemies, and even they are not powerful enough to take on an attempt such as that.

"But let's leave this talk until a later time, when Arley himself can prove the truth to your words. For now I am to treat you as any other strangers, caught in proximity of our lands. After all, you could also be Imperial spies, especially since we have caught quite a few of them in the past few weeks."

"I assure you that we are not with the Empire," stated Elson firmly.

"That is not for me to decide. I have no other choice but to escort you to the castle. There you will be able to clarify the matter, and if you are lying there will be an appropriate place for you to spend some long hours, awaiting trial of the Count's court." The sergeant turned to his subordinate and made a quick gesture I did not catch.

"My men will take you to the castle," said Rosso. "I suggest you comply with my request. We will use force if necessary, so unless you want some blood-shed, I expect you to refrain from any resistance. If there is no problem, we will allow you to keep your horses and your weapons, but at the first sign of trouble, my men will see that you do not see another day."

We had little choice but to surrender to the will of his men, some of whom balanced their hands on their bowstrings.

"No objections, I guess," said Elson at last.

"Good, if you wait here, I will assemble my men. Your escort will be ready shortly." The sergeant finished and left toward one of the huts.

Just as Rosso had said, an escort of twenty men was amassed in just a few moments. The horses were saddled and the soldiers were ready to lead the way. After few more instructions the procession took off. As expected we were kept in the middle of the group, with six men ahead, four men at each side, and six more in the back, watching our every move. We did little to alert them and tried to keep up with the vanguard, sending our mounts into a steady trot.

Chapter 45

THE ROAD turned south. I tagged behind Elson, who struck up a conversation with one of the Lombardians. For a while I listened to their stories, but then let them be and turned inward to reflect on the present state of the quest. Although we had managed to pass through one kingdom with only minor problems, our journey came to a halt at the southern borders of the Northern Empire. It so happened that we were not welcome in Lombardia, and to remind us of this we had twenty armed soldiers, surrounding us. Yet things were not too grim. We were halfway to Azoros, alive, and near the castle that belonged to the count, whose son we had saved back in Bonneville.

A while after leaving the hidden camp inside the woods, we ventured out of the wild grass fields and onto the cultured pastures, bordered by long woven fences of thick dried vines. Further away, where several large hills touched the low-hanging clouds, thin smoke pillars rose into the sky.

"Here we are," said one of the soldiers, who rode next to me. "His highness' grand estate."

"Another two leagues or so we will be in the castle," said another soldier. Two other riders agreed.

"Where is the castle?" I heard Ike asking over my shoulder. He was staring ahead, standing high on his stirrups. His face showed a glimpse of excitement.

"You cannot see it from here. It is on the other side of the town," replied the young Lombardian.

"A town?" asked Ike again, twisting backwards in his saddle. "What town is it?"

"Orencia. It is the biggest city in this locale, the wealthiest too, and it belongs to the count. Although most counts live away in the countryside, his highness prefers the city and so has set up his private estate at the western side of Orencia, next to the large fairgrounds, where his honorable subjects attend seasonal carnivals and tournaments."

"You have tournaments too?" Ric asked in a surprised tone.

"Of course we do. The Lombardian tournaments are the best in all of Ethoria. I bet you have never seen such tournaments in your entire lives." The young soldier exclaimed, waving his hands in the air.

"I think we have. We come from the land of knights where we have many great tournaments too; some last for days, even weeks. And the annual tourneys at the capital—that is a whole other story. Hundreds of knights come to the city to test their courage and skills," rebutted Ric.

"Yeah, but do you have dueling pits with slaves fighting desert cats, or mercenaries squaring off against black bears?" asserted the soldier. He did not wait for a reply, but continued. "I do not think so. Here we have it all. Twelve fighting pits and three arenas, all set up for battles of every sort." The young Lombardian's voice was instructive. He clearly enjoyed telling us about the tourneys of Orencia, and once asked, went on talking about it for sometime. Meanwhile the road ahead got busier, as more locals joined in, making their way to the city, which was slowly sailing into the view.

When the path eventually came up to a low stone wall, our escort met with a group of guards, who stood near a wooden hut that sat at one side, just off a seemingly empty street. There four soldiers dressed in dark blue vests stopped us, and one of them went on to discuss something with the men from our escort. Afterwards, the guards stepped aside and let us in. At last we were in Orencia.

At first glance the highly praised city of northern Lombardia was a disappointment. Although it was bigger than Villone, it faded in comparison to other places we had come across in our travels. Needless to say there was little to look at. Most of the city was made of timber. Rows of logged houses lined wide unpaved streets. At the front of each building stood a wooden deck, which served both as a boardwalk during the raining days, and as a storage place for firewood and water. At some corners, usually next to some larger crossings, rose tall towers. They were guard posts, placed so that the local sentries could oversee the safety of the streets from the high point above. In addition there were also several chapels, a few stone eating halls, and some parks that were nothing more than large circles, made of green rosebushes, placed in and around small wooden wells.

Such was the plain picture that accompanied us as we crossed one city street after another. After a while I began to wonder if the count's castle would be any different. But as we passed another guard tower, the city's look began to change, losing its brownish tan of treated wood and transforming into a more ample place, suitable for some decent living. Stone houses became more frequent, and the crossings started to show signs of rocky pavement. Yet luxury and comfort continued to elude the streets, until we came to a set of ornamented gates, made entirely of iron plates, which displayed elegant curves of splendid mystic trees and flowers. The large doors were opened, and several guards paced back and forth, carrying short halberts on their shoulders.

Unlike the men at the edge of the town, they did not stop us, nor did they say anything. Throwing inquisitive looks they let us pass through the archway and into another plaza, which stood in contrast to those intersections we had seen earlier. Its ornamented floor was tiled with several ceramic overlays, each of a different color. Forming a particular design they surrounded a large white statue, probably made of some mountain rock that stood in the very center of a high, equally white pedestal. It was a figure of a horseman in full battledress, brandishing a large two-handed sword. Riding a massive warhorse, his clad figure towered over a group of grotesque creatures, which only vaguely reminded one of human forms. Their crouching bodies showed fear and confusion, and their stone eyes were focused on the powerful rider looming over them. Beneath them, on the side of the pedestal, in a curved stone frame, rested a metal plaque, which read—Simor Der Simor, Arus Ni Rossil. The words sounded foreign and I turned to the Southerner, who rode next to me, also studying the finely made monument.

"What does it mean, Simor Der Simor?" I asked pointing to the writing.

"A great man will always be a great man," said Elson.

"A great man? Who is that great man? Is it him?" I pointed at the horseman.

"Yes him. Arus of Rossi, the Great Lombardi General. The founder of Lombardia."

"Arus of Rossi? I do not recall such a name. How long ago did he live?"

"He lived in the middle of the first age, when the four Great Empires ruled the world."

"First Age? How can he be the founder of Lombardia then? I thought Lombardia did not come to exist until the first half of the Second Age."

"That is right, Lombardia became a kingdom only after the Great War. But it does not mean it did not exist. Until the fall of the Old Empires, it was a part of another nation of Liousous. Although it was but a province then, it acted very much like a singular state, with its own kings, laws, and armies. Back then it was called Lombardi Arus—the land of Arus, the man who had freed the lands from the ancient race, called Uruks."

"Uruks? I never heard anything about Uruks."

"They were human-like creatures who lived in this region many years ago. When our ancestors came to settle the region, they met with Uruks, who immediately went to war with them. Uruk tribes gathered a huge host and advanced against the human settlements. For several years they drove our forefathers south. That was until Arus of Rossi came, bringing his massive armies along with him from the valleys of Brusono, the land that now holds the ruins of Magnicia. The two sides met in the fields of Lan and there fought their three battles. Some books say that Arus won them all, but some insist that Arus lost the first two, then rallied his troops and took the victory in the last one. Of course it is hard to say for sure what really happened then. Only when it was over, Arus emerged victorious, routing the Uruks east toward the Great Forest, and as the last of the creatures fled, Arus claimed his prize, the throne of a new kingdom, which he had forged with his own sword. Since that time, he has been viewed as the father of Lombardia, its creator, and its hero, and that is why anywhere you go in Lombardia you will see his image, in metal, stone, or wood, his two-handed sword, and his faithful steed, Rimos."

Listening to Elson I looked at the stone figure of a man, the great man, someone, who had singlehandedly forged an entire kingdom. I wondered if such men truly existed, or if they were just images from fairytales. I wanted to ask Elson about it, but by then our column had already descended down a gentle slope and at the bottom came up to a completely different Orencia. While before, the buildings cramped together, the upcoming view presented grand beautiful houses spread far apart, with a lot of green grass fields filling the gaps in between.

"Do you think this is where the count lives?" I asked Ike, who rode just ahead.

"I do not think so," he replied. "There is no castle. No lord lives in a house; they have forts and keeps, remember?"

I nodded. Ike was right. In Normandia every lord had a castle; it was the same in the Northern Empire and Westalia. But in Orencia I could see no towers, no battlements or high stone wall—only large manors and tall chapels near them.

Spinning in our saddles, taken by the splendor of the passing buildings, we traveled along a wide-open lane of yellow gravel and at the corner of a large white house with many thin tall pillars along its facade turned left, immediately coming to a stretch of grass, trimmed neatly to look like an even, live carpet. Next to it, some cubits away from the road, ran a tall fence, made of iron spikes, and behind it—a row of thick old pines, which shielded the view of anything beyond them. The road continued for some distance along the grass strip, and then split into two—one track continuing down the wall, the other turning right and coming to a set of ornamented gates, made of the same steel bars and decorated with images of animals and flowers of some unknown kind. Before the closed massive doors rested four guards, all dressed in the uniforms of the local garrison that consisted of steel armor shined to perfection, similarly glittering helms, blue tunics, red trousers with metal leggings, and long leather boots, which also had rows of metal strips, either for protection or adornment.

It seemed that the guards expected us, and when the first of our company reached the gates, they swiftly opened the doors and let us into a splendid park, hidden earlier by the wall of trees. Plants of all shapes and size, fountains, and scores of sculptures were placed along many narrow paths and wider lanes, which ran through the green grassy floor, also seeded with flowers of all colors. Although there were no buildings anywhere in sight, I knew that it was all a part of the count's private residence, for only a highborn noble could afford such luxury. Soon enough my contention was confirmed. As our company came out of an island of aged oaks, a large mansion appeared before us. It was not a castle, at least not in a sense that I came to know it. Instead it was a marvelous three-storied mansion made of white polished stone. Split into several distinctive sections, marked with its own entrance and different designs, the house was embellished with many sculptures, frescos, and pillars, and with rows of large brass windows spread along its sides, each furnished with long metal grates.

"Is this—" I started with the question, but before I could finish Elson nodded. "Yes, it is. Count Erbeis' family estate—big, tall, and full of splendor."

The entryway we were led to was at the far left side of the building, placed in the middle of a long section with a distinctive glass roof, and columns shaped like human warriors. A wide staircase was leading to it. Once at the bottom of the stairs, we dismounted. After surrendering our weapons, which we did without reservations, we then followed our escort up through a set of large oak doors and into a large foyer, round in shape and swathed in many red silks curtains. From it ran several hallways, each with its unique design and decorated with many paintings, carvings, and statues, done both in stone and metal. Taking one of those corridors, our company passed several closed doors and then entered a grand hall, several hundred cubits wide, with the entire ceiling made of glass. In the center stood several men; some wore military outfits, others were dressed like city dwellers, very well-off city dwellers. They waited for us to come closer and then one of them, a man in a dark regal robe with golden stars affixed to its collar, raised his hand and spoke.

"I am told you are visiting us from the North," said the man and scratched his chin several times.

"Yes, Sire, we have come from Normandia and are heading to Azoros on orders from our lord, Sire Rone of Sirone, the sworn knight of the Duke of Bois, Sire Tem," I reported loudly, yet not yelling.

"I see," replied the man, and he walked up a bit closer. "But why this way? The main roads are off to the west. Surely it is much faster to use them, instead of these back routes. Do you not think?" He asked sharply, giving us a stare full of distrust.

"The main routes are blocked by the Imperial army. We had to take a slight detour," interjected Elson before I could utter my explanation.

"The Imperial army, you say? Where did you see it?"

"Closer than you might want, just a few leagues off the border," replied Elson.

"That is indeed very interesting news, but do you have any proof?"

"Nothing that can tell you for sure. All I have is my word and my honesty. But if that is not enough, I suggest you send your faster scouts to investigate, before it is too late."

"Your word? I know nothing of you to take your word for the truth, and as of the scouts, let me decide on that."

"As you please," replied Elson, moving back into line, his face red with anger. Still the Southerner kept his composure and let the man continue with his questioning.

"So now, you three, you are the squires, right?"

"Yes. We are," I answered firmly.

"Tell me then, what business do the Normandian lords have so far south? What reason do they have for you to take such a long journey to Azoros?"

"I am afraid I am not at any liberty to tell you this. All I can say is that it is of good faith and a just cause…and it has nothing to do with this kingdom."

"Huh…What if you are spies, working for the Northern Empire and this squire-talk is your disguise?"

"We have told you about the Imperial forces gathering just north of here, have we not?" protested Ike, but then he was quick to stop.

"You did tell me that, but it does not mean that I believe you. These are dangerous times. We are on the verge of war with our northern neighbor. Bandits pillage our lands, and our people are getting more scared with every passing hour. Under such circumstances we cannot take any chances. And in your case it all sounds very strange. To see a group of Normandian squires venture into Lombardia, using the back roads is strange to say the least, but—you tell me."

"Again I must assure that we…"

"Stop with your assurances. I am the head protector of this estate, Simodumo Gapo and my job is to make sure that nothing happens to the count and his lands. You are trying to persuade me of your good intentions, but you have no proof to support your tales. It leaves me little choice, but to conduct my own investigation. While I am doing so, you will be confined to quarters in our lockup. If I find that you are who you say you are, you will be set free. But if I find any glimpse of the Imperial mud on you, you will have to answer many more questions. And trust me, you will."

The man turned around and started for the door at the other end of the room. The soldiers around us unsheathed their weapons. The situation was suddenly getting worse and we had to do something.

"Before you walk away with your entourage, I want you to know that we are the men who saved the life of Arley Erbeis. I believe he is the son of your lord, Count Erbeis." As I said these words, my hand reached into my bag and pulled out the letter for everyone in the room to see.

"What did you say, young man?" The chief protector stopped and glared directly at me. Then he said something to one of his men and walked back.

"Yes. My friends and I met the count's son in Bonneville under some peculiar circumstances."

"How did you know he was in Bonneville?" The protector sounded surprised.

"As I said, we saved his life there, and we have a letter to prove it." I handed the letter to Gapo, who immediately started to read it, with several others joining him.

"This is indeed his highness' signature," said a man dressed in green robes.

"And he was indeed attacked on his journey through Normandia," added another.

Gapo wanted to say something too, but before he could do so, the far door opened, and a young man walked into the room. Immediately all the noise died out, and everyone was looking at the newcomer, who casually strolled toward our company, smiling and whistling some cheerful tune.

It was not long before I recognized his features. He was the man we had found bleeding in the dark alley near the Valiant Knight. He was Arley Erbeis and he was looking much better now. His face had color; his clothes were perfectly fit and fashioned. His walk had a slight limp to it, but it did not seem to affect his mood, which was bright and joyful.

As he quickly crossed the room, the protector bowed deeply and stayed in such a state until the young noble let him rise.

" Gapo," Arley said loudly, "I have just heard. Those men who saved my life, they are here. Oh, I cannot wait to meet them." He smiled again and looked at our company. "These are some new faces. Who are they? Are they my saviors? Are they the heroes of Bonneville?"

"Your highness, so nice to see you in a good mood today. How was your morning meal? I hope you have found everything to your satisfaction?"

"Oh, Gapo, away with your silly questions. Tell me are these men my brave saviors?"

"I am not sure, your highness. Our scouts have found them crossing the border in the northern valley. They claim to be from Normandia, and they have a letter with your stamp on it, but we are not sure if they are indeed the men you wanted to see."

"Let me see the letter, let me see it," insisted Arley, so the protector had to comply.

"Yes, yes. My letter. I left it with the captain of the city watch back in Bonneville. I told him to give it to my saviors. If they have it they must be the ones."

"I would not be so hasty, your highness. They may be somebody else."

"Do not be silly, Gapo. Why else would they have my letter?"

"For one, they could have stolen it from the real heroes."

"You and your constant suspicions. When are you going to stop?"
"I am sorry your highness, but this is my duty, and I..."

"I know, I know. Father has entrusted you with the safekeeping of his estate. It is your sacred duty, blah, blah, blah. I have heard it all so many times. You should not be so edgy. But if it pleases you I can test these gentlemen. I will ask them a question, and if they are actually the ones who had saved my life, they will know the answer." Arley tapped Gapo on the shoulder and turned to us. "My friends, would you mind a little test? You know, to satisfy Gapo's suspicion."

"Not at all, your highness," I answered firmly and threw a quick glance at the protector, whom I had already come to dislike.

"Okay then. Let's see...Oh, I know. When I was brought to the tavern, what was the name of the healer who patched my wounds?"

"This is easy!" Ike exclaimed. "Master Az, and L'iote was the owner of the Valiant Knight."

"That is absolutely correct." The young noble smiled again and extended his hand to me. I shook it. "You see, Gapo, they are the ones. You were worrying for nothing."

"But they can still be the spies," insisted Gapo.

"No," replied Arley. This time his voice held little cheer. It was a polite snap.

"They are Normandians, and Normandia is not the enemy of Lombardia—the Northern Empire is. If they are here, they must have a good reason, and I take their word for it. If you do not stop with your stupid allegations, I will see that my father knows exactly how you have treated the people who saved my life."

"Yes, your highness. I humbly apologize." The protector bowed and backed away; his entire staff followed, each of them bowing to their toes.

Paying them little more notice, Arley returned to us. "My apologies for Gapo. Do not take it personally." He waved at the protector, not even looking at him. Then suddenly he shook his head and exclaimed, slapping his forehead. "Where are my manners? Please follow me to the meeting hall. This room is not suitable for a talk with friends." The young noble gestured for us to follow and set out toward the other end of the hall. Strolling by Gapo and his lackeys I could not help but look at the protector one more time, smiling straight into his face, defying all of his distrust toward us. I was an honorable guest, and only the most unusual of circumstances could change that.

Chapter 46

THE PLACE Arley referred to as the meeting room was a small comfortable chamber, dressed in light blue colors with golden trim at the ceiling. Despite its size, it did not feel crowded. The many mirrors added to the width of the chamber, and two large windows brought even more breathing space, presenting us with a wonderful view of the green yard, spread around several water cascades that illuminated a feeling of tranquility and peace. Settling in cushy seats around one of the low tables, with glass tops and five brass legs in the form of wolf paws, we waited for Arley to take a large chair next to an elegant stand and pour a reddish liquid into several glasses from an elegant crystal jar.

"Welcome to my home," said Arley, after finishing with the last cup. "Well, not mine, of course, my father's. But it does not matter. His courtesy is as good as mine, so feel at home here." The young noble handed me the first glass. I thanked him and took the drink, which had a sweet taste to it.

"Please, excuse my curiosity, but can you tell me about your heroic act? My memory has failed me so far. I cannot recollect anything that had happened to me that night. I will be very thankful if you help me get the whole picture," Arley said when he was done pouring his own drink.

"If you desire I will be more than glad to do so," I replied and set the glass on a wide armrest, big enough to seat a grown man. The story, which I told Arley with some help from Ike and Ric, was the full account of the events, from the moment we had stepped into the alley until we had gotten his letter from Sire Jim a day after. Throughout the young count listened carefully. He asked some questions, but did not interrupt too often. And when the tale was over he sat in silence for a while, breathing slowly, leaning back in his chair.

"That is some tale," he said afterwards. "I knew that I was badly hurt, but I had no idea that it was so bad. Once again, I am very grateful for your service. I am forever in your debt."

"Consider this debt repaid. Your protector, Gapo, was about to throw us in jail, but your appearance had fixed everything. If it were not for you, we would have been stuck in a cell somewhere under your castle." I smiled and lowered my head in a gesture of appreciation and gratitude.

"That was nothing. Gapo is always like that. I am sure it would all have been straightened out soon enough."

"Better sooner than later," I noted, and everyone agreed.

For the remainder of the afternoon we stayed in the room, trading stories and talking of the current situation in the region. We had a good time and did not notice how the day turned into evening and the moon's crescent had ventured into the sky. Only when a light knock on the door broke through our voices did we realize it was late evening. The knock repeated itself a few more times, then the door opened and an old man, dressed in white tunic and black trousers, stepped inside, bowing deeply before the young noble.

"What is it, Lazo?" asked Arley.

"Master Arley, your father says it is time for the evening meal. Everyone is already seated. They are waiting for you." The old man looked from under his gray brows. "Your friends too. Your father wants to have a word with them afterwards." The man bowed again.

"Very well, Lazo. Tell my father we are on our way." The servant nodded a few times and backtracked into the hallway, quickly vanishing in the shadows there.

"Will you join me for dinner this evening?" asked Arley as the door closed. We immediately accepted the invitation and, after fixing our outfits, followed him to the dining room, where several dozen men seated around a long oval table, met us dressed for dinner. Almost all of the chairs were taken, and I noticed some familiar faces—Gapo and some of his aides. One of the men from our escort was also there. He sat at the far side of the table, next to two lovely ladies and looked at us kindly, smiling a little. But another man quickly took our attention, a large elder with a dark beard and long hair. His expansive golden cape had a white fur collar, and several large chains of different metal dropped down his black leather vest, adorned with silver studs and colored pins. It was the count himself. He sat in a high throne-chair, watching our company with interest.

When Arley had escorted us to our seats, the count nodded slightly and raised his hand. All the talk ceased instantly and everyone looked toward the lord, who remained silent for a moment, studying the guests. Then his hand dropped and he began to speak:

"Today we have new guest joining us for the evening meal. These men are those who have saved the life of my only son and the heir to the seat of Orencia, Arley Erbeis. They have come here all the way from Normandia and it is a pleasure that they have decided to pay us a visit so I can have this chance to thank them personally."

The count raised a metal goblet in his hand and addressed us directly. "It is nice to put faces to the people. I am very grateful to you, and so I bring this first cup of our best sweet wine to you, the men brave enough to risk your own lives to save my son's. Hail to you, young squires, hail to your courage."

The count lifted the glass and drank it full. The entire table did too. A loud burst of cheer rushed through the room. The moment was such that I felt I had to say something, so I did, even though I did not know if it was proper conduct in Lombardia.

"Thank you, your highness. It is an honor to be here and I am grateful for this toast and this invitation. But I must say that we have not done anything courageous. Any good man would have done the same. We are just glad we could be there to assist your son."

The count smiled and took another glass, already filled by one of the servants. After emptying it he said, "Brave and humble. It's a good combination. We should drink twice for that."

Before I knew it I had another full cup of wine, which I had to drink. It was the start of a meal I could never forget. There was so much food and so much drink that I could not remember all of the names of the dishes served. But what I did remember was excellent—roasted ducks, a seasoned grilled boar, sizzling fish of many kinds, and cold cuts of beef, fresh bread, and cakes, and steamed vegetables. Before I knew it I was full, but continued eating anyway, so by the time the servants brought in sweets I could not swallow any more, for my belly started to hurt and I had to loosen my belt to allot some freedom to my waist.

When the dinner finally ended and the table was cleaned, we were invited to another chamber, where the count and some of his men asked us about our homes, our ranks, and our journey. We gladly told them everything. But for the most part the count was interested in the Imperial army and its position, numbers, and movements. Elson was quick to answer those questions. Even though we knew very little, the answers seemed to satisfy the count and his councilors, who wrote down everything we said. When all the inquiries were done with, we were allowed to leave.

It was almost midnight when we left the meeting room and met with Lazo in the hallway. At the sight of our group the old servant smiled with his toothless mouth and bowed several times.

"Master Arley has ordered me to take you to your quarters," he said, and bowed again.

"Good. It is rather late," replied Elson and let Lazo take us to our room, which was located on the third floor, at the end of a corridor dressed in green drapes.

The chamber itself was very big and well lit. Four beds sat in each of the corners, along with chairs, desks, and vanities. Next to a fireplace was a door, which hid a spacious bathroom. There we found four metal tubs, filled with warm water, some soap, and crispy clean towels, which I did not wait to use. Jumping in one of the tubs I enjoyed the pleasantry of the steam that rose from the water. When I felt tired enough to fall asleep, I dried myself up and went to bed. My eyes closed fast and I drifted away. I did not wake up until the next morning.

Chapter 47

MY VISIONS continued.

To Minia's own surprise his recovery was quick. With each passing day he felt stronger, and soon could walk and sometimes even help Sala with her chores around the room. Once he tried to get out into the hallway, but the young maid refused to let him go. Despite his pleas he had to obey her orders and stay inside, where all he could do was look out of the window, observing the commotion below. Ark and Rob stopped by often, bringing him news of the upcoming expedition, and fresh berries they so kindly picked up at the local market, which stood near the castle walls.

Indeed it was busy time for Bonneville. Aside from the usual inflow of traders and seasonal workers, the city was full of armed men. Almost all of the Bois lords took on the challenge and headed to the provincial capital, eager to test their might and skills in the forthcoming campaign. Although some of the knights came with just a few of their fighting men, many brought entire garrisons, and nearly all took their sons along.

With many of the lords still on the way, those who had already arrived, occupied almost every available room in the castle, filling the inner court with much bustle and noise. Their men-at-arms and squires were housed outside the castle's walls, within the city's many taverns, where soldiers could spend their time drinking, singing, and awaiting the Duke's final word on the departure. Along with the soldiery, lines of carriages, wagons, and pushcarts also streamed into the city and packed the streets beyond the limit. Food, armor, weapons, and water, everything was brought in abundance, all for the needs of the departing war party. Some of the supplies were then stored onto huge six-wheeled war wagons, built by the local carpenters specifically for the occasion, and the rest were sold at local markets, much to the satisfaction of the local folks, who saw the prices drop considerably from just a few days before.

Everyone in Bonneville felt anxious and very excited, including the Duke and his captains. Tired of their boring life as the guardians of the province, they saw the upcoming campaign as their chance to prove their worth as fighting men, a chance to be real knights, a chance to rid the land of the wicked false believers. Although they wanted to set out as soon as possible, the King's late reply delayed their plans. The messenger from the capital had not arrived yet, and almost every passing day the Duke sent out his scouts to look for the courier. But it was not until the eighth day since Minia's awakening that the King's message finally came.

Early in the afternoon a royal page galloped into the city and delivered the word of King's approval that spread quickly amongst the people and marked the final day before the departure. The following morning the entire war party was to depart north to the mountains of the Land's Edge. Until then, there was just rest and storytelling of things that had happened during previous campaigns and things that could take place during the coming one.

The night hours went fast and, well before sunrise, human lines began to form in front of the gates of the castle. While the knights, dressed in their battle gear, commanded the men-at-arms, squires and servants toiled amongst the horses and carriages, busy with the last minute preparations. Yet, by the time the first rays of the sun peered over the horizon, everything was ready. Columns of soldiers stood in place, war wagons assembled, and battle horns ready to sound the departure. Everyone was waiting for the Duke, who appeared in due course at the top of a hastily constructed podium, escorted by his captains and the guards. Sire Jim was amongst Sire Tem's entourage, and so were Rob and Ark, who stood timidly in the back, overlooking the busy courtyard below.

The only one missing the gathering was Minia. He was in his room, trying to find a way to sneak out of the infirmary. Although Uncle Srola prohibited him to go, he ignored the healer's advice. Well before dawn, when all the servants had been called to the yard to help with the preparations, Minia collected his gear, put on his armor, and made his way out of the room, limping. Doing his best to be as quiet as possible, he took only a few steps before Sala's watchful glance spotted his crouching figure at the end of the corridor. Unhesitatingly, the young maid rushed toward Minia and, grabbing onto his sleeve, dragged him back to the room. Minia tried to reason with her, but she did not listen. Her grip was of a persistent cat, and he had no other choice but to return to his chamber. A while later, he tried to leave again, but found Sala in the hallway near the door.

Meanwhile outside, the ringing of metal and the squeaking of the war wagons intermingled with cheers and the clapping of many hands. Everyone was joyful, but Minia, who was stuck in the infirmary, alone and away from all the action. Feeling miserable, he dropped to his bed. But suddenly a daring idea came to him. Blocking the doorway with the bulky bed, he snatched all the sheets and curtains he could find, and cutting them in several long strips, made a thick rope. One end he tied to the grate of a small fireplace that was screwed to the floor, and the other he threw out of the window, dropping it down the side wall of the tower. After checking the fastening several times, Minia climbed onto the ledge and looked down, taking a deep breath. His improvised ladder looked feeble, but he began his descent anyway, holding firmly to a piece of cloth, which once made his comfortable blanket. With his feet planted firmly into the stones, he moved slowly toward the ground, but halfway down the cord tore, and the low snapping of the fibers sounded an alarm. Luckily though, the distressing noise soon went away, and Minia managed to clear the rest of the distance, reaching the sandy floor without any complications.

The part of the castle's inner grounds around the infirmary was empty as all the people were huddled at the other side of the court, watching the procession that had already begun its advance, announced by many drums and horns, all sounding at once. Afraid that he was too late, Minia let go of the rope and hurried toward the noise, around the corner, and into a thick mass of bodies that blocked his way. Further ahead he could hear the war party marching. Afraid again that he would miss the whole thing, Minia pushed his way through the crowd. Passing one row of spectators after another, often earning curses and shouts from those he hit, he soon emerged at the front of the crowd, where several cubits away an almost perfect column of mounted soldiers were passing by, their march accompanied by the clanking of their armor and weapons.

While Minia tried desperately to find his friends, the battle horns sounded again, the drums picked up the tune, and many colorful banners shot into the air. Those were the knights' flags, which meant that the lords were starting their voyage too. Jumping at times to see further along the lines of soldiers, Minia rushed down the length and soon saw the Duke amidst his entourage, and further away, riding slowly behind Sire Jim, he spotted Ark and Rob. Without thinking twice, Minia left the crowd and darted across the lane. But before he could take a few steps, several hands grabbed him at once, and the cold steel of swords pressed against his chest. The castle guards had him, and did not want to let him go. It was impossible to explain anything to the armed men, and so for the last time Minia jumped up as high as he could and yelled to Sire

Jim, whose plated figure was about to pass by. Despite his wounds, Minia's call was loud, and the second captain turned his head, quickly noticing Minia amongst the guards. Sire Jim's commands were brief, and before long, Minia found himself free from the restrains and on a horse, riding alongside Sire Jim, Rob and Ark.

One after another more regiments left the castle grounds and streamed down the main street out of the city and to the road north. A vanguard of mounted soldiers was followed by a column of knights, some forty of them, all accompanied by scores of their squires. After the lords came footed men-at-arms, their rows moving tightly, their silver helms glittering in the sun. The Duke and his host rode in the middle of the procession, inspiring applause and cheers from the common folk, who flocked to the sidewalks to watch the High Lord depart. Minia, Rob, and Ark let their horses trot right behind Sire Tem and his personal guards. The expedition was finally on the move. As Minia had imagined, it was a great sight, colorful and fervent—the fighting men of Normandia riding to fight for their people, their land, and their king.

Chapter 48

IT WAS the sixth day of our stay at Arely's estate. Although we did not intend to remain with the count for so long, Arley's father insisted on it, and we could not refuse. It was not an internment, yet it was understood that we would not be allowed to leave, even if we asked, not until all suspicions about our characters were cleared. Even so, during our forced sojourn we had found the mansion to be a comfortable, peaceful place. Everyone was always courteous, even the nobles, who were always willing to talk to us, giving our company some insight into life at the Erbeis estate. The only one who remained untrusting was Gapo. He continued to question our intentions every time he saw us, and even assigned several of his men to follow our group. I disliked such treatment, but it was a minor worry, compared to all the advantages we got from being the guests of the young count.

Trying to ignore Gapo and his lackeys, we spent much of our time chatting with Arley, feasting on some fine foods, and sharpening our combat skills. For our convenience Arley had employed several masters of arms, renowned southern mercenaries, who were kind enough to teach my friends and me a few lessons, which ranged from horseback riding to fencing—a funny way of sword fighting, where opponents tried to sting each other with thin long rapiers. I did not understand how such weapons could win against hard iron-plated armor. But one of the masters told me that a slim blade was indeed a very effective tool in close combat, and had many advantages that the heavier weapons did not. In training we spent many of our afternoons squaring off in the courtyard, learning new moves and maneuvers. My brother joined us at times, but more often he spent time at the local observatory, tagging along with the sages, who introduced him to a new science. It was the study of stars and constellations, a weird teaching as to how little green dots hid all the answers to the questions about the world. Although it sounded foreign to me, my brother grew fond of it, and spent hour after hour looking into a strange-looking huge spyglass, searching through the night sky, or drawing unusual maps that to me were nothing more than a bunch of dots and straight lines, put together on one parchment. As for Elson, he preferred to stay outside of the estate, often departing to the city for several days at a time. When asked, he said that he was looking for some wares, but somehow I did not believe him. And when he did stay at the estate, he devoted his time to long walks alone, always inspecting the grounds, checking the gates at night, and talking to the guards.

After devoting the entire daytime to more training, we spent the evenings in the open, sitting on the stones, talking. It was then, at dusk, a messenger arrived at the mansion, carrying news from the border of a massive Imperial host moving toward Lombardia. As soon as the report was known, the whole place burst into a commotion. Everyone began doing something, and only we sat idle, our usual evening walk in the park with Arley called off. Then, sometime after the evening meal, scores of armed men started to arrive, bringing along with them several dozen large wagons covered with dark thick furs, which hid something big, stashed inside. Later Elson told us that those were war engines, large long iron tubes which, once loaded with several sacks of fire sand, could shoot big round stones several hundred cubits into an open field.

The newly arrived soldiery stayed only for a little and soon were off to the other side of town, where a large camp was assembling, lit by many large fires, which marked the outlines of Orencia's fighting force. In the mornings all these men were gone, but by the next evening many others came. That continued for three more days, and somewhere in the midst of it, we discovered three armed guards, standing outside our door. To our inquiries the soldiers answered little, saying that such were the orders from their master, who was concerned for our safety during such troubled times. But everyone knew that it was not entirely true, and that there was some other reason for the soldiers guarding us day and night.

It was then I started to wonder if it was indeed time for us to depart. I sought Arley's audience and asked him as to the day we could leave the estate and resume our journey. To my surprise the young count told me that we had to postpone our departure even further. He said his father had some more questions for us, and that he had ordered his men to keep us on the premises. When I inquired as to the reasons behind such instructions, Arley gave me no answer. He only said that he regretted such a change, and hoped that everything would be resolved soon enough. Resolved—I did not like this word. I knew that the count had his reservations about our visit, but I did not know that the situation had gotten so much worse so quickly. One thing was clear— we were not as welcome as we first had thought.

From there on some other changes started to take places at the estate too. At first it was only visible at the dining table, where the people grew less responsive to our questions. Then we were asked to eat at another chamber altogether. Although the food was still very good, and the setting was as lavish as before, the adjustment concerned me greatly. But it was not until Arley started to avoid our company that we had our last clue that we had to find some way to escape Orencia, before it was too late. After three days of weighing our options we finally settled on departing the estate as soon as possible, which happened to be the very same night when such a decision had been made.

After retiring to our beds, we suddenly heard strange noises from behind the door.

"What is going on?" I heard Ike's voice in the dark.

"I have no idea," Ric replied.

I looked to the door. The sounds were coming from the hallway. Listening carefully I then went to the window that overlooked the backyard. Outside I saw many torches moving around the dark alleys. Several men dragged long wagons, and someone in the distance was yelling out quick commands. Further away, the sky was brightening, and distant sounds that reminded me of thunder rolled through the land.

"What do you see?" Ike asked me from across the room.

"Something is going on there."

"Yes, but what?"

"I do not know but I am sure we will find out soon enough." With those words I went over to the door and cracked it open, just enough to see most of the hallway. To my surprise I did not find our usual escort. The corridor around our door was empty and dark. But further away, closer to the stairs, I saw people running from one room to another. Servants, maids, and common folks were moving various things—furniture, lamps, and large metal chests—out into the hallway, and then down the stairs to the first floor. From the open doors I could hear loud talk and the crying of children, and from some other place, probably a floor down, the yelling of soldiers. The scene was one of complete chaos. Something was definitely amiss here.

For the first few moments I stared at the bustle, confused. But soon I realized that the situation was to our advantage, as in the midst of all that disorder nobody would notice our escape. It was our chance. I closed the door and turned to the others. "Pick up your gear," I said promptly. "I think it is time to say our farewells."

Nodding, my friends hurried to their belongings, and with our bags packed, we started for the door, ready to go. We did not know where yet, but we had to leave.

"Wait." I heard Ric's voice behind me. "Where is Elson?"

It was a good question. Looking through the dark room I did not realize that the Southerner was gone. His gear and his weapons were missing too.

"Where is Elson?" I repeated the same question, more out of surprise than anything else. Ike shrugged his shoulders, and Ric just shook his head.

"He was there when I went to bed. He must have slipped out during the night. Oh well, we will deal with him later. Right now we should find our way out of here before Gapo can do something stupid."

I walked out into the hallway and headed quickly for the lit portion, where people were still working on extracting every piece of furniture from the rooms. Sneaking along the wall, we slid past the first set of closed doors. Sounds of a hasty departure were coming from inside. Then, suddenly one of the doors opened and a group of young servants rushed by us, scrambling for the stairs, with heaps of clothing in hand. They were in such a hurry that I could barely see their faces. All I heard were their frantic voices and heavy breathing. Ignored we waited for them to vanish upstairs, and then proceeded further, going by several more open doorways that presented us with the same images of complete disorder. Along the way we met some more people, but nobody wanted to talk to us. To any of our attempts to find out what was going on there, they only waved off their hands.

Then almost at the stairs, we came up to a large doorway that led into a spacious round room, which once served as a music hall. There, several men and women, all of the house serving staff, tried to pack three large cases with statues and vases of thin white glass. Throwing everything they could lay their hands on into the crates, they ran around the room. One woman was sobbing, another had dirty streaks down her cheeks. Three men were a bit more composed, but their hasty movements and shaky hands betrayed their worried state. Although they were ignoring us I managed to get one of them to talk.

"Excuse me?" I yelled out and grabbed one man by his wrists. He raised his eyes and stared at me. "What is this all about? Why is everyone acting like the Barrier has been broken?"

An elder fellow, with almost all of his hair long gone, straightened up, still holding a vase of fine silky white porcelain, and sighed. "You do not know?" he asked with a note of surprise, then threw the vase into the box without even bothering to wrap it up, and added, "The Imperial army crossed the border some hours ago. Our scouts have reported thousands of their soldiers closing in on the city. It is an invasion and we are the first ones in its path." The man threw his hands up in the air and started to shake his head.

"Why?" he asked, looking up to the ceiling. "What did we do to them?"

He shook his head again and then returned to his work. I wanted to ask another question, but it was useless. The man did not say anything. The other servants did not talk either, and I motioned for my friends to get back into the hallway.

"Invasion!" exclaimed Ike as we headed for the stairs. "The war, the knights, great battles."

"It is all very exciting when you read about it hundreds of years later, but being there in the midst of everything, I do not think we will be so excited for too long," I replied thoughtfully. The news disturbed me. The Imperial invasion was another obstacle to our journey. Although the conflict had nothing to do with us or our kingdom, it did not make it any less dangerous. Being caught in the middle of it left us fewer chances of making a safe trip to Azoros. I sighed.

"We obviously cannot stay here for long. If the Imperial army comes here, they will not care if we are from Normandia or not. They will treat us like everyone else, and only Spirit knows what they do to their prisoners. Do you remember where the stables are? I will it hate if they have claimed our horses to transport all that junk."

"I think it is down the main lane, the second building on the right," said Ike, pointing in that direction.

"What about Elson? Should we not wait for him?" Ric asked, trailing some steps behind me.

"As I said, we will worry about him later; we cannot go looking for him now. We have no time."

Past the last of the opened doors, we took the stairs several floors down and halted at the edge of a round room, which had three different hallways running in different directions. Looking at the open archways I struggled to remember which way the front doors were.

"This place is a maze. Where should we go?" I asked my friends, when my memory failed me.

"Take a next left, and then a right, I think," said Ike.

Following his directions, and passing several broken furniture pieces that lay scattered on the floor, we ran through the corridor until we came up to another corner. But as we were about to turn, we were met by with three armed men, who appeared at the other end of the hallway, some forty cubits away.

They seemed to care little for the commotion around them. Instead, when they spotted us standing at the other end, one of them said something and all three ran toward us.

"Hey, outlanders," an older soldier, whose face was covered by a visor, continued as the men came closer. "His lordship, Arley Erbeis wants to see you as soon as possible. He is awaiting you in his room."

"Arley?"

"Yes, Arley Erbeis."

"Then we will go," I said. "Lead the way."

Chapter 49

WALKING FAST after the soldiers we crossed several hallways and then up two floors, all the way to a large oak door, guarded from the outside by four men in full battle gear. In contrast to the lower levels, that part of the castle was unusually quiet. Although there were still a lot of servants and soldiers, who we met along the way, none of them rushed anywhere. Everything seemed to be well organized and orderly.

"His Highness is inside," said the soldier once we reached the entrance and knocked several times. Almost immediately the familiar voice of the young count answered from the other side. Then the door opened and we walked in. Arley stood at the open window, staring at the dark clear sky. He remained quiet for some time, then turned around and greeted us with a grim smile.

"Come in, friends. I want to have a word with you." The young count pointed at the chairs next to the window and himself sat down into a comfortable armchair made of red wood.

"Can you tell us what is going on around here? We do not seem to get any clear answer from anybody." I started as soon as I sat down.

"That is the reason I have summoned you here." Arley sighed deeply. "I am afraid your stay at this castle is over. You have chosen a terrible time to come here. It seems that your report of the Imperial forces, sitting just outside our borders, has proved to be correct. A little before dark, two of the Imperial vanguards crossed the front line northeast of here. Our forces have taken a position ten leagues from Orencia and now are trying to repel the attack. But it seems that there are more Imperial troops on the way, and I am afraid that those few soldiers we have there will not be able to hold off the enemy for long."

Arley thought for a moment in silence.

"What are you going to do? If what you say is true, the enemy will be here in no time. Are you preparing the defenses, is there going to be a siege?"

"A siege?" Arley laughed. "Have you seen this place? This is no ordinary castle. The only thing it has in common with a real fort is the name, nothing more. We have no walls, no battlements, and frankly we do not have enough men even if we did. All we have is a small contingent of soldiers, a few mercenary bands, and a hundred militiamen. That is no match for a real army of the Empire. It hurts to say, but there will be no fight for Orencia. This place is already lost to the enemy. It is just that the enemy has not yet arrived to claim it."

"But what about all those soldiers who were camping here some days ago, and war engines, and…," I asked, remembering the scores of Lombardian armed men passing through the city many times during the last few days.

"Those men were the advance regiments of the Lombardian border legions. Like I have said they are too few to stop the invasion. Their goal is to stall the enemy, while the main forces, sent by the queen's generals, prepare the defensive positions. Only their orders are not to protect the city. The officers say that the city is impossible to defend, that the landscape around it is not suited for a major battle. Instead they will assemble the troops southeast of here, near the low banks of the Winter Rivers. So as you can see Orencia is destined to fall." Arley sighed again.

"But what about your father, and you?" asked Ike, the concept of giving up without a fight was foreign to him.

"We will leave this place as soon as our wagons are ready. The commoners will probably stay. But if there is no fight, the town will be spared. It is too valuable a place to destroy. The Imperial army will use it to run its own supplies through here. For my father and me it is disaster, but for the regular folks it is a simple matter of trading one master for another. I bet you some of them will not even see much change.

"As for the nobility, along with us, they will leave the county and travel south to Lorio. It is the next largest city to the south of here. It has a real castle and a strong garrison. Our family has a house there and some lands around the city. So it will not be too much of a strain on us. Our soldiers will go with us and if needed will join the army there."

"Will you fight, yourself?" I asked the young count.

"Yes, I probably will. It is expected of a Lombardian noble to take up arms once his kingdom is under attack. I am sure my father has already found a position for me with the coastal legions. It is where he had served back in the old day, and it is where I will probably go too.

But let us stop talking about me. There is an important matter that I must tell you. As you know, Gapo is not too fond of you. He has not done anything about it yet. But with the Imperial army just a few leagues away, I suspect he will try to implicate you in the invasion. You have little time. I have already arranged for your horses to be put outside, at the back entrance. Elson is there too. He will take you out of the city. I must say you are lucky to have a companion like him. With his assistance you will make it to Azoros without any problem. Leave now, before Gapo realizes you are missing. I hope you have your gear with you."

"We are ready to go," I replied and pointed at the bag next to my chair.

"Good, then let's not waste any time on farewells. I am sure we will see each other again someday. Right now, you should take your leave. Gapo and his men cannot be too far behind."

"Thank you, Sir. We appreciate all you have done for us." I got up and bowed to the young count.

"Nonsense, it is I who am forever in your debt. You saved my life, remember?" Arley laughed and waved at us. Our bags on our shoulders, we headed for the door, but the young count stopped us almost at the exit.

"Do not use this door. Take the one behind those curtains to the left. It will take you straight to the yard. Elson should be there, waiting for you. Good luck."

"Good luck to you too." I saluted the young count and slid after my friends through the opened doorway and into another corridor, dim and narrow. Outside, the air was cold. We left the mansion quickly and right away came face-to-face with Elson, who stood in the shadows, waiting, with all our horses next to him.

"Hurry up, fellows." I heard the Southerner's cheerful voice. He stepped into the light and threw a quick glance over his shoulder. "Come, your horses are over here."

Our steeds ready for departure, we fixed our gear, checked the saddles, and following Elson, rode out toward the fence.

We had gone little more that few cubits, before a loud yell attracted our attention. The howl came from the castle. We slowed down a little bit and looked back. Standing on the front stairs I saw a small group of men, who shouted something and pointed at us.

"Something is wrong?" asked Elson, pulling hard on the straps.

"I do not know, but I sure do not like it," I noted, looking at the group near the house again.

The people at a distance seemed agitated and continued to wave their torches. All of them were commoners, but then another group appeared from around the corner. Unlike the others, they were armed, and amongst them, dressed in his distinctive blue robe, walked Gapo.

"That is the cursed protector. I think we may have a serious problem," I commented right away.

"Gapo and his friends?" asked Ike. "I say we run."

"I agree." Elson turned and hit the bridle. Picking up the pace, we sent our horses into a gallop. Meanwhile the men by the house started to run, giving us chase. But soon they fell behind. With their figures lost in the cover of darkness, we crossed the wide-open grounds of the park and came up to the front gates, which were closed and guarded by five men, who stood anxiously peering toward the castle.

"Who is that?" one of the guards shouted, as they heard our approach.

"It is me, Elson. Open up, we have to leave this place," said the Southerner.

"Sorry, lad. Cannot do it," replied one of the guards. "We have just received orders from the protector not to let anyone through, not even the count."

"Oh, great." Elson spit. "How can we leave then?"

"Everyone is using the western gates. But I do not think you should go there. The protector has his men watching the road."

"Is there another way out?"

"You can take the stream. It is about half a league east of here. If you follow along the wall, you will run straight into it. The fence breaks by the water, and you should not have any problem crossing it." The soldier pointed with his spear in the direction he described and added, "Do not worry it is not deep, one cubit, maybe less."

"Thanks." Elson saluted the men and started along the wall of trees, heading east. We followed. As we left the lights of the front gates, I went up to the Southerner.

"Why did they not stop us?"

"Gapo is not the most popular person around here. Most people hate the protector."

"So is that why they helped us?"

"That or maybe the three gold plates, which I had so kindly given them a day ago." The Southerner grinned.

As the soldier said, the stream was a shallow creek that ran across the estate and into the valley, banking around the town. Full speed we rushed into the water, splashing it all over our clothes. Slicing through the once calm surface, we trotted along the shore, heading for the nearest low slide in the bank, which appeared several hundred cubits behind the fence. It was a sandy slope that ran straight into the water. Although too steep for a man, it was an easy climb for the horses, and soon we were back on firm ground, heading away from the estate, down a narrow path that ran around the city.

When the last of the houses disappeared, we came to a large trade route and took it south, venturing further and further away from Orencia, passing through the nighttime lands of Lombardia, distracted from our thoughts only by the flickers of light in the distance. Time passed slowly, each hour dragging like a year. Eventually the last of the city fires went away, and we came up to a crossing, where we turned east.

"How do you know this place so well?" I finally asked the Southerner somewhere along the ride.

"I have been here before," he answered, staring ahead into the darkness.

"Before you came to Normandia?"

"That too...," he thought about something for a moment. "I was born here."

"Here, in Lombardia? Where is your home? We can visit it if you want."

"My home is gone," said the Southerner after a pause. "I lived in a village south of Orencia. Muru, it was called, a small parish, maybe a hundred families. My father was a farmer there and my mother was a maid at a count's summer house."

"You said that it was gone. What happened?"

Elson sighed loudly, suddenly not himself. He grew quiet and the always cheerful voice turned sad.

"I do not think I want to talk about this anymore," he said sharply, and we continued for a while in silence, reflecting on our own thoughts.

"It was early spring," said Elson unexpectedly after several more leagues of a wordless ride. I turned around. Although I could not really see his face, I heard his voice, and it was full of grief.

"I was ten years old. We lived in a nice house near the center of the village. There was a small pond nearby. I used to fish there with my friends. Even in the wintertime it never froze. That day I had a fight with my father. It was a stupid thing, but I got upset and ran away. Two of my friends joined me. They just wanted to get out of the village and explore the nearby lands. Of course we could not get too far. After three days we ran out of food and our clothes were soaked from rain. With little to go on we headed back. But when we returned we found the familiar noisy parish gone. Instead of houses there were just ashes and smoke. The entire village was burned to the ground, and the people were gone, all of them. For hours, the three of us searched through the ruins, trying to find someone, anyone, but everyone had vanished, and everything was destroyed.

"Still we hoped our parents were alive; that was until we made a terrible discovery in an old barn, about a league away from the village. The old building was also burned to the last log, but unlike the houses in the village, there was something different about the ashes that covered the floor. At first the strange shapes looked like sacks of grain, but then, as we examined them closer, we realized they were figures of people, piled up on top of each other. Children, the elderly, even pets, all who lived in our village were there, and they were dead, my parents too.

"Crying until we had no more tears, my friends and I buried the bodies and left for the nearest town, where we hoped to tell the soldiers of our gruesome discovery. Walking for several days and nights, knowing little of the lands we had been crossing, we reached the gates of Luzo, a midsize town that belonged to an old baron and his three sons. There we found some soldiers from the legions and told them everything. They promised to help, but never did. Nobody did. For days we wandered the dirty streets of Luzo, searching for someone who would listen. But our pleas were left ignored, and soon there was no hope left for us. Sad and alone, we left the town and headed down the road, just walking, not really caring where we were going. Somewhere along the way, my friends departed in their own directions, and I found myself in the Amber Empire, serving as a stable boy in one of the taverns in Azul, a small port city near the border."

Something moved at the side of the road and we both looked there. It was a wild dog. A skinny hungry creature stared at us, but finding no interest in our company, turned around and fled into the tall grass.

"So, what happened then? Have you ever found out who burned your village?" I asked, anxious to hear more of Elson's tale.

"Oh yes," he said quietly. "It happened many years after I had left Lombardia. While with the company of Brave Heads, I was hired by a count in the northern parts of Lombardia to escort his daughter, who was to be wed to another lord from a nearby county. The trip was quick and the job was easy. But it brought me to a town where I had once tried to find the truth. Luzo met me with the same indifference, but it so happened that there I found my answers after all. When I was done with the escort duty, I was immediately paid to be a bodyguard for a merchant at the wedding party of my recent client. It was the usual revelry, lots of local nobles, booze, and gossip. Wandering amongst the various chat groups, I came upon a discussion about teaching servants and peasants respect and admiration for their masters.

One of the younger nobles was telling a story about his father, who had some problems with a small village in northern Lombardia, which went by the name of Muru. Once I heard the name, I had to find out more, so I got closer and listened to the rest of the tale. According to the young lord, his father owned a summerhouse near Muru. One day—the mansion happened to catch fire. It was an accident—some servant left a candle lit. It got tipped over and the whole building burned to the ground. When the lord found out about it, he became furious. Although he had ten houses like that, he could not let such a misstep go unpunished; he thought to make an example of Muru's inhabitants, so his other subjects would never dare to destroy the noble's property again. The lord had little time to waste on finding out who to blame. He simply declared the entire village to be guilty and set a punishment for them, which came in the form of a mercenary band ordered to erase the village from the face of Ethoria. The day I ran away, those cutthroats attacked my home. They did their job perfectly. After rounding up all the villagers, they brought them to the barn and executed them one by one. When all was done, they piled the lifeless bodies and burned them. With that task completed they torched the village and left."

"Is that not a crime? That count should have been put to sword for something like this," I exclaimed in protest, picturing the evil described to me.

"Those were different times. Besides, Lombardia is very different from your home kingdom. Here the counts own their lands and their men alike. If you are born into some village, which belongs to some noble, you are his property and he can do with you whatever he wants. Of course in the last years more and more counts granted freedom to their folks. However, there are still a lot of people who are slaves to their masters, though they are not called so."

"But these are people we are talking about."

"Welcome to the real world, lad," replied Elson, and he spat on the grass that passed quickly underneath the hooves of his mount. "It is a bitter, cruel place we are living in. Injustice and insanity are as common here as leaves on the trees."

The Southerner sighed deeply, slowly releasing the air from his lungs, and added, "You have yet a great deal to learn. At least you have a chance to prepare yourself for the darker things. I did not have such a choice. Not that it matters anymore."

The silence fell again.

In the meantime we made yet another turn and moved aside from the road, and went into the tall grass field, striving to reach the edge of the scarcely visible forest before dawn. I was not sure how long we spent in the vale, but when I looked back I saw a reddish line of flickering light. It came from the north and filled the entire sky with a soft glow, which jumped up and down as if dancing to a silent tune. At first I thought it was morning, but I quickly realized the sun did not rise from the north. The light was something else.

"What is that out there?" I asked the Southerner and pointed toward the red streak.

"Will you look at that?" Ike halted his horse next to me. "I have never seen anything like this before."

"That is Orencia," replied Elson.

"Orencia?" I repeated, startled by his words.

"What you see in front of you is the sight of a burning city," clarified Elson, and he turned his horse away from the view and toward the forest.

"So this means…"

"The city is being put to the torch."

"But Arley, he said that the Imperials will never ravage the city. He said that…"

"The Imperials are not the only ones who could set the city on fire."

Nobody said anything else.

Chapter 50

THE PALE morning sky crawled out from the east, crowded with heavy thick clouds. We had been traveling all night, stopping only briefly to check the road ahead. After reaching the edge of the forest, we went alongside the lines of trees until we came upon a small road, a single track of yellowish soil that emerged out of the woods and ran south, veering from time to time. Even with light, our sour mood did not improve. For me it got even worse as I also fell prey to the weariness of our unplanned journey.

"Is there an inn we can stop at?" asked Ike at last. He was shivering from the early cold, and enveloped himself in his cape, so that only his face was visible.

"There should be a village a few hours ahead. We can stop there for a quick breakfast. But we cannot stay there for long. There is an entire Imperial army on our heels, and I am sure some of Gapo's men are looking for us too. To tell the truth, I do not think we should stop until we reach Piorio."

"Piorio?" I asked from underneath my hood, which slid down to my nose, shielding most of my face from the bitter wind that had accompanied us ever since we left Erbeis' castle.

"It is a city, two days worth of travel along this road. If we hurry we will make there just in time to catch some rest and get some supplies before they close the gates, for I am sure the news of the attack has already reached the city."

"Why bother, we can just skip it too for all I care." I heard Ike's murmur, and I did not blame him. Our situation was dreadful—some crazy protector was giving us chase, and a real war was being fought just a few leagues away. Elson was right though. We had to be very careful.

Unfortunately Elson's memory of the land was not too accurate. Instead of a promised village we found only an abandoned trade station—a couple of half-ruined stone houses that stood like ghosts on the side of a roadway, offering little comfort or shelter. Yet we decided to stop there anyway, as the aged walls of naked granite offered us some cover from the chilling wind. There, amongst the rubble, we ate a stale hard meal of wrinkled apples, dried-out cheese, and pieces of wheat bread, which showed signs of mold. Our horses enjoyed even less, having to settle for a small patch of hard grass and prickly plants with tiny blue flowers and no scent.

Already far enough from Orencia, we did not abandon our idea of traveling that day, and after our bodies had rested enough, climbed back into our saddles and resumed the journey. When evening came, we scouted the surroundings, and soon spotted a decent place for a camp in a narrow stretch of young forest. Hoping to get there before dark, we hurried toward the trees, but as we stepped into the grass, someone appeared on a lane a little more than half a league south of us. A large dust cloud made it hard to see anything, but as the wind picked up the sand, several figures of horsemen rose in the distance. At first I only saw five riders, but as their silhouettes grew larger, many more men appeared behind them. In all I counted over a hundred horsemen, who made up a tight column, which moved swiftly toward us.

"Lombardian guard," announced Elson and stopped his horse.

"Should we move closer to the forest?" I asked him, although I already knew that the men had seen us, and that we would not find refuge in the woods. If those men were after us, we were doomed.

"No, it is useless," noted Elson, agreeing with my thoughts. "If we flee they will chase us for sure, but if we stay they may let us be."

While the men continued in our direction, I tried to think of the best way to communicate with the Lombardian guards. But with the image of Gapo fresh in my mind, I grew more and more unsettled. What if that mutt had alerted others in the nearby cities? What if these soldiers were here to arrest us?

I shook my head, trying to brush off my unpleasant thoughts, but they refused to leave me. The closer the guards got to our position, the more nervous I became. My palms were sweating and I had to wipe them several times. By then the front of the column had reached us, and I could see the riders well. All of the men were dressed in the uniform of the Lombardian guards. Their trousers and jackets were of dark blue color, decorated with bloodred stripes on sleeves and cuffs. Bright steel breastplates covered their chests and showed golden buttons, arranged on their tunics in two rows, which went from stand-up collars to belts. The shiny steel helms were also trimmed with gold; their visors were lifted, showing ranks and ranks of tough clean-shaved faces. At each soldier's side hung a long sword and a long wooden lance, which sat in a large leather cup, attached to a saddle.

Although the riders looked at us with curiosity, none of them stopped. Instead their column proceeded straight north, leaving us with a feeling of relief. But then, as our eyes were following the rearguard, several of the riders separated from the group and rode back to us.

"Hey you over there," yelled one of the soldiers. He was a tall man, wide in the shoulders and thick in the arms. His chest plate bore a golden symbol of three talons, and on his helm, a figure of a descending eagle was fixed just over an open visor. Three of his companions also had talons on their plates, but their helms were plain, with no adoration or symbols.

"We are just commoners, traveling to Azoros," Elson hurried to explain. I noticed that his accent changed and now took on a distinctive Lombardian flavor, not present earlier. "We are coming from Orencia, fleeing the invasion."

Elson looked at the soldiers, who by that time had already stopped their horses just a cubit away from him.

"Orencia, you say. How long ago did you leave the city?"

"A night and a day. When we heard about the Imperial army moving in, we packed our things and left, and we have been on the road ever since."

"Have you seen the Imperials?"

"No, but we did see some fires in the distance. Even before we departed from Orencia, we heard sounds of a battle some distance away. And then, once gone, we also saw a huge bright glow rising over the city."

"Cursed Northerners," spat one of the riders in the back. "They must have put it to the torch."

"Are you sure about the glow?" another rider repeated.

"Oh yes, it lit up the whole sky."

"This may be worse than we thought," said the man with the eagle. "We have had reports of the enemy crossing into our kingdom. But we did not know it had already captured Orencia."

"So what next, your highness?" asked a chubby older soldier.

The man with the eagle on his helm thought a moment. "We go north. The General is waiting for us by the river. I am sure he will fill us in on the situation."

The man then snapped the bridle and turned to head back to his troops. Halfway down he turned around and yelled, "Be safe on the road, travelers! There is a war going on. If you remember anything, report to the nearest military post. We need as much information as possible. The Northerners took us totally by surprise."

The man snapped the bridle again and, along with his two companions, galloped after the column, which had already disappeared into the shadows cast by the darkening sky.

When their figures finally vanished in the distance, we recommenced our own journey.

"Are they going to Orencia?" asked Ike, looking back at the road.

"I am sure they will be able to put up a decent fight. There were at least a hundred of them," added Ric.

"I doubt they will fight alone. That was a single regiment, probably from Piorio. They will not last a moment against the Imperial army. My guess, they will join the rest of the Lombardian forces by the Winter Rivers. In these lands, it is not an army until the count is at least four thousand men"

"Wow, four thousand. I cannot even imagine seeing so many people in one place!" exclaimed Ike, taken by such numbers.

Elson laughed. "That is nothing. If you want to hear of real armies, open a history book. During the First Age, the opposing armies counted tens of thousands of knights alone, and twice that of regular soldiery. Just in one battle at the Amber River, during the Great War against the Horde, there were fifty thousand dead."

"How do you know all this?" asked Ike again.

"You would have known it too, had you bothered to read the scrolls that the old sage gave us back in Villone," I commented.

Everyone laughed. Our better mood was slowly returning to us, and once we settled for the night amidst the trees, jokes and laughter sprang to life, making our ordeal a lot easier, at least for the time being.

Chapter 51

THROUGH MY Fore Sight I continued to receive news of the expedition, assembled by the lords of Bois. When, in my sleep, I rejoined the troops again it was the final day of the advance. Everything was going as planned. The expedition had made good time, and scouts had returned with the news of several large encampments, found on the shores of Lake Azul. During the march, which had started six days before, the Duke's army grew by another hundred men, mostly brought in by those of Bois knights who had missed the initial assembly in Bonneville, and the nobles from Puno, brought in by Sire Zuros, along with their soldiers, banners, and supplies. With the new arrivals the column extended even more and now stretched over a league, looking much like an animated giant snake on a grassy meadow, with the Duke riding in its very center.

Minia, Rob, and Ark were there too. Riding several rows behind the knights, they followed a wide choppy route, plagued with large sharp dips and broken tracks of dried mud. At times the bumps were so deep that my friends found themselves holding tight to their saddles, trying not to lose their grips and plunge to the ground in front of all the soldiers, lords, and fellow squires. And though they managed to stay in their seats, their bodies endured much battering, and all of their limbs were starting to hurt.

Of the three, Minia felt the worst. His recent wounds were still far from being healed and reminded him of it frequently, bursting with pain after every jerk or turn. For a while he tried to distract himself by looking at the passing landscape, but the upcoming scenes became too dreary too soon, and he had to turn elsewhere to make himself forget about the pain. After talking to his two friends for some time, he joined a pack of young squires behind Sire Jim and listened to their tales of past campaigns. But even stories of Great Wars and brave heroes did not save Minia from his torment, and so he had to struggle through the day, hoping that the night would bring him some relief. Yet, when the evening finally came, the troops did not stop. Instead the perfect lines of soldiers continued to march on, their long procession lit by many torches. From a distance, the moving column looked like a glowing stream of floating fire that ran ahead toward another set of yellow glimmers outlining the Duke's main camp, which was made up of three wide circles placed around a barely visible hill, one on top of the other.

Set up several days before by the forward parties, the encampment was split into three different sections. At the top of the mound, several hundred cubits up a grassy slope, rose four large pavilions, all adorned with rows of vivid banners, many of which were painted dark blue and red, the colors of the Duke's house. Several dozen wooden frames hung over the tents' thick walls, all shaped like triangular shields and affixed with noble symbols, which probably belonged to those knights who had decided to take part in the present campaign. In between the timber screens, just several cubits apart, tall metal grates were placed around each of the pavilions illuminating the site with a bright yellow glow, making it hard to believe that it was in fact nighttime there.

Even at a distant the orderliness of the upper section of the camp was hard to miss, and left no doubt that the summit of the hill was reserved for the Duke and the lords, who, even in times of war, did not give up their way of life, infused with plentiful meals, made beds, and numerous servants, many of whom were already attending to their masters' needs, scuffling busily amongst the horses and wagons. In fact there were so many serving men who had arrived with the expedition that a separate section of the camp had to be allocated just for them. Erected several cubits down the slope, the servants' part was composed of dozens of wide tents and fenced cubicles, amidst which ran grown men and boys of all ages, filling the air with much noise, clatter, and constant shouting that probably could have been heard from leagues away.

Yet, it was the lowest and the largest section of the camp that was the busiest and the noisiest of all. Assembled to house the fighting force of the Duke's army, the soldiers' campgrounds were set at the bottom of the hill, swelling far into the nearby fields, counting over a hundred tents, placed in such a way so to form a thick defensive line around the entire mound. Inside that line along a wide-open lane of straw and sand that ran across the middle, dozens of bonfires were burning high; their blazes, though not as grand as at the hilltop, providing plenty of light that left not a single cubit of the ground to darkness.

Soon after the glow of the camp's fires came into view, my friends concluded their journey and rode through large, freshly-cut gates of a short logged wall, finding themselves surrounded by dozens of soldiers, who were already attending to their tents and gear. Swept by the commotion, Ark and Rob thought about breaking formation too, but Minia signaled for them not to, and instead took them after the other squires, up the slope and to the summit, where, attended by a host of servants, the Duke and his noble peers were already entering one of the pavilions. Only when the last of the knights disappeared behind the draped door, did Minia allowed the other two to dismount and walk around their horses, stretching their legs and arms, numb from a long and tiresome ride. The squires around my friends left their saddles too. Some walked back down to the soldier's section; some took their mounts to the stables, set up in between the pinnacle and the servant's quarters; and some settled right there by the lords' pavilions, warming their hands by the large grates, talking to the servants and each other.

Slowly getting some feeling back into their limbs, Ark and Rob surrendered their horses to a pair of stable boys and walked over to Minia, waiting for further instructions. But their commander had nothing to say. The whole experience of a real war campaign was new to him too, and frankly he had no idea as to what to do next. Luckily, as soon as his companions reached him, he heard their names being called from across the opening, where, standing at the entrance to one of the pavilions, a white-haired soldier was waving and telling them to come quickly. My friends complied immediately and rushed to the flapped door, which the soldier moved aside to let them inside a splendid spacious hall. Simply decorated, the grand chamber was designed solely for waging war. In the very center, surrounded by several high candle stands, stood a large square board with a large map of Puno nailed over it. A long table rested empty nearby, but stacks of scrolls and leather boxes were visible under it, suggesting that it would soon be cluttered with much paperwork. Two rows of plain tall chairs were placed evenly along the tent's thick leather walls, and in between them, cast-iron lamps, at least twenty of them. Although there were no other visible fittings in sight, the free space was modest as a crowd of men filled most of the space—knights, servants, and guards huddling in a circle around the board, where the Duke and some older lords were talking to a young noble dressed in plain plated armor.

"How much resistance can we expect?" asked a knight in a green vest with a symbol of a rising sun.

"Our scouts report a large force of several hundred men, standing several leagues north of the lake. As far as we know this is their main host, but we think there are more men in the caves further up," answered a younger lord.

"The main host, you say. How much of that host is made of local peasants or prisoners or slaves? Do we know anything about that?" asked another knight. He was much older than most of the men in the room and wore a vest of red color with an emblem of a black crow, the symbol of the province of Puno. And with his golden cloak and an abundance of gems on his vest, my friends could easily guess that the man was Sire Zuros, the High Lord of Puno.

"I cannot tell you, Sire. The enemy has set up many posts along their camps and our scouts could not get past them, not without running the risk of triggering an alarm."

"The risk of sounding an alarm, you say?"

"Yes, Sire. We could not—"

"And what about the risk of losing our men in battle tomorrow, all because we do not know anything about the enemy? How many swords do they have? How many bows?" The lord in the red vest snapped angrily and spat on the ground.

The young officer lowered his head and nodded, his face turning dark crimson. The red-vested knight did not seem to notice; his anger grew and he raised his voice again, but Duke stopped him.

"My old friend, Sire Zuros," the Duke said in a calm but firm tone. "I ask you to cool your anger. The enemy is across the field, and it is with him we have to fight, not with our own." Sire Tem tapped the red knight on his shoulder gently and continued, addressing everyone in the room, "Still, Sire Zuros speaks the right words. What we know, my fellow lords, is but a fraction of what we ought to. In times of war such poor preparations could cost us many lives. To put it mildly—this is unacceptable. We have a hostile force just a couple of leagues away, and we do not know anything about it. Or do you suggest we forget about everything and just attack?"

The Duke frowned and threw a glance at the young knight, who started to turn from red to pale. "I do not hear the answer."

"My lord, we can send a new group at dawn," another young noble in green armor uttered, but swiftly withdrew, put down by Sire Tem's harsh gazes.

"Another group, you say? You had four days to do your job. You knew the location and the layout of the compound. You had as many man as you had asked for; I personally gave you the best horses and the best gear, including my own spyglass. And what have you come up with?…Nothing. But now you want to send another team when our forces are already here. How long do you think it will be until the enemy realizes that we are at his doorstep? We have no time for another scout run. We must act now and act quickly, before they retreat into the mountains where we will never find them."

The Duke gave the younger knight in green armor another tough stare and turned around. His furred cloak slid from his shoulders and dropped to the ground. But the Duke did not seem to notice. Instead he walked up to the board and slammed his hand onto the leather pane at a spot where a large dark outline of the lake peered out of the skin, his fingers pressing hard into the surface of the map.

"We will act as if we have no scouting reports," he said loudly. "Morrow morning we will attack. Sire Loule and Sire Rigor, you and your men will take positions at the edge of the forest. You will be our right flank. When the time comes you will strike at the enemy's eastern camp and cut off any routes of escape. Let's just hope that the mist from the swamps will cover your movement, and by the time you hear my signal, the enemy will not see you coming."

The Duke then turned to another group of knights who stood around Sire Zuros.

"My old friends, Sire J'ioma, Sire Hogiour, Sire Fray, old brother Ferios, and you, lord Zuros. Your task will be an important one, as always. You will command the center. You will place your troops outside the ridge, and will advance first, taking on the largest of the outer camps. Your goal is to draw as many of the enemy's forces as possible. While you do so, the left flank under the command of Sire Ross and Sire Dioser, will remain behind the hills and then advance to the western camp that blocks the way into the caves. As you, Sire Ross and Sire Dioser, will be the closest to the mountains, when you attack, you will delay your assault until the enemy is drawn to the center. Then and only then will you strike. Your movement has to come unexpectedly and fast, as after destroying the western camp you will have to get to the caves. So take only the mounted men with you, squires, scouts, and a regiment of light cavalry. Two more units of bowmen will also give cover until you clear the enemy's positions. Those of your men who are on foot will join Sire Zuros in the center, since that is where most of the fighting will take place. I will join the center lines too."

"But my lord," protested some knight in the front row. "We need you here to command the troops."

"No. I am a knight, and this is my campaign. So I will not sit still while my men are fighting on my orders. I must be there with them."

"My lord, but his majesty's dispatch, it said that—"

"Away with the dispatch. The king probably did not even read it when he signed it. Some of his royal relatives who have never seen a real fight before, composed the letter, so when the time comes they can themselves sit safely in the rear of battle. But me, I will not do such a thing. My place is with my men, and this is it."

The Duke granted the crowd another sharp glance, and when no response came, resumed, keeping his voice as firm as ever. "Now, as I have said we will start at dawn. Two flaming arrows will be the sign to move out. First goes the center. Then as it reaches the main camp, I will give a sign for the left flank to advance—one flaming arrow. Sire Loule, Sire Rigor, as our right flank, you will circle around the swamps and wait there. Should you hear a horn blow three times, you will join the center group for it will mean that we need help. Otherwise, wait for the horn sound once and then move swiftly toward the western camp and then in between the mountains and the forest. In doing so, make sure none of the enemy escapes you.

"Finally, for all the knights here, once in the caves, your main goal is to find and seize as many of the followers, who call themselves the Alavantars, as you can. It is essential to take them alive, for we must question them afterwards."

Rob continued to listen as the lords talked strategy. He tried to follow their words, but when the Duke started to assign each remaining knight his place on the field, he got lost, quickly realizing that battle plans and tactics were truly noble tasks, which he, a commoner, could never comprehend. And those were not the only things he did not understand; a question of why the three of them were summoned there was also a mystery to him. Was it a mistake that the white-haired soldier made? Or was there a reason for them to be inside the Duke's pavilion?

Rob wanted to ask someone, but everyone in the room, besides Ark and Minia, were ignoring him, and so he continued to wait, standing by the door for several hours until the counsel was over and many of the knights departed outside, taking some of the guards and servants along with them. With only a few nobles left, Rob's doubts about their presence there grew, but then the flap behind him moved and Sire Jim walked inside, greeting everyone with a quick glance and a nod.

"Ah, there you are," he said, seeing my friends before him. "I have been looking everywhere for you." The second captain gave Minia a brief smile and motioned for the three to follow him outside, which they did, walking into the open, a chilly breeze making them shiver.

"I guess old soldier Grus made a mistake. Instead of summoning you to my quarters, he took you to the Duke's tent. Oh well. It did not hurt for you to hear our battle plan, though you were not supposed to hear about it until morrow morning. But let's talk about why I wanted to see you."

The second captain took my friends closer to one of the grates so they could get some warmth from the blaze, and resumed. "With the approval of our Duke and your master, Sire Rone, who, unfortunately, was unable to join us in this campaign, you have been assigned to Sire Tem's garrison, which means that you are now under my command.

And since you are the ones who know the most about the Alavantars, my first order will be for you to help us pick out the foul believers amongst those we fight in the morning.

"For this reason I have assigned you to the company of Sire Ross, on the left flank. Once our troops breach the compound in the caves, you will assist the men in seizing those Alavantars you have told us about. Before then though, you are to stay away from any fighting. It is an order, not a request. Do not try to be heroes; your job is to find the true enemies and those who lead them. When you find them, Sire Ross will take them prisoner and bring them to the Duke."

"But Sire," interjected Minia. "How are we to find those Alavantars? We have never seen them."

" That may be so. But you still know more about them than the rest of us. Besides, it is a chance for you to prove your worth to Normandia." The second captain smiled briefly again and concluded, "Now men, get some rest. It is an early rise tomorrow, and a long day after it. One of Sire Ross's men will give you more details in the morning."

The lord quickly turned away and vanished inside the tent, leaving my friends startled for words.

For a while, standing outside, Rob tried to gather his thoughts about the new assignment. To find and catch the Alavantars was a task worthy of a knight, not a squire, not even tens of squires. How would the three of them be able to recognize the Alavantars amongst the others? And what if those men inside the camps were not Alavantars at all? Rob had no answers to those questions. Taking a deep breath, he looked at the Duke's tent one more time and then hurried after his friends, who had been already far down the slope, heading toward the soldiers' section, where a tent was allocated for them near the base of the hill.

After veering through rows of marquees and fences, my friends finally reached a small triangular pavilion of dark blue color. Saying only brief greetings to several unfamiliar youngsters, who grilled pieces of meat on the rising flames of a nearby fire, they slipped inside a plain undersized chamber, fit with eight narrow beds and a black cauldron filled with murky water. At first Rob thought it was there to drink, but Minia promptly explained that the water was for washing only. Thankful that he did not take a sip, Rob quickly moved away from the pot and picked his place in a corner, next to Ark, who was already in bed. Keeping his clothes on, Rob lay down too. He thought he would never go to sleep, not after receiving such an important assignment from Sire Jim. But dreams came to him easy and soon he was snoozing away.

Chapter 52

ARK AWOKE early with everyone around him still asleep. Shivering a little from the morning cold, he lingered under the covers for some time, but then climbed to his feet and staggered outside, where a low thick mist swathed most of the ground and made it hard to see past several cubits. Still Ark could hear the camp already coming to life around him. Some low voices were sounding from a distance, accompanied by the shuffling of dozens of feet and the clatter of metal. Further away, war dogs were barking at something, and the thumping of many hooves was coming from the sanded lane ahead. Breathing deeply, Ark listened to the commotion, staring at the clouded sky above. But when a cold wind picked up from the west, he quickly hurried back inside and into his bed in the corner. Feeling the warmth of the covers, Ark closed his eyes again. Alas there was no time for sleeping, for shortly after, a call of many war horns came rolling through the camp, announcing the start of the important day.

Inside the tent, everyone got up and hurried outside, fixing armor and weapons as they walked. With the cloth flap sliding open continuously and the cold air rushing in, Ark had to rise too. Yawning, he put on his battle gear, given to him by Sire Rone, and followed the others back into the mist. By then though most of the white haze had retreated toward the mountains, and the line of calm dark green waters of Lake Azul became visible in the west. To Ark, the sight of the lake so close to the camp was a surprise, as, in the darkness of the night, he did not see how the Duke's column had ventured from the lower valleys of Puno and come up to the shore of Azul, the largest of Normandian lakes that crept at the very steps of the Land's Edge mountains.

From a distance the green waters reminded Ark of the Seven Seas, and he immediately recalled those days when his companions and he had come to see the coast for the first time; he also remembered their visit to Pullie, and then the moment when they had to take their separate paths. Seemingly distant now, those memories were always in his mind, and looking at the lake, Ark did

406

not want to let them go. Alas he had to. Breaking through the ranks of soldiers, a young lord rode up to their tent and ordered everyone to move to the other side of the camp, where the Duke and his captains were already waiting for the troops to take their positions for the assault. While the other squires scurried after the knight, Ark and Rob took after Minia, who had turned for the stables, thinking about the horses. But as the three of them were about to start up the slope, two stable boys emerged from behind one of the tents and brought their mounts along with them. Thanking the lads for the service, my friends quickly jumped into the cold saddles and trotted after the rest of the men, across the camp, to where the perfect lines of soldiers were growing fast, getting ready to move out toward the enemy's compounds.

When all the troops were in formation, another blow from the horns announced the departure and the column moved out, marching steadily down a wide road, through a narrow stretch of trees, and to the edge of a narrow dale, tucked in between the lake on the west and the thick swamped forest on the east. Above, glimpses of red and yellow brightened the sky, and a barely visible tip of the sun peered over the horizon, its first thin rays reflecting on the perfect files of men who advanced forward and then split into three groups. While the majority of the footed soldiers continued north down still misty fields, several regiments of those on horses veered off, some following a group of knights east to a distant line of woods, and some, including my friends, heading west, toward the shore of the lake, keeping a little behind the center.

Although at first, my friends took up positions at the front, they were quickly ordered to the back, and had to move alongside the brigades of bowmen, who paid them little grins and smirks as they walked. Some half a league away the Duke's host finally made its stop, bright colorful banners waving in the wind over the helms of the fighting men of Normandia. And further across the field, almost invisible to the naked eye, the right flank was moving fast, its lines disappearing into the thick vale that rose up from the shallow swamps.

After passing another quarter of a league into the tall grass, the left flank's column finally halted at the edge of a narrow wooded ridge, with a view of the mountains peering straight ahead. The Land's Edge, the great barrier, which separated Ethoria from the Northern wastes, stood before them. White distant peaks ascended in a dominant wall and stretched in one lone massive line of stone, proving once again to be indeed the most impressive monument, left from the days of the Ancient Times, a source of countless legends, told throughout Ethoria from generation to generation. In Villone alone, there were at least a dozen songs, and many more tales, all devoted to the great mountains and the Barriers, those who built them, and those who fought for them. And that day, my friends were standing before it, looking at the threshold of the civilized world, the place famed by all races, living and dead.

Down in the field, the troops continued to wait for the signal to move out. Time dragged forever, and every time a sound came from the Duke's company to the right, the men jumped up and peered at the sky, searching for two flaming arrows. But for a long while, all they saw were a few birds flying high over the dale, apparently unaware of the dangers that lurked below. My friends felt tension building within them. Their breathing was getting harder, and their eyes started to hurt a little from the strain. Yet, when they suddenly spotted two distinctive black shapes cross the sky in the distance, leaving barely visible trails of smoke behind them, their stress receded and blood rushed through their veins.

Suddenly the entire host came into motion. The lords put down their visors and took long lances from the squires. The bowmen strained their bows, first arrows falling quickly into the slots, and the riders snapped their bridles, letting the mounts take them further into the field. The remnants of the fog cleared and presented a view of the enemy's encampments—three sets of barricades, each one made of a logged wall and towers. The largest of the three forts stood opposite the center group, another one some half a league further east, and straight ahead the smallest. It was that camp on the left flank my friends were ordered to attack.

Remaining in the back row, Ark, Rob, and Minia studied the barricade and the various structures that composed it. Made up of several dozen tents and long boarded fences that ran around the camp, the only formidable edifice was a single tall tower, which stood in the middle of the camp, rising several cubits into the morning sky. On top of it Ark noticed some movement; but before he could determine what it was, he heard the sound of a horn coming from the enemy's position, a sign that their foes had seen the signal too.

While the enemy was preparing their defenses, Sire Ross and Sire Dioser held off the attack, keeping their troops still, watching what transpired in the center, where the Duke's company was proceeding with its assault, its lines shining in the sunlight and banners flapping in the wind. More horns sounded from the enemy's camp, and were immediately answered by the many drums from the Normandian side, joined then by loud commanding yells from the lords, who rode at the front lines, cheered by the troops that followed.

The pace quickened, and soon the first regiments of the center group were at the enemy's wall, clashing hard with the defenses of the larger barricade. Slamming their spears into the logged wall, the Normandians pushed inward and swiftly broke through, opening a large gap into which poured knights and their squires, slashing and hacking at the defenders' ranks. Amongst the mass of men and horses my friends saw several of the footed soldiers fall to the ground. A bit further a group of squires became separated from the rest of the regiment and were fighting furiously with a host of foes who had surrounded them from all sides. Their silhouettes waved desperately from side to side, but then their numbers dwindled and one by one the brave youngsters disappeared from sight, dragged from their horses by dozens of hands. Yet, the defenders' resistance was no match for the many swords and spears of the Duke's forces, and before long, the Normandians made their way further and further into the camp, pushing the enemy away toward the mountains and the caves visible there, black holes on a grayish rocky surface.

By then the left flank came into motion too. Sire Ross and Sire Dioser gave several quick orders and the first files of horsemen started forward, trying to stay safe from friendly arrows, sent in numbers at the defenders' positions. "Lower weapons, raise shields," my friends heard the closest of the knights yell and dropped their visors with one hand while balancing their long lances with the other. The lord then dug his heels into the sides of his mount and galloped toward the front, where the other knights, ten of them in all, were coming closer together to form the tip of a spear, completed behind them by rows of squires and light cavalry. Above, more arrows flew. This time many of them came from the other side, seeding the ground around the advancing ranks with small but deadly razor-sharp blades. Although the firing was not too accurate, some of the bolts managed to take out several of the squires, a few horses, and one knight, who caught an arrow in his shoulder and had to fall back to patch his damaged plated armor. Still the losses were small and did not slow the advance.

At the other end of the stretch, the once innocent-looking figures transformed into a crowd of armed men, who flocked to the logged wall, ready to repel the assault. Although they did not look anything like a real army, they still posed a threat, for even without uniforms, banners, and drums, they had plenty of weapons to cause some damage. While many enemies looked peasant-like, hastily dressed in cheap rusted armor, there were others who appeared well equipped and organized. Their distinctive foreign look made them stand out from the rest of the crowd, and their particularly well-formed lines marked them as mercenaries from abroad. Ark and Rob and Minia still remembered their run-ins with the hired swords in Bois and Pullie, and so knew well that the upcoming fight would be anything but easy.

Almost at the encampment's fence the Normandians broke the formation. While one band of squires dismounted and rushed to the low wall, others remained behind and shot arrows from the short bows that many of them always carried into battle. A few cubits further away moved the knights, stirring their mounts constantly to avoid the continuing stream of arrows and darts. The bowmen came closer too and now were making more accurate shots, picking one defender after another, and freeing some room for the footed squires to storm the barricade of logs and carriages. Still the resistance was furious, and more Normandians left their horses, rushing into battle to support their comrades. The continuous streams of men came from both sides, like two mountain rivers, hurling toward each other. Ark, Rob, and Minia wanted to run too, but they were still too far from the fight and their orders were not to cross the wall until the way was cleared. Still the three of them made their way through the friendly ranks and toward the front lines, where they could hear the battle raging on. Around them the other soldiers were chanting an old Normandian battle cry, and automatically my friends' voices joined with the others.

At last the footed squires by the wall managed to push back the defenders, enough to start picking up the barricade. The enemy tried to regain ground, but was too late, as several of the broken logs had already fallen to the floor, leaving a wide passage in their place, through which the knights rushed right away, followed by the rest of the mounted men. In time Ark's mare reached the edge of the camp; the fighting was far from the wall and close around the wooden tower that continued to stand in the center. All around him bodies and weapons covered the ground. Most belonged to the enemy, but there were a few of the Duke's soldiers, distinguished by once clean colored uniforms and metal marks on the helms. Broken swords, spears, and lost armor were everywhere, but Ark moved past them without stopping. His attention was fixed ahead, at the center of the camp, crowded with the enemy. He planned to follow Sire Ross and his two friends through the encampment, but as soon as he reached the fight, he had to halt and parry a hail of random attacks. Holding tight to the straps, he spun in one spot and swung his horse, trying hard not to lose it.

The fight was furious, and Ark could feel his arms becoming numb too quickly. His hands began to sweat and his grip was loosening. Luckily he did not have to fight for long, as soon it proved that the poorly trained bandits were no outmatched by the formidable armored soldiery of the Normandian Kingdom. Even the skilled mercenaries could do little to change the course of battle and after another failed attempt to push back the lords and squires, the enemy's ranks broke. First fled the seemingly well-organized mercenaries. Using the others as shield they abandoned their defenses and ran for the mountains, taking as much gear with them as possible. Some of the squires wanted to chase them, but the few remaining pockets of the resistance took away the attention from the fleeing hired swords. Of those, who insisted on defending the camp, only few managed to escape, as the majority was quickly taken up by swords and morning stars of the Normandian knights. Only at the base of the tower, the fighting continued. A dozen footed squires had already died there, and even one knight fell victim to a random strike, which killed his warhorse, trapping his clad figure underneath. But with the other foes gone, the Normandian losses were quickly avenged. One by one the remaining defenders were cut down, and then the way was cleared for Sire Ross and Sire Dioser to order their men into a fast gallop and rush across the hill's summit, past the rows of buckskin leather tents, and down a stretch of grass, which lay before the base of the mountains, where several large caverns peered out like toothless maws.

Again Ark tried to keep up, but fell behind, slowed by his not too strong mare. When he finally reached the next barricade that blocked the way into the caves, the men had been already scaling the cordon. This time Ark did not stay behind. Instead under a threat from the enemy's bows, along with some forty men, he leapt toward the wall. The lack of heavy armor and shields proved to be deadly at first for the squires. Before they could even get over the barrier, several of them fell. Ark passed a number of bodies of his comrades—he did not know how many—chasing after Rob and Minia, who despite their orders had also refused to stay idle. Once at the wall everyone climbed. Ark climbed too. As he tried to pull himself up, he realized that he was tired; a prolonged sprint had exhausted him. Yet he refused to give up. Gathering all his strength he pushed himself over the edge and slid onto the stone floor of the cavern.

At first Ark could only see shapes, moving sporadically in front of him. Then as he adjusted to the dim light, he depicted details of the place and the combat that engulfed it. Unlike the outside camp there were fewer defenders. Most of them did not even look like fighters; they looked like—monks or scribes. "Alavantars," Ark thought to himself. "They have to be." Immediately he remembered Sire Jim's assignment—to catch the followers of the wicked sect alive. And so he rose slowly up, searching for Sire Ross, or any other lord, still not too sure whom he had to find. But no matter where he looked, he could not see a single knight. Surprised he looked back and then realized that despite the progress that his fellow squires had made inside the caves, the barricade that blocked the path was still intact and held off all of the lords and many more soldiers. For a moment Ark thought about what to do next, but quickly recalling his poor fighting performance at the first camp, he ran to the cordon and grabbed one of a pushcarts, which lay upside down, supporting several long longs. Yanking it with full force, Ark ripped the boarded side from the base of the hurdle and fell back. The logs at the top did not move at first, but then trembled and rolled down, almost crushing him beneath.

When the clatter stopped and Ark opened his eyes, he could see that his effort produced a gap in the wall, enough for two men to walk abreast, and through which the knights were already passing quickly. Ark called to them, trying to remind them about his orders, but nobody listened. The lords moved forth quickly; their battle cries resonated through stone passages and echoed off the rocks deep in the caves. All Ark could do then was run after them.

The chasing proved even more tiresome than the dash toward the caves. Ark lost his breath and slowed down, eventually halting to rest a little. As he did, he continued to watch as his fellow countrymen battled the defenders, those few who were still alive. Again Ark could notice how different the people inside the caves were from those who manned the outer camps. Their figures were often thin and had no armor to protect them. The weapons were long daggers and metal staffs, with which they tried to keep the angry soldiers away from them, praying for their lives. However, their efforts were pitiful, and before long their resistance was crushed, bringing more cheers from the coming soldiery. Ark thought he would be glad too, but he was not. As the last of the Alavantars died or fled deeper into the caves, Ark realized that somehow the Duke's orders were ignored. With most of the upper sections of the caves cleansed, there were no prisoners to take back outside. Only corpses covered the stone floor, with no one to tell their names or purpose for being in those caves. Ark sighed loudly and sat down on top of a hollow crate, breathing heavy, sweat dripping from him. The victory belonged to Normandia, but was this the sort of victory they needed? The question remained unanswered.

Chapter 53

SIRE ROSS stood by the half-broken wall, helm in hands, his gray-haired head drenched with sweat. Wiping out wet sticky lines from his face, he observed the carnage, slowly shaking his head as he turned.

"Listen up. That was good work. Now we need to press on." The lord encouraged his men. "We must catch their leaders, who I suspect are hiding in one of those tunnels." The knight pointed toward the belly of the cave, lit only by a single row of torches affixed to the wall.

"My fellow noblemen of Bois…" He looked to the remaining lords. "We well split our company so we can start the search. Sire Muro, take several of your men and count our losses, check the place for wounded, and send word to the Duke, telling him that we have the caves." The other knight replied something inside his helm and went outside, escorted by a dozen or so squires.

"Since only three of us know anything about the Alavantars, we will divide our strengths in three. Each group will take on a tunnel and sweep it. We will start at this level and move down. Make sure you inspect every room carefully, and for the Spirit's sake, watch out for any traps."

With those words Sire Ross assigned the men to the different groups, and assuming command over one of them, led them into the nearest dark sleeve, taking Ark along with him. Rob went to another tunnel, following a young lord from the south of Bois, Sire Higus, and Minia left with a dark-haired noble by the name Sire Guils, accompanied by eight of the other squires.

The trip to the underworld, which many of the Normandian folks considered to be cursed, was grim. For three long hours Minia's group went from one passage to another, always turning, always scaling stairs. Throughout their advance, the discoveries were few. Except for some open crates and broken jars of wine, the underground chambers were empty or collapsed, and none showed any signs of human presence. After clearing another long hall of dark gray stone, the group descended to the next level, filled with already familiar damp air. Following the fires of the first torches, Minia tried to guess how far deep they had gone, but it was no use. Nobody knew that. The tunnels that lay beyond the Land's Edge were as mysterious a place as the mountains themselves. Constructed thousands of years ago, the web of catacombs was long forgotten by the living. Many were afraid of them, and only very few ever dared to explore them, often disappearing forever amidst the darkness of the stones. Indeed, being inside those ancient corridors gave Minia an uneasy feeling, a mixture of fear and excitement. On one hand he wanted to get out into the open again, but at the same time he wished to see more of the underworld.

Concentrating solely on the path, laid out with many smaller rocks glued together with some grayish milky substance, Minia's group came to another wide spiral staircase and at the end of it, entered a long tunnel, which swerved like a snake into the blackening darkness. In the distance Minia could see rows of low entryways, each blocked by a small round door made of some rough metal, and further away portions of a collapsed wall. After studying the layout of the corridor carefully, Sire Guils gave orders to check the rooms. But just as on the levels above, all they could find were silence and stone.

Soon they examined the last of the rooms and turned back, heading for the stairs. Minia walked last, dragging his tired feet a little, feeling the effects of his wounds. The pain in his shoulder had returned, and made him stop at times to catch his breath and gather strength. A moment of rest gave some relief, but not for long, as every new step made him feel the ache. He did so for a while, but by the time he reached the middle of the tunnel, the pain became unbearable. Suddenly he felt dizzy and stumbled, falling to the ground, facedown. The fall brought him back, and after lying still for a moment he lifted his armored torso off the floor. By then the others were way ahead, but seeing Minia had disappeared, they turned around and walked back to the place where Minia was sitting, his back leaning against the cold wet rocks. The squire refused to believe that he was tired and weak, but more than that, he hated to let the others see him like that. So taking a deep breath, he gathered all his strength and pushed himself off the wall. For a moment his body swayed back and forth, but he kept his balance, and holding on to a door, focused his eyes.

Concentrating on the thin light from the small lantern in his hand, Minia was about to start walking again, when he noticed something odd about a reflection his lantern cast on the wall. Straining his eyes, he then realized that it was not the reflection that was strange, but the wall itself. The way it took the light was abnormal. It looked as if the wall, which was wet from dripping water, did not glow like the rest of the tunnel. Instead it consumed the light.

He made a step toward it just as the others arrived yelling questions. But instead of answering them, Minia just pointed at his find.

Sire Guils was first to take notice of the squire's discovery. He quickly approached the wall and studied its hard surface, tracing the rocky lines with his fingers. While he did so, everyone else watched. After inspecting the wall some more, the lord called in three squires, and together they shoved their shoulders against the rock. At first the stone did not move, but when three more men joined in, something jolted inside the wall. Suddenly a cracking sound came from behind the rock and a portion of it moved inward, revealing an entrance into a hidden passage. Narrow and dark the corridor ran up the low stairs, counting many steps, which stretched for several hundred feet and led to a set of doors made of solid iron plates. Through a thin gap between the slits a tiny yellow streak was visible in the dark—and some moving shadows. Someone or something was inside. Sire Guils' orders were brief. The group quickly crossed the hallway and took positions by the door.

The door might have been locked. It might have been barred shut. It all might have been, but the Normandians tried anyway. As quiet as possible the squires grabbed the large metal rings, and after counting to three, yanked them hard, several men to each side. To everyone's surprise the lock broke easily, and the doors swung outwards. A bright light came through the slit, and Sire Guils rushed through the opening, keeping his battle yells to himself. The rest followed, Minia being the last to enter.

As soon as the Normandians were inside, they halted, startled by a strange scene. Before them stood a dozen hooded figures, forming a wide circle in the middle of a large triangular room, its floor laid with long marble plates of black. Despite the intrusion, the strangers did not even glance at the intruders. They remained focused, unconcerned with events around them. Then Minia heard a low hum. At first he thought it was the wind, but soon realized it came from the hooded figures. They were chanting. The humming noise lasted for some time, then abruptly stopped when Sire Guils raised his voice.

"Hey, you there," the lord yelled loudly. "What in the world is going on here?"

The strangers did not answer. The lord asked again, and again there was silence. The knight shook his head. "Suit yourselves. You are all under arrest—so are the orders of the Duke of Bois and our King Philip the First. Give yourselves up willingly and you will not be hurt. Resist and you will be put down like the others."

Still there was no response, and so the knight gave orders to start moving again. Walking cautiously along the clean polished walls, the Normandians surrounded the strangers, who continued to ignore their presence. Then for a while everyone stood still, until a squire took a step toward the center and tried to grab one of the men by the sleeve. Before the young soldier's fingers could even touch the other, everything changed. In an instance the hooded shapes dispersed around the room and long thin blades appeared in their hands.

The alert sounded too late. The first two squires had already fallen to the ground, blood streaming from their necks. Several more men dropped down just a moment later, all Normandians. The rest jumped back, retreating toward the door. As the squires stumbled, trying to form their defenses, Sire Guils decided to take on a challenge. Probably inspired by his oath of chivalry he walked forth and attacked the closest of the enemies. But his armored body proved too heavy and too slow for fast strikes from the opponents. Every time the lord swung his weapon, his armored plates received a dozen blows. If it was not for the excellent marksmanship of the Bonvillian blacksmiths, Sire Guils would not have lived through the first few attacks.

Seeing his commander overwhelmed by the enemies, Minia forgot about his fatigue. He lifted his sword up and charged, but his strike fell short. The foe was just too quick, and Minia had to retreat to start over. The man dodged the next blow too and then took charge himself, cutting Minia's hand just below the wrist. It was a scratch, but it hurt, and Minia jerked back. By then the other enemies were on the offensive. Quickly Minia moved left, then right, then forward. All the time he tried to get closer to Sire Guils, who was giving up slowly to the constant blows from the enemies' daggers. But every time Minia made a step toward the knight, he was pushed back. Meanwhile, to Minia's right another squire fell prey to a sneaky strike, and then the knight too finally dropped to his knee. Immediately three daggers pierced through his metal joints. The lord cried out in pain, rose back to his feet, but quickly stumbled and crashed to the ground. He did not move again.

The Normandians were losing the fight. Out of ten men who wandered into the hidden room, only four remained, all young squires, green lads of fifteen, and Minia, wounded and tired. The enemy lost only one man, and even he was not dead. With the odds against them, Minia knew well that there was little chance. They could not retreat and they could not attack. Defense was all that was left. The four remaining men huddled closer together and formed a half circle, watching the enemy moving around them. Their own heavy breathing was deafening, and all they could see was the enemy in front.

Minia was so focused that he did not notice that the passage behind him lit up, and many shadows appeared in a distance. He also did not notice the clatter of metal, and files of his fellow countrymen streaming past the secret door. Minia only saw the enemy retreating. He could not understand why, not until he saw several of the Duke's men appear by his side. A feeling of relief came over Minia. He lowered his weapon and stepped away from the entrance, allowing the others—soldiers, squires, and knights—to get inside. Much of Normandian reinforcement took position around the enemy, but did not attack, and only pushed the black robes toward the far wall, cutting off their way of escape. It seemed that the marble chamber could not hold any more men, but more soldiers came; then came the Duke himself, escorted by his guards, Sire Jim and Sire Zuros. At last Minia gave out a sigh and leaned on the rock. His eyes closed, and he thanked the Spirit for saving his life once again.

"Hey lad, are you all right?" Minia heard a low voice, addressing him. He looked up. An unshaved soldier towered over him. The man's once white vest was covered in dirt, and his chain mail was stained with blood. Minia stared at the soldier, blinking. The man smiled, then patted the squire on the shoulder and added, "You did good, lad."

Minia nodded in reply and let himself be lifted by the arms.

At the other end of the hall the hooded men were unwilling to give up. They stood, pressed against the wall and stared from underneath their clothed covers. The Duke looked back at them, his eyes fixed and calm. He studied the enemies vigilantly, then lifted his sword and spoke. His tone was of a victor, earned rightfully so.

"I am the Duke of Bois, the rightful ruler of the province and the honorable sworn knight of King Philip the First. We are here to place you all under arrest. As you can see there is no reason to be stupid. You cannot win. So I suggest you spare us the time and lay down your weapons. Be advised though that any false move and you will be dead before you know it."

This time the enemy answered. One of them, a taller figure, dressed in a particularly black robe, replied calmly. His face was shielded from the light, but his voice was clear. He spoke the Northern tongue, but his accent was a thick one.

"You—fools!" the man exclaimed. "How dare you break into our sacred place of worship? How dare you interrupt our link with the master?" The man threw off his hood and exposed his face, thin, bony, but not old. His short dark hair was shaved, and only a trace of it was left to form a thin rim, a circle just over his forehead. There was something very evil about him. It was something about his gaze; his eyes were completely white, or so it seemed to Minia, who had managed to make his way up front.

"Do you even know what you are dealing with?" the man continued. "You are challenging the Master of the Old, himself. And do you know what he does with those who stand in his way? Oh. You cannot even imagine what he will do to you, stupid, simple creatures. You think you have won. Fools. You can lie to yourselves, but beware. Your punishment is already set, and the time will come when you must answer for your acts, for your unworthiness."

The man fell into a crazy laughter. He threw back his head and chuckled. "Yes, yes, I see it now. All of you fools—on the stakes, pleading to die fast. But no…there will be no mercy. You will get what you deserve, no exceptions."

Another burst of laughter accompanied his words. "Not even you, a highborn ruler of Bois. For you we have a special treat, a death unworthy of your kind. Yes, yes. I know it, I have seen it in my visions. You will die a slow, pitiful death, cast away, broken and alone, isolated in a dark cell with you and your wicked mind as your only companion."

"I do not care for your hollow threats, worm," replied the Duke firmly. "You foul thoughts are yours to ponder, and your predictions do not interest me. I am here to judge you for what you have done to my land, for all those innocent lives you have taken, for all the sorrow you have seeded in my kingdom. Surrender, answer as a man, and repent; maybe then your death will be a quick one."

"Mindless old brat, so poised in your false beliefs. Repent, you say. Ha! I will repent for my mistakes, but not to you or your false kings. And as for those you say we have killed…they were the enemy, and we are at war, so consider them fallen soldiers,…huh, consider them whatever you like, but know this, killing us will not save your little kingdom. This is just the beginning."

"Enough of your mumbling, fly. You are finished here. Alavantars are finished, and we are done talking."

"Alavantars cannot be finished until our master wishes so. But you are right in one thing. We have no more business with you. We are done talking."

The man turned around, yelled something in an unknown tongue, raised his two hands, laughing madly. The other hooded men did the same. They threw back their hoods, and resumed chatting. Their mumbling turned into singing, then cheering, and then shouting. Instinctively the Normandians moved back. Even the knights, Sire Jim, and others took a step toward the door. Only the Duke remained, his face unchallenged, his right hand on his long sword.

The strange tune continued to ring inside the room until all of the Alavantars stopped and lifted their knifes. The soldiers lowered their weapons, expecting an attack. But the hooded men did not attack. The strangers then spun around several times, waving from left to right, yelled another cheer, and sank the daggers into their own chests. Blood poured down from underneath their robes. For a moment they stood motionless, with daggers in their hearts, and then, as one, dropped to the ground, dead, killed by their own will. Those who witnessed the odd scene stood frozen. The followers were dead, their hideout destroyed, and the threat eliminated. Minia wanted to feel relieved, but he did not. Something was missing, something was not right. He looked at his friends, who had made it into the room. Their faces reflected dark thoughts too. Somehow the three of them knew that the crazy man was right, that it was not over yet, that in truth it was just beginning.

Chapter 54

THE NORMANDIAN victory was complete; the prize—three battered camps and a caved compound, with its many inner chambers and tunnels. From the Duke's army four of the lords lost their lives: Three were young lordlings who fell prey to their inexperience and hotheadedness, and then Sire Guils, who died underground at the hands of the Alavantars. Fifty some soldiers also perished in a fight, and so did forty squires. In all it was a low count, as the causalities were but a fraction of the total number of the attacking force, well over a thousand men. On the other side, a meager seven hundred men—mostly hired swords from across the region—assembled for the defense of their headquarters, were completely destroyed, beaten, and routed by the Duke's well-organized troops. Although half of the combatants fled the field of battle, leaving behind their masters and the offered pay, over three hundred men were dead, their bodies scattered all around the valley.

There were also those who became captives of the campaign. There were a hundred prisoners, almost all outlanders hired from the southern regions, lured by the promise of an easy job and good money. Pushed together at the edge of the cavern, they sat on the ground, guarded watchfully by the Duke's men, whose expressions gave out their readiness to dispose of anyone even remotely wishing to break free. But there were no sign of such attempts. The prisoners had already accepted their defeat, and only hoped for a humane punishment, which had been predetermined even before they lay down their weapons. Those without too bloody a trail were to be sent to the walls as barrier guards, their duties lasting for at least ten years, after which they would be free to leave as they wished. True criminals, those with blood-spattered records, were to be put to the sword or hanged before the upcoming tournaments, and a few others were to be ransomed back to their mercenary companies, bringing some good coin into the provincial treasury. Such were the rules of the kingdom, and everyone knew it, the soldiers, the prisoners, and the lords. The only exceptions were a handful of captives in black robes who had been extracted one by one from the low levels of the catacombs, where the Duke's men continued to search for hideouts and secret chambers.

For those remaining Alavantars who did not die during the attack, there was a different fate. As the only standing proof of the existence of the sect, they had to travel to Bonneville, where the dark cold cells of the Duke's jail awaited them, along with hours of interrogation, torture, and pain—something none of the honorable lords of the kingdom had ever acknowledged, but often used when needed. But, even with all the weight of inquires falling on them, it was obvious they had little to reveal. Young acolytes, scared boys from the western regions of Ethoria, they were but followers, pawns in someone else's game, abandoned by their patrons, left in the midst of the foreign realm, captives of the Duke. They did not know what to do, and only looked at everyone confused and scared, finding some refuge amongst themselves, huddling together, whimpering and trembling.

Away from the prison cages, pacing angrily along the summit of a nearby hill, the Duke and the older lords were holding their counsel. Frustration boiled inside them. The senseless slaughter inside the caves was what made Sire Tem so furious. Alas there was little he could do about it now. Many of his soldiers and lords were too young and inexperienced; most never saw a real fight before, and none had known a true enemy. Their knowledge of battles came from the older comrades who were few in numbers, and rare lessons learned while spending leisure seasons in training, devoting much of their time to drinking and slobbering. Even though they bore arms and displayed the symbols of the noble houses, a lot of them were far from being real soldiers. In truth all they were was a rowdy bunch of poorly trained men, often not too smart and not too skilled. It was only natural that in the heat of the battle, almost all of them fell prey to their enthused fervor, and let their witless weapons chop to pieces everything that stood in their way. While the older lords subdued such blind efforts, many of the younger knights encouraged these actions, and so the slaughter was not stopped in time, and out of some hundred and fifty followers in black robes, only thirty survived the assault.

Standing not too far away from the Duke and Sire Jim, my friends remained quiet, listening to what the High Lord of Bois had to say.

"How can I possibly work with this cattle!" Sire Tem yelled as he turned again and walked away toward the battered remnants of the enemy camp. "What kind of an army is this?" He looked at the other knights, who stood quietly beside him. "I will tell you. It is not an army. It is a mob that happened to wear my colors. *My colors.*"

The Duke stopped and took a long deep breath. "This is a disaster. First, those crazy masters of the north cut their own throats, and then I find out that most of their followers are dead too. Only they did not kill themselves. Those witless soldiers of yours slaughtered them." The Duke shifted his gaze to a group of young knights. "And you, the noble warriors of Normandia, tell me, how did it all happen? These are your men. You have recruited them, trained them, and brought them here. What does it say about you? I am asking you."

The Duke's question remained unanswered. The High Lord threw his gloves on the ground, mumbling a few not too friendly comments, and headed to his horse. His guards and the captains went after him, leaving the rest of the lords and the squires at the top of the hill.

My friends stayed still too, watching as the Duke galloped away toward the Normandian base camp. The rage of the old knight was vivid. The common men knew well such lord's fury. They had seen it many times before, especially during the lavish tournaments and fairs. Then, throughout the gatherings, amongst the many nobles, every knight wanted to be perfect. When the high-brows did not get their way, or if something went wrong, they always blamed their servants. Poor squires, stable boys, and maids were often beaten and jailed; some even lost their lives, all because their master's helm was not shiny enough, or a warhorse was not ready in time. Sometimes it happened without any reason at all; a flare of lord's anger—nothing more.

But it was different with Sire Tem. His rage was well deserved by his subordinates. His men had failed him, and for that he was sure to receive his penalty from the royal court. Yet that was not what bothered the High Lord of Bois. It was the lack of answers. Just like my friends, the old knight knew very well that destruction of the compound was but a setback for the sect. In no time, the Alavantars would return, set up a new camp, and resume their doings, bringing more terror to the lands. The real threat was not amongst the dead peers of the sect, but someplace else, a place of which the Duke had hoped to learn with the capture of the compound. With most of the Alavantars dead now, such a chance was almost impossible.

Of course there was still hope of uncovering something amongst the enemy's scattered belongings, chests, books, and broken parchments, but that required time. Still, as soon as the battle was over, the Duke ordered a search of the entire stronghold. Almost five hundred men took part in scouting the camp grounds, picking anything that might hold something of any importance. All the finds they stored at the base of the cave, setting several distinguished piles, books and scrolls, war gear, and other equipment. But as the sky dusked there was no end to the hunt. The place was just too big, and the lords had to call their men off for the night, during which each of the knights spent time grill-ing, yelling, and punishing those soldiers who had taken part in the killings. Sure enough, when the morning dawned and it was time to resume the effort, several dozen men did not show up for work. Instead they were seen amongst their former foes, stripped of their colors and weapons, pushed into a separate pen, where they had to wait for their turn to be sent to a castle to stand trial.

Ranks cleansed, the rest of the expedition force continued with their in-spection of the enemy's camps. Soon after midday of the second day, all of the outer grounds were done with, and the effort shifted solely to the caves. The deep intertwined tunnels were no easy task, even for hundreds of men. The many rooms, corners, dens, and hollows were everywhere, and only a fraction of them held anything of any interest. Spending long hours underground, as-sisted only by the light of lanterns and torches that often burned out too quickly, the soldiers and squires worked through each day. When a low hum of the war horns sounded from above, the work stopped and everyone retired for the night, only to start again in the morning.

Sometime during the third day of the search though, the Duke received another dispatch from the royal court. It had to be important because Sire Tem left soon after, taking many of his captains with him. In his place he left Sire Zuros, whose strict composure made everyone work even harder. But then the Duke of Puno had to leave too.

Two days after Sire Tem's departure, came another message from the royal capital. That time it instructed that the prisoners be moved to the city of Can-ton, a small town on the border of Chantue province. Since the task was very important, Sire Zuros took charge of the escort, to make sure that none of the remaining followers escaped along the way. Under his watchful eye the cap-tives were pushed into a long column, and by nightfall the lines of tired and dirty men started their march south, accompanied by almost three hundred guards and a score of heavily armed knights.

When Sire Zuros and the prisoners were gone, many other lords also de-cided to depart from the deserted valley and said their farewells to the distant mountains of the Land's Edge. Along with them they took all of their men, which cut the contingent of the remaining expedition force to a meager num-ber of a hundred men, a host of squires, several young lords, and a group of the Duke's own guards, who continued to patrol the grounds day and night, al-ways keeping their eyes on the tall mountains above.

Despite their wish to go home, my friends had to stay and help with the search. Considered to be the utmost experts on the defeated enemy, they barely had a moment to rest. Except for the few brief hours at night, they spent their entire time underground, searching through the rubble of the dark tunnels. All three of them were placed under the command of a very young lordling from Bois, by the name of Adim of Urianos. Although he bore the title of a lord, the lad was but a child of thirteen and his leadership was only a formal one. In reality an old gray-haired soldier, the noble's master-at-arms, Rtem, took charge. While he let the lordling speak the words, everyone knew that it was not the boy, but the elder arm's master who led the search. Such an arrangement was best for everyone, as the young nobleman had no experience to do much either. Minia was not even sure if he had been fighting a few days earlier. He suspected that the youngster had arrived with one of the dispatches to look at the carnage of a real battle that his father, Lord Aster of Urianos, wanted the boy to see so he could get a feel of what it was like to be in battle. But then the orders came to deliver the prisoners to Canton, and so the father lord had to depart, leaving the youngster with Rtem. To occupy his time, Lord Aster gave his son the simple task of searching through the ruins, something that held little danger and some fun. The boy enjoyed the assignment and tried to look very important and very noble-like. It was funny to look at, but such was the arrangement, and no one could object.

On the morning of sixth day of the search, the horns sounded early, and the half-awakened men dawdled back to the tunnels, dragging their weapons and mining tools along with them. Some went more slowly than others, and nobody hurried to resume their duties. Minia went after his friends. He did not even bother to wash his face. It was of no use anyway, as it would get dirty with dust inside the passage. Past the tall heaps of gathered ware he lit his torch and descended several flights.

As before, results were poor, and a growing feeling of boredom was slowly descending on the men. My friends felt jaded too, and at times had to fight a strong desire to leave the darkness of the low corridors and go home to the warm fields of Villone. Many others shared similar wishes, and often, when the tapping of the hammers ceased, one could hear whispers from the soldiers, who complained to each other of their poor fortune.

The lights under the mountains were dim, and the silence was almost perfect in places, spoiled only by random footsteps resonating off the rocks. Minia, Rob, and Ark went through several small chambers. All were empty, not even a patch of straw to look at. There were also no secret doors or levers. The walls were smooth and solid, without even a little crack. It was the same level after level, tunnel after tunnel. Again Minia's mind started to wander off, and only the few comments from Ark and Rob brought him back. It was then, in his state of daze, he heard someone's feet beating a quick stride off the wet hard floor. Minia looked back and unsheathed his weapon. Peering into the darkness he saw a light dwindle in a distance, and then a tall figure appeared in the archway at the top of the stairs. When the man spotted Minia's group he hurried down, taking several steps at once. Halfway down he bent forward and yelled out, as if he were standing tens of feet away.

"Help! Help! Oh Spirits, Help me!" The man dropped several more steps.

"What is it? What happened?" asked Adim's faithful master-at-arms.

"My company, they are all trapped. Please help me get them out."

"Calm down, lad. Tell us what happened first."

"We were all searching through a tunnel several levels up, when a wall collapsed on us. I was at the end of the group so the stones did not get me, but everyone else got caught. I cannot help them alone. I need you to help me get them all out."

"I said, calm down," replied Rtem. "We will help you. Just tell us where to go."

"This way, friends, follow me." The soldier, whose clothes were dirty and ripped, turned and ran back up the stairs. It was a fast dash several floors up, then three or four sharp corners, and a sprint through a long and narrow corridor that got even narrower toward the end. At the last corner the man stopped and pointed to his right. There, amidst the murky reflection of the lanterns Minia spotted a collapsed wall, a stack of boulders and broken beams that blocked the passage ahead.

Rtem immediately started to examine the rubble. Minia joined him. It was a fresh slide; the rocks were still loose and small streams of water ran through their cracks, making the barricade even more unstable. Minia pressed his hands against some rocks and gave them a light push. The stones budged and sank inward. It was a bad sign. Although Minia knew little of the mines and tunnels, he had a feeling that those trapped under a mass of turf and rock were doomed.

"Everyone!" yelled Rtem, done with inspecting another crack in the wall. "Move back. This passage can collapse further. Sire Adim, I suggest you return to the stairs. It is not save to be here, not for you."

Although the boy refused at first, a tough stare from the old soldier made him swallow his objections and take some steps back. Everyone else did too, watching Rtem's focused face, his eyes narrowed on several large gaps at the top corners. The soldier's head then shook a little and he turned to the man who had brought them there.

"This was no accident," he said with a note of suspicion in his voice. "Someone dropped these walls on purpose. This beam," Rtem pointed to a broken thick log that peered out of the rubble. "It was cracked in two places. Those are clean cuts made with an axe or a sword."

"What is going on here?" asked one of the squires, and everyone looked to the stranger. The man did not answer. Instead an odd grin graced his face, a wicked smile that made Minia want to yell. But it was too late. Before he could even say a word the man leapt to one side and picked up a large object that in the dark resembled an axe. He then swung the thing well over his shoulder and dropped it onto a wooden frame that stood in the middle of the corridor, supporting the rock plate, which composed the ceiling of the tunnel. Immediately the timber split, and a loud cracking sound rushed through the pass.

"What are you doing, halfwit?" called Rtem from the back. Two of the squires sprang forward, trying to stop the man. Minia jumped too, though it was of no use. The ceiling shook and a large gap grew fast just over his head. Minia threw himself to one side, away from the collapsing shower of rocks and water. The noise was thunderous; the dust flew every place, covering everything in one large cloud. Minia could hear cries and shouts, he could taste soil on his lips, and his eyes were full of sand. He shielded his face and stumbled some feet back, stepping on something soft. When he turned he saw Sire Adim, crouching by the wall. The boy was crying, his eyes full of fear. Not thinking, Minia hurled himself on top the boy, covering him with his torso, and clenched his jaws. Something hit him in the back, then a sharp pain ran through his legs, but he did not move. He kept himself pressed against the small figure of the young lordling. Somewhere during the chaos Minia managed to take one last look toward the end of the tunnel, where the strange man stood watching them die. The man was yelling some words. The noise was so loud that all he could pick out was "You will never disturb us again." Then everything went black.

Chapter 55

IT WAS in the midst of the night when we went again. We had slept for just a few hours, but my dreams were cut short by Elson's soft voice, which told me it was time to go. The road led us straight south, and by the time the morning came we were traveling down a paved road, laid with brown stones, which took us to the town of Piorio, one of the four major cities in the central part of Lombardia. After traveling several leagues, we came to the low level of the city, packed with many small houses reserved for the poor and less fortunate.

Further away, situated on the side of a large hill, we could see another, better part of the city, separated from the lower section by a tall gray wall and four large gatehouses that blocked the way. After crossing several open market squares already filled with people, we came to one of the gates. A group of guards stood near the pass, watching the crowd and the moat that ran below. Giving us but few disinterested glances, the soldiers quickly browsed through our scarce belongings, and let us into the inner grounds of the upper part of the city, where, disoriented, Ike, Ric, and I trailed after Elson, trying not to loose him in a thick traffic that was everywhere.

In a single file, we went along several streets and alleys, and then arrived to a wide flat square with five large buildings situated around it. Some houses looked like merchants' stores, a few were of a residential kind, and one had a familiar shingle hanging next to an open porch.

"Zimbora Mira? What kind of a name is that?" exclaimed Ike, reading the familiar letters that composed strange words on the sign.

"You are far away from the Northern parts. Most folks around here do not speak the Northern tongue. It is the old Lombardi dialect that you will hear in and around these lands," replied Elson.

"I have never heard of a Lombardi tongue," announced Ike and he shrugged his shoulders.

"I am sure you have not. It is not the Southern Way, yet it is also different form of the Northern Way. There are some words that are similar, but for the most part it is a distinct language, which I happen to know well. So if you want to avoid any problems, while being here, you should do what I tell you."

With those words, Elson sprang from his horse and walked inside the tavern, leaving the steed with Ike.

"Should we follow?" asked Ric once the Southerner was gone.

"No. I say we wait here," I replied and climbed down. But even before my feet touched the ground, a small girl of twelve or eleven ran out of the inn and, almost hitting me with her head, grabbed the straps to Elson's horse. Ike yanked the straps back, dragging the girl with them.

"What are you doing, lady?" he cried loudly.

"*Simura bila ma, zappa!*" the girl yelled back, also unwilling to give up. She looked angry, and her puffy cheeks, pricked with freckles, turned red.

"*Zappa, zappa*, I do not care, it is my friend's horse, and you are not getting it," shouted Ike in return.

"*Nora ma, zappa!*" shouted the youngster again. She lost one of her sandals, and after struggling for another moment, renounced possession of the steed and let it go.

"*Roma, nara,*" she said angrily, picked up her sandal and ran back inside, emerging an instant later in the company of the Southerner. The girl was telling Elson something in the foreign tongue. When she was done, he gave her a copper coin and walked up to us.

"What kind of a country is that, people just grab others' horses without even flinching," stated Ike, proud of himself. The Southerner smiled even wider.

"And what in the world is *zappa?*" added Ike.

"*Zappa* is 'Sire' in Lombardi. That kid was about to take our horses to the stables." Elson started laughing.

"Fine, *Zappa* or no *Zappa*. If these people spoke the normal language…"

Mumbling, Ike came down from his horse and handed it over to the same young girl, who, still red in the face, appeared from behind Elson. She grabbed the leather straps from my friends and grunting loudly turned to lead the animal around the corner. Ike did not say anything, but rolled his eyes, clearly dissatisfied with the first encounter in the city.

When the matter was resolved we walked into the tavern, which looked just like every other eatery we had been in. Apparently it did not matter where in Ethoria you decided to lodge, all the accommodations were the same. Even the smells of cooking were similar.

"What does *Zimbora Mira* mean?" I asked Elson as we helped ourselves to a table.

"It is easy," answered Elson. "*Zimbora* means 'local' and *Mira* means 'inn.'"

"Oh, it is easy. Now I know two words in Lombardi. Who knows, by the end of the trip, I may be able to speak a foreign tongue. Our sage in Villone will be proud." I smiled and sat down, passing my glass to Ike, who was already pouring warm ale of a dark brown color.

After we were done eating, we went to our room. It was a large chamber of a square shape with four beds, some chairs, and a kiln dressed like a fireplace, which hosted a sizable pile of burring logs that radiated a soothing warmth all across the floor. Tired, we quickly put out the few candles that were scattered around the room and went to bed. Soon all were asleep, but me. After staying in bed for a while, I got up and headed for the door. I did not know why, but something drew me to it. With my clothes on, I slipped past my sleeping companions and opened the door. But instead of the dim corridor, I found myself swathed in a bright white light, which filled the space around me. It was the same light that came to me in my dreams before. It was another vision.

Chapter 56

"MISHUK," THE familiar voice called my name. "Mishuk. It is me, A'tie."

It was the A'al woman again. A feeling of relief came quickly. I stepped into the void and rushing through the tunnel of whiteness, flew with lightning speed. My head was spinning, and I had to close my eyes to keep my focus intact. When I opened them, I was inside the green hall, facing the memorable A'al. The same chair sprang out of the floor, and I sat down. A'tie was as beautiful as ever, with the same warming smile, gracing her slender face.

"We meet again, my young warrior," she started softly. There was something about her voice that relaxed me. Maybe it was the tone, which was so gentle and so pleasing to my ears.

"I have summoned you because your journey is about to take a new turn. You have been true to your quest so far, despite all the obstacles that have come rushing onto you. But this is far from over. There is much more to be done." A'tie raised her hand and made a circular motion, producing a bluish sphere that floated in midair.

"Watch…and remember what you see," she said. The sphere started to move up and down, then the color changed from blue to white and suddenly a clear picture appeared within its circumference.

There was the face of man, someone very familiar, someone I had met before. I looked harder and recognized Gapo, the first protector of the Erbeis estate. He sat in a chair, behind a large table filled with food and drink. Next to him stood a man whose face was vague and I could only make out his large frame, covered by a thick dark black cloak. The two were talking. There was no sound at first, but then the voices became vivid. The sphere grew larger, so I could no longer see A'tie, nor could I see the green hall. Instead I was in the room, standing next to Gapo, listening carefully to what the two were talking about.

"How did you know it was them?" asked the stranger.

"At first I did not recognize them, master. Although I have received your descriptions, the dispatch spoke of a company of seven, not four. But when I learned that they were from Normandia, and that one of them went by the name of Mishuk, I immediately realized they were the ones described in your message, and sent out a word to you. If it were not for the invasion, I would have had them here for your arrival. But they escaped. It was that damn young count who helped them—oh, and the Southerner too."

"A Southerner, you say?"

"Yes, a mercenary from Azoros. He came with them too."

"Are you sure he was from Azoros?"

"Pretty much so. He looked like a cutthroat."

"And what about the boys?"

"There were three squires, all young lads. I did not get all their names, but the leader called himself Mishuk."

"Mishuk. Huh. Yes, it is them. The squires from Bois. They have already caused me a great deal of trouble, ever since they started on their stupid quest."

"A quest, my master? You have not told me about a quest. Does it concern us?"

"Oh yes, it does. Those young bloods have uncovered more about our plans than anybody else has in twenty years."

"Are they that smart?" asked Gapo.

"No. They are not smart. I sense that someone is helping them, someone very powerful. Besides, too many of our associates in Normandia have gotten too careless. They thought if nobody was asking questions about them, they were safe. Well, that proved to be wrong. Those youngsters plowed through our entire structure in just a few weeks."

"So is it true then, what people are saying…that the Northern Chapter has fallen."

"I am afraid it is so. That part of us has ceased to exist, raided by the Normandian knights who, by the way, got their insight from those squires you have failed to secure for me."

"I apologize for such a misstep, but that sneaky lordling outstripped me. Who knew those squires actually saved him from the men whom I had hired to dispose of that noisy youngster? Before I could get to their miserable little souls, he warned them and helped them escape. But he will pay for it."

"Do not be so harsh on yourselves," said the stranger. "You did not have enough to go on. But…next time be more resourceful….We cannot afford to loose another chance like this."

"Yes, Master, yes. I am working on it as we speak. I have labeled them as spies, responsible for the attack on Lombardia. Soon every guard within the kingdom will have their description on hand—and hired swords too. They will not be able to stop anywhere without my men waiting for them. They will be caught soon enough, and then I will deliver them to you as you have requested."

"I hope your plan will work, because if it does not, I will have to find somebody else."

"No need to do so, master. I have everything under control. My people are in every city in Lombardia. By the time these few days are over, they will be ours."

Abruptly the image started to shrink, and then transformed back into the sphere, quickly vanishing in one simple flash. I was in the presence of A'tie again.

"Do you know any of these people?" she asked me after a short pause.

"The bold one, his name is Gapo, he is the first protector with the estate of Erbeis."

"So you know him. It is good, because he is one with the enemy. Beware of him. For he is a spider and his web is a sticky one."

"How can I avoid him?"

"Follow your instinct and trust your companions, they will not betray you. As for the other one, he is yet the trickiest of your foes. He is trusted by others and has many friends. Yet, I do not know who he is, or where he comes from. It is a mystery to me, and for that I fear him greatly. One thing I know though— you must reach Azoros before he finds you. Be swift and be stealthy, time is running out for all of us."

A'tie lowered her head a little and added, "Alas, this all the time we have for now. Still, as before, I can grant you one question. Do you know what you want to ask this time?"

"Those two, they talked about the Northern Chapter being destroyed...All I saw was true then, was it not?...Then my friends, Minia, Ark, and Rob..."

"Yes, the Northern Chapter of our enemies has been destroyed, but it is just a minor setback for the Alavantars. And of your friends..."

"Are they all right? I saw them in trouble, someone tried to bury them alive..." I yelled out, but the vision blurred and I woke up a moment later, lying in bed surrounded by my companions who were sound asleep, unaware of the obstacles that had been mounting with the speed of a gusting wind.

Chapter 57

"GAPO? THAT mutt. I knew he was fishy," called Ike from across the table. "Frankly, it does not surprise me he works for the Alavantars."

Ike took a couple of sips from a wooden mug, and asked, "So how do we get to Azoros without risking being caught?"

"We stay low and do not attract any attention," said Elson. "If the protector is looking for us, he will have his men everywhere. It is our luck we have made it as far as Piorio without any complications. Let's hope that it remains so, but we need to hurry. Word travels fast in Lombardia. Before you know it, every mercenary band in the region will be seeking our company."

"That is right. We should get ready today, buy as many provisions as possible, and leave by nightfall, keeping off the main roads until we reach the border," I agreed and started to check the coins in my purse, hoping that we had enough money for a sizable refill of food and gear.

"How sure are you about those visions?" asked Elson, while I was preoccupied with counting the coppers. "I do not want to be rude, but it is all very new to me, the visions, the A'als, magic…"

"Well, I have had these dreams for a while now, and they have not failed me so far. As for the A'al, she has appeared to me many times before. Every time she warned me about things that seemed odd, but they all came true. Her warnings saved our lives, you know. As a matter of fact, she was the one who told us about Sire Matt and his treachery."

That was all true, yet there was one thing I did not mention to my friends. I did not tell them about Ark, Rob, or Minia, nor did I say anything about the falling of the Northern Chapter. It was something I was not ready to reveal. Not yet.

We spent the remainder of the morning and the rest of the day preparing for our trip. At some of the local shops we got more supplies. The stable boys washed and fed our horses, and we fixed our gear. Only by the end of the

433

afternoon did we managed to have everything ready and after settling all the accounts with the owner, set out toward the front gates of the city, cautious of any unusual attention toward our company. Fortunately nobody cared about us too much, and we passed quickly through the upper section of the city and to the gatehouse at the eastern part of the wall. While getting there was easy, leaving Piorio was not. By the order of the chief guardsman, all four city gates had to be closed at sunset; so everyone, who wanted to leave afterwards had to wait until the next morning. Although, when we got to the doors, the sun was still up, the guards were already lowering the heavy iron grate, blocking our way out. We tried to pass anyway, but the soldiers refused to allow it. It took Elson much talking and a few silvers to change the guards' minds. But in the end, with coins changing hands, we were out of the inner city and into the poor districts that sprang around the outer walls, with no more guards to give us trouble.

Keeping a good pace, we had gone some leagues before dusk finally caught up with us. After the recent warning, we felt it was safest to travel at night again, at least for a couple of days. As before, Elson led our company, always along less traveled paths, away from more crowded routes further west. Soon the first stars peered above and guided us to a crossing, where we turned south and, traversing through a long wide field, headed toward the Great White River, which ran from the ruins of Magnicia, down the eastern parts of Lombardia, and then across to the coast of the Seven Seas.

All night we stayed on our course, and when the first light of day rose over the horizon, we found a perfect spot for our camp, a small clearing just at the edge of the forest, with a tiny pool of clear water nearby. There we stayed for the day, keeping a sharp lookout, splitting in pairs to carry out the watch. But there was no sign of pursuit, just some noises of the awakening forest and the prolonged squeaking of restless insects. During that time, we slept and talked and slept some more, hidden in the foliage that surrounded us. But when the twilight returned we immediately set out, riding further away from the main trade routes and closer to the Great Forest of Ethoria.

Occasional glimpses of distant villages, and sightings of faraway towns went by; their outlines marked by many small yellow dots, giving us only a vague smear of the surrounding landscape. It continued so for three more nights. But on the fourth night, we came to an impediment that we could not avoid. It was the Great White River, or Grima Blako Sursa as the Southern Lombardians called it. Being almost as big as the Bound, running from the Grom Bay of the Blue Sea to the brink of the Great Forest, it was as wide as a narrow sea in the south and as deep as the waters of the Abyss, or so people said. Those, who wished to cross the mighty stream had to spend at least a day on the water—two, if the weather was bad. Although for regular travelers the river did not give any reason for concern, to us it presented a serious problem, since all of the nearby crossings were located within the limits of towns, which we were trying so desperately to avoid. To go to any of those large parishes meant too much risk; so somehow we had to find another way to get across.

Jumping off our horses, Ike, Ric, and I walked up to the edge of the abrupt bank and stared into the blackness that enveloped calm waters several cubits below. Meanwhile, Elson unrolled a small leather map and making a humming noise, studied it carefully. Then he hid it back under his vest and uttered, "There is a village called Luks several leagues upstream. If we hurry we will be able to get there just in time for everyone to get out of bed."

"Do you think it will be safe there? If the visions tell the truth, there might be people looking for us too," I noted.

"I think we will be fine. Even if Gapo has already mounted a pursuit for us, we still have a good day to outrun his men," Elson rebutted.

"What if he has sent dispatches ahead of us?" asked Ike as he climbed back up into the saddle.

Elson smiled. "Any message has to be delivered, then it has to be read and acted upon. It all takes time. We left before Gapo could do anything. All the dispatches he has been able to send out are still on their way. I am sure that some of the notes have already reached the bigger cities. But the small places are still free of the protector's grasp."

The Southerner turned his horse and started off in the eastern direction. "Let's get going, or we will have to worry about Gapo after all," he added and galloped forth.

With the first rays of the rising sun lighting up the route, we followed the stony bank all the way to a host of wooden houses surrounding long docks, which harbored several small fishing boats.

"There is no ferry here," exclaimed Ike, once we were at the piers.

"Who said we would take a ferry? Wait here, let me see what I can do." The Southerner dismounted and hurried back into the village, which consisted of some open yards, rows of huts with straw roofs, and a few disinterested fishermen, who were already up and busy moving loads of fresh fish from long wheeled carts and into large wooden boxes. Almost at the center, Elson stopped and knocked on a door, which opened quickly. A man appeared on the steps, half-naked and sleepy. The two talked for a while, then the man nodded and followed Elson back to us. At the docks we waited for them to come and once they did, listened to their conversation.

"So, Captain Rex, how much?" I heard Elson say.

"Ten silvers," replied the chubby fellow and he rubbed his floppy cheeks.

"That is absurd. There is no way I will give you that much. You better name a different price or I will find someone else to take us across."

"Huh, maybe eight will satisfy you, outlander?" asked the portly man.

"Still too much. I bet you one of those fishermen will give me a better deal without thinking twice about it," insisted Elson. He pushed a hard bargain, but it seemed he knew exactly what he was doing.

The man sighed and scratched his forearm.

"Six silvers, and that is my last offer," he stated firmly. He kept a straight face, but his eyes were running from side to side, occasionally halting to look at the Southerner's belt that held a sizable coin bag.

"I tell you what...." Elson sighed as if tired of talking. "It is better if I name the price. I will give you four silvers for us and three coopers for each of the horses. You can take it or leave it. Frankly I do not care."

The man's forehead frowned as he debated weather the deal was worth taking. Then he looked at Elson, and at his palms, which he opened and closed several times. His lips moved and he replied, "It is robbery, you know. But with business so dreadful lately, I will take your offer."

The man waved his hands and walked away, heading toward a group of sailors who had appeared at another pier and watched the conversation from a distance.

"Can we trust him?" I asked, when the man was far enough away.

"You can trust no one, lad. But we have little choice. This man is a local trader from across the river. Two days ago he brought a load and now he has to go back. Only there are no goods to transport across, not these days, with all the supplies moving north because of the war. And these guys hate to ride empty-handed."

"I guess he really did not have any luck with customers if he agreed to take us on board," Ike joked and rocked on one of the boards that got loose from the side of the pier. By then the captain had returned and told us to take our mounts onto his ship, which was a bigger boat with a large open deck, a single mast mounted right in the center, and a two-storied cabin in the back, that probably served as sleeping quarters for the crew. The crew consisted of three men—a ten year old boy with a shaved head, an old rugged man with long gray mustaches, and a middle-aged fellow whose eyes told that he was too fond of heavy spice wine, a strong brew made of hard grain and sugar.

After the money changed hands, we were allowed on board. While the horses were left on the deck, our company went downstairs through the open hatch and inside a roomy storage place, which was completely empty and damp. At first I thought the place was designated for us, but luckily we did not stop there. The youngster took us further toward the back where we came through a narrow doorway, and emerged at the entrance to a small room that held six bunk beds attached permanently to the wall, and a dresser laced to the floor with several thick leather belts.

"Your room," announced the boy. "The bedsheets and the pillows are in the dresser. I will bring the candles once we set sail. Dinner is served at nine. Until then you are free to do whatever you want, just keep the deck hatch closed at all times. We cannot have any water in the storage room; it ruins the wood. Oh one last thing....My name is Sid. If you need anything I will be in the cabin on the deck."

The boy bowed, holding a small red hat in his hand, and ran off leaving the door open.

After throwing our bags to the floor, we inspected the room, and then climbed back up into the fresh air. There we watched our boat leave the pier, and roll through the low waves toward the open waters of the Great White River. When the crew was done with their duties, we chatted with them for a while. For the evening meal, everyone gathered in the upper cabin, picking seats on hard plain benches, which ran alongside of a similarly plain table, filled with even simpler food and drink. It was no dinner at the count's estate, but it suited our needs—some soft bread, pieces of boiled meat, and fresh vegetables composed our dinner, which we devoured in due course. When the food was gone, we were off to the lower deck, where we quickly gave in to the fatigue, hoping to make it to the other side sometime before morning.

Drifting through the night, the boat crossed the river and with the first sunlight, reached the southern bank. I was still in my bed, when a sudden bump almost sent me to the floor. But I managed to grab onto a side of the mattress, holding tight until the boat stopped jerking. When everything calmed, I let go of the rough quilt and slipped into my clothes, a little rugged from the days of traveling. My friends were already gone, so after throwing the bedding into the dresser, I hurried upstairs. Everyone else was already fixing the saddles, getting ready to venture onto the deserted beach.

Brushing off the morning dew that immediately settled on my face, I examined the strip of land before me. Indeed we had reached our destination. Most of the bank was steep, with a large hillside blocking much of the view. Straight ahead though, a small stretch of sand extended a dozen cubits along the waterline and enclosed four small houses, which were linked together by wooden lanes that ran from one hut to another, forming one large square, with a lonely pier sticking out into the river.

While we waited for the boat to dock, the crew was busy securing the lines and fixing the sails. At last a loud creaking noise announced that the ship was docked, and a narrow boarded bridge slammed on to the logged pier. I was the first to exit. My horse was a bit confused by all the commotion and refused to yield to my jerking. But I managed to subdue the beast and after some stalling dragged the bemused animal after me. Ike and Ric were a step behind, while Elson was still on the deck, talking.

"Hey, Mishuk…Do you see anything strange around here?" I heard Ike and turned. He nodded toward the beach, so I looked around. Immediately I saw that there were no people besides us and the crew. The houses, the pier, and the shore were empty. I remembered that at the Bound, and on the other side, there were people running around—fishermen, kids, and farmers. But here I saw no sign of human presence, nor any hint that the parish was a living one. Since it was our goal to avoid much contact with strangers, I should have felt relieved, but I did not. Instead alarm came over me. Startled I glanced at Ike and my brother, who both stood still, also studying the surroundings.

Our alarm grew fast. With one motion of my hand I freed my sword, just in case, and stepped further toward the land. Halfway down I looked back again. There I saw Elson finish his chat with the captain and lead his mount onto the pier. While the Southerner picked his way, the owner of the boat counted the money again, then yelled something to the crew and jumped back onto the deck. The bridge went up and the ropes disappeared overboard. Then came the sound of strained wood, and the boat slowly drifted away.

Following the single sail of the ship moving away from the beach, I turned to Elson. "Did you ask them to drop us off here, in this place?"

The Southerner looked around and frowned. "Yes, I told him to get us to the southern shore away from any big cities. This looks like a decent place, quiet and deserted."

"Does not it look too quiet though? " I pointed at the empty houses at the end of the pier.

The Southerner peered harder, first straight ahead, then to the sides. He did it several times, then turned back to the boat. As he did, his face changed. The smile disappeared, and his eyes focused on the empty buildings. Swiftly he pulled out his two swords and pushed the horse in front of him.

"This does not look good," he said, kneeling down, so he could see from underneath the mount. His gaze was studying the black holes of the open doorways. Suddenly he jumped back up and pushing his steed aside, started running toward the shore. As he dashed across the pier, he gave out a loud yell. "Ambush. Take cover."

The warning startled the rest of us and we halted in confusion. But when a whispering sound of an arrow ripped through the morning air, we knew that we had to follow the Southerner's call. The first few shafts landed astray, splashing water around us. Several more slipped through wide cracks between the boards, and some struck the wet aged wood of the pier.

"Turn your horses. Stay behind them." I heard Elson again from afar. He had already reached the end of the pier, and jumped into the sand vanishing from sight. As another arrow flew by me, I ran after him. I could feel more shafts pass over my head. Ike and Ric also realized what was going on and raised their weapons, spinning their horses around, seeking cover from the menacing shower of metal, which continued. Luckily for them the darts were blown east and crashed into the river several cubits away. Yet, a few lucky shots found their target. One pierced Ric on the forearm, leaving a sizable long bloody streak, and another hit the saddle of Ike's horse, sending the animal into a frenzy. The mount jerked the straps and roared. Ike tried to hold onto the bridle, but his footing slipped, and he fell from the pier, plunging into the cold water, along with his gear and weapons. My brother tried to grab his hand but was too late. My friend had already gone underwater, dragged down by the weight of his load. Back on the berth Ike's horse continued to leap from side to side. Ric made every effort to keep his own horse steady, but it was impossible. After another violent push, Ric's mount broke several boards, and one of its legs got stuck between the planks. Trapped, the frightened animal panicked, throwing its upper body in all directions. Ric could do little else, but jump away to avoid being hit by the furious beast. Like Ike, he dropped down, sending a huge splash after him.

I was the only one left, standing. The rain of wood and metal was getting dangerously close, and in one long dash I cleared the last few cubits, leaping to the base of the pier, hitting the sand with my entire body. As I rolled to my knees I caught a glimpse of something lurking inside one of the houses. Although it was only a blur, I was positive there was someone in there. I yelled to the Southerner, who had reappeared at the other side of the beach, and pointed at the buildings ahead. He nodded and ran forth toward a set of crates, while I head for a fence next to the closest house, making sure to stay out of the clear line of sight. Fortunately the netting that was stretched everywhere served as a decent cover, as occasional arrows hit its metal weaving and bounced back.

During the run, I lost track of the Southerner again. The others were nowhere in sight either, nor did I have any time to look for them. My focus was on a building ahead. Clearing the last cubits in several long leaps I jumped forth and dropped to the ground behind the back wall of the house, which was solid, with no doors or windows. For a while I remained still, just lying there, trying to catch my breath. When my heart stopped beating so fast, I sat down and immediately heard noises coming from the inside. The situation was worse than I thought. There were at least two distinctive voices, and they spoke a dialect that sounded very much like Lombardi.

Keeping quiet, I remained by the wall, listening. But I could not do so for long. Sooner or later the men would realize that I was there, and would do something to get me. I had to do something, and fast. Then, suddenly a bold idea came to me. Resting at the base of the shack lay a large round boulder and next to it were two rotting boards, which hung loose on a couple of rusted nails, with chunks of failed wood scattered on the ground beneath them. Without thinking twice, I put down my sword and picked up the rock, which was heavy and slippery. Still, I managed to pull it over my head, and aiming for the failing wood, dropped it into the wall. Immediately, the sound of cracked timber rang through the sand and someone yelled something inside the house. Only I was not listening. Instead, after snapping back my weapon, I rushed around the corner and through a door-less entryway. It was a little dark within the shack, but my eyes adjusted quickly, and I saw two men standing over the large gap made by the fallen stone. Both held short bows in their hands and on the floor lay several dozen arrows, stashed in three separate piles.

My arrival was a surprise to the strangers, as they were still looking at the hole when my first sword blow reached one of them. The first man was quick to fall down, with a gashing split in his neck. Blood poured violently onto the floor, his limbs twitching uncontrollably. His partner stood frozen. His hesitation was all I needed. In one swift motion I spun around him and threw my blade outwards. The sharp edge struck the foe in the arm and he screamed. It was a light wound, but enough to startle him and give me time to execute the next attack. The strike that followed was a hard one. Leaping forward, I thrust my sword into man's chest, putting all my strength into it. The blade slid through the leather armor easy as a needle, sinking deeper into the man's chest. The foe did not yell. The only sound he made was a soft sigh. Then he slid down to his knees and leaned forward a little, his head dropping down onto his shoulder. He was still clenching his bow. For a moment I expected the enemy to get up again, so natural was his position, but he did not. For him it was over—he was dead.

Victorious, I crawled up to one of the windows and peered cautiously into the clearing. But as soon as my head appeared in the opening, three shots hit the wooden frame, close to my face. I jerked back and fell on the floor, staying there for some time. When I recovered, I slowly got up and crept to the doorway so I could finally take a look at the surroundings.

I peered cautiously, barely sticking my head out of the opening, and spotted Ric and Elson at the other end of the clearing. They were together and hiding behind an overturned fishing boat, pinned down by several archers who hid from my view within one of the houses next door. Several dozen arrows were stuck in the bottom of the rotted planks, and more flew whenever Ric or Elson tried to get a quick glance out. Glad to see the two of them alive, I took a chance and searched for Ike, but my childhood friend was nowhere to be found. I wanted to go back to the pier, but could not—first I had to do something about those other archers. My brother and the Southerner were still crouching behind the boat, pressed hard by the deadly shots.

The hole in the wall that the rock had made served as a perfect way for me to sneak out of the empty house unnoticed and get to the next shack without detection. It was the best plan I had, so picking up an extra sword from one of the slain opponents, I stepped outside and carefully circled around the hut, halting at the corner. Some ten cubits away stood a similar-looking structure, with four small windows and a single open doorway. There was a shadow lurking inside—the enemy who besieged my brother and Elson

For a few moments I looked for signs of movement, and once seeing none in the nearest windows, prepared to rush forth. But as I was about to leave my refuge, I noticed someone crawling toward the same house, taking cover behind larger rocks on the bank. Covered in sand the figure was barely noticeable, but it did not take long for me to see through the sandy disguise. The man was Ike. By the time I realized so, my friend had seen me too, and was giving me quick signs with his hand. Once knowing that I had seen him, he rolled along the rocks several times and disappeared around the far corner. A moment later came the sound of a struggle, but it was brief. I looked back at the windows of the house, but there was no longer any movement. I turned to the spot where Elson and Ric had been hiding; they were gone too. A bit perplexed, I gathered all my courage and leapt across the dune toward the house. At the wall I halted, floor, lay the body of a man. The blood was still oozing from underneath his poorly crafted brown robe, and his face showed fear and pain.

"Just one?" I asked my friend, staring at the body. "I had two in the other house."

"Hey, he was pretty tough…," commented Ike, looking outside. "But all those days we have spent in training at the count's estate seem to have paid off."

I nodded in agreement, and joined him in peering through the wide crack at the bottom of the wall. There were two more buildings on the opposite side, but only one concerned us. In the glare of the sun, between the slits of long-gone windows, more shadows loitered. Some twenty cubits away, still shielded by the boat, Ric and Elson reappeared once more and were free to move. Yet the remaining foes posed a serious threat; their arrows were as deadly as ever, and any awkward move on our part could cost us our lives.

It was Elson who acted first. Leaving his shelter, he came closer to the leftover hut and announced, shouting his words across the clearing, "I think all of your friends are dead. If you give yourselves up, we will not kill you. What do you say? Shall we continue this useless bloodshed?"

At first nobody answered, but then a low deep voice, polluted by a thick Lombardian accent, responded, "How do we know you will keep your word? If we give up now, nothing will stop you from killing us later."

"As far as I am concerned, you only have two choices here," replied Elson. "You can either trust my word and stay alive or you can continue to resist and then you will be dead for sure. It is up to you."

Another pause lasted for some time, and then I saw two bows and some blades soar from the darkness of the windows, and the same voice yelled, "We take your word! We are coming out!"

Two figures appeared in the doorway and slowly stepped outside, holding their hands wide apart to show that they did not conceal any more weapons. The men walked forth and stopped, not far from the Southerner.

"I rely you are a man of your word," began one of the strangers who had a bright bald spot that ate away most of his scalp, leaving only a small patch of hair around his ears. He and his companion wore the familiar plain brown robe and light leather boots, dirty with wet sand and dried-out seaweed. Yet, unlike the other bandits, who lay dead, their clothes did not look cheap. On the contrary, the outfits were made of a superior piece of wool, adorned with lines of choice leather. Instead of ropes, their waists were wrapped with fine belts that held a small bag and a well-crafted sheathe.

"Fear not," said Elson. He walked closer to the men, studying them in-quisitively. In the meantime Ike and I left the crooked shack and, after walking over to the prisoners, picked up their abandoned weapons, throwing them aside, making sure they were out of the strangers' reach.

"What are your names, men?"

"Old sword, Bross, and my brother, Mithy. I do not suppose you want to know the rest of my crew, since they are dead and all."

"No, it is enough. But what I do want to know is the reason you have attacked us," said Elson, now staring straight at the bold fellow.

"What do you think?" replied the man. "A robbery, of course, what else?" He sounded surprised at the question. And his tone suggested that he took offence at Elson's words. The Southerner did not seem to notice it.

"Will you be so kind as to tell us more?" Elson stared at the captives, playing with the hilt of his sword. "I think we deserve that much."

"There is really nothing to tell," answered the prisoner. "That trader you came with, he is the one who had organized the whole thing. It is all very simple; we have done the same so many times before. Usually he would pick up lonesome travelers on the other side and bring them to a deserted beach on this side, where we would do the job. Afterwards he would meet up with us and we split the loot."

"I see, and what do you do with the victims? Kill them?" That time Elson's voice was anything but gentle.

"Oh no. We do not kill no one. Once the poor souls leave the boat we scare them. Several shots from a bow are usually enough to frighten most folks. When people see arrows flying, they get so terrified that they are ready to give us anything we want. Of course there are those who resist, but only until the first wound, and that does not happen often. But I swear we have not killed anyone, not us."

"I find that hard to believe. You must have had some tough fights, have you not?"

"You must understand that those whom the captain brings are rarely of the fighting kind. The captain is very careful about selecting the right victims. Never have we had a real fight—that was until today of course."

"I guess this is your unlucky day," noted Elson sarcastically. His smile was devious, but well deserved.

"If you do not kill anyone, what do you do to the victims after you have robbed them?" I asked.

"After we seize their belongings we blindfold them and take them a few leagues away from the river. The lands here are deserted, so we do not have to worry about anyone trying to bring Lombardian guards to catch us. I am sure some search parties had been sent out through the seasons, but we are usually gone long before that. Besides, we never stage an ambush in one place. That is all we do. We have not hurt anyone. Not physically at least."

The man took another deep breath. "So are you going to take us to the nearest town and claim your reward? I am sure you will get a few silvers for us."

"I would not mind collecting the prize, but lucky for you we are short on time. Of course we cannot just let you go either. So what shall we do?..." The Southerner turned and looked at me. I shrugged my shoulders. Ike and Ric did too. The two prisoners became uneasy. Their faces began to show signs of fear, and their eyes passed amongst our group. It did not seem to bother Elson though. For a while he remained quiet, pacing back and worth before the captives, occasionally pulling his sword a little out of its sheath. At last he stopped and declared, "I think I found a solution. Ric, Ike, tie them up. There should be a rope in my bag somewhere. Mishuk, gather the horses. We should leave as soon as we are done."

The men complied without question. While I hurried to the mounts, which were scattered along the stretch of sand, Ike and Ric threw the ropes over the bandits' hands and legs and tied them hard, so hard that the men jerked from pain.

"Now," the Southerner addressed the prisoners, "since we cannot take you with us; or simply leave you wandering around, we are going to leave you here. Mishuk and Ike, take the younger one, gag him, and throw him inside one of the houses over there. Eric and I will take the bold one. Any questions? Good, let's do it."

Ike and I seized the younger prisoner and carried him inside one of the huts. The poor fellow thought we were going to kill him. He pleaded relentlessly and even cried. Only when we stuck a rag into his mouth did he shut up and just shook his head in despair. Ignoring his weeping, we secured the prisoner to an iron pole inside the house that seemed stable enough and after checking his restraints one more time, walked back outside, where Ric and Elson were already attending to the horse and fixing the saddles, wet and broken during the fight. Luckily all our beasts escaped unharmed and aside from few arrow tips that got stuck in thick leather padding, did not seem too frightened or distressed. Soon everything was ready. Whatever supplies we could salvage from the water, we placed back on the horses, and then set off, leaving the two prisoners behind.

Chapter 58

AWAY FROM the cursed beach our company went. During better times, we would have taken the captured bandits to the nearest military post, but circumstances dictated otherwise. We, ourselves, were on the run, possibly labeled as outlaws, and had to shun local folks and towns. Although the fight drained much of our strength we pressed hard, and some leagues away from the river ventured onto a small but well-traveled lane. The morning mist had finally dispersed and the open view of a yellowish valley stretched before us. It was decided that we would take the trail east to the small parish of Rooks, and then turn back south, heading toward the town of Roval, located near the border with Azoros.

By high noon we arrived at the village, which peered through thick lines of full-grown fruit trees lined up along the roadway. Some folks joined us on our approach. Most went with us, and only a few walked toward us. Veering amongst slow moving carts and wagons, we passed a low-hanging wooden archway and entered the small rural community consisting of a dozen or so houses, plentiful orchards, and a few large barns, where scores of men loaded heavy sacks onto long wheeled trailers.

Our clothes in need of cleaning and our stomachs craving a meal, we decided to stop at a local inn for a little while. After finding its two-storied logged building near the village center, we dismounted at the front door. A group of rowdy youngsters were quick to take our horses to the stables where they were to be fed and washed. And we, a lot more tired now, proceeded into a square dining hall. As it was too early for bigger crowds, the place was empty, but clean. Only two persons stood at the tall counter. One looked like the owner and the other a servant or a cook. Absent of any other patrons, they busied themselves with washing stacks of clay plates, dipping them into a bucket of foamed water, and then wiping them off with long dirty rags. The scene was not appealing at all, and I decided to refrain from eating anything in that place that was not cooked.

Halting at the doors just for a moment, we went to the nearest table and settled around it, stretching our limbs. The owner was quick to visit us. A middle-aged man with patches of gray in his hair, he took our orders and immediately disappeared behind a pair of swinging doors, along with the other fellow. Soon after, the food arrived and we ate it as if we had not had a crumb of bread for days. Meanwhile another servant, a girl of ten, cleaned our capes and for an extra copper polished our boots, already beaten by the lengthy journey. When all the food was gone, a drowsiness came over us. But we could not sleep there, so we had to go. After the girl was done with our gear, we paid the bill and returned to the yard, finding our horses also ready for departure.

Then it was off on the road again; our next stop—the border town of Roval. The trip there was three days through heavily populated lands spotted with many villages, trade posts, and farms. It was both good and bad. For once we did not have to ride alone anymore. But at the same time there was a greater chance someone would recognize us. Of course there was a detour we could have taken, skipping Roval entirely, instead traveling through the western regions of Dvorenia, but that would have added another week to our travels and that we could not afford. So we chose the risk over time.

Luckily, during our trip to Roval nothing happened. During hours of daylight we mingled with a crowd of other travelers, riding past villages and tended fields, and at night we camped in the open, each time settling away from the ever busy lanes, either under cover of thick undergrowth, or in the shrubs of fruit orchards that were so plentiful in those lands. Throughout we kept our mouths shut, and stayed away from any idlers and long caravans that streamed up and down the lanes, carrying everything from hay to people. The others on the road did not bother us much either, nor did the weather. Occasional drizzles were short, and more often the sunshine made us company, turning the air hot and humid.

By the first light of the third morning, our company finally reached the outskirts of Roval. The darkness was long gone and the early morning fog started to thin, letting us see the road, already filled with travelers. Unlike Normandia or the Border Regions where we often traveled days without seeing anyone, the routes of southern Lombardia were always busy. Day and night someone journeyed somewhere, and closer to the town the traffic became denser, soon turning into a continuous torrent of people, carriages, and animals that moved at a very slow pace. A few times we tried to veer off to the side, but found people there too. And what looked like a fast trip to the city gates, quickly turned into a long crawl, lasting twice the time we had hoped to spend.

Only after we had cleared a slum surrounding Roval did the crowd recede a little. We were able to pick up some speed and arrive at the massive outer walls, which stood at least twenty cubits tall, split into many sections by dozens of battle towers that presented travelers with an impressive view of the grand architecture of southern Lombardia, imparted with triangular pillars, oval arches, and long lines of curved statues. From afar I thought Roval to be average in size, as big as Bonneville perhaps, but in reality it was much bigger, even bigger than Pullie. Like many other Ethorian municipalities, the border city was made up of several separate districts. In the very center stood the mighty castle of the local count, Axim Long Horn of Arisi. The tall stone fort was shaped as a large star, five grand towers marking each of its corners, and the sixth—the center keep of the count himself. Around it lay the inner city, interlaced with many streets and packed with hundreds of houses, sometimes so tall their roofs peeked over the outer wall, beyond which stretched the slums, a collection of wooden huts, barracks, and tents clustered together for some leagues out.

Where the road we had taken came to the wall, a large tall archway rose at least ten cubits up the stone barrier and was equipped with four sets of doors, ranging from a simple wooden grate to cast-iron solid doors, which were locked from inside by three large beams, each as thick as ten human hands. At the base of the entrance, dressed in familiar navy blue uniforms, stood a dozen men. Unlike the guards in Piorio and other places, the sentries checked everyone who came through, paying particularly close attention to the carts and wagons. Each new search took time, and as a result, a long line formed, extending for half a league, weaving along the road.

We stood in line too, waiting our turn for hours. The sky had already started to darken, and many fires lit the town and the poor borough below. At last, irritated and tired from sitting in the saddles, we finally came to the first set of doors, where a tall broad soldier blocked our way with his torso, his long sword drawn. Another soldier stood a cubit behind him, and two more a little further away. Since the guard spoke Lombardi, Elson did the talking. Their conversation lasted for some time, then the soldier laughed at something the Southerner said and stepped aside, letting our company through a wide passage and onto a street paved with large stone bricks of a distinctive gray color. Beyond the walls life was as busy as in the poor section. People and wagons packed the lanes and the squares, snaking around the many houses, which started almost at the walls and lined up along the street, sitting on top of each other. A lot of the buildings were slender in appearance—most some ten cubits wide, but tall, at least four stories high, and adorned with numerous small balconies made of thick iron bars of various shapes.

Each of the knots of dwellings ended at a crossing, which usually formed an uneven plaza busy with street performers and small bazaars, where town folks went about their daily lives, bargaining with vendors over every imaginable thing. Aside from being a source of excitement, each square also functioned as a center for different neighborhoods, and so had a unique design with its own distinguishing colors, represented by hosts of banners and ribbons hung everywhere. Such an abundance of color, noise, and movement was spectacular, and did not let me sit still even for a moment.

Taken by the fuss around us, our company crossed more intersections, getting closer to the central castle that grew larger with every step. But almost at its walls, Elson turned right and following a much narrower alley that led us to a large house that looked no different from the rest of the structures on that street. There the Southerner stopped and dismounted.

"We can rest in here," he said abruptly and ran up the low stairs.

"Do you know someone in here?" I asked curiously. The place did not look like an eatery or an inn. It was a simple house, its windows closed, and with no people in sight.

"This is the best place for us to rest, given the circumstances of course," Elson answered, and he knocked several times.

"What is this place exactly?" I insisted, climbing down from my horse. "Is this a tavern?"

"Sort of. For those of us who have chosen to take up the life of a hired sword, the common establishments may not always be the best or the safest places to spend a night. Sometimes our duties demand a much quieter place, where we can gather our thoughts and rest. For such purpose there are places like this."

The Southerner knocked again—three short beats and one long. Some noise came from inside and then door cracked a little. Standing taller than Ric, a man came out and started a quick conversation with the Southerner. The two exchanged handshakes and the host invited us in. As we entered, three more men showed up from around the corner and without saying anything took our horses away. We made a move toward them, but Elson stopped us and motioned to follow him instead, which we did.

Behind the simple door we found an ordinary setting, usual for an average house—two small rooms, some simple furnishings, a small fireplace at the back wall, and the smell of cooking. Off to the side, across the room, a small staircase led up to the second floor, where the sounds of children playing resonated loudly. Puzzled I looked at the Southerner, but before I could ask him anything, the tall man walked up to a towering bookcase at a side wall and pushed something. Right away, the shelves moved with a surprising ease and revealed a small stairwell that ran down several floors, lit by several lanterns. The man said something else to Elson, who nodded and hurried down the steps. We trailed after him.

In contrast to the upper floor, the cellar looked just like a tavern. There was a dining hall with five tables, a counter with barrels of local brew, and a set of doors at the back wall. The place was bright and carried the stuffy scent of herbs, roasting meat, and smoke, which hung over the room in one thick cloud. Some twenty men, not counting the serving staff, sat at the tables. None of them looked anything like the regulars of usual city eateries. Their faces were hard and often scarred, their bodies toned, their weapons numerous, and their armor well made—a clear sign of hired swords. They sat in several groups, and once we came in, studied us wearily. Amongst us, only Elson got a positive reaction from the patrons—some salutations, a few handshakes, and occasional nods.

Unlike, Ric, Ike, and I, the Southerner did not seem to be bothered by the strange company. After sitting us at a faraway table, he went over to the counter and talked to a large fellow who was pouring one mug of ale after another without stopping. We got some brew and a simple meal as well. As the evening grew older, more people arrived, all mercenaries. The noise around us picked up. Some people were shouting, and a few tables were singing, but we kept silent. Frankly I did not feel much like talking. Surrounded by shady characters, most of whom seemed to stare directly at me, I wanted to get out of the dining hall as quickly as possible, away from unwanted attention and the hostility.

"Did we get a room in here?" I asked Elson when a rough-looking girl snatched my plate before I could finish a portion of boiled beef.

"Yeah, it is one floor down, on the left-hand side. I think it is number eight." The Southerner looked at a large key attached to a piece of wood, and flipped it around. "Uh-huh. Eight. Why? Do you think of leaving us? I am disappointed. I thought we would have a night on the town."

"No offence, but this place gives me creeps," I whispered. "Personally I prefer regular inns, with normal people for guests."

"Ah, do not worry. Most of these guys are harmless."

"I am sure they are. It is that I would rather sleep without having my weapon by my pillow," I replied sharply, but then realized that it was exactly what I had been doing ever since my friends and I had become involved with the Alavantars. I shook my head and sighed.

"Hey, do not worry, lad, I do not take any offence. Here…take the key. I will join you later on. There is some unfinished business I have to attend to." Elson threw me the key and smiled. I nodded and walked to the stairs. Ike and Ric hurried to join me. The three of us cleared the few steep steps and walked into a wide hallway, deserted and quiet. Small candles lined up along the right side and gave the place a dim yellowish light. Many closed doors stood along each of the walls, each with a number carved at the top.

"How big is this place?" Ike asked halfway down.

"I have no idea. It looked like a normal house from the outside," I replied, taking a sharp corner and coming to a dead end with three doors. Our room was the one in the middle, with a big number "eight" drawn on it.

"Here we go." I inserted the key. The lock clicked and the door opened. To my surprise the room was clean, well furnished, with plenty of light. Right under a large chandelier was a long polished round table and five padded chairs. A jar of ale, and a plate of apples rested on top. Five beds were placed against the back wall, each with its own tall nightstand and a set of pillows, blankets, and sheets, clean and fresh. At the other end between a set of chests and a wooden rack, used to store weapons and armor, peered a narrow doorway with a cloth curtain instead of the door. It was pulled to a side and showed a portion of a small tin tub and some large buckets.

It did not take long for us to abandon our chain mail, heavy boots, and dirty pants, and substitute clean light white tunics that hung on the side of the beds. The robes were comfortable and soothing, as were the bath and the red wine, which we found in one of the chests. Soon I felt very drowsy and went to bed, falling asleep as soon as my head touched the soft pillow. Yet, to me it was another night of visions and Fore Sight.

Chapter 59

TRANSPORTED INTO the memorable hall of trees, I met with A'tie, who spoke to me yet another warning.

"You are on a verge of a new turn in your destiny, young warrior," she said kindly, once I was seated. Immediately the hall filled up with a soft light, which seemed to stream from everywhere. "When you reach this crossroad, you will have to make a decision, a choice as to which way to go. It is very important you make the right choice, for the fate of Ethoria will depend on it. Unfortunately I cannot prepare you for it. You will have to decide on your own. Yet, before you can do so, there will be perils. A few were crafted by forces even I cannot understand. Some will be hard, others not so, but it is important you pass them all, for if you do not, you will be lost. Think of these obstacles as trials, something that you have to do in order to succeed in your quest. Fortunately, here I can help you, though only with advice.

"The first of these trials will come very soon, well hidden from your eyes. If you overcome it you will not even know you have done so, but should you fail—you will die. More than ever, your enemies will try to weaken you, break your company apart, seeding mistrust and deceptions within your ranks. At times the tales you hear will be the truth, but you should ignore them, as the companions you have now are your closest allies. Without them you will not succeed. Although it may be hard to spot the trickery, I will give you three clues. If you watch out for them, you will live through this trial."

The A'al closed her eyes for a moment, whispering some strange words, as if meditating. I did not understand anything and only watched as she began to move her hands up and down. Her lips did not move, still I could hear her voice clear in my head.

"This is my help to you. Three things you watch for, three things you stay away from—Yellow Cape, Green Fire, and Words of Truth filled with blood.

451

Do not trust those who bring you these things, and do not take them as true, although they may be filled with truth. Because if you do, you will perish along with your friends."

Unexpectedly the sound of A'tie's voice stopped and the images of the hall vanished. The darkness filled my mind. I opened my eyes. The same room in Roval lay before me, only there was something wrong about it. Suddenly I heard someone else speak.

"I hope you do not believe everything she tells you," the stranger's voice sounded across the room. I jumped from my bed; the darkness made objects barely visible. My eyes struggled with the poor light from a single candle that was still burning in the bathroom. On the far side, almost by the door, I saw some movement. Indeed someone was inside, a dark figure of a man, a tall, slim man.

"Who are you?" I yelled out. My sword was in my hand. "Identify yourself." I took a step forward.

"Oh, Do we need to use violence this lovely night?" said the voice. "I am not here to fight, not yet at least. I am just here to deliver a message."

"Answer my question first, and then we will talk," I insisted, peering hard into the dark shadows that became even thicker.

"Put your weapon down, fool. I said I am not here to fight." The voice sounded a bit irritated; the man whispered something and a sharp burning sensation rushed through my arm. Like a snake it wove its way down to my hand and into my blade. Suddenly the hilt of my sword became ice cold. It was so cold that it hurt my fingers. I tried to hold on to it, but the pain was too strong. Screaming, I dropped the weapon to the floor. My hand was red, as if dipped in boiling water. To my surprise once the sword touched the ground, the pain receded and after some rubbing, I could feel my fingers again.

"Now, as you see, we do not need swords to talk. I assume you will be more reasonable from now on."

"I will," I snapped angrily, holding onto my hand.

"Good, then sit down and listen. I do not want to spend too much time in this hole."

I lowered myself onto the side of my bed, staring at the dark man who stood quiet for some time. He did not move, but I could hear his rhythmic breathing clearly.

"As I was saying, I have been asked to convey a message to you." The man went on after the pause. "My employer, who prefers to stay in the shadows for the time being, is very interested in your progress. He has been watching you for some time now, and let me tell you, he is impressed thus far. If you continue with the same zeal he will probably want to meet you in person. Until then though, I will speak for him. This time he wants me to tell you that the A'al woman who visits you so often, is not your friend, though she may say so to the contrary. You should know that she has her own agenda about you and it has nothing to do with your little quests. Do you think that it was your decision to come to Azoros? No, young one. It was the A'al who masterminded your trip half-across Ethoria. She did not do it because she wanted to help you, but because it suited her needs.

"I know what you think—she has not failed me yet, she has saved my lives a few times. And you are right, she did all that, but only because she has a personal interest in keeping you safe and moving. But there will come a time when her plot takes a sharp turn and she will abandon your cause. When she does, you will not find her as friendly as you do right now. My master wants you to know that such a change will come, and will come soon. Be prepared, and do not say that you have not been warned. I suggest you think carefully about my words. It may be a while before I can contact you again.

This is all I have to say for now. Remember your quest has sparked a lot of attention throughout the world. Many are watching, and many more will be. So be careful, and do not trust everyone who claims to be your ally. The world is full of trickery and deceit."

The voice ceased and the silhouette of the man started to fade. I got up and moved forward toward the spot where the dark figure had been sitting. But when I reached the chair, it was empty. There was no one there. I called to the stranger several times, but nobody answered. The room was quiet. Confused, I lit a candle. Its soft glow illuminated the room, but quickly grew brighter, and soon was so bright that it hurt my eyes. Then came a flash and I was blinded. I closed my eyes, and when I opened them again I found myself back in my bed, looking straight at a serving girl who was moving nearby, picking up some of my scattered belongings. When she noticed that I was up she bowed and ran out, closing the door behind her. Alone I lay back and thought of what I had just seen. A strange vision it was, alarming and unsettling. Unable to sleep again, I put on my clothes and walked into the hallway, where Ric and Ike were standing by the stairs, talking to each other. When they spotted my arrival, their conversation stopped and smiles graced their faces.

"You cannot sleep either?" said Ric. I nodded.

"This place just does not feel right," added Ike. "Shall we go upstairs and drink a few?"

The idea sounded good, so the three of us climbed to the next floor, where we found a suitable unoccupied table.

"Did you have another vision?" asked Ike suddenly, when we ordered a round of cold brew.

"How did you know?"

"Come on, I can tell when someone has a nightmare. You were talking and moving and shaking in your sleep."

"You are right, Ike," I agreed. "I saw A'tie again, but that is not all."

My friends' attention was on me. I was telling them of my dream.

"Are you sure those were indeed visions?" asked Ike once I was done.

I thought a bit. "Which one, A'tie or the stranger?"

"The stranger, of course," interjected Ric before Ike could say anything.

"I am not sure. I have never had such visions before. But it felt real, and the pain, the light, the breathing." I rubbed my hand. "It really hurt."

"Did you recognize him?" asked Ike

"No, I could not see his face. He was always in the shadows."

"Huh, very interesting," said Ike. "If he is as real as the A'al, who should we believe then?"

"A'tie," replied Ric thoughtfully. "For now at least. I mean, she has been helping us for a while now. We can't just dismiss that, and she is willing to do so again."

"Yes, but why? Why does she help?" Ike's voice carried a fraction of a doubt. "Do not you find it strange that all of a sudden an A'al sorceress, if there is one, has decided to help three commoners from Villone. And remember when she first appeared."

Ike looked at me.

"It was when we found the Alavantars' tome back at the abandoned monastery," I replied.

"Exactly." Ike leaned back. "But why? Why did not she come earlier, when we were still in Villone or when you first learned about your father's convoy gone astray?"

"She gave us many answers. Remember?" interrupted Ric again. "She said we were to save the world."

"Save the world. Yeah, right," said Ike. "Do you not think they would have found someone else to do such a thing? I mean no offence, but we are just farm kids from a small remote town in Normandia. If we were knights or hired swords, or soldiers, that would have been a different story. But..."

"Ike, you cannot ignore all that has happened to us. Yes, we were nobodies when we first started. But we are the squires now. We have uncovered the

Alavantars, exposed Sire Matt, and now have traveled half across the world, following the orders of the Duke of Bois himself. Does that not count for anything?" I rebutted.

"Think what you want, my friends, but say that advice we got may be worth considering. I do not know if that A'al woman exists, but if she does, we better be careful about entrusting her with our lives. All I am saying is that we should take everything with caution. It will be safer for all of us." Ike rubbed his nose and sneezed as if to prove his point.

"Let's not fight over this, all right? Nobody says that we should ignore the warnings. We will consider them all. In the meantime we have to figure out what we are going to do once we get to Azoros. Do you think we can trust the Southerner?" I looked at Ric and Ike.

"I would," said Ric at once.

"I did not expect any other answer from you!" exclaimed Ike. "You will trust anyone."

"I want to agree with Ric," I insisted after some forethought. "Elson seems like a decent fellow, a good fighter, and a fine storyteller. But let's keep our guards up, just in case. You never know what can happen once we are in Azor."

"I know I will," stated Ike firmly, and as he did, I noticed the Southerner appear at the bottom of the stairs. Soaking wet, he waved at us, and after discussing something with another patron, came over to the table.

"Good Spirit, what has happened to you?" the three of us asked him at once.

"Oh just a little rain. I would not recommend going outside for some hours, it looks like the storm is in for good." He threw his wet cape on the floor near the fire and sat down.

"Did you finish all your dealings?" I asked Elson after he was done ordering some warm stew from a short, blonde serving girl.

"Yes. And now I need some rest. Do not worry, it will not take long. We will be back on the road in no time. I suggest we leave early in the morning, before dawn." The Southerner took off his muddy boots and handed them to another serving girl, who immediately took them downstairs, probably to get cleaned and polished. Relaxed, the Southerner finished his food, and after paying for it, got back up.

"Well, I am off to bed. You should be too. It will be a long ride tomorrow."

We agreed and followed him downstairs. To my surprise, once in my bed, I fell asleep easily, as if nothing had happened.

Chapter 60

MINIA FELT pain in his entire body. Although the sharp stinging had become his constant companion throughout the last weeks, the throbbing was too strong now and spread further down from the shoulder to his stomach and onto his thighs. His tried to move his feet, but stopped almost immediately. It hurt too much. Sometime later he tried once more. It hurt again, but not as much, which was a good sign. Slowly he felt his legs with his half bandaged hands. His fingers pressed into the wet cloth of his trousers in several places. There were some superficial cuts but the flesh underneath seemed undamaged, no broken bones or rampaged skin. One thing was certain—he was alive. Thanking the Spirit for that, Minia opened his eyes. Yet all he could see around him was darkness, a pitch black blanket that hung everywhere, without a single trace of light. He could feel dried blood on his lips, and many bits of gravel from the broken rock on his teeth, but that was all.

Slowly Minia swallowed the sand and tried to get up. But he could not. There was something underneath him, something soft that barred him from pulling up his feet. He felt the strange object with his hands. It was warm, shivering. It was...suddenly the images flashed before Minia's eyes—the collapsing wall, a man with a mallet, and the young lordling who was crouching by the wall. Minia pressed his palms into the soft flesh of the young noble and pinched it a little.

"*Aouch!*" exclaimed a thin voice. It was the young lordling. It was like music to Minia's ears. At least he was not alone in that hole.

"Are you all right?" Minia asked quietly. Somehow the darkness made him whisper. He did not know why, but it just felt right.

"Aye, aye. I think so." The boy coughed. "My legs hurt and I cannot see anything. What happened? Where are we?" The boy was starting to sob.

"We got trapped in a tunnel," replied Minia, and he pushed himself up a little. "Can you roll onto your side?" he asked the youngster.

"I think so," the boy replied and shifted. He did not move much, but it was enough for Minia to free his legs and get to his knees. But as he tried to rise further, his head hit solid rock.

"Oh, that hurts," he said loudly, and kneeled back down.

"Are you all right?"

"Yeah, I am fine. I guess we do not have much room here."

"Where do you want to go? I want to go home. Will you take me home? Will you?"

"I will, I will," said Minia, and started to search the ground floor for anything—a lantern, a torch, or his pouch with some firestones in them. "Stay still, I will try to get us some light."

"No, Sire, please, no. Do not go. I am—"

"I said sit still," Minia cut the youngster off. He had no time for tending children. He had to act quickly to get them both out of the ruined tunnel. It was the only way to survive.

For some time his hand felt nothing but sand and rocks. He crawled some distance, touching the walls and the rough floor and the ceiling, banging his hand and ripping his knees bloody. At the dead end, he turned around and started to make his way back, when he felt something firm and slick under his foot. It was the squire's kit, a metal cylindrical container used to stores some of the smaller gear, which Normandian soldiers often carried on their belts. If Minia was lucky there would be several small black cubes inside the tube, a set of firestones each squire usually carried with him. Moving his fingers quickly alongside the can, he found a thin leather strap and yanked it, but it did not open. Something was pressing on the can from above. In complete darkness Minia tried hard to examine the outline of the casing and soon came across a large sharp rock, which sat on top of it. With all his strength and ignoring the pain in his body, he pushed the rock off and extracted the tube. Though dented it opened nonetheless, and in it Minia found the so desired firestones that could be used to start a small fire. Hastily placing the cubes in his palms, he rubbed them together until yellow sparks began to spring into the air. It was enough. Pulling out a small patch of straw, which he also found inside the casing, Minia caught one of the flickers and started a tiny fire. Immediately the darkness retreated to the walls, and a dim blaze illuminated a portion of the cavern. The first thing Minia saw was a torch, which lay nearby—another stroke of luck. In one swift motion Minia set it ablaze and holding it tight, examined the place he was trapped in. At first Minia only saw black shapes and sharp angles of rocks, but when his eyes got used to the light he made out several items scattered on the floor, amongst which he distinguished a half broken lantern. Though its metal shell was broken off, the filter and oil canister remained intact. Shaking the lamp a little, Minia lit the small fuse with his little torch. Immediately more light streamed into the hollow.

The place where Minia found himself after the fall was indeed a small cavern some five cubits in length, formed by large rocks stacked one on top of each other. Luckily for Minia and the boy, the black stone plates did not break in small pieces, but hung over his head in several huge plasters. Yet it was of a little help, as all around them were only stone and fallen rocks.

Inspecting the walls for any visible ways of escape, Minia returned to the boy, who crawled into a small ball, sobbing. The light of the lantern made the young lord stop his weeping and look up. His face was black from dust, and long streaks of dried tears ran down to his chin.

"Good Sire, you have found the light. Oh, great, now we can go, can we?" The boy asked with a note of hope in his voice.

Go where? Minia thought to himself, but did not say it. Instead he patted the young lord on the shoulder and helped him to his feet. "We will find a way out, we just need to see which rocks are loose enough to move."

Minia knew their only chance was to pick apart the less heavy boulders and crawl out to the undamaged part of the tunnel. It was a dangerous plan, because the rocks were very unstable and could collapse further in. But Minia had to try it. Otherwise they would die in the hollow within a few days.

"Hold the lantern, I will try moving these stones over here." Minia handed the lamp to the boy and placing the torch into a narrow crack, crawled over the collapsed wall. He pushed several rocks one at a time, but none of them budged. He tried to pick up some smaller stones, but it was of no use either. The wall was solid. Then he went to the other end and tried again. It was the same. None of the stones moved, and Minia only cut his wrists on a sharp edge. Feeling the pain the squire sat down by the wall, holding his hand. Frustrated, he was losing hope, and to let his anger out he kicked the wall in front of him with both of his feet. He booted it so hard that his heels sank into the side. Minia closed his eyes, then immediately opened them. The slight dents in the wall just under the ceiling gave him an idea.

"Hey, boy," Minia yelled at the youngster. "Come over here. Do you know how to dig?"

"I, I think so."

"Good, do you have a knife or a dagger, anything?"

"I have a pocket knife."

"Good. Take it and start chipping at this side. I will go find something too." Minia remembered seeing a sword somewhere. Sure enough he found a half broken blade under a boulder. He quickly pulled it out and joined the boy by the wall. Together they started to work their way inward. While the initial walls of the tunnels were made of hard rock, past it was a clay-like stone, which after some pounding crumbled into many small pieces. Minia's plan was simple—to dig a passage around the collapsed portion of the tunnel and find their way to the other side.

To save the leftover oil from the lantern for as long as they could, Minia and the young lord put it out, and using just the torch, which they watched carefully, worked on the wall, chipping away more and more of the soft soil. As they could not tell the time, they did not know for how long they worked, but when the fatigue was unbearable they stopped. After resting a little they resumed again, and did not stop until Minia's sword struck something hard. It was another plaster of solid rock. Quickly they cleared the rest of the clay and gave it a push, but the plate did not move. With a dead end before them, Minia cursed loudly, but refused to give up. Instead he pressed his hands to the hard surface and pushed as hard as he could.

Suddenly the slippery cool plate budged. It was just a little, but it was enough for Minia to try harder. Together they drove the rock further and further inward. In the dark Minia could not see much, but he could feel the rock move. Then he felt it wobble slightly and fall. A loud cracking sound echoed off the stone and ran into the distance. There was an open space ahead, and a tunnel too. Gathering his strength, depleted by the long dig, Minia crawled through the opening. On the other side his hands found a hard floor, and he collapsed on its cold surface. The boy slid next to him. A light chilly breeze hit them in the face, and their breathing resonated through the darkness. A while later, when Minia's heartbeat returned to normal, he lit the lantern again. As the light twinkled in the small cage, Minia saw that they were in the middle of a wide-open tunnel, undisturbed and empty. Yet it was not the tunnel he had seen before. Unlike the other tunnels he had gone through in the past days, the new passage was well made, wider, with large polished plates evenly placed one after another.

"What is this place?" Minia heard the boy's voice.

"I do not know lad, I really do not know." The squire answered and peered into the distance where the darkness ate the light. Unable to see past several cubits he turned around and looked toward the other end, which also disappeared into the black vale of the underworld.

"It is so dark here," said the young lord after a pause. "Which way should we go?"

"Do you feel the breeze?" Minia lifted the lamp to let the light wind play with the little flame.

"Yes, it is coming from over there." The boy pointed to the left of them.

"This is where we will go. There has to be some way out."

The boy nodded and climbed back up. Shuffling his feet he went over to Minia, and they started slowly against the wind.

Chapter 61

ROVAL WAS behind us. Its houses disappeared in the morning mist, leaving our company alone, riding down a deserted road toward the border. Ahead the nation of Azoros awaited us and so did answers to many questions. The coming realm was indeed an unusual creature. With much wealth and splendor in the markets, Azoros had no official language, no standing armies, or any single ruler. Instead it was divided amongst four casts of merchants—the four houses—each holding a major city and lands around it. House of Glory ruled over Nacitav, House of Pride—Oniram, House of Valor—Omoc, and House of Coin—Azor. A council, consisting of the wealthiest and most powerful members of the merchant guilds, ran every house. In turn the leaders of each council formed a more grand assembly, called the Great Union, which supervised the entire country. Yet the Great Union was more of a formality since the real power was with the city councils, as they were the ones who controlled the levies and taxes of their subordinates.

Such a loose organization made Azoros into a most free-minded society, where all were welcomed, so long as they did not commit any crime against the nation or any of its inhabitants. With almost no restrictions on travels, the realm was frequented by all sorts of folks, ranging from the finest craftsmen to the most ruthless mercenaries, who always found plenty of work within the realm, hiring out their services to those who paid the price.

Ike, Ric, and I were very excited to actually get there, to see the true essence of the free markets, carnivals, and fairs so famous around Ethoria, but most of all, Elson's mysterious employer, Revor, who lived somewhere in the nominal capital of the nation, the city of Azor. Although I had heard a lot about the city, its inhabitants, and its marvelous bazaars, it was all but fantasy to me. I was yet to find out what it was like to see the most diverse and unusual city in the world.

After hours of hard riding, we finally reached the borderline, marked by a small guard post, which consisted of a boarded hut, a watchtower, and a tall wooden bar that ran across the road and went up or down to let the traffic pass. At that time the thick shaft was lowered, and several armed men sat near it, leisurely resting on the stone steps. They were Azor's customs guards. As it was, every House collected duties from all the goods that traveled in and out of its lands, making it one of the best sources of gold. I was impressed to see, that although the road was empty up to the post, beyond the station, wagons, horses, and people formed a long line, which veered down the lane, vanishing beyond the summit of a distant hill.

"What are all those people doing over there?" I asked Elson, pointing toward the crowd ahead.

"Oh, those are merchants waiting for the border crossing to open," replied the Southerner and he sped up toward the gates.

"How come there is no one on this side? Do not people want to get into Azoros from here?"

"They cannot. All caravans to Azoros have to take the lower road, a couple of leagues south. This is the place where they let the caravans out—an exit from Azoros so to speak."

"Then why are we going this way? Should not we take the lower route as well?"

"This rule applies only to the men of coin. Since we do not have any goods to declare, we can come and go without paying any duties. This road is as good as any, and we do not have to wait in line, unless, of course, you want to spend a day or two socializing with the merchants." Elson laughed.

At the other side everyone was waiting for the gates to open. We galloped straight past it, not even stopping to check with the guards, who, though they stared at us, did not do anything to stop our intrusion. Instead they slowly rose to their feet, and after picking up their weapons, went up to raise the pole, allowing the first few wagons to get by. Immediately a wave ran through the line, and it came to life. Suddenly the valley was filled with noise, the squeaking of many wheels, the moaning of animals, and the shouts of men who were preparing their loads for inspections.

While the first few convoys rolled into Lombardia, we were already a ways into Azoros, but the line was still going. Even after we put another league behind us there were still people persistently waiting their turn. It seemed odd to me that folks would subject themselves to such long delays, but apparently it was a price they had to pay if they wanted to trade in Azoros. Elson, for one, was convinced that it was a fair deal, saying that Azoros offered both the highest and cheapest price for various goods, which any well-trained merchant always cared to exploit to his own benefit.

Some times later the line dwindled and disappeared altogether, giving way to a less populated area. Yet the road was never empty. Every half a league or so we passed some village or town. Their streets were always busy, occupied with numerous shops and taverns, ready to serve anyone. After one of such parishes the route became wider, and turned into a well-maintained, three-lane road, which, although filled with traffic, had enough room for us to travel freely, without worrying about stepping over anyone.

By high noon, we reached the outskirts of Loral, a good-sized inland town, which Elson described as one of the best and quietest places to rest and get good meals.

The first thing that set Loral apart was an absence of a central castle that regularly dominated the skyline of all Normandian municipalities and served as refuge during sieges and other misfortunes. In its place Loral sheltered six or seven smaller citadels spread throughout the city. Not one of them matched the magnitude of the forts of Pullie or Bonneville. Yet they were of a fair size and provided decent protection to their inhabitants in time of crisis. Around the towering walls of the citadels lay the town itself with its numerous houses sitting on top of each other. The streets, narrow alleys, and wide boulevards pierced districts like razors, allowing a continuous flow of traffic through the city. Once two or more streets joined together, large plazas served as marketplaces. These were often packed with numerous stands and counters where traders of all sorts made their best efforts to sell goods to the eager, spoiled crowd.

And a crowd it was. People of all sorts were everywhere. Many of them spoke unfamiliar tongues, and a lot looked so different from the Northern folks that I could not help but stare at them with my mouth open. There was a group of men of dark color. They stood over two cubits tall, bare chested, and muscular, their toned bodies reflecting the sun. Although a few of them wore nothing but a skirt-like cloth on their hips, most had strange outfits made of skins and feathers, colorful and odd. For weapons they carried short spears with clean white tips, probably made from some animal's dried bones. Elson later told us that those were men of the Sarie Desert, free tribesmen of the sands.

Then there were men of pale, almost blue color. They had unusually bright golden hair and dark blue eyes. Also tall, they were slender but athletic. Wearing some of the finest silks of tan reddish colors, they strolled around the city in bands of five or six, always watching everyone who happened to look at them. One of such a group caught my attention too, and before I got myself in any trouble, I had to look away. All to good reason, because as the Southerner said, those were the dwellers of the Isles, the fighting men from the Island of the Claw. Arachies was there name, and often it was spoken in a whisper, for those pale men were some of the most skillful swordsmen in the entire Ethoria, standing rival only to the Great Blades of the Free Cities, the best of the best amongst all mercenary companies.

In due course, we made our way toward the center of the city, where amidst a wide plaza, three of Loral's many eateries stood. After reserving a room in one of them, called Notlis, it was off to the city. While Elson immediately disappeared as soon as we had stepped outside, saying again he had some business to take care of, we spent our time wandering through the maze of streets and corners, always sticking together so as not to get lost. When the darkness came, we found our way back to the inn, where the Southerner was already waiting for us, sipping on a tall glass of red wine. We joined him, ready to enjoy another evening in the company of a small crowd of quiet patrons.

Little happened afterwards. We ate and talked and ate some more, and then got up to leave to our room, located just off the stairs on the third floor. But as we rose from our chairs, a loud slam of the front door made us halt. At the doorway stood five tough-looking brutes. They studied the crowd for a moment, then one of them laughed loudly and strolled inside, followed by the others. Right away I knew these men meant trouble. Their faces showed ignorance and stupidity, and their behavior was rude. While two of the brutes chased away some solitary guests from their tables, three others harassed one of the serving girls, who, although quiet, tried everything to get away from them.

Such a scene of insolence made me furious. I could feel my blood boiling, and I felt my fingers closing tighter on the hilt of my blade. To my left, Ric and Ike were ready to fight too. My friend pulled out his sword and sat shifting in his seat. Next to him, Ric looked calm, but I could sense the tension brewing within his huge fists. Elson was the only one who appeared to be distanced from the ordeal. Distracted only by a small fly buzzing around his plate, he chewed on hard bread, paying no attention to anything that transpired just several tables away. Meanwhile, as several more guests left the room, the thugs continued to insult everyone, throwing things at the serving girls and spitting onto the tables next to them.

"Are we not going to do something?" I finally whispered to the others.

"No," replied Elson firmly. He took another bite, at the same time waving his hand at the insect.

"Why not?" asked Ike angrily.

"Because we are just two days away from Azor, and it would be stupid if we get in any trouble now. I think it will be a setback if one of us gets killed here, do you not think?" The Southerner looked over his shoulder, and then back at me. "I know it is not what you wish to hear from a hired sword, but let this one go. We have more important tasks ahead. As for the brutes, things like this are common to Azoros. In truth it is nothing but a show of force. Someone will yell and scream and push others around, but in the end, leave."

"But what about this poor owner and his servants?" Ike insisted.

"Oh, do not worry about the owner. He will file a complaint with the city watch and will get his compensation. As for these thugs, they will probably get arrested, and after paying a hefty fine, will be kicked out of Loral for a few days. In the end everybody is happy. So, let's eat. We have a long day tomorrow."

No matter how sad it sounded, Elson was right. We were too close to our destination to get involved in an ordinary brawl. There was nothing worse then catching a quick blade in the ribs just days before reaching Azor. Sighing several times, I turned away and focused on my plate, trying not to listen to the increasing rowdiness of the brutes. But while we thought we got out of a fight, the fight found us.

I was brushing off some crumbs from my pants, when the sound of approaching footsteps came from behind. I could not see who it was, but something told me those were the thugs. Following Ike's glance, I spun in my seat and came face-to-face with the five men, who were standing next to our table, looking down at us with their small squinting eyes. Their unshaved faces looked rough and pierced with scars and warts. Dried ale was on their lips. All of good size, broad shouldered and thick through the arms, they promised to be tough opponents, and I only hoped that they were slower than us, and not as skillful with their swords, which hung loosely on their belts, clipped with large metal rings.

Without introduction, one of the men walked around the table and toward the Southerner, who continued to devour his food with ease and calmness.

"Long time no see," started the man. He was much bigger than the rest of his friends, standing almost as tall as my brother, with a shoulder span that could double mine easily. His attire looked cheap and consisted of a light leather vest, a chain mail tunic, and leather pants with bolted spikes on each side. High boots finished the outfit and concealed a pair of throwing knifes, a usual attribute of every mercenary's arsenal.

"How come you do not say hello to your old friends, huh?" The thug grinned wide and stepped closer to the Southerner. Elson continued to ignore him, carrying on with his meal. The Southerner's face was unchallenged, as if there was nothing wrong. But his eyes told me a different story. I could tell he was preparing for a brawl, so I began to study the other thugs, who had taken positions around our table, with one standing directly behind me.

"Oh hello, Asson," Elson finally replied and raised his head, leaving an unfinished piece of onion on the plate. "I did not recognize you with all the new scars on your face. I have told you to be more careful when sewing, have I not?"

The Southerner smiled and kicked back in his chair.

"Funny as always," rebutted the brute. "But heck with it." He looked at his men and resumed. "I believe we have some unfinished business to discuss. If my memory does not fail me, there was a question of a reward that you were supposed to share with us."

"I think that your memory is getting worse, Asson. I do not recall any rewards, nor do I remember owing you anything."

"Oh how funny, ha ha." The man smiled again. "Let me remind you then. Ten seasons ago we had a job together. You took the money and left us be, not giving us a penny of it."

"Ah, You are referring to the Free Cities' raid. I remember it now, and I also remember that whatever we made then I split evenly with you. Do not tell me you have not made a small fortune working with me."

"I want to believe you. And you know what—I did, I did until I found out some things about that job, which you, somehow, forgot to mention. I know how much the Imperial merchants gave you. It looks to me that my boys and I were underpaid by twenty gold plates. Will you prove me wrong?"

"As I said, you got all that you deserved, no more, no less," replied Elson and this time his tone was serious.

"Whatever. The way I see it—you can either give us our money or we will have to take it from you ourselves. It is your choice of course."

There was a brief pause. Elson stared at the man from his chair, then suddenly slid back. Two blades appeared in his hands, and leaping swiftly toward the thug, he switched the swords in front of Asson, barely missing the tip of his long blistered nose.

"I am tired of such a foul tone," the Southerner stated ever calmly. "So let me give you a choice of my own. It is either you leave my friends and me alone, or I will be forced to make you leave this place if not in one piece than in several. Now…What is you choice?"

The thug jerked back from the Southerner and yanked his own sword. The four others did too, and so did we, jumping off our chairs and spinning quickly to face the foes. With our weapons raised we watched carefully as the enemies spread out, preparing to launch their attack.

"Ha, I see you have found other fools to do your deeds," said Asson, hiding behind his long sword. "How resourceful of you. The poor brats probably do not even know a single thing about you. Well, why do we not share it with them before they commit their swords to your defense?"

Asson took another step back and addressed us. "Hey, you three. I see that you still have your mother's milk dripping down you chins. You should be at home with your mommy. So I suggest you leave this place. That way you will get to live another day, and we will have less work to do."

"Who are you to tell us what to do?" snapped Ike in return.

"This dispute does not concern you, fool. All you need to know is that I have killed many youths like you, long before your mother crawled in bed with your half-witted father. But today I have no desire to do so. I have more pressing matters, so I will let you live, that is, of course, if you lower your weapons and get out of here."

"It does not sound too persuasive." Elson smiled and took a step toward the enemy; in turn Asson retreated.

"Then let's tell them a little story, shall we?" Asson looked at Elson, and back at us. When he resumed, his tone changed—it became angrier. "That man, whom you know by the name of Elson, is not who he claims he is. His real name is Aromun Lirosu, the son of some lowlifes, poor farmers from northern Lombardia."

"His parents were murdered. We know. If this is all you have let's get on with it," I exclaimed and swung my sword, slicing the air in front of me.

"I do not care if his parents were eaten by goats. What I want to tell you is another story, a story about why our friend changed his name, why he became Elson Rian. Judging from the looks on your faces you have not heard this tale yet, so listen then, before you rush to your deaths.

"Years back, when Elson grew up to become a mercenary, he came back home as some lord's bodyguard. There he found out the truth about his parents' death, that they were murdered by some noble years back. So what did Elson do? He paid a visit to that lord. Under cover of night he sneaked into his mansion and killed him, but not just him, his entire family too. And I do not mean just grown sons. He murdered every living soul in that house. First he disposed of the guards. How many were there, Elson? Ten? Fifteen? It does not matter. When all the guards were dead, he went upstairs and sliced the lord himself, along with his young wife and four of their children. The youngest was no older than two, but Elson did not care. He snatched that baby's head like an apple, ripping it from the boy's tiny shoulders with his bare hands. Or so they say. After that he took care of the rest of the noble family, the elderly aunt, two uncles, and three guests who happened to be lodging at the mansion. He killed all of the servants too. In all, some forty men, women, and children died that night.

"The murder was so gruesome that it took several days to bury all the dead; their graves alone made up an entire cemetery. If you do not believe me, travel to Ariso someday and see for yourself. Their graves are still there, all of them. Word of the slaughter spread quickly through the lands. A neighboring count dispatched a whole regiment of heavy cavalry to hunt down Elson, but it was useless. He was largely gone, galloping to Azoros as quick as he could. There was even a reward posted for his head, but since there was no one left alive from the count's family, nobody could pay up the money, and so there was no interest.

"But that is not the end of it. Years later Elson came to the city of Hugis, a small parish in the south of the Amber Empire. The village itself belonged to a peer of the realm by the name of Fruis Guijis, who happened to be a distant relative of the murdered Lombardian count Elson hated so much. Once our friend found that out, he sought the old brat's death too, butchering his entire household along with him, just like he did once before. Afterwards he tried to flee, but was caught scaling the walls of the peer's mansion by a passing patrol. He was thrown into jail, then tried and sentenced to die in one week's time, but before the punishment could be carried out, he escaped from his cell. Until this day nobody knows how he managed to pull that trick, but he did, and after he was clear from pursuit he ran to Azoros again, where he has been hiding ever since.

"Unfortunately for him, some of the relatives of the killed peer survived and claimed Elson as a wanted man, posting a reward, which this time was to be paid in full. The prize was not big, yet it still presented Elson with a challenge, as there were plenty of hotheads who needed money, and were not too uptight about killing a lonesome hired sword. To avoid the hunt, our friend changed his identity, and that was how Aromun of Lombardia became Elson Rian of Azoros, which by the way was the name of a longtime dead mercenary from Arabia, a legend in some places.

"So now you have it. You are in company of a wanted criminal, a killer, a murderer of children and women, a man who has seeded fear in so many hearts that some folks are still afraid to say his name aloud. His savagery and hate are renowned, and his lust for bloodshed is famous. Now I ask you again, are you ready to die for him? Because if you are, remember this, he does not have any friends, he will betray you soon, and when he does, you will be in a whole lot of trouble."

The tale stunned me. Doubt started to consume my mind. Yet I could not allow for it to spread. The situation at hand demanded that I stayed focused, and so I did, chasing away the dark thoughts, knowing well that once free from the immediate danger I would come back to them.

"Your words may have some truth to them, but it is not for me to abandon a friend. Should there be any doubts we will deal with them later. Right now I stay with Elson." I stepped forward and faced one of the men, who although determined in his expression, moved back away from my weapon. A bit more hesitant Ike also shook off whatever concerns he had and joined me on a flank; Ric did too, his eyes fixed on a skinnier man to the end of the table.

As silence fell again, the tension grew. The five of them and the four of us stared at each other like two packs of wolves studying every move and every jerk. It went on for a while. Then Asson, who was measuring his chances against Elson, suddenly took two steps back and lowered his sword.

"Ah, heck, it does not worth it. I will see you some other time, when you do not have your crazy friends with you. As far as I am concerned you all deserve each other. You are all mad or stupid, whichever it is. But know this, you have just made another enemy today. Better watch yourselves next time you pass by me, because you might find a dagger stuck in your backs."

He motioned to his men to take their leave.

"Let's get out of here before the guards show up. I know another good place where we can get some ale and cheap women."

Relieved, Asson's thugs put away their weapons, slapped a serving boy one more time, and left, slamming the front door so hard that a small horseshoe hanging over the entrance fell down.

At last the confrontation was over. The fight was no to be. Our weapons found their resting places, and Ike, Ric, and I gazed at the Southerner, who stood at the side of the table, thumbs tucked under his belt.

"Is this true? The things Asson has said about you?" asked Ike afterwards.

"I wish I could tell you that it was not, but it is. Everything he has told you is true; my personal vendetta, the murders, and the warrants, all of it did happen. I am still wanted in the Amber Empire and Lombardia."

The Southerner took a deep breath. "I am sorry I did not tell you, but it is not something someone wants to share. If you want to leave now and take your own path, I will understand. There is little I can say. I did terrible things, and I have to live with that for the rest of my days. If I could take it all back, I would, but I cannot. What is done is done, and all I can do now is try to pay back as much as I have taken. Your quest is indeed a virtuous one, and I sensed a need to help you. Of course you do not have to tolerate me any longer. Just say it and I will depart and never bother you again."

The Southerner lowered his head and sat down on the stool. For the moment he seemed vulnerable. And I did not know what to say. The things he did were horrible, evil, and savage. But at the same time he looked like a different person now. He had helped us uncover the conspiracy in Pullie, and led us through the Northern Empire and Lombardia, and saved us from Gapo. Maybe he had changed, maybe he was a new person, someone I could trust and rely on.

Abruptly a recollection of my recent vision revisited me. The words of the A'al sorceress streamed into my mind and gave me the answer I was searching for. In her warning, she said that I should be cautious of the Words of Truth that deemed to make me doubt my companions. Could it be that the truth about the Southerner's dark past was what A'tie talked about? If so, one piece of the puzzle fit. Although with difficulty, I made my choice

"Someone has warned me that this would happen. That someone also told me that the truth would not be my ally, but my enemy. I understand it now. What has happened in your past is yours to deal with, but to me you are a true friend and a valuable companion. I would be lying if I say that it does not bother me, but I will learn to cope with it. The quest that has brought us together is too important, and so, despite of what the others say, I believe you, and will not mind having you in our company. You have my vote."

Ric slowly nodded and said nothing else. It left Ike, who clearly struggled with his decision. He looked at me, then Elson, then Ric, and back at me. Then, slowly he uttered, "If it is good for Mishuk, it is goof for me. You have my vote too. I just hope I will not be sorry for it later."

"You will not," I answered for the Southerner and raised my half-full cup. "Let's drink then for our bond, our quest, and us. May the Spirit be our guide."

Everyone repeated my words and downed the warm ale. Then we did not talk about Asson's tale anymore. Instead we paid some coins and walked out into the yard to resume the journey. Somehow we did not feel like staying in that inn any longer.

Swiftly we led our horses past some rows of houses and out of the city, soon taking a back road southeast toward Azor. To our surprise the route was empty, with only wind to serve as company. The sky above was darkening with clouds, but other than that nothing promised to disturb our journey, not until we were stopped by group of men, who waited for us behind the summit of the first low hill. At first I did not recognize the group, but soon detected familiar features in their rough faces. The strangers were the same brutes we had faced back at the tavern—Asson and his lads.

"Hey, you there." I heard Asson's voice again. "I have changed my mind. I think I will collect my debt now. You can try and fight if you want, but I will have it my way."

"Asson, Asson, I see that you have kept your stupidity flourishing." Elson rode straight for the large thug. "You have not learned a single lesson life has thrown at you. If it takes another lesson I will be more than glad to grant you one."

"Say what you want, I want my money and I want it now." The man lifted himself off the saddle and yanked a short-handed sword, raising it high over his head. He wanted to yell something to his friends, but did not. Like lightning, Elson's hand moved up and something flew toward his opponent. A light sound pierced the air, and Asson jerked back. He sat still for a moment, then his head tilted and he slid down from the saddle. His heavyset body dropped down, and I saw a large dagger sticking out of his chest. The remaining brutes, who had not even seen the attack, stood in confusion. They looked at each other, then at their leader, then at Elson. Suddenly one of them spun his horse and sent it galloping into the field. He was followed by another fellow, which left only two others remaining.

"Rat's tail! I will not take any beating for Asson. It was his debt, not mine," one of the men yelled loudly so that we could hear him clearly.

"Yeah, and the money was not that good anyway," agreed the other.

"I say we forget everything."

"Yeah, let's let them pass."

"You can pass, we need no money from you." The men backtracked from the road, opening a gap for us to get through.

"Good. I am glad that you have wits, not like your leader," said Elson, and he started down the road without throwing another glance at the thugs. We went after him, letting our mounts pass the two men, who turned and fled into the fields, never to be seen again.

"I say we hurry, before anyone blames this murder on us," said Elson afterwards, and he galloped forth.

Chapter 62

SIRE JIM'S hopes to return to his duties in Bonneville were put off for some more days. Along with the unexplained suicide of the leaders of the sect and Duke's hasty departure, more troubles purged the expedition. Unexpectedly several patrols that toured the outskirts of the base camps vanished without a trace. Some days later their armor was found two leagues away, hidden underneath some dried-out leaves on the shore of the lake. The men themselves were never seen again. Although many of his fellow soldiers started to talk about the surviving Alavantars avenging their masters, Sire Jim was sure that the missing soldiers simply left their posts and ran home, tired of the boring life at the camp.

But desertion was a minor problem, compared to another misfortune. Six days after the search of the underground had began, three main tunnels collapsed unexpectedly. Over thirty men were left buried alive, and what was worse, Sire Rone's squires, those who had uncovered the evil plot of the Alavantars, were amongst the trapped. Efforts to extract them from underneath the rubble were rendered useless, as the broken rock and large boulders were too heavy for the men to lift with their hands. The rescue required special mining equipment and many more horses. Alas the expedition had not such tools. Although a message had been sent to the local lords and mining camps to deliver the necessary gear, the time in which it would arrive would be too long for the men inside.

As if such dire news was not enough, after the departure of the many knights, the troops that stayed at the lakeside were in disarray. The remaining lords were confused, and their men were unsure of their duties or purpose being there. Seeing morale dropping, Sire Jim took charge. Gathering as many men as he could, the second captain resumed the rescue. But before he could complete the task and save his men, a new set of orders arrived from the royal court. According to the instructions the remaining part of the expedition force was to abandon the camp by the lake and start a march to Runo, the second largest city in Chantue province. Such a destination startled many, and so the rumors so flew. Some said that they were going to join another campaign further west. Others thought of medals and honors, but nobody knew for sure. The knights did not do anything to clarify the gossip, but kept it to themselves, divulging few bits of information, mostly related to the past battle, and not much else.

Even after the remnants of the expedition had reached the city walls of Runo, the purpose of the visit remained unclear, even for Sire Jim who, along with the many other Bois lords, was kept in the dark throughout the journey. Absent of any explanations, they led their men to the inner grounds of the local castle, where two large barns were hastily turned into barracks. There the soldiers, squires, and servants were allowed to settle in, while the lords took up several upper levels of the castle's keep, already crowded with other noblemen, those, who had arrived earlier with the Duke of Bois, and those who had come with Sire Zuros from Canton.

As space was scarce, Sire Jim had to share a room with two other knights from the western part of Bois who spent most of their time talking about the recent events. The second captain joined the discussion at times, but the fatigue quickly overwhelmed him and soon he fell asleep, not waking up until the next morning when the sound of a battle horn summoned everyone outside.

Wet from the early dew, the inner grounds quickly filled with half-sleeping men, who hurried to form several long lines facing a small wooden platform, where a group of men observed the commotion below. Sire Jim came out too. After greeting some of his squires, who stood some cubits away, he squeezed past several knights from Puno, and took a spot near the pedestal. When the last of the soldiers found their spots and silence was restored, a local ruler of Runo, Sire Drisne of Trios, explained that the royal court had found the recent campaign in Puno to be a failure and so had sent a group of its inquisitors to Runo to investigate the matter further, to find the guilty parties and those responsible for the poor performance of the Normandian troops.

Once the announcement was over, the soldiers were dismissed, but the knights, along with Sire Jim, were asked to convene in the castle's meeting hall, where a large table full of foods awaited them. During that meal the lords of Bois and Puno finally learned details of their summons to Runo. It appeared the dispatch that had called off the Duke from the caves of the Land's Edge was no ordinary message, but a summons from the royal court, signed by the King himself, almost as soon as the battle at the Lake Azul was over. In it the Duke was ordered to come to Runo, where the royal questioners were to ask him about his actions and duties during the campaign against the Alavantars. Although such solemn matters were the responsibility of the King, Philip the First was a young king of only twenty years of age. His interests were with a grand tournament that was about to begin in the Normandian capital, and so the matter was entrusted to his royal councilors, amongst whom Sire Liore was the chief. Being one of the nephews of the old King, Sire Liore, was also a young lord, whose many scandalous endeavors had earned him the nickname "The Regal Fox." He took the assignment of questioning the Duke very seriously and after arriving to Runo with his extensive entourage, immediately began the questioning.

First he sent for the Duke's trusted men, his captains and squires, whom he questioned for several hours, defying their every word with doubt and suspicion. When he was done with them, he called in the Duke, whose interview lasted for two days, during which the Regal Fox and his young lordlings from the capital asked Sire Tem so much that soon there was nothing left to ask. Yet it did not stop there. After learning about the prisoners reaching Canton, Sire Liore decided to question them too, and so ordered Sire Zuros to bring the captives to the city.

As Runo's two small prisons had no room, when the captives arrived they were settled on the outskirts of the city, in a burned field inside two large pens, used until then to hold pigs and cattle. There the men were guarded day and night, supplied with little food and few barrels of water, which was barely enough for them to last for a day under the hot rays of the sun.

Interrogation of the captured men went on for some more days. When it was done, Sire Liore was not satisfied and decided that he wanted to see the entire expedition force before him, so he could talk to the remaining soldiers and the lords, all those who took part in the campaign. It was for that reason the remaining troops were order to go to Runo and, on the third day of his stay in Runo, the second captain and two other lords found themselves sitting inside a small chamber, awaiting an audience with the Regal Fox.

At the base of the stairs that led to the second level, the Bois nobles were met by the three soldiers. From the symbols of the golden crowns on their blue tunics, it was clear that they were members of the Royal Guard, probably sent from the west along with Regal Fox. The soldiers did not say much. After giving quick salutes to the lords, they escorted them up and into the castle's common room, a stone spacious hall with many windows, long hanging banners of all colors, and pieces of decorative armor from the old times. Around the gray walls stood more armed soldiers, all Royal Guards, all still and fit. If it were not for the slight movement of their breath, they could have been mistaken for statues, so common to the many keeps in Normandia. But they were real, and very aware of things that took place inside in the room, where in the middle sat several nobles. From the look of their clothes, soaked in splendor, Sire Jim knew that the young lords were royals. But amongst the array of colors and jewelry displayed, one figure stood out more than others. Young and slender, he had fine sharp features, a distinctive sign of the royal bloodline. Thick brown hair covered his forehead, and his dark eyes were full of indifference and boredom. Sire Jim knew that face, the Regal Fox himself, Sire Liore of Burgunion.

Unlike the lords of Bois, who lived and depended on their lands, the royals were always ignorant and snobby and cared little for anyone but those who stood above their rank. To them young and not so young men of the provincial nobility were a nuisance, an awkward, time-consuming matter they sometimes had to deal with. There was no respect, no sympathy, no honor, just ignorance and insolence of a sort. Sire Jim hated such an attitude; he hated the royals and the entire regal stance, so fake and shallow to him. And standing before the Regal Fox, he began to despise it even more.

For a while, the Bois lords stood at the entrance in silence, waiting until one of the guards finally yelled their names and brought them close to the table, halting several cubits away from the draped velvet covers. The questioners continued to chat for a little longer, then a red-haired fellow on the corner put aside his white silk gloves and gave a brief explanation as to what was needed from the summoned lords, namely, to answer questions about the campaign.

Of course, the Duke and Sire Zuros were the main targets of the investigation. Although poor results of the expedition were the pretext, Sire Jim understood the true reasons behind such a thorough query were of a different ilk. After spending many years with the Duke's garrison, the second captain had learned that although calm on the surface, the Normandian nobility was upset by a hidden conflict between the old knights of the kingdoms and the young lords of royal blood. Since most ranks and high seats in the provinces were taken by the older knights, who had received their honors from the deceased king, Arat the Third, many younger lords had little chance to advance in ranks. Such a situation displeased them greatly and with their hunger for power growing like wildfire, they tried everything to remove the old knights from their posts, proving their own worth not in the fields of battle, but in the royal court, appealing to the young king and his trusted aids.

Sire Tem and Sire Zuros both were of the old blood and also held the High Lords' Seats in Bois and Puno—a combination for which they were despised by many royals who had been long searching for any motive to remove them from their posts. It so happened that the campaign against the Alavantars, which yielded such poor results, was such motive. Although the true reasons for mistakes made at Lake Azul were hidden within the weak state of the Normandian army, the royal court was ready to accuse the Dukes and their sworn men, for if Sire Tem and Sire Zuros were found guilty, they would have to be removed. Still, to place a blame on two High Lords was no easy task. Sire Jim understood it well, he also understood that to divulge the information was to help the Regal Fox and aggravate the situation for the Dukes even more. It was something none of the local lords wanted to do. At the same time they also had to answer the questions. To refuse the royals was to lose their noble title and earn expulsion to the Barrier Wall. It was a very harsh price to pay, and not too many knights were ready to pay it.

Sire Jim told the examiners his account. When he was done, he had to answer several questions, and then was ordered to leave, which he did gladly. There were no thanks, no farewells, just a handful of cold glares and dry unpleasant grins, images that stayed with the second captain all the way down to the courtyard, where the familiar faces and the friendly choruses let him loosen up and forget for a moment about the unpleasantries of the recent inquest.

The second captain expected the ordeal to repeat the following morning, but for the next several days there were no more questions. Everyone was left alone, though none were allowed to leave the castle. The mood amongst the troops was foul, and the only refuge came from songs, which could be heard throughout the camp, jumping from one fire to another like a grasshopper on a summer day. Along with tunes came talk and rumors. The soldiers disliked the investigation and those who conducted it. The fate of the Dukes and his captains became the center of many discussions, as men weighed in their doubts about the kind of justice served by the royal court. To make the situation worse, there was still no real news about the two High Lords, who were somewhere within the castle in Runo. It brought more suspicion into the ranks, and some even started to wonder if they would ever see their commanders again. Many of the knights shared their men's concern and often joined them on their short walks around the castle grounds, spending hour after hour talking about the situation. Sire Jim wondered too. Though he said nothing to the others, the second captain worried much about his lord.

That very day, after the questioning, the expedition troops were called to formation. When the men assembled their lines, a column of the Royal Guards came out and formed a human wall around the podium. After some time Sire Liore, along with his entourage, made his way into the center of the stage. The royals were in good disposition, smiling and joking amongst themselves. Their leisured manner disgusted many, but the high borns did not care. Instead they continued to entertain each other with more talk for a while. Then one of them, a tall fellow in a green robe, stepped out of the group and began to speak, not to the soldiers but to a crier, who then relied the words to the men below. A boy of twelve or thirteen made brief introductions, paying the expected honors to the lords on stage, and only after that announced that the investigation was to continue for several more weeks, and that during the time the Dukes were to remain in their quarters without leave. For a brief moment the troops stood confused, but then some shouts sprang through the crowd and trouble started to stir. First individual murmurs came from the back, then someone yelled a rude remark and several other joined in. Soon the entire yard was consumed with a roar. The clanking of metal was deafening; the soldiers' anger was almost at the boiling point. Everyone demanded to see their lords.

The turmoil amongst the soldiers and squires immediately worried Sire Jim. Even though he had never seen a revolt, he was a witness to its consequences. Once, some years back, Sire Tem had been called in to assist another Duke in putting down a local rebellion in another province. Although the uprising was of a peasant's sort, nonetheless it hosted some threat to other lands. So Sire Tem made a pledge and set on a short march, taking a small contingent of his men with him, including Sire Jim. But by the time the troops arrived at the rebellious small town, the uprising was over. Still its aftermath was everywhere. Scorched fields and gardens, destroyed houses, and slaughtered cattle told a grave tale of the recent battle. The many dead bodies of the rebels showed all the harshness with which the revolt was put down. But it was just the beginning, for in the days to come the surviving dissenters were brought before the lord's court. The punishment was swift. Those of the inciters who did not die during the fight were beheaded, right in the middle of the town square, with all the people gathered to watch. The defeated men pleaded for their lives, but there was no mercy. A large axe did its job a dozen times, and soon a row of sticks emerged just outside the castle wall, displaying the deformed heads of those executed. It was a lesson and a punishment in one. A horrific scene, a reminder of the reality of the less pleasant side of Normandian life.

Standing amidst the crowd of angry soldiers, these pictures of devastation and sorrow revisited Sire Jim. He knew what would happen, should the troops take arms against the royals. They could win the fight in the courtyard of

Runo, but the aftermath would be a brutal one, as the King would surely send an army to deal with the problem. Sire Jim could not allow such senseless bloodshed; so he quickly gathered as many lords as he could, and led them to the podium, where the royal questioners were watching the fuming mob. More shouts and threats came from the men below. Some of the ranks started to break too, but Sire Jim did not care. Jumping onto the pedestal, he rushed straight to Sire Liore, whose face expressed a glint of worry.

"Your Lordship," said the second captain in a rigid tone, "You must do something to calm the troops."

"What do you suggest?" asked one of the royals, a tall thin man in red armor.

"I do not know but we must do something quickly, before it is too late." Sire Jim looked at the Regal Fox.

"Why do not you order them to calm down? They are your men, are they not?" asked another royal.

"I wish it was that easy. My words would calm some of the men, but it would not be enough. They will only listen to Sire Tem or Sire Zuros."

"That is out of the question," snapped Sire Liore. "The Dukes are under investigation. They will remain where they are. As for this bunch of half-witted peasants, they can try and attack us. We will teach them a lesson. Those fools…If they want a fight they will get one. Sire Greiuy, tell the guards to take a defensive formation."

"Your Lordship, this may not be wise," interjected the man in red armor. "They have over three hundred men here, our numbers are three times smaller."

"So what? I bet you half a pouch of gold plates that one Royal Guardsman is worth five peasant soldiers."

"That may be, but it is a dangerous call. And…a fight amongst our own, will only aggravate the situation further. Should they win here, and should the other Dukes take their side, we may have a civil war on our hands. The king would never approve of this."

Sire Liore thought for a moment then waved his hand and turned around, his cape swaying after him. When he was about to descend down the stairs he looked over at Sire Jim and said dryly, "Fine. Tell them anything you want. I do not care. Oh, and Sire Jim, why do you not stop by my private chamber once this little ordeal is over?"

"But what about the Dukes, will you let them speak to their men?" asked Sire Jim in return.

"No, the Dukes will not be allowed to leave. As for their fate, we will talk about it later. For now calm your men. That is an order." The Regal Fox spat on the ground and ran down the stairs, quickly disappearing behind a metal door of the keep. Sire Jim returned to the edge of the podium and raised his sword. The commotion below halted. The shouts ceased, and the men got quiet. Everyone turned their attention to the lord. The second captain looked satisfied but there was sadness in his gaze. He stood in silence for a bit and when he spoke his voice had a slight tone of grief. He told the men that the investigation was not yet concluded, that the royal questioners were to continue with their inquiry. Meanwhile the expedition force was to be dismissed, and the knights were to take their men back home. The hardest part came at the end—the Dukes and some of their closest men were to stay in Runo, for such were the orders from the King himself. Another wave of discontent rushed through the ranks. Sire Jim waited. When the shouts ceased he spoke again.

"I know that you do not like this. I do not like this either, but these are orders from the King and we must comply. The Dukes are still our lords and we must do everything to make them proud. If we try to resolve the matter with arms, it will not help them. This battle cannot be won with swords."

His next words were firm.

"Now men, follow your lords and return home to your families. They are waiting, for you have been gone far too long."

It was the order that nobody tried to challenge. Slowly the rage died out and the men returned to their tents. It was their last night in Runo. In the morning, the knights were to gather their men and leave, each heading for his own domain. Sire Jim was preparing for the departure too. He did not have too many men to lead back. Most of them had already departed, and some were still at the caves, trying to rescue the trapped men. Of them, there was still no news, but Sire Jim did not have time to pursue it. He had to leave Runo and return to Bonneville. His squires, servants, and soldiers he instructed to get ready for the morning, and he himself took a little stroll beneath the castle walls.

He did not understand most of it, nor did he want to. His upbringing was one of valor and chivalry, and honor, but what he observed in Runo was a disgrace. For the first time in his life he was ashamed of his kingdom and his king. He wanted to cry, but he was a lord and lords never cried. So instead he continued to walk in silence, grim and focused. Then he remembered that Sire Liore wanted to see him in his quarters and quickly headed back. He decided to stop by his room first so he could put on his best suit of armor. He also wanted to wash his face, but when he got to the door he realized that he would have no time. Inside the room five guardsmen awaited him. They bore the sign of the Regal Fox's House, their weapons ready at their sides.

"Sire Jim of Ogar, the youngest son of Sire Rimdor?" asked the man in the yellow tunic, with a large silver chain dangling on his chest.

"Yes, how can I be of assistance?"

"We have orders from Sire Liore to take you to the court hall."

"I thought I was to meet him in his quarters?"

"Sire, we just have our orders. Will you please abide willingly?"

"Certainly, there is no need for confrontation."

Sire Jim turned and stepped into the corridor, walking after the men, quietly. There was only one thought on his mind. He knew why the men had waited for him in his room. He also knew why he was summoned to the court hall instead of the private chamber. The royals wanted to arrest him, but why? He did not have a clue. Before he stepped into the large chamber, he was convinced he would not see Bonneville for quite some time.

Chapter 63

"PULL THEM up."

"Hurry! Grab the rope."

"I said hurry up....We do not have all day here."

"Be careful, do not drop them."

"I told you not to drop them."

The voices ran through the darkness of an empty mind. I heard the fuss, but I knew it was not me who heard the talking. Although the sounds were loud, as if it were somewhere nearby, I sensed that it was my Fore Sight. It was a vision. After listening to the strangers for some time, I began to detect some shapes. Then the picture cleared and I saw several figures huddled over me, two of them leaned forward and looked straight into my eyes, though those were not my eyes and it was not me who concerned them. Before I could understand their words, I rose up several feet so that the entire scene opened before me. As I floated in the air, like a spectator of a sort, the men below continued to cluster in the center of a freshly dug hollow that looked like an excavation site.

Eager to find out more I peered closer and soon spotted three long stretchers laid out near a round hole in the ground. On them rested three figures, dirty and motionless. A thought ran through my mind and suddenly I had to get closer. As if taken by some strange force, my focus changed. When I blinked again I was amongst the men, looking down at the covered silhouettes, two of which I immediately recognized. The dirty figures were Rob and Ark and someone else—and all three were alive.

Their limbs moved bit by bit, and Rob, whose once fine clothing was covered in dust and white powder—probably from the fall—opened his eyes. He looked confused, and his pupils moved from one face to another, searching for a clue as to what had happened to him.

"Do not worry, lad," said one man from the crowd that packed a small clearing around a large hole in the floor. "You are safe. You are not in the tunnels any more."

"What—where—but—" Rob tried to speak, but his voice was very weak. He moved his lips, but no sound left his mouth.

"Do not talk. We will take you to the infirmary. The old healer will take care of you and your friends too."

Rob turned and found another man next to him, also dirty and unconscious. He did not recognize him at the first, but the familiar features soon emerged and Rob saw his friend. He wanted say something to Ark, but could not. Instead he lay back and took a deep breath. Fresh air felt nice inside his chest. It hurt a bit, but that was nothing. He was alive.

As he gave himself to the fatigue, someone picked him up and carried somewhere. He did not care nor did he have any strength to ask. He stayed still and let the wind brush down his dry cheeks. Before he drifted away he heard somebody say, "Lucky youths. Just three of them. Three…out of almost forty men. Oh, wait, no, two…"

When Rob opened his eyes again, he found himself lying on a straw bed inside a large tent. There were no people inside, just a dog sleeping on the floor, barking in its sleep, probably dreaming of chasing some of its biggest prey. After staying motionless, Rob moved his feet a little and then stretched out. To his surprise he was fine. There was no pain, no weakness in his body. He felt fresh. After inspecting himself and finding no wounds, except for two small bandages on his hand, he got up and walked to the door flap. Almost at the exit he halted and stretched again, at which moment the door swung aside and Ark strolled inside, caring a bucket of water.

"Oh, I am glad you are awake. I was about to pour this bucket over your head." Ark smiled and lifted the pail, spilling some of the water onto the floor.

"Ark, how are you my old friend? I am so glad to see you," replied Rob cheerfully.

"Ha, same to you. I guess we lucked out in that tunnel?"

"We sure did, do you know what happened there?"

"The men say that as we were searching through the leftover corridors of the compound, several of the lower tunnels collapsed. Some forty men got trapped underneath, buried under a rubble of stone. Nobody really knows how or why the tunnels dropped; only it happened so quickly that nobody escaped. There was so much ruined rock piled up there that the first attempt to dig us out did not bring any results.

Apparently you and I were lucky that we got caught in the upper reaches of the caverns. How we survived for so long without water or food no one knows, but I do know that two days ago the men managed to break a hole and get to the first collapsed tunnel—that was where they found us."

"And Minia, Sire Adim, and the others?" Rob asked remembering that there were three survivors.

Ark lowered his head and shook it. "No. They found Rtem and some other men from our group. I hate to say it but they were all dead. Minia and the young lord are still missing, and so are other men from the lower levels. I want to think that they are alive, but with so much time already passed, no water, no food…"

"What if they are alive, what if they have survived, just like us, what—?"

"Rob," Ark looked straight at his friend. "They pulled us out of there three days ago. It was a miracle we lasted for so long."

"Three days…"

"I came to my sense a little over a day ago. Since then all I have been doing is helping the diggers. We pulled out several more bodies, but they were out of life, dead. We have been pounding stone day and night, but have made little progress. Considering there are only some forty men here, we—"

"Forty men," exclaimed Rob. "What has happened to the expedition, Sire Jim, the Duke?"

"If you remember, the Duke went to Runo several days after the fight; Sire Zuros escorted the prisoners to Canton. As for the remaining men, almost everyone has been pulled back to Runo, there is some sort of a royal court assembled there. They are asking questions about the expedition. There is a big rumor going around, about the Alavantars and how they have gotten into the many noble houses of the kingdom. People say that royal councilors are accusing some lords of conspiring with the sect. It is some crazy purge that the men are talking about. Some even say that the King himself suspects the Dukes to be amongst the worshipers of the North, which is why the expedition was a disaster."

"Are they crazy? If it were not for the Duke…"

"I know, but there is little we can do…"

"We can go to Runo and talk to someone, we can tell them the truth."

"No, we cannot," replied Ark. "We will travel back to Sirone. The local lord, who has been left in charge of the dig, has ordered everyone to leave his land as soon as possible. That goes for us too. Tomorrow is the last day of the dig; after that it will be off to Bois. Do you think you will be able to ride?"

"I think so," replied Rob. It was all he said, the rest he left to silence.

So it was. The rescue efforts were abandoned. All the equipment was brought out of the caverns and put away in the wagons. The men reassembled at the remains of the mercenary main camp and moved out, following the road east. The remaining soldiers from the expedition, about fifty of them, headed home. Confusion was in their mind, and new rumors they picked up along the way only strengthened their bad mood. It appeared that the Duke and his captains had been accused of conspiring with the Alavantars to overthrow the King and seize the throne. In turn such talk made the men in Bois very angry, sending the province into turmoil. The last rumor proved to be wrong though, as after crossing the border to Bois, my friends found no disorder within their homelands. The local folks went on about their business as usual, and nobody talked much about the campaign, the Duke, or the investigation.

Somewhere beyond the border, most of the soldiers turned west and only my friends headed south. Although Rob wanted to go and speak to someone in Bonneville, Ark assured him that it was of no use, and instead took his friend to Sirone, where he hoped to explain everything to Sire Rone and use his noble status to clear the situation. Still he was not sure if Sire Rone could even do such a thing. These were difficult times, and it bothered Ark. Yet he kept his worries at bay. He wanted to get home first. So he rode, cheering up his friend, and remembering better days when he was still living in Villone. Those were pleasant memories, and they helped him get through the journey. At last the towers of Sire Rone's castle rose before them. Much time had passed since they had last seen the place. They had left it as green lads, and now were returning true fighting men. But they were not the only ones who had changed—the city was different too.

Chapter 64

REFRESHING REST restored our bodies and minds. With memories of Asson and the events of the preceding night pushed back, all the focus shifted to more immediate duties, such as finding a suitable place to restock our depleted supplies of food and fire stones. In the next parish we visited a decent shop, where we found everything we needed. With our saddlebags full again we resumed the journey.

The hours passed quickly. Traffic was light and the road was flat. With the dry southern wind chasing us, we picked up the pace, but as we veered around an island of trees, we came upon a group of soldiers moving in our direction, marching in one long well-formed column. There were at least two hundred men, almost all on foot. Each soldier wore a green chest plate, a round helm with an imprint of a broken sword on the side, and a small round shield, also green, with a picture of a broken sword displayed in black. On their shoulders they carried long metal spears with triangular tips, wrapped in dark brown cloths. At the top of the column, riding large black steeds, trotted a group of ten men. Just like the foot soldiers their uniforms and armor were of a green color, and their shields also showed a picture of a broken sword.

"Who are they?" I whispered to Elson, as we stirred out horses to the side of the road, letting the soldiers pass.

"These are the Maurisians, a freelance company from the Free Cities—probably got hired by the House of Coin."

"How many of them are here?" inquired Ike, and he moved closer to get a better look at the hired swords.

"About two hundred men, one regiment I would say. As to the size of the entire company, it is hard to say. The number of men any freelance company employs varies greatly. But there is never less than a thousand men."

"Wow, this is an army. With so many men they can conquer almost any kingdom!" Ric exclaimed in the back.

"I would doubt that. They are no match for a standing army. But joined together with other companies they can pose a serious threat."

Elson wanted to say something else, but unexpectedly one of the horsemen split from his group and rode up to us. He gave a quick salute and lifted his heavy visor, revealing an unshaved, scarred face. His dark brown eyes stared at us.

"Fair be your ways, travelers. I see you are heading for Azor." The man threw a glance over his shoulder.

"Yes, we are," replied Elson.

"If I were you I would think of changing your mind."

"Why?"

"There was another raid on the city. The attack came two nights ago. This time the poor side got hit the worst."

"Azor was attacked?" asked Elson, surprised. "How can this be? Who dared to attack the House of Coin right in its home?"

"Grass Folks, at least three tribes from the lower plains. Nobody knows how so many of them got to the city. I think they sneaked into the kingdom in small groups of five, ten men. The guards caught a few, but it was impossible to stop them all. When their numbers counted several thousand, they attacked. The city of Grumos was first. It was a tough fight there, but the walls held and the wildlings only destroyed the slums around the city. About the same time, another wild band launched an assault on Lupos, a lesser parish west of here. Unlike Grumos, the garrison there was small and could not stop the attack in time for the Brave Company to help it. After some hours of fierce fighting, the village fell to the enemy. Nothing of it stands today. Then, some days later, the wildlings appeared near Azor. They used the sewers to get inside the city."

"The sewers? I thought it was impossible to get through there," Elson said.

"Everyone thought so, everyone but the Grass Folks. They caught us completely by surprise. Before the guards could form their defenses, half of the poor side was destroyed. We were dispatched to the center, where the armory was. One of our regiments got hit hard. In all we lost thirty men dead, and seventy wounded. It was brutal."

"What about the western districts, did the wild men get there too?" asked Elson.

"No, only the poor side and a bit of the eastern district. Still if you plan to get there, you might have a hard time getting through the rubble. Most of the streets that lead up to the inner gates are still barricaded. There are a lot of collapsed buildings too. You will want to go around the poor side and try the northern gates. I think the doors should be opened for traffic. There were a lot of people fleeing the city too, so the roads are jammed. Everybody is afraid of another invasion. Who knows how many more wild men are hiding in the forest?" The man paused, at which time another soldier from the column yelled something at him. He turned and waved, then returned to us and lowered his visor.

"I have to leave you," he said abruptly and spun his horse.

"Thanks for the warning," said Elson. "Where are you heading now?"

"To Furosi, a small town on the western border. We have a camp there, and we need some rest. I have a feeling we will be fighting many more battles soon." The man waved again and rode off, galloping back to the front of the column. We remained still and waited for the remaining soldiers to pass. When the last of them was gone, we returned to the road, consumed by the news.

"Grass Folks!" exclaimed the Southerner as our company resumed the journey. "There has to be something wrong indeed with the world, if those wild men can reach Azor undetected."

"Who are those Grass Folks you speak of?" I asked Elson, taking my horse closer to him.

"The strange people of the Plains," replied the Southerner. He did not look at me, but ahead, toward the horizon, where new shapes appeared on the road. "Huge hordes of them, organized in loose tribes, roam the Great Plains south of the Free Cities. Usually they dare not cross into Ethoria, but occasionally a tribe or two will come together and launch a raid against one of the Free Cities in search of gold and slaves. More often than not the mercenary bands will repel these attacks, but sometimes they fail and then the cities are destroyed, every living soul enslaved, and every single building burned. Some of the Free Cities try to negotiate an alliance with the wildlings, but seldom they succeed, for the tribes' leaders change often, either killed in battle or overthrown by their own. Once an army of the Amber Empire marched into the Great Plains, instructed to rid the land of the wildlings. But no matter how many men the Imperial troops killed, twice as many came to fight them the next day. It was not long before the Amber armies had to withdraw, without as much as destroying a single tribe."

The Southerner did not say anything else, and I did not ask any more question. Meanwhile, along the way we met more people. Many were common folks, traders, craftsmen, and peasants, but there were also other mercenaries amongst them. Some walked in small bands, and others, like Mauritians, formed long columns, small armies, with their own command, supplies and wagons. Their faces were sour, their armor stained and dirty—marks of a heavy tiresome battle. I wanted to ask them if they were coming from Azor too, but Elson sent his horse into a frantic hurtle, making us chase him, running our horses toward the city.

By midday we arrived at a wide crossing. A long pole with wooden plaques stood in the center. Although I did not understand the letters written on the boards, I knew they were directions to the different parts of the city.

"North Gate," repeated Elson, after studying the signs. "Let's go." He snapped the bridle and turned. We followed. The path the Southerner chose was a side rode that ran around the poor side of Azor and up to the northern gates, letting us skip the devastated parts of the city, which most probably were closed to outsiders like ourselves. Since Revor's mansion was in the Western District of Romul, the new route promised to save us time and effort.

As we reached the outskirts of Azor, the devastation caused by the recent invasion became visible. The poor side, reserved for the indigent folks, indeed suffered much damage. Stacks of black smoke still rose up before the wall that encircled the rest of the city. Like ghost towers they swayed amongst burned skeletons of once sturdy houses, standing witness to the fury of the wild men's hunger. Soon a large fort, which stood in the middle of a long stretch of stone wall, came into the view. It was the northern gates of Azor.

Although I noticed some people manning the battlements and the four round towers, there was no one outside the gates. Heavy metal doors were opened and unguarded. A few common men went in and out through the stone archway, all worn-out and grim. Preoccupied with their own duties, none of them bothered us and let us pass into the inner grounds of Azor's common part, where piles of rubble and a stench of extinguished fires welcomed us. Though scores of the townsmen were doing their best to clean up the street, most of once open lanes remained blocked by the debris. Many more people ran frantically, some dragging large long barrels of water; others carrying long stretchers filled with various belongings. Although we could not see any dead, a sense of death was present, and getting stronger as we went further into the city.

Once we passed a large three-story building where several men, dressed in black leather suits moved bags of brown cloth, which held something resembling corpses; the stench became worse, and to escape it we had to make a quick turn and gallop through several intersections, almost knocking some passing folks off their feet. Only when we reached a narrow alley, which ran along the back walls of houses, did we slow down. By then another tall wall, which ran inside the city, blocked our way and we had to ride along it until we reached another set of gates that separated the western district of Azor. Unlike the northern gate, the upcoming entrance was blocked by thick wooden doors, closed shut from the inside. Again there were no guards anywhere in sight. But it did not seem to bother Elson, who had already dismounted and headed for the large archway, strolling casually across an open stretch of beaten soil.

Almost at the base of the gate, he yelled something in a foreign tongue and stepped back, looking up. At first nobody answered, so the Southerner yelled again. Then several figures appear at the top of the fortifications, sticking their heads out of the stone parapets. They studied our group for a few moment; then one of them yelled something back at Elson, and the two exchanged a few words, of which I did not understand any. Once they were done, the Southerner returned to us and climbed back to his horse. By that time I heard a loud click from behind the wall and the doors moved inward.

Through the gap we entered a short wide tunnel beneath the gatehouse and stopped again, this time halted by a large grate that rested before us. Several guards clad in iron armor were lingering behind it, pulling on thick ropes. A moment later the heavy grid jolted and moved up. Click, click, click. Finally, the grid stopped at the top, its black sharp teeth hanging menacingly over the paved lane. With our eyes up, watching the grate over our heads, we cleared the tunnel and entered the western district.

Immediately a group of soldiers, whose tired faces showed signs of sleepless nights, greeted us. Their armor was covered in dirt and their once white tunics stained in blood. The men gave us weary glances, and one of them, a short wide-shouldered lad in his late teens, resumed the conversation with the Southerner. They talked for some time, at times shaking their heads, and spitting on the ground. As before I could not understand a single word. But I was sure that they were discussing the recent invasion, of which I hoped to hear more.

Before long, we let the guards be and rode into the western district, turning and weaving through its busy streets. In contrast to the poor side, and the eastern part, reserved primarily for common traders and craftsmen, the better section of Azor was left unscarred. Except for some minor damage, confined mostly to the rooftops of the larger barracks that were adjusted to the inner wall, the quarters exuded lavish glitter and affluence. Most of the houses were well-built, often surrounded by gardens and parks. Fountains and statues decorated almost every corner, and marble plates covered the sidewalks. While by the gates a lot of smaller buildings were situated in and around large plazas, hosting many shops and eateries, each of its own design and coloring, further into the district the plazas became rarer, and then disappeared altogether, giving way to much larger and more luxurious mansions and smaller keep. It was amongst these lavishly decorated houses that we hoped to find Revor's home.

As much as we had traveled in the past months, the last stretch of the road was the longest by far. Every house we passed seemed to be the one, but we went on, making more turns, circling south. Then, clearing another long tall fence, we came up to a figured wooden gate, where Elson halted and dismounted again. While we remained on horses, the Southerner grabbed one of the metal rings and banged it on the wooden boards several times. The answer came almost immediately.

I heard some voices and the sound of footsteps, mingled with the clanking of metal, which could only mean chain mail and weapons. Then all the noise died and someone yelled out in a firm deep voice, "Who goes there?" It was spoken in the Northern Way, which surprised me.

"This is Elson. Did you people forget my voice already?" answered the Southerner, his head shaking.

"Elson, you say," continued the guard. "How do we know it is you? We need some proof."

"Proof? You need proof, you fool!" yelled the Southerner. "I will give you proof. How about I climb over that fence and show you what I can do to your face with my fist. Maybe it will refresh your memory, eh?"

A short pause followed. Several voices whispered something, then the same man spoke again, his tone a bit different this time. "Now you sound like a true Southerner. Welcome back, friend."

The locks moved quickly, and the door slowly floated inward, revealing a view of a large garden, seeded with grand statues, bricked lanes, fountains, and magnificent trees of unusual shapes. Five men stood at the other side, all dressed in heavy sets of plated armor, their heads crowned with polished round helms, adorned with symbols of a descending bird that resembled an eagle. As I have suspected they were house guards, mercenaries, hired by the owner to provide adequate security to his dwelling. They were all young, big in the shoulders, and cheerful, their faces carrying an expression of toughness and arrogance. They studied our company with interest, especially Ric, who stood three heads taller than they. But when they saw the Southerner, they quickly formed a line and straightened up, their eyes focused on him.

Elson did not seem to take notice of any of it, but just waved at the guards in a casual manner, so common to his southern manner.

"I see you have been enjoying the ales, Olas," the Southerner grinned, addressing one of the guards, a shorter lad with a pointy beard. His big tanned belly was sticking out from underneath his plate. "You know you cannot carry all that extra weight if you want to be a real hired sword." Elson slapped the man on the shoulder and laughed. Olas turned red in the face and lowered his eyes.

"Where is the old man? I have urgent business I need to discuss with him," the Southerner continued

"He is in his study. He has been working on his new manuscript ever since you left. He says it will be his best work. Truly, we have not seen much of him the past few weeks. He only asks for food and ink, and does not go outside at all. It worries me. He needs some fresh air," replied Olas and sighed.

"Fresh air," repeated Elson. "I am not sure that a walk through the city is such a good idea, especially when the place is being sacked by the Grass Folks."

"Oh no, I did not mean that," the guard hurried to explain. "I just wanted to—"

"Do not worry," the Southerner stopped him. "I know exactly what you mean." He gave the guard another light shove. "I will see to you men later. Now I have more pressing business."

Elson turned and started down one of the lanes, then stopped and added, "By the way, these three men are with me. They will be master's guests, in case you are wondering. Oh, and close the gates. We do not need any wildlings running around here. While at it, also strengthen the patrols along the walls. Something tells me we may have some unexpected visitors soon. I want to be ready. Get some extra hands if you need, but keep the estate sealed."

Elson saluted the men and resumed his walk. He halted again and added, without turning back, "And get my chest from the basement. I am tired of these old rags."

Chapter 65

REVOR'S MANSION, his humble home, as Elson described it, was a huge three-story building of light blue color. Long white pillars ran across the facade, spaced evenly between large windows carved out of fine aged pine, a distinctive deep brown color. At the top and the bottom of the outer walls, two rows of continuous frescoes stretched across, portraying scenes from various aspects of city life. On the roof, colored in a bright shade of green, five spiky towers, one large in the center and four small at each corner, held rows of narrow windows, and at the top, tall standards decorated with many large colorful banners. In the center, located between two giant stone carved wolves, was the grand entrance. As magnificent as the rest of the manor, the entry started with an open foyer, supported by large spiral columns arranged in a half circle. Wide expanding white stairs ran up to the front doors, sculpted out of large wooden plaques, displaying a unique design of wildflowers and birds. The doors were left open, and behind them, resting several cubits inside the house stood the second set, made almost entirely of treated glass. Completely translucent, they let the sunlight stream inside the mansion.

At the other end of the stairs, extending well into the park, was a clearing in a shape of a half circle, made of reddish powder, probably ground red brick, so popular in the Southern lands. It served as the parking place for the arriving carriages and horses, allowing the guests to come up to the mansion without bothering to leave their comfortable seats and saddles. And in the middle, straight across from the front entrance a large fountain of black stone completed the composition. The cascade was marvelous, depicting a scene from some old tale. In the very center, standing on a large pedestal raised over the water, was a figure of a bare-chested man with a short curly beard and long hair. He stretched his hands up to the sky holding a large round shield, where a beautiful maiden sat timidly, her own hands up toward a small dragon-like creature, which instead of fire breathed water that ran down onto the girl's hand and then into the pool beneath.

Near the fountain and at the front entrance stood more guards. Unlike the men at the outer gate they did not say anything, nor did they move. They only watched us carefully and nodded when Elson passed by, leading his horse up to the stairs, where we dismounted and followed him up and into a spacious oval hall, equal to the outside decor.

A cathedral plaster ceiling stretched high above, and held one large painting, which pictured several scenes from a great hunt, with images of horses, men, and wild beasts racing across an open valley, caught in a moment of chase. Straight ahead rising between two open corridors stood another staircase of white polished stone, with four statues of unusual beasts resting at the bottom, watching visitors as they passed by. I studied the statues as we headed to the next floor, walking over thick red carpet that covered almost the entire staircase, standing in sharp contrast to the walls dressed in green satin cloth. The same color scheme was present in the hallway that we took at the top of the stairs.

The long corridor ran across the house, eventually veering to the left, bringing us to another smaller stairwell, which took us to the third floor and a triangular door. Elson knocked on it several times and then opened it. We entered a sizable round room, filled with strange objects, odd-looking frescos, and tall shelves, packed with many books and scrolls, piled everywhere in disarray. As we walked in, a distant voice came from behind a large rack of bookshelves, which stood at the far side of the room in the afternoon shadows. I could not understand what the voice was saying, but I was sure it was talking to us. Elson said something back, and the secluded mumbling continued.

"*Shorum, sara,*" said Elson a moment later. He shrugged off his cape and walked up to one of the shelves. "*Shorum alar,*" replied the voice.

"*Asir mara sarush,*" said Elson, that time with a smile on his face.

"*Loria morus suri mana.*" The answer came, and a small pile of books moved slightly. From behind it, dressed in long blue robe covered in dust and sand, a dull aged figure appeared. The man was in his late years, but not yet elderly. His hair, hidden under a plain leather cap retained its original black color and curled around his large ears, covering some of the wrinkles that ran across his reddish cheeks. And on his nose, just beneath thick dark eyebrows, he had a pair of glass disks, similar to the ones I had seen on the old hermit, Irk the Wise, back in Bois. Through these two tired eyes looked at us, studying our company with a visible meticulousness. In his hands the man carried a large leather book, which he quickly closed and put aside.

"*Shorum aser,*" started the man, then he stopped, scratched his forehead, and smiled. "Oh, my sincere apologies," he continued in the Northern tongue. "Where are my manners?...By your looks I can tell you do not speak the Southern way. How rude of me...Sometimes I completely forget which tongue I am speaking. My years have not been too kind to me; my mind is not what it used to be. Once again I apologize for this inconvenience."

The man bowed slightly and slid to a low desk near the window, pulling a wooden armchair, closer to him.

"My name is Revouar Rey'noland Mi Noiry. But everybody calls me guru Revor. It is not exactly accurate, but I do not mind." The man coughed loudly then slapped his chest several times, clearing his throat.

"I am the owner of this estate, and the employer to this man." Revor pointed at Elson and bowed his head a bit. "You probably think of me as some sort of merchant, a man of coin. But I am not. I am a man of science, a man of knowledge and wisdom, or that is what I tell myself. He he he." Revor laughed. "Some call me a sage, others a tutor, and a few even call me a wizard, though I know nothing of the lore of magic. But that's what they say, I do not mind it, as long as they leave me be."

Revor paused, leaned back in his chair and addressed the Southerner. "I see you have returned safely, my young friend. It brings me great joy. You do not know how worried I was when I got news of your capture. But now, as I see you here before me, I assume everything has gone well for you."

"In the end it all played out fine. There were some obstacles along the way, my capture would be one. But those were minor setbacks, the job is done, just as we had planned," Elson replied cheerfully.

"And your friends. Something tells me that they are the Northerners you have told me about. Let me see." Revor rose from his chair and walked up to us. "Huh. Very interesting indeed. Frankly I have expected a much older company." He spoke to the Southerner and then turned back to us. "They are just boys, no older then eighteen or nineteen."

"They are young in flesh, but strong in spirits. I am almost sure these are the lads you have been looking for," replied Elson.

I shook my head. "Wait a moment here. What are you two talking about? Do you care to explain this to us? You told us this man would help us with our quest. You never said you were looking for us. I wonder what could be the reason for such interest. Oh wait, I can probably guess myself. It has something to do with the Alavantars. But let me tell you if you are with them, we will not give up without a fight."

To validate my words I grabbed the hilt of my sword. I could not see my friends, but I could hear their weapons leaving their resting places in a swift preparation for battle. Elson and Revor remained calm and unmoved, though they watched as we moved back and took the defensive formation. When we were done, Revor raised his hand and smiled kindly.

"You do not have to worry yourself with thoughts of betrayal. We are truly your friends, allies if you wish. I understand your concerns. But if you give me a few moments I will try to explain everything. Please," said Revor and he sat back into his chair. "Lower your weapons, there is no need."

I looked around, first at Elson, then Revor, then back at my friends. Although I was ready to fight, I did not feel like crossing my sword with Elson, who had become a true member of our group. Remembering A'tie's words, I put down my anger and lowered the sword. My friends followed my example, and Elson, who did not stop smiling, gave us four small stools. When all settled around him, Revor took off his glass disks, cleared them with the tip of his sash, and put them back on.

"It is true," he started slowly. "It was my intention to get you to Azoros, but it was not until I learned of your struggle against the Alavantars. Do not be alarmed though. I can assure our that my goals are the same as yours. We have a common enemy." Revor took a drink of water and resumed. "You have already learned much about the Alavantars. I have too. Unfortunately we are the few. Most people are unaware of the sect. Even those I warn of the dangers wielded by the group, do not listen. Those fools answer me with jokes and laughter. They think I have lost my mind. Their little brains cannot even comprehend all the grief perils that are waiting our world in the years to come.

This is why to find someone, anyone, who is equally aware of the Alavantars is irreplaceable. You cannot imagine, how long I have been looking for allies, people who are ready to stand up against the Alavantars and their crazed masters. When I received a note from Elson, telling me that he had heard of a band of adventurers who opposed the Alavantars, I had to meet you. Alas I could not come myself, so I instructed Elson to try and bring you to Azor where we could meet in person.

Now, as you have arrived we should not waste any more time. We have already lost too many days, allowing our foes to grow stronger. I understand your mistrust. If it were me, I would have acted in a similar manner. But let me talk. Maybe afterwards I will regain your trust."

Revor glanced at us. Everyone was quiet. The old sage pulled one of the large tomes closer to him, blew off a thick layer of dust, and opened its heavy leather cover.

"Unfortunately, the world we live in today is full of ignorance. In all their cries for knowledge and enlightenment our fellow Ethorians refuse to see what is unfolding right before their eyes. While so-called scholars and sages search for some forgotten mysteries of ancient times, they fail to notice the most evident things, things that can answer their many questions. They claim to take their wisdom from ancient texts. Yet they pay no attention to the words those texts hold. Like fools they clang to their settled ways, studying only what they can see and hear.

"Alas Ethorians will not change, at least, not until the day comes when the sky rains fire and the old enemy comes back from across the Land's Edge. Only when an old forgotten feud is renewed will they come to understand that they were blind, ignorant, and stupid. But it will be too late. The time of terror and sorrow will descend upon the world. The rivers will take on the color of blood, and the sky will turn black from smoke and ashes. Many will die, many more will suffer greatly. No standing army of men will be able to halt the invading force. Entire nations will fall, their dwellers cast in chains and iron, led away as slaves and servants to their new masters. And all because we did not learn from the past.

"Fortunately, there is still a chance, a chance that will depend on one man—the Chosen One, as Arac calls him. That man—a warrior, a leader, and a savior—will be entrusted with safe-keeping of Ethoria, and bringing peace back into the world."

Revor paused and sipped from the glass again. A chuckling noise ran across the room. The sage then took another deep breath and pulled the books closer. He lowered his head and read small lines of fine text. His boney hand ran down the pages, turning them with an amazing speed, then he continue.

"Today, we stand on the brink of time, when chaos returns to Ethoria after many years of waiting. Across the Land's Edge a great Northern army will come, led by another great man, a leader, a warrior, a god to his followers, and a tyrant to his enemies. He will command a vast host of wild men and beasts, endeavoring for his only goal—the utter downfall of all the human realms in Ethoria. If he is successful, our world as we know it will cease to exist, and all the kingdoms and empires, including your home realm of Normandia, will disappear forever.

"That man, the Northern ruler, is also called the Master of the Old. Regrettably, we know very little of him. Prophecies of Arac serve as the only texts where we can find any descriptions of him, telling us that he is the son of Alin, a descendent of the fallen Keepers, imprisoned beyond the Land's Edge by his own kin. The prophet says that the Master of the Old wields great powers, both in his body and in his mind. He will be able to travel the world without taking a single step, and will be able to persuade anyone without saying one word. Compassion and justice will not be his virtues, as only everlasting lust for absolute power will drive him. Strengthened by defeating his foes, he will not tolerate any resistance. Those who decide to stand in his path will perish, and those who survive will be put to sword, so as to teach the others a horrible lesson. If he is not stopped in time, he will rule Ethoria one day, marking the worst of times for all.

"But, as I said, this dark force will have a worthy adversary, the Chosen One. The protector of Ethoria will rise from the ranks of the common men and stand up against the invading horde, leading his own armies to battle, of which there will be many, each more immense than the previous. Steel and iron will come together as thousands of soldiers clash, turning soil into a sea of blood, sweat, and fire. And in the end, it will all come to one final standoff, a great battle, when two armies meet for the last time. There on that field, the fate of Ethoria will be determined. Sadly Arac does not talk of the outcome of that battle. Many think that the final pages of the prophecies, which describe the aftermath of the fight, have been lost, that by finding them it will be possible to know the end of the conflict, but after studying the texts for many years, I am convinced that there are no lost chapters in Arac's Verses. The prophet did not know the outcome himself, nor do we now. "

Revor became silent again. He returned his glance to the book in front of him and froze. The story was familiar to me. I had heard it before, from Irk the Wise, and from A'tie. So taking advantage of the intermission, I voiced my thought. "I must tell you that we already know this story. We know all about the prophecies, Arac, the invasions, and the Great War. We even know about the Chosen One. But what does it all have to do with us?"

"Huh," replied the sage, taking his eyes off the book. "This is a most intricate question indeed. What does it all have to do with you? I will try to answer. As I have suspected, you are familiar with Arac and his words of the future, so I will not waste any more time explaining to you the significance to these predictions. I will not talk about the ancient history either. I sense you have heard it too. Instead, I will tell you of things that I think may link you to it.

"I will start will the Alavantars. I have no doubt that they are responsible for the many troubles in Ethoria. But they were not always like that. Once, a long time ago, they were true scholars, who devoted their time to the search for knowledge and wisdom. Driven by a desire to learn more of the origin of the world, a small group of young sages from across the world traveled to Magnicia, where they spent years picking through the old stones of the ruined cities, looking for scrolls, books, and artifacts. When they found something, they studied it carefully, recording their finds in many journals, which they later stored in underground compounds, deep beneath the wilds of Magnicia. It was in those days that I first came to the forsaken realm, seeking the true meaning of life. Young and full of energy, I journeyed hundreds of leagues across Magnicia, visiting dozens of ruined sites, picking through the rubble in hopes of uncovering a mystery of some sort. Somewhere through my travels I met the Alavantars. They took me in as their own, sharing their discoveries, teaching me many secrets of the ways of the ancient races. A new world of knowledge opened up to me. Intrigued, I sought their company, and before long became one of them. Yes, yes. Do not be surprised. I was once an Alavantar too.

"For many years to come I served the common goal of the group, which was a pursuit of wisdom lost. It was a time of sheer joy, a time when as a devoted member I was happy to risk my own life for the benefit of the others. That was...until the arrival of Agraz, when things began to change. At first there were only faint changes. Many did not even notice them—a few new ideas, new people, new goals. But when the prophecies of Arac were discovered, things really started to change. Since the ancient text was written in the old tongue, called Uru, long dead and forgotten, it took much time to translate the Verses. Little by little, all the search for knowledge was abandoned, and everyone focused on the newly found texts. Day and night everyone in the group deciphered Arac's words. The Alavantars no longer sought enlightenment. Many old precious books were throw away, piled up in old dusty cellars. The only task that everybody cherished was our translation of Arac's prophecies.

"Meanwhile, the ranks of the sect were being cleansed. The old leaders vanished one by one, and new men took their place. I was promoted too, all because of my progress with the Verses' translation. From the second brother of Arac, I became a member of the first council and by the order of Agraz was instructed to perfect my interpretations of the prophecies.

"I remember it like yesterday. An old, crumbling stack of parchments sat on my desk. A single candle lit my small room. The yellow leaves of thin tree crust were so aged that I was afraid they would fall apart right in my fingers. Oh what a feeling it was—to touch the ancient relic, to read straight from the past. Although I succeeded in translating almost the entire work, there were still passages that eluded me. But the challenge only inspired me more, and I dug deeper into the pages, trying to decode the inscribed symbols.

"To tell you the truth I was so consumed by my work I cared little of the daily life of the sect. But when I finally emerged from my daze, I was a stranger to my own brothers. The Alavantars had become so different that I could not recognize any of them. Even my best friends were no longer sound, their minds corrupted by Agraz teachings, based solely on the translated parts of the Verses. The new leader preached a new faith, a faith to follow a new master, the Master of the Old. Where once I saw scholars, stood uncompromising fools. They became the slaves to the false faith, puppets in hands of Agraz. They denied enlightenment, choosing to devote their lives to serve the dark lord of the North instead. Those fools believed so blindly that with the coming of the Master of the Old they would become his great disciples and trusted aids, that they began to despise the world they lived in. They no longer cared for Ethoria. Instead they sought its destruction. Their only goal was to help the Master of the Old.

"At first I thought such beliefs would fade, that they would never last. But I was wrong. Agraz ideas proved to be too popular not only amongst the brothers of the sect, but other folks as well. More people joined the group, and as the Alavantars grew in numbers, they expanded outwards, seeping into the many realms, unnoticed by the local sovereigns. They formed the council of Jeg Aazes, and saw it's members open chapters throughout the lands, building an interactive web, like spiders in a warm dark cellar. Before long, there were hundreds of chapters, thousands of Alavantars, and many more supporters scattered all across the world, each serving one common goal.

"Such changes frightened me. I questioned my ties to the sect. I no longer felt part of the group. I was an outsider, and the clouds started to gather over my head. First I lost my position with the council, demoted back to second brother. Then I lost my journals, and then Arac's scrolls as well. Only my former friends did not suspect that I was prepared for such a course of action. Before surrendering my work I made a copy of the old texts, the replica I gave away and the original I kept for myself. Those fools never noticed, nor did they realize that I tampered with the copy. Sensing the dangers that the Alavantars could pose for the world, I altered the copied text, switching words and symbols, changing the meaning of some passages, so to sway the Alavantars away from the true message of the prophecies.

"Then one night, an old friend of mine, Auro, came to me with a warning that my brothers were set to kill me soon. There was little for me to do, but leave the sect and take a hasty journey south, to Azoros, a place where I knew it would be easier to hide from the Alavantars. Packing only a few personal things, my journals and Arac's scrolls, I took a secret passage to Dvorenia. There I reserved a carriage and rode south, keeping close to the edge of the Great Forest all the way to Azor. Once there, I changed my name and settled in a small house in the slums of the poor side, renting my services as a tutor. After many small jobs, I found a wealthy merchant who was willing to hire me full-time as a teacher for his two children. The two young boys were as stupid as pigs, but their father insisted on their education. I tried my best, but the results were mediocre. Eventually the merchant had to give up all his efforts and sent the lads to the Amber Empire to attend a military academy. For some reason he continued to retain my services for several more years, according me a humble salary, which in turn allowed me to buy this house and the services of a few men, such as Elson.

"But in all the time I spent in exile, I never stopped studying Arac's scrolls. Several years ago I made a breakthrough in interpreting the parts of text, which until then had remained unconquered. Amongst newly translated passages I found the answers that the Alavantars had sought so desperately. Indeed there was a weapon I could use against them."

"If your words are true, sage, then we may find a way to work together," I noted, still a bit distrustful of Revor and his tale.

"Good," the sage replied quickly, and smiled. His glass disks slid down his nose and he nodded several times. "I am glad we understand each other. It makes everything much easier. Now, if you do not mind, I would like to continue with my story. As I have already mentioned, the Alavantars have only one goal, which is to see the Lord of the North succeed in his conquest of Ethoria. When Agraz declared himself as the supreme leader of the Alavantars, he claimed to receive his powers from the Master of the Old himself. Although I doubt this, there is something unnatural about him. Somehow, no matter how far he is, he seems to see and know everything, making it almost impossible to deceive him. Out of fear or lust or admiration, the others follow him without question. In return he promises them whatever they desire—rank, lands, gold, and wisdom.

"Seeing only promised riches, the fools try to do everything in their power to bring to life the prophecy of the Great War. So far they have succeeded in penetrating into every realm, in some places reaching as high as the ruling families. Do not be surprised, but minds of many lords, merchants, knights, and soldiers have been tainted by the false preaching. The ranks of the Alavantars continue to grow, and their powers continue to expand, weakening the kingdoms of Ethoria.

"Not long ago there was a new order from Jeg Aazes, instructing every Alavantar with the mission of eliminating the adversary of the north. They decided that they could change the course of events and remove a threat to the Master of the Old by killing the one who can challenge him. In his prophecies Arac has described the Chosen One in great detail, and the Alavantars took that depiction as the guide. I must say that I am partially to blame for it. By translating Arac's manuscript, I inadvertently led them closer to finding the Chosen One and destroying him.

"You are probably wondering what Arac has said about the savior of Ethoria? I will tell you."

Revor turned another page and started to read, monotonously taking sips from his glass, smacking his lips afterwards. "Arac has told us that the Chosen One would come from the Northern parts of the world, the regions which border the Land's Edge mountains. Once a part of the ancient empire of Titul, the home kingdom of the Chosen One will hold the last true treasure of the world, a deep blue lake, sealed deep within the aged thick trunks of the ancient forest. In those lands, the future savior would live his life until the time comes for him to start his journey. Arac points out that the Chosen One will be a firstborn child, raised by a family keen on gold, good fortune, and respect. Sheltered from the perils of rough life, he would share his home with many siblings, of whom one will be his true brother. Exactly twenty three cycles after the last great battle, he will depart and take on a quest of his own that will take him many places, all in the search for the true meaning of his soul."

"Excuse me, but I though the last great battle took place thousands of years ago," I asked, confused by tale.

"Back in the days of Arac, there was a different calendar. People used a different time line, borrowed from the A'als and D'ars. Then, in those times, they did not have years, they had cycles, worth several hundred years each. When I did all the calculation and deductions, the date that Arac talked about corresponds to the year 1220 of the New Era of the Second Age."

"But this is only five years away," spoke Ike.

"Exactly my point. I am sure that Alavantars came to the same conclusion too….Anyway…Once you put together everything that the prophecies tell us, it will not take long to realize why people began to disappear in Normandia. There is no doubt in my mind that the Alavantars are responsible for all the vanishings. Following Arac's words, they are set to hunt and kill anyone who resembles the description of the Chosen One. But they do not know all. Roaming across Normandia, the Northern Empire, and Westalia, they search for their victims in the dark. Because of my doings, they do not have the full description. Some parts of the portrait are missing, and so the sect cannot locate its target. Yet my tampering proved to be a two-edged sword. I distanced the Chosen One from the dangers of the sect, but at the same time endangered hundreds of others. Not knowing who to pursue, the Alavantars strike at everyone. Nobody can tell how many young men and boys have already fallen prey to these crazed fanatics.

"Of course, when I first heard about all those incidents I was not exactly sure if it was the Alavantars. But I had to find out. To do so I had to find a way to check out the disturbances, to gather evidence, facts, accounts. Since it was impossible for me to travel myself, I sent my trusted friend Elson, who journeyed to the Northern Empire, then the Barrier, and then Normandian. Throughout his voyage he collected information, talked to local folks, and studied every unexplained disappearance involving young men or boys. Then he reported back to me, sending several birds a day.

"In the meantime I continued my work on the translations, especially the passages I had concealed from the Alavantars. Slowly decoding the remaining symbols I uncovered several crucial details about the Chosen One, which the Alavantars had never known. My findings led me to believe that although the Chosen One was indeed a firstborn, it did not mean that he was the son of the man who had raised him. The prophecies tell that a child who is destined to save the world, will not in fact be the son of the man he calls father. Rather he will be a child of a human woman and a Keeper."

"A Keeper?" exclaimed Ike, jumping out of his seat. "I thought the Keepers were dead."

"Yes, the Keeper, the last surviving relic of the distant past, the last member of his ancient race."

"Are you saying there is a true, living Keeper, somewhere in Ethoria?" I asked, equally astonished.

"I do not know. It is what I have read. Arac says that it will be a union of the two races, that through the veins of the Chosen One will flow blood of the ancient race. It is this heritage that will make the Chosen One—the chosen common man—a hero and a great warrior."

"Still I do not understand. How does all this make the Alavantars wrong in their pursuit?" Ric looked at the sage, then at me.

"You are too young to see it. I will try to explain. If the Chosen One is a son of the Keeper, and not his foster father, it means that he may not necessarily be the oldest of the siblings, which in turn means that by hunting down only the young men they believe to be the firstborns, Alavantars are looking for someone else, and thus allowing the true redeemer to escape."

"So you are saying that the Alavantars have been chasing the wrong man all along?" my brother asked again.

"In simple words, yes."

"Then, it means that anyone can be the Chosen One, anyone at all?"

"Not really. Remember the Chosen One has to be the son of a Keeper." Revor smiled slightly.

"How can you tell who is truly the Chosen One? Is there a way to find out? Like a test or a trial of some sort?"

"Indeed, there is such a test, though it is not really a test. To find out if someone is the Chosen One, he has to evoke one of the Spirits. It is believed that some Keepers concealed themselves within the waters of the lakes, so as to escape death. Those who decided to do so, lost their bodily form and transformed into Spirits. Although back in the days when Arac wrote his prophecies there were many such lakes all across Ethoria, today I know of only one such pond—the Lake of Wonders in Normandia. The prophecy says that when the moon is full, the Chosen One has to come to the Spirit's resting place. Then a secret passage will open, leading him into the dwelling of the Spirit. I do not know what will happen afterwards, but when the Chosen One emerges onto the surface he will know his destiny, and his true name—the true savior of Ethoria."

"Huh, interesting. Lake of Wonders. We should stop by there someday." I smiled. "Who knows...maybe one of us is the Chosen One. Won't that be something? Ike the Great, the Savior of the World...what do you think?"

"I wish it were true." Ike sighed. "But I do not have any brothers, just sisters."

"Who knows, maybe you do have brothers and you just do not know about them yet?" Ric laughed loudly.

"You talk crazy, Ric." Ike turned red.

"Crazy or not," interrupted Revor, "he may be right. The identity of the Chosen One is yet unknown."

"I still do not see how it will help us find Father and Ave. Back in Pullie Elson said that you might know how to find them. Do you know anything of their fate?" I asked the sage the question that was in my head ever since we had agreed to join the Southerner on his journey to Azoros.

"Not yet. But do not be discouraged. Azor is a unique place. You would be surprised what you can learn here by just visiting one of the local eateries. No matter where things happen, here people know about them. Give me a few days. Maybe I will find out something."

Revor rose up and addressed the Southerner. "My good friend, it seems that I will need your assistance once more. Can you ask around about Mishuk's father? Use your sources, see what you can come up with."

"Of course, master Revor," said Elson, and he climbed from his chair and left the room.

As the door shut behind him, I turned to the sage. "What about your former friends,…won't they figure out everything you have just told us?"

"Those infidels who call themselves the prophets of the North are nothing but self-centered, mulish fools. They are so absorbed with pleasing their leader that none of them even care to see if they are heading in the right direction. At present time all they want is to kill as many young Northerners who fit the description as possible. They do not question why, they just do it. So blindly do they pursue their false beliefs that they would never admit to being wrong. After all Agraz talks directly to the Master of the Old, and with such great power within him, there can be no mistake. It is why we still have time. We can still spoil their plans, and rid the world of their poisonous presence."

"How do you suggest we do it? So far only a handful of people know about their existence. You said yourself, the Alavantars have nobles amongst them, they have gold and armies of mercenaries and many supporters. What can we do against such force?" I raised the next question.

"Do not be so gloomy. You may not know it yet, but your seemingly innocent investigation into the disappearance of your father's caravan has stirred up suspicion amongst a lot of people. Several lords from your home realm were alerted by your findings. You will be glad to know that the Dukes of Bois and Puno sent out an army to eliminate the threat of the Alavantars in Normandia. It was a successful campaign too. Mercenaries and local bandits were no match for the mighty knights of Bois. The chapter was destroyed, so it was our first victory, the beginning for which you are solely responsible."

"How do you know about the campaign?" I was curious about the expedition I had seen in my visions. I was not sure how true they were; I was still getting used to the Fore Sight. But when I heard Revor's words, I was convinced that what I had seen in my dreams was true. Did it mean that everything else was true as well? Such a revelation scared me. But past the fear I sensed excitement, because if true, the Fore Sight granted me an ability to travel great distances and see things that others could not, a marvelous talent indeed.

"I told you—Azoros is a unique place. You can learn everything here, almost as fast as it happens elsewhere. And the news of the campaign against the

Alavantars in Normandia has been told in locals taverns for quite some time." Revor paused. "But it is just the beginning. While Agraz is still alive, the Alavantars will not be defeated. We need to strike at the heart of the beast, their stronghold hidden within the ruins of Magnicia. It is there the true enemy lurks."

"But how do we know where to find them? You have left the sect many years ago. Since then they could have moved some other place," asked Ike.

"Finding Agraz is not your biggest problem, defeating him is. He is a sly foe. He knows and sees all. I am sure your endeavor has not gone unnoticed by him either. You will need an army to defeat the Alavantars. And to get an army you will have to persuade your lords. It should be easy enough by now. Normandian lords already know about the sect. Besides those nobles are always ready to prove their worth to the King. To them it will be a question of honor and courage."

"A good proposal. But how are we to make the lords join us? They are nobles, they do not listen to the likes of us." Ike sighed.

"This may be, but remember you have already made them listen once. A Duke himself has acted on what you have told him. He may listen to you again. The least you can do is try. Besides, I may be able to assist you."

To tell Sire Tem—that was easier said than done, I thought to myself, recalling some of my latest visions. If the Fore Sight had told the truth, the lords of Bois had more important matters to worry about—a civil war, for one. "I cannot leave Azoros without finding out something about my father and Ave," I said, troubled deeply by my own deliberations.

"Give me some time and I will get you your answers," replied Revor. He said something else, but it was mumble that soon turned to silence. We sat quiet for some time. Then his voice rose again. "It is getting late, and I see that we all are tired. You have just heard so many new things that you want to think them over. As for me, I am an old man and need rest. Let us adjourn this talk until later. For now, consider my house as your new home. I have already arranged for the rooms to be ready. There you will find all the necessary things— hot water, towels, and clean clothes. Dinner is served at seven. I will see you downstairs then."

Revor nodded and pulled a rope that hung at one side of the window. A distant bell rang several times. Soon two young fellows appeared in the door and escorted us into the hallway, talking to us in a broken Northern way. "We now go and show you rooms. Your things with us. We clean them, and give back later. Rooms nice, you like them. If you want baths, they are ready too, hot, very, very hot. We sorry."

Rumbling, the men hurried, taking long strides, first to the stairs, and then to the second floor, also lavishly decorated and well lit.

Several wide hallways ran parallel to each other, occasionally linked together by shorter, equally wide passages. Along the corridors, on both sides, stood tall polished doors carved out of deep brown wood. All the entrances were closed, and some had guards sitting near them. At one of the doors, the servants finally stopped. "Your rooms. I hope you like," they said almost at once. Then one of them turned a knob and let us enter a large chamber, divided into three parts by two rows of columns. The pillars were wide, but set apart at a good distant from each other, enough for us to see through from one end to another. Each section of the room had a large sturdy bed, plenty of furniture, a bath, and several open chests packed with various colorful items of clothing.

The servants left us amongst the luxury, letting us relax and talk about all we had heard and seen in Azoros. Time went by quickly. Before I knew it, the sky darkened, and soon after a couple of other servants came in and invited us for the evening meal, which was served in a dining hall on the first floor of the mansion—another grand display of luxury and splendor.

Amidst the marble chamber, at least fifty cubits long and twenty cubits wide, stood a heavy oak table covered with green silk cloth. From one end to the other it was crammed with food and drink. Rows of metal plates, brass glasses, and thin elegant silverware formed perfect lines, all glittering in the light of the many lamps and chandeliers. In the very center sat a huge tray, and on it rested a whole steaming roasted carcass of a wild boar. Around it, placed in large bowls, were fresh herbs and fruits, piled up high so that some pieces fell onto the table, splashing clear drops of water onto the cloth. Dishes of tasty poultry, cold meats, and freshly baked bread, loaves of it, warm and full of aroma, were mixed with jams, and spices, and fresh fruits, and everything else imaginable, which completed the colorful display.

As we walked in, Revor, who himself had appeared from one of the side doors, gave us a welcoming jest and took his seat, a cushioned thick armchair placed conveniently at the head of the table beside a large glass jar of bloodred wine. He seemed to be pleased with the efforts of his cooks, and was smiling widely, overlooking the foods before him.

"What are you waiting for?" he asked, looking at us with a hint of a laughter on his face. "Are not you hungry? You must be hungry, after such a long journey."

Ric, Ike, and I nodded in response, and took a few steps toward the table.

"Ah, do not be shy. Come, take thee seats next to me. We shall chat as we eat." Revor took in the wonderful aroma of the food and sank a knife into a large piece of a chicken. Instantly scores of servants, all dressed perfectly in white tunics and green trousers, crowded the room, each quickly attending to our persons. The feast reminded me of Arley and his father the count, only at Revor's it was even richer, more extravagant, and tastier. It was a banquet I would never forget.

Chapter 66

RED WINE, southern cuisine, and a cheerful mood were a pleasant change to our long voyage. When we were done eating, Revor invited us to another room, which looked like a small library, with shelves of books covering the walls from the ceiling to the floor. Settling on top of many soft pillows thrown over a thick red carpet, we resumed our chat, sweetened by a jar of warm wine brought by one of the servants. Nobody noticed time passing, but when a light knock came from behind the door, it was very late. Escorted by a single servant Elson strolled in, greeting everyone with a quick smile. He was still in his street clothes. His cloak, dirty at the bottom, swayed on his shoulder.

"How are you?" Revor asked the Southerner, waving for him to take a seat next to us. Elson gladly accepted the invitation and dropped to the floor.

"Do not delay, tell us everything you have learned." The sage grabbed a poured glass and gave it to the Southerner. Elson took the metal cup and downed it in one gulp. "It was unusually hard," he said afterwards. "For some reason my usual sources have not been all that forthcoming with the information, which means that someone very powerful and wealthy must be behind this. Yet, I did find someone who seemed to know a little about your father's caravan, Mishuk. The problem is that I was unable to find out what he knows. For that we need to pay him."

"How much?" Ike and I asked together. We had some money left, and we could sell our mounts if needed.

"A thousand gold plates," replied Elson. The number made me speechless. A thousand gold plates! I repeated silently. Where in the world could I get so much gold? Even if I were a lord I would not have that much money. Surely Elson was joking.

"A thousand!" Ike cried out my words aloud. "I do not think I have ever seen anyone with so much money. It is ridiculous. No...it is stupid. How are we supposed to get a thousand gold plates? Even if we sell everything we have, we will never get even a tenth of what is needed." Ike sighed and added, "Who is this man? Maybe we can get that information some other way, let's say…we can talk to him with our swords. I am sure he will be persuaded."

"I seriously doubt it." Elson grinned, swallowing another gulp of wine. "Unless you intend to break into a mercenary stronghold and dispose of several dozen guards, I suggest you think of some other way."

"Elson is right. Violence is not a solution, at least not here in Azor. Money and favors are the ultimate tools of persuasion," the sage noted in a calm voice.

"Then we can forget about asking that source of yours any questions. We do not have the money." Ike was still fuming.

"Wrong again," the sage replied. He glanced at me and bowed his head a little. "I will give you the money. A thousand gold plates may be a lot, but it is a meager price to pay for a win against the Alavantars. Elson…When can we expect to meet with this man?"

"Whenever we have the money. He will be waiting for us by the southern gates."

"Then it is settled. Tell him to meet us at the southern gates in four hours. Also tell him that we will have the money."

"How safe will it be?" I asked the Southerner and the sage.

"It will be safe enough. People here respect such dealings. If something should happen tonight, it will not go unnoticed. But just in case I suggest you put on your war gear. I do not think you will need it, but it is better to have the others see that you are prepared." The Southerner got up from the pillows, as did Revor. The two quickly headed for the door.

"The servants will escort you back to your rooms," added the sage. "We will see each other by the front doors in three hours."

Revor then dismissed us all, and himself left the room, trailed by the Southerner. We were taken upstairs to our quarters, where we found our sets of armor and weapons neatly placed on top of large wide chests, cleaned and glossy.

Even though I was excited about the news, some questions held back my enthusiasm. How true was all that I had heard? Was I to trust the sage or the Southerner? Were we to take his proposal and meet with a mysterious source? Or was I to prepare myself for a betrayal?

At last I was close to the conclusion of my quest. Yet I did not feel confident. I just did not believe that it would be so easy. Maybe it was time for it to come to an end. I caught myself on a thought I wanted for my voyage to conclude. The three hours passed quickly.

As I put on my chain mail I heard the door open, and the shadow of a tall man appeared in the entryway. The figure stayed there for a moment, then swayed to one side and stepped in As the light glided over his face I recognized Elson's features. The Southerner was cheerful.

"Everything is set. Master Revor is waiting outside." Elson clapped his hands several times, rubbing his palms together a little. "Let's go."

The Southerner waved for us to follow and went back into the corridor. We immediately followed. At the front entrance our company was met by the sage and together we walked outside, where two large, closed carriages were promptly pulled up to the bottom of the stairs. Saying nothing, Ric, Ike, and I climbed into one of the coaches and two pairs of large brown horses started to pull.

We rode through the dark alleys for a long time, passing lonesome lit windows, which disappeared almost immediately, swathed by the black shapes of the buildings. Although the trip was rough, it was nothing compared to the worn-out saddles, which had endured quite a beating since we had left Normandia. The thick leather cushions that covered the wooden benches inside the carriages felt soft and comfortable, and after some shifting allowed for some rest. Leaning back against the wall, also covered in leather padding, I let my limbs relax and stared out of a narrow opening. I did so until the carriage stopped, and a thickset man dressed in a long cape that covered him from neck to toe, opened the curtained door. The bright light of a lantern lit the way, and we promptly climbed out, joining the sage and the Southerner, who immediately started walking along a narrow alley running between two tall windowless buildings, each at least five stories high.

At the corner we turned and went across a wide street toward a three-story wooden house, illuminated by a row of torches placed high over the entrance. At the front door we turned again and entered a large plaza, with a fort rising at the far end, its high walls and thick guard towers lit with many torches. At the center of the front wall was a single entrance, a gate of metal and wood. The doors were closed, but as we came to them, they opened and we were allowed in. The corridor, made up of dark green plastered walls, went slightly upward and ended with another door, which opened as soon as we reached it. There, a tall bold man, dressed in a long wide dark blue cape, greeted us, and after giving the Southerner a light nod, stepped aside, letting us through into a tended round courtyard.

At first the place looked deserted, but as my eyes moved away from the fires of the torches, I saw figures standing some distance away in the cover of the green plants of the garden. Four men stood in the shadows, their faces shielded by wide hoods. They remained silent and unmoving until all of us were inside. Then one of them came out into the light and gestured for us to follow him toward the other side, where past a small pond towered a long one-story house. Its windows were lit, and in them I could see several moving shapes.

Our arrival was expected. As soon as we entered the house, two men blocked our way. They inspected us with cautious glares for a moment, then moved away. We moved further into a spacious hall decorated with large shields and suits of armor, which hung on the walls. In the center of the room stood an old long dining table. Several dozen chairs surrounded it, lined up in perfect rows, all covered in white cloths. Another group of armed men stood along the walls, ten or twelve of them in all, dressed in capes, hooded, with loaded crossbows in hand. They never once took their eyes off our company, not until the front door opened again, and a tall slender man walked in.

Once past the doorway, he threw off his hood and exposed the fine featured, slim face of a middle-aged man. Brief in his salutation, he moved around us and settled in one of the chairs, looking up at Revor and Elson. The three exchanged nods, and the man switched his attention to Ric, Ike, and me. He looked at us for a while, then leaned back, crossed one leg over the other, and raised his voice, which had a thick accent to it. "So my old friend Elson tells me you are searching for a caravan that has gone missing in Bois early last season." The man glanced over at the Southerner, then returned his focus to us.

"Yes, that is correct," I replied quickly. "My father's caravan vanished last season, and along with it my father, Brune Loyde, my brother, Ave, and a dozen other men. We have traveled a great distance to find out something of their fate, and so far our search has brought us here to Azor."

"Indeed it did," the man replied and smiled. It was a thin, dry smile that made me feel a bit uneasy. "You came to the right place. Azor is where information is bought and sold, and it is here you can learn much about things that happen in other places. It so happens that I may know something about the caravan that you are speaking of. Unfortunately the information is expensive and in your case, the cost is exceptionally high, proportionate to the risk I am to take for divulging it to you. I have already named my price, and it remains the same—a thousand gold plates. If you have the money, you will get what you have come for. Otherwise, we have little else to discuss."

"They have the gold," said Revor and he pulled out a hefty satin pouch. He weighed it in his hand and handed it over to one of the strangers, who took the bag and without opening it, passed it to another fellow by the door.

The man examined the contents, then nodded once; and the gentleman at the table resumed. "Now that this is settled, let's move to the main aspect of your visit." He switched legs and cleared his throat.

"You see, I am a mercenary, a true soldier who rents out his services for a good cause and a good prize. In all my years I have ventured to almost every corner of this world, often visiting places unseen by other human eyes. I took part in many wars, went on several campaigns against the Grass Folk in the Great Plains, and sacked four of the Free Cities. General Riz Asmar is my name. Ask around if you wish, but if I were you I would take my word for it. Why do I tell you all this you ask? I will answer—I want you to know I am a serious man, not some cutthroat or thug. Now, let's move on to the subject of your father's caravan.

"I first heard about the caravan you speak of two seasons ago. A man came to me, a very wealthy man, once the richest merchant in Azor and now one of the councilors, a patron to the Saffron Guild of Trades.

"Master Revor, I think you know him. His name is Oris Lexandro. He came to me with a rather strange request, looking for someone to ambush a single caravan somewhere in the eastern parts of Normandia. But it was not the cargo that interested that man of coin—he was looking for some men who were supposed to be traveling with that caravan. He wanted those men to be brought to Azor and delivered to him.

"The offer was worthy of my consideration. But I was reluctant to agree, and after thinking about it I decided to decline, for reasons that should not concern you. Let's just say that I have a reputation here, which I have earned with my own sword. I am a general, a hired-sword, not a thug from the slums. So I refused, but I did not lose notice of the matter, for to have a member of the council express an interest in a simple caravan meant that there had to be something more to the deal than the merchant would admit.

"Intrigued, I kept my senses sharp. Alas, for some time I could not uncover much, except that Oris had found another group, the Silver Suns of the Free Cities, to take the job. For many weeks I heard nothing, but then, not long ago, word reached me that the Silver Suns had been ambushed while crossing into the Border Region. The news interested me, and so I gave an order to find out more. It so happened that one of the Silver Suns, their leader, survived the ambush. My men did not fail me and a week later found the man, who was so dispirited that he could not talk or walk straight. I was afraid it was his mind, but luckily the man was just drunk, and after a few days of rest he was able to talk again, revealing a tale, which now I am passing on to you."

The general paused to adjust his long sleeves that caught accidentally in between the cushions. Then he continued. "The former leader of the Silver Suns told me that his band went to Normandia, on the orders from Oris himself. It did not bother them that they had to travel across Ethoria, or that they had to deal with Normandian lords. They saw the money and that was all they needed. After they received two hundred silvers they headed north, all twenty of them. Led by my unfortunate acquaintance, Iggs of Pirr, by the beginning of the spring season they reached the Normandian city of Pullie. There they got more supplies, some extra hands, and after wasting more money on ale and women, set out south to the city of Bonneville.

"There they were approached by a stranger, Oris's personal aid. The man had a mark from the merchant, and a set of papers that instructed the hired swords to follow his orders without question. Since the dispatch proved to be authentic, the Silver Suns had to obey. The stranger, who never divulged his name, then escorted the mercenaries to some isolated corner of the province, where the sought caravan had already settled for the night. Eager to get done with the task they attacked. As instructed by the stranger they seized the wanted men. As for the rest, they killed them, probably afraid that they would sound an alarm. It was a stupid thing to do, but not all the hired swords are smart or trained or cautious of their actions. Some are just plain stupid and follow any order given to them. In any case, after disposing of the bodies, they took the prisoners and the cargo and headed back. Somewhere along the way, Oris's aid left the Silver Suns, all much to the satisfaction of the hired swords. The nameless stranger appeared ruthless and harsh and rarely talked to the others. His company alone made the mercenaries feel uneasy and, so when he was gone, the men were relieved. Near Bonneville one of the captured wagons broke and so the Silver Suns abandoned it, hiding the cart in the woods some leagues away from the road.

"Certain they had pulled off the easiest job of their lives, the happy brigands traveled back to Azoros. Without problems they left Normandia and rode through the Northern Empire. But when they thought they were safe, they lost it all.

"On one of the eves, as they settled near Lombardian border, their camp was attacked by a sweeping force. The assailants were quick and deadly. In a few short moments they killed all the guards, and then surprised the main company, leaping out of the shadows, slaying anyone who tried to resist. Before the Silver Suns even knew what happened, all of them were dead, all but Iggs, who managed to fake his death, crawling underneath one of the corpses.

He was lucky that the attackers did not check for wounded. They were only interested in one of the prisoners, a young man named Ave. It was for him they came, and it was him they took, leaving Iggs and his dead comrades alone with the other prisoners and the cargo.

"Iggs insisted the assailants were not human. Instead he called them shadow people, or the A'als as you may know them. Frankly I do not believe such a tale. Yet if it is true, there may be a mystery to what the foreign kin were doing so far west from the forest, or why they took the young captive with them, but let the others be. Alas, no one knows the answers. As for Iggs, there was little left for him to do but to continue south with the other captives, hoping that Oris would still pay him the full prize. But his hopes were gone as soon as the merchant heard the news. Oris refused to pay a single coin, and when Iggs tried to threaten him, the merchant's men threw the rowdy man out, stripping him of all weapons, armor, and jewelry.

"A few days later Iggs persuaded some other fools to help him raid Oris's estate, eager to get as much gold out of the house as possible. Although his sneak attacked was a success, Iggs did not get too far with the loot. At the gates his band was attacked by the merchant's guards. Again, all of his men were killed, the booty was lost, but Iggs escaped, hiding in the slums. But it was only a matter of time before he would be dead. His band was gone and he was a wanted man with no money and no friends. He was done, and that was how I found him and offered him sanctuary in exchange for his tale.

"Afterwards, Iggs begged me to help him get out of the city. Frankly, I did not care if he lived or died. He would be dead soon enough one way or another. But it was for my own protection, I had to help him. After I had heard Iggs' story, I became an unpleasant witness for the merchant's dealings. So I could not let Iggs back onto the streets, for he could tell others of our meeting. I also could not kill him. Do not ask me why, I just could not. So instead I arranged for him to get out of the city and hid away some safe place in Dvorenia. Since people there do not mind new faces and ask few questions, the place was an ideal hideout for Iggs to melt away amongst the local folks, though something tells me that it will not save him.

"With Iggs gone, the only person, who concerned me was Oris himself. The caravan was just one of the many things that made me suspicious of his plans. In the past season alone, he hired over a hundred men, and every one of them left north with assignments that none were brave enough to divulge. He also purchased several large estates in the western part of the city, raising large garrisons to protect them, each over two hundred swords strong. All my attempts to learn more about the count's dealings brought me nowhere. The security around his strongholds is so tight that I have already lost four of my scouts. Everyone in the city is silent too, even my best sources have nothing to say. They all tell me the same thing—it is too dangerous, too risky to talk. And I believe them. But Oris could not manage such order on his own. There is no doubt someone is helping him, someone powerful and rich, as the entire enterprise requires strict collaboration, which leaves me to wonder who the merchant's true allies are."

"Why does it bother you so much?" I heard Ric ask suddenly, interrupting the mercenary. To my surprise, the self-proclaimed general answered calmly as if he had expected such a question.

"Personally the merchant himself does not interest me; he never did and probably never will. But things that he is involved in do concern me a great deal. The reason for it is such that the realm of Azoros exists because of a very complicated and fragile balance of power. All of the cities in Azoros, including Azor, are equal in their wealth and power. Of course each of the municipalities has its strength and weakness, but none of them has an advantage strong enough to topple the others. To attract money and people, each city tries to exploit its strengths—and rivals' weaknesses. In such a complex game of politics and intrigue, the realm exists, reaching the prosperity that you can see today.

"Look around you, this city has been just attacked by a horde of the wild men, and only a fraction of it is destroyed. The rest remains untouched, for the most part because of the mercenaries who crowd this place. To keep them here, the city needs a lot of money, but if the money leaves, so will the mercenaries, and then the city will remain defenseless. The cities need mercenaries and money. They need to compete to stay alive. They need their rivals to prosper. Should one of them acquire just a tiny advantage, the implications will be enormous. The power balance will shift, and so will the stability. In turn the equilibrium will break apart, and so will this entire nation."

"Is that not what you want? War—so you can rent out your army and make a profit?" Ric asked again, and the general paused, thought for a moment, then smiled and spoke.

"You are right in that I need wars to live, but not that kind of war. How much do you think the rival cities will pay once a war starts amongst them? In the beginning the price will be similar throughout, but as some of the cities fall, the price will drop, as there will be more arms to go around. Few cities will mean less demand, which in turn will mean less money for my company and me. And do not forget—mercenaries do not like to lose. If their campaigns are tainted by too many defeats, they will abandon their master's cause and switch sides, leaving the patron defenseless. If there is to be a war in Azoros, it will be a short one. One, maybe two cities will come as victors. Their councils will take the realm for their own. If and when it happens my services may not be requested any longer. Then, where will I be? Free Cities? Or maybe the Border Regions of the Northern Empire? No. I like everything just the way it is."

"Why tell us all this? We do not know anything about Oris, or Azoros' politics. All we want is to find the men from the missing caravan," I said, eager to get answers.

"You came here to learn about the fate of the convoy. So you did. Now you know what has happened, and you also know that Oris is the one responsible for the ambush and kidnapping of your father and your brother. You know they were amongst the prisoners, the two men from Villone—Brune and Ave Loyde. Your brother Ave might have been taken by the shadow people, but your father is still here, probably held prisoner in one of Oris' compounds. So you see, our paths cross. You want to rescue your father, and I need to learn more about the merchant's dirty deeds. Together we can help each other. I will assist you to free your father, and in return you will get me the information I so desperately lack. I think it is a fair deal, do you not?"

"I say that you are out of your mind, if you think that we will trust you. We do not know you, nor your motives for telling us all this," I said firmly.

"True, but do you really have a choice? If you ignore my offer, you will return to your fruitless quest. You will never find your father without my help. You do not have the money, nor the skills, to face the merchant or anyone else who stands beside him. Only with my help will you be able to get into the stronghold and then escape out of Azor unscarred. Remember: You need me more than I need you. I will find others to do my task, but you will not have another chance to reserve the help of someone like me. Now, I await your answer. Do you want to take my offer?"

"Before I answer, I would like to know what exactly is to be expected of us," I replied, looking straight at the general.

"Like I said, I need you to find clues, letters, scrolls, books, anything that can tell me about the count's plans. Should you be able to hear something, remember it, and then tell me. As for your father, try what you must. It is up to you. My job is to get you inside. The rest is yours to act upon."

"But did you not say that Iggs tried to get into the merchant's house? Look what happened to him. What makes you think that the guards will not catch us too?" Ike spoke this time, probably tired of standing idle.

"Do not mistake me for Iggs, young man," the general retorted. "I know what I am doing. I have organized and executed more daring plans then you can ever imagine."

The mercenary smirked. I looked over my shoulders to where my companions stood. Both Ike and Ric remained focused on the general. My thoughts were heavy, the questions were tough, and the choice had to be made. Still, I needed some help. So I turned to Elson. The Southerner stood calmly in the back, listening quietly. When he saw me look at him, his face warmed up and he shrugged his shoulders. Sighing, I switched to Revor. The sage was quiet too. He gave me a light nod, but not much more. To make the matter even more difficult, Ike and Ric did not say a word. It was clear—the choice was mine to make, and so I did.

"We take your offer." I gave him my decision. "But I want to ask you one thing first."

"Go ahead," replied the man.

"Why did you take the money from us, if you wanted to ask us to work with you?"

"Simple, that money is not for me. I do not need a copper from that pouch you brought. The gold is for you. It will pay for your gear, your pass into the count's compound, and your escape from the city. Did you think you would be able to stay here once you raid the merchant's estate? As soon as you set foot onto his land you will become wanted men. There will be a prize put on your heads. You will need to leave the city as soon as you are done, and it costs a good coin to make sure that you do."

"When are we expected to act?"

"That I will tell you later. I need some time to arrange everything. Meanwhile return with Revor and enjoy the few brief days of peace. Try not to venture too far off the sage's estate. It is best that nobody sees you while you are in town. We do not need any unwanted attention, for the mission is a sensitive one."

The man rose to his feet. The guards who stood nearby came up and halted next to him. The general nodded once, said a brief farewell, and walked out, followed by his men. We left after him. Past the bridge, the general veered into the shadows and disappeared. We retraced out steps back to the street, where two carriages awaited us. After dallying a bit, we climbed in and traveled back. The ride home was humdrum. Every so often, lights passed in the small open windows of the carriage, and gusts of cold wind hit me in the face. But I cared little for it all. Consumed with heavy thoughts I stared onto the dark streets. If all was true, Father was in Azor, held against his will by the local merchant. I hoped he was alive. I wished I could save him and bring him home to Villone. But it was all uncertain. And Ave?…I was full of questions. Why did the A'als, the shadow people, seek him out, and where did they take him? If it was true, why did A'tie not tell me anything about it? My head hurt. I felt tired, and my eyes closed. I do not know how long I was asleep, but when a familiar jerk awoke me, we were back at Revor's estate. The curtain doors opened, and I got out.

I remember little else of that night. Somehow I made it to my room and into my bed. The next day promised to be equally important. It had to be.

Chapter 67

MINIA AND Sire Adim peered into the gloom, eyes squinting. The flickering light from the two lanterns was enough to see a few cubits ahead, but the darkness claimed the rest, slowing their advance. Yet they kept on walking, hour after hour, day after day. It had to be days, because they had been moving along the same wide corridor forever, stopping only when fatigue took them. The oil canister was all but empty, and the torch was burned almost to the grip.

Still there was hope. The light wind that had lured them in that direction was getting stronger, and it was all Minia needed to keep himself from giving in to despair. Along the way they had come across several large caverns, some round and some a weird triangular shape. At first, all the rooms looked empty, but later some of the walls began to display writings, strange symbols inscribed in long lines over large rock plates, placed at the ceiling and arranged so as to form different patterns—half circles, long columns, and squares. Minia had no idea what those words said, or who exactly inscribed them there, though he suspected it could have been the D'ars, one of the ancient peoples from the Old Era.

Sometimes there were also pictures, images of strange things—odd-looking creatures, unusual plants, and human-like figures dressed in armor, ready for a battle. None of the scenes looked familiar to Minia, and it made him frightened. But it also made him excited, because, despite the dire situation, he had managed to see and touch something no other human soul had touched before.

One after another, dark chambers skipped past the two stranded shadows that made their way further down the tunnel, soon reaching a crossing where three similar-looking corridors came together. It was a large round room, with a high ceiling and a tiled, dusty floor. The smooth walls were covered with text and pictures. Tall statues, all depicting the same strange human-like people, stood by the entrance, guarding them with their stone spears. Illuminated only by the dim light their dark faces looked pale and cold, as if frozen in a span of time.

Unlike the other intersections they had passed before, this crossing had an uneasy feeling about it, and Minia wanted to leave it as soon as possible. But the tiredness that had accompanied them ever since the start was too strong. They needed rest. Not even bothering to check the chamber for hidden dangers, Minia and the young lord sat down on a broken flagstone, which stood in the very center of the room. Minia extinguished the flames to save the precious oil, and covered in blackness, started to sing. The youngster picked up the tune, and together they sang an old song of a great hero, Storm of Liosen, the man who drove away the numerous Westalian armies from the southern Normandia with only three hundred knights at his command. The Storm's revenge, as people called it, was one of the greatest Normandian victories. When that song was over, Minia sang another one, and another, and then fell asleep, without even noticing.

It was a strange dream Minia had that night. He did not see anything, but heard soft sounds, the shuffling of many feet and low voices. He tried to understand what it could all mean, but then suddenly he realized—he was not asleep, but awake, and peering into the darkness, at a spot where he remembered seeing two open archways of the adjoining tunnels. There was someone there, or was it just a trick of his imagination? Minia moved his hand to grab the lantern. He remembered putting it next to his bag. But the lamp was gone. The bag and the torch were missing too. A sudden rush of fear made Minia's heart stop. His nerves became taut as string, and he remained still, terrified. Then he sensed some movement very close to him. The squire jerked back, but the familiar voice made him halt. "What is going on?" asked the young lord, almost whispering.

"There is someone here," replied Minia softly, his voice trembling a little.

The boy gasped, but his sound died in Minia's palm. There was someone or something there, and the squire could feel it. Yet, a long time nothing happened. The silence was pure and the darkness perfect. But then, the noise returned. It was louder this time, and closer too.

Holding tight to his sword, Minia peered harder. At one moment he thought he saw a shadow, but that was impossible—it was just too dark to see anything. He immediately recalled the words of an old master-at-arms from Sirone, who said that eyesight was just one of six senses given to men, and that a true warrior needed only four to fight well. Minia tried to use his other senses, but somehow he needed his eyes most. Without them he knew he had no chance.

But suddenly a single cone of greenish light sprang up some cubits away. It looked like a tiny dot on a black mantle, yet it was bright, almost blinding. Minia jumped to his feet, his sword in front of his chest. But he still did not see his target. It was just one green cone, then two, then three, then four, a row of cones, which grew longer and longer with every passing moment, until the end of it was lost in the distance.

"What is this?" My friend heard himself asking, and when he did, several of the strange lights broke from the rest and moved toward him in a slow dance. Once, almost within arm's reach, the small glowing cones came together and burst into a flash. Minia, who was not used to such a contrast, shielded his eyes. For a while brightness was all he saw, but bit by bit his eyes adjusted to the light, and he saw a group of men around him; only they were not humans, they were something different, something Minia had never seen before. Dressed in odd dark clothing, their figures were slender; their skin almost purple, and their eyes deep green. The strangers were staring at the squire, studying him cautiously. Minia's first thought was of a fight, but he quickly discarded the idea. No matter how good a swordsman he was, he stood no chance against the strangers. Trusting his life to the Spirit, Minia lowered his hand and dropped his sword to the ground. The young lord did the same. The foreigners watched them in silence, none of them moved and Minia, who did not know what to think anymore, took charge. Clearing his throat, he spoke. "Greetings, friends," he said loudly. "We are the men of Normandia, and we mean you no harm."

Minia waited for a reaction, which did not come, so he resumed. "We have been lost in these tunnels for days. All we are seeking is safe passage to the surface, nothing more. If you can be so kind as to direct us to the exit, we will appreciate it greatly." Minia bowed slightly, at which time one of the strangers stepped forth and lowered his staff-like torch, which was not really a torch since it had no flame, but rather a glowing orb made of some unknown crystal.

"You speak an odd version of an old tongue," the stranger said in a dialect similar to the Northern Way. There was not really an accent to his speech, but rather a manner in the speech itself.

"We have heard of your kin, the surface dwellers, but none of us has ever seen any of you, none of the new bloods at least. It worries us that we find you here, so far deep into the Verge of the World. So we will take your arrival with caution."

"That you may," replied Minia. "But it has not been our will to come here, rather it was to strive to find a way out of this maze that drove us here. We have no idea how we got here, and we do not intend to intrude any further. Just show us a route to the surface and we will leave you be."

"You will let us be no matter. But answer me this—how many of you are here in the reaches of the dark world?"

"As I said there are just the two of us. We were exploring the upper tunnels of the caves near the Lake of Azul, when one of the corridors collapsed and we got trapped inside."

"Lake Azul, you say. This name is unfamiliar. But if you speak of the open caves that hold the tunnels, then the two of you have made progress no other has ever made, which in itself is out of the ordinary. Your arrival here may be a sign. But let the old bloods decide, for only they will know your true purpose—"

"Who are you?" the young lord interrupted the stranger unexpectedly.

"A young and haughty man," replied the green-eyed man. "He must be of a higher seat. Yes. I can sense it well within your blood, nestling. How interesting, very interesting." The stranger mumbled something else, then stopped and gestured for several others to come forth.

"Come. We will see what awaits us now." The green-eyed man waved his hand and the other strangers formed a circle around the young lord and Minia.

"Do not resist, surface dwellers. It is all for the best." He started off, his feet moving fast, yet gently and soundlessly. Minia had no other choice but to give in, and he walked after the new companions into one of the hallways. The new corridor, full of twists and turns, led them down an incline and eventually ended in a blind alley, blocked by a single solid boulder. There, the man who seemed to be the leader reached underneath his cloak and took out some sort of a glowing circle, which he then inserted it into a small opening in the boulder. Immediately a soft noise came from somewhere inside, and the giant rock moved to the side, revealing a view of a large staircase that led even deeper into the underworld.

"You follow us closely now," said the man. He pulled out the medallion from the opening, quickly hiding it under his mantle.

"Where are we going?" Minia's distrust was growing, and he was hesitant to walk through the newly-opened doorway.

"To Rah Vor Dr'asrs of course. The great city of the dark, the home of the D'ars race."

"D'ars." Minia was speechless. D'ars, the forgotten kin, the race that had disappeared thousands of years before the first kingdom of men was born. Ever since their defeat at Brown Mire's Pass, during the third of the Blood Wars, little had been known about their existence. What Minia could recall were meager passages from some old book, and even those texts told very little about the mysterious race, just that once the Da'rs were the same as A'als, and claimed large territories of Ethoria for their Empire, which stretched for thousands of leagues and at times counted millions of inhabitants. But in time the one race split, the D'ars were born, and the time of devastating civil wars began.

The conflict between the opposing sides lasted for thousands of years and came to be known as the Blood Wars, referred to in some texts as the Great Wars of Sorrow. During those days, the A'als and the D'ars battled each other fiercely, for causes long since forgotten. It was only known that in the end the A'als pushed the D'ars north to the mountains of the Land's Edge, and after seizing the victory at the battle of Brown Mire's Pass, routed the enemy into the caves of the Land's Edge, sealing them there with giants gates of rock and iron. Since then, the D'ars were a dead kin, never seen or heard of again. That was the history Minia knew; that was what he used to believe.

The great depths of the tunnels beneath the Land's Edge, which stretched before Minia, made the squire doubt all that and more. As he adjusted to the dim light, the reality of where he was slowly began to sink in. He was in the realm of unknown, the land of those who claimed to be the D'ars. The wide stairs opened by the secret door, led his young companion and him into another corridor, which then took them several leagues down in a gentle slope. It seldom veered, yet each turn was sharp, and at times it seemed like they entered a completely new tunnel. But the passage was the same, and continued for hours.

After a while Minia started to wonder if they would ever stop and rest. But they did not, not until their strange company emerged in front of a large opening, lit by several dozen long orbs, similar to the ones held by the D'ars. Locked in a smooth, polished arch, the opening started as a short tunnel, but then quickly grew into a cavern, a huge hollow with a massive stone wall and giant gates at its other end. Just one look at the towering entrance made Minia breathless. Over fifty cubits tall, two glossy stone plated doors stood shut between two large pillars, each as thick as an average Normandian keep. On each of the doors, huge images of two figures were carved. One was a depiction of a D'ar standing with his weird sword raised, and another of a strange creature that resembled a mix of a wolf and a man. The two forms were facing each other and in the middle was a large tree, its thick trunk surrounded by a spiral shape that at a closer look appeared to be the tail of some mystic creature, a flying beast that, itself, sat at the very top, gazing at the ground below.

Around the beast were more pictures, but Minia could not see them all, as they were just too high to see. Instead he turned his glance to the floor, which was covered with heaps of rubble. At first, he thought it was garbage, then realized it was the debris of many battles, some old and some recent. Although there were no bodies, much of the ground was covered with broken weapons, brown stains of dried blood, and deformed skeletons.

"What has happened here?" Minia heard the young lord's voice.

"Our lives here do not know peace. The underworld is a dangerous place," replied the closest of the D'ars without even throwing a glance at Minia or his companion.

"What sort of troubles do you face?" the squire asked again, studying the soil under his boots carefully. "I thought the underworld was deserted."

"You could not be more wrong, surface dwellers. The Verge only seems peaceful and quiet, but it is not. The things that live here are many times more terrifying than anything you have encountered on the surface. There are deep crawlers, fire-spitters, and blind hounds—and the dark ones. What you see is just from the last of their incursions."

"The dark ones? What are they, some sort of animal?" Minia was curious.

"They are no animals. Yet they possess a beast's savagery. They are no D'ars either, if that is what you are asking. They are ancient creatures that had lived here even before our forefathers first came. You see that beast on the great doors of Moor? It is one of the dark creatures. Our legends say they had been created by the first masters themselves, so as to guard the underground passage from intrusion by their enemies."

"First masters? Do you mean the Keepers?"

"Yes. I am surprised you know of them. I did not think that the lesser surface dwellers possessed such knowledge anymore. But we have not ventured into the sun for years. Many things must have changed since our last time in your world. I hope it is a better place than the one we left."

The D'ar nodded and immediately took a large horn from one of his comrades. Placing it into his mouth, he blew into it. A low humming sound left the large conical bone and ran through the cavern, resonating through the darkness. Before the last of its echoes disappeared, a similar noise came from behind the wall. Then some lights appeared on top of the gates, and the doors opened inward. Through the growing gap Minia saw another passage, wide enough for ten men to walk abreast. The handmade gully had tall walls on each side, carved out of the rock and forming lines of fortifications and towers, seeded with many narrow slits. Behind it, several hundred cubits into the tunnel stood another gate, a set of iron grates, all as thick as three human arms, and further away, some strange parish lit with thousands of glowing orbs.

Indeed it was the D'ars city, which lay at the bottom of a huge dip several leagues wide and twice as long. Pierced by the green light stood rows of buildings and grand statues, displaying majestic and grotesque architecture of the ancient race. The streets, which ran in long straight lines, came together at a huge square decorated with pedestals and pillars of different heights, all displaying pictures of the D'ars and of the wolf-like creatures, either locked in battle or getting ready for a fight. And at the far end of the widest of the avenues, a grand structure rose. Covered in many green orbs it was a huge half-dome of stone. Extending several hundred cubits into the air, and some quarter of a league across, the building of exceptional craftsmanship came out of the side of the cavern's wall and curved down, descending to a wide pedestal, supported by rows of columns and statues, each twice the size of an average human. Around it, forming the base of the structure, stood several towers. These were tall and ample, their rooftops pointing toward the ceiling, all lit by thousands more soft large green spheres that seemed to be suspended in air. That of course was an illusion. In truth the spheres were attached to long metal strings that ran up to the ceiling.

The sight was magnificent and Minia could not help but stare. The fact that it was built many leagues underground made it even more fascinating.

"This place?" Minia pointed at the half-dome, unable to take his eyes of the structure.

"*Tazrlossera,*" replied the D'ar. "The House of Light. It was built by the first D'ars as a tribute to the days our people had spent on the surface, under the sun, where day changes to night. There we had first emerged from the dust of the creators and it is there we should return to reclaim what has been taken from us. Thus it has been foretold in the great prophecies of the ancient thoughts. Our journey home will begin here in the underworld, in the great halls of Tazrlossera, but only when its secret is uncovered, and its surface is lit with the light of the sun. That will be a glorious day. We all live for that day to bring the past back to us. Until then, Tazrlossera serves as home to our council of seven, the wisest of our kin, who make sure that we do not forget, that we do not loose our ways, that we survive to see the true light of the sun."

The D'ar stared at the dome for a moment and then resumed his stride, taking Minia and the young lord deeper into the foreign city, somewhat busy with folks, all of whom looked the same—purple-skinned, green-eyed, and dressed in either robes or chain mail of black iron. Some Da'rs also carried large curved two-bladed swords, but most had strange-looking metal circles that hung on their belts next to knifes and bridles. There were both male and female Da'rs that Minia met along the way, but no children. That was strange, but then, everything about the D'ars and the tunnels was strange.

After crossing another open plaza, the D'ars escort turned right and, passing several wide houses that bordered a narrow stone carved lane, came up to a dead end shaped like a round arch, which had no door, just a thick black curtain dropping down to the floor. A low whistle sounded quickly, and the mantle slid to one side, revealing three purple-skinned men behind it. They gave Minia's guides slight nods and then stepped back, allowing the squire and the young lord to walk inside.

Minia was greeted by a spacious room full of D'ars. Some wore robes, long gowns of red and blue; several had capes thrown over their shoulders; but most were embraced in armor, shiny and slick mails of black. The D'ars stood in a half circle, facing the entrance, looking straight at Minia and the young lord, who were left alone in the center of the room. The voices were many —whispers, gasps, and some cheers that came from the back of the crowd. Soon enough, the noise died out, and one of the D'ars, who wore a blue cape, came forth. After greeting the gathered with a short hail, he turned to the humans and spoke.

"You will not hear any words of invitation here," the D'ar started in a solid voice. His thick accent made it hard to understand yet my friend listened. "We do not know who you are or why you are here, but we intend to find out soon. The faces you see before you are the wisest and the bravest of our kind. They are members of the council of seven, masters of their houses, and leaders of their outer clans. They have come here from across the underworld because of you, surface dwellers.

"You may think of your arrival here as an accident, but we do not believe in accidents. Everything has its purpose and everything has its reasons. And your arrival has a purpose too. We are determined to learn what this purpose is. If it is that you are the ones of whom the ancient verses speak, the D'ars are standing on the verge of a new era, a most glorious moment when we rise back to the surface, back to the sun."

"What are they talking about?" muttered the youngster to Minia.

"Be quiet," my friend whispered back and turned to listen, but it was too late. The D'ar was silent. He stared at the squire and his companion. Everyone else in the room was too. For a moment Minia thought they were doomed, but to his relief, the D'ar turned back to the crowd and resumed his speech.

"*Barsitq'erd yuis'd,*" he proclaimed loudly. "Be praised the Light and the Dawn, be praised the humble D'ars who have come from it, and be praised the future that is foretold. I am the high channeller of the Grand House of Stone, the pronouncer of the sacred verses, the narrator of the holy texts. Once again we gather here in this hall of our great ancestors to determine whether it is yet time for us to walk into the light. All D'ars are waiting for our decision; our people are eager to know what awaits them. Should they prepare themselves for the light, or should they continue to dwell in darkness, hoping? This time we decide again, and these are the keys we must test." The high channeller pointed at Minia.

"The verses say that a surface dweller will hold the key to our future. Soon we will see if these two can unlock the mystery of Tazrlossera. Should they do so a new era will begin for the D'ars, yet should they fail our hopes will burn even brighter, for every failed attempt brings us a bit closer to our goal."

The D'ar addressed the two humans. "You do not know what to say, and you do not have to. There is nothing for you to decide; your destiny has been decided for you. The masters of the world have brought you here, and now you will take a test, a test to see if you are the ones with the key. Trials await you in the scared place of the D'ars. If you pass the trial you lead our people back to the surface; fail and you become another false prophets, and thus will have to find your luck in the maze."

"A maze—what kind of a maze?" exclaimed Minia at last. "Listen. We are no prophets, we have no keys and we do not know anything about you. Your prophecies are yours, and they do not concern us. All we want is to get back up to the surface…"

"That is our goal as well. Only for us it is a daunting task. You will have time to get your answers. It is not yet time. You are here to listen. This is how it has been written and it is how it shall proceed. Now you must depart. You will find your refuge suitable for all your needs. There you will rest, think, and prepare for the trials. We come in two sands. *Arshd'der'sradf,*" the channeller pronounced.

"Take them to D'uroms," he commanded next and two other D'ars, not the earlier guides, came forth and led Minia, along with the lordling, back outside. Minia did not protest; it was not the way he wanted to act. Of course, Minia was not too fond of such changes in his situation. His hopes for a quick departure dwindled, and the thought of captivity, servitude, or even death dawned in his mind. He knew one thing though. If he was to die amidst the foreign folk, he would make sure to take a handful of them with him. But before he could do that he had to find out what the D'ars meant by their strange tale. He needed some time to figure out what to do. He was sure he could find a way out of the strange underground city.

From the meeting hall, the Normandians were escorted across several streets, through dozens of intersections, to another dead end. There, a similar-looking curtained door moved to one side, and the tired and subdued humans walked inside, where, illuminated by the same greenish light, a set of stone benches, an altar filled with some clay pots, and a large pool of water carved out of the floor in the very center, met their eyes. The men who brought them there did not follow. Instead they remained outside and observed the captives for a while. Then the curtain dropped, and they were gone.

Somewhat surprised, Minia immediately ran up to the door and slid aside the thick black cloth. He was right. The D'ars had gone and there was no one in sight, just a deserted street and a few lights in the distance. Minia smiled and stepped outside. But as he did something threw him back. It was more of a jolt than a push, but it sent Minia stumbling back, away from the doorway. Unsure as to what had just happened, Minia tried again. The same invisible force pushed him back again. Strange it was, but he could not get out. "Magic," Minia said loudly with a sigh and stepped away, shaking his head.

"Magic?" repeated the youngster. "Please tell me, what is happening to us? It is all so strange. Please tell me what it all means. Please, Minia, tell me."

"Surely, my lord," said Minia quietly, and he dropped to one of the benches. "These people we have met are the D'ars, the ancient people from the old epoch. Nobody knows anything about them. Even so they have always been known as the Dark Folks, mostly for the hue of their skin. Before the Blood Wars they were believed to dwell in the jungles and hot forests of the south. A warlike proud folk they fought to dominate the world. Amongst their fiercest enemies were the A'als. The two sides never ceased to battle; only when the Wall was in danger did they come together to fight the North. In the last of the Blood Wars the D'ars were defeated and then were gone. Everyone thought they were dead, but it was not so, as you can probably guess. I think all of our texts and books have been wrong."

Chapter 68

DAYS SPENT in a small stone cubical dragged like ages. Sitting on a straw patched bed, looking at a single barred window placed high over his head, almost at the crest of the ceiling, Sire Jim was left to himself. Although the investigation was still pending and the council had not rendered any decision, the second captain was convinced that afterwards he would be stripped of his rank, relieved of the command of his men, and dishonored from his claim to his father's lands. He had expected it all, preparing himself for the worst, but no matter how hard he tried, it was still very hard. Hour upon hour he struggled to understand how it came to be that he had become a prisoner, a suspect, and a traitor.

He was not the only one. Word had reached him that many more of the Bois lords and soldiers had also been detained, all placed under guard, their weapons and armor taken away from them. Sire Jim lost his battle gear too— his father's sword, the plated suits he had gotten from his great uncle, and his great helm. But the second captain did not care for those things. It was the humiliation he could not let pass, not a humiliation due to his present state, or his imprisonment, but the humiliation for his kingdom, for the Normandian army, or what it had become in the years of peace. He knew that the expedition failed in some respects, that they did not catch any of the sect's leaders. But that was not the reason for such scrutiny from the royal council. They won their battle, losing only a few men and horses. They ridded Normandia of the Alavantars' threat, and they did so for the King, and for the kingdom. There were mistakes along the way, but they were minor compared to the punishment that the royal questioners proposed. Indeed, these were grim times; he knew it better than anyone.

On the second day of the third week one of the Royal Guards came in and brought another summons from the royal examiners. It was a formal letter signed by the Regal Fox himself, which could mean only one thing: the questioning was to be public, and for that Sire Jim needed some time to prepare. Even without his sword and his armor, he was still a knight and he wanted to look like one. After reading and signing the letter, the second captain handed the scroll back to the guard and asked for some clean clothes, a razor, and a warm towel. All the items were given to him, and he spent the morning cleaning his face, shaving, and getting ready for the upcoming meeting with the examiners. When the guards came back, they brought him his armor and his sword, which Sire Jim slid on his belt. Sire Jim felt almost like his old self again. His posture was straight and his expression firm. He gave a brief salute to his escort and left the dark cellar of the castle's prison, heading quickly upstairs to meet his accusers.

The meeting hall where the hearing was to commence was small but crowded, with guards, spectators from the ranks of the royal court, and chief examiners, taking many seats and benches on one side of the hall. The last sat behind two long tables opposite each other, facing one single chair placed in the center, next to a small round table where a young skinny scribe prepared his tools to record all that was to be said. When Sire Jim walked in, all eyes turned to him. Startled by all the attention, the second captain halted, but someone from his escort gave him a light push and he went forward. As he measured his steps across the white and black tiled floor, he studied the men who were to question him, and the Regal Fox amongst them. The royal lord rested in the middle of the table, sitting on a large throne-like chair, which probably belonged to the local lord.

"Ah, Sire Jim," said the Fox, when Sire Jim stopped in front of him. "We have been waiting for you. Please, come take a seat." He pointed at the chair with his finger, then leaned back and smiled. Sire Jim granted the examiners a light grin and sat down, his eyes focused on the Fox.

"This, as you know, is a public hearing ordered by the King himself, so to investigate the accounts of the recent campaign, organized by the late former Duke of Bois. Oh wait, my silly memory—not the former, but still active Duke, Sire Tem."

Regal Fox laughed softly, then cleared his throat and continued. "We, the royal examiners, appointed by the King's highest decree; are here to ask questions." Sire Liore's aristocratic accent made Sire Jim want to spit, and his eyes gave out a sharp glance, so cold and tough that the Fox had to shift in his seat, leaning even further back, as if putting more distance between the second captain and himself. Sire Jim, however, was calm. He had no doubt the public hearing was anything but a spectacle for the amusement of the noble crowd.

"Sire Jim, you are aware of this investigation, are you not?" the Fox went on. "You also know that I have been appointed as the chief inspector by the King himself, and it falls to me to tell you that of the findings that we have come upon during our inquiries, I find none that make much sense. No matter how hard I tried to find any reasons in Sire Tem's or Sire Zuros's actions, I could not. So maybe today, you, Sire Jim, will clear up some of the mysteries."

"As I have said before, I will tell you anything you wish to know, my lord," replied Sire Jim without sympathy.

"Good. Then let's proceed. My first question is of the so-called Alavantars. The Duke has stated that you have done some investigation in that matter, and that your men collected evidence of an evil plot, put together by these so-called Alavantars. Is it so?"

"Yes, this is correct. For the past several seasons we have had a number of unexplained disappearances and kidnappings in our province. We did everything to solve the problem, but our efforts failed. We did not know why it happened, or who was responsible for it. Then a group of squires from Sire Rone's garrison came across some clue, which they reported first to their lord, then the Duke and me. What they had uncovered in their search was an evil plot against Normandia, put forth by a group that called itself the Alavantars. Those so-called followers of the Master of the Old, they consider themselves to be the servants of the great northern lord, who, they believe lives beyond the Land's Edge and is preparing to invade Ethoria, avenging the defeat of his forefathers during the Great War. In Normandia, a group of Alavantars has set up a chapter, and begun their deeds: a spree of murder and kidnapping. Their targets? Young men and boys."

"So you claim the secret sect does exist?" interrupted the Fox.

"I know so. We have evidence, places where they have planted their agents, people they have paid, and men they have murdered. I am sure you will find all the information as trustworthy as I did."

"Huh, this is what I actually want to ask you next. You see, we have looked through these so-called findings of yours, but did not see any indication of an evil sect, which as you say, has worked its ways into our realm. If there were any written words to support your claim, they are missing now."

"Missing? That cannot be. The Duke had everything scribed and copied, everything—the journal, written accounts of the squires, along with letters from the Duke of Pullie, and from the other lords."

"Hmmm. Interesting. We have searched through the Duke's papers several times, but did not find anything that mentioned Alavantars or their conspiracy plots."

"Even so, I saw the false believers with my own eyes. I fought against them in Puno, and I saw those crazy Alavantars kill themselves in front of the Duke and two dozen men. I was there."

"Your eyes you may trust, I have no doubt, but your eyes might have seen what they wanted to see, and not the truth. Our people have inspected the compound your soldiers so bravely and savagely ripped to pieces. We have listened to the accounts as to what happened in that underground chamber. And we did not see any trace of a so-called sect. Did the enemy you so bravely dispatched say who they were? Did they call their names aloud?"

"I did not hear, but I was—"

"Did they reveal their identities to you, or did they talk of their plans?"

"Again, we have—"

"Did you ask them, did you interrogate them, break them? Oh, I forgot they killed themselves. Twenty some men just put daggers into their own hearts, and everyone else—soldiers, lords, the Dukes—stood and watched. I am sure at least one of you could have done something to stop the madness."

"I cannot agree with you. You were not there. You did not see the chaos and the strangeness of the place. The people who opposed us were not normal, they were…"

"They were what? Were they not men, like us? I saw their corpses, they looked like any other humans. Dead, but normal. And please, spare me any talk of magic or sorcery, I am tired of such heresy. Now, what is your answer?"

"You may think what you desire, Sire Liore, but I stand firm in my beliefs. The Alavantars do exist and they were there in those caves, fighting us. We did make mistakes, but they have nothing to do with the outcome. None, not I, not the Dukes could have predicted the madness which we found."

"Enough of these empty words. Let us talk of facts, not things of imagination. If you still stand by your claim then I would like to meet those squires who uncovered the plot you speak of."

"It…it is not possible. Several of those men are on their way to Azoros, and the rest…they were trapped in the tunnels at the Land's Edge. Unfortunately we had a hard time picking apart the fallen rocks. When I left the camp, they were still underground."

"Gone or dead, how convenient, do you not think? Let me think—you have no papers to verify your words, you have no squires who could have explained everything to us, and you have no captives who we could have gotten answers from. Sire Jim, I will be frank with you. All this sounds very strange to me, will you not agree?"

"But what about those men we did capture? Did they not say whom they served?" exclaimed the second captain.

"They were foreign mercenaries and local thugs, whose limited accounts had nothing to do with any sects, or Norther Lords, or Great Wars," replied the Fox.

"Still, if you—"

"If you do what? Imagine things, make up stories?"

"I am of noble birth, my blood is of descendants of the royal line. I am a knight and a captain of the guards. My word is of the truth, and it offends me that you question it."

"I do not question your word; I question the purpose of your actions. What you tell me may be the truth for you, because it was told to you as such. But in reality it could have been a trick, used by someone else, to make you believe in some conspiracy, to make you take part in an expedition, whose true goals had been obscured. The real reasons have been hidden from you, and from the others. Do you see what I am trying to tell you?" The Fox looked at Sire Jim, then leaned forth, and continued.

"The story about the Alavantars was a tool to inspire the expedition, but in truth it was made up to organize a raid so to destroy a mercenaries camps in Puno. Why? That is what we are trying to find out and so far the true reasons elude us. Maybe, the Dukes wanted favors from the Kings for a successful victory; maybe some of the older knights grew boarded of peace. Or maybe, just maybe, those mercenaries knew something that the Dukes did not want others to know. You said yourself that many men went missing in your Province, that all the clues led you to Puno. What if the Duke knew something about those kidnappings? What if—"

"Do I understand you? Are you accusing Sire Tem of treachery?"

"I am not. It is you who have said the word. I merely stated the facts."

"I cannot believe this. The Duke, you cannot question the Duke, he is the High Lord of Bois, put in his rank by the King himself. He fought in the border wars before you or I were even born. Even as the chief royal examiner you have no right to accuse him of such actions."

"Oh, we are not accusing anyone yet; so far we are only investigating, nothing more. But I see that my questions have angered you. Let us pause for a moment and cool down a bit. The fresh air should suffice. Sire Jim, will you walk with me?"

The Regal Fox got up and went over to the second captain. The guards stepped in, but the Fox halted them with a slight wave of his hand. Then he pointed at the door and let Sire Jim pass him outside into the small courtyard set up inside the castle, covered by a glass roof that was left opened that day, letting the fresh air fill the walled space. With everyone remaining inside, Sire Jim and the Fox paced in circles, their voices sounded softly in the breeze.

"I hope you understand the seriousness of the task we are faced with here. I know that my inquires can be harsh at times, but the role that I have been appointed to by the King is an important one. This matter of the failed expedition has started a rather serious turmoil within the royal family and some there want to see the guilty parties punished. My job is to make sure that those parties are the right ones, and that no innocent soul suffers injustice. The King himself sends me couriers by the dozen, all with the same questions, for which I rely on you. I just hope you understand my actions. I am not the villain here."

"It is funny, but I started to get that exact impression," replied Sire Jim.

"You have all the right to such words, but I must assure you that your anger is misplaced. You see, the recent—should I say 'scandal'?—has touched many noble houses in Bois. The Duke himself is under tough scrutiny. Few can understand his actions, and it just may be that he is too old for his responsibilities. He has been a good knight and a faithful servant to the King, but his time has passed. The wars are over, my friend. We do not have enemies pressing at our borders, and there are no raging Hordes behind the Land's Edge. Still the old knights are eager to sharpen their swords and charge some enemy, even if the enemy is just a crowd of low-paid mercenaries."

"You say what you want, I will not change my position. We were there to seize the Alavantars and we did, only not many of them survived to answer our questions."

"None of them survived, to be exact," the Fox corrected him and coughed. "Did you know that I met your father when he came to the capital? Yes, I did. He is a good man, a great lord, I might say. But do you know what impressed me most about him? His wits, he had a great use of logic in his decisions."

"My father always claimed to be a sober thinker. Pragmatic he was indeed."

"Yes, exactly, pragmatism. Can I say that the same traveled with his seed? Do his sons possess the same skill?"

"I cannot tell you, though I never complained as to the ways my mind works."

"Great, because if your logic is strong, you will see through the mantel of posture and courtesy and spot the true things that are unfolding here. The time of the old lords is coming to a close. The king is young and he wants to see young nobles around him. This trial is but the beginning of a new era, with new blood substituting for the old. The gray-haired knights will not hold for long. We, the new generation, will soon take every position in the army. And it is up to us to use it to our advantage, to the advantage of our great kingdom. Soon the investigation will be over, and trust me there will be some familiar names on the guilty list. Lords and soldiers, squires, and even servants, you will find them together in one cell, listening as we announce the charges and the punishment. I can tell you right away it will be the Wall. Some say it is harsh, but I say it is better then death, do you not also say?"

"I surely do," replied Sire Jim. "I sense there is proposal in the air?"

"Of course. I will be open. Join me, help me find the truth, and I will help you."

"Help you find the truth? Which truth do you seek?"

"The one that serves the kingdom best of course."

"Who am I to betray? Oh wait...I think I know. You need the Duke, do not you?"

"Smart words, and correct ones too. Yes, the Dukes will probably suffer, but they were the ones who took responsibility for the campaign. Both of them knew the consequences, good and bad. Your job is to follow Sire Tem, I understand. But is it he you should follow, or the official title he holds? I say your oath is to the seat and not to the man who holds it. Today Sire Tem is the Duke, tomorrow it will be someone else, and one day it may be you. Someone will take the High Seat of Bois. It will happen sooner or later, better for us it happens sooner. If you agree to assist me, and attest to the Dukes' mistake, no one will get hurt. Well, the Dukes will, but they will lose their position anyway, so there is really no harm done. Your loyalties will not suffer either; Sire Tem does not have to know, we can make it sound all very nice and innocent. So what do you say?"

"I say...you speak sweet words, which...disgust me. You are a disgrace to your noble title and to the knighthood of Normandia. Never before have I seen such a dirty mind in the body of a lord."

You ask me to betray my commander, the man I have served for years, the man who took me in and gave me the position of second captain, the man who is a hero to his people. To your offer I have only one answer—I will never do what you ask and I will not stand quiet when you try to ask the others. I am sure some of the lords will take to your proposal. I suspect that some have already done so, but I would rather spend my remaining days as a Barrier guard than betray the Duke.

"Huh, I see that all the logic has been left to your father. Too bad. I had hoped we would find common ground. Alas, with such a position as you insist on I must end our chat. It is getting chilly anyway. Guards, escort Sire Jim back to the hall. We have some more questions for him to answer."

Out of the open door came three large soldiers wearing the royal insignia on their chest plates. The second captain did not say anything. He just gave the Fox his last stare and walked back inside. Sire Liore stayed outside. His eyes were closed and he was thinking. Sire Jim wanted to know what, but he was already past the doorway. A little later the Fox returned and the questioning resumed. It was no different from the first part of the session. Throughout Sire Jim answered firmly, not giving in to the fatigue. He took the rest of the interrogation standing like a true lord. Although his legs hurt and his throat was dry, he did not budge, not even a notch. His position was relentlessly strong within him. He was the Duke's man and he would remain his man, even if it meant death for him.

Soon after sunset the meeting ended. The guards escorted the second captain back to his cell and then came a long and restless sleep. Strange dreams hunted the second captain. He woke up often, always reaching for a cup of water, which stood by his bedside. Hard times were upon him indeed, but he did not regret anything. He was happy that he had enough strength to refuse the Fox. He worried only for the Duke, Sire Tem, of whom he had not heard in quite some time.

Chapter 69

FOLLOWING THE dried-up tracks in the road, Rob and Ark entered Sirone. At last the undulating houses, their rooftops parched by the hot sun, lined up before them. It was a welcome sight to both of my friends, as they were glad to come home at last, leaving all the perils of their long journey behind. But as they joined the moving crowd, heading for Sire Rone's castle, they overheard much of the latest rumors, which brought them dreary news of their lord, who had been struck by a sudden and unexplained illness. For some unknown reason a little before the campaign in Puno, Sire Rone fell ill and within a few days time had to be carried to the infirmary, unable to care for himself. His wife, Lady Cathir, took charge of the estate and declared that her husband's condition was to be blamed on a treacherous heat, which had settled in the region. The lord's healers agreed with her, but common folks suspected otherwise. Although none said it aloud, amongst the whispers Ark and Rob could hear accusations toward the noble lady, whose family's desire for Sire Rone's lands had long been known. Ark was not sure what to think of such allegations, but the fact that his lord had been taken by some mysterious illness made him cautious. Rob felt uneasy too, and when the two finally reached the first gates, suspicion grew even more.

At first glance everything looked just like my friends remembered, yet the feeling that there was something different did not leave them. With the darkness closing in, the gates were shutting. Several soldiers were working hard to push the metal door into position, their shield and spears stacked in a corner. When my friends came to them, the men stopped and quickly picked up their weapons. At that time several more soldiers, armed with two-handed swords, walked out from inside the gates and joined their comrades, all staring at Rob and Ark. The guards' faces were unfamiliar.

"What business do you have here?" asked one of the men. He had a large head, too big for his half-helm.

"We are squires in service of Sire Rone, coming back from the Puno campaign," replied Ark proudly.

"What are your names? I do not seem to remember any squires of your appearance around here," the same guard insisted.

"Ark Aclendo and Rob Ard of Villone. We have served in the company of Minia Emile. I am sure you know him, do you not?"

"Minia Emile. Huh, that does sound familiar," said another soldier, who was no taller than a half-man. He was short, but his thick sturdy forearms, naked of the chain mail, hinted that he was not as weak as he seemed.

"Maybe they served with the old garrison," suggested another guard.

"That it may be," agreed the big-headed fellow. "Hey, Asil, bring me the old roster." A young soldier passed a stack of parchments, fixed together with two metal rings. The big-headed guard took the papers and started to flip through them slowly, licking his fingers each time he turned a page.

"Huh, Ark and Rob of Villone…Let' see. Huh…No….No." The guard turned several more pages. "No and no." When he came to the last page he lifted his glance to my friends. "I do not see your names in here. Sorry lads, maybe you got the wrong castle." The other soldiers laughed.

"Shut up, you men," snapped the short fellow. "They probably do not know of the changes around here. When did you say you left Sirone again?"

"It was last season, and that was just a day after our initiation."

"Huh, then you have definitely missed the changes Lady Cathir has ordered around here. If you do not know yet, Sire Rone has fallen prey to a strange fever. The healers say it is because of the bad sun this season. Anyway, when the knight got sick, his wife Lady Cathir took over his daily duties."

"Lady Cathir?" asked Ark. "I though that Sire Rone had a grown son."

"Yeah, Sire Rollan is still the heir to the seat, but he is not here. Before Sire Rone fell ill, he had gone to the capital to serve with the Royal Guards. I think it was his mother's idea, but Sire Rone did not object. So he has been gone for half-a-season now."

"Was not there another son?"

"Young Lord Timor. He is only a toddler, a boy of five. He has no place ruling the lands. Besides Lady Cathir does a good job. She has paid all the debts that Sire Rone had accumulated through the years, and hired new paymasters. She also changed the garrison. The lord's captains have been sent back to their families, and most of the men went to Simor to join the garrison at Lady Cathir father's castle. In their places came our regiments. Lady Cathir's men we are. So you can see why we do not recognize any of you. But we do have some soldiers from the old watch. Why do we not ask them?"

The short guard raised his hand and the other guards stepped aside, though not too willingly, allowing my friend's horses to pass. Behind the gates another set of guards met them and after my friends dismounted, took them to the barracks, where more armed men sat at boarded tables, playing an odd game where each player had to deal with several large square pieces of paper, which depicted various numbers and animals. Although the game seemed to be interesting, Ark and Rob did not have time to get into it, as their escort brought them to a large fellow, whom Ark immediately recognized as Ao, a tough-looking, hard-spoken chief guard.

"Ah, young brats from Villone!" exclaimed Ao even before any question could come to him. "How have you been? Did you find the caravan you had been looking for? Or was it a merchant? Oh I do not remember now....Ah wait, where is Minia?"

"So you know these men?" interjected one of the other guards.

"Yeah, yeah, I know them. They were squires with the old garrison. Sire Rone initiated them himself," said Ao, irritated by the guards.

"So you verify that they are Sire Rone's sworn men?"

"Yes, I do. I do. Now where is Minia? I really need to talk to him." Ao waved off the soldiers and focused on Ark and Rob.

"I am afraid our commander is not here," replied Ark. "It is just the two of us."

Ao studied my friends for a moment with an inquisitive look.

"Huh, it does not sound too good. Not good at all." The chief guard shook his head, and without looking at the other men, said, "You can leave, soldiers."

"As you say, chief." The guards turned around and left, and Ao resumed his questions. Ark and Rob tried to answer as best as they could, but they knew very little, and none of their answers seemed to satisfy the large chief master. Yet, in the time the three spoke, my friends managed to tell the chief an entire account of their adventures in full.

"Thank you for this story," said Ao afterwards. "At least now I know the truth. We do not get too many truths around here. The whole thing about the campaign in Puno is not to be spoken aloud, such were the orders from Lady Cathir." Ao paused. His eyebrows lowered, and he stared at the floor for some time, then added, quietly so only my friends could hear. "I cannot believe they got the Duke. No matter what they say out there, he is a good man, a very good man, and a fair lord too."

He paused, then uttered again, "The word is that our province is up for some changes. The Duke is not dead yet, and in Bonneville new lords are already organizing a huge tourney, as if nothing happened, and here in Sirone,

Lady Cathir is trying to do her husband's job." Ao's voice turned to a whisper. "Since you have sworn fealty to Sire Rone and served with Minia, I have no doubt that your loyalty lies with the knight, and not his wife. And to you I may say that what she is doing with Sirone is wrong."

As Ao whispered, two soldiers walked by and the chief froze. When the men were gone, he leaned forward and said, "Let's talk someplace else. This is not the best place to discuss Lady Cathir anymore. Come, I know where we can chat freely."

With those words, Ao picked up his sheathed sword from the table, fixed it on his belt, and strolled into the yard. My friends followed. Together they left the castle grounds through a small door in the side of the gates' door, along a narrow path that emerged at the nearest street. They followed it to the other side of the town, where a small crooked building stood alone, a tiny tavern with three tables and a fireplace that exhumed puffs of smoke and fumes from overcooked piece of freshly cut goat. Half-drunk patrons ignored everyone, and unnoticed the three of them took spots at a far corner, resuming their interrupted talk.

"So as I said, I am not afraid to say what I think about Lady Cathir. I do not know you all too well, but you were from the old garrison, and there are not too many people left from it. Almost everyone was ordered to Simor. It is a move our Lady enacted to ensure the safety of her husband. You see, while she tells the commoners that the lords' sickness is due to some bad heat, within the castle she claims that someone has given our lord a poison. She does not have anyone to blame for it yet, but she accused the guards of allowing such a thing to happen. Personally I think so too, I mean that Sire Rone was poisoned. I do not think it was our fault though. The guards under my command were good men, and loyal to our lord. None of them could have harmed Sire Rone. They also saw no intruders nor any suspicious characters anywhere around the castle. This leads me to believe that whoever poisoned the lord lived inside the castle and was close to him."

"Do you think it was—" started Ark.

"Yes, I do," interrupted Ao. "I have no proof of it, but looking at all that has happened right after the lord's illness put him in bed, I think she did it. First she assumed Sire Rone's place even before he stopped talking. Then she hired new paymasters and jailed the old. She claimed she had repaid all of Sire Rone's debts, but none had seen any deeds signed. The money is gone, but where—no one knows. My sources also tell me that the Lady has sold most of the armor and the gear from the armory. And the garrison—that is another story. Right after Sire Rone fell to unconsciousness, she dismissed the captains and sent away almost all the men from the old garrison. In their place she brought in her father's men. Now there is just me, two old masters-at-arms, and you two who remain sworn to Sire Rone. I really hoped to see Minia but if you say that he died in Puno, I guess that leaves just the six of us."

"Is there anything we can do?" asked Rob.

"Not at the moment. You have just gotten here. After such a tiresome journey you need some rest. When you have your wits and fists together we will talk more. Until then I suggest you watch your step. Remember those men at the castle are not your friends. They do not care for the lord; their fealty is with the Lady, and with such, we are not with them. If I were you I would think of leaving the service. It so happens that I can grant you such a wish, since I am still the chief guard."

"How did you manage to maintain your rank?" asked Rob.

"Huh, I see where your questions are going. Do not worry. I am no traitor. It just so happened that Lady Cathir needed someone to teach the new guards about the defenses of this place. She chose me, probably because I was the only one whose name she could remember. But I am sure that once I am done with the training I will be shipped off like the rest of Sire Rone's men."

"To Simor?"

"Yes, to Simor. Though something tells me that there may be a different destination, reserved for me."

"Where?"

"I think that my men are not in Simor, but someplace else."

"Which place would that be?"

"The wall, my friends, the wall.…Yet, let's not talk about it now. Stay here for the night. In the morning we will meet by the gates. Now, I must leave. Farewell."

Ao took off right after he finished his ale. My friends remained inside. They cleaned their plates and went to bed, to catch up on much needed rest. But it was not rest they got, but a night full of worries and suspicion. Everything sounded strange. Everyone acted weird. Ark and Rob did not know what to do, or who to trust. They just hoped that the next day would bring them clarity. Until then they needed to sleep, and so they did, although they had uneasy dreams.

Chapter 70

MY BROTHER stopped at the door. He stood still for a moment, thinking, then turned around and looked at Ike. The two stared at each other, quiet and pensive. Ric waved his hand and returned to the table, pushing a tall seat away so he could lean back and stretch his long legs under it.

"What about Ave—why did the A'als need him?" he exclaimed, looking at the floor.

"Why do you not ask Mishuk's sorceress. The two of you seem so convinced that she is helping us." Ike's voice was full of sarcasm.

"I understand why the Alavantars would want to kill our brother. I can even guess why Oris wants him, but the A'als…" Ric ignored Ike's comment as he continued with his deliberations. "Aren't they supposed to stand against the Alavantars?"

My brother looked at me.

"Frankly I do not know anymore. Everything seems to be so out of place. It is as if someone broke a mirror and small pieces scattered everywhere, and now we are trying to put them all together," I replied.

"And what interest does Oris have in the caravan?" Ike responded to Ric's comment.

"He may be one of the Alavantars himself. They probably have people everywhere now, Azoros, Normandia, maybe even Villone," said Ric.

"It does not make sense," I said. "If he is one of the Alavantars, why did he want Ave and Father alive? It would be much easier to just kill them and not worry anymore. But to hire a whole bunch of mercenaries from Azoros, then send them to Normandia to get Father and Ave—it is too strange. There is something different about the merchant, something we do not know yet. That is why we need to get to that compound and find out more. If nothing else we will get Father out of there."

"How will we do that? How will we get through the merchant's men? You all heard the mercenary general— Oris has over two hundred guards at each of the compounds. And we have—what?...four, five men—" Ike's words were bitter.

"What are you saying? Do you want to quit?" I cut him short, unable to keep my frustration at bay any longer.

"No, I do not want to quit. I am just trying to make sure that we survive. So far we were lucky, but it cannot go on like this forever. Someday, we will really have to fight, and some of us will die. That day may very well be tomorrow or it can be the day after tomorrow. We must be prepared. We cannot simply rush into every endeavor that may or may not bring us closer to finding your father, Ave, and all those other missing men. We must stop and think. And now is the time to do so. If you ask me we should hold off on the mercenary's offer, and find some other way."

"Ric? You think so too? Shall we find another way?"

"Do we really have a choice? I, myself, do not see one. I want to find Father and Ave, and the caravan. If it means that I need to trust my life to some southern general, so be it. I am with you, brother."

"You two, listen to yourselves. You do not know the first thing about the general. You do not know who he really is, or what he wants with us. Maybe he is working for the Alavantars, maybe he is along with the merchant. Or maybe this is all one big ruse—"

"Ike," I interrupted him. "It may be a trap, it may be a plot to get us killed, it may very well be anything. But I must take this chance. It is too important for me to ignore. If you do not want to go, then do not. I will never hold it against you. Spirit is my witness. I am already in your debt, for all you have done for me. Do not think that you are obligated to follow me this time. No matter what you choose we will always be friends."

Suddenly Ike was quiet. He stood thinking for a moment, then looked at me and spoke. His voice sounded less angry. "Do you really think I would leave you here? Not a chance. Even if you decide to do the stupidest thing in the world, I will go with you. Why? Because I am your friend, and as your friend I must tell you that you are wrong this time." Ike raised his chin and continued. "Do not worry about me. I will not leave, nor will I say anything else. It is enough that you know my outlook."

Ike nodded and turned, and his voice grew lower, but I could hear his whisper. "They do not want to listen to me." Ike was silent after that. I did not say anything either.

The three of us sat in silence. But soon the familiar voice of the servant who had been given to us, sounded in the hallway. Then came a light knock, and the same voice asked us if we wanted clean towels and hot water. The thought of a nice bath soothed me, and I opened the door.

"Come on in," I said to the young lad, who immediately brought in two big buckets and a heap of fresh towels, so white that they looked almost light blue. The man went into the bathroom, and once done there, returned to the door. Bowing several times, he took his leave, but soon returned and timidly invited us to join Master Revor for a midday meal, served as usual in the grand hall downstairs.

A plentiful, delicious meal had been already set up, and the tasty aromas filled the air. I thought I could eat it all, yet I barely touched anything on the table. That afternoon we spent talking. We had many questions for the sage, but before we could ask any of them, Revor spoke himself. His tone was serious. We all listened carefully.

"There is something I need to tell you." The sage's face grew grim. "The merchant of whom the general has spoken…it so happens that I know him."

"You know Oris? I almost jumped off my seat."

"Calm down, young man." Revor raised his hand. "I did not say we were friends, although years back some would have called us that. The merchant's name is Oris Lexandro de Jadin, a member of the council of Azor, and a successful trader. Before he was a count, he was a successful trader. Truth to be told, he was the one who hired me to tutor his children when I first got to Azor. He paid good money, gave me half of his mansion, and allowed me to work on my studies. There came a time when we started to spend many hours together, talking of different things. As years passed I became fond of his company, and eventually grew to trust him. But then came a night, when after too many cups of fine wine, I first told Oris of my past. I told him of my previous perils as a sage, and as an Alavantar, of Arac's prophecies, and of the things that may yet come. He seemed curious to learn as much I wished to tell him, and afterwards asked if he could read some of Arac's prophecies. I refused, and he did not mind, promising to keep my secrets safe.

"But some weeks later he asked me of Arac's work again, and again I refused to show him the texts. That time Oris did not take my rejection too well. He left my chambers furious. Though he excused his behavior the next day, I noticed a change in him. He no longer invited me for evening talks. His visits to my study became infrequent, and soon he asked me to travel to the Amber Empire, where I was to escort his dimwitted children to a festival held by one of the royals. Back then I thought of it as an innocent request, but what a fool I was.

"I failed to see the true reason behind the merchant's seemingly harmless appeal. A man who was so cautious for so many years, I let myself be tricked like a child. Blinded by luxury and money I left for the Amber Empire, leaving most of my work unattended. Many of my translations, notes, and books remained at Oris's estate, while I spent weeks away. Upon my return I found how grievous my mistake really was. As Oris explained, while I was absent there was a robbery at the estate. A band of thieves attacked the mansion, taking many of the valuables, and not surprisingly almost all of my work. The merchant promised to find the intruders, but never did, and so my writing, my books, and my notes were gone. Now I suspect that there was no robbery. It was Oris who took my notes. Luckily he did not get the most valuable of the writings. The original text, the one written by Arac himself, remained with me. Yet, what Oris did take from me was enough; for it is from those pages he learned about the Chosen One."

"Is he one of the Alavantars?" I asked with a sense of deep pain. Everything I had been working for was on the brink of collapse. The sage's revelation upset me so much I wanted to cry. But I was a squire and tears were not the way of a warrior.

"I am sure he has nothing to do with the Alavantars," the sage answered quickly. "For one, I would not be here to tell you so. My former friends want my death so much, they would not miss such a chance. Also it looks like he did not intend to kill your brother, or your father. He wanted them alive, which is not what the Alavantars want, for the sect strives to eliminate the Chosen One, not to seize him. Why did Oris need your brother? I do not know. Only he can answer that. But there has to be something very important about your father and your brother that he has spent so much time and money trying to bring them here."

"What about the general? Will you tell us something new about him too?" I asked again, angry but composed.

"I know nothing of the general. He has a good reputation, much respect, and a lot of support amongst other freelance companies. Under any other circumstances I would not trust him, but do we really have a choice? To get inside Oris' estate we need help from someone like him.

"And the general needs us as much as we need him, or he would not have contacted me with his proposal," said Elson, who had walked into the hall unnoticed and settled at the head of the table, helping himself to a large, juicy piece of chicken, which lay steaming on the table. "But just to make sure, if he decides to betray us, I have made sure that his distrust of the merchant would be known to some of the general's enemies, and trust me, he has a lot of them."

"How will you do that?" asked Ike, chewing on a chicken leg.

"It does not matter. I will and that is it." Elson chuckled a little and switched his attention to a jar of warm wine.

"So, what now?" I turned back to the sage.

"We go to the merchant's stronghold, after we make all the necessary preparations of course. As the general said, it will not be easy."

With those words the sage rose to his feet, and pushing himself off the chair, called to the servants. Two of them hurried to their master and helped him walk away from the table. Halfway to the back door Revor halted, thanked the men, and looked at us. "I will let you know when we go." He waved his hand again and left the room.

Chapter 71

ARK AND Rob dismounted and took their tired steeds to a small trough, located under a patched straw roof, adjoined to the outer wall of the tavern. As the horses drank warm stale water, they walked up to the single door and entered the familiar smoky dining hall. It was what they did almost every day. As a matter of fact for the past days my two friends had been leading a strange life within the castle of their lord. They were still in the service of Sire Rone, but they did not feel like his sworn men anymore. The lord himself was long absent from his duties, and his wife, Lady Cathir, refused to see them even once since their arrival from Puno. Brix ore Das, the new first captain, one of the Lady's father's sworn men, who had taken charge of the garrison, ignored them too. Although Ark and Rob saw him often—either in the company of the Lady or amongst his fellow men—he never spoke to them, always busy, giving them nothing but brief glances. Yet my friends were not left alone. They had to deal with Brix's two deputies, hard-faced, bearded lords with rows of yellow teeth and scarred cheeks, which made them look old, much older than they really were. The two men commanded all of Sire Rone's squires, including Rob and Ark, assigning them to various tasks, many of which seemed absolutely pointless and boring.

At times my friends had to patrol the lower parts of Sirone; or ride to the surrounding hills, scouting the outer borders of Sire Rone's domain, looking through many dens and creeks, scattered within nearby forests, never knowing what they should be looking for. One time Rob asked a deputy about the purpose of their missions. But the officer only barked that it was not Rob's concern, and that my friend had to mind his own business if he wanted to remain with the garrison. Furthermore, all of my friends' request to travel to Villone, even for a day, were denied. No matter how many times they asked for a leave they were sent back to the barracks, entrusted with a new pointless duty.

To dispirit my friends more, the men of the new garrison shunned their company too. Almost all of the guards were Lady Cathir father's men. As such they were not openly hostile. They simply ignored my friends. A few words, some nods, and a couple of glances were all that Ark and Rob got from their fellow soldiers. The only one who remained friendly was Ao. In the evenings he met my friends at the tavern, and there the three spent hours talking about things that bothered them.

While some weeks before Sire Rone had been in a sound state of mind, as of late he lay unconscious in his bed, sometimes talking in his sleep. The lord's worsening condition continued to spur rumors; talk of strange things taking place behind the keep's tall walls grew fast. The common folk began to suspect foul play and some even whispered of Lady Cathir's involvement in the whole ordeal. After a while the tension grew to such a degree that the Lady herself had to announce through her town criers that Sire Rone had fallen prey to an infested wound and not the bad sun's heat. She also said that though the injury itself was minor, the infection that polluted his blood was too strong for the local healers to remove. The clerics and sages did everything in their power to find a cure, but had little luck. Such explanation did not work though, and more rumors surfaced every day, all while the lord was slipping slowly into the realm of the dead.

There were other changes that made the local crowd weary and unhappy. Levies grew, as did duties placed on the passing caravans. Despite traders' complaints, Lady Cathir insisted on taking one copper from every loaded wagon, and half a copper for the empty ones. Such stringency made many traders skip Sirone, and though the flow of goods was still coming to Sire Rone's domain, it shrank fast as displeased merchants took their business elsewhere, leaving Sirone under-supplied. Still it did not bother the Lady and her paymasters, who continued to collect the money. Then there were also strange trips, which the Lady took under cover of night, when most of the city was asleep. Nobody knew where she went, but people often saw her ride in the northern directions, accompanied by a score of personal guards and loaded wagons. My friends knew that they could not ask the guards of the journeys, and so they took their questions to Ao.

The chief master seemed to be aware of the late-night trips, and though he did not know anything specific he had his own opinion, convinced that the Lady was meeting with some rouge traders, to whom she sold things from Sire

Rone's household. Of course the chief had no proof, but he did not care. He was assured of his belief, and shared it with my friends on every possible occasion.

When my friends entered the dining hall, the chief master was already waiting for them. He sat at a corner table, away from the others, drinking brown ale and eating dry crumbling bread. As the front door closed, the chief master turned. His face lit with a cheerful smile and he gestured for the squires to join him. For some reason Ao looked particularly happy. He was joking often and laughing a lot, ordering several more drinks through dinner. When Ark asked the chief master about his joyful mood, Ao only nodded toward the other guests and pressed a pointed finger to his lips. Then he winked and returned to his glass, taking several large gulps so that some of the ale ran down his red beard, dripping onto the table below. He did not say anything else until the other folks left.

Once the door closed behind the last of the patrons, Ao finally put down his cup and leaned forward so that his chest was almost lying on the table, dirty with spills and crumbs. He grinned again and whispered.

"You will not believe what I have found out." The chief master looked over his shoulder, making sure there was no one else left in the room. Nobody was, and so the chief master unbuttoned his vest and pulled out a small tube, sealed with several red laces. "A friend of mine, a servant with Lady Cathir, got it for me."

"What is it?" Ark studied the tube in front of him.

"Proof of Lady Cathir's plans to dispose of our lord, Sire Rone. This is a letter that she received some days ago from her father."

Ao rolled out the tube on the table. "Her entire plan is here; everything that we have suspected her of is true. It is all her doing."

Surprised and confused, Ark took the scroll, which was burned at corners and had a yellowish tan color to it. "Are you saying that this implicates the Lady in the sudden illness of our Lord?"

"Yes, and much more. Here, look for yourself. Tell me if I am wrong." Ao waved his hands and moved back, letting Ark study the letter, which my friend did. Indeed it was a piece of parchment—yellow paper, rich black ink, and, of course, with an insignia of a noble house engraved at the top. Ark traced his finger over the raised letters, then brought the scroll up to his nose and sniffed it. The scent was of burned wood, but through it he could also sense dried flowers and ivory. If it was a fake—it was a good one, an expensive one at least. Ark looked at the letter again and started to read, loud enough so that Rob could hear.

My Dear Little Cathir,

My councilors have informed me on the poor state of your husband's health. My condolences to you, my little daughter. His sudden sickness has been shocking news to us all here at Simor, and we grieve for your troubles. Although we hope for the best, Sire Rone's illness maybe too serious and he may not last for too long. For that, we have you to thank. As I have always said—who needs a son when he can have a daughter like you? Our work is almost complete now. The claim to your husband's domain is yours, ours if you wish. Thanks to you the house of Crom will rule Sirone again. Congratulations.

As of your eldest son, he is cared for as you have requested. The young lord is so infatuated with the capital and the knighthood of the royal court that he rarely thinks of anything else. His days pass in festivals and tourneys. Soon he is to start his training with the Royal Guards, and I am certain he will take the duty with the royal court very seriously. If so, we can be sure that he will take the service and so his claim to his father's estate will pass to his younger brother. Since Lord Tomir is only five, you, as the rightful guardian, will have the rule.

Now of your late husband—my sages say that his suffering should end soon. Still some time should pass before it happens. Although I know how eager you are to assume your new duties, I think that you should not expedite Sire Rone's tragic end. There are already rumors that implicate you in his illness. My advice is for you to wait and let the black water work its course. You have been patient long enough, but wait a bit more. We will have our prize.

While you wait, I will arrange for the money to be sent to you; it should arrive with the next courier. Use the coin to hire more men from Simor. Also make sure to get rid of those from the list I have given you. And please, do not waste anything on your stupid jewels and gowns. I know that you want to look your best, but it is not yet time. We will have much more soon. Until then be careful with what you buy. And by all means, keep the duties high; we do not need any foreign traders in the lands. Let them complain—those fools cannot do anything about it anyway. If any of them threaten to cease trading in your lands, let them. Those fat old brats will regret it later.

Oh well, the drums are sounding, I am off to a hunt. I hope you get this letter in time, before you do anything stupid. Remember, soon we will have all the gold we need to live like royals. I am proud of you, my sweet little daughter.

Your father,

Sire Simiors

Burn this letter once you read it.

"Where did you get it?" Ark asked Ao when he was done.

"I told you a friend of mine got it for me. He is Sire Rone's man, like us. Three nights ago a messenger came to Sirone. He brought this letter along with him. My friend was in the room when the Lady received it. He knew that it was important because the Lady sent everyone out. Luckily she was in a hurry. After reading the letter she threw it into a fire and left without bothering to wait for it to burn. When it was safe, my friend returned. By then the envelope was already ablaze, but the note inside was untouched. So my friend saved it and gave it to me, not even knowing what it meant. The poor lad cannot read nor write."

"What do we do about it then?" Rob took the letter and studied it carefully.

"That I do not know. With the province in turmoil, there is really no one we can go to. The Duke is gone. Almost all of the Bois lords are busy choosing sides and declaring fealties. It will be weeks before Bois returns to normal again."

"But we must do something," Rob insisted.

"I have heard that Sire Jim was supposed to be back soon from the questioning. Maybe we can go to him. He knows us. And I am sure he will help," Ark noted.

"We may very well do this, but first we must think of how to get out of Sirone unseen. If the Lady finds out we are trying to depose her, she will have our heads on stakes." Ao shook his head.

"We need a plan," agreed Ark. "It will be hard to get out without a leave."

"You are right, it will." A strange voice came from the back. My friends jumped. In the shadows of low-hanging curtains, which blocked the way into the kitchen, stood two figures dressed in common clothes. Their faces were kept in the shade, but when Ao took a step toward them, the men stepped forth—Lady Cathir's personal guards they were. My friends never knew them personally, but saw the men often within the court of the castle, always in the company of captain Brix.

"A nice little company you have here," said one of the men. He flung his cape to one side, exposing a shiny chest plate engraved with an insignia of Simor, a broken sword and a rose placed over a shield split in two, one red and one white. "I am sure you have a good explanation for such talk. Though I care little for your reasons, I have heard words of treason, and for that I must place you under arrest." The two reached in and unsheathed their swords.

Ark, Rob, and Ao backed away a little, and the chief master glanced at the front door. It was closed, but unattended. Ao took a quick step toward it, but one of the men shook his finger.

"Eh, eh, eh, I do not think you will get out that way, chief master." The man pulled out a small silver whistle and blew into it three times. Immediately the door swung inward and ten more armed men burst into the dining hall. They held long swords and spiked clubs in their hands, and some had round shields with the same symbol of a broken sword and a rose. The men moved swiftly along the walls and surrounded my friends, blocking their way to a pair of large windows. There was also a back door, but it was too far and my friends would have to scramble through at least four of the guards to get there. It became even less possible as more enemies got in. Their numbers were growing quickly. Their swords were many. There was no way out.

Ark and Rob searched the enemy's defenses for any signs of weakness. Suddenly they saw Ao place his right hand on his sword. The chief master pulled out his weapon and moved some steps toward the nearest enemy. His weapon, a short shiny sword with a grip shaped like a hawk's talon, rose up and froze. My friends prepared to fight. But a fight did not happen. Ao held the sword over his head for a moment, then threw it on the floor.

"I yield!" he yelled loudly. "I will go willingly, but I will not say a word to you. I will only talk to the captain or the Lady." Ao pointed at my friends. "They are innocent. They were merely my listeners. They had nothing to do with whatever you might have heard."

"It is not for you to decide. You are all under arrest for treason. Come, we will take you to the castle. There is someone who would like to ask you a few questions."

Ark and Rob stood in confusion. They did not fight though. Standing still they let some guards come over and take their weapons. Then someone else slid thick metal rings around their wrists and pushed them outside onto the street and into an open cart. With them inside the wagon, a large whip slapped the pavement several times, and two large mules pulled the wagon up the hill, toward the lights of Sire Rone's castle. The trip was short. Soon they arrived at the keep. Then several soldiers led the prisoners down a spiral staircase and into a cold cellar, where a small wet cell was ready for them. The heavy metal door then closed, the light disappeared, and my friends were left alone—no fire, no food, nothing, just cold stones and damp straw beds.

Ark and Rob spent three days in the dungeon of the prison, or so it seemed as there was no way of telling time for sure. But Ark thought it was in the evening hours of the third day, when he heard the rattle of chains and clumping of heavy boots. At first the noises came from above but then died out, only to return again, this time coming much closer to my friend's cell. When the footsteps were almost at the door, several voices sounded too. Locks clicked a few times, and a large square iron door squeaked open. The light from several lanterns rushed into the chamber, chasing the shadows into the corners of the little cubical, which was no more than two cubits wide. Blinking rapidly Ark and Rob rose up from the floor. They rubbed their eyes and tried to see who was paying them a visit. Soon they were able to distinguish a large silhouette of a man. He moved into the entrance and halted, his bulky frame blocking almost the entire doorway.

"Squires are you?" the man asked in deep voice, his eyes glaring into the cell, not really focusing on anything.

"Yes?" Rob answered.

"You do not ask questions," the man barked. "I am the only one who asks questions here. Come, the captain wants to see you now." The large man moved back into the corridor and let my friends exit the cell. In the hallway four more guards stood waiting for them. When my friends came before them, they slid the iron rings onto their wrists, escorted them to the upper levels, and into a large round room.

In the center of the chamber stood a single desk next to a wide fireplace, accompanied by two tall columns in the form of half-naked maidens who clasped large dimly glowing orbs. Behind the table, resting in a leather armchair, sat Brix. The captain was leaning over some slips of paper laid out in a row in front of him. In one hand he held a candle, and in the other a quill. When my friends came in, he stopped working and looked up. Making a chuckling noise, and bouncing the tip of the quill's feathers on his lips, he studied Ark and Rob for a while, then put down the feather and took two pieces of paper instead.

"Ark Aclendo and Rob Ard, of the village of Villone," the captain said as he read from the scrolls. He leaned back and his feet slid on top of the table, the metal patched heels of his boots reflecting the light of the candles. "Sworn men to Sire Rone, the proud squires of Sirone who managed to persuade the old fool, Sire Tem, to organize the infamous expedition to Puno. How did it come to be that you are accused of plotting against our fair Lady Cathir ?"

"We have never plotted anything against anyone," Rob snapped, and when he felt Ark's hand on his shoulder, stopped. But by then the captain's face had already changed from indifference to irritation. He withdrew his feet from the desk and returned to the upright position.

"No talking until I say so," Brix barked loudly. "You stay here and listen while I tell you whatever I need to tell you, then you will leave, and there will be no talking on your part. You have spoken all the words you wanted back at the tavern, now it is my turn."

He rose up and strode to the fireplace, hands behind his back, clasping a swagger stick. After staring at the fire for moment, he turned around and resumed.

"I am here to tell you two things, squires. The first is that your service is no longer required here. Since you are Sire Rone's sworn men, I cannot take away your squireship, only Sire Rone can do so, and he is in no condition to. So you remain his squires. But you have no fealty to our Lady Cathir. That you have proven already, and for that you will be punished. Therefore under a personal order from her highness Lady Cathir, you are removed from her service and no longer belong to this garrison. You will receive no more payment, nor any privileges. You will also lose your weapons, your horses, and your armor. You will not need them anyway, because as of yesterday you have been found guilty of treason. Whatever you may want to say in your defense is pointless. The Lady's court has rendered its decision and set the appropriate punishment, which I am to announce to you duly. Since the former chief master insisted on your innocence the court could not prove your direct involvement in the conspiracy. Nevertheless you had long known of Ao's plan, and did nothing to stop it. This makes you his accomplices, so says the Lady's court, established under the rules of justice, issued by his highness, King Philip the First. You retribution for such a crime is service at the Barriers. The time of such service starts now and should last for no less than twenty years. You are to surrender to my authority at once and take these written slips, which, from now on, identify you as Barrier guards. You will take them to the Great Fortress, where you will give them to your supervisor, who will then assign you to your tasks.

Do not think that I will let you walk to the Barriers on your own, hoping that you will obey my order. There is a caravan, which will arrive here in three days. It is heading for the Land's Edge. Along with it go all those who have been sentenced to the wall. You will join the convoy and will go to the border, and then to the Great Fortress. I suggest you do so willingly, because if you don't, you will never see your home again."

The captain spat into the fire, walked back to the desk, and picked up two slips of paper, freshly written and sealed with a waxed stamp. He checked the writing and handed the papers to Ark and Rob.

"Here are your passes. Keep them safe, without them you are not only convicted criminals, but outlaws—fugitives who will be hanged upon capture. And believe me when I say that you will be caught, should you decide to flee from the caravan. So I suggest that you tuck the passes away and not lose them."

Brix sat back in his chair. "I am done with you. Be gone."

He was quiet after that. But as Ark and Rob were walking out of the door, they heard the captain's last remark. "Fools they still think that they will live."

There was a smirk too, but my friends did not see it; they were moving downstairs, back to their cell.

When the iron door to their chamber closed, and the sounds of guards' footsteps faded, Ark turned to his friend. "What just happened to us?" he asked quietly.

"I do not know," replied Rob. He paused for a long time before adding, "I think we have just shortened our lives by twenty years."

Together they sighed. They did not say anything else. There was nothing to say.

Chapter 72

THE SOUND of footsteps was louder this time. First strange pounding came from above, but then moved downward into the hallway, where Sire Jim could hear it much more clearly. The noise continued until it was almost at the cell door, but then stopped. The silence returned, and Sire Jim could hear his own heartbeat again. It was a sound he grew to hate in the days he had spent underground, locked beneath the castle grounds, away from the sun, the wind, and his comrades, of whom he knew nothing. The life of a captive was tough for the nobleman, not because it was wet, cold, and sticky inside a little stone cube, but because there was no one to talk to, no one to share his thoughts with, no one to comfort him. In the beginning Sire Jim was glad that he did not have to share a cell with anyone else, but as time passed he became forlorn. He slowly started to lose track of time and his thoughts. His mind grew bored, and his limbs became numb. But he did not care. All he wanted was to see the sun again, to feel the cool breeze on his face, to exchange a few simple words with someone. If he had to travel to the wall, he would have taken it, as along as there was no darkness or silence.

When the thumping returned it was very close, just cubits away from the door. Someone was in the hallway. Sire Jim listened to it for a little bit, then climbed to his feet and went to the door, pressing his ear to the cold metal plate. More noises came almost immediately. This time it seemed as if something fell to the ground, and dozens of footsteps and voices entered the corridor.

"Ah, cursed lamps," someone snapped.

"It is so dark here, I barely see my own hands," another voice agreed.

"Hurry up, you two; we do not have much time," said the third voice.

They do not sound like regular guards, Sire Jim thought to himself as the men outside continued to talk amongst themselves. "Who can they be? Are they here to kill me?" Sire Jim made his hands into fists and moved away from the door, but before he could even make a step, the lock broke and the door swung inward. A dim yellow light streamed into the chamber and along with it, came three figures.

Sire Jim only saw black silhouettes. "They will not get me," the second captain whispered, tightening his muscles, ready to leap forth. He did not have to—the stranger in the doorway called his name, and not just his name, they called him lord.

"Sire Jim, my lord, are you here?" One of the men yelled into the darkness of the cell, his torch searching through the hay and stone. "Sire Jim, we are here to rescue you." The strangers got inside, behind them there was more light and more men. The fire from the torches lit their figures and Sire Jim could finally see the men. Armed with long swords, they wore iron plates with white tunics thrown over them. On their chests they had a symbol of a leaping rabbit. A familiar sigil, Sire Jim thought again. At least they are not the Royal Guards.

"Sire. We are here for you," the man repeated. "Sire Barron sent us; he and several other lords from Bois came to Runo to get you out of here."

"Sire Barron?" the second captain asked. He knew that name. Sire Barron was a renown knight, a sworn man of Sire Tem, whose family held a small plot of land at the southwest corner of Bois province, on the border with Westalia. The two lords had been good friends for a long time, coming together numerous times to join campaigns or to attend tourneys. Alas the old Barron was dead, stricken by the ague three seasons back, and the only other Barron was his son, Hur, a skinny boy who rarely left his land.

Although Hur continued to honor his father's oath to the Duke, sending supplies and men to Bonneville when needed, he never took part in any campaigns, nor did he ever visit the Bois capital. To hear his name in the dungeon beneath Runo was indeed a surprise.

"My lord, please. We do not have much time. The royals may be here soon. We need to leave this place as soon as possible." The soldier came closer and extended his torch so that the light fell onto Sire Jim. Sire Jim stood still, saying nothing.

"Are you sure it his him?" another soldier whispered.

"Yes, I am sure," the first man replied and turned to the second captain. "My lord, do you not remember me? I am Ennes Rus, the chief guard of Sire Barron's garrison. We met several times when you came to visit my master in Dures. You even gave me a few tips on how to train new recruits. Do you not remember?"

Ennes Rus—the name sounded familiar too. Sire Jim's mind was fragile, his memory was wanting, and he struggled to remember. To help himself he closed his eyes, and soon the familiar scenes flashed before him. It all came back to him. Two seasons ago the Duke had ordered him to lead a party to the southern border of Bois to inspect the safety of the borders with Westalia. Amongst the stops Sire Jim made along that trip was a small town by the name of Dures, which belonged to the Barron family. It was there he met the young Barron, and his chief of the guards, Ennes. Yes, yes. He remembered then.

"Enes, you fight with two swords, no shield, and no visor on the helm," Sire Jim announced slowly.

"Yes, yes. You remember!" the man exclaimed and brought the torch up so Sire Jim could see his face. Over his large wrinkled forehead sat a round helm, a half-helm to be exact, with no visor, just hinges that marked its formal place.

"What are you doing here, Ennes? Are you not supposed to be back in Dures, guarding the border?" the captain asked.

"We were, but then we got orders from our lord to come here, and so we did. But let's talk of this later. We really need to leave. Please Sire, follow us." The soldier came over and placed his gloved hand onto Sire Jim's shoulder. "Trust us. We are your friends." There was something in his voice that made the second captain relax. He lowered his arms and stepped forth, stumbling over a large stack of hay. But before he could fall, several pairs of hands caught him and put him back up to his feet. Already in the hallway someone gave him a chain mail, which Sire Jim put on quickly, and someone else handed him a sword, his sword. The familiar feel of his own weapon made the second captain feel like his old self again. He squeezed the leathered hilt and smiled.

"Lead the way, chief," he said firmly.

Together with the soldiers, he rushed to the stairs, then several levels up, and into the large foyer of the prison, left in disarray. A fight had been fought there recently. Debris and bodies covered the floor, furniture was thrown around, and blood pools were every place. Several dozen men walked around, checking the dead and the wounded. Some of them wore the insignia of Sire Tem, others were Sire Barron's men, or other lords of Bois whose symbols Sire Jim recognized. But most of the bodies had symbols of the Royal Guard. Outside, the picture was even more devastating.

The castle grounds were lit with many torches and fires, some still burning and some smoldering. Several wooden buildings along the walls were ablaze and so were parts of the main fort, yellow and red rushing out of the slits like snake tongues. There were many dead on the ground too, and again, most wore sigils of the Royal Guard. Amongst the bodies, over them and around them, walked soldiers, common folks, and lords, displaying their damaged armor and dented helms. Constant shouts, yells, and cries completed the scene, coming together in one low rumble, which Sire Jim could not understand.

Observing the sight, the second captain followed his escort almost to the open front gates, where several dozen knights stood in a half circle, their armored suits reflecting the light from the fires. They huddled around a large improvised table made of two large crates, talking loudly amongst themselves. When they noticed Sire Jim, their discussion stopped and everyone stared at him. All of them were the young nobles from Bois—Sire Barron with two of his younger cousins, Sire Druso and Sire Giors, Sire Verien from the northern part of the province, and Sire Fruios from the east. There were others too. But Sire Jim could not recall their names.

"Sire Jim, how good of you to be here with us," said young Lord Barron. He waved his plated hand and smiled. He was no older than twenty, but had a commanding look. A true knight, Sire Jim thought to himself, saluting the lords.

"Would you care to explain what is going on here?" the second captain addressed the young Barron, skipping the formal introductions.

"We are here to rescue our fellow knights of Bois."

"Yes, but how…What has happened here?"

Another knight, also young of face, wearing green armor, lifted his visor. "The Spirit knows we did not intend for it to end like this. All we wanted was freedom for the Duke and his fellow men, whom the royals have kept captive here. We came in peace, urging the royal councilors to listen to our pleas. We told them to let the Duke go, to let him stand trial as a knight, not as a common criminal."

"Indeed we did," agreed Hur Barron. "But those royal lackeys refused to listen. They sent us away, telling us that if we wanted to keep our titles, we should forget about Sire Tem. And then they said that the Duke was a doomed man, and nothing would save him. They also told us to run back to our castles and hope that no one takes away our lands. Those fools left us no choice. When nightfall came, we ordered our men to attack the fort. Luckily for us some of the local guards were loyal to Bois. They opened the eastern gates for us, so our attack came as a surprise for the Royal Guards. They stood no chance. After we killed a few of them, the rest gave up and now we hold them prisoner, locked in the very same cells our comrades once sat in."

"What about the Regal Fox and his council—did you catch them?"

"Five of the councilors are in our possession, but three have fled. I am afraid the Fox is amongst them. Along with a handful of his bodyguards he fought his way to the outer moat. There they seized some of our horses and fled. Our chase was fruitless. They escaped. But take my word, if he stays anywhere near Bois we will catch him. That scum of a knight does not deserve to live."

"Raising arms against the royal kin. This sounds like treason," Sire Jim said after some thought.

"Sire, of all people I thought you would understand. Those royals accused the Duke of terrible crimes. They made him sit in a cold cell without food or water, took away his family sword, and burned his banners. How can you talk of treason after all that has happened?" exclaimed Sire Barron.

"I did speak of treason, but I did not say that I, myself, consider it so. If there is no fealty, there is no treason. I am afraid that my own fealty has changed. When the Regal Fox tried to bribe me to his side, while we walked the gardens of the meeting hall, I realized that I gave a mistake oath when I took up knighthood. My fealty was not to the royal family, but to my friends, my land, and my commander, Sire Tem, not some Regal Fox or Philip the First. Maybe at the start of the Puno campaign I would have thought of you as rebels, but now I think of you as my comrades, men who are not afraid to stand up against the wrongs that plague our realm. If you want me to join you, I do so with pleasure. But I also want you to join me in a crusade against the injustice that the royal court has seeded in Normandia. Before you do, though, know that my fight is not just one battle; it is a war, which may last long and end in defeat. You may lose much in the process—lands, titles..."

"Who needs titles if they mean nothing?" A familiar voice came from behind. Sire Jim turned and saw Sire Zuros. The old knight's head was bleeding, half of his fingers were broken. Yet he did not look weak or in pain. His eyes were full of fire, and so were Sire Jim's, though he did not know it then.

Sire Zuros stepped into the center of the group and raised his healthy hand.

"I am proud," he said when everyone was looking at him. "So young and so brave. I am impressed. With you Normandia has hope." He turned to Sire Jim. "I have spent a lot of time in a dark cell, not the best place for a knight to be. There I was left to ponder with myself and I realized many things. With my conscience as my most fearsome judge, I understood that much of what filled my life was false. Somehow hollow values sneaked into my mind, blinding me, making me follow the wrong path. But no more. I am not going to be a fool anymore. Sire Jim is right. There is no treason when there is no fealty. Abandoning your commander will be treason, but fighting to save him is not. So let us take up arms to protect our land, our people, and ourselves."

Even before the last word left Sire Zuros' mouth, the entire yard, lords and soldiers alike, burst into one loud cheer. Everyone, even the former opponents from the garrison, were chanting, all chanting the same things: Hail to Bois! Hail to Sire Zuros! Hail to Puno! Hail to Normandia! The chanting grew louder, and soon it was impossible to hear anything. It was so loud that to talk to Sire Zuros, Sire Jim had to shout in the old knight's ear, repeating his words a few times.

"Where is Sire Tem?"

"Safe," Sire Barron replied instead. Sire Zuros only shook his head in silence. "But well he is not. We found him in the lower reaches of the prison, left without food or light for days. The time spent in the nasty hole had proved to be devastating for him. He is alive but in very bad shape. We are afraid he will not survive for long. Our healers are doing everything they can, but…"

"He is dying," added Sire Zuros in a low voice, almost a whisper. Such words made Sire Jim frown, not in sadness, but in anger. The second captain was very angry indeed. The Regal Fox had to pay for what he had done to his commander, and to him. Yet, there was little he could do at that moment. He slowly swallowed and asked, "Can I see him?"

"Yes, of course," replied young Sire Barron. "You will find him on the second level of the main tower. My men will escort you."

Sire Jim did not waste any more time. He thanked the lords and ran for the large archway, carved out of the thick stone wall of the main tower of the castle, parts of which continued to exude puffs of smoke. Quickly he made his way through the thick crowd of soldiers and commoners, and climbed the wide spiral stairs to the second floor, where amidst a large hall, he found a group of men dressed in white robes, huddling around a tall bed. In it, covered with layers of satin blankets, lay the Duke. Thin and pale, his face was hard to recognize. His once strong muscular features had vanished, and in their place were boney lines that outlined the Duke's drained visage. His chin and cheeks were covered in patches of white, almost silver hair, and in deep sockets rested two half-closed eyes, which moved slowly from side to side, studying everyone in sight. For some time the Duke's glance passed over Sire Jim, who had moved up close to the bed, standing within arms reach of his commander. But eventually Sire Tem found the second captain. The Duke's face expressed a sign of delight, and his right hand moved up. Sire Jim quickly took his commander's hand and kneeled, holding it gently so as not to hurt the old man.

"Rise, my sworn knight" the Duke whispered when Sire Jim's lips touched his boney wet wrist. "You do not deserve to stand on your knees—none of us do."

A cough interrupted him. It was loud and violent, and to stop it one of the healers placed a steaming bandage onto the Dukes chest. It seemed to help and the Duke's voice returned, though it was weaker this time.

"I am afraid this is not my best appearance. I am not the commander you are used to seeing. Now I understand how old I really am."

"Sire, everything is going to be all right. A few days of rest and you will be back on your horse, leading us again."

"I am afraid I need more than a few days. Truth to be told, I do not think I will make it through this. Oh, please, do not be sad. I am not. I have lived a good life, I am glad I…." Another violent burst of cough sent the Duke to the other side of the bed; his head bounced on the pillow and his eyes rolled up. The healers rushed to attend to the patient. Someone pushed Sire Jim aside, then someone else made him step back to the door. "Leave, please leave," one of the healers said then and closed the door.

Sire Jim remained outside for a moment and then went back to the yard, where more people hurried to fill the many wagons with food and weapons taken from the castle's armory. Halted by a passing group of soldiers Sire Jim looked up at the tower he had just left. Tears were in his eyes and he turned, only to find another grim sight. Before him lay a view of the burning city. Runo was ablaze. The mob, encouraged by the lack of guards, was looting the stocks located on the other side of town.

"Why does anyone not stop them, Mother?" He heard a thin voice next to him. He turned and saw a young boy sitting on the ground near to a broken chest. A young woman was standing next to him; in her hands she held another child. Both were staring at the fires ahead. "Mother, can we go there too? A man at the wall said that we could get some food there."

"No. We cannot. Only bad people go there. When other lords come they will punish them. Do you want the lords to punish us too?" replied the mother.

The boy did not answer. Instead he climbed from the dirt floor, and rose on his toes so he could see better. "Silly commoners. No matter what you do, the other lords will punish you," Sire Jim thought to himself. "Better flee this place. When the royals come they will hang everyone."

Sire Jim looked at the two one more time and then walked away. There was little he could do for them. There was little he could do for himself either. He was a traitor now, and so were half of the lords in Bois. Tough times lay ahead. The scent of civil war was in the air, and Sire Jim was liking it, though he tried to deny such a thought.

Chapter 73

THE IDLE days we had spent preparing for our daring endeavor counted twelve. We had devoted this time to training, and in the evenings discussed our plan. Elson's experience proved to be particularly useful, as he taught us how to fight indoors, seek cover, scale walls, and hide in shadows. I tried to remember everything the Southerner told us, and as I did I slowly began to realize how risky our trip to Oris' estate actually was. Although we often went to bed early, I could not sleep, and when one night a sage's servant invited us to his master's study, I was the first to walk into the hallway, with most of my gear in hand.

Revor waited for us in the company of the Southerner—no servants, no guards. A lonely candle lit a small portion of the room, where an empty table hid shadows of stacked books. The sage sat in a chair next to the window; Elson stood by his side. Both were silent and composed. When the door closed they turned.

"Are you ready?" The Southerner looked at us. We nodded.

"Then let's do it." Elson clapped his hands once and walked out, the sage followed, and so did we. Outside, two black coaches waited for us. Elson took a seat on top of the first carriage, and we settled in the second one, alone with Revor who immediately began to read his scrolls, mumbling something as his fingers ran through the yellow pages. Then I heard the loud snap of a whip, and the carriages moved.

The trip seemed long. In the open window the familiar scenes of the sleeping city passed by swiftly. Houses changed into plazas, which then turned into fences, and then into houses again. The view was dull, yet no one spoke a word. Everyone was thinking of things to come, and so did I, trying to recall everything I had learned in the past days.

As a cruel joke, somewhere near the gates to the poor side, the weather turned worse. The wind became stronger, and thick drizzle poured from the black starless sky, which promised a wet and miserable night. But the weather was the least of our worries. The questionable offer of help from the mercenary general still bothered me. Within myself I agreed with Ike—there was something very tainted about the general, and I did not trust him. But at the same time I had little choice. I had to try to get inside Oris' compound, for I had to find Father. Besides, there was little I could do then. I had made my decision, and there was no way back.

Past the gates to the poor side, we continued forth, then made a sharp turn and stopped next to a tall four-story building, surrounded on all sides by a tall metal fence. The house was of deep green color, its front entrance illuminated with two large streetlamps. Four men dressed in black guarded the way in. When we got out of our carriages two of them ran up and took us inside. There they transferred us to an older sentry, who seemed to hold some rank within the freelance company.

"The general is awaiting your arrival," said the white-whiskered guard as he escorted us into a meeting room, a round chamber lit with many candles and packed with some two dozen people. Most of the men were strangers. They wore suits of scaled armor, long swords hung at their hips, and shiny full helms laid on a bench by the wall. They stood in a half circle, leaning over a large desk, covered with several leather maps. And in the center, holding a golden helm in the shape of an eagle's head, rose General Riz Asmar. His polished steel plates gave him much more size and made him look menacingly big and dangerous. A large two-handed sword with its decorated hilt dispensed with any doubt about the general's status. Indeed he looked like a warrior, worthy of his title. As we came in he was explaining something to the others. But once he noticed us, he stopped and lifted his head.

"Ah, the Northerners!" he exclaimed loudly. "Good, you are finally here. Come. There are a few things we need to discuss."

When we were at the table, the general pointed to the other men around him and continued. "I want you to meet my loyal comrades, my captains. They will join us as we go to the compound."

"What do you mean by 'us'?" I asked. "I thought we were to go there alone, just the four us." The general looked at me, and a big smile ran across his face.

"Did you think I would let you boys go there alone?" the general exclaimed, laughing. "Poor lads. You know nothing of the ways of Azoros. There is much more to our plan than four swords and a starless night. To get to Oris' compound you will need money, connections, a small army, experience, and with all due respect, you do not have any of it. But I do, and since I will have to employ it to aid you I will have to make sure that the job is done right. Therefore, I have decided to go with you. That way I will know that there are no problems."

"But is it not a bit risky for you?" I heard the Southerner in the back. "I mean your reputation, your safety."

"My reputation and my safety can be jeopardized, and this is exactly why I want to go with you. I want to make sure that all the risks for me are minimized." The general straightened up and threw his cloak back behind his shoulders. The cloak - it was of a stranger yellow color, which made me feel cautious. Why? I could not understand.

"There is nothing else to explain." The general's tone was firm. "I am leading this expedition, and this is it. Now. Everyone, listen up. You all know what we are doing tonight. It will not be easy, but you are already aware of it. First I want to tell you of the rules. Rule number one—I am the leader here. I am the sole commander, and there will be no deviations, no initiative without my approval. Everyone does what I say and how I say it. If anyone tries something different I will make sure that he does not see the light of day again. Are there any questions? No? Good.

"Rule number two—Each group will follow their objectives. They will not leave their posts or improvise. If the order is to hold a line, you hold a line. And finally rule number three—no pillaging or stealing. Any loot taken from the compound can be traced to us, and that I will not tolerate. You steal—you die. Understood?

"With this out of the way, let's move on to the operation. For several weeks now I had my scouts study all of the merchant's estates. Out of the four compounds, only one raises suspicion. The estate I speak of is located inside the western borough and was purchased by the merchant two seasons back. Ever since there have been strange things taking place near it. My scouts tell me that almost every night Oris's men bring in closed carriages, several at a time. Nobody knows what is in those wagons, but some folks say they have seen scores of men inside the wagons. I cannot verify such reports, though it does not matter—there are other signs too. In the past season alone Oris' paymasters ordered huge supplies of bread and water. They also hired extra guards, and a new blacksmith from the Great Plains. All this suggests that something is going on there. My guess is that the merchant has built his own personal prison, and our goal is to find out what and who is held there.

"The man in charge of security there is a fellow by the name of Rozor. I do not know him personally, but I have gathered some information about him. He comes from the Free Cities. A leader of a small freelance company he took service with the merchant two seasons ago. Although he brought his company with him, most of the men are long since gone, and in their place Rozor has hired others. So now the garrison makes up a colorful bunch. Still they will not be easy to defeat should we assault the compound head-on. The place itself is located at the westernmost point of the district. It is surrounded by two walls and a spiked fence. There is also a moat dug around the central building and three watchtowers, which are manned at all times. Luckily we do not have to worry about any of it.

"The stronghold is an old A'als keep. While the upper parts have been rebuilt numerous times, the deeper reaches of the dungeons below remain almost unchanged. Since most of the tunnels were abandoned long ago, nobody really has explored them much. Still there are a few old maps, which show the layout of the dungeons below the mansion. It so happens that my men have acquired one of such maps. It shows that there are several escape routes into the compound that extend under the sewers and all the way to the edge of the forest, several leagues from the city. I have already dispatched my men to investigate the passes. So far they found two of the entrances. Alas one is collapsed, but the other is still open. We can use it to get into the merchant's compound.

"It is not possible to send a large brigade though. The underground is too narrow, and should we have to retreat, too many men would cramp the tunnel. Instead I have decided to take two groups of six. The first group will include the three squires from Normandia, the Southerner, my Captain Silo, and myself. We will follow the map to the dungeon beneath the compound, and then inside the mansion itself. The second group, led by Captain Ris, will go after us, but stay inside the dungeon, so as to make sure that we have a clean route of escape. Twenty more of my men will remain at the entrance to the tunnels. Master Revor, you will stay behind too.

"If all goes well we will be in and out of there before the guards know what has happened."

The general packed the map, which he had studied as he spoke, put it into a large skin handbag, and headed for the exit, escorted by his men. The ringing of metal from their armor resonated off the stone walls. Left alone in the room we looked at the sage, who stood quiet, looking at the fireplace in front of him. He remained still for a while, then jolted his head and turned.

"There is little else to say." The sage sighed. "He already has a plan. I wonder why he forgot to mention it before." Revor thought some more. "I am sure he has spent a lot of coins to get it all in order. I just hope he paid the right people to do it." He looked at the fire. "What is done is done. Let's go. We do not want to keep the general waiting."

In the courtyard we met up with the general's staff. Some of the men were already riding away, and some were pulling out their horses, fixing saddles and trying straps. The general himself was sitting on a large black horse. The steed stood still and waited while his master gave out orders. Once satisfied with the progress of the preparations, the general yanked on the bridle, and rode up to us, yelling something to the passing servants, who started to run in disarray.

"Get in your carriage. My page will show you the way." The general turned again and galloped off. At the same time a young blonde boy of thirteen of twelve appeared before us. He sat on top of a gray pony and in his hand he held a long torch.

"Good night to you all," the boy said in a thin voice. "Master general asked me to escort you to the cave. If you do not have anything else here to do, please follow me. The general said it is urgent, and he is not too kind when he has to wait."

Our carriages were ready, and so we took after the boy, keeping to the general's orders. As we rode down the streets, I could hear the gray pony strolling a short distance ahead, its little hooves knocking monotonously on the paved lane. The sound stayed with us until we reached the outskirts of the poor side. There the pavement ended and turf lanes began. It got darker too. The lights of the city were left behind, and the black outlines of the countryside yielded nothing of interest.

Still I continued to stare out of the window, and when our carriage veered left, I noticed a thin glow coming from behind some dark shapes. It was a mercenary outpost. Distressed by the latest invasion of the Grass Folks, the council of Azor set out guard stations around the city, so as to be ready for any future intrusion. The post which we passed was one of them. It was a small camp, which included a hastily raised wooden tower, several tents, and two large fire pits, each burning high with flames standing two cubits tall. A brigand of forty sentries crowded the place. Although most of them seemed to be preoccupied with their own business, a group of them noticed our procession and halted us. The boy did all the talking, and soon we were allowed to continue forth.

When we stopped again, it was at the rendezvous point, situated on a high bank of a shallow river. Surrounding us stood tall pines, and straight ahead many torches moved by the water. To get there we had to follow the page down a sandy slope. On the beach, which was a stretch of sand about ten cubits wide, several dozen men—all general's men—moved around, following the orders of their commanders. Several of the men had suits of heavy armor, long swords, and heavy round shields. But the majority had only light leather suits, one or two short swords, and a small pack, which they had fixed behind their shoulders.

They were expecting someone—not us—though our arrival did not bother them. Then I realized….Everyone was waiting for the general, who arrived soon after, walking down the beach in the company of five bodyguards. He got rid of some pieces of his armor, keeping only a steel helm and a breast plate, which covered a fine set of chain mail. As soon as he reached his men he gave out several quick orders and then looked at us.

"I see you made it here in time. Good, I hate when people are late. I have everything ready. My men are in position. If nothing else, we are ready to proceed." The general gave another command to his men and turned back to us. "As I said, the Northerners and Elson will go with me. My Captain Silo will join us too. He is a great scout, and has the eyes of a cat. I do not know what wicked magic he uses, but I swear he sees better in the dark than in daylight. Silo and I will go first, the squires will take the middle, and Elson will have the rear. Another seven men, under Ris' command, will go after us. They will hold the passage while we go into the compound."

The general stretched his arms, and groaned. "Shall we?"

Not waiting for an answer, he brushed off light drops of his gloves and started down the river, away from the light of the main group. We followed him to a heap of twigs and twisted roots that came down from the top and hung over the side of the embankment in a wicked arch. Underneath it I could see a narrow slit peering out of the sandy soil. Although wide enough for one man to pass freely, the entrance into the cave was hard to detect, as its black color blended in perfectly with the dark brown colors of the live wood. But as our small lantern dispersed some of the blackness, the passage inside became discernible. Some of the general's men were already inside. Their torches flickered in the distance, and their voices sounded in a low hum.

"Scouting party. I sent them ahead to see if there are any collapses in the tunnels," explained the general. He stepped up to the entrance, whistled, and the voices stopped. Three men emerged from the tunnel, brushing off some dust from their shoulders, and immediately reported to the general. They spoke the Southern Way. I did not understand anything, but when they were done, the general smiled and entered the tunnel. We went after him, carefully picking every step so as not to trip over the entwined roots that made up the floor of the passage.

The soft but wet air made it somewhat difficult to breath. It was not foul, just different. It was dark too. But we had enough light with us; six torches cleared the way through the darkness. The tunnel appeared to be straight.

After a while its walls, first made of soil, soon turned to rock, and the distance between them widened, allowing three men to walk abreast. Yet we continued in single file, following the general and his captain. Clearly handmade, the tunnel slowly took on a square shape. Once smooth, the ceiling had long deteriorated and some portions had given in to the heavy weight, hanging dangerously close to our heads. The crumbling old stones also became victims of the many years, and some of them had dropped to the ground, blocking the path. But as we got further into the tunnel, the more refined it became. By the time we reached the first opening, the walls, floor, and ceiling looked completely intact, with only some cracks and hollows. The clearing itself was of a round shape and wide enough for a dozen men to fit perfectly. Before us stood three archways, each supported by wooden beams. We took the one in the middle.

The new passage was a bit wider. Slanting downward it took several sharp turns into another clearing. This time there was just an entrance at the other side. Without stopping we went through. As we continued forth I suddenly realized that the floor under our feet was no longer made of rock and soil. Instead it was rows of wooden boards, darkened but solid. Undoubtedly, the wood was cared for. How long it had been there, I did not know.

For several hundred cubits our path remained clear, but then we came to a small iron gate. Half the size of an average door, it was shut tight. Our attempts to open it proved useless, as the iron hinges and locks were sealed from the inside. It promised to be a serious obstacle, but not for the general's man, who quickly extracted some strange potions out of his bags, and while we remained behind, poured some bluish liquid onto the metal work of the door. Then he moved back and threw something forward. A bright flash disturbed my vision, and I could hear the noise of the metal hitting the floor, resonating through the empty dark corridor. Indeed, when my sight returned, I found the door on the ground and Silo packing his tools. Wasting no more time we passed the demolished door, and as we left the twisted metal pivots, eaten away by some invisible force, I thought of magic. "There is no magic in Ethoria. Probably black powder or something," I thought to myself.

Soon though another hatch blocked our way. This time it was made of oak boards and sat at the top of rough stairs. Although there was no sign of a recent visit, half-rotten rags and burdened torches fit into the walls, suggested that the tunnel had been used a while back. When—it was hard to say. While we studied the woodwork, Silo did his trick again. Without trouble he removed the door with the same bluish liquid, only he did not move away that time. Instead he held the door with his hands, and when the flash came, he lowered the door carefully onto the floor, so as not to make any noise. He did a good job, because aside from a hissing sound everything went quiet.

On the other side, we entered a large stone chamber. In its center stood a stairwell, narrow and seemingly flimsy. Made of old wooden boards, it was a questionable route, but it was also the only way to the upper levels. To my relief the staircase held, though it moved and screeched as we climbed. At the top, we came to the start of another corridor. Large polished stone plates covered most of the floor and walls. Although our lanterns gave plenty of light it was impossible to see the color of the stone, concealed beneath layers of dust, dirt, and spiderwebs that hung like shawls, so thick in places that we had to use our swords to cut through them.

"This is an old dungeon, right under the merchant's compound," the general said, standing before an open hall, pierced by many dark tunnels and caves. "Nobody knows what we might find here, so watch your step. Walk after me, and do what I tell you. Hopefully there will be no one down here."

"How do you know that there are no guards here?" I asked, as the general was about to head down one of the corridors. "I mean, if we know about these secret passages, so will Oris, do you not think?"

"Good question. But did you think I would risk my life without doing some investigating first?" The general spit, not in anger, but in irritation, the mesh from the webs was all over his face and he tried to remove it with his gloves. "The lower reaches of the dungeon are empty of the merchant's men. It is impossible to guard this part. There are just too many tunnels in here, so the guards settled in the upper levels, where the tunnels are few and it is easy to watch over the halls. So worry not about finding any sentries."

"But what about the upper levels, will we not have to go through there before getting into the compound?" I insisted. Something was odd, yet I could not say what. The general looked straight at me. The grin left his face. His tone was serious.

"Why do you think I asked for a thousand coins from you? Information is an expensive thing, but not that expensive. A good portion of your payment went to bribe the guards at the compound. They are mercenaries after all. It so happens that I have arranged for a free pass for us through the dungeon. Those men who are supposed to patrol the upper reaches will not be there to see us. Instead they will attend to other duties. It has been orchestrated that a diversion will attract their attention elsewhere. The deal is that as we are about to enter the upper section of the dungeon, several of my associates will break into the compound from above, and set some of the merchant's stables on fire. Of course before they do so, some of the best steeds will go missing. In turn the entire garrison will chase after them, trying to retrieve the stolen goods, and while they do, we sneak into the compound and see what we can find. If all goes as planned, we will have plenty of time to do our job and leave without ever being noticed."

The general looked at me. "I hope that answers your questions."

I did not say anything, but just followed him to a wooden staircase, which had been hidden by some columns. It took us to the next level.

Just as the general had said, the entrance into the dungeon's upper section was unguarded. The doors that blocked the way were left unlocked, and the grate, although lowered, was easy to lift, secured afterwards by a piece of wood that Silo slipped under the rusted bars. Past the doors we found another inter-active web of passages and chambers, built from the black stones. The first distinction I noticed was the presence of light. All the caves, rooms, and corri-dors were filled with low-hanging oil lamps, which exuded a reddish light and puffs of black smoke, giving them a scorched look. The passages themselves were empty, and the silence was everyplace.

We quickly crossed several of the corridors, and after taking a sharp left turn, halted. Further away we could hear strange noises. They did not sound like voices, more like clanking of metal and shuffling of feet. The sounds were very distant, yet they were very distinct.

"Be careful. Some of the guards may still be here," the general whispered and waved at Silo. The man nodded and took off his backpack. Leaving the bag next to us, he then picked up his swords and ran ahead, using the many shadows for protection. The general's man was away for a while. When he returned, his breathing was fast. He said something to the general, after which we all got up and moved quickly, crossing more passages, each time seeking cover of the black rock. At some point we came to an open room that looked like a storage place. Boxes, shelves, bottles, and sacks were put into pallets and arranged along the walls. I noticed that one of the bags was ripped and several small seeds had fallen onto the floor. I reached over and grabbed them. Wheat. Indeed there was plenty of food in stock, at least a hundred sacks of grain, enough to feed a town like Villone for the entire winter.

Meanwhile the strange noises got closer, and then at the far end of the corridor I saw a group of men, five or six of them, walking slowly, talking to each other. They had to be the merchant's guards. Immediately my heart started to race, and the blood rushed to my head. I realized that I was afraid. Suddenly I heard another sound, the loud but distant ringing of a bell. It was an alarm. Had they found us? I looked at the general, but he remained calm. It seemed he had expected it. Then I remembered—the diversion!

All of a sudden, disorder filled the tunnels of the upper sections. Far off, yet clear, more voices, the clatter of metal, and footsteps, a lot of them, ran through the dungeon. Yet, where we hid, everything remained unchanged. A single rat appeared for a moment from under one of the sacks, probably curious to find out what it was that disturbed its evening meal. The small beast sat on the floor, peering with its small red eyes, then slowly moved across the room and hid under a crate. By then the commotion had already moved above and then stopped all together. With silence restored the place felt empty again.

One by one we left our hideout, and moving slowly along a wall, made our way to a circular chamber with six open gates. Each of the passages looked identical, dim and quiet. Silo, who was in the room before anyone else, chose the corridor to the south and led our group into another short tunnel, which quickly brought us into a grand hall, so big and long that I could barely see the other end. It was consumed in a dark vale, despite rows of oil lamps, which hung low from the cathedral ceiling. Along the stone walls, shaped in wide arcs, I could see small openings located almost at floor level. The openings looked like sewer drains. Yet they were not. As I got closer I realized that they were holding cells. The general's scouts were right. The dungeon was some sort of a prison.

The closest of the grated holes was empty. But in the next cell, amongst dirty haystacks and old rags, I noticed someone sitting at the far wall, crawled in a little ball. In the dim light it was impossible to see the features of the poor man, just a pair of bony dirty feet and dark ripped trousers.

"There is someone in here," I exclaimed, kneeling down before the grid, which was chained to the wall and locked with a bulky dead bolt.

"*Jero, der Vir,*" whispered Silo, and came up next to me. Speaking to the prisoner inside, he used the Southern Way, but Elson translated his words to us.

"Hey, you. We are no guards," Silo repeated and checked the iron bars, shaking them several times. The prisoner remained quiet.

"Listen, if you want to stay here, then stay quiet. Otherwise, you better start talking." At those words the jailbird shifted, and a thin voice answered in the Northern Way without an accent. Whoever he was he was our countryman. I had no doubt.

"Do not beat me, master." The stranger started to cry. "Oh please, do not beat me. I will do anything you say, I just do not understand your words." A lad crawled up to the door, and as the light came over him I saw his face. To my surprise, behind the grate I saw a young boy of twelve or thirteen. His hands and bared chest were seeded with razor-like burns. Black streaks ran down his cheeks, and his puffed eyes were full of tears. The boy was scared, trembling, and confused.

"We are not going to beat you, young man. We are no guards," said Silo, this time in the Northern tongue. Hearing a familiar language, the boy's face lit up. He crawled closer and smiled. "You, you are not with Sero. But…Who…who are you?" The boy looked at us with tears trailing down his cheeks.

"It does not matter who we are. We are here to help," I said quickly. "But to do so we need your assistance. Will you help us?"

"Oh, I will do anything, anything you say, just take me away from here, I am so scared, I cannot stay here any longer. Please, please. I—"

"All right then. I have some questions for you," the general said before I could do anything.

"Yes, yes, I will tell you anything."

"Good, then." The general was about to continue, when I interrupted him. "Let's get this poor boy out of his hole first." The mercenary gave me a sharp look, but did not say anything. He gave Silo a quick nod, and the captain extracted another blue potion. He then sprinkled the destructive liquid onto the chain and stepped aside. A small flash illuminated the cell for a moment and the grid fell outwards. The boy sat still, but once realizing that the blockade was gone, crept into the open, looking at us full of hope.

"Who are you, lad?" The general asked quickly.

"Me, oh, I am Suho, Suho of Remour. My family lives in Risole; it is a small village, in the southern part of Chantue. Sire Serge is our lord."

"How long have you been here?"

"I do not know, many days, many, many days. But there are some boys in the other cells who have been here even longer. It was late winter season when they took me. I was playing with my two friends in the woods. There is a small pond. It is quiet and no one goes there. But that morning just after we came there, four men jumped out of the trees and grabbed us. They threw me in a bag, and into a wagon. And then they brought me here. I do not know anything else, good sire."

"Those men who took you—do you know who they were?" I interjected my own question. The general was getting even more irritated, but I did not care.

"I do not know who they were, but they were not from our lands. They spoke some strange tongue, the same language the guards speak here in the dungeon."

"Were there any other boys with you?"

"When we traveled here I saw some other boys. They were not my friends; they were from other towns. But we could not talk much; the men beat us when they heard us talking. And here there are a lot of boys too. I do not know how many, but I have seen at least forty of them. And there are more coming almost every week, two or three at a time. Some are put in cells further down the hall, and others are taken someplace else. I wish I could tell you more, but we are not allowed to talk in here either. Once, I heard some boy cry at night and so I talked to him. But the guards caught me and beat me bad, so now I talk to no one. It is so horrible in here, sire. Please take me away. Please, take me home."

The boy broke down and started weeping.

I felt anger building within me. "How could someone treat children like this? How evil is that Oris!" I spat in disgust.

Meanwhile, the general rose up, and patting the boy on the head, said something to Silo, who immediately picked up his gear and hurried across the hall, where more grids peered out of the wall. Halfway down he turned and suddenly vanished. Something was wrong. But before I could understand anything, a very loud whistle came from some distance away. Ike, Ric, Elson, and I tried desperately to find the source of the disturbance, yet could see nothing. Then, suddenly, the general shoved the young boy back into his cell and leapt away from us. A large sword appeared from behind his shoulders and his face twisted in a wicked grin. Instinctively I sprang back. So did the others, pulling out their weapons, facing the general. No one had time to say anything, as a streak of white light appeared at the other end of the hall. The line grew wider, and soon I realized that there had been a door hidden in the dark shadows. Swiftly the wooden gate swung outwards, and several dozen men streamed inside the hall. It was an ambush. The general had betrayed us.

There were four or five foes for each of us, including the general and his right-hand man, Silo, who had reemerged along with the others from the general's company. To fight them would be suicide, but to give up without a battle was not an option either. If it had to be, it had to be. We would die beneath Azor.

Pulling out my A'al blade, I waved it in the air and stepped back toward the entrance we had walked in. Ric, Ike, and Elson were by my side. In front of us, the enemy pushed forth. They did so unhurriedly, forming two rows of spears. They knew that we had no way out. We realized so too once we reached the door, which was closed and blocked from the other side. It was a trap, and we had walked right into it. Anger came over me. I hated Azor, the mercenaries, and the wicked general. But most of all I hated myself for being so naïve and trusting. I should have listened to Ike, but it was too late now. Then, again, my eyes saw the yellow cloak that swayed behind the General. Indeed it looked very familiar. It was—suddenly my memory cleared and I remembered the night when A'tie had told me to watch out for three things: Words of Truth, Green Fire, and Yellow Cape. Of course, how could I have missed it? The Yellow Cape was a warning. A'tie tried to tell me about the General and his betrayal. But I failed to see it in time, and now Ike, Ric, and Elson had to die, all because of me. I was so angry with myself that I wanted to leap at the advancing foes. Yet, before I could make a single move, the enemies halted and the General addressed us in a loud, demanding tone: "Give up your swords, Northerners. You do not stand a chance. Look at yourselves—a handful of peasant boys from Normandia, and one ill-fated mercenary. Please, spare me some time and lay down your arms. Oh, and if you please, take one of these cells. I would really appreciate it. If you do as I say I promise you will live."

"What makes you think we want to listen to your rotten words? You are scum, and we will have nothing to do with the likes of you!" Elson yelled back, his voice angry. His eyes glittered with fury.

"I could not care less for your judgments. You are my prisoners, and this is it." The general said back. "Take my advice give up your swords."

"Never," I yelled out next. "You have betrayed us. There is no honor in you, and I would rather die than surrender."

"Enough of your empty grumbling. This is my last warning. Surrender or die!"

"Come and take us," I snapped again.

"You may kill us all, but believe me, before you do, we will take some of you with us." Ike picked up my yell. "It is up to you to figure out who will die today from the hands of the peasant boys and who will live. Personally I do not care. I will die anyway."

My friend laughed and swung his sword. The general laughed too. He waved his hand and the guards behind him started to advance again, their spears lowered toward our chests.

The metal tips were getting dangerously close. But then the unexpected happened. The wall to the right of us suddenly trembled and a bright flash illuminated the hall. A cloud of dust and broken rock filled the room, along with the smell of burning wood and melting metal. I was thrown to the ground, but not hurt. When the noise subsided I climbed back onto my feet. Around me the enemy and my friends were stumbling too. Shaken by the blast they walked around in disorder, dazed in the gray mist. I looked at the spot where the wall once stood. A part of the stone barrier was gone, and in its place I could see a large hole, through which scores of men were pouring in.

First I thought they were also Oris' guards. But when the first of the newcomers slashed a disoriented soldier, who was about to attack us, I knew they were on our side.

"Who are they?" I heard Ike's voice. I did not know, nor could I find out because by then, the fight was all around me.

To my left two men clashed swords, and to my right one of the general's men charged me. His attack was ill-fated. Trying to reach me, he extended his torso too much, and caught a passing arrow right in his chest. While his lifeless body hit the floor, another foe was at my face. Big in shoulders he proved to be no better than his fallen comrade. After dodging his attack I slid aside and hit him back. My blade made a graceful swing and sank into his neck, leaving a very nasty gash, which made the man drop his spear and run away screaming as though crazy. Free from the fighting for a moment I surveyed the scene. The battle raged with wrath. The once-empty hall was thick with fighting men, amongst whom one figure stood out more than any other. The general was in the middle of the swarm, swinging his large two-handed sword like a toothpick. Indeed he was good swordsman. His movement was graceful and his attacks accurate. He was fighting four men at the same time, and winning. Yet it did not stop me from dashing toward him.

Jumping over the dead and wounded I raced through the crowd, my eyes focused on the general, who saw me too. After pushing away his opponents he turned around and waited. Without stopping I sent my first blow, which the general parried with ease. A grin settled in the corner of his mouth and he chuckled loudly. He enjoyed watching my awkward movement. In turn I got even angrier. Hotheaded I swung my sword again, but the hasty attack fell short of its target. The blade sliced the air and hit the ground. The impact was so strong that I lost my grip, and the weapon flew out, landing a cubit away. The general chuckled even more loudly, but not before he dropped his own sword onto my neck. It was a miracle that I managed to scuttle off. Leaping to one side I rolled on the ground, picked up someone else's sword, and stood up.

One mistake was enough for me. There was no room for anger in a fight. I needed my mind to work straight, and my body to listen to my will. Moving slightly backwards, safe from the general's reach, I stopped and took a deep breath, letting the fuming anger leave me. Soon my thoughts returned, and I was ready to launch another attack.

This time I did not run directly at the general. Instead I circled around him, studying him, his pose, and his eyes. The general followed me, turning slowly, keeping his sword before him. My plan was to make the general come to me, which he did. When I was about to start another circle, the general dashed forth. His blow was hard and heavy, but missed me. The two-handed sword passed near my shoulder and hit the floor, extracting several bright sparks from the stone tiles. Still I did not attack, but moved further to the left, where I had more room to maneuver.

The general was after me. Quickly he raised his sword once more, but a passing man attacked him. It was a swift blow, but the general parried the strike, and with a free hand hit the young warrior in the face with his plated fist. The poor man's head exploded and streaks of blood ran down his chest. The stranger lost consciousness and dropped, his hands still clenching his sword. The general did not even look to see if his hit disabled the enemy. His focus was on me again. He took one step closer, at which time I leapt at him and then kneeled down so that the edge of my sword struck the general's armored thigh. Although my weapon bounced back, the iron legging dented and split in the middle. Surprised, the general stumbled. In disbelief he looked at his damaged armor, shaking it from side to side. As soon as his eyes let go of me, I let my sword fly again. This time I hit the general in the shoulder. The blow was not strong enough to pierce the well-wielded armor, but it made the general drop further back. Angry, he stared at me again, then lifted his weapon, and yelling something, swung it full force. His blows hit hard and my hand was soon numb, jolted by the vibration of the steel. The hilt of my sword was slipping, and I knew that if I did not do something I would lose the fight.

Luckily for me Ike came to my rescue. Appearing out of nowhere my friend sneaked behind the general and struck him in the back, giving him a light but painful wound. Grinning in pain, the general spun around, ready to chase my friend, but Ike was already gone, disappearing in the cloud of smoke. This was a mistake on the general's part, because before he could turn back, I managed to recover my shadow dagger and with it charged full force. Summoning all the strength left in me, I jousted the sword into the general's side. The A'al's sword broke through the chain mail, slashed the leather tunic, and dug into flesh. Something warm touched my fingers. It was blood, deep red, streaming along the blade to the hilt and down to the floor. Then I looked up. The general was staring straight into my eyes. His lips moved slowly, yet he said nothing, nor did I care to hear anything from him. I yanked the sword out and stepped back, breathing hard. Meanwhile the general slid down to the floor. He was not dead. In truth he did not even look wounded. His face expressed more tiredness than pain. Yet I knew that life was leaving him. I wanted to finish him, but before I could come close, his body fell and did not move again. That was the last I saw of the general who had betrayed us.

The victory was mine, but the enemy was still plentiful. More men came from both sides, fueling the fight, and the number of dead and wounded grew with every passing moment. My friends and I were right in the middle of it. After disposing of the general I found my companions, and together we held our ground, trying to come up with some plan to escape the mess. Then, through the noise of battle, I heard a familiar voice.

Looking over my shoulder, I saw Revor struggling through the crowd. His face was covered in dust, the once perfect robe was dirty, and in his hands he held a long staff with a metal tip, covered in blood.

"You!" the sage yelled at my friends and me. "Get out of here. We do not have much time." He turned and surveyed the scene of battle. "We will not be able to hold them for long." Revor turned again. "Hurry. Go."

"But where shall we go?" I shouted back.

"Through the hole in the wall, through the secret passage, and into the merchant's mansion."

"Why in the world would we want to go into the mansion? We need to get out of this dungeon, out of Azor," Ike said angrily.

"Mishuk, the general was right in one thing. Your father, he is here in this compound. I believe that he is held in the upper levels of the stronghold."

Speechless, I froze. It was my brother who asked the next question. "How do we know that this is the truth? We have been betrayed already."

"I cannot give any proof, just my word. Do you think I would have come down here if I wanted your death? No. I need you to stay alive. I need you to continue your struggle against the Alavantars. Go. Find your father; take him back to Normandia. Tell as many people as you can about the threat of the foul sect. Tell them everything you know, everything…"

"What about you? Why do not you go with us? Your tale will surely persuade the lords in our kingdom."

"I would," said the sage. "But we cannot escape this dungeon together. I must stay with my men. I brought them here and I must stay with them until the end. Should I survive this fight I will find you. Right now, it is your time to leave this underground hall. Go to your father. Go."

He searched for something underneath his robe; then extracted a leather case and opened it. Inside was a rolled map. Made of treated buckskin, it was of a yellow color, and on it a layout of the underground passes was burned in deep black lines. The sage looked over the map and handed it to me.

"This is the plan of the dungeon and the mansion above. I got it this morning from a very good friend of mine. No one but I know of its existence. Here you will find a secret passage, which will take you to the upper levels. From this hole, take the first left and follow the tunnel all the way to the end. There you will find a small hatch. It is the entrance into the secret tunnel. To open it twist a small torch holder to the right-hand side. When the lock clicks three times, let go of it, and the door will open. Follow the secret passage to the stairs and then up to the very top. There will be another door, which will let you into a storage room within the compound. The chamber where your father is held should be somewhere near it. Be careful though, there may still be some guards there."

"But…how did you get all this information? How—" Words left my mouth slowly.

"Remember," the sage interrupted me, "I used to work for the merchant. I know him like no one else. And I also know people who despise him. They are the ones who are helping me. Now leave. We will see each other again sometime. May the Spirit be with you."

The sage turned and ran back to the open door at the other end, where the fighting was most intense. "But what about the other prisoners?" I exclaimed, chasing him with my question. The sage turned his head quickly and yelled, "I will see to them! I promise you." And with that he was gone, his bony silhouette disappearing in the cloud of smoke, and his voice died, consumed by the loud sounds of battle. Elson hurried after Revor too, giving us nothing but a quick nod, and was gone soon too.

Standing some distance away from the nearest enemy, we had a moment to think of our next move. As my brother kept his eyes on the fighting, Ike and I opened the map and studied it. Quickly we found the place in the dungeon where we were, and then the tunnel we had to take. Just as Revor had said, the way to the upper levels was through the newly opened gap in the wall, and it was there we ran, leaving the fighting crowd behind. Outside the sounds of battle were muted. Making a few turns, we reached the first intersection and turned left, taking the tunnel all the way to a dead end. Unfortunately there was no sign of a secret hatch. The stone plates around us were smooth, no gaps in between the rocks, no cracks, no hints of any passage. Our torches lit the walls, and our eyes were searching for a lever, masked as a torch holder. To our misfortune there were dozens of cast-iron cones, spread on each side of the tunnel. Which one did we have to press? We did not know, and so we hurried to try them all. At first, none budged, but as we worked our way closer to the end, one of the vessels broke off and turned slightly. A screeching sound ran through the tunnel, then came the promised clicks. "One, two, three," I counted, then let go of the lever. The cone slowly returned to its original position, and a part of a large stone plate moved inward, presenting us with a view of a dark tunnel.

As soon as we stepped through, the gap closed, cutting us off. Having no choice but to follow the new corridor, we walked down a straight line for some time until we came upon a spiral staircase standing in the middle of the hallway. Rough iron strings looked flimsy, but we climbed them anyway, holding tight to a thin railing, which moved up and down, yet did not break. It was hard to tell how high the stairwell had taken us, but when we emerged at the top, we could not see the bottom. In front of us was a wall, and a small button pressed into the stone. After examining the switch, I pressed it and again a portion of the wall moved aside. Behind it was a room, just as the sage had said.

The place looked like a storage facility, packed with some sort of boxes, barrels, and sacks. Unclean and unsorted, it looked like the room was left unattended, given to the mercy of dust and vermin. Yet, through the junk I spotted another door across the room, and underneath it a thin line of light. Some shadows were moving, and the sound of footsteps clear and firm. Afraid to incite an alarm, we put out our torches and dropped them back onto the stairs, and hid behind a stack of half-filled satin bags. Darkness filled the room, yet we could still see a white streak in the distance. Soon though the noises died, and the shadows left. Still we continued to wait for a while longer, then crawled up to the door. Pressing my ear to the cold boards, I listened. There was nothing. After listening some more, I finally dared to open the door. A glimmer of the same bright light streamed through the gap, also letting in distant sounds of voices, some singing, and the tapping of a hammer or an axe perhaps. Yet, the hallway itself was empty, and after surveying the corridor a few more times, I slipped out of our hideout, sneaking carefully along the decorated wall. Ric and Ike were behind me, and together we journeyed forth. Somewhere behind one of the many doors seeding the walls, I was to find Father. I was not totally sure if it was so, but I hoped for it to be true.

Chapter 74

THE BIG room was lit by two sets of lamps, which stood in rows along the far wall, and bordered by a large window shut with long dark blue drapes. Furnished and carpeted it looked like sleeping quarters, adorned with light green silk straps, which hung loosely from the ceiling in long graceful arcs. Although the chamber looked empty, I could sense someone there, and so we continued to study the place carefully.

Suddenly, one of the curtains moved a bit, and someone's face leaned out briefly. Although the stranger disappeared right after, we saw him well and made our way to the window, keeping our weapons ready. Then Ike's voice broke the silence and called to the man in a threatening tone. At that moment the curtain opened again, and the same fellow walked out. Because of the shadows I could not see his face at first, but when he moved a little closer I was speechless. Before me, dressed in a loose brown robe, stood Father. Had I finally found him? It was the only question in my mind, and as the answer to it my old man stood in front of me.

An impulse of joy came over me, my face lit with a smile, and tears filled my eyes. I wanted to say something, but could not. Words simply did not leave my lips. Father did not say anything either. He stood still and looked at me, then Ric, Ike, and me again. And so we stood, frozen in a moment, surprised and shocked. It was Ike who broke the stillness. He quickly waved his hand and greeted, and as he did the curtain moved for the third time. We took several steps back, and as we did, a stranger came into the light. He was an older man, bold and fat. His eyes were small and his left cheek was misshaped by a scar. Once he realized we were not the guards, he leapt for the front door. His mouth opened to scream, but before he could do anything, Ric grabbed him by a throat, lifting him off the floor. For a moment the man tried to fight my brother's grip. His short legs beat violently in the air, and his entire body twisted and turned in all directions. But soon his face turned blue. He stopped fighting, and stared at my brother in fear and despair. At last subdued, the man was still and Ric put him down, at which moment Father suddenly spoke. His voice was odd; there was a strange sadness to his tone, mixed with disbelief.

"Mishuk, Ric, Ike…What in the Spirit's sake are you doing here?"

"We came here to rescue you and Ave," I replied.

"But…how…"

"It's a long story, Father. We will tell you everything later. Right now we must leave this place as soon as possible." I turned and headed for the door, but then halted, realizing that Father was not moving. He stood where he was, looking at me.

"I…I cannot, " he said. "I must stay here, but you need to leave. If the guards find you, they will kill you. It is…It is too dangerous in here.…"

"Father, what are you talking about? Come, we need to go," insisted Ric.

"Come with us, Uncle Brune," Ike pleaded too, and grabbed Father by his robe. But he refused to move.

"No," he said firmly. "I must stay…"

"But why? Why are you acting so stranger?" Ric's voice was starting to break.

"You will never understand…it is too complicated." Father spoke softly and lowered his head. At the same time the stranger, whose neck was still squeezed by Ric, started to mumble something. Ric, Ike, and I turned to him. The stranger wanted to say something.

"You want to talk to us?" I asked the man.

The man nodded.

"Well, if I let you speak, will you promise not to shout?" asked Ric then.

"Uh-huh."

"Do not worry," said Ike as he came up to the man. My friend raised his sword and pressed it against the man's chest. "If he decides to yell, I will cut his heart out before he makes a sound." The man glanced at my friend in fear and nodded.

"Let him go," I commanded. My brother removed his hand but remained at the stranger's side, just in case. Free from Ric's grip, the man coughed several times, and rubbing his neck, started to speak, making frequent glances at Ike's sharp blade.

"Are you really Brune's sons?" he asked me, continuing to clear his throat.

"Yes, we are. What is it to you?" I shot back.

The man did not answer. Instead he turned to Father. "How could you?" he exclaimed. "You never told me you had two other sons. The deal was all our male children, and you lied to me. I gave up my two little boys, and you told me Ave was your only child."

"What is the meaning of all this?" I asked the stranger. When he did not respond, I turned to Father. "Please, Father, say something."

"Go ahead, tell them, Brune," the stranger said with sarcasm. His tone angered me and I leapt to him, my sword in hand.

"Oh, no, please. Do not hurt me." The man recovered quickly. He raised his hands in front of his face, his eyes closed. When no attack came, he opened them again and sighed. "I am not the villain here. Well, I may be, but not to you. Just let me speak and you will understand. Please do not kill me."

"Do not listen to him, Mishuk. He is lying; he is just trying to get out of here alive." Ike pressed the blade closer to the man's chest.

"No, no. I am not lying. Though I do wish to get out of here, I do not intend to use lies to do so. Believe me."

"Yes, Mishuk, let him speak," Father uttered slowly.

The stranger nodded, swallowed hard, and began. "My name is Rulio. I am a trader from Normandia. Your father and I used to be partners. He brought me Westalian spices and I sold them in my shops. We did so for years. Everything was going well. That was until a gambling party came to town. Although betting is prohibited in Normandia, once in a while foreign traders open gaming holes where interested folks can spend a few extra coins. It was one of these places your father and I decided to visit one day. Located in the slums of Pullie, it was hosted by a group of southern merchants who came to Normandia under the patronage of Oris Lexandro of Azor. Everyone played there, and so did we, spending a few gold plates and some silvers.

"We gambled for a few days, nothing big, lost some and won some. But then one of the merchants showed us another game, a serious game where bets and risks were very high. At first we watched as others played, but then decided to try ourselves. The first few games we won with ease, making so much money that we could buy a small keep somewhere in western Normandia. But soon our luck turned and we started to lose. We wanted to leave, but the guards there made us stay, telling us that we had to play a dozen games at least. Under the threat of their swords we did, and lost. When we had no more money, we borrowed it from the merchants and played again. It went on until we found ourselves in such debt, we could not repay it. We tried to flee, but the guards caught us and threw us in a cell. Several days later one of the merchants came down to speak to us. He informed us that our debt was a thousand gold plates, and that we had to pay the whole sum in three days' time.

"We could not do that; we simply did not have that much money. So then, the merchant offered us a deal. He said that his master, Oris Lexandro, had been recruiting young Northerners for his personal guard, training them from an early age to serve as his bodyguards. Since most of the local families were very weary of the southern lands, none wanted to give up their children, and Oris could not find enough men to fill his needs. Even the money did not help. Normandians simply refused to go south. It was a problem for the merchant. For some reason he needed boys with the Northern blood.

"The deal Oris's man offered us was that we were to give our male children into the merchant's service. In return he would forget our debt, and would provide for our sons, paying them a salary as his guards. Back then it seemed like a reasonable offer, and we took it. Only…"

The man looked at Father again. "Your father lied. Instead of giving up all of his sons he brought only one. How could you?"

The stranger stared at Father, tears in his eyes. "At least you could have told me. I would have understood." The man was crying. "Now I know why you did not want the merchant's men to come to Villone. Now I know why you arranged to meet them in the forest, away from your house." The scar-faced man turned to us. "If you did not already know, your father was the one responsible for his own kidnapping. Afraid that they would see his other children, he told the merchant's men of a place and a time to meet his caravan. He did not know though, that those hired swords who waited for him in the forest had something else planned for their meeting. The mercenaries took your father and Ave prisoners. As for the others, they killed them.

"Alas, my story was somewhat similar. As agreed I brought my two sons to the hovel in Pullie. Though we came willingly, the same treachery was waiting for us. Once we entered the room, some men jumped us. We had no time to resist. Before we knew it, we were chained inside a closed wagon, riding someplace we did not know. Lost, we rode for days. As if that was not enough, one night our caravan was attacked. The assailants came unexpectedly. They acted quickly and precisely. Slaying several of the guards they got inside the carts and snatched Brune's son, but left mine be. I wish I could tell you who they were, but I cannot. Everything happened so fast that none of us could describe them. I wish they had freed us too, but they did not, and so we remained prisoners.

"After the attack our journey continued. We rode and rode until we got to this place, where we had been ever since, held prisoners against our will."

"By the looks of these quarters you do not look like prisoners to me," interrupted Ike.

"You look more like guests," I added.

"This is what the local guards call us too," replied Rulio. "After we had arrived to Azor, the guards placed us in here. Several times Oris's aids, or so they claimed, came and spoke to us. They apologized for the actions of the hired swords back in Normandia. They also said that while Ave was still missing, my sons were starting their training with Oris's guards, just as agreed. As for us, they said that until they found out who had attacked our convoy on the way to Azor, we had to remain in our quarters, for our own safety. They called us Oris's honorable guests. Only we do not feel like guests. We cannot go anywhere, cannot talk to anyone but each other, and I cannot see my sons. I know what you want to ask next. And I will answer you. We do not know why the count holds us here, or why he gives us food and clothes. All we know is that we are somewhere in Azor, leagues away from home, alone, and beaten. At least I hope my sons are doing better."

"I am afraid it is not so," I said with sadness in my voice. "I am almost sure that your sons, along with dozens of other young boys from Normandia, are held captive, locked in the dungeon below."

"No, this is not true. You are lying, you…"

"I wish that was true, but we have just been there. We found a whole prison full of young boys. We even spoke with one of them. If you do not believe us go down and check for yourself. I warn you though, there is a battle going on. Some of our friends are fighting the guards, fighting for your sons."

"If it is so I must go there. I must help free my boys. Please let me go. I need to see them."

Suddenly, the sound of many footsteps echoed through the corridor, followed by some voices, several of them, all speaking in the Southern Way. At first they were in a distance, but soon got closer, and finally were in the hallway just outside the door. Inside the room we stood still, waiting. Then someone started pounding on the thick wood, and all of us stepped back, our eyes focused on the door. At that time someone in the hallway yelled in a thick southern accent, "Hey, you in there! Is everything all right? We had an intrusion; someone attacked our post in the dungeon. We have been ordered to search all the buildings, so open up. We need to check the room."

When the voice stopped, Father whispered, "Mishuk, Ric, Ike, hide in the closet. We will try to make them leave quickly."

"Do it," added Rulio. "This is your only chance." At that time the pounding resumed, and we ran for the larger closet, situated next to a fireplace. The wardrobe was big enough for the three of us to get into, and so we did, covering ourselves with heaps of cloths, leaving only a small gap in between the garments so we could see what was going on. We did so just in time, before the front door swung inward and several armed men strolled into the room. They wore the uniform of the merchant's guard and carried short swords and round shields.

"What is going on here?" One of them asked Father, who did not answer.

"Why did not you answer when asked?" Another man roared and walked up to the window, lifting the curtains with his sword. "Are you hiding something?"

"No, no. We were asleep, we did not hear." Rilo started to mumble, but was cut short by yet another guard. "Arg, shut up you Northern waste. I sense there is something wrong in here. Boys, check the room. Make sure there are no visitors hiding in here."

The other guards started with the search and quickly dispersed around the room. It was a bad twist of luck. Holding my sword tightly, I readied myself for an attack. At some moment, one of the men came up to the closet door. His hand reached for the door, and he was about to open it, when Father jumped toward him, hitting the man in the face. With his other hand he grabbed the man's sword and yanked it up, freeing it from the enemy's grip. The guard was caught by surprise. He let go of his weapon easily and fell to the floor. His body twitched as Father thrust the weapon into him. The guard was dead even before his friends understood what had happened. But I did, and while Father was drawing the weapon back, I leapt out and charged the nearest foe. The man was quick to follow his comrade, and soon was joined by two more guards, slain by Ric and Ike, who were swift and without fear. The last of the enemy tried to flee, but did not get too far either. Just as he reached for the door his head exploded in one red gory burst. He sank down like a bag of stone, with Rilo towering over him, a huge half-broken obelisk of a sitting eagle in his hand.

"Go on, leave. You do not have much time. Their friend will return soon; you will not have another chance," said Father, wiping the blood from the blade. Rulio hit the man over the head one more time and dropped the broken statue, saying, "Your father is right. You must go now. Hey, if you ever meet Simo or Sulo of Rame, tell them that their old man was sorry for what he did, and that he tried to be the best father he could. Tell them that I tried to fight for them."

Although I promised to do as asked, I did not know if I would ever see the poor lads. Most probably they were already dead, and I was afraid it was the same for my own brother, Ave. And Father —I was not sure what to think. I did not know what to say either. My mouth opened, but I had no voice. My throat was choking with tears.

Tears ran down Father's face too; his cheeks were red and his hands were shaking. He stared at me for a moment, then lowered his head and said, "Go, Mishuk, leave." He wiped the tears. "Forgive me…I did not think it would turn out this way. I was a fool to do what I did, and so I will die a fool. I only have one request, do not tell your mother anything. Tell her you did not find me, tell her I vanished without a trace. The truth will kill her."

I did not reply, as more footsteps came from outside. It sounded like at least a dozen men. We had to leave. I looked at Father then at the door. My brother and I were on our toes, ready to slip out into the hallway. For the last time I turned to Father and suddenly noticed how Ike pulled something out of his pocket. It was his sister's ring, the same ring we had found in the clearing near Lulione, many days before. He showed it to Father and asked, "Why did you leave this ring then if you did not want us to search for you?"

Father glanced at the elegant loop. "Ike, I did not leave any ring there. Besides, I sold this one last season in Bonneville on request from your father."

Ike did not reply. Ric and I did not say anything either, as the noise outside was getting closer. I sighed and ran out the door, with Ric and Ike following, all without another word.

We emerged into an empty hallway. For a moment we stopped and listened. The footsteps were some distance away, and so we sprinted for the secret passage. The storage room was just as we had left it, dark and messy. We had no light, yet we made our way to the far wall, and found a loose torch holder. After I twisted it several times, the wall extracted several clicks and opened. Through the gap we ran to the stairs, where we found our torches still smoldering. After lighting them up again with our firestones, we hurried down to the lower reaches of the dungeon.

The way back along the dark tunnels went unnoticed. Yet, as much as we had been through, the last few cubits to the surface seemed the longest stretch by far. My relief at seeing the dim moonlight ahead was palpable, but a feeling of constant treachery persisted. Although the general's rearguard could still be there we did not care. We were too angry and exhausted to hide our approach. But as our small company stumbled out of the tunnels, we found the low shore in front of us empty, dark, and calm. The place was silent, but for the sound of the water hitting large river stones, sent there by gentle gusts of the spring night wind. There were no guards, no hired swords, no one—just us and the stars above. Tired and relieved we dropped our swords and slid onto the sandy floor. Suddenly the life force left our limbs. Unable to move even a finger, I stretched out on the ground, staring at the dark sky, my eyes still full of tears. Everything around me looked as if nothing had happened underground, as if there was no battle, no betrayal, and no revelation of Father's true deed. A large part of my quest was complete. I had found Father and uncovered the truth about the disappearance of his caravan. Yet there was no joy. And so it was. I was beaten, exhausted, and with a large gap in my heart.

Chapter 75

THE STREETS were dark, unfamiliar, and full of danger. Our small tired band of Normandian squires made its way past rows of unlit buildings, trying to find a way to the sage's mansion, where we hoped to take our horses and leave the ill-fated city for good. But getting to Revor's estate proved to be a rather difficult task. Left without Elson or the sage, we found ourselves lost amidst the maze of streets and alleys of the great city of Azor. Yet we knew the general direction and so headed there, following the two bright stars that marked the western edge of the clear night sky.

Finally, after much walking, we reached the dividing wall, and after walking along it for another few hundred cubits, came up to the main gates of the western district. Although the wooden doors were left open, the inner grate was lowered, and some guards paced on the other side, beating the stone pavement with their metal heels. By then we could guess that the merchant and his men had been already looking for us. Surely the men at the gates would have been warned; so instead of going straight for the gates, we veered left and after walking for another hundred cubits, found a dark spot where the wall looked particularly low. There we scaled the barrier, and once on the other side, quickly hid in the shadows of a small park.

Like the rest of the city, the western district was asleep. Though well lit, the broad avenues were seeded with many trees, which served as perfect cover for our movement. Running from one patch of green crowns to another we slowly crossed most of the borough and reached familiar territory, just off the sage's estate, which looked like any other domain, calm, dark, and peaceful. Yet, after some examination, we noticed some commotion at the gates. Hidden in the darker shadows, a group of men armed with long spears and shields, huddled at the front doors. It was too far to see any symbols on their suits of armor, but I could discern the color of their tunics, which were the same as those of the city watch patrols. The men talked casually to each other, their spears leaned against the wall. Immediately I remembered Revor talking about the council of Azor. Maybe the sage had warned its members of Oris' mischief and they had sent their soldiers to help. The idea seemed sound to me, and I was quick to make a move into the open, ready to meet up with the city watch, when a sudden hiss stopped me in mid-step. I quickly turned to where the sound had come from. It was too dark to see, but I picked out the silhouette of a man standing beneath a large oak tree, leaning against its trunk.

"Who is there?" I whispered.

There was no answer.

"Come on out, before we attack," snapped Ike. Ric raised his axe, and I clenched my blade.

"I would get away from the light if I were you," the familiar voice finally replied, and Elson emerged before us. He looked different from the last time we had seen him. His once shiny chain mail was covered with specks of blood, and several large cuts had ripped through his metal tunic. His face was dirty, and a large bump shone on his forehead. He was missing almost all of his gear; his sword was the only thing he had left, and even it was dented and chipped.

"What happened? Where is Revor?" I asked surprised.

"We lost the fight," said the Southerner grimly. "We had started to get the upper hand, when more guards showed up. This time they were city watchers. When we first saw them behind the enemy, we started to cheer, but when they began to loosen their bows at us we realized they were the enemy too. Then we stood little chance. We were doomed, and yet we fought, until almost everyone amongst our company was dead. We tried to retreat into the tunnels, but the enemy surrounded us before we could make our escape. It was then, Master Revor used his black fire dust. I do not remember much what happened afterwards. Suddenly everything went dark. All I could hear was rumbling and screams. When I finally came to my senses, I found a large portion of the dungeon collapsed, the ceiling caved in, large rocks thrown across the room, and dozens of men, friend and foe, crushed beneath the rubble. I could hear some of them crying for help; most were gone. Revor was gone too. I sought him amongst those around me, but could not find him anywhere. He had vanished, probably blown to pieces by the blast. I wished I had more time, but the stones were getting shaky and I exited. Thank Spirit there were enough holes inside that room. As soon as I made my way onto the surface, I came here, only to find more city watchers waiting for me."

The Southerner contemplated the men who rested on the street some distance away.

"The council's bodyguards. They have been camping out there for a while now. While waiting in my hiding place near the gates. I overheard them talk about you, the sage, and me. According to their story, the council of Azor, which Revor was so fond of, has taken Oris' side. Even before our assault began, the merchant declared Revor and his men as conspiring with the Northern spies to assassinate Oris, for reasons unknown. And when we were ambushed in the dungeon, by the general, Oris sent out messengers to notify all of our intrusion. The council of Azor then labeled all those participating in the attack on Oris' estate as 'enemies of Azor,' the worst of all designations given in the realm. So now you and I are outlaws; the council declared us so. From this moment on, every hired sword in Azoros will be looking for us. I would not be surprised if there is already a price placed upon our heads."

The Southerner paused and listened. Then satisfied there was no one near us, continued. "Of course it helps us that everyone considers us dead in the blast. But soon enough they will learn that we are not down there, and then the hunt will begin. For Spirit's sake—they already arrested all the servants, and stole most of the valuables from Revor's mansion."

"Enemies of the state?" Ike repeated the words slowly, thinking, "But why? Oris is the true enemy of Azor. He is the one who has imprisoned so many innocent men; he is the one who tried to kill us; he…"

"I know, but he is also very rich and very powerful. His connections go far beyond this city and this realm. I would not be at all surprised to find out that he had something to do with the latest invasions of the Grass Folks. Why do you think the poor side was hit the worst?"

"Poor side?" I asked, confused. "But only the poorest live there. Why would anyone want to attack them?"

"The poor are no threat to the council or Oris. But the underworld is. Numerous guilds of thieves, assassins, low-paid mercenaries, and simple thugs are located in the poor side. Their living accommodations may be simple but many of those groups are very powerful indeed. I am sure Oris had a few problems with some of them, and what better way to get rid of your enemy, but to send a horde of wildlings into the city? That way the merchant is free from any accusations while the job is done."

"What about the prisoners then, why does he need the young boys from Normandia?" Ric joined in, also keeping a close watch on the road.

"You have heard the sage. He is looking for the Chosen One, just like the Alavantars are," replied the Southerner.

"But why? What does he want from the Chosen One?"

"Ultimate power, my friend, absolute control. Why do the Alavantars try to kill the Chosen One—because they are afraid he will defeat their Northern master. If he does so, the entire world will be at his feet. Ethoria will be his to rule, and he will be the true king of the world. How much do you think this would be worth?"

The Southerner paused, looked at me, and sighed. "Revor did not want to tell you this, but since the sage is probably dead, you deserve to know. Oris is a very cunning man. First he used Revor to learn about the Chosen One, where and how to find him, and then tried to find the future hero himself. But he did not know that Revor did not tell him all; that the true description of the Chosen One was left with the master sage. Just as with the Alavantars, there were just too many candidates that fit the vague picture known to Oris. Picking through so many men became a daunting task. At first the merchant tried to persuade the parents of the young lads to let them go to Azoros. To some he offered money, to others deals of trade, gems, food, or services.

"But in the end it proved to be too costly. There was also a question of time. The count did not have much of it. The Alavantars were becoming more active, and were killing the candidates by dozens. So after a while Oris chose to act differently—instead he hired mercenaries in great numbers and sent them north, instructing them to kidnap the youngsters and bring them to Azor, where he would place them in his dungeon, keeping them there until he could determine the true identity of the Chosen One. When it so happened, Oris would then decide on what to do with the Chosen One. As for those other prisoners, he could sell them as slaves to the Free Cities, paying off all the expenses he had incurred."

"What a scum!" exclaimed Ike.

"Did not you say the city watchers had raided the sage's estate?" I asked, as chill ran down my spine. "What about Revor's texts, the originals of Arac's Verses, and their translations? Where are those writings?"

"Alas, I can not say. Revor always kept them in some secret room inside the mansion. No one knew where, not even I. Let's hope that the city watchers did not find anything, or that the sage had hid the texts some other place outside the city," replied Elson slowly.

"Let's hope it is the last. We do not want our enemies to find the Verses," Ike noted after a pause. Everyone agreed.

"So what are we doing now? We cannot allow Oris continue with this mischief, can we?" I looked at the Southerner.

"First we must leave this town. It is not safe for us to be here. Once we are out of the merchant's sight we will think of some plan. Until then let's concentrate on making our escape."

"And how do you intend to do so? Any ideas?" asked Ike.

"I still have some friends here. There are a few of them working at the outer eastern gates tonight."

Without waiting, Elson turned and hurried down the darkened lane of shadows, away from the sage's estate. We went after him, passing through a small garden, a few narrower streets, and a wide creek. Soon enough we were standing at the dividing wall, forming a human ladder. Then we quickly climbed over the barrier and emerged at a neatly trimmed lawn. The soft grass silenced our falls. No human eyes saw us, and we continued through the eastern district toward a set of closed gates. Two lonely guards stood there passively. They immediately recognized Elson amongst us. After talking to him for a few moments, they let us pass, opening a narrow slit for us to get through. We did so quickly and then disappeared into the dark again.

The poor side proved to be much safer for us—no light, less attention, and a denser night crowd, in which we melted in an instant. Several street corners away from the gates, Elson made a sharp turn, and brought us up to a shaggy one-story building, where to my surprise we found our horses, saddled and ready for the trip. I knew that the Southerner had something to do with it, but I refrained from asking. There would be a better time for that. At the moment all I could think of were the count, his men, and the reward on our heads.

The flight from Azoros was swift. Our horses carried us out of the poor side and into the open fields of Azor's countryside, galloping back toward the southern part of Lombardia, and then to the Kingdom of Dvorenia, where none of the mercenary's bands would dare to attack us in the daylight. Luckily the border was just three days away, and with decent weather we could get across before the merchant learned of our departure. It was only then, safe from Oris and his men, that we could decide on a further course of action. Before that time, all we did was ride as fast as we could, away from Azor, and away from Father, of whom I tried not to think much.

The night went quickly, and so did the day after it, and another night, and another day. Throughout we traveled with very few stops, alone, taking the back roads as much as we could. It was on the eve of the third day that we finally reached the borderline, composed of a stone fence, just a cubit high, old and collapsed in places. Where the crooked wall met the road a gap was seen, and through it we went, making our way out of the realm of Azoros, and into

Lombardia, not even halting for a moment to look back. Around us the scene remained serene; sounds of moaning cows came from a distance; crickets sang their monotonous song, and the invisible birds flapped their wings, flying close to the ground, which was a sure sign of an upcoming rain. Swathed in such music of the evening, we rode for some leagues and then stopped near an old tree at the top of an open hill, where we settled to rest. There was no fire that night, barely any food, and few words. Everyone was too tired to talk, so we slept instead, each consumed with his own thoughts and fears.

The dream I had that night was another vision, which brought me back to the edge of the memorable green meadow, just outside the A'al sorceress's grand hall. It was a pleasant sight, for I needed answers. Hurrying to meet with the A'al I passed through the invisible gates of long branches and succulent foliage, and entered the chamber, taking a seat near the high throne, where A'tie had been already waiting for me. As always everything about her was beautiful and graceful; her features, her gestures, and her smile radiated warmth and kindness, and brought me a much sought-after sense of comfort and safety. Like a child of only a few seasons, I was staring at the beautiful visage before me, hoping to hear A'tie speak, and so she did, greeting me kindheartedly in her soothing soft voice.

"I see you have completed a large portion of your quest. You have learned all about the disappearance of your father's caravan; you have found your father, and have obtained new clues as to the fate of your older brother. Tough tasks they were, but you have succeeded in accomplishing them, all to the surprise of many. Not me of course—I always had faith in you, my young warrior.

"Yet there is much more that you must learn. I sense that you continue to harbor many questions, of them the fate of your brother concerns you the most. You still do not know of his whereabouts, if he is dead or alive. Although you have heard some accounts in the past weeks, none of them answered your inquiries. But it is time you learn the truth, and I will help you in this.

"Whatever you have heard about the mysterious ambush of the mercenaries' party is true. Their camp was indeed attacked one night, and your brother taken, freed from his captives and brought to a safe place, where none could hurt him again. How do I know this? Because the ones who rescued him from those ruthless mercenaries were my kind, the A'als. Acting on my orders, a party of A'als wardens traveled to Lombardia and searched out the caravan. They followed it for several days until they thought it was best to act. Under cover of the night they sneaked into the enemy's camp and took your brother along with them. So now your brother is with us, resting comfortably in the depths of the Great Fortress. He has suffered some, but—do not worry—he is all right."

"Why did you not tell me this before? You knew about Ave all along and yet you kept it from me. You made me travel all this way to Azoros. You lied to me."

"Careful with words, my young warrior. I never lied to you. Never once did I say I did not know where your brother was or what was happening to him. In truth I followed him ever since he was taken away. I knew who took him and where he was taken to, just like I knew of your father's deed. The reason I did not tell you any was that it was not safe, not for you, nor me. I also was not sure of your true intentions, or if your Fore Sight would mature. Until I was convinced, I could not risk telling all that I knew, not with others watching you closely. Or did you think that your visions were only for you to see? The others often see them too, and some of them even try to interfere, stirring you away from the true path. Do you remember the dark visitor? He came to you once and told you not to trust me."

"Yes, there was such a visitor once. But I do not know who he was. He was very keen about hiding himself from me."

"That was his intention—to remain unseen. Secrecy is his ally. Even I cannot break through the veil he shrouded himself in. He uses very strong magic, unlike anything I have ever seen before. His magic is very old, very powerful, and very violent. A dangerous man he is, and you should fear him, for I fear him myself. In time I will be able to uncover his true identity, and then I will know what to do. Until then we must continue to be careful in what we are saying in our sessions. So now you understand why I did not tell you all. But tonight the time has come for me to open some of the secrets. You have completed your quest, and passed the trial. Your intentions are true, your path is righteous, and your Fore Sight has grown much since our first meeting. Soon, very soon, you will be ready for the true quest, far greater than anything you have faced so far.

"You see, my young warrior, we, the A'als, know everything about the upcoming conflict in Ethoria. To you Arac's prophecies of the forthcoming war between the forces of Ethoria and the Northern Hordes maybe but the prophecies, a tale of some sort. To us though these divinations of the future are as evident as the present. Although we do not posses the articles ourselves, we know everything about them. We know what they say is true, that the events the articles describe will happen. We also know that there is no way to avoid or prevent them. But we do not know when or how it will happen, or what will be its culmination. These things remain a mystery to us too. So we continue to look for clues that can tell us more about the future. Amongst the things we search for is the great hero of whom Arac speaks. Yes, my young warrior, you have heard me right. We too are looking for the Chosen One.

"We spent many years going through ancient text, trying to piece together the accurate description of the great man. And not too long ago we finally succeeded in putting together a picture that helped us narrow our search. I cannot tell you much more, though. Our channel is not safe. But I encourage you to visit me. Come to the Great Forest and see your brother. See me as well. I need to tell you much."

"But how? You are somewhere in the Great Forest, and I am in Lombardia, leagues away."

"Still, you should travel to my home. Consider this a formal invitation."

"Do I really have a choice?"

A'tie ignored my question, and the pause lasted until I spoke again. "Of course I will come. What shall I do?"

"First you travel to Dvorenian, and then to the town of Briek, which is located at the edge of the forest. Once there go to Red Silk Tavern and ask for Arok. He is a human scout, who has been long regarded as a friend of our people. Tell him your name, and he will lead you to the meeting place where my guides will pick you up. Do you have any questions?"

"Yes, one. My friends, they may not understand when I tell them of our new voyage. They do not say it, but I suspect they do not really believe in you. How can I persuade them to come with me?"

"Do not worry about your brother. He will go with you no matter what. As for your friend and the Southerner, they are your true companions and so they will go too."

"But what about my father? Is he alive, is he well?"

The answer did not come. The image of the sorceresses, her grand hall, and the trees vanished as soon as I uttered the words. In their place came the blackness, and I woke up, only to go back to sleep again. I was still very tired.

When the morning came I told my friends of my latest encounter with the A'al sorceress, and then revealed the plan to travel to Dvorenia and then to the Great Forest. To my surprise none of them objected. A'tie was right once more. I did not have to worry about my companions. They were with me, and for that I was thankful, but not for much else.

So it was. Our company of four started a new journey and a new quest. All of a sudden the tiredness vanished, and our goal became clear: our destination—the mysterious realm of A'als. There was no time to waste, the enemy was all around, and friends were far away.

Chapter 76

IT SEEMED to Rob that he had dozed for only a few moments, but when he awoke he found the sun setting and the warmth of the day gone. Ark was back at the tent too. He sat next to an open door flap, preoccupied with fixing his boots, which had started to fall apart from long days of constant walking. Sending a long needle in and out of the broken leather, Ark was whistling a simple tune. It was a familiar song, yet Rob could not recall it. In truth he could not recall a lot of things. Faces and dates were slowly being erased from his mind, and he could do little to stop it. Instead he tried concentrating on the present, memorizing names of places they had passed and people they had met. It helped him stay focused, and it was what he intended to do, no matter what the circumstances were. Although Ark had little talent for singing, the sound of his melody was soothing, and Rob remained under his cloak for a while longer, listening. But the song was soon over, so then Rob had to get up and crawl outside, where a cold breeze and an odd cooking aroma hit him in a face. Shivering, he stood still in the opening of his tent, surveying the scene around him, which had changed little since that afternoon.

The caravan my friends had joined days ago made camp on the bank of a low river, between two beds of mountain rock. Since their departure from Sirone, a number of men sentenced to the Barriers had grown by handfuls and now counted over three hundred, all separated into four groups, each guarded by at least a hundred armed guards, mostly freelance soldiers from the Southern parts of Normandia, hired to watch over convicts and cargo. Besides the prisoners and the guards there were also hundreds of commoners, men and women and children, who had tagged along with the caravan and were now spread across a dale, setting up numerous tents, and filling the place with bustle.

Just like very other day, Rob and Ark were placed at the far edge of the camp, close to the guard post, where some ten hired swords watched over a host of prisoners, paying close attention to a small band of outlanders in the back. The foreigners were a particular source of worry for the guards. Although the men looked calm and passive, they were a handful, to say the least. Thrice throughout the trip they had tried to break free. Two of their attempts ended just at the outskirts of the camp. And once they succeeded to slip into the wild grass, where they hid for four days until a group of local men-at-arms found them and dragged them back to the convoy. After their return three of the outlanders were executed and the rest beaten with sticks. The punishment seemed to work, and afterwards there were no more escapes, as the sight of their dangling bodies proved to be a good lesson to all.

For a while Rob stood quietly, looking at the commotion around him, but when the fires started to spring up throughout the camp, he moved to the next tent, closer to a small blaze started by one of their fellow prisoners. The warmth of the fire brought some comfort and my friend extended his hands to the heat, which was a rare thing in the highlands of the northern part of Normandia. When the cold finally left his sore limbs he lay back, chewing on a dry thick piece of beef jerky and chatting of things he cared little about. Still, just talking was enough. Slowly Rob's mood began to rise, but not for long, as an hour or so later the sound of a horn rolled through the camp. It was a command to get back inside the tents, and it was not to be fooled with. Saying brief farewells, Rob returned to his small clothed shelter and slid behind the draped door just a moment before the arrival of the guards, who were always eager to beat someone just because they could. Ark was already under his cape. His eyes were closed, but when Rob crawled up to him, he smiled, and moved a little, freeing a narrow stretch of the floor for his friend. Rob lay down there. The cold grass was uncomfortable and rough, but the two youths from Villone had gotten used to such bedding, and soon were sound asleep, only to be awakened in the morning by the same loud horn.

The next day marked the last part of the tiresome trip. Chased by loud commands from the passing guards the camp was quickly dismantled. The caravan was moving steadily up the road, heading toward the township of Jiuyes, a large village situated at the foot of the Land's Edge, which officially belonged to Normandia. But since the place served as the only way in and out of the Great Fortress region, the parish was run by the council of a local lord and a high ranked officer from the Barriers. Although its strategic location made Jiuyes very important, it was not a military installation. Instead it was a simple supply depot, where much of the stocks came through before being delivered into the Great Fortress or the Barrier Walls. It was also a place where all the sentenced men were brought first and handed over to the local lords, who then took them further into the heart of the Land's Edge, where the Great Fortress itself stood, cut off from the rest of the world by two walls and high mountain peaks.

Although to the men of the prisoners' caravan Jiuyes was just a stop on the way further north, to the convoy's masters it meant payment for their labor, which made them push forth even harder. Wagons and men formed two long lines, struggling to keep themselves close together, so as not to fall into the many caverns that often appeared on either side of the weaving road. Surrounded by thick fog, for half a day the caravan climbed up the wide lane of crumbled rock. Sometime during the ascent the green colors of the lower valley disappeared, and in their place came dark brown shades of sand and stone. It was only in late afternoon when at the top of a steep slope, which ran up to the edge of the plateau, the mist receded the men saw a row of small triangles, roofs of buildings, the first site of the promised village.

As the caravan went higher, the view became clearer, and soon my friends could see almost the entire village, which turned out to be quite big for such an inconvenient location. Occupying a side of a mountain, Jiuyes sat on three rocky platforms, which rose in an almost vertical slope like giant steps of an old staircase. At the bottom the place was occupied by larger buildings and stretches of cultivated land, packed with the golden color of the flourishing crops. Further up stood several lines of smaller buildings. Two and three stories high they ran along the mountainside, at one end coming to a large cavern, and at the other to a wide-open staircase, which led to the upper platform. The top level hosted four stone citadels, which looked as if they had been cut out completely of bedrock. Very similar to smaller Normandian keeps, the structures were seeded with rows of slit windows, some square and some oval in shape. Along the citadels' sides ran several wooden galleries and at the top, arch bridges connected each of the forts, also equipped with slender towers, visible from the bottom plateau.

"Famous Dark Prisons of the Great Fortress," whispered a man behind Rob, by the name of Hui. He was a smaller lad in his early twenties with red hair and small whiskers. Always quiet and calm, he had joined the caravan not long before; his crime—petty thievery. Like many others in the ill-fated company, Hui thought of himself as a very unlucky man. And there was some truth to such a stance. Where a man with some coin would have gotten off with just a fine for stealing a basket of bread, Hui was sentenced to ten years at the wall, a very unfortunate ordeal indeed.

Earlier in the journey he shunned the company of others, spending time by himself or with the animals, but as the days passed he became more used to his situation and soon befriended Rob and Ark, who, though not in the best states themselves, accepted the loner and spent much time with him, telling him of their recent adventures, often having to repeat the same episodes from the Puno campaign several times a day.

"Dark Prisons?" asked Rob staring at the gray shapes above.

"They say this is the place where they keep those, who try to escape from the Barriers. Folks around my village say that if someone is sent there he is never seen again. They also say that at times the guards throw some of the prisoners into deep pits, where giant dogs rip them to pieces. And at night, when the mountain winds are asleep, you can hear the weeping of poor souls crying for mercy."

"These are just stupid stories you fool," interrupted another prisoner, Gois. He was an older man, short and stocky. He got into the caravan because he killed two horses that belonged to his lord's stable. Afterwards Gois claimed that he had to do so, because the animals were demons. But such a story did not impress the lord's court, and so he was sentenced to the wall, though a better place for him could have been a distant hostel or a monastery somewhere in the western reaches of the kingdom.

"They do not hold humans there. There are demons in those cells. Yes, demons. I know so, because I have seen them in my dreams. And those sounds you hear are not weeping men, they are demon calls. Yes, calls. Calls to their fellow evils to come and rescue them. Demons live beyond the walls, you know. Usually they stay there and do not bother anyone. But sometimes they climb over the walls and hunt for human flesh. Those who get caught by the guards are brought there. Why do you think they are called dark prisons? Because the walls are black from smoke, which the demons exhume."

"Shut up, you idiots." A passing guard interrupted Gois' tale. "Back in the line."

The soldier raised his gloved hand and everyone quieted. Satisfied, the guard smirked and walked further down.

From there on no one said anything and just walked up the slope until the first wagon reached the gates of the village. Then the procession stopped. While the free folk were allowed to walk into Jiuyes, the prisoners were forced to line up along the fenced wall, pushing close together three men deep. Rob and Ark were put in the middle of first row, with Hui behind them. For a while nothing happened. The men just stood there, shivering from the cold winds, particularly strong and bitter. Rubbing their hands together, my friends breathed hard into their freezing palms, trying to bring back some sense into their numb fingers. The others did the same. Some started to whisper a few brief words to each other. But all the murmuring ceased as soon as a group of men appeared at the gates. The men were clearly of a noble stance and wore distinctive colored capes, thrown over shiny chain mail, with cloth scarves wrapped around their necks. Unhurriedly they moved down the line of sentenced men, often stopping to inspect the prisoners and say something to a host of young boys, who ran after them carrying large books in hand, in which they wrote a few lines each time they passed a man.

"Who are these men?" whispered Hui, peering out of the column so he could get a better look.

"Supervisors, who else?" replied a skinny tall man to the right of Rob, whose name was either Dumos or Dumas. Though Rob an Ark did not know him well, they knew that it was his strange lust for women's small clothes that brought him to the wall. Too fond of petite ladies' garments, Dumos stole them any chance he got. Caught once, he tried to do so again, and again, until the local council tired of him and sent him off to the Barriers. A harsh sentence it was. But Dumos did not mind, and only wished that there were women at the Great Fortress, whose private clothing he could take when the chance presented itself. A sick thing he was, but there was rarely any normality amongst the sentenced men. Rob and Ark came to realize this early in their journey.

"How do you know?" asked Hui again, this time staring at Dumos.

"Do you see those cloaks?" Dumos pointed at the group ahead. "You can tell if someone is a supervisor by the cloak he wears. The color of the cloak shows the supervisor's rank; the highest is red and the lowest is blue."

"What colors do you see there?" Hui looked at the start of the line, but could not see anything. Aside from his less than average height he also had bad eyes.

"One yellow, two greens, and seven blues," replied Ark, studying the men ahead.

"Is that good?" Hui's voice was shaking a little.

"I do not know. I have never been to the Wall before," snapped Dumos. "Although some say that if you see a red cloak that means you are going to the First Barrier. And nobody wants to go to the First Barrier. In the winter it gets so cold out there that fingers just fall off your hands. And then there are Nords too, the wild men of the North. Sometimes they scale the Wall and kidnap unsuspecting men, taking then to the bare plains for food and slaves."

"Oh, no, I do not want no wild men. I just want to serve my years and come home. I do not need to fight. I, I—." Hui was about to cry, when Ark interrupted him.

"Those supervisors—are they lords of some kind?"

"You may say so. Most of them are exiles like us. The ones who wear blue are junior supervisors. They are common men. Some of them came here on their own, but the majority were sent here years back. After serving their term in full they chose to remain at the Great Fortress. As free men they could not be equal to the prisoners, so they became junior supervisors. They are the ones whose faces we will see the most. They will command us, train us, and watch after us, so none leaves this dreadful place before his time is up. Sometimes a few of the blue cloaks, those who earn much respect from other supervisors, then go on to become greens, or senior supervisors. But that does not happen often, because green is reserved primarily for the noblemen, those lords who are sent here to pay for their own crimes. Since even in prison the nobles are no equals to common men, when they arrive they take green, which means they do not have to work like us. Instead they are charged with overlooking the mines, making sure that the work is done properly there. Those greens who choose to stay after their sentence is over, receive a yellow cloak—the mark of the head supervisor. Those are big birds. They live in the Great Fortress and are entrusted with different parts of the land between the two Barrier Walls, responsible for much of the mining operations in the region. Then there is red—the ultimate color of power here. In all there are only twenty red cloaks in the entire Great Fortress area. They are the true lords here, and amongst them there is the one, the high commander of the Great Fortress—he is like a king."

"How do you know so much about this place?" Ark was surprised to hear such a detailed account from someone who had just arrived at the Land's Edge.

"My father. He was to the wall. I was not born yet when he was taken away, but when he returned I made him tell me everything."

"I guess this runs in the family," noted Hui, but Dumos did not have time to reply. The company of supervisors was upon them. After studying a prisoner next to Dumos, the man with the yellow cloak came over to Ark, then turned to one of the young boys who lingered nearby.

"Former squire of Sire Rone of Sirone. Bois Province," the boy read from the book.

"What is his crime?" the man, asked in a dry tone.

"Treason," replied the boy.

"Treason, treason, treason." The yellow cloak sighed. "It seems that almost nine out of ten men who arrive from that province are traitors. How can that be?"

"These are tough times, you know. People are getting edgy," the man next to him, with a bright green cape, noted. "What is his age?" he asked the little scribe.

"Not yet twenty," the boy replied.

"At last some young bloods. We need young bloods." The green cloak waved his hand at another boy. "Sign them up for the twelfth tower. They need more strong men out there." With those words the men turned away and moved further down the line. Meanwhile, the boy came over. His head was shaved and on his forehead was a tattooed symbol of the Great Fortress—two towers, linked by a single bridge.

"Your slips?" The boy raised his hand not even looking at my friends. Ark and Rob handed over their pieces of paper, which disappeared quickly inside the boy's stack of scrolls. The lad then opened another book, wrote something in it, and ripped out two other slips.

"These are your passes. Do not lose them. When you know your supervisor give it to him." The boy closed the book and ran after the cloaks.

"The twelfth tower," Ark repeated aloud.

"Does anyone know what it means?" Rob asked the others around them. Nobody knew.

Chapter 77

THE DAYS the sentenced men had spent in Jiuyes finally came to a close, and on the dawn of the fifth day the prisoners were ordered to leave spacious barracks and were pushed into a column by a group of guards, some of whom wore blue cloaks. Chased by the freezing gusts of the ever-cold mountain winds and the constant barking of the guards, the men moved quickly through the lower levels of the village and up the stairs to the third platform, where the Dark Prisons stood. The closer the prisoners got to the citadels, the more slowly they went, challenged by the sight of ice that climbed up the black polished walls, making the gloomy structures look even gloomier.

Eventually, after much stalling, the rows of convicts reached the top, where another group of guards met them with more shouts and immediately led them into a large hall, inside the first citadel, empty of any fixtures, except for a set of columns at one end and a small fire grate at the other. In the center, forming a half circle, stood more colored cloaks—a dozen blues, three greens, and one yellow. When the last of the sentenced men was inside, the yellow cloak raised his hand and the large doors closed behind the last row of the prisoners, making a nervous bustle run through the ranks. Some men began to yell, others pleaded for mercy, and many more just stumbled back. But all that came to a quick end, when the sound of a battle horn thundered across the room. In an instant all the noise stopped, and while the men stood still, the yellow cloak spoke, his voice loud, his tone firm and commanding.

"Listen well, men. My name is Lexan Duvalio. I am the commander of the lower garrison here in Jiuyes, and I am in charge of transporting you to your final destination, wherever it may be. Before I do so though, let me explain a few things to you. First of all, this fort is not a Dark Prison. The towers you have seen from below are guards' towers, set up to watch over the land before the Second Barrier. Although these structures were once part of a larger prison, these days they serve as a sorting ground for the likes of you, which means that

604

it is here you will receive your assignments, your uniforms, and your instructions. So listen carefully because I will not say this again.

"Whatever your crimes might had been, we have no interest in them. No matter what you did in the lower lands of the free world, here you are all the same. You follow the same rules and live the same lives. You work, obey orders, and do not cause any troubles. Should you decide to do something stupid, like try to find an early route out of here, you will be punished. Otherwise, you may find the Great Fortress to be a rather generous place. It is not the most pleasant of the realms, but it is not the worst either. My advice—forget about your past lives of freedom. Those times are done with. From this moment on you have a new life, life in the Fortress—serve your term and go home a free man, or die before that."

The yellow cloak chuckled. "Now. Move out, men. We do not have all day."

He raised his hand again. Another set of doors opened at the far end and the sentenced men were hurried through the low archways, past a set of iron grates and into a short, wide hallway, blocked at the other side by a metal door, which was locked. With the last of the prisoners inside, the first doors closed too. Huddled together inside the stone sleeve, the men gazed in confusion at one another and at the doors. The sense of fear was all too obvious. In disarray the crowd moved from one end to the other, but then a screeching sound came from above. Something in the ceiling turned and suddenly streams of cold water rushed down like a waterfall. Many men tried to jump aside, but there was no room. And so the water fell, soaking the prisoners to the last stitch. When it was over, the wet crowd was allowed out of the corridor and into yet another grand hall, where along windowless walls stood rows of plain tables stacked with gray clothing. As each man passed the tables, a guard threw him a bundle containing the uniform of the Great Fortress—rough cotton trousers, a long-sleeved tunic, a brown leather belt, a hard gray mantel, and a pair of plain boiled-skin boots. Also for every prisoner there was a small medallion with an inscription on it, a name of some sort.

"Look at your marks," said the blue cloak as Ark and Rob took their bundles from him. "These are your names now. Remember them well, for none of the supervisors will call you anything else." The man smiled and turned to somebody else.

"Furo. I guess I will be Furo from now on," said Ark, reading from his medallion.

"Nice to meet you, Furo. My name is Kimo," replied Rob, already done with his outfit.

Dressed in gray, with name-tags dangling on their chests, my friends moved after the others through one more set of doors and into the open courtyard. Similar-looking gray men surrounded them. No one was talking, and there was no time to talk either, because very soon another command came and everyone moved again. This time the column headed down one level to where the open cavern was. There, the men stopped again before the entrance.

A green cloak walked up in front and said, "Men, you are about to leave Ethoria and enter into the land of the Great Fortress. This tunnel is the only way in or out. So if you had any ideas about fleeing, forget them. The pass closes after dark and there are plenty of guards to watch it during the day." The man waved his hand and the column moved into the wide dark handmade corridor that ran through the mountain, around the Second Barrier Wall, and into the Great Fortress' realm. It was a lengthy march, but in time a white light peered ahead, and the procession walked out onto a spacious marble platform that overlooked a long stretch of flat land locked in between two walls and mountains of rocks. Thin lines of roads ran across the valley, and further away, in the center of the dale rose a massive dark shape.

Bathing in the rays of the rising sun, the great fort stood unchallenged, its tall conical towers extending far into the sky, long colored banners waving in the wind. One of the oldest fortresses in Ethoria, the Great Fortress had been constructed along with the Second Barrier, a few years after the Great War. It was designed to be a part of the Barriers' formidable defenses, and for many years served as headquarters for the Barriers' once numerous garrisons. But as interest in protecting the pass through the Land's Edge dwindled, so did the importance of the fortress. Slowly the garrison that once guarded the walls transformed into a clan of supervisors, who though continuing to claim their duties as the Barriers' defenders, in truth were reserved for running the numerous mines that dotted the mountain slopes. To them—controlling the output of red ore had long become the most important task. With that, the Great Fortress lost its purpose as a formidable defensive outpost against the North, and instead was turned into a place where supervisors dwelled in their wealth.

While much had changed since the earlier days, the citadel itself remained as it had always been, still dominating the landscape, counting at least twenty main towers and over forty small ones, arranged along three descending rings of stone walls, each taller than the tallest castle in Normandia. The site was indeed a magnificent one, and my friends could not take their eyes off of it. They stared up at the stone lines, even as they descended a steep staircase, which took them down into the valley where some twenty carts awaited the prisoners.

At the bottom, Ark looked back, and again his eyes met a grand site—a massive wall that shot over a hundred cubits into the sky. Laid with huge bricks of black rock, the fortifications stretched for several leagues from west to east, with many towers reaching even higher, topped with flag posts and fires. The whole structure was clear of any steps or lifts, yet at the top a few small figures of men were visible, walking slowly back and forth.

"The Second Barrier," Ark whispered and sighed. Under different circumstances he would have enjoyed the view, but being a sentenced man changed it all. His time in the shadows of the great walls was just beginning, and already he disliked it much. After a pause, Ark sighed again and returned his attention to the group cloaks, who split the prisoners' column into several smaller groups and were pushing them onto the wagons, a dozen or so men at a time. My friends found themselves loaded onto the sixth cart, along with Gois, Hui, and Dumos, whose tall slender finger did not fit any of the uniforms and so he had to wear a smaller one, which made him look funny. Yet no one laughed, there was no time to laugh, because as soon as the last of the carts was loaded, a new command sounded and the wheels began to squeak.

The piercing noise gave Ark a headache. He tried rubbing his temples, but it did not help. He tried to sleep, but the road was filled with bumps and ditches, which made the carts jerk constantly, giving no rest for its passengers. He tried to talk to the others, but no one answered him. Even Rob was quiet, his face grim and cold. So Ark let his friend be and instead made his way to the front of the carriage, where, settled on a high bench sat two men, one a commoner, a servant perhaps, and the other a blue cloak. Ark did not know if he could talk to the supervisor, but he wanted to try.

"Can I ask you a question, Sire?" my friend asked politely.

"Sure, lad," the blue cloak replied cheerfully. There was not a hint of hostility.

"Are we going to the twelfth tower?" Ark smiled and sat behind the man.

"We sure are. Why?"

"I was just wondering, which one of them is the twelfth tower?" Ark pointed at the Great Fortress, which slowly rose as the caravan continued to roll down the dirt lane.

The blue cloak looked at the citadel, then at my friend. For a moment his face expressed a sign of uncertainty, but then his eyes lit up and he started to laugh. "Do you think we are going to the Great Fortress?" he asked, still laughing. Ark nodded. The blue cloak shook his head several times and added, "Boy, the twelfth tower is at the northeast end of this valley." When Ark did not reply, the man added, "The First Barrier, young man, the end of the world, as they call it."

The cloak stopped laughing and thought about something for a moment, then returned his attention to Ark and uttered, "Do not worry, boy. It is not so bad. You will see…you will see." The last words were a whisper, but Ark heard them anyway, and they made my friend frightened. For the first time since his arrest back in Sirone he was truly afraid, afraid of what lay ahead. Suddenly he did not want to talk anymore. Quietly he thanked the blue cloak and returned to his seat. Afterwards he spoke very little. His mind was pressed with one single thought—they were going to the loneliest and most dangerous place in Ethoria—First Barrier Wall, the place where the world ended and the Northern wastes began.

Give the Gift of

Ethoria's Chronicles

to Your Friends and Colleagues

CHECK YOUR LEADING BOOKSTORE OR ORDER HERE

❑ **YES**, I want _____ copies of *Ethoria's Chronicles: The Shadows of the Past* at $24.95 each, plus $4.95 shipping per book. Canadian orders must be accompanied by a postal money order in U.S. funds. Allow 15 days for delivery.

My check or money order for $_____ is enclosed.

Name _____

Organization _____

Address _____

City/State/Zip _____

Phone_____ E-mail _____

Please make your check payable and return to:

ICLS International, Inc.
107 West Sumner
Harvard, IL 60033